WHEN THE SPLENDOR FALLS

Laurie McBain

sourcebooks
casablanca

Published by Sourcebooks Casablanca, an imprint of Sourcebooks,
Inc.
P.O. Box 4410, Naperville, Illinois 60567–4410
(630) 961–3900
Fax: (630) 961–2168
www.sourcebooks.com

Originally published in 1985 by Avon Books, a division of the
Hearst Corporation, New York.

Printed and bound in the United States of America
RRD 10 9 8 7 6 5 4 3 2 1

*With love for Elizabeth, Leigh, and Will McBain,
who, when very young, believed in fairy-tale castles and
happily-ever-afters, may all your dreams come true*

Characters

TRAVERS FAMILY OF VIRGINIA

Stuart Russell Travers, master of Travers Hill; gentleman farmer and breeder of Thoroughbreds.

Beatrice Amelia, mistress of Travers Hill; wife and mother, and one of the Leighs of South Carolina.

Stuart James, firstborn son; attended Virginia Military Institute. Married. Grows tobacco at Willow Creek Landing, a plantation on the James River south of Richmond. House and lands inherited from paternal grandmother, the former Althea Alexandra Palmer, only daughter of a Tidewater planter family.

Althea Louise, firstborn daughter; attended finishing school in Charleston. Married Nathan Braedon and lives in Richmond. One daughter, Noelle.

Guy Patrick, second son; graduated from University of Virginia. Reads law in a great-uncle's law practice in Charlottesville.

Russell Eamon, died in infancy.

Palmer William, youngest son; attending VMI.

Coralie Elizabeth, died in infancy.

Leigh Alexandra, third daughter; attended finishing school in Charleston.

Blythe Lucinda (Lucy), youngest daughter; attending finishing school in Richmond.

Thisbe Anne, mistress of Willow Creek Landing; wife and mother, and formerly Thisbe Anne Sinclair of Philadelphia.

Stuart Leslie, only son of Stuart James and Thisbe Anne.

Cynthia Amelia, only daughter of Stuart James and Thisbe Anne.

Stephen, majordomo at Travers Hill; arrived from Charleston with his young mistress, Beatrice Amelia, when she wed Stuart Travers.

Jolie, maid, cook, and confidante to everyone at Travers Hill; married to Stephen.

Sweet John, head groom at Travers Hill and son of Stephen and Jolie.

Braedon Family of Virginia

Noble Steward Braedon, master of Royal Bay Manor; gentleman farmer and breeder of Thoroughbreds.

Euphemia (Effie) Margaret, *née* Merton, mistress of Royal Bay Manor; wife and mother, formerly of River Oaks Farm.

Nathan Douglas, firstborn son; graduate of Princeton. Lives in Richmond, where he practices law and represents his home district in the state legislature. Married Althea Louise, *née* Travers. One daughter, Noelle.

Adam Merton, second son; expelled from VMI. Lived with relatives in South Carolina and managed to graduate from South Carolina College before leaving on an extended European tour. Part owner in a coastal shipping firm.

Julia Elayne, only daughter; attended finishing school in Charleston with best friend, Leigh Travers.

Braedon Family of New Mexico Territory

Nathaniel Reynolds Braedon, younger brother of Noble; left Virginia to make his fortune in the West. Settled in the New Mexico Territory. Married, widowed, remarried. Raises horses, cattle, and sheep at Royal Rivers, ranch where he lives with second family.

Fionnuala Elissa, *née* Darcy, first wife of Nathaniel Braedon.

Shannon Malveen, firstborn daughter of Nathaniel and Fionnuala. Kidnapped by Comanches when she was twelve years old. Shannon's Comanche name: She-With-Eyes-Of-The-Captured-Sky.

Neil Darcy, firstborn son of Nathaniel and Fionnuala; kidnapped by Comanches when eight years of age. When fourteen, rescued by father. Sent East for schooling. Graduated from Yale, traveled in Europe. Owns land, and the original homestead of Braedon family, Riovado, northwest of Royal Rivers. Neil's Comanche name: Sun Dagger.

Camilla Elizabeth, *née* St. Amand, second wife of Nathaniel. St. Amand family fled slave uprising on Santo Domingo and settled in Charleston.

Justin St. Amand, firstborn son of Camilla and Nathaniel; attending VMI and staying with aunt and uncle at Royal Bay.

Lys Helene, only daughter born to Camilla and Nathaniel; attended finishing school in Charleston for a year before returning to New Mexico.

Gilbert Rene, youngest son of Camilla and Nathaniel.

Serena Ofelia, wife of Neil Braedon; eldest daughter of Alfonso and Mercedes Jacobs, nearest neighbors to Royal Rivers.

Prelude
Territory of New Mexico—
Early Autumn 1859

O wild West Wind, thou breath of Autumn's being,
Thou, from whose unseen presence the leaves dead
Are driven, like ghosts from an enchanter fleeing…
Percy Bysshe Shelley

A Land of Legend

Close to the sun in lonely lands.

Alfred, Lord Tennyson

THERE WAS A TIME WHEN ONLY *THE PEOPLE* ROAMED THE enchanted lands of the setting sun. High atop mesas that rose in majestic solitude out of the dust of canyon and desert below, these children of the sun prayed to the gods. Corn ripened golden in the sun. Clouds rained shimmering silver upon the earth.

A dagger of sun striking the earth through stone slabs marked the changing of the seasons, celebrating the coming of the spring equinox and forewarning of the winter solstice. When darkness fell across the land there was no fear, for the myriad fires glowing softly in the night sky watched over the children until the morning star beckoned the sun to spread its enveloping cloak of light and warmth. The children prospered and their cities became great. They were the Makers of Magic. Their magic brought the clouds and the rains and turned the earth green.

One day the Sun Father and his sister, the Moon, frowned down upon them, and the painted maiden's chants to the god of rain went unanswered. The golden-edged clouds were a reflection of the Sun Father's pleasure, but now when the children cast their eyes upward, the towering clouds grew dark with the thundering wrath of the angry gods.

Ceremonial dances and sacrificial rites to the gods were held in the sacred caves. But the chanting *kachinas*, the masked spirits, could not protect them from ill fortune. The Plumed Serpent and the Corn Father, the spirits of mountain, water, and wind, and all the lesser deities remained unappeased. Soon the despairing children felt the displeasure of the Great Earth Mother. Drought and famine and death followed, and the prayers and drumbeats, the rattles and bells of the frightened shamans stilled.

There was only the lonely echoing of the wind.

Where once the favored ones grew strong and mighty, the wolf now stalked the canyons and the coyote scavenged through the abandoned villages. The eagle and the hawk soared high above the forsaken cliff dwellings.

Despoblado. The desolate land. Unpeopled and treeless.

From the High Plains the nomadic tribes—Navajo, Apache, Ute, Comanche—raided the children of the Ancient Ones, who had scattered across the desolate lands. But the children survived. With the coming of each season they grew stronger, and gathered together along the banks of the great river that flowed from the heart of the snowcapped peaks of the north and disappeared into the wastelands to the south. The valleys were fertile and their corn grew tall and green under the warmth of the sun. They prayed to the gods and their villages prospered. The weavers and potters, the masters of silver and turquoise, the farmers and hunters, and the *kachinas*, who kept the old myths alive deep within the *kivas*, knew again the almightiness of the wise, life-giving spirit that had guided them on so long a journey.

But it was prophesied that one day bearded warriors in gilded armor and riding strange beasts that caused the earth to tremble beneath them would appear magically out of the desert to the south. *The People* would once again know despair, and conquered, their gods would be lost to them. But the legend of the conquerors, as well as the myth of the fair-haired who would come from the east with the rising of the sun, had almost been forgotten when the *conquistadores* crossed the Sierra Madre and the deserts of Chihuahua and Sonora.

The unexplored lands of the north beckoned them to greater conquest. The gold-rich kingdoms of the Incas, Mayas, and Aztecs had been conquered. Moctezuma was dead and his great island-city, Tenochtitlan, looted of its fabulous riches and heritage, was destroyed. There was a fire in the blood of these *conquistadores*—a flame kept burning bright by the ancient legends.

Quivira, a land where golden ships with silken sails were rowed upon a great river of gold. The people ate off plates of gold and silver and were serenaded by golden bells singing in the wind.

The Seven Cities of Gold, a kingdom where the streets were paved in gold and emeralds sparkled above every golden door. Surely this was where the "gilded man" of fable, who had thus far eluded capture, ruled as king.

El Dorado, an Indian chieftain so wealthy that when crowned before his people, his loyal subjects anointed his skin with perfumed oils and covered him in a coat of gold dust that he washed away in a sacred lake.

With the gold and silver, emeralds and pearls of earlier legends bringing them wealth and fame, these adventurers continued to believe in lost cities and hidden treasures just out of reach. Their lust grew feverish after a party of shipwrecked explorers, who had wandered for years through the wilderness of the great northern lands, spoke of having seen seven great cities that glowed golden beneath the sun. Among those survivors was an ebony-skinned Moorish slave. His name was Estevanico. Estéban and the others told wondrous stories of golden-hued, many-storied houses with greenish-blue stones bordering each door. Their vivid descriptions of all they had seen on their fateful journey across the unknown lands were intoxicating and conjured up fantastic imaginings in the minds of their listeners who hungered for the glory of Cortés and Pizarro, the greatest of the *conquistadores*.

Soon a party of adventurers, guided by the Moor, went in search of this fabled kingdom of gold. They returned to the seven legendary cities accompanied by a gray-robed Franciscan monk, Fray Marcos, who went in search of lost souls. But they were met with hostility by the wild tribes of the north. The Moor met his death in Hawikuh, one of the seven cities, but the friar escaped, returning to Mexico to tell of the greatness of the golden cities he had seen from afar. Francisco Vasquez de Coronado, governor of Nueva Galicia, a northern province in Mexico, listened to this tale and dreamed of greater glory in the unconquered land now known as *Cibola*, and where he would find the Seven Cities of Gold. With great expectations, Coronado led an expedition of over two hundred horsemen glinting with armor, and followed on foot by soldiers armed with crossbows, pikes, and harquebuses. Indians, friendly to their Spanish conquerors, and teams of mules carrying the provisions and cannon into this promising land of riches trailed close behind.

Coronado never found the fabled golden cities or the fabulous treasure of the gilded man.

He discovered a new land for Spanish conquest and dominion. From the sunbaked adobe pueblos along the fertile valleys of the Rio Grande to the snowcapped *sierras* and great *cañons* of the northwest, to the grassy plateaus of the High Plains rising far into the northeast, across the burning white sands to the west and the vast sweep of prairie and rolling hills to the east this *despoblado* was claimed in the name of the Spanish crown.

The sound of mission bells replaced the shamans' chanting, and church spires rose beneath the sun in holy challenge to the heathen gods. The cities, Taos high in the mountains to the north, Santa Cruz de la Cañada, Santa Fe de San Francisco, Albuquerque, and El Paso del Norte bordering the southern wilderness, were peopled by the children of God and grew prosperous. The soldiers stationed in the *presidios* protected the children of God from the wild tribes that roamed the wastelands, and the *ranchos* knew no boundaries as sheep and cattle grazed the fertile grasslands and valleys.

The seasons changed and the ancient myth of the fair-haired, long forgotten by most, came to pass as Spain's empire in the New World crumbled and a fledgling nation along a distant eastern shore began to spread its wings westward toward the wealth and promise of unexplored lands.

Surrounded by desert, prairie, and mountain, the Territory of New Mexico had remained isolated. Mexico now claimed sovereignty over the territories north of the Rio Grande. Separated by endless desert and impenetrable jungle, the trading caravans made the long, arduous trek only twice a year between the annual fairs in Chihuahua and Taos. Imported from the Old World via Veracruz, a port city on the Gulf of Mexico, goods from Mexico were exorbitant. The New Mexican traders were left with little profit and the colonists with even less satisfaction by the time the caravan left Taos on its return journey.

But to the east, beyond the Pecos and across the Staked Plain that Coronado had seen darkened by herds of buffalo, from the wide waters of the Mississippi came the French traders, eager to barter. In the mountains where the Rio Grande and her sister rivers began as crystalline streams the waters were full of beaver. In exchange, the French brought guns and powder and liquor to trade with the Indians for the right to trap and hunt on the slopes without fear of attack.

Following in their footsteps came the Americans, exploring the lands newly purchased from France. News of this wondrous territory west of the Red River traveled fast. It was rich in furs and hides, and in Santa Fe there was a profitable market for textiles and dry goods. An enterprising Yankee trader could make a fortune. From Ohio and Missouri and farther east they came. Across the grassy plains of Kansas to Fort Dodge, they crossed the big bend in the river and followed the Arkansas's course toward the mountains rising starkly in the distance, and from that rocky terrain into the Territory of New Mexico. The heavily laden packhorses bringing manufactured goods for trade were replaced by wagons groaning under loads of towering freight and drawn by teams of well-muscled oxen and sturdy mules.

Soon the great wagon trains were leaving from all along the Missouri River. Franklin, Arrow Rock, Fort Osage, Independence, Westport, and other small towns that had basked lazily in the sun were now crowded with strangers. The adventurers, traders, and trappers, hunters, mule-skinners, and merchants were eager to travel the trail that crossed the plains despite the dangers. Beyond might lie death, or great wealth to be found in the lands of the western wilderness. Disease, hunger, thirst, violent storms, flash floods, prairie fires, and the misfortune of accident awaited. They would be preyed upon by marauding tribes of savages that roamed the wilds, with only the soldiers back at Fort Leavenworth for protection until, if they were fortunate enough, they reached western Kansas and came under the protection of the guns of the newly built Fort Larned.

Council Grove, with its shady groves of oak, hickory, walnut, and other valuable timber, was the last outpost of civilization. It was here that the wagons began the westward trek that might take over four months to cross the inhospitable plains. By the time they reached Cottonwood Creek, many would have wished to return as they gazed at the treeless plains that seemed to stretch beyond the horizon.

Upon reaching the Arkansas, they followed the river westward, moving ever closer to Fort Larned. Before they reached that safe haven, they had to pass Pawnee Rock, where many a train had been ambushed.

Miles of endless prairie stretched ahead before they even sighted the hazy outline of the distant mountain range barring their path, but at the foot of the mountains was Bent's Fort, sanctuary for those who'd made it safely across the plains. Yet, for those grown weary of the trail, a cutoff that would shorten the journey beckoned to the south across the Cimarron. But the route also crossed perilous desert where lack of water and threat of Indian attack was an ever-present danger.

From Bent's Fort the train traveled through Raton Pass. The long journey was nearing an end as they entered the Territory of New Mexico along this mountainous route and were welcomed with celebration and cheerful cries of *"Los Americanos!"* in the plaza at Santa Fe.

While this enterprise was opening up a valuable trading route between the New Mexico Territory and the ever-expanding American nation, Texas had declared and won its independence from Mexico and was anxious to establish its authority over the lands and people east of the Rio Grande, its western boundary. Mexico was becoming increasingly nervous about the influx of American citizens into its territory, and when the United States accepted Texas, their former territory, into the Union as a state, hostility between the two nations increased. Soon, with boundaries being disputed and blood shed on both sides of the Rio Grande, war was declared by the United States.

Mexico was defeated and her territories north of the Rio Grande were annexed by the United States. The trail that had been opened between Santa Fe and this emerging nation by the early traders became a busy highway between the two cultures as more Americans braved the dangerous crossing and dreamed of making their fortunes in this wild land west of the plains.

Despoblado.

Sangre de Cristo. Blood of Christ.

The mountain range was bathed in an unearthly glow from the bloodred of the sunset. Above, the sky was molten copper.

The burning sun sank lower behind the mesa, sending a shaft of golden light across the red-streaked rock of the deepest canyon and gilding into gold the yellow of a sagebrush-covered plain. The bluish-green slopes of the mountain range darkened into purple as dusk fell across the eastern horizon.

A lone rider made his way down from the high grassy plateau, the big bay he rode picking its way carefully along the loose shale of the narrow trail, but the horse's hooves slipped precariously close to the edge of the cliff, sending a shower of rocks tumbling into the canyon far below.

Cañon del Malhadado. Canyon of the Unfortunate.

The scent of pine and spruce lent a sweet pungency to the air. Below, on the lower slopes, the aspens were like brightly burning flames among the thick stand of evergreen. The rider tracked the mountain stream winding through the forested valley, his searching gaze catching the silvered glint of water through the cottonwoods bordering the ravine. He followed its meandering path until it disappeared into a narrow canyon; when it reappeared it would be no more than a trickle through the mesquite of a dusty arroyo in the scrubland of the foothills.

A distant rumble of thunder disturbed the silence. Glancing back at the ragged peaks of the mountains towering behind him, the rider knew that by sundown the storm rolling in from the High Plains would bring rain or even the first snowfall of the season.

The rider's gloved hands tightened on the reins as he caught the sudden movement of a shadow traveling swiftly across the land. He glanced upward, his eyes narrowed against the blinding brilliance of the sun as he watched the soaring, gliding flight of a hawk on the wing. Silently it dropped from the sky, diving down into the thicket of piñon and juniper on the lower slopes, striking like a dagger from the sun. A moment later the hawk was climbing high into the sky, its hapless prey caught in its talons. The hawk, its great golden-tipped wings outspread, flew back into the sun it had been spawned from, toward the high rocks of the mesa where it had made its nest among the ancient ruins.

The rider's buckskin-clad knees touched the bay's flanks with gentle pressure and they continued down the trail.

Suddenly he pulled sharply on the reins. He waited, his narrowed gaze searching for something that eluded him. Then he urged his mount forward again.

It had been only the lonely echoing of the wind through the canyon.

There was no one. Not even ghosts. Dust rising beneath the bay's hooves, the rider rode toward the darkening skies, feeling the *despoblado* surrounding him.

Part One

Virginia—Summertime 1860

Eternal summer gilds them yet,
But all, except their sun, is set.

George Gordon, Lord Byron

One

Olympus, where they say there is an abode of the gods, ever unchanging: it is neither shaken by winds nor ever wet with rain, nor does snow come near it, but clear weather spreads cloudless about it, and a white radiance stretches above it.

Homer

CAROLINA YELLOW JESSAMINE TRAILED OVER THE WHITE, split-railed fence bordering the green pastures of Travers Hill. The sweet-scented jessamine was a favorite of Beatrice Amelia Travers, mistress of Travers Hill. Beatrice Amelia was one of the Leighs of South Carolina, and jessamine and azaleas, benne wafers, and the daily ritual of sipping her syllabub were comforting reminders to Beatrice Amelia of her girlhood days in Charleston.

Fortunately her family enjoyed chicken curry with rice, another of Beatrice Amelia's favorites, because they had the dish every Sunday, along with crab soup, honey and cinnamon-candied yams, corn fritters, baked ham, garden stuffs, and brandied peaches. Except for Mr. Travers's bourbon pecan cake, which was always prepared with ceremonial care the afternoon before, Sunday dessert was subject to the seasons. The Travers children, however, had always been very fond of Jolie's caramel custard, which was a treat for year-round enjoyment. But on this particular Sunday late in July, blackberry cobbler had been planned for the family's delectation.

Beatrice Amelia Travers was also very fond of roses. That was why the garden before the entrance to the house had been planted entirely with roses. Beatrice Amelia was especially fond of her *Rosa gallica aurelianensis*, one of her prized French roses. But it was an old damask rose, lost amongst the China, sweetbriar, and cabbage roses, with its heady scent of cloves that lent such a spicy sweetness to the air when one entered Travers Hill.

Travers Hill sat upon a wooded knoll overlooking the river

and was a pleasant day's carriage ride from Charlottesville. The curving lane swept up a gentle slope from the river where sweet bay and loblolly grew wild with the willows along the banks. Scattered through the landscaped grounds, the sourwood was heavy with white blossoms, and the camellias and gardenias were in full bloom. A field of sun-bronzed daylilies stretched toward the blue-green pastureland where blooded mares and their foals grazed peacefully in the shade of a gnarled oak. Even the long row of stables, the heart of Travers Hill, showed little sign of activity this sleepy afternoon. A solitary, stately chestnut with a canopy of leafy green branches divided the narrow road halfway up the knoll. One of the lanes led to the sawmill and lumberyard just upriver, and the other curved up to the house and around to the big barns, servants' quarters, and coach house behind.

The lower slopes to the east were planted with orchards, the fruit turning amber, scarlet, and purple as peaches, pears, apples, and plums ripened under the summer sun. The valley floor that surrounded Travers Hill like a sea of green was lush with cultivated fields of crops. The master of Travers Hill had proudly predicted a bountiful harvest this year.

Westward, toward the Blue Ridge Mountains, wooded slopes and tiny hamlets dotted the rolling hill country. The Travers family's nearest neighbors were downriver at Royal Bay Manor, home of the Braedons, and the finest example of Georgian architecture outside of Richmond. The ties between the two families had become even closer since the eldest Travers daughter, Althea Louise, had wed Nathan Douglas, the firstborn son of the Braedons and the first in line to inherit Royal Bay.

The Travers family lived in an unpretentious style; the manor house being of modest proportions, the brick facade mellowed with time. The house was tastefully decorated in a comfortable manner that seemed to welcome visitors. Which was perhaps why Travers Hill was always filled with family and friends, and no stranger had ever been turned away from the emerald green door with its pineapple-shaped brass knocker. A row of green-shuttered windows flanked the entrance and overlooked the covered veranda, the slender posts marching along the front thickly entwined with rambler roses much to Beatrice Amelia's satisfaction.

It was in the shade of the veranda that part of the Travers family now sat in companionable relaxation and casual conversation, the gentlemen enjoying their cooling mint juleps, while the ladies indulged in a pitcher of sweet lemonade and lace cookies. It was a moment of peace before the week's busy preparations for the celebrations that were to begin on Friday with the sixteenth birthday party for Blythe Lucinda, youngest of the Travers. Althea Louise and her husband, Nathan, and their only daughter, six-year-old Noelle, had driven over from Royal Bay that morning in order to spend Sunday with her family. They had arrived two days earlier from Richmond, where Nathan had a law practice and just this past year had been elected to represent his home district in the state legislature. They planned to spend the week visiting between Travers Hill and Royal Bay, dividing their time equally between the two families—the Braedons especially anxious to spend time with their only granddaughter.

On the morrow, Stuart James, the eldest Travers son, and his wife, Thisbe, and their two children, Leslie and Cynthia, were due from Willow Creek Landing, the family's plantation south of Richmond, and fronting the James River. Unless, of course, they stayed over in Richmond and accompanied Maribel Samuelson and her party on Tuesday. That was when Maribel, Stuart Travers's sister, and her husband, J. Kirkfield, were supposed to leave Richmond for Travers Hill. Family and friends were expected any day from Charleston and Savannah, and the friends and neighbors from Charlottesville and the surrounding county would start arriving during the latter part of the week; and half of those coming on Saturday just for the horse auction, followed by the race on Sunday.

And sometime midweek, Palmer William, the youngest Travers son, was due home, and he might have half his class from school accompanying him as he had at Christmastime, much to his speechless mother's dismay. And the Traverses' in-laws from Royal Bay, especially Euphemia, Nathan's mother, who was also Maribel's best friend from childhood, were likely to be dropping in and out all week. Euphemia always had a special recipe she wanted to share. All of these thoughts and far more disturbing ones—concerning the menus for each meal, the dresses and gowns that should have been laundered by now and hadn't, where everyone would be put up for the week, and who was talking to whom and should or shouldn't be seated next to each other in the seating arrangements, and had Stephen polished all the silver—were racing through the mistress of Travers Hill's mind and belying the outwardly serene expression on her face as she tended to her sewing.

Beatrice Amelia was very carefully stitching a delicate pink rose on one of her fine lawn handkerchiefs, which she intended to tuck inside the lace-edged sleeve of her favorite rose pink foulard gown on Wednesday. Her pale blond head with its heavy, netted chignon was bent low over her embroidery as she examined her workmanship with a critical eye.

Mother of eight children, the eldest twenty-six, the youngest fifteen, with only two not having survived infancy, Beatrice Amelia still retained much of the beauty that had made her a famous belle of Charleston in the thirties. Her flawless profile had been the inspiration for many an artist when creating a likeness to grace a cameo, and many of her dearest friends claimed Beatrice Amelia could still wear her first ball gown if she so chose; although, privately, each thought she must have let out the waist at least an inch or two, surely?

"When is your cousin supposed to arrive, Nathan?" Stuart Travers, master of Travers Hill, asked, accepting another mint julep from the tray being proffered by the majordomo. "Ah, that's nice, Stephen," he told the ebony-skinned man, who'd been standing quietly beside him. "Nobody, and that means nobody on this good earth, and certainly not in the Old Dominion, makes a julep better than Stephen. Takes a fine, steady hand and a sharp mind to mix it this tasty."

"Not too sweet then, sir?" Stephen asked, his words coming as slow and rich as blackstrap molasses. There was just a hint of a French accent, which startled those who didn't know that he'd come to Travers Hill from Charleston when Beatrice Amelia had come as a young bride. He and his wife, Jolie, had been given to the young mistress by her father as part of her dowry. Stephen was the son of Jean Jacques, the most highly prized majordomo in all of Charleston, and to part with

Stephen, who'd been trained by Jean Jacques, had cost Beatrice Amelia's father dearly.

Colonel Leigh hadn't really minded parting with Jolie, a mulattress. The colonel had never been easy around her. Bad blood. That's what came of an African mother and a Cherokee father, the colonel had predicted, for Jolie, tall and long-necked, carried herself with a queenly dignity that at times bordered on insolence—as if she knew something he didn't. And more than once he'd sworn that Jolie had been at the root of the disquiet in his home. He'd never had any trouble until she'd come under his roof with her voodoo charms and chanting to strange spirits, and when she'd been baptized a Christian she'd become even more eccentric in her beliefs. But Stephen hadn't minded his wife's oddities, claiming he'd never shake the fever from a love potion she'd given him. But Colonel Leigh knew Jolie would die before she'd allow any harm to befall her young mistress, having cared for his daughter since Beatrice Amelia had been in the cradle. And so with mixed emotions the colonel had bid farewell to his only daughter and one of his most prized slaves, sending them into the wilds of Virginia with Jolie.

"Neil said sometime this week," Nathan replied, declining another julep. "He wrote in his letter he hoped to leave Santa Fe by the end of June. It's a long way, and even Neil might meet up with the unexpected."

"The crossing from England is safer, I'd wager. I hope he makes it in time for our celebrations. Palmer William is due to arrive on Wednesday or Thursday, and I would imagine he'll be riding down with young Justin Braedon; they've become good friends at school. He'll probably be over here at Travers Hill as much as with his cousins at Royal Bay. I'd bet we've seen as much of young Julia as your folks have since she and Leigh returned from school. Never heard the house so full of silly giggling or seen it so crowded with beaus," Mr. Travers said with a sigh of exasperation. "Never thought I'd have to introduce myself to strangers in my own home. Of course, I'm not the one those young bucks are interested in since Leigh came sashaying home from Charleston, and a saucier and sassier young minx I've yet to meet. Should never have let her leave Travers Hill," he grumbled beneath his breath, wondering what had happened to the sweet little girl who'd been fond of climbing trees, riding bareback, and going fishing with her father on a hot summer's afternoon.

"Now, now, dear," Beatrice Amelia interrupted, quite pleased with the results of the Charleston finishing school. "Leigh Alexandra was quite incorrigible *before* we sent her away to school. She is exactly what a proper young lady should be *now* that she has been trained in the proper pursuits for young ladies. I am truly beginning to have the highest hopes for her."

Mr. Travers took a long swallow of his mint julep, emptying the tall glass, his ruddy-complexioned face becoming ruddier. Damn, he'd hardly recognized the furbeloved female who'd greeted him at the door of Travers Hill when she and her mother had returned from Charleston. Surely Beatrice Amelia had brought home the wrong girl. "I suppose this Neil Braedon has planned his trip to Virginia in order to see his brother and bring any news from home?" he commented politely, thinking it would be good to see his youngest son again. At least he could take some pleasure in the change in *that* member of the Travers family. Since they'd sent the boy away to the Virginia Military Institute at Lexington, he'd seemed to grow into a man overnight, not that he had much beard to show for it yet. It had caused much consternation for his mother, since Palmer William, with his fair hair, soft blue eyes, and gentle ways, had always been his mother's favorite.

"Justin won't need to hear news from home. Aunt Camilla, his mother, is one of my mother's dear friends and an untiring correspondent. Neil and Justin would have nothing to discuss other than family, and Neil has never considered himself part of my uncle's second family. I feel sorry for Neil sometimes," Nathan said, frowning slightly. "He seems so alone, although he makes it damned hard—forgive me, ladies—to get close to him. Of course, from what I've heard from my father, Neil always has been a loner. Except for his sister, Shannon, who was always there for him, he has never had anyone who cared about him. She almost raised Neil by herself, especially when Uncle Nathaniel would have nothing to do with him. Their mother died giving birth to Neil. It's a pity, seeing how

Uncle Nathaniel and Neil are so much alike. If only Shannon had lived. I think that was the final blow that caused the rift to widen between them. And then when Uncle Nathaniel remarried and had another family it left Neil outside again. Now I think about it, I believe it was my own dear mother and Maribel Samuelson who introduced Uncle Nathaniel to his second wife. The poor man didn't stand a chance, being a wealthy widower and having all of the eligible young females thrust in front of him as if at auction."

"Sounds like my busybody sister, always sticking her nose where it shouldn't be. Think Neil would be interested in our little auction? Might do them prairie ponies good to have some pure blood running in their veins."

"He might be interested. Neil has a good eye for horseflesh and he's interested in improving the breed," Nathan allowed. "Of course, he might claim that some of our Thoroughbreds at Royal Bay actually came from good Spanish stock, and that is why our Virginia bloods are so famous today."

"Nonsense," Mr. Travers said, eyeing Nathan over the rim of his glass.

"Indeed, sir. I believe your own grandfather bought Andalusians, bloods from fine Arabian and Barb stock, from the same French trader and Pawnees in the Santa Fe trade that my great-grandfather did. Patrick Henry was governor and even back then he knew to look to the West. Yes, sir, mighty fine horse trader too. My cousin will, of course, want to see what Royal Bay has to offer first. Neil still rides one of Royal Bay's best."

"Naturally," Mr. Travers agreed, with a wide understanding grin that didn't fool anyone. "Patrick Henry was also a lawyer," he added softly.

Squinting, for she would only deign to wear her spectacles in private, Beatrice Amelia looked up from her embroidery, her mind still on the first part of their conversation. "Justin Braedon and Palmer William? Well, I just hope he's more civilized than that brother of his or I don't want him having anything to do with my son," she declared, remembering the other Braedon who had visited his relatives at Royal Bay years ago. "Surprised any of us still have our hair," she said, frowning at one of her stitches as she held the cloth up to the light. "I declare, I nearly miscarried because of the trouble you, Nathan Douglas, who should have known better; that brother of yours, Adam Merton, who will never know any better; and, most especially, that uncivilized cousin of yours got involved in that summer. Still have nightmares, I do indeed, remembering that bloodcurdling howling you Braedon boys all used to scream at the top of your lungs."

"Ah, the war cry," Nathan murmured with remembered pleasure.

"A war cry? What is that, Papa?" Noelle Braedon demanded, her brown eyes wide with interest. "What does it sound like? Like a baby? Like Leslie when he doesn't get what he wants?" she asked, remembering her young cousin's constant bawling at Eastertime.

Althea Louise, who'd been reading to her young daughter from an illustrated book of fairy tales, looked imploringly at her husband, silently urging him to hold his tongue. Except for her brown eyes, inherited from her father, she bore a strong resemblance to her mother, possessing the same fair hair and delicate features. She need not have worried, though, for Nathan would do nothing to upset his lovely wife, or his mother-in-law—and certainly not by demonstrating what a war cry was to his imitative daughter.

"Neil is not a savage, Mrs. Travers, even though he spent most of his childhood with Indians," Nathan said with a smile as he defended his cousin. "He has too much of my uncle in him."

"Apaches, weren't they?" Mr. Travers asked, taking another mint julep for himself and his son-in-law from the tray being held steadily at his side by the ever-patient Stephen.

Nathan nodded his thanks as he accepted the tall glass and stirred the topaz-tinted liquid with a sprig of mint. "Comanche, sir. They kidnapped Neil and Shannon when he was eight and Shannon was about twelve."

"Heathen savagery!" Beatrice Amelia murmured, jerking impatiently on a silken thread that had tangled before she bit it neatly in two with a quick snap of her teeth.

"His sister died in captivity, didn't she?" Mr. Travers questioned.

"Yes, years before my uncle rescued Neil," Nathan responded. "Old Uncle Nat never gave up. He hounded those

Comanche through every canyon in the territory, chasing them back into Texas, then across the border into Mexico, then back into the territory, until even they began to believe they were being chased by their own devil gods, and finally they abandoned Neil, leaving him wandering alone across a desert called *Jornada del Muerto* in the southern part of the territory. It means Deadman's Passage, and I gather it is a place even more desolate than the Cimarron. I remember my Aunt Camilla—she married Uncle Nat during the time Neil was held captive—thought he'd brought home a savage when he returned to the ranch with his son. Neil looked like a young Comanche brave except for his long braid of blond hair. She said he was wearing only a breechcloth and buckskin leggings. He was as brown as an Indian, and had a golden eagle feather and some barbaric charms stuck in his hair. He had only a knife to defend himself, which, apparently, he had, using it on several members of the search party before Uncle Nat took it away from him."

"Doesn't surprise me any," Mr. Travers said. "Nathaniel was wild just like that. As a young'un he was always out hunting in the hills, even got as far as Tennessee one time before his father sent out a search party looking for him—he was only ten and he claimed he wasn't lost. Never knew anyone who could shoot as straight as he did. Nearly got himself killed in five or six duels, though.

"He always puzzled me. Said dueling wasn't challenging enough for him. Scandalous behavior for a gentleman, even then, but Nathaniel was a hot-tempered young buck with nothing better to do since your father was the eldest and would inherit Royal Bay. Never thought he'd settle down with one woman. The ladies wouldn't leave him alone. I suspect, even though they claimed they'd strike his name from the family Bible if he did it, that his folks were rather relieved when he headed west, bound for Texas, for a little adventurin'. Never was quite the same around here after he left," Mr. Travers said with a sad grin that quickly became a deep laugh. "Now you mention it, I remember Nathaniel always was fascinated by those wild Spanish ponies his grandfather bought. Or, perhaps, it was the land they raced through free as the wind that intrigued him the most. So you think your cousin Neil inherited the worst from both Nathaniel and the Comanche?"

Nathan shrugged good-naturedly, lazily running a big hand through his dark brown hair. He was a large man but managed to move with a quiet deliberateness that often disguised the alertness in his keen gray eyes. His patient expression, which sometimes seemed to border on lazy indolence, had often misled an opposing attorney or difficult witness in court. "I'm not certain, sir, that there is much difference between the Comanche and Nathaniel Reynolds Braedon when he has a grievance. My father says his younger brother is the most hardheaded Braedon of the lot. He always did what he pleased and was unforgiving when people crossed him. But he had a good sense of humor, could tell a joke that would have your sides splitting, and if he looked kindly upon you, as he did his first wife and Shannon, he was a very warm and loving man. A devil with gold curls, my father always called him. But after his first wife died, he changed. Never smiled except for Shannon. Apparently she was the living image of her mother and he adored her. I'm afraid he always blamed Neil for his mother's death. Couldn't stand looking at his own son. He was a constant reminder of his loss. It was always Shannon he was determined to find when she and Neil were kidnapped. That is why he never gave up looking for them. He wanted Shannon back, and then he found Neil, not little Shannon. He did not rejoice in bringing Neil back home to Royal Rivers, even though he was his own flesh and blood. Uncle Nat believed he had lost everything."

"I remember Fionnuala Darcy. She was a real beauty. Nathaniel was back at Royal Bay, his first visit home since heading to Texas. She was visiting with friends in Charlottesville. She was from Boston. I remember thinking she had a mighty funny accent despite how pretty she was. Of course I was rather young to appreciate fully a beautiful woman's charms."

"And what exactly did this Fionnuala Darcy look like, dear?" Beatrice Amelia inquired, interested to know what her husband considered to be "a real beauty."

"Midnight black hair, and the brightest blue eyes you could

imagine. Just like a slice of the sky," her husband responded, unshaken. "Of course," he continued diplomatically, having taken note of the slender, tapered fingers with their well-cared-for nails tapping against the arm of the chair in growing irritation, "I've always preferred dark blue eyes. They have mysterious depths, like the sea, or perhaps like the hidden fires in a sapphire draped around a lovely woman's throat."

Beatrice Amelia smiled slightly, but not enough to warm her dark blue eyes. "I never knew you were so poetic, dear. And after over a quarter of a century of marriage, here I am just now finding out that you are a poet."

"Justin is a fine young man. I've heard from several of his professors at VMI and they are quite impressed with his academic record as well as his qualities of leadership," Nathan said, changing the subject.

"Do you think he'll continue with a military career? Being born in the territories, he would have the advantage over other officers and he could use that to get a good post in the West. That's where you make your name and your promotion nowadays—Indian fighting," Mr. Travers remarked, wondering if his wife knew that Palmer William had been thinking about joining the army when he finished his cadet training.

"I don't know," Nathan admitted frankly. "He has mentioned something to me about going into the law, which, of course, I urged him to do. No self-respecting lawyer would do anything else. After all, the law is a splendid profession, especially as a springboard into other professions."

"Like politics?"

"I speak only from very limited experience," Nathan deferred with a smile.

"I'm expecting to see you run for senator next, Nathan. I'll back you, son. Call in some old debts to make sure you get the nod from Richmond," his father-in-law promised. "We need some steady voices in Congress now that the Republicans have nominated this Abraham Lincoln as their presidential candidate and the Democrats couldn't even come up with one. Half of the delegates walked out of the convention in Charleston, and I don't feel any easier about what came out of their reconvening in Baltimore. The party is split, and this Breckenridge, although he was vice president, is a Kentuckian. I don't know too much about this Douglas fella, except that I like his ideas on letting the people of the states and even the territories decide whether or not they want to vote for or against slavery. Know things are changing. Travers Hill has very few slaves and soon I'll see that there are none. I've always found the selling and buying of human beings to be barbarous, so I won't do it," he admitted. "Of course, I don't grow cotton, tobacco, or even rice at Travers Hill, so 'tis easy enough for me to speak thusly. All I need are enough hands to bring in the crops we do grow for our own table, and I hire out for most of that. I raise horses, Nathan. That's my business. I'm blessed to have Sweet John handling my beauties, or I'd be paying an Irishman double just to have him training my bloods. But that would be paltry compared to what my grandfather would've had to pay to get his tobacco picked at Willow Creek."

"I understand, sir. I am deeply concerned about this peculiar institution of ours, and yet, I cannot condemn my own brethren because of the beliefs that have been necessary to the survival of our way of life. I believe that, eventually, we will right this wrong, but unless we are given the time, and left alone to change, then there will be irrevocable harm done. Indeed, sir, I fear the worst," Nathan admitted, voicing aloud for the first time his most nightmarish thoughts. "I'm beginning to doubt if we will ever be able to settle peacefully this question of the disposition of the territories. It is the burning match, sir, to the powder keg. I've listened to the voices on both sides becoming angrier and angrier, growing more unreasonable in their demands every day. Armageddon will be the outcome if the ardor of some isn't cooled soon. I wish there were more who were at least willing to talk about change."

"I am not optimistic, Nathan. I expect to hear any day now that South Carolina has seceded from the Union over this question of whether to keep the territories free soil or let a man take his property, including slaves, into them without fear of breaking the law or having his property confiscated. I can understand both sides. There were a lot of good Southerners who fought in the war and helped win those new lands from Mexico, and now they are to be denied their rights because of a few hotheaded Northerners. Trouble indeed, Nathan, when you have a Senator from Massachusetts beaten over the head with a stick by a Representative from South Carolina who didn't like his abolitionist talk. Not surprising to find this madman John Brown raiding and killing when that goes on in the Senate by supposedly sane men. Of course, some things never seem to change, since I recall that this was the very same talk in Charleston even when I was courting Mrs. Travers. Let's see, that was about the time of the Purchase, wasn't it?" he said with a wink.

"I believe, sir, you refer to my great-grandmother's time," she said.

"My pardon, ma'am. Of course, I do remember quite vividly that there always has been a Leigh, perhaps even the old colonel, with one of the loudest voices in the crowd calling for secession," Mr. Travers declared. "But then you Leighs always have been a rebellious lot. First to call for poor mad King George's bewigged head, I believe."

"Actually, sir, I believe there were several prominent Leighs who were Tories, and that is why we have cousins in England today. However, that is beside the point. I declare, all I ever hear anymore is this abolitionist talk. And it is dangerous talk, you mark my words," Beatrice Amelia warned them. "Why, it caused my poor Great-Uncle Louis Wilcox's death."

"Great-Uncle Louis's death? I thought he choked on a catfish bone?" Mr. Travers asked, wrinkling his brow in memory.

Beatrice Amelia sniffed as she wound the silken thread tighter around her slender fingers. "He did," she replied evenly, "but it was only because he turned apoplectic at the dinner table over all this abolitionist talk, and unless you wish me to follow in my great-uncle's footsteps over dinner this eve, then you will cease this instant, Mr. Travers."

Beatrice Amelia's son-in-law was clearing his throat from a sudden huskiness when he caught his wife's eye and knew he hadn't succeeded in masking his chuckle.

"Did I tell you we met Neil Braedon in Europe when we were on our honeymoon?" Althea said, speaking to no one in particular and hoping her mother hadn't heard her husband's muffled snort.

"Really, dear?" Beatrice Amelia responded, genuinely interested.

"Neil was in Paris. I have to admit he is a very handsome man, and now I think about it, your description of your Uncle Nathaniel seems quite appropriate in describing his son," Althea said.

"What did I say?" Nathan asked, concerned that he might have been indiscreet, for whatever might have seemed appropriate in describing Neil surely couldn't have been mentioned with ladies present, and he hoped he hadn't been disrespectful to his uncle.

"You spoke of 'a devil with gold curls,' which I believe very nicely describes Neil Braedon. I was pleased to be introduced to him as your wife, dear," Althea added.

"Not really? I've never thought he was that threatening," Nathan declared in surprise.

"You are not a woman," she said with a delicate shiver.

"What does that mean? He's irresistible to a woman, or dangerous?"

"One and the same when you meet those eyes of his," Althea surprised her husband by answering. "His gaze is so intent, and patient, as if he knows he will get what he wants if he waits long enough."

Nathan laughed. "Then I am glad I met you first, my dearest."

"Actually, I decided upon you first, so you need never have worried, even when Neil came here that summer and you Braedon boys were quite horrible to me."

"Never!"

"You might thank Neil and Adam for being so obnoxious, because you always came to my defense, and that was why I fell in love with you."

"Did I really?" Nathan asked, pleased at the thought.

"A woman never forgets," Mr. Travers commented at great risk.

"When we were in Paris we also met Neil's wife," Althea continued, remembering that encounter as though it were yesterday.

"I do recollect you mentioning something about her now, dear," Beatrice Amelia remembered. "Foreign, wasn't she?"

Nathan smiled. "Of Spanish descent on her mother's side of the family, but her father was originally from Ohio, I believe, definitely an American. He went out to the territories about the same time Uncle Nathaniel did. He married a woman from one of the oldest families in the New Mexico Territory. This Alfonso Jacobs owns the land nearest to Royal Rivers."

"She was exquisite," Althea recalled. "Black hair, black eyes, alabaster skin, and a profile that was very aristocratic. Although haughty, she was quite charming. She said very little. And when she did speak, she had quite an accent, so I assume she preferred speaking in Spanish. What was her name, Nathan? I remember we said it fit her perfectly."

"Serena."

"Hmmm, sounds foreign to me," Beatrice Amelia declared, not impressed.

"She was wearing the most incredible jewels."

"Oh?" Beatrice Amelia's attention was caught now.

"Biggest emeralds I've ever seen," Nathan admitted. "From her mother's family, I believe," he added quickly when he caught his mother-in-law's speculative gaze on him. "When she and Neil walked into the hotel the most amazing silence descended on the lobby. Every eye was on them."

"You have to admit they made a striking couple. I was quite concerned for a while that your cousin might find himself involved in a duel with one or two of his wife's more ardent admirers."

Nathan grinned. "He's got the Braedon temper, so I had good reason for concern too, but after the first few minutes, I relaxed."

"Why?"

"Because it seemed to me that Neil was more amused than angered by the lustful stares his wife's beauty caused."

"Being married to a beautiful woman, the man obviously had come to expect such a reaction," Mr. Travers said with understanding, for his own Beatrice Amelia had been a great beauty and he'd come close to dueling many times when an admiring gentleman had become too familiar.

"Yes, but I've always wondered…well, it is too late now," Nathan said with a shrug, leaving unsaid the rest of his thought.

"What?"

"It doesn't matter. It is over now, and whether or not Neil was happy no longer matters."

"You don't think Neil was happy with Serena?" Althea asked, a curious expression in her soft brown eyes.

"Whether he was, or not, it ended tragically for him," was all Nathan allowed.

"What ended tragically?" Beatrice Amelia demanded, her interest held by Nathan's oblique comments.

"Serena died. It was one of those tragic accidents. She had been out riding and something happened to frighten her horse. It bolted, throwing her to the ground. She was left abandoned and lost in some godforsaken canyon. They didn't find her body for months."

"How perfectly terrifying," Beatrice Amelia murmured, feeling a twinge of pity for the unknown woman who had died so horribly.

"Poor Neil. It seems tragedy stalks him. I hope you are wrong. Even for the short time they had, I hope he knew her love," Althea said.

"When was this?" Mr. Travers asked.

"A year ago. Many blamed Neil, but it's just talk. They think he's more Comanche than white, and it scares them. They don't understand."

"Were there any children?" Beatrice Amelia questioned, thinking this half-savage Neil Braedon probably had caused his wife's death.

"No," Nathan replied, his thoughts drifting back in time. "I haven't seen Neil since Paris. I remember him far more vividly from that summer when he came to Royal Bay for the first time. He scared me to death playing those Comanche tricks on Adam and me. We played knights in combat and he'd beat us every time. No one could ride like Neil, even when he was sixteen. I never knew if he was on his horse or not the way he'd hang halfway to the ground on one side. I nearly broke my arm trying to copy him. And the first time he cut loose with that bloodcurdling howl, I had nightmares. In the very beginning, when we first met him, we really were enemies. He frightened me at times, because he didn't think the same way we did. But after we came to an understanding, I had him on the ground and threatened to beat his brains out, we began to play a never-ending battle, albeit a good-natured one, of surprising one another by secret attacks. We rode all over the countryside and found the most likely places for ambush and secret hideouts. We even found the most secret of secret hideouts," he confided with an almost boyish expression.

"Where was that?" his father-in-law asked, curious now how those three Braedons had managed to elude capture all of those years ago.

"I am afraid that I am under oath not to reveal the secret," Nathan declared. "We all swore on our honor never to tell. We even took a blood oath, becoming brothers rather than cousins that summer. I'll never forget my surprise when Neil pulled out that wicked knife of his and slit our wrists and his before either Adam or I could protest. Our blood mingled and we recited a vow of loyalty much like the Three Musketeers would have. It was all very exciting. Of course, Adam, with his devil-may-care attitude, always managed to even the score with Neil, which earned Neil's grudging respect."

Althea smiled, although she did not find it especially amusing, since she had been the object of Adam's practical jokes since she'd been a child. One never knew what he was up to, but it was wise to be on guard whenever he was about. For even now, full grown man that he was, Adam was just as likely to put a frog in your picnic basket or a snake in your garden hat as kiss your hand with gentlemanly courtesy. He didn't have a serious bone in his body, and Althea wished someone would get the best of him one day.

"At least, dear, you grew up, and it would seem as if Adam is still in his childhood," Althea commented, pleased her own daughter didn't have an Adam Merton Braedon to torment her. "I think it is time for your nap, darling," she said, smoothing Noelle's dark brown curls.

"Oh, Mama, not yet, please."

"I should not admit this, but Neil and I managed to come close to expulsion several times when he was attending Yale and I was at Princeton."

"I always knew there was more to you than just the

Braedon name," Mr. Travers said with new appreciation of his son-in-law. "By the way, where are those daughters of mine? It seems unusually quiet around here."

"Leigh and Blythe, and Julia, have all gone on a picnic," Beatrice Amelia informed him complacently, thinking it an appropriate afternoon's excursion for her daughters.

"When I was leaving the kitchens earlier, I heard Leigh offer to fetch the blackberries for dessert," Althea added absentmindedly.

"Blackberry picking," Mr. Travers exclaimed with pleasure. There was still hope for his daughter yet. He hadn't completely lost her.

"*Blackberry picking?*" Beatrice Amelia repeated in a less exuberant tone.

"Looks like we will indeed be having blackberry cobbler for dessert tonight if Leigh is doing the picking," he chuckled, thinking this would be the best blackberry cobbler ever. "That girl has the best eye for horses and blackberries in all of Virginia."

"I realize now that I was more fortunate than I thought when I married into this family. Because I was acceptable to Althea was the only reason I was allowed to have one of Damascena's foals. I've never been subjected to such scrutiny from so wee a lass to prove I'd be an acceptable owner for a horse," Nathan complained with a laugh.

"You are indeed fortunate. Did you hear that Leigh turned down Dermot Canby's offer for Capitaine? He offered an outrageous sum for that colt, but she wouldn't even consider it. The man turned purple in the face when she turned up that little nose of hers at his offer. Not that I would sell to the man either, too heavy-handed with the whip, but it isn't likely she'll ever part with the little lad," Mr. Travers said with fatherly pride.

"She is too much like her father," Beatrice Amelia said, shaking her smoothly coiffed head. "I seem to recall a certain Stuart Travers who has allowed each of his children on their tenth birthday to select any horse of their choosing at Travers Hill, despite what its worth might later prove to be, considering Travers Hill only has the finest bloodstock in Virginia. And upon graduation from college, were not each of this same

Stuart Travers's sons again granted so great a privilege, and were not each of his daughters upon their marriage to be given the same privilege?" Beatrice Amelia inquired, her needle and thread weaving in and out of the fine lawn with each word.

"How did you expect me, madam, to get any of my children to stay in school, especially Guy, without holding a tempting carrot out to them?" Mr. Travers demanded. "I've no regrets. They've all turned out winners."

"I would have suggested a firmer hand on the reins, sir," Beatrice Amelia responded.

Catching sight of his father-in-law's harassed expression and fearing his mother-in-law was about to begin one of her long-winded recitations, Nathan sighed with exaggerated pleasure and declared, "I'd wager all my worldly goods that Mrs. Travers has the best recipe for blackberry cobbler in three counties."

"I have always suspected that cobbler was why you married me in the first place, Nathan Braedon," Althea said. Eyeing her complacently smiling husband thoughtfully, she added, "That…and marriage to me brought you Belle Rosa, and she just happened to be the dam of Dahoon Holly, that father sold to Jasper Drayton before you had a chance to bid on him. I'm surprised you didn't break our engagement over that. Holly beat every two-year-old racing that season. You wouldn't, by any chance, be hoping that Belle's latest foal will turn out to be another Dahoon Holly?"

Nathan Braedon's smile widened. "I am thankful I do not have to meet you in court, my dear. I fear I can deny nothing. When it comes to tasty cobblers and fine horses, how can a man resist such temptation?"

"I certainly couldn't, and I'm certain it was the reason he married you, sister dear. I did warn you against marrying a Braedon," declared a handsome young gentleman walking up the path beside the veranda. He was leading the roan hunter he'd selected as a graduation gift only last spring, and which was now limping noticeably.

"And some people know better how to care for their valuable property," Mr. Travers said with a worried frown as he noticed the limp and hurried to examine the roan's foreleg, his steps hindered by the pack of hounds that had accompanied his son and always seemed to be close on his heels.

"I've already looked at it, Father," Guy Travers told his parent a bit defensively, "and it looks no more than a slight tendon sprain. There is no heat in it yet," Guy informed him, but he couldn't meet his father's stern eye.

"Tried to jump the fence near the mill again, didn't you?" Mr. Travers demanded, and upon seeing the guilty look in his son's eye he snorted derisively. "I knew it! I've told you before, Guy, it is far too high. You take too many chances, boy, and this is all you have to show for it. Lucky it wasn't your fool neck that was broken! Not that I wouldn't have broken it myself if you'd broken this lad's leg," the master of Travers Hill warned, his voice raised with anger and growing louder as he tried to speak over the excited barking of the hounds.

Mr. Travers paused for a moment, staring around him as if counting noses. "I'd swear there are more hounds here than yesterday," he said in surprise. "I thought I told you, boy, to get rid of that last litter."

"I've tried, Father, but...I seem to remember you broke your arm taking that same fence ten years ago," Guy reminded his father, meeting that old gentleman's fiery eye with a challenging glint in his own now.

"Really! Such impertinence. Guy Patrick, you will apologize to your father this instant," Beatrice Amelia demanded with outraged parental dignity, but her indignation was soon turned on her husband when she heard his muffled laughter turn into a wheezing cough.

"I'm sorry, Bea, but the boy's right. I can't scold him for something I myself have done too many times in the past. You've patched me up enough to know I speak the truth. And if I hadn't gotten as thick as a bale of cotton with the middle hoop busted I'd still be trying to make that jump. Damned if I wouldn't!" he vowed, then coughed apologetically as he noticed his wife's pinkening cheeks and tightening lips.

Althea and Nathan exchanged knowing glances. Stuart Russell Travers, gentleman horse breeder and farmer, was far too lenient and generous with his family and friends. Besides her father—and perhaps her mother—only she and Nathan, and the local banker in Charlottesville, knew how heavily in debt the Travers family was. Stuart Travers had even taken out a mortgage on Travers Hill in order to get money to pay his most outstanding debts.

Althea could still hear her father's angry curses when a man he owed money had demanded payment with ungentlemanly short notice. It just wasn't done in polite society. What was the world coming to? he'd demanded with gentlemanly outrage. Apparently some men were not gentlemen and would not take a gentleman's word of honor that he was good for the money—perhaps not today, or tomorrow, but a gentleman always paid his debts. To demand payment was not only ungentlemanly, it cast a slur upon the other gentleman's honor.

Unfortunately, being too much the gentleman was Stuart Travers's worst enemy. Too often he would sell one of his prized horses on the promise of payment once the horse won a race for the eager, and too often out-of-pocket, buyer, or collect a stud fee from a prospective horse breeder only after the mare gave birth to an acceptable foal the following spring—and then, more often than not, he would have to accept a promissory note of payment, for he was, after all, a gentleman.

"Well, if you ask me..." Guy began.

"Which no one has," his mother reminded him, still out of humor with her son.

"Then I'm betting there will be plenty of disappointed buyers moping around the county when they learn that Leigh has no intention of selling that colt of hers. Of course, once the truth is out, I fear the homestead will be besieged with suitors, and were not my dear little sister Leigh an acclaimed beauty, we would still have no difficulty finding her a proper husband."

Leaning negligently against one of the veranda posts, his booted legs crossed comfortably, a mint julep held in his hand and already half emptied, he expounded further. "What a horse race this will turn out to be. Talk about a race to the finish, I don't know how I'll ever handle all of the bets," he laughed, anticipating the jockeying for position by the eager young bucks.

"I declare I'm already beginning to question the motives of those who would make my acquaintance, for as surely as I stand here before you today they eventually manage to mention the unparalleled beauty of Leigh Alexandra Travers of Travers Hill, and could I, by any chance, be related? Hardly, I respond with an appropriate guffaw of incredulity, since they obviously believe me some hick from the backcountry. However, someone is going to be a very lucky gentleman, so we should be especially particular about screening Leigh's beaus. I think we should have pick of the litter. At least half, if not all, of the state is trooping up our path. Your prized roses, Mother, will never survive. So, lest we be too hasty and come out on the short end of the stick, let us exercise caution. After all, we should all benefit handsomely because of this fortunate circumstance of Leigh's grace, beauty, and possession of Damascena and little Capitaine. She always has had the best eye for picking the true bloods—even when she was little," he said with a disbelieving shake of his head, the chestnut curls falling into casual disarray.

"Well, really! You have gone too far this time, Guy Patrick Travers!" his mother exclaimed, outraged anew by her son's vulgar talk. "Why, one would believe you were speaking of breeding our mares and collecting stud fees," she said, fanning herself more rapidly.

"I knew I should never have allowed you to tour Europe with Adam. Forgive me, Nathan, for I do not mean to dishonor your good name, but..."

"But Adam prides himself on his rakish reputation. My brother is not your choice of tutor, and rightly so, sir, for your impressionable son," Nathan said, unoffended by his father-in-law's opinion.

"I can see I shall never be taken seriously by any of you."

"I certainly shan't as long as you stand here enjoying yourself instead of getting this lad to the stables," his father reminded him.

"I will, Father. Let me finish my drink. Worked up quite a thirst."

"That is your second glass already. Rambler has a thirst too."

"I can hold my liquor, sir, never fear on that score, and I'll see to ol' Rambler, don't you worry. And, to set everyone's mind at ease concerning Leigh, I suspect it is the gentlemanly

Matthew Wycliffe who has captured our Leigh's heart," he confided, patting several of his favorite hounds and hiding his grin.

"*Wycliffe?* Do you really think so?" Beatrice Amelia murmured thoughtfully, easily diverted from her earlier annoyance with her son by this pleasing revelation.

"What is this?" Leigh Alexandra's father demanded, apparently not as pleased as his wife in hearing this startling news. "Wycliffe said nothing to me of his intentions when we spoke last month. And no gentleman would dare to approach a young lady of good family with such a proposal without speaking to her father for permission first. Would have expected far better of Wycliffe. Comes of good stock. Hmmm," he muttered to himself, "makes sense now, his generous offer to help. Although, 'twas a good business deal for him. Well, if that young buck has acted improperly, I'll have his"—Mr. Travers choked off the last of his threat just in time to spare the ladies the indelicacy of his comment and sputtered instead—"I'll geld that young stallion if he's touched Leigh. Should never have agreed to packing Leigh off to Charleston. But you insisted, madam!"

"We sent Althea Louise 'off to Charleston,'" Beatrice Amelia reminded her husband. "And she married our dear Nathan here."

"That was different. Althea's always been easily managed, but Leigh is a high-spirited little filly and will stray unless handled carefully," he said, his anger beginning to simmer as he thought of those randy young bucks in Charleston.

"You do have the most irritating manner of speaking at times, *Mr. Travers*, and, for your information, I am not a broodmare, so please do not refer to my children in that manner."

"*Mrs. Travers*, I'll have you know that—"

"Please, Father, really, Matt has been a perfect gentleman, as indeed he always is," Guy was quick to explain, calming his father's fears and dousing what was quickly becoming a heated argument. "Actually, since Matt and I are old friends, and I am Leigh's brother, I was taken into his confidence when in Charleston last," Guy confessed. "He was very interested in hearing all about our family, and, indeed, said you and he had become involved in a number of business ventures. Said he felt like a member of the family already.

"He told me he was going to approach you this weekend and ask your permission to speak to Leigh. He believes his suit would be welcomed by my dear little sister. And she was asking me quite a few personal questions about him when last we spoke. And she danced almost every dance with him the night of the Craigmores' barbecue. Ah, young love... However, Matt has neither tarnished his good name or sterling reputation nor sullied ours," he said reassuringly, knowing his quick-tempered father would waste little time in confronting an innocent Matthew Wycliffe. "Told Matt I'd be proud to welcome him as a brother-in-law. And I would."

"Now I recollect, he has visited more often of late than ever before, and Wycliffe Hall has one of the finest stables in the Carolinas. They were famous even when I was a girl," Beatrice Amelia remarked, thinking Matthew Wycliffe would be a splendid match for her middle daughter, and making a mental note to have a serious chat with that young miss.

It had been quite the gossip in five counties when Althea had managed to catch the eligible Nathan Braedon; even if they had been sweethearts since youngsters and there'd never been any doubt in her mind that the marriage would take place, nevertheless, until Althea Louise Travers had become Mrs. Nathan Douglas Braedon of the Braedons of Royal Bay, nothing was certain, and it had done their family proud that day when she'd said her vows. Such a lovely bride...the reception had been unsurpassed...everyone, including the governor himself, had been there...and now, if Leigh were to marry a Wycliffe from the Carolinas, well...no more wild berry picking for her. A scratch on the cheek could ruin all of her chances, Beatrice Amelia fretted, thinking of those unfortunate freckles that were certain to appear across Leigh's nose if she took off her straw bonnet, which she was certain to do. Leigh Alexandra could be so very difficult at times. Not nearly as agreeable as Blythe Lucinda—who was such a well-behaved little dear, much like her sister Althea, who'd always acted with such decorum and made such a splendid match.

Setting down her embroidery with a suddenness that sent

the neatly grouped silk threads she'd been winding with mechanical precision for the last half an hour into a jumble, Beatrice Amelia decided to make up another bottle of lemon-and-cucumber lotion immediately. The sooner the better, she thought, a glint in her eye as she envisioned the party and imagined the competition to her girls, for Blythe would be turning sixteen on Friday and was already showing promise of great beauty. Her youngest daughter would capture her share of beaus before the week was over, the former Beatrice Amelia Leigh vowed with the same determination that had made her mistress of Travers Hill.

Of course, it was to be expected, for hadn't she herself been an acclaimed beauty at seventeen and had her dance card filled for months in advance of any ball? Why, it had been almost scandalous the way all the eligible gentlemen, and some not so eligible, had sought her favors, Beatrice Amelia remembered with a slight smile of pleasure curving her lips as she thought of that Season so long ago. That had been the very same spring, when she'd been attending Madame Talvande's French School for Young Ladies, that she'd first caught sight of Stuart Travers. She could still remember hearing about that handsome young gentleman from Virginia, rumored to be one of *the* Travers family, famous for their Thoroughbreds, and had decided without hesitation that he was to have the honor of becoming her special beau. And later, after an exciting Season of tea parties, and race parties, and hunt parties, and picnics, and balls, and masques—after all, it had been her very first Season—she would graciously accept his offer for her hand in marriage, for Beatrice Amelia Leigh had no doubt at all that Stuart Travers would become her husband one day. It was always so nice when things turned out the way one planned, she thought, glancing around at her family gathered close about her—and each having fulfilled her dearest wishes. But one couldn't count on good fortune always lending a hand; 'twas far wiser to plan every detail very carefully, then there could be no unpleasant surprises waiting around the corner—that was Beatrice Amelia Leigh Travers's maxim on life.

"Better add an extra tablespoon of lemon," she murmured beneath her breath, politely excusing herself as she hurried inside, her smile tight as the unwelcomed thought of black-berry juice staining her daughters' pale, delicate hands struck her. Of course, they would be wearing gloves, she thought, momentarily relieved.

Beatrice Amelia did not see the amusement flicker across Althea's face. But Althea had seen that look of consternation suddenly cross her mother's formerly serene countenance, and, having seen that determined expression many times before, she knew none of them would get any rest until after the party. Praying that her sisters were acting with propriety, Althea returned her attention to the conversation at hand, but in the back of her mind she couldn't help but remember the last time Leigh had disappeared for the afternoon. She'd gone in search of honey and brought a hornets' nest down on her head instead. Althea sighed, and placing a kiss on top of Noelle's soft curls, she wondered if the afternoon could possibly continue so peacefully.

Two

HER ARMS FULL OF WILD LAVENDER, LEIGH ALEXANDRA Travers was strolling gracefully through the tall green grasses of the meadow. It appeared the perfect pastoral scene: a lovely young woman, the feathery blue flowers of love-in-a-mist catching at the hem of her gown of light summer muslin, a chestnut mare following beside her while a frisky colt raced ahead, and the only cloud in the deep blue sky, a fleecy one that had already drifted by without casting a shadow. Beatrice Amelia would have given a thankful sigh of relief could she have seen her daughter, because the wide brim of Leigh's straw bonnet was shielding the rose petal creaminess of the ivory complexion so treasured by ladies of leisure.

The young Misses Julia Elayne Braedon and Blythe Lucinda Travers were seated comfortably in a two-wheeled cart being drawn by a sturdy Shetland pony. No guiding hand was needed on the reins. The fat little pony had followed this path across the meadow many times over the years as the Travers children had explored the countryside. More often than not his services had been needed to haul back the children's treasures, whether they'd been picking blackberries, hunting crawfish, or searching for Jolie's special healing herbs. The cart and pony had served well over the years. The cart had lost one of its big wheels only once, sending the squealing children tumbling onto the ground. And the pony had rarely displayed his temper, since Leigh usually handled him, but on one occasion he'd taken a punishing bite out of an impatient Stuart James when he'd tried to prod the stubborn pony forward.

"Are you certain, Leigh, this is where we'll find blackberries?" Julia inquired, and not for the first time since they'd left the lane and followed the narrow path into the woods. "I don't think this rickety ol' cart will go any farther without losing a wheel, and I'm not getting out and walking," Julia warned as she stared at the field of undulating tall grasses and wondered what snakes might be lurking in the tangled undergrowth.

"This is the very best place for blackberries. The Travers family, since before even my grandfather's time, has always found the juiciest, sweetest berries in this meadow," Leigh told her, glancing toward the thick brambles at the far end of the meadow with a professional eye. Leigh dropped her bundle of lavender in the cart next to the woven split-oak basket that held the picnic lunch carefully packed by Jolie. Wrapped inside a green-checked gingham cloth were the treats Jolie could prepare so well—shrimp-stuffed tomatoes, sausage rolls, pâté and biscuits, crabmeat pasties, pear tarts—and which would entice three young misses to eat properly and temporarily forget to worry about how tiny their waists should be. Next to the basket, empty pails, waiting to be filled with glistening blackberries, rattled together noisily as the cart rumbled along the path.

As they drew closer to the far end of the meadow, a white-tailed deer bolted from concealment in a grove of maple. Its sudden flight startled the daydreaming Julia, and her high-pitched squeal cut across the peacefulness of the afternoon, reverberating through the trees and sending a flock of wood pigeons scattering into the sky.

The mare neighed nervously and Leigh patted her velvety muzzle reassuringly. "There, there, girl. He won't hurt you, Damascena," she said softly, quieting the mare with her gentle touch. "He's far more frightened than you are, my beauty," Leigh told her, and the mare, named for one of Beatrice Amelia's roses, as most of the horses at Travers Hill had been, nudged her young mistress's shoulder affectionately, but Leigh wasn't fooled and pulled off her bonnet just in time to save it from a crunching bite. "I've got an apple for you in the basket, so you will just have to be patient."

"I'm famished too, and thirsty, and I'm not nearly so patient as that ol' horse of yours, Leigh. This isn't enjoyable at all. I'm certain we're lost. Why, I'm being baked like a field hand under this sun. Certainly not like going for a stroll along the Battery," Julia complained, thinking of the handsome young gentlemen who would surely have been in attendance, if she and Leigh had been in Charleston this Sunday afternoon and not lost in the backwoods of Virginia. "I don't know how I let you talk me into this, except that you can talk the devil out of his tail and horns when you want something. I had forgotten how hot and sticky it gets in Virginia, but a picnic sounded so nice. And I do hope Jolie remembered how fond of pâté and buttermilk biscuits I am. I have to admit I didn't find any to compare with hers in Charleston. Of course"—she sighed—"Jolie did come with your mama from Charleston. You will be pleased to know that I remembered to bring some of my mama's deviled eggs and sponge cake."

Trying to fan herself and tip her parasol to provide better shade for her flushed cheeks, while balancing the basket on her lap, Julia continued sadly, "We did have the nicest sea breezes in the afternoons. Do you remember, Leigh, how wonderfully delightful it was to sit on the veranda of your cousins the Benjamin Leighs's house and watch the ships in the harbor?"

Leigh glanced back at her friend in amazement. "I don't recall you ever showing that much interest in the ships, Julia," she responded, remembering only too well Julia dragging her along the Battery at an unladylike trot in order to catch up to a couple of blue-uniformed sea captains. "If I recollect correctly, it was the crew aboard ship you were more interested in."

Julia giggled, twirling her parasol with remembered pleasure. "Well, of course, silly, who cares about some horrible, smelly ol' boat. And I nearly fainted when you wanted to go aboard. Thank goodness your cousin, Mr. Leigh, thought it entirely improper. You will, of course, remember the captain who was so insistent we come aboard was considered quite disreputable and to have been seen in his company—despite how handsome he was—well…'twould have been the ruin of both of our reputations. Besides, who needs to go aboard to meet the crew? I've never set foot off dry land, and I can count three captains and any number of handsome young officers, five of them British, as my beaus, and they are all gentlemen because I made their acquaintance at very proper soirees.

"I declare, I do feel so sorry for Blythe having to attend school in Richmond instead of Charleston. She'll never meet anyone interesting there. 'Tis so…so provincial, don't you think, Leigh, to attend finishing school in Virginia? I dare say she hasn't learned French with a proper accent. Mademoiselle Dubois, who tutored us in French, was originally from Martinique. And I dare say there isn't a single British officer in Richmond, perhaps even in all of Virginia! How will she ever expect to learn about the world? Poor little Lucy," Julia said, using Blythe's childhood nickname as she sighed with commiseration over her friend's misfortune.

Blythe Lucinda remained quiet, knowing it would do little good to assure Julia that she was very happy attending school in Richmond and seriously doubted she'd ever have need of a proper French accent. She hadn't been in the least disappointed when her parents had broken the sad news to her that they couldn't afford, this year at least, to send her to the same finishing school her sister Leigh, and Althea before her, had attended. Her mother had been heartbroken, unable to speak without dabbing at her red-rimmed eyes with her lace-edged handkerchief as she tearfully informed her of the tragedy. Watching her mother's ineffective efforts to dry her tears with the damp, delicate piece of lace, Blythe had felt momentarily ashamed of herself. The news that she wouldn't have to leave Virginia had gladdened her heart, but when her mother had been forced to retire early to her bedchamber, with Jolie drawing the shades and administering a soothing mint balm for her moaning mistress's migraine, Blythe had felt a twinge of conscience—after all, her mother only wanted the best for her, as she had for all of her children.

A smile, that might have seemed sly had it not been dimpled, tugged at Blythe's lips as she caught her sister's eye. Only she and Leigh, not even Julia, knew how happy Leigh had been to return home to Virginia from Charleston.

"I could just gaze for hours upon hours at that beautiful painting of Charleston that your mama has in the foyer of Travers Hill. I declare, Leigh, tears come to my eyes when I think of all that we're missing. I wonder if any of my beaus even remember me. That spiteful cat Libby St. Martins was always trying to steal them away from me," Julia fretted, her full-lipped mouth forming a petulant pout as she watched with a disagreeable eye the dragonfly hovering over her flower-trimmed bonnet. "La dee, but I've been so excited, Leigh, since Mama's been feeling under the weather. It's this heat. Mama swears she will expire, and I do believe she is serious. You should see the way her hair cannot hold even the tiniest curl. Well, she will not accept it another day! Papa says we'll be going to Newport sometime in August. And you'll never guess, Leigh, but Papa is planning to take Mama and me to England! Isn't it just too wonderful for words," Julia exclaimed, clapping her hands and causing her parasol to tip precariously close to the pony's fat rump before she jerked it back, nearly poking Blythe in the eye. "We'll take the boat from Charleston, of course, so I'll get to see all of our dearest friends again. I suppose you couldn't sweet-talk your papa into allowing you to accompany us? It would be so amusing if we could both be in London at the same time. Think of the secrets we can share. I think we'll even cross the Channel and visit Paris, and in the spring, Leigh! Can you imagine the romance of it? All of our dreams will come true."

"I dare say I'll have my portrait painted by a handsome, dissolute young English lord who has been disinherited by his father, the duke of something-or-other, and has been banished to the Continent. He will be maddened by my unparalleled beauty and won't be able to stay away from me. Why, I could return to Virginia a duchess! La dee, that Libby St. Martins would turn pea green with envy, wouldn't she. I'd even marry a fat ol' duke, ugly as my second cousin, Harmon Cawley, on my mama's side of the family—you remember him, don't you, Leigh?—he has such bulging eyes and he's always gulping between words...well, I'd do it just to see Libby St. Martins's face turn all red and mottled trying to catch her breath. She'd be so ugly then she couldn't catch even a fish, or even poor ol' Harmon," she said with a laugh of wicked delight. "Why, come to think of it, Harmon does look like a fish. But then, all the Cawleys do. You ought to see my cousin Eulalie, Harmon's sister. Her mama just despairs of ever finding that girl a husband. And if they do, I wouldn't be at all surprised if he isn't in trade. It will be quite the scandal and I dare say the Cawleys will never be invited to Royal Bay again.

"I do believe Libby St. Martins thinks she's going to wed that Matthew Wycliffe," Julia continued, casting a curious glance at her quiet friend, but Leigh had her face slightly averted and Julia couldn't see her expression. "Not that I'm interested in him, even if he is one of the wealthiest gentlemen in the Carolinas, because I'm only going to marry a handsome, titled Englishman. Oh, Leigh, I've just got to be engaged by Christmas. I don't know what I'll do if I'm not. Grandmama was married by the time she was seventeen and she was in the family way before she was eighteen. I'm almost eighteen, and so are you, and I haven't *even* received a proposal. At least not one I'd accept. I'll just die if Libby St. Martins gets engaged before I do. Mama didn't marry until she was almost an old maid. I won't wait that long, I just won't!

"Leigh! Did I tell you about my gown for the party?" Julia cried out as she suddenly remembered the package that had arrived at Royal Bay just the day before. "Why, it just took my breath away. It arrived yesterday—and unfortunately so did Adam—and from Charleston! I told Mama upon my arrival home that I insisted on keeping that French dressmaker or I would never leave my room! And she knew I meant it. Even though I've had to return to Virginia, at least I will still be dressed in the height of fashion. Blond lace, Leigh," she told her friend with a widening smile, her light gray eyes wide with the wonder of it all. "Yards and yards of it! And it is quite décolleté. Scandalous, even. Cream satin, flounced all around the skirt and draped with bunches of blushing pink satin rosebuds and ribbons! And I'll be wearing my necklace of pearl beads that I got for Christmas last, and I'll have my hair arranged à la—oh, and you'll never believe what Adam said when he saw me yesterday eve! I had to try on my new gown so Mama would have time to sew the alterations if need be, but Simone is such a fine seamstress that not an extra stitch had to be taken, although I was quite despairing that Mama was going to add an extra inch of lace to my bodice.

"And Adam, standing there with that grin of his, well, he can say the most outrageous things! I'll have you know I had ol' Bella check my linens before I got into bed last night. Well, I was close to tears worrying about what trick he had up his sleeve. I dare say he's lurking around here somewhere right now waiting to pounce on us. He threatened as much. You will remember."

Blythe glanced over her shoulder, hiding her yawn as Julia continued with her usual patter about anything and everything that came and went in her head. In the last few days, Blythe had come to the conclusion that she'd liked Julia far more before she and Leigh had gone off to finishing school in Charleston—especially since Julia had returned wearing one of the roundest steel-hooped crinolines Blythe had ever seen, and if that was what Adam Braedon had jested about, then she could certainly understand. Julia hadn't even been able to get through the front door of Travers Hill. Poor Stephen would never be the same, Blythe thought, remembering the expression on his face when Julia had gotten caught half in and half out of the doorway, her crinoline flying high in back and baring her pantaloons for all to view. And trying to share a small seat with Julia, fashionably dressed in her prized crinoline, was anything but pleasant, Blythe thought as she pushed down the wave of striped muslin, fluffy petticoat, and rigid crinoline that spread out around Julia and threatened to engulf the cart.

Leigh, however, had come home from Charleston the same beloved sister who'd left, and still wearing the same unfashionable crinoline she'd left home in, much to Stephen's relief. Although, for the first couple of weeks, Blythe had known a certain consternation when her sister had used French phrases when asking for potatoes at the dinner table, but their mother had been delighted. Leigh had even declined to play croquet on the lawn in favor of reading a book, *An Essay*…or something equally dull, Blythe remembered with a grimace, and then her sister had made an incredible fuss over the childish bodice of one of her favorite gowns, which had sent their father into an ominous silence when he'd seen the new cut of the décolletage of Leigh's once modest blue gown.

But last week, when Leigh had grabbed a sweet roll on her way out the door, unable to linger for a proper breakfast in her haste for a ride across country with Guy, and Saturday last, when she'd stayed up until well past midnight helping with a difficult breech delivery of a foal, and this morning, when she'd suggested they go blackberry picking, Blythe had known that her sister's sojourn in Charleston had not had any damaging effects.

"Oh, la dee, but this is nice," Julia murmured as the cart rolled toward a sun-dappled creek, shaded by hemlocks and sycamores that beckoned the three girls with its soft murmuring into the cool shadows of the glade. "We can have our picnic over there," Julia directed as the cart came to a halt in the shade of a tall sycamore. To their right, and indeed the perfect spot for a picnic, was a gentle rise of bank carpeted with meadow-sweet grasses and wildflowers, the overhanging boughs of one of the hemlocks creating a natural canopy above their heads.

"I am absolutely parched," Julia said with a dramatic sigh. Climbing down from the cart, she had no idea of the comical figure she appeared as she tried to gather her billowing skirts and stiff crinoline, keep her parasol shading her delicate complexion, the basket of stuffed eggs and sponge cake from tipping its contents, and all the while maintain her ladylike dignity as she blindly searched for a safe footing on the uneven ground. And it proved no easy feat, for by the time Julia had stepped away from the cart, she was flustered and out of breath from the effort, her fancy bonnet askew, and a delicate strand of pale blond hair dangling untidily across her cheek.

"I hope Jolie remembered to pack a refreshment, Leigh," Julia said faintly, eyeing the cool waters of the stream with little interest.

"Lemonade," Blythe told her cheerfully, jumping down from the cart with annoying ease and grace, her long, dark brown hair tied with a satin bow and swinging freely around her shoulders. Her saucer-shaped straw bonnet was tipped at a rakish angle and seemed to mirror her gaiety. Ignoring Julia's sniff of superiority—after all, there were certain discomforts a lady had to suffer to be fashionable—she squeezed past the voluminous skirts threatening to wrap themselves around the tree. Her own layered petticoats were far more practical for blackberry picking than wearing a crinoline, but Julia had seemed doubtful of Leigh's suggestion to take off her crinoline and leave it in their bedchamber at Travers Hill. She had also refused to borrow one of Leigh's old muslins, obviously believing she would encounter one of her hearty sea captains strolling through the woods. Blythe smothered a laugh at the thought of encountering a ship under full sail entangled in the honeysuckle and quickly set the basket down, but her hazel eyes twinkled with humor as she spread out a quilt snatched from the linen closet. The fragrance of lavender and roses still clung to the soft folds; delicate aromatic sachets, prepared by their mother's own hand, scented all of the linens at Travers Hill.

"Shall we eat first, or look for berries?" Leigh inquired, unhitching the pony from the cart and sending him with an affectionate pat on his rump into the meadow to graze with the mare and the colt.

"Eat!" Julia said with unladylike vigor. "Well, at least I believe we will do a far superior job picking berries if we keep our strength up. And I do not intend to wander far even then. I'll have you know this is my best pair of kid slippers," she told the Travers sisters as she tried to settle herself as comfortably as possible on the outspread quilt. Her careful descent to the ground would have earned high marks and praise in Madame St. Juste's proper deportment class, but when Julia's shoulders and head disappeared beneath the rustling mound that had enveloped her, Leigh and Blythe started to laugh, at first softly, then loud enough even for the missing Julia to hear inside her silken cocoon.

"La dee," came the faint voice from inside the crinoline, "I swear this is one fashion I could do without," Julia declared, a sheepish grin on her face as she peeped from the folds. "Very well, help me from this cage," she pleaded, her hands reaching out for help.

Blythe stared at Julia in surprise, pleased that their friend hadn't completely lost her sense of humor in Charleston.

"Never will I doubt your advice again, Leigh," Julia admitted as she was pulled to her feet, looking like a giant flower opening its petals. "Unfasten me, dears," she said, sounding like the grand dame she'd been playing for the last few weeks. "If it were not that I am half-starved for those stuffed eggs, which are just out of reach in my current predicament, then I would suffer this torture, however…since we aren't in Charleston supping on the lawns of the Craigmores' house overlooking the Ashley River, with my faithful beaus surrounding me, I will forgo fashion for the moment."

"Welcome home, Julayne," Leigh said, unfastening Julia's crinoline and smiling with satisfaction as the offending object rolled away and Julia's skirts returned to an almost manageable size, and allowing room now for everyone to sit on the outspread quilt.

"Except for Adam calling me that, and he does it to tease me, I don't think I've heard that name in years, at least not since we went away to Charleston," she stated, seating herself with far more ease this time. "La dee, but I'm so hungry I'm even looking forward to your mama's chicken curry and rice tonight," Julia said, digging into the basket from Royal Bay as she pulled out the stuffed eggs that had so tantalized her.

"I thought you liked curry and rice," Leigh said as she knelt down, the skirts of her plain muslin gown spreading out around her. She began to unload the basket, setting the china plates and silverware, napkins and goblets out on the blanket.

"Oh, dear, I didn't mean that the way it sounded, truly I didn't. But we had curry and rice all the time in Charleston, Leigh. It used to seem so exotic and foreign when I'd have it at Travers Hill, especially the way Jolie fixed it and with your mama being from Charleston, and descended from the French aristocracy. All we ever had, and still do, at Royal Bay are butter beans and plain ol' ham. When I got to Charleston, though, it didn't seem so wonderful anymore, especially since we seemed to have rice with everything! I declare, I thought we'd have it at breakfast even," she said, watching as Leigh loaded her plate with an assortment of delectables. "Another biscuit with pâté, Leigh, please," she entreated, smiling widely as another biscuit found its way onto her plate. "Of course, I do believe I really am looking forward to that curry and rice this eve, now that I've returned to Virginia."

"I put the jar of lemonade in the stream, it'll be cool in a few minutes," Blythe said as she dropped down beside them and accepted her plate with a wide grin of pleasure, forgetting about the final fitting for her ball gown on the morrow as she gave in to her healthy young appetite.

"You are a sweet dear, Lucy," Julia said, sounding as if she were far older than she was—but two years makes a big difference in a girl's life, especially if she has been away at finishing school. "Naturally you will be wearing a new gown for your sixteenth birthday party," she said matter-of-factly. "I seem to recall vaguely that I had a pink gown for mine," she remembered with a slight frown of concentration, as if the event had occurred a century ago.

"I'm going to wear a pale green silk with ruffles. I was fitted for it in Richmond just before I left, and Althea brought it with her when she arrived," Blythe said, and thinking about her beautiful gown, she decided against another sausage roll.

"Oh, la dee, how wonderful, Lucy. Green truly is your color," Julia agreed. "Of course, I am rather more fortunate, because Simone says I can wear any color. 'Tis the fairness of my complexion and hair. I really do not think yellow would be a proper color for you."

"I suppose your cousin Justin Braedon will be arriving when Palmer William does?" Blythe asked, fiddling with a half-eaten stuffed egg.

"Oh, la dee, I s'pose. Mama and Papa are expecting him, and his brother from the territories. I hardly remember him, but from what I've heard I am certain I shall not like him at all. I can tell you I am not looking forward to having to put him up, especially with Adam home too. It might be nice, though," she said as a sudden thought struck her, "if Justin brought along a few of his cadet friends to stay over the weekend. Of course, I imagine that Matthew Wycliffe will be arriving shortly. He was invited, wasn't he?"

"I believe so. He is interested in some of our stock which will be auctioned on Saturday, and then the race is on Sunday. Many are betting on Sea Racer to win, and he came out of the Wycliffe stables," Leigh told her.

"Horses! Really, Leigh, is that all you can think about?" Julia demanded in exasperation. "Of course," she continued in a different tone of voice, for she knew her friend, "he must truly love horses to have bred such fine stock and have such famous stables."

"He is a very fine rider," Leigh agreed. "I've never seen him take his whip to his mount, nor has he ever lost his seat as far as I know," she said, which was high praise indeed.

Julia bit her lip in vexation. "Yes, that would seem to indicate he is very well-bred."

"He converses quite well," Leigh added, taking a sip of the lemonade Blythe had retrieved from the stream and poured into the goblets.

"Oh, yes, indeed," Julia was quick to agree, although, privately, she thought Matthew Wycliffe's conversation rather dull. "You do like him, then?" she asked hopefully.

"Hmmm, I s'pose," Leigh responded, glancing away for a moment, and only Blythe saw the smile that curved her lips.

"Oh, Leigh! Please!" Julia cajoled, straining to catch sight of Leigh's face, but when her friend looked back, her expression was one of innocence. "You know I won't breathe a word of it. You are my very dearest friend, and I do mean that," Julia said with great solemnity, and she did mean it, for she and Leigh had been friends since they had taken their first tentative steps out of the nursery.

"Well," Leigh said, relenting in her teasing of Julia, and knowing she could indeed trust her with any confidences, for although Julia could be exceedingly irritating at times, and rather silly, and selfish even, she was a trusted friend, and they'd stood together against many an adversary, "he is rather handsome."

"Oh, most certainly," Julia agreed, nodding her blond head and licking a dab of crabmeat from the corner of her lips. "And..."

"And very much a gentleman," Leigh allowed.

"Not a word spoken against him." Julia was in complete agreement, for if Leigh married Matthew Wycliffe and went to live in Charleston, then, as Leigh's very best friend, she would be invited to stay and would accompany Leigh and Matthew to every important party of the Season. "And..."

"And he is very soft-spoken and he seems a very considerate man," Leigh continued, remembering his patience with a confused and crotchety old gentleman who'd known his father and wanted to reminisce, and his kindness in comforting a frightened young boy who'd been thrown from his mount.

"You've already said he's a gentleman, Leigh," Julia

reminded her. "And?" she prompted, her mouth full of pâté and biscuit.

"And?" Leigh asked, curious, for it seemed she had described Matthew Wycliffe reasonably well.

Julia swallowed the mouthful of half-chewed food, nearly choking in her haste. "Why, he's rich! I declare, Leigh, how Matthew Wycliffe is situated in life is to be considered above all else. Naturally, it would be hoped that he is handsome, but then, that is why we are considering him in the first place. We don't have to choose just any ol' body. We can be selective."

"*We?*"

"Well, of course, silly, you don't think I'm going to let you choose your husband? I'm family now with your sister married to my brother. You've too soft a heart. As your very best friend, which I trust you will always remember—especially when I come to visit you in Charleston—I really must look out for our best interests," Julia declared, although she wasn't too concerned because Mrs. Travers had a keen eye when it came to matrimony and doing what was proper. Mrs. Travers would never allow Leigh to make a mésalliance. And Matthew Wycliffe as a son-in-law was hardly that, Julia thought with a sigh of deep satisfaction as she planned their futures in Charleston, her thoughts drifting dreamily away into the warm afternoon.

"Actually, I think I will never wed," Leigh stated, thinking Julia had far too smug a look about her. "I will become another Rebecca, who can never know the love of her knight, Wilfred of Ivanhoe," Leigh predicted, pleased by the momentary start of surprise on Julia's face. "I shall pine away with unrequited love, leaving this land to journey far."

"La dee, then I'll be the Lady Rowena, I am as fair as she, and then I'll be the lady of the manor," Julia decided, wishing she could spy a knight in shining armor come riding through the trees to sweep her up in his arms and carry her off to be ravished.

"You would be the lady of the castle. Ivanhoe had a castle."

"Hmmm, I declare I like that even better."

"Even if named Udolpho or Otranto?" Leigh asked with a shudder as she remembered the castles of those Gothic tales of old.

"Even then, for I might meet up with a very mysterious,

handsome prince who would hold me captive until I fell in love with him."

"Or you could end up like poor Clarissa," Leigh said, reminding Julia of Richardson's classic, while holding her clasped hands against her breast, "dying because she has been held against her will and cruelly violated."

"Oh, Leigh, really!" Julia said with a look of outrage on her blushing face. "The scandalous things you say."

"Which are not unknown to you, I suspect, since you were raised on a horse-breeding farm the same way I was," Leigh reminded her, surprised by Julia's sudden missishness, for unless she had been blind her whole life she must have seen a stallion mount a mare in heat.

"Well, I think I will be Evangeline," Blythe said softly, "and I will search for my true love, only to find him on his deathbed, then I will die tragically of a broken heart."

"Oooh, la dee, I do so hate unhappy endings," Julia exclaimed. "At least little Jane Eyre found her Rochester, although, 'twas a pity he was nearly blinded in that fire and he was never considered quite handsome. I'm sure I don't know what she saw in him. He was quite disagreeable and she was far too much the mouse to suit me. I dare say, I would not have had the patience to put up with his ill humor."

"But if you loved him, you would stay by his side despite whatever happened to him," Leigh said.

"I most certainly would not, because, I would have the foresight not to choose him in the first place. I declare, Leigh, you have me worried. A lady *always* knows when a gentleman means trouble. You can spot it a mile away. Never marry a man with a swagger. It's a sure sign. What do you think we've been learning at school? How to find a proper husband and make an ideal match. You don't want to be another Catherine Earnshaw, do you? Oh, she made the right decision, and married her proper Edgar Linton, but then she tormented herself pining away for that Heathcliff. A dark-visaged gypsy. Nothing good can come of such a mismatching. You have got to be coldhearted about matrimony. Love, my dears, has nothing to do with it."

"But I think of the noble sacrifice some heroines make for

love. Like Marguerite Gautier? She gave up Armand because she loved him, only to face his wrath, know unhappiness because of his contempt, then die knowing she had made the greatest, most unselfish sacrifice for love."

"Well, pooh, who wants to die and leave your lover? What pleasure is there in that? We should never have read so scandalous a story, except that Madame loved it. It's French," Julia declared, taking a slice of sponge cake.

"What about his love? He might die of unhappiness," Blythe said, defending the hero of *La Dame aux Camelias*.

"Oh, la dee, Lucy dear, don't you believe that. Heroes are never the ones who have to sacrifice anything in romantic novels. It is always the heroine. If she doesn't die of a broken heart because she didn't capture the hero's love, then she dies in childbirth because she did and has to suffer the consequences of their illicit love—because it usually is. He, of course, rides off to great adventure on the last page, certain to find a new love."

Leigh stared dreamily at the sky, the pear tart on her plate untouched. "'Twas on an afternoon, much like this, when Daphne fled Apollo, and I am certain that Atalanta stopped in this very glade to pick up one of the golden apples dropped by Hippomenes."

"Oh, Leigh, you do know I never enjoyed reading that stuffy ol' Greek mythology," Julia reminded her with a frown. But when Leigh remained silent, she added, "So?"

"Atalanta had to wed Hippomenes, because he had outraced her and won her challenge. She was very fleet of foot and thought no one could catch her, but he tricked her by tossing three golden apples, which were quite irresistible, in her path. She could not resist them, and stopped to capture them for her prize. Alas, no more would she roam the woods alone, because he won the race and claimed her as *his* prize. And poor Daphne, well, she was turned into a laurel tree in order to escape from Apollo, who was determined to possess her. But a maiden who is loved by one of the gods is to be pitied, for a child of that union is doomed to death, and the maid to exile. She wished for neither, and chose instead another fate. To honor her, Apollo chose to wear a crown of laurel leaves whenever victorious."

"Really," Julia breathed, thinking the Greeks had been more romantic than she remembered from her studies. "La dee, but I am sleepy," she said with a sigh of contentment, her plate empty.

"Oh, no, we have work to do, so you'd better not get comfortable," Leigh reminded her sleepy-eyed friend.

"Oh, Leigh, you know I can't go blackberry picking in this," she said, holding out the fine muslin of her skirt. "It'll be ruined. Mama will be so displeased with me if I come home with it snagged and stained," she explained unhappily, yet hopeful of being excused from the purpose of their picnic. "Simone, my *modiste* in Charleston, she sewed this gown for me and it cost a fortune. And my slippers, remember them," she added just in case.

"I did offer you one of my old dresses to wear," Leigh reminded her, unimpressed by Julia's argument.

Julia eyed Leigh's slender shape with a look of envy. "I declare, you eat the same things I do, yet you never even put on a pound. Only to you will I admit this, and I'll deny it later, but I was afraid I might not be able to fasten your gown around my waist. It would have ruined the whole week for me, Leigh, to learn that your waist is smaller than mine," she confessed with such a heartbroken expression that Leigh took pity on her.

"There are many who think I am too thin, and unfashionably tall," she said. "You know you are an acclaimed beauty, with countless beaus, and you've one of the smallest waists in the county," she reminded Julia.

"Yes, that is true, Leigh," Julia said, pleased to hear as much even if she knew it was the truth, for she was quite proud of her figure and fair complexion. "Of course, your waist *is* tinier, and for someone who is not in the least bit plump, you are quite nicely rounded in all of the proper places," Julia added, thinking it must be inherited from Mrs. Travers, who could still wear her wedding gown. "You are a trifle taller than I am, but not unfashionably so, truly," she added generously, eyeing the length of Leigh's skirts. "I'd have tripped over the hem of your gown anyway."

"Here're the pails," Blythe said, tossing one to Leigh, then, thinking better of the temptation, placed Julia's pail with undue care before her.

"Thank you, Lucy. Always so helpful," Julia said sweetly, her expression looking as if she'd bitten into a sour berry by mistake. "Why, whatever are you doing, Leigh?" she exclaimed, her attention drawn to her friend, who'd kicked off her slippers, and was now unrolling her stockings.

"I don't want to ruin my shoes either," Leigh said, and taking the hem of her skirts she crossed and draped them around her hips before tying them together in a bulky knot at her waist. "There!"

Leigh turned around to show off her handiwork. Putting on her bonnet and picking up her pail, she said, "No stains or ruined slippers now. And I bet I'll have a pail full of the biggest, blackest, juiciest berries before either of you," she challenged, glancing over to where Blythe was already following her lead and removing her slippers and stockings. "Julia?"

But Julia had already kicked off her finest pair of kid slippers and unrolled her silk stockings, gathering all of the material of her voluminous skirts was another matter, though. But with Blythe and Leigh giving her a hand, they were soon searching the thick brambles for the prized blackberries.

Three

How sweet I roam'd from field to field,
And tasted all the summer's pride,
Till I the prince of love beheld
Who in the sunny beams did glide.

William Blake

"I JUST HOPE YOU HAVEN'T BEEN PICKING FARKLEBERRIES instead of blackberries, Julia," Blythe said, eyeing with some suspicion the full pail Julia held up so proudly.

"I do know what a blackberry looks like, dear," Julia responded smugly, making a face at Blythe, but she glanced down just in case a stray farkleberry had found its way into her pail. "Well, I don't care if there is a farkleberry in there, I won't take another step from under this tree," Julia vowed, collapsing onto the quilt and dragging her bonnet off as she rolled over and crossed her bare legs as if prepared to remain in so relaxed a position for some time.

Fanning herself lazily, she watched the Travers sisters with a wary eye, especially Leigh, who was busily loading the pails of blackberries into the cart, her hair hanging in untidy strands down her back. "La dee, but your mama is going to be fit to be tied, Leigh," Julia remarked. "Just look at you. Your hair is sprouting twigs, and I just hope you haven't gotten any freckles. Oh, and your hands! I declare, they're so purple with juice stains one might mistake you for a kitchen maid, or a *fille de joie* with your skirts tucked up and your petticoats and bare legs revealed so shamelessly," she said, giggling, and momentarily forgetting she'd been picking blackberries too, and in much the same state of dishabille.

"Whatever would Madame say if she could see one of her prized pupils now? '*Oh, mon Dieu! Vous êtes horrible, incorrigible, et peu digne d'une dame!*'" Julia said, clucking her tongue in mock disapproval and perfect imitation of Madame, who would have fainted at Leigh's unladylike behavior and Julia's unladylike language.

"Well, I can't pick berries with gloves on, and even Madame would understand that," Leigh said, frowning when she saw the purplish-blue stains that so delicately outlined her nails and highlighted every line running across her palms. "Oh, dear…" she murmured, momentarily startled by the damage.

"I declare, Leigh, you've even got a stain across your cheek. Or is it a scratch? Let me see your tongue," Julia ordered, sticking out her own for view. "I bet yours is purple! No wonder you have half as full a pail as I do, you've been eating every other one you picked."

"I was very selective in the ones I picked, Julayne," Leigh said, for she'd seen quite a number of small, reddish-green ones in Julia's pail.

"More likely, selective in the ones you ate," Julia said, tapping her fingers together complacently, but her mouth dropped open when she saw the dark purple stains on her own pale hands. "Oooh, no…" she cried, holding her hands up to the sunlight in disbelief, "this is just awful, What if my hands are still stained on Friday?"

"You could always wear a big purple ribbon in your hair," Blythe said, ducking behind the cart as Julia tossed one of her best kid slippers at the sly wretch.

Leigh ignored them and walked to the edge of the shade and whistled softly, staring across the meadow. Patiently, she waited, then smiled when she heard the answering neigh. A moment later, she spied Damascena's shiny chestnut coat through the leafy green of the brambles. The mare broke into a trot when she caught sight of Leigh's outstretched hand and the apple sitting squarely in the center of her palm.

"That's my girl," Leigh said, patting her lovingly, her fingers combing through the long tangled mane before she scratched the mare behind her ears affectionately.

"Here boy, I haven't forgotten you," Leigh said, pulling another apple from her looped-up skirt when she felt the warm breath of the colt against her arm. He snorted and shouldered his way closer between Leigh and the mare, his teeth quickly closing over the apple being held out so temptingly by his mistress.

Then he was racing away, kicking up his hind legs playfully as he circled the meadow, his tail held high. Leigh shielded her eyes as she followed his progress, noting with interest the measured, easy pace and the long length of his stride. He was going to be a winner, her little Capitaine, she thought proudly. She was still watching the colt when she was startled by a gentle nip on the soft flesh of her upper arm and jerked around to see the pony standing beside her, his velvety muzzle sniffing against her skirts as he searched for his treat.

Leigh rubbed the spot on her arm as she quickly sought the last apple she'd tucked away in the folds of her skirt. Moving her arm out of the way just in time to avoid a more painful bite this time for her slowness, she was about to deny the naughty pony his treat when she caught sight of his soulful brown eyes gazing up at her.

"All right, Pumpkin," Leigh said, relenting. She had hardly found the apple and held it out before the pony had claimed the prize. The little pony, fat as a pumpkin, was in no mood to share his meal, and he stalked off on his short, stubby legs to a safe spot beneath a tree. There he kept an eye on the frisky colt, whose long-legged gait and curiosity were bringing him closer with each circling of the meadow.

"Don't worry about those stains, Julia," Leigh said as she returned to where Julia was frantically trying to wipe away the purple stains from her hands with a cologne-soaked handkerchief, but the more she rubbed, the darker they seemed to become.

"Not to worry?" she squealed, staring down at the purplish-pink skin that covered her hands. "You may have Matthew Wycliffe so blinded with love for you that he might not notice anything amiss, even purple hands, but I am hardly so fortunate. How can I give my hand in marriage when it looks like this? I had intended to receive several proposals this week, Leigh. And now I cannot attend little Lucy's birthday party! I would become a laughingstock. The whole county will know, and when the gossip starts there will be no end to it. Why, Libby St. Martins will probably hear of this in Charleston and laugh her foolish blond head off," Julia cried, her voice rising shrilly. "And Libby is always claiming that her hair is fairer than mine," Julia stormed, the old grievance seeming all the more important with this latest threat to her beauty. "La dee, but hers looks quite brassy!"

Leigh, however, did not seem overly concerned as she sauntered back to the cart. She was well used to Julia's ravings, and seldom took them seriously. Reaching beneath the seat, she withdrew a bundle. "Jolie thinks of everything, even before Mama does," she said with a grin of satisfaction as she pulled a bottle stoppered with a cork from the bag and held it up for Julia to gaze upon.

"What is it?" she asked faintly, hardly daring to breathe lest her hopes be shattered. "Not Jolie's highly prized, secret skin balm? Oh, Leigh!" Julia exclaimed when Leigh nodded, for salvation was at hand. "It has never failed and everyone agrees that your mama, even for a woman her age, has the softest, palest, and most translucent skin in all of Virginia."

"Jolie thought Mama's lemon and cucumber lotion might not be strong enough, and she didn't want to cause my mother a fit of the vapors when she saw our hands."

"And what is that?" Julia demanded when Leigh held up another, smaller bottle that contained a delicate pink-tinted lotion.

"Roses and lavender," Blythe told her. "Mama's favorite, and guaranteed to leave your skin soft and sweet-scented after it has been scoured down to the bone by Jolie's voodoo mixture."

"Voodoo? Not really? What do you think is in it?" Julie asked, her gray eyes wide with horrified speculation that did nothing to lessen her determination to rub some on her stained hands.

"'Eye of newt, and toe of frog...'" Leigh quoted with Shakespearean seriousness, sidestepping Julia's other kid slipper as it flew past her head. "Actually, I think it has almonds in it, and oatmeal, and..."

"I hate oatmeal."

"...and lemon juice, and sour milk, and Jolie's secret herbs, which she gathers only by the light of a full moon."

Julia's mouth fell open. "No, not really?" she breathed, truly impressed. "It *is* very potent, isn't it? After all, Jolie took those horrid grass stains out of my best Sunday gown with it, remember? It must be magical," she declared, a complete believer in its powers.

Hearing a strange sound, almost like a muffled snort, Julia glanced with haughty disdain at Blythe, but Blythe, with an innocent-enough-looking expression, was lifting the last of the pails of blackberries into the cart.

"I recall it also ate a hole in the seat of one of Guy's finest pair of riding breeches," Blythe added on a helpful note.

"We'll have to wash this off as soon as we use it or it might cause an irritation," Leigh warned as she uncorked the bottle, wrinkling her nose at the odor that wafted forth before she poured some into Julia's eagerly outstretched hands.

Julia glanced up in surprise, her expression of pleasure becoming a frown. "A rash?" she said, thinking of the creamy, unmarred loveliness of her shoulders, especially when shown off to perfection in her new gown.

"It only happens to people with very delicate skin—"

"I have very delicate skin," Julia informed her, eyeing the liquid dripping from her palm as if it had suddenly turned into blood.

"—but I have seldom seen that happen," Leigh continued, pouring a fair amount into Blythe's hand and her own, then rubbing her hands together until the thick, grainy liquid had almost disappeared.

Julia gave a squeal. "It's coming off!"

"Your skin?" Blythe asked in genuine amazement, thinking there was no end to the tragedies that befell Julia.

"No, silly, the stains! The blackberry stains are gone!" she breathed in awe. "Quick, Leigh, where is the water?" she cried, glancing around for the carafe.

Leigh pointed behind Julia at the stream, the water looking invitingly cool.

"Oh, Leigh, no! If Blythe splashes me, then my dress will be ruined. The water spots will never come out of this material."

Blythe opened her mouth to protest, but then thought better of it when she remembered the last time they'd been on the riverbank and she'd splashed Julia's gown with a drenching spray of muddy water.

"Surely you are going to take your gown and petticoats off, Julia? I intend to, even if this is an old gown. And these petticoats—it will take forever to dry them out if they get wet. And I think that likely, for have you looked at your feet?" Leigh asked, turning around so Blythe could unhook her in back.

Julia stared down at her greenish-red toes, and for once in her life she was speechless—but not for long. "My toes! Oh! Leigh Alexandra Travers, I hate you! If you hadn't insisted we go blackberry picking, none of this would ever have happened! I declare, this is an afternoon I'll not soon forget, or forgive you for," Julia said with a tearful sniff, placing the full blame for her predicament on Leigh.

"Now, now, Julayne," Leigh said soothingly, and Blythe grinned, thinking Leigh knew how to handle Julia even better than plump little Pumpkin. "Let's unhook you, then rub some balm on your feet, then we'll wade into the stream and wash it all off. Remember how much fun we used to have wading, and it is so hot, don't you think?" Leigh said in a persuasive tone as she unhooked Julia's gown and untied her petticoats and poured more of Jolie's special balm into Julia's palm.

"Well...'tis rather hot," Julia allowed, and it did feel good to be out of her gown and petticoats and standing in the cool shade in only her chemise and pantalettes. "La dee, I do wish I hadn't had Bella lace me so tight this morning, but I do declare I've been having trouble getting into my best Charleston gowns since I came home," Julia fretted, wishing she hadn't had that last stuffed egg as she tried to loosen the laces of her corset. She started to giggle when she caught sight of Leigh and Blythe, who'd draped their gowns and petticoats over the side of the cart.

"Oh, dear, whatever would Madame say if she could see us now? We look worse than gypsies. I dare say we couldn't go for a Sunday stroll along the Battery dressed like this," she said, feeling slightly giddy at the thought of such a scandalous scene—and yet, the thought of standing before a gentleman in only her chemise and pantalettes caused Julia's heart to quicken its beat.

"I do believe you are blushing, Julia," Blythe said as she ran down the slope and splashed into the stream with complete abandon, just as Julia had feared she would.

At a far more circumspect pace, Julia followed, looking for all the world as if she were indeed out for a Sunday stroll—in her finest lace-edged pantalettes and best straw bonnet, her dainty parasol held aloft to shield her from the sun.

Leigh, after hanging Julia's petticoats and gown on the cart, was the last to enter, and by then Julia was perched on a flat rock, her bare feet dangling in the clear waters of the stream.

Leigh waded into the middle, the frill of lace on the legs of her pantalettes becoming soaked as she went deeper. Bending over, she dunked her hands into the water, washing away Jolie's balm, then rinsed her feet and calves. Straightening, she glanced around curiously, expecting to see Julia or Blythe watching her, but Blythe was wandering along the far bank and Julia was intent upon her own thoughts.

"We really must do this more often, Leigh," Julia said, flicking a bug from her foot with the tip of her parasol. "It truly is quite refreshing."

"Why don't you come back in, Julia. This mud feels wonderful squishing between your toes," Blythe said, her attention caught by a frog leaping into the grasses on the far bank.

"It really is such a pity that Blythe hasn't had the pleasure of meeting Madame. I suspect she could do wonders with the child," Julia said with a heartfelt sigh, her own attention held as she admired her reflection in the water. "You do remember I am going to be staying at Travers Hill tonight, since Althea and Nathan are staying over. I just hope I don't have to share a room with Noelle."

"You'll be sleeping in our room," Leigh assured her, glancing down at her feet, which were now free of grass and berry stains. She held up her hands, smiling at the results of Jolie's special balm.

"Did you remember to bring that lotion, Blythe?" Julia asked, glancing down at her own slender hands. "I don't want my skin to become chafed."

"It's behind you on the rock, Julia," Blythe told her, making a grab at the frog. "Don't bother, Julia, dear, I'll get it for you. I believe it is out of your reach," Blythe said, hurrying over to where Julia sat daydreaming on the rock.

"There. Hold out your hand," Blythe requested, placing the frog in Julia's innocently outstretched palm.

The squeal that followed was gratification enough for Blythe, who had quickly made her way to the opposite bank. Her laughter became uncontrollable when Julia jumped off the rock. The frog leaped even farther, and Julia, trying to keep her balance, dropped her parasol into the water.

Leigh stared at Julia's silk-fringed parasol floating away

downstream. Muffling her laughter as she waded past Julia, unaware that she splashed her even more as she hurried past, Leigh caught the parasol before it sank.

Holding it up, water dripping from the fringe, Leigh returned to where Julia was standing, cheeks pink with outraged indignation.

"Your parasol, Julia."

"Thank you, and I'll have you know that I will get even with Blythe Lucinda Travers, and at her sixteenth birthday party. Beware, Lucy, for I am Adam Braedon's sister, and I will even the score in a manner which you will never suspect," she promised, and taking her ruined parasol from Leigh, she stomped from the stream, splashing more water over her already damp pantalettes.

"I shouldn't have done that," Blythe said, feeling a twinge of remorse and even more concern over Julia's promise of retribution.

"No, you really should not have," Leigh agreed, her voice soft, but before Blythe could move out of the way, a wave of water swept over her, soaking her.

Julia's laughter drifted across the bank, but before Blythe could even the score with her sister, Leigh had waded into the middle of the stream, where a deep pond had been formed by a natural dam, and disappeared into the water until just her head and arms showed. She sighed with the pleasure of the cool water surrounding her, a challenging glint in her eye as she met her sister's speculative glance.

"Leigh! Whatever are you doing?" Julia exclaimed from the bank where she was hurriedly gathering her petticoats and trying to restore her maidenly modesty.

"You are going to outsmart yourself one of these days, Leigh Alexandra," Blythe warned, for Leigh always seemed to be a step ahead of her—and the splash she had intended sending her sister's way.

"Better I do it than you, little sister," Leigh said, her smile widening into one of devilish satisfaction. "Umm, this feels wonderful. I was so hot and sticky. Why don't you both come back in for a swim? Our underclothing will dry fast enough in this heat."

"Not me!" Julia declared adamantly. "You really are

behaving most improperly, Leigh—even if we are on Travers land and no one's likely to see you, except your mama when you try to sneak back into the house, and dripping across her fine carpets. Well, I just hope you don't get chilled and have to be confined to your bed on little Lucy's birthday. And you'll never untie your laces now," Julia said, her voice muffled as she struggled into her petticoats. "They'll be in knots."

"They'll dry," Leigh said, drifting dreamily through the caressing waters, her eyes closed against the glare. "Besides, Jolie is the only one who can ever untie them anyway."

Leigh opened her sleep-drowsy eyes and stared up at the deep blue sky that didn't have a cloud in it.

Mrs. Matthew Wycliffe. The Mrs. Matthew Rutherford Wycliffe. Leigh Alexandra Wycliffe of Wycliffe Hall Charleston, South Carolina.

Leigh sighed, wishing it were Virginia rather than South Carolina. Of course, she'd always known that one day she would have to leave Travers Hill. Despite the sadness of that day, it would also be her wedding day, and Leigh's lips parted with pleasure as the vision of Matthew Wycliffe as her husband-to-be floated before her. His black hair was thick and shiny, and his brown eyes were wide-spaced and thickly lashed, and bright with intelligence. He possessed a firm jaw, and his mouth was nicely proportioned, his teeth quite even. He had a fine-looking nose. He was taller than her father, and could sit a horse as well as any—even Guy. And, Matthew was a gentleman. He was everything a young lady—and a young lady's family—could hope for in a suitor. When Matthew asked for her hand in marriage, her father would give his permission and she'd have her mother's blessing. *Yes*, she would say yes when Matt asked her to marry...

"Leigh!" Julia's voice called out. "You're going to end up floating downriver into Richmond *en déshabillé* if you don't wake up."

"On disabeel? What's that? Something like a barge?" Blythe questioned, staying well out of Julia's reach.

Leigh kicked her feet and paddled back toward the bank, her arms moving in slow, deliberate strokes through the water. Her dreams of Matthew Wycliffe were temporarily forgotten as she stood up and walked toward the bank where Julia and

Blythe were sitting in companionable silence. Julia was rubbing the creamy lotion over her arms and legs with a lavish hand while Blythe wove wildflowers and grasses into fragrant braided wreaths.

"Leigh!" Julia squealed. "You're dripping all over us."

"Sorry," Leigh murmured, stopping by the bundle Jolie had prepared and pulling out a brush. Leigh dried her arms and shoulders with the skirt of her gown, then pulled the silk net and hairpins from the untidy chignon that was hanging lopsided against her nape. She began to brush the long strands free of tangles as she walked past Julia and Blythe, coming to stand on the edge of the meadow, her eyes searching for Damascena and Capitaine. The lazy pony was grazing peacefully beneath his tree and showed no signs of wandering off, and she suspected he might prove stubborn about being hitched up to the cart again.

Leigh whistled softly, but there was still no sign of her horses. She waited, brushing her long hair until it fell in a smooth, silken veil across one shoulder, the ends curling past her hip to midthigh. Her gaze wandered over the tranquil glade, lingering for a moment on the shadowy copse beyond the blackberry brambles, where she thought she saw a movement. She whistled again, expecting to see Damascena come racing from cover, but the copse remained undisturbed and silent.

Suddenly, from the opposite direction, Leigh heard the familiar hoofbeats and turned to see the mare and colt racing toward her. With a low laugh, she opened her arms to them.

In the cool shadows of the copse where Leigh thought she had seen a movement, a lone rider had sat watching the woodland nymphs. A slight smile of pleasure had softened his lean, sun-bronzed face as he gazed upon the romantic scene of three lovely young women bathing with seductive innocence in the cool waters of a gently murmuring stream.

The rider had watched them for some time, unwilling to disturb their idyll, or forfeit so rare a privilege of viewing the three beauties without their knowledge. He had come upon them in the act of disrobing, his keen eye not having missed the pails of blackberries in the cart. On so warm a summer's day, and after so arduous a task, it had seemed only natural to wish to take a refreshing dip in the stream—which had been his intention when spying the stream from across the meadow. But he had put aside his own wishes and, with considerable patience and pleasure, had enjoyed their childish pranks in the stream, their ladylike decorum forgotten as they frolicked on a midsummer's afternoon.

It was apparent by her actions that the fairest of the young women had aspirations of becoming a great lady. Affected and indolent, she was the perfect image of the pampered lady of the manor, her every wish or whim instantly gratified. He had laughed softly when the dark-haired one had placed the frog in her hand. The little dark-haired one, still more girl child than woman, seemed determined to cause mischief. He had noticed a defiance in her actions—as if she sensed this would be her last summer of innocence and was rebelling against leaving the carefree world of childhood.

The rider's gaze narrowed as one of the young women stepped from the shade. *She* had been the one who had caught his interest the most. He was surprised that she held such a fascination for him. But there had been something so elusive about the way she moved, the water hardly rippling around her as she'd walked from the stream. There was a natural grace and beauty about her, nothing affected or calculated to attract. And her smile seemed to come as quickly as her laugh, even when seeing to the needs of her spoiled mistress, on whom she waited hand and foot.

As she stood there staring out at the meadow, she began to brush her long hair. The man felt a warm stirring in his loins as he watched the slow, rhythmic movements of the brush through the silky strands. How far more seductive a woman was when half-dressed, with the glory of her hair unbound, he thought, than when dressed in her finest silk gown, her hair confined in tight curls atop her head. And as he continued to watch her, he felt the strange enchantment of the moment and knew it would never be enough just to gaze upon this young woman's beauty from afar. There was a warmth about her that drew him to her as surely as a moth to a flame, and he wanted to feel the sensual pleasure of touching her, to know the satisfaction of arousing her to a fiery passion that would match his own.

And yet she continued to stand before him, innocent of his desire while she revealed herself to him with a wanton's disregard of the consequences. How many men had she tempted with her beauty? He couldn't believe she could be so ingenuous. Some man would have lain with her by now, have made her his. The man was startled by the sudden jab of jealousy that made him resent that unknown man, for he would have wished to have been the first man to have awakened her to passion—to feel the warmth of this woman in his arms, to have her hold him close to her heart. What would it feel like to possess her, to know her love, he wondered idly.

A shrill whistle pierced the silence, drawing him from his thoughts. He heard the hoofbeats before he saw the mare and colt. Strangely enough, he wasn't surprised when the young woman opened her arms to them. Almost enviously, the man watched as the colt insinuated himself close to her, his velvety muzzle pressing against her warmth with the self-assurance of a beloved pet. Dropping the brush, she climbed on the mare's back with incredible gracefulness, sitting astride, with no saddle for support or reins to control her mount. With a slight nudge of her bare heels, she sent the mare into an easy trot around the meadow, the colt galloping alongside.

The man had never seen so magnificent a sight. If he had believed the young woman beautiful before, she was bewitching now. With her hair hanging down to her hips, and the same rich chestnut shade as her horse, she rode as if one with the beast. Her thick, shining mane flowed over her shoulders as she rode, seeming to blend with the mare's. Golden strands of hair, like captured sunlight, glistened in the heavy, silken tresses. The man's breath caught when she suddenly stood up on the mare's back, balancing with an ease he'd seldom seen.

As the young bareback rider drew closer across the meadow, he could see that she was small-boned and delicate-featured. The damp linen of her lacy pantalettes and chemise clung to her flesh, revealing it as truly as if bared naked to his searing gaze. Her shoulders were thrown back, arms outstretched for balance, and her breasts were high, their firm roundness pressed against the thin chemise. The nipples were hard, as if her breasts had been cupped in his hands and the soft peaks hardened into passion beneath his caress. Even with a corset laced tight, he could tell her waist would be tiny, and easily held captive between his hands as he brought the soft, womanly curves of her hip and belly against the hardness of his. The linen covering her buttocks molded their shape, enticing him and drawing his eye along the curving line of translucent material. Her thighs were slender and smoothly muscled from riding. He could see the gentle rippling of taut flesh and knew they would hold him tight, after having yielded and parted against the pressure of his own, their soft length wrapping around him and enfolding him as he took her to him. Her calves tapered down to small ankles and feet that were high-arched, the delicate curves destined for the touch of a man's lips. *His lips.*

What would her lips, her kiss, taste like? To feel the silky softness of her hair tangled in his hands, and the heat of her flesh against his, branding him with her scent.

The rider's smile suddenly became cynical at his own lustful thoughts. The warm expression in his eyes cooled into a glittering iciness as he wondered if she would be a warm, loving woman in his bed. Or would she become cold and unresponsive, suffering his touch because she was his wife and had a duty to perform, or was a whore who wanted to be paid for the evening's pleasure she had sold him?

Could this woman be any different? Was her beauty true? The rider's gloved hands tightened slightly on the reins of the big bay he rode as he continued to sit beneath the trees, enjoying the vision of loveliness despite the old doubts and disappointments warring within.

He had speculated on her relationship to the fair-haired miss, believing she might be her ladyship's personal maid, but watching the way she rode, as if born to it, he wondered if she might not also be a groom's or trainer's daughter from one of the horse-breeding farms nearby. As the bareback rider circled the meadow, the dark-haired girl came to stand just beyond the shade. As the rider neared the tree, the dark-haired girl held out a wreath of flowers, which the bareback rider caught easily over her arm, twirling it as she rounded the meadow again. With a laugh that drifted to him on the warm, meadow-sweet breeze, she placed the flowery crown on her head—soft and fragrant, the flowers were far lovelier than a crown of the most priceless jewels.

One more time around, she came, and the man found himself gazing more closely at her face, trying to discover what color her eyes were, but they remained a mystery to him. If he had been close enough to see their color...

Regretfully, however, he watched as the spirited bareback rider halted the mare in front of the dark-haired girl, who had been viewing the acrobatic feats with cries of pleasure and encouragement. Dismounting, the beauty with the unbound hair patted the mare on its rump and sent it and the colt back out to graze. She accompanied the dark-haired girl to where the fair-haired one had almost managed to complete her toilette, except for hooking up the back of her elegant gown, the voluminous skirts threatening to consume everything in sight.

Sadly, he watched as the other two pulled on their petticoats and then their gowns, which, not surprisingly, were far less elegant than the fair-haired one's. Soon, they had hooked themselves inside the concealing folds of linen and muslin and propriety, their carefree abandon seeming to disappear along with their tender flesh. For several minutes, they seemed to be searching for the remaining articles of their clothing, because the dark-haired girl, who had disappeared somewhere behind the cart, held up a slipper with a cry of triumph.

Suddenly a shrill cry of terror reverberated across the meadow. The man instinctively reached for the rifle at his knee. Pulling it from the holster and cocking it, he had already taken aim, ready to pull the trigger, when he suddenly began to laugh softly.

The fair-haired young woman's screams had turned into shrill, angry words. Out of one of the baskets, a harmless garden snake had slithered across the quilt, causing the fair one's initial fright. When the dark-haired girl, who was obviously far more stouthearted than the others, had captured the snake and held it up for their perusal, the fair one's voice had become piercing with her objections.

He was surprised to hear the laughter of the other two, who seemed interested in taking a closer look at the snake, but the fair-haired one refused, preferring to maintain a safe distance.

The danger past, especially when the dark-haired one had freed the frightened snake, the rider uncocked the rifle and slid it back into the leather scabbard hanging from his saddle. Far too quickly, they had loaded the baskets into the cart and folded up the quilt. With the pony hitched to the cart, and the fair-haired one and the dark-haired one settled inside, they began to cross the meadow, the mare and colt walking docilely beside their mistress as she guided the pony with a gentle yet firm hand. The shadows were lengthening and the shafts of sunlight slanting down through the trees had deepened to a burnished gold as the afternoon fled.

The rider's gaze never left the cart's progress across the meadow—or the beautiful young woman walking barefoot through the tall grasses, her unbound hair fiery with the touch of the sun, and crowned by a wreath of wildflowers. In the afternoon light, she was warm and golden, and he longed to reach out and touch her and know that she was real.

Far too soon for his peace of mind, the little caravan disappeared into the trees on the far side of the meadow. Leaving the shadowy confines of the glade where he'd remained hidden from view, the rider, with a packhorse following on a lead behind, crossed the meadow—silent and empty now that the three young belles had left. Despite himself, the rider began to wonder if it had all been an illusion, especially as he reached the place where the vision of loveliness had stood brushing her hair.

"Thirsty, boy?" the rider asked softly, patting the big bay as they neared the stream that had first attracted him to this enchanted meadow.

Suddenly, the rider grinned, for his hawkish search of the area had rewarded him. Within arm's reach, caught on a bramble bush was a single stocking, the finely spun silk of the palest shade of blue. Holding it to his face, he breathed deeply of the sweet scent of lavender and roses, careful not to snag the delicate material on the rough leather of his gloves.

Hers. She was real, he thought, remembering her walking barefoot across the meadow. He stared down at the prize with as much pleasure as any conqueror of old would have when claiming the spoils of victory.

Dismounting, he walked beneath the canopy of branches, the bay following close behind. The rider moved quickly, and silently, his steps light as he crossed the bank where the three young women had waded into the stream. His gaze missed nothing of his surroundings: not the footprints in the muddied bank, the grass still matted down where the quilt had been spread beneath the tree, the wheel tracks from the cart, or on the far bank, the underbrush and trees that crowded close and would offer cover to someone.

Remaining on the bank for a moment longer, he stared down at the blue stocking he still held gently in his gloved hands. As if becoming aware of his own attire, and the dirt and sweat clinging to him, he eyed the cool waters that only a short while ago had lapped so sensuously around his vision's hips.

"Come on, fellas, drink up," the rider said, allowing his horses onto the bank.

Throwing the blue silk stocking over his shoulder, he began to unsaddle the bay, tossing his gear near the base of the tree, but keeping the rifle close at hand. The mounds of supplies followed, relieving the packhorse of his load as the rider allowed the two to graze on the tender, sweet grass of the meadow.

Spying several blackberries that had spilled from the pails, the man picked them up. They were sweet and juicy. The delicate scent of lavender reminded him of the stocking and he carefully folded it up and placed it in one of the canvas-covered bundles. Quickly shedding his clothes beneath the tree, he walked to the stream and waded into the cool waters.

The man began to feel the tired ache of his muscles fade as the water soothed his flesh. Lying on his back, he allowed himself to drift as he stared up at the blue sky, his thoughts on the young woman with the unbound chestnut hair, of her floating beside him, her soft body touching his as her lips came close…

The chestnut-haired beauty of his dreams, the long strands of her unbound hair now twisted into a prim braid that hung down her back, was riding back through the glade toward the meadow, the retrieval of her blue silk stocking the only thing on her mind.

Leigh lightly touched her bare heel to the mare's flank to hurry her along the shadow-dappled path, thinking of Blythe and Julia waiting impatiently for her back on the road. She had only discovered her stocking missing after they'd reached the road and she had stopped to put on her stockings and slippers.

It was Adam Merton Braedon's fault, Leigh thought, a glint in her eye as she thought of evening the score with him. If he hadn't planted that snake in their picnic basket, she wouldn't have scattered her clothing, losing her blue silk stocking when Julia had screamed. And that he was behind the prank, she had no doubts, although Blythe had seemed a bit too innocently shocked, for seldom had she seen a snake with a ribbon tied around its middle. And Adam had returned to Royal Bay just last evening, well in time to try his hand at mischief. Adam could not have borne the disappointment had they thought the snake had accidentally slithered into their picnic basket. He took great pride in his pranks—and in taking credit for them. Indeed, he might even have been hiding in the trees during the whole episode, and laughing uproariously, just as Julia had predicted earlier, Leigh realized, glancing around.

It was then that Leigh became aware of the strange horses grazing in the meadow. Halting Damascena beneath the trees, she hopped down, leaving the mare waiting patiently beneath the branches.

Moving cautiously, Leigh approached the two horses. Although the one horse, the bay, was unknown to her, its bloodlines were not. It was from the stables at Royal Bay. She would recognize one of their bays anywhere. And from its color and blaze on its forehead, she'd bet its dam was Royal Blaze.

Curious, a suspicion gaining strength in her mind, Leigh kept to the edge of the meadow, just within cover of the trees, as she approached the stream. Reaching the blackberry brambles, where only an hour earlier she'd been picking berries, she halted, staring in amazement at the stream, where not more than half an hour past, she'd been swimming.

As she watched, a dark golden head disappeared beneath the surface of the deep pool near the opposite bank. Reappearing, the man gave a shake to his longish hair and flexed his wide shoulders, as if banishing the tiredness from his body.

With a widening smile on her face, Leigh carefully backed away, moving stealthily along the outside of the brambles, where she wouldn't be seen from the stream.

She had recognized that golden head, and Adam was in for a big surprise, she vowed as she neared the tree where they'd had their picnic. Beneath the tree, in an untidy pile, were Adam's clothes. Cupping her hand across her mouth to smother her laughter, Leigh hurried over and quickly gathered up his clothing. Keeping watch on the stream, where Adam was still bathing with his back to her, Leigh carefully backed away, hurrying back to her hiding place in the blackberry brambles.

Glancing down at the clothing held close against her rapidly beating breast, Leigh knew an instant of surprise as she stared at the buckskin. Odd, she'd never seen Adam wearing anything so strange. In fact, it was hard to imagine Adam looking anything but the well-dressed gentleman. He had always taken pleasure in the fashionable cut of his trousers and the mother-of-pearl studs for his fine linen shirts. And the last time she'd seen Adam, he'd played continually with the fancy fob chain dangling from his silk waistcoat. No, this did not seem like Adam at all, Leigh began to doubt, looking down at the rough buckskin beneath her hand. Of course, Adam had been away, and now fancied himself a seafaring man, so she should not be surprised to find Adam wearing such clothing, she reassured herself.

Reaching the blackberry brambles, Leigh suddenly froze, the sound of a twig snapping beneath her foot echoing like a gunshot in the quiet glade. Leigh crouched down, unwilling to have Adam discover the prank too soon. It would hardly be amusing to be caught in the act of stealing his clothes. How much more amusing to have him believe that a common thief had sneaked into the bushes with his finery, Leigh chuckled, determined to win the hand and have the pleasure of surprising Adam for once.

She would have her revenge against him for planting that snake in their basket, Leigh vowed, prepared to savor it as she peered through the leafy branches that effectively hid her from view—her gaze seeking the dark golden head of her enemy.

Leigh Alexandra Travers gasped. Never had she been so surprised in her life, for the man staring intently at her hiding place was *not* Adam Merton Braedon—the man was a complete stranger!

Leigh swallowed hard. She couldn't understand her mistake, she thought in disbelief. She would have sworn it had been Adam swimming in the stream. The sun shining down on this stranger's head had turned the dark gold of his hair to the same burnished shade as Adam's, but it also made the hawkish-featured face all the more forbidding. Never had she seen such a harsh and unforgiving expression. With a sinking of her heart, Leigh wondered how she could ever explain her actions. He might even believe she was a thief who had been rummaging through his clothes in search of valuables.

Suddenly there seemed incredible strength and power in his muscular arms as he swam ever closer toward shore, his narrowed gaze seeming to penetrate through the brambles to capture her where she crouched like a frightened rabbit cowering beneath a hawk's shadow.

Like that rabbit, Leigh was too frightened to move. If she did, then he would surely spot her, for she doubted he could really see through the thicket to where she remained safely hidden, she comforted herself with the thought. However, if he came out of the water…

Leigh closed her eyes in growing embarrassment before opening them again to look down at the buckskin breeches she clutched so tightly. Leigh risked another glance at the pool, her worst fears realized as she watched the stranger slowly wade from the pool. Water was dripping from his broad-shouldered frame, down the bronzed chest rippling with muscle, where the golden hairs were thickly matted, to trickle along the tapering leanness of his naked hips, before disappearing into the water that was now low enough on his body to reveal his bold maleness and thighs hard and sinewy.

Whether she revealed herself or not, she couldn't remain where she was any longer, Leigh decided, suddenly determined not to wait another second before fleeing. Fearing more for her threatened modesty than her safety, she found the courage to move.

But before Leigh revealed herself to the searching gaze of the man, a loud crashing noise sounded directly behind her, causing her to glance around in fear. Losing her balance, Leigh fell to her knees as Capitaine raced out of the trees behind her, his playful neighing masking her cry of surprise. Intent on being naughty, he galloped past, his tail waving like a streamer, his hooves sending clumps of dirt flying. Breaking through the bushes, he startled the man as much as he had Leigh only seconds before.

But Leigh did not wait a second longer, and still under cover of the brambles, she crawled through them, then raced as fast as she could into the safety of the trees while Capitaine kept the man's attention turned away. Praying the man was not in hot pursuit, she nevertheless ran faster than ever, oblivious of the branches and tangles slapping against her face and grabbing at her ankles, and forgetting about the buckskins she still held in her arms.

Reaching the tree where she'd left Damascena, Leigh's skirt caught on a bramble; losing precious seconds, she freed the snagged material, then pulled Damascena after her through the trees. Halfway down the forest path, Leigh stopped and quickly mounted, the buckskins nearly dropping from her grasp as she pulled herself onto the mare's back.

Only then did Leigh rather belatedly realize that she still had the man's clothes. She could hardly ride up to Blythe and Julia with a pair of man's buckskin breeches in her possession. With considerable reservation, she quickly stuffed the buckskin breeches and shirt beneath her skirts, tucking them securely between her legs and the mare. At least she wouldn't have to answer any embarrassing questions from Blythe and Julia. She would return the clothes to the pool the first opportunity she had, Leigh promised herself. She was no thief, despite what the man might be thinking right now. Of course, from the condition of the buckskins, he did not look as if he were a man of great wealth. How could she possibly steal anything from him—except his clothes? He must be furious, especially if he had nothing else to wear, and it was beginning to grow chilly. With an uncontrollable smile beginning to curve her lips, Leigh sadly thought of the man's predicament.

Hearing a crashing sound in the bushes, Leigh looked back, dread filling her, certain she would see the naked man come racing down the path. Relieved, Leigh laughed, for it was just Capitaine, tired of his game and trotting back to find them.

Leigh patted the colt's back. "Thank you, little one," she said softly, urging the mare down the path and away from the stream.

In the woods, standing beneath the tree, Neil Darcy Braedon was cursing his own stupidity. He knew there had been someone there, watching him, he'd felt it, but when the colt had shot from the trees he had allowed himself to believe there hadn't been anyone after all, just that frisky colt. And it had proved just as elusive as its mistress.

He had been wrong, he thought in disgust as he stared down at the place where his clothes should have been. Nothing.

Stolen.

Damn, he thought again, wishing he could get his hands on the thief and wring his treacherous neck. Gone. His clothes had been stolen. And, *it* was gone too. The soft leather pouch that he wore suspended from a rawhide thong was missing—and inside that pouch his most treasured possessions. And most prized of all, the delicate silver dagger—his talisman.

A good luck charm to ward off evil spirits? Perhaps he believed in its power—perhaps not. But it was one of his few possessions from another time and he cherished it. Almost everything else from those seven years of captivity had been destroyed by his father.

Neil Braedon glanced around in distaste at the golden shadows of the glade. Only a short while ago it had seemed so enchanted. And for just an instant, he had let down his guard and allowed himself to dream. And that had been when something very precious had been stolen from him. Neil cursed himself for the fool he had been as he pulled out the clothes he'd planned to wear after his bath. He hadn't wanted to arrive at Royal Bay dusty and disheveled, and looking half the savage in his buckskins.

But now...now he would wait...and he would search the glade and beyond until he found the thief who had stolen from him. He would take infinite pleasure in the punishment he had planned. But even as Neil savored that thought, he couldn't quite banish the image of the girl with the long chestnut hair glistening in the sun, and he found himself wondering again about the color of her eyes.

Four

Blue, darkly, deeply, beautifully blue.

Robert Southey

REACHING TRAVERS HILL HAD BEEN FAR EASIER THAN Leigh had anticipated. Still breathless from her escape, she had rejoined Blythe and Julia on the lane, the stolen buckskins safely tucked beneath her damp posterior, and none-too-comfortably since something sharp kept stabbing her tender flesh. But not one suspicious glance or question had come from the two busily chatting occupants of the cart. And neither of them had noticed Leigh's frequent backward glances, but since the road behind had remained empty Leigh hadn't seen the need of informing them that they might be in serious danger of having their maidenly innocence compromised by the sight of a naked man.

The situation, however, had become slightly more difficult as they'd neared home. Upon reaching the curving drive leading up to the front of the house, Leigh had seen most of her family sitting on the veranda. Under the guise of stabling Damascena and Capitaine, and changing into another pair of stockings, Leigh had ridden around back unobserved. Blythe and Julia, reclining as if seated in a royal coach-and-four, had been pulled up to the front of the house by the shaggy little pony trotting as fast as his short legs could step, a wreath of flowers adorning his proudly held head. The pails of blackberries, and Julia's overly excited and extremely exaggerated version of the afternoon's activities, would guarantee her family's interest long enough, Leigh had hoped, for her to enter the house and hide the buckskins with no one being any the wiser. Then, changing into a dry pair of pantalettes and chemise, she would join her family on the veranda as if nothing out of the ordinary had occurred on this warm summer's afternoon.

Leaving Damascena and Capitaine in the hands of a capable groom, who seemed to see nothing odd in the bundle of buckskin tucked beneath the young lady's arm, Leigh had hurried along the flagstoned path from the stables. She passed the kitchen gardens with hardly a glance, nor did she give much attention to the washing hanging on the line on the other side of the path. Her goal had come into sight: the half-opened door to the scullery, which would give her access into the kitchens, pantry, larder, and laundry. Once inside, all she would have to do is hurry along the covered passageway between the kitchens and the big house, avoiding the open stretch of yard, where she might easily have been seen from her mother's bedchamber window. Every afternoon, about this time, her mother would sit at her small slant-front desk next to the window, her spectacles perched low on her nose as she went over with Jolie in the minutest detail the menus and lists of chores for the following day. And Jolie standing ever vigilant at her mistress's shoulder had a clear view of the yard below and observed all who came and went.

It was on the thought that she would have to be especially careful when passing by her mother's bedchamber door that Leigh came to a sudden standstill. Standing in the middle of the kitchen yard, a tall, thin, coppery-skinned woman stood surveying her small kingdom, and the busy maids laundering the family's linens.

Jolie!

Leigh sighed at the hopelessness of it all. To have come this far without detection, and all for nothing—because *nothing*, beast or human, would get past those narrowed, strangely tinted yellowish-brown eyes.

Still partly hidden by the long line of washing, Leigh stayed where she was, trying to decide the best course of action. She couldn't reach the house without being seen, and Jolie would be certain to spy the bundle of buckskin. And she couldn't retrace her steps now, because Jolie had moved to the far end of the yard, where she had an unobstructed view of the stables across the greensward. And there was no place to hide either herself or the buckskins, Leigh thought as she eyed the freshly turned earth of the newly planted herb garden adjacent to the stone wall that paralleled the path. She was trapped. Leigh looked down at the buckskins in her arms, wishing she could toss them over the wall, but it was too far away. Hearing Jolie's voice moving closer, Leigh knelt down, the buckskins hugged close against her breast. Gradually, she became aware of the almost overpowering odor of leather, horses, and sweat that permeated the man's clothes—there was also the faint fragrance of lavender and roses from where she'd sat on them in her damp pantalettes.

Leigh grimaced, damning the buckskins even more as she stood up, but holding them at a fastidious distance from her person now. Glancing back into the yard, she wished she could drop the offending buckskins into a tub of soapy water. She had forgotten the washing would be done today instead of tomorrow, the usual day, since there was so much cleaning and baking to be done this week in preparation for Blythe's birthday party. As long as she stayed hidden behind the gently swaying row of clean drawers and lacy chemises, Jolie might not see her, but she couldn't stay behind the wet laundry forever, Leigh fretted. She heard giggling, followed by hastily hushed whispers, and glanced between the frilly legs of a pair of pantalettes.

Spread out across the yard were various-sized washing tubs. Each had a washerwoman bent over its rim, arms elbow-high in soapy lather as the piles of soiled clothes were being meticulously scrubbed of stains before being rinsed several times in another tub of clear water. Finally placed in the big copper furnace, the linens would be boiled to a pristine whiteness before being wrung and hung out to dry. It was an endless chore that came all too soon every Monday, and the whole household was in an uproar as Jolie gathered her troops and tracked down all of the dirty linens and clothing, then sorted and counted and checked every piece for spots and stains and mending chores. And tonight, Leigh knew that half of the maids would be standing over the ironing boards in the laundry pressing the intricate ruffled collars and cuffs and frills on the finest garments.

The mistress of Travers Hill was very particular about the family's linens and clothing. Although some articles might have been mended many times over, never would a guest discover a soiled and torn, unpressed sheet on a bed, or a family member be allowed to wear a garment that hadn't been properly laundered. Perhaps a person might be clad in darned stockings and mended cuffs, but they still had their pride, Beatrice Amelia was fond of reminding her family.

Slowly, Leigh moved along the path, staying hidden behind the wet clothes. Once or twice she risked another glance, but Jolie seemed to be everywhere, and constantly eyeing everything. Leigh was still standing indecisively behind a pair of her father's drawers, when one of the youngest laundry maids came walking around the far end of the line of washing, a big basket heavy with dripping linens balanced on her hip. As Leigh watched, she began to hang the assorted collars, cuffs, handkerchiefs, and stockings, carefully secured with wooden pegs, along the length of flaxen line.

"Jassy," Leigh said softly, glancing over the pair of drawers to where Jolie now stood beside a harassed washerwoman, the cuffs she'd been scrubbing apparently not meeting Jolie's high standard of excellence.

Jassy gave a small cry of surprise, then smiled when she recognized the young mistress. "Oh, Miz Leigh, you scared me so! It's that Jolie, sneakin' up behind me, I was thinkin'. Don't want no more of her pinches. I worked harder this day than I ever have. An' still that ol' Jolie comes a-pinchin' an' a-slappin' an' a-puttin' that evil eye of hers on me. An' now, I've finished this batch, an' then she'll give me a bigger batch to do, an' I'll never get dinner tonight, 'cause I've the ironin' to do an' then the foldin' an' then the puttin' up, an' it's Sunday an' we have biscuits, an' maybe some fried catfish. Dan'l an' Sweet John been fishin', Miz Leigh. That Jolie, she's a mean one. It's that savage blood from her papa, I reckon."

Leigh grinned, thinking she had just discovered the solution to both of their problems. "Would you wash these, Jassy?" Leigh suggested, shoving the bundle of buckskin toward the startled girl. "They won't take long. And Jolie will be pleased and she'll leave you alone."

Now she could walk leisurely into the house without making Jolie any more suspicious than usual, Leigh thought, and she would have the stranger's buckskins washed before she returned them—which, considering their condition, was a great kindness on her part—and Jassy could avoid Jolie's wrath.

Jassy frowned as she stared down at the buckskin breeches she now held out in front of her. "These men's britches," she said in amazement. "An' a mighty long-legged one at that. Where'd you get these, Miz Leigh?" she demanded, looking them over with a critical eye. "These aren't a gentleman's britches!" she suddenly exclaimed, lifting her nose with a disdainful sniff.

"Shhhssh!" Leigh hushed her, cringing down even lower.

"How'd you get hold of these, Miz Leigh? Yer mama's not goin' to like this any if she finds out," Jassy said wisely, for everyone knew that the mistress of Travers Hill was a proper lady.

"Please, Jassy, just wash them for me," Leigh pleaded, peeking across the washing to where Jolie still stood, hands on her hips, but Leigh would have sworn Jolie had moved a tub closer. "It is a secret."

"A secret?" Jassy asked, a doubtful look on her face as she held up the shirt. "They must be Mister Guy's? That's it! Always doin' somethin' he shouldn't be. But I don't know where he's goin' to wear somethin' like these ol' britches. An' they're too long fer him anyway. He's almost as short legged as Mister Stuart. What's this? You want it washed too?"

Leigh was just as startled to see the leather pouch drop to the path when Jassy shook out the shirt. It was the first time she'd seen it, but when Leigh picked it up and felt the shape of various items within—and one particularly sharp item—she suspected it was what she'd been sitting on.

"Don't you worry about this, I'll take it with me," she said, hardly able to contain her curiosity about its contents. "Hurry now, Jassy, and wash those buckskins for me before Jolie finds out and has you washing all those bed linens instead. I'll do something special for you," Leigh promised, and since Jassy knew her word was good, she nodded, placing the buckskins in the empty basket as she turned and ambled toward the big tub, her gaze steady on Jolie as she waited her chance to sneak the dirty clothes into the soapy water.

Seeing Jolie with her back turned slightly, and the buckskins now safely immersed in the soapy water, Leigh hurried toward the house, certain she had successfully made her escape yet again today.

She had almost reached the house when she heard her name called out. Glancing around, Leigh managed an innocent look as she greeted Jolie, but never stopping as she continued toward the house, keeping the buckskin pouch hidden beneath a fold of her skirt.

Fortunately, Leigh didn't see the look of dumbfounded surprise crossing Jolie's high-cheekboned face when she caught sight of Leigh's bare legs. She was also spared the glint that came into Jolie's eye as she watched Leigh's slender figure disappear inside the house with undue haste.

Hurrying across the rough brick flooring of the scullery, and not easily sidestepping the big iron pots and pans that were stored and cleaned there, Leigh entered the kitchens. The room was hot and airless, but cheerful with its white walls that reflected the sunlight pouring in from the two big windows. Bright red geraniums and Jolie's special medicinal herbs were spaced along the deep sills in small clay pots. A fat calico cat that guarded the kitchens at night from marauding mice was curled up asleep in a spot of sunlight that bathed the sill in a warm golden glow. Bunches of rosemary, thyme, saffron, sage, parsley, dill, tansy, and assorted cooking herbs from the garden were being dried from the rafters where baskets of every weave, shape, and size dangled from hooks. The kitchen was redolent of savory aromas rising with the steam from the copper pots swinging over the fire in the great fireplace. Freshly baked beaten biscuits, browned to a light golden color, were being lifted from the oven on a long-handled wooden paddle. Earthenware bowls of creamy churned butter, eggs, honey, walnuts and pecans, lemons and oranges, flour, a pitcher of sweet milk, a cup of brandy, chunks of chocolate, and small bowls of cinnamon, nutmeg, mace, cloves, and ginger were crowded together at one end of the big table sitting square in the center of the kitchen. Rosamundi, the only kitchen maid Jolie trusted to measure out a recipe and prepare it without step-by-step supervision, was busy at her task. While still warm from the oven, the pecan and orange-nut bars, cinnamon squares, brownies, and brandy balls she was making would be carefully packed into tins. The treats were bound for luncheon baskets at the end of the week when many a guest faced a long journey home—the brimming picnic basket a tasty reminder of Travers Hill's famed hospitality.

Leigh wrinkled her nose as she caught a whiff of the pungent odor of vinegar as she neared a smaller table near the window where freshly chopped snap beans, cauliflower, cucumbers, peppers, onions, and special seasonings were grouped in piles, ready to be pickled into Jolie's famous chowchow. Many of the highly prized jars covered in green-checked gingham cloth were bound for favorite guests' baskets, along with jars of peach chutney and apple butter—a tradition at Travers Hill. In her haste, Leigh bumped against a basket of white corn, ready to be husked, then nearly sat on top of a smaller basket of green tomatoes. When coated in seasoned cornmeal and deep fried in bacon drippings, the tomatoes would be served at dinner accompanied by chile sauce. It was a favorite of Guy's, and whenever he was home Jolie made certain the family had it at almost every meal. Finding her balance, Leigh nearly fell over one of the maids. Down on her hands and knees, she was scrubbing at a sticky mess of sorghum that had spilled from an overturned jug. Leigh automatically glanced up at the wall where the waffle irons usually hung next to the oyster roaster, long-handled skillets, trivets, and fancy shortbread molds, but the space was empty, and she knew they'd be having waffles tomorrow morning for breakfast.

The hickory-smoked ham, the pride of Travers Hill's smokehouse, was sitting pink and succulent in the center of the platter that would grace the head of the Sunday table. The matching tureen would be filled with chicken curry and rice and placed at the corner nearest her mother, who ladled a healthy portion into each person's dish before Stephen removed the tureen from the table and replaced it with another course. Stacks of blue-patterned china, destined for the long mahogany dining table in the big house, were being carefully carried from the kitchens by the most sure-footed maid. In the back of the cupboard, and the only items collecting dust in the kitchens, were several cookbooks, the most valued a copy of the eighteenth-century edition of Mrs. E. Smith's famed *The Compleat Housewife*. Leigh had been studying it of late, carefully turning the yellowed pages of the fragilely bound book. Handed down to her mother by her grandmother, whose own mother had brought it over to the Colonies from England, it occupied a place of honor on the shelf. But Leigh had found Mary Randolph's *The Virginia Housewife*, and a newer volume called *The Carolina Housewife*—a gift from her mother's cousin in Charleston after she had enjoyed a month of Virginia cooking—far easier to comprehend. Jolie, however, hadn't missed them. Even if Jolie could have read, she would never have glanced at the books, for she knew by heart every recipe that was prepared, garnished, and served at table at Travers Hill. Leigh eyed the dusty tomes without pleasure, for trying to understand the recipes and prepare them had been frustrating, especially when she'd never seen Jolie measure anything—it was always a pinch of this and a dash of that.

Leigh was tempted to pinch a pecan off the top of her father's bourbon pecan cake as she passed by the table where it was sitting in solitary splendor, but one of the maids would probably be blamed, for every pecan half and candied cherry was counted when placed in decoration. Besides, she didn't like the taste of bourbon that the pecans soaked up when the cake was wrapped in a bourbon-soaked cloth to keep it moist. As the days passed, and the cake aged, the bourbon flavor became even stronger, which seemed to please her father, for there was never even a crumb left by the end of the week. Nearing the door, Leigh passed the row of stone jars filled with fermenting blackberries, currants, and dandelion blossoms, which in another two months would become wine worthy of being poured into crystal decanters and served to feminine guests visiting Travers Hill. The copper still, which occupied the far corner of the kitchen, and was not to be touched by anyone but Stephen, worked steadily producing corn whiskey and brandy for the master of Travers Hill and his thirsty friends.

Leigh almost ran along the passage to the big house, entering without a backward glance as she hurried along the paneled hall and past the silent library. On a side table, arranged in one of her mother's prized Sevres vases, a fragrant bouquet of roses and blue delphinium caught Leigh's eye. She sniffed curiously, then spied the box filled with cloths, dusters, and polish sitting on the floor beside the table, the linseed oil and beeswax overpowering the scent of roses. The double doors to the great hall were standing opened, but the elegant room was quiet. The side chairs and sofas, upholstered in pure silk woven in soft, mellow colors, the tea table, and the spinet and harp had been pushed against the walls. The floor had been waxed to a shining brilliancy the day before in preparation for the ball that would be held Friday, when the gilt-framed looking glasses spaced around the hall would reflect the dazzling light from the wall sconces and the crystal chandelier as ladies in their colorful gowns danced past on the arms of handsome gentlemen.

Leigh tiptoed past the door of the dining room when she heard a tuneless whistling coming from within and saw Stephen doing a last spot of polishing on the silver before it was laid for dinner. Her barefoot steps on the Oriental carpet covering the pine planking of the floor made no sound, and it was with a sigh of relief that she found the parlor empty. Leigh smiled unconsciously as she looked up at her grandfather's flintlock fowling piece above the doorway. Next to it was a powder horn engraved with a map of Virginia. She'd always suspected that the long-barreled weapon kept people from lingering too long in polite conversation. Leigh glanced across the hall at the opposite wall. Displayed above the door to the reception room, where her father and his gentlemen friends always gathered for brandy and cigars and a friendly hand of cards after dinner, was a brass-hilted German sword with a long and tapered, diamond-shaped blade. Its counterguard embossed with a running horse seemed an appropriate symbol of Travers Hill. In reality, it had been surrendered to her great-grandfather by a Hessian officer he had captured during the Revolutionary War, but it complemented nicely the cavalry saber that same great-grandfather had taken from a British dragoon he'd wounded at Yorktown. As easy as winging a turkey in a shoot, her grandfather had claimed when reciting the story of his father's experiences when the red-coated enemy had been trapped by sharpshooting Virginia militiamen and riflemen. He had often declared with a cackling laugh that he'd wished he been around to see Lord Dunmore, the last Royal governor of Virginia, sent packing in the middle of the night with his tail between his legs and Patrick Henry's damning oaths ringing in his ears. Through the opened windows Leigh could hear voices and laughter coming from the veranda and knew Julia was well into recounting her own particular adventure of the afternoon.

Leigh nearly cried out in surprise when the tall-case clock next to the hall bench struck the hour. Her mother's wide-brimmed garden hat was hanging from the arm of the bench, the silk-ribboned bonnet strings fluttering softly. Glancing at the front door, left open to allow the breeze to flow through the hall, Leigh wasted no time in climbing the stairs and walking softly past the doorway of her mother's bedchamber. She did not need to look inside to know that her mother would be sitting in her favorite rose damask upholstered chair and working diligently at her sewing before returning downstairs to supervise the cooking of the Sunday dinner. Although it was her father's bedchamber as well, the room seemed a reflection of her mother. Decorated in delicate shades of rose and cream, with the furnishings in warm cherry wood and the fragrance of roses and lavender always strong whenever one entered, the room was where her mother oversaw all of the activities of Travers Hill. From her small desk she handled the daily accounts and records, paid the bills, wrote letters to friends and family members, made entries in her diary, gave her orders to the house and yard servants, and disciplined her children.

Leigh gave a sigh of relief as she safely passed by, although she couldn't help wondering what her punishment would be should her mother learn of her behavior of the afternoon. Putting it out of her mind, she hurried past Althea's old bedchamber, then Stuart James's, both of which were now used by her sister and brother and their respective families when they visited Travers Hill. Leigh was sorry to see Guy's bedchamber empty. The colors of brown and green dominated the room, and hunting prints and marine paintings shared space on the walls with an extensive pistol collection. A model of a three-masted brigantine, cannons poised, and a pair of Staffordshire figures of noted pugilists, standing with fists raised, were ready to do battle on the mantelpiece. She would have liked to have shared the exciting story of her near escape at least with Guy—he would have found her mistaking the man for Adam amusing. But perhaps it was better that no one, not even Guy, know of her encounter with the stranger.

Across the hall from the room she shared with Blythe was Palmer William's, but it would be empty until midweek. Leigh reached her bedchamber, hoping Blythe and Julia wouldn't come upstairs too quickly. Gingerly, Leigh held the leather pouch out in front of her, eyeing it as if something distasteful might be hidden within. Hearing a step in the hall, her breath caught sharply, but it was just the house creaking in protest of the heat. Leigh glanced around, wondering where she could hide the pouch until she could return it, which would be as soon as possible—after she'd looked inside. A floral-patterned quilt was folded across the foot of the four-poster. She'd hide it there, but no, Julia would be certain to feel it on her feet tonight since she would be sleeping in their room. And the winter bed hangings and window draperies had been removed and replaced with light dimity, so there were no heavy damask folds to hide a leather pouch behind. And there was no place on the night table to conceal it. And she couldn't wedge it between the table and the bed now that the big four-poster had been moved to the center of the room and the headboard removed so she and Blythe would sleep more comfortably during the hot nights. And Blythe was certain to discover the strange pouch if she hid it in the high chest of drawers, Leigh decided as she found another pair of pantalettes and stockings. Tossing them onto the bed, Leigh had just pulled out a dry chemise when her gaze came to rest on the blanket chest at the foot of the bed. It would be the perfect hiding place for...

"Miss Leigh!"

Spinning around, Leigh met the gimlet-eyed gaze of Jolie. Momentarily startled, Leigh was unable to say anything. Afraid her expression was giving her away, she managed to turn and hide the leather pouch in the fold of her skirt at the same time she walked casually toward the window.

"Miss Leigh! You get back over here. An' don't you go turnin' a missish shoulder on me like I was one of yer beaus. You aren't goin' to think up a fib to fool poor ol' Jolie into believin' 'twas gospel truth. I'm not goin' to swallow none of it. I saw yer face when you tried to sneak in the back door. I was out back, countin' linens just in case any of them girls got light-fingered with Miss Beatrice Amelia's finest. An' I know you're the one who gave that no good Jassy them buckskins. Thinks she can fool ol' Jolie. She learned different when I boxed her ears good an' hard. Reckon she ought to be thinkin' about more 'n that good fer nothin' Dan'l. An' I warned that girl if I find out she's been makin' cow's eyes at Sweet John I'll send some of my kinfolks, an' on my papa's side of the family, after her. I already planned fer lil' Rosamundi to marry my Sweet John. So I told Jassy that ol' Colonel Leigh called my papa Reynard. That means fox in French. That's what Steban says. To my papa's people, he was Creepin' Fox. He was that good a tracker. Why'd you think no runaway ever got more 'n a step or two off the colonel's land? Creepin' Fox. He scared them so they believed those yellow eyes of his were taken from a fox he hunted down an' stole the soul from," Jolie said with an emphatic nodding of her head with its tight wrapping of fine black braids, and Leigh knew Creeping Fox's daughter believed it because she had inherited those eyes—and Leigh certainly knew Jolie could see in the dark.

"Now, no honey-tongued words are goin' to keep me from knowin' what you've been about. But I know this much, it hasn't been good. You can't fool me, missy, I raised you since you were no bigger 'n a sucklin' babe." The voice came soft, but insistent behind Leigh's stubbornly turned back. "Now you tell me right this instant, lil' honey, where you got yer hands on those buckskins, or I'll have to tell Miss Beatrice Amelia, an' yer mama'll be sure to have some kind of fit when she learns you stole some man's breeches.

"Hah! You can't hide anything from Jolie. I saw you flinch like an up-to-no-good varlet. Ye're goin' to be the death of yer mama yet, an' when we have to revive her with the salts, yer papa is sure to hear about it, an' then…well, I just don't know what will be happenin' in this house. Figure the roof'll blow sky high, what with little Miss Lucy turnin' sixteen on Friday, an' all the fancy goings on that we've been doin', an' yer Aunt Maribel Lu comin', an' all them nice folks from Charleston an' Savannah. An' here, just a lil' while past, yer mama comes in here a-worryin' herself sick, that poor lady, that yer hands were goin' to be stained purple, an' I find you sneakin' in the backyard with a man's breeches!"

Leigh looked heavenward. If only she had reached her room before Jolie had spied her, but no one yet had ever gotten into Travers Hill without Jolie somehow knowing about it, and if she didn't like what she saw, then she was hot on the miscreant's heels.

"Jolie."

Turning around with one of her sweetest smiles, her dark blue eyes full of entreaty, Leigh met the topaz-eyed stare of Jolie, the leather pouch now held protectively behind her back. Behind her smile Leigh was fuming, but against herself, for her only mistake had been in not slamming shut her bedchamber door. Unable to resist discovering what was concealed inside the pouch that had bruised her derriere, she had momentarily, and foolishly, forgotten Jolie.

"Now, Jolie, you know I've been out blackberry picking with Blythe and Julia, and we found such big, juicy berries. That cobbler is going to be the finest one this whole summer. And we had such a nice picnic. Julia especially enjoyed your pâté and buttermilk biscuits. I declare there isn't even a crumb left. And we don't have any stains on our hands at all. Mama will be so pleased. How can you possibly believe that I've—" Leigh began, wondering how she would extricate herself from this latest predicament.

"Don't you go all mealymouthed on me, miss. I know exactly where you should've been an' what you should've been doin', so how you got yer hands on a pair of buckskin breeches, I want to know."

"Jolie, please—"

"An' no amount of sweet-talkin' is goin' to budge me from this spot till I know what's goin' on. Look at yerself. Why, I was thinkin' that I saw some thief sneakin' in the back door. What if the neighbors was to see you standin' here barefoot, yer gown an' petticoats damp, an' yer hair hangin' down yer back like poor white trash that doesn't have even a lil' ribbon. Yer poor mama would never recover from the shame. Lucky ol' Jolie can tiptoe as soft as lil' Miss Leigh here, or yer mama'd be in here right this instant. An' lucky ol' Jolie knows that butter won't melt in this lil' child's mouth, so after I have that first answer, I'm goin' to know how come ye're standin' here in wet drawers."

"I don't have to tell you a thing, Jolie," Leigh brazened, unwilling to admit to her crime, or meet Jolie's fiery eye for much longer.

"Oh, we'll see about that, missy," Jolie warned, thinking Miss Leigh had gotten a trifle too big for her breeches since going away to Charleston, and on that thought she remembered the reason for the argument, her fingers itching to grab hold of a bit of that buckskin Leigh was keeping just out of reach. "I don't s'pose lil' Miss Lucy or Miss Julia will be so tight-lipped about what happened. Of course, once I start askin' questions of Miss Julia, there's no way we're goin' to keep it quiet. An' then Miss Effie is goin' to hear about this, an' you know she can't keep a secret any better than her daughter. So you might as well be tellin' yer Aunt Maribel Lu too."

"Go ahead, but they don't know a thing about those buckskins," Leigh admitted, pretending unconcern, but the last thing she wanted was for Blythe, and especially Julia, to find out and start asking nosy questions and giggling and gossiping about a naked stranger—then her mother would surely hear and she would never hear the end of it.

"We're goin' to see about that," Jolie said, her arms folded across her thin bosom as she turned around, prepared to track down the other two, and Leigh knew it was hopeless, for Jolie never gave up.

"Oh, all right, I'll tell you." Leigh gave in with a sigh, just as Jolie had suspected she would. "But you have to promise you won't breathe a word of this to anyone, Jolie. Especially not to Mama. Promise!" Leigh pleaded, reaching out her hand to grasp Jolie's arm.

"I'm goin' to do no promisin', missy, till I know what you've gone and done," Jolie responded, standing firm now that she had her miss cornered and had captured the slender hand that had grasped her arm. Now she would have her confession, for Miss Leigh wasn't going anywhere.

But even Jolie wasn't prepared for the admission that followed, and Leigh began to think her actions sounded even worse now than they had seemed at the time. She could certainly understand the expression of disbelief on Jolie's usually impassive face, which convinced Leigh more than anything else could have of the magnitude of her crime.

"Oh, Lord help me," Jolie murmured. "I'm not goin' to live to see any more gray hairs on this poor head of mine," she muttered, her eyes shuttered and showing none of the concern and affection she felt as she stared down at Leigh's chestnut head, bent slightly now as if she were indeed repentant of her actions. Jolie sighed, unable to stay angry at her, for next to Guy, Miss Leigh Alexandra had always been her favorite—even if she and her brother had caused the most trouble in the family. It came of having the same colored hair as their papa, who was a hell-raiser if she'd ever met one. She'd had more than her fair share of sleepless nights since her sweet Miss Beatrice Amelia married into this family.

"Hmmmph!" Jolie muttered, and although she still had a tight hold on Leigh's hand, she patted it soothingly. She never could look into those dark blue eyes without being reminded of Miss Beatrice Amelia at that tender young age. Although Miss Beatrice Amelia had never caused her the worry that this young miss had.

"This man of yers is no gentleman, honey," she said, repeating Jassy's astute observation of only minutes before. "I saw those buckskins you gave Jassy, an' I haven't seen that kind of beadwork since my papa's kin come down out of the mountains backcountry way in Georgia," she said, a worried frown forming on her wide brow. Holding out her hand, she added, "What have you got behind yer back, honey?"

"He can't be a Cherokee, Jolie. He has golden hair, that's why I mistook him for Adam Braedon," Leigh responded, ignoring Jolie's request. She had no intention of giving up her prize without finding out what it was first.

"What've you got, child?" Jolie asked again, determined there would be no secrets from her.

Leigh sighed. Slowly, she revealed the leather pouch she'd been hiding behind her back. Jolie reached out to grab it, but Leigh was quicker than Jolie and, since it was her find, she folded back the flap and reached inside before Jolie could take it from her. "What is this?" Leigh asked in surprise.

"Now don't you go openin' that, Miss Leigh, it's none of yer business an' what's inside best be left a mystery to gently bred folks," Jolie advised, but her warning came too late, for Leigh had already emptied part of the contents of the pouch into her outstretched palm.

"Oh, you've done it now, missy," Jolie said, taking a quick step back when Leigh held up a single feather, then an arrowhead, pieces of flint and steel, tobacco, a curl of black hair woven into a tight braid and decorated with colorful beads, some reddish dirt, a tiny pine cone, a small switch of something that looked suspiciously like horsehair, and lastly, an animal's yellowed fang.

Leigh glanced at Jolie in surprise. She'd never seen her frightened, but the look in her eyes was definitely one of fear, or perhaps dread. Shrugging, Leigh felt inside the pouch and found one last item—but it captured all of her attention and praise.

"Oh, look, Jolie," Leigh breathed, holding up a delicately wrought silver dagger. "Ouch!"

"What have you done, honey child? Bless me," Jolie said, shaking her head as if banishing what had just happened. With a look of genuine concern on her face, she said, "I knew this wasn't goin' to bring any good. Jus' knew it! Felt it in my ol' bones this mornin' an' I warned that Steban. No good's goin' to come of this day," Jolie said repeating her warning of earlier. "But all that Steban's been worryin' 'bout is if he's got enough mint fer the juleps. Sometimes that man doesn't see past that turned-up nose of his. He's as fussy as an ol' maid. Oh, lil' honey, I just don't know what we're to do now. Reckon by nightfall we're goin' to have thunder. Spirits get awfully angry when they've been disturbed, an' then they start cursin' somebody."

"Cursed?" Leigh squeaked in surprise, looking up from the blood seeping from the scratch where one of the sharp-pointed, ornate rays of a sun on the hilt of the small dagger had cut into the soft flesh of her palm.

"This man of yers must be a savage. An' to think my sweet lil' honey child was alone with this man. I don't want to think what might of happened if he'd gotten his hands on you. Might have scalped you," Jolie crooned, her thin hand gently smoothing Leigh's long chestnut braid.

"Oh, Jolie, we're in Virginia," Leigh said, laughing, but there was a slight trembling in her hands as she put the stranger's possessions back inside the pouch she had stolen. She'd been around Jolie her whole life, and was concerned enough to heed at least some of what Jolie said. "What is it, Jolie?" she asked timidly.

"That's juju, honey," Jolie said in an even softer voice than Leigh's, her eyes closed as if in prayer. "It's meant to protect this man from evil spirits. It's his totem, his charms fer calling the spirits to help him when he's in trouble. It's not good fer us to be seein' these charms of his. He's goin' to be mighty angry. No one's s'posed to see them. Warriors wear them into battle."

"They do? Around their necks? Like some people wear crosses, or a locket of hair from a loved one?"

"That's right. Sometimes they wear it 'round their neck, but most wear it from the waist. It dangles down beneath their breechcloth. Warriors figure it's mighty safe there, good medicine next to his, well, where his—" Jolie tried to explain, her coppery cheeks becoming brighter as she met Leigh's curious gaze.

"I don't know if my voodoo'll be strong enough to protect you, lil' honey. Jus' knew today was goin' to be a bad one. All the signs have been there."

"Jolie, you are a Christian," Leigh reminded her, eyeing the pouch with distaste as she thought of where it had been.

Jolie sniffed. "I am, missy. I've been baptized. But it's never wise to mock the powers that be. An' I know there be plenty out there that civ'lized folk don't know about. An' it's a good thing they don't, those that's God-fearin', 'cause it'd scare them senseless, but they're out there. Now, let's get you out of these wet underthings. Then I need to help your mama in the kitchens. I jus' hope you don't catch yer death of cold."

"Not if those angry spirits get me first," Leigh jested, wincing when Jolie jerked on her laces. "You aren't going to tell her, are you, Jolie?" Leigh said, her voice muffled as Jolie pulled the damp chemise over her head.

"I haven't decided. Figure we'll jus' have to wait an' see what happens."

"I'm going to return those buckskins and this pouch tomorrow," Leigh promised.

"No you're not."

"I am, Jolie, I have to," Leigh insisted, her chin set in stubborn lines.

"You get one of the gardeners or grooms to. Won't matter if they get scalped. But you're not goin'."

"I'm the only one who knows where I found the buckskins and where to put them back," Leigh said, determined she would do this herself, although she wasn't quite certain why. "It is my responsibility."

"You're not steppin' foot from this house!"

"I'll take Sweet John. No one, not even these spirits of yours, will bother me then," Leigh said, for Jolie and Stephen's son stood tall and broad, and although he had a gentle hand with a horse, there was no one who could beat him in wrestling or boxing.

Jolie frowned. "I don't know," she muttered, not liking to have her plans changed, but Leigh had already hidden the pouch deep beneath several comforters in the blanket chest.

"If I return the buckskins and the pouch, then no one will ever need to know, especially Mama. You know how upset she would become. And it might appease the spirits I've angered," she added, the corners of her lips curving upward in a smile.

"Sssssh, girl. Don't you mock them," Jolie whispered, looking around nervously. Then she sighed as if in resignation. "All right, but I don't like it. An' you can take that smug, cat's that licked the cream smile off yer face, missy, 'cause I'm goin' to be watchin' you like a fox," Jolie warned. "An' don't you run off. Goin' to put somethin' on that scratch," she said, thinking it would be just as well if Miss Beatrice Amelia never found out about this, and it wouldn't hurt to do a little conjuring of her own this evening when certain other folks were safe in their beds.

Whatever conjuring Jolie had in mind, it wasn't strong enough to silence the thunder that rolled across Travers Hill just before dawn and awakened Leigh from a sound sleep.

Five

> *The wild hawk stood with the down on his beak,*
> *And stared, with his foot on the prey.*

Alfred, Lord Tennyson

"DID YOU HEAR THE THUNDER LAST NIGHT, STEPHEN?" Leigh asked, startling him when she entered the dining room, her step so light that he hadn't heard it.

"Miss Leigh! You gave me such a scare, sneakin' up on me like you were Creepin' Fox. An' why're you up so early? Ol' rooster still in bed, why aren't you?" he asked, lifting the cover from one of the silver chafing dishes on the sideboard, the aromatic steam rising tantalizingly as he gave the contents a professional stir.

"I've something I must do this morning, and I am afraid it cannot wait," Leigh said with a self-assurance she wasn't feeling as she tucked two apples she'd snatched from the centerpiece into the pocket of her gown.

"Hmmm, don't I know that, Miss Leigh," he replied, the looking glass over the sideboard mirroring his perceptive glance.

Leigh looked up in surprise. "You do?" she demanded, thinking Jolie couldn't keep anything to herself anymore.

"Goin' down to the stables to see to ol' Rambler. I told Sweet John that young Miss Leigh wouldn't be able to stay away once she heard 'bout Mister Guy's tryin' to jump that fence again, but Sweet John, he just smiles. Yer papa sure was angry with that boy of his. But Mister Stuart's real proud of him anyway."

Leigh breathed a sigh of relief as she walked over to the elaborate, domed birdcage sitting on a table between the two windows that overlooked the veranda. "I see Mama's songbirds are up early," Leigh commented as she watched the colorful birds flitting from perch to perch inside their gilded cage, their melodic song filling the room with a pleasant cheerfulness.

"Ever since yer mama was a child, she likes to hear those little chirp, chirpins in the mornin'. Colonel Leigh, now, he hated those little birds, an' threatened to pluck every last one of them of their tiny feathers, but the mistress, yer gran'mama, she did love them so, just like Miss Beatrice Amelia. An' even if I'm not hearin' good as I was, I'm not completely blind yet, Miss Leigh," Stephen said, gesturing to the faded blue gown she was wearing. "Knew you wasn't plannin' on callin' on those uppity Canby girls."

Leigh glanced down ruefully at the pale blue calico gown that was sadly bereft of any trimmings, and woefully shorter than when she had first worn it three years ago. With her white-stockinged ankles showing, and her long, chestnut hair flowing loose over her shoulder and tied with a blue ribbon, she could have been that fifteen-year-old of three summers before—except that the blue gown now hugged the gentle roundness of her breasts and left no doubt that she was indeed a young woman.

Her favorite mauve-striped muslin would have to wait until after she'd completed her errands of the morning. She had left it hanging on the door of the clothes press, along with a lace-trimmed petticoat and fine pair of silk stockings folded across a chair. When she had tiptoed out of her bedchamber, Blythe and Julia had still been sleeping peacefully. Not wanting to disturb them, she had taken little time with her toilette, having to be satisfied with brushing her hair and splashing lilac water on her arms and face. And if all went as she planned, then she would be back in her bedchamber before either Blythe or Julia had awakened. "Doesn't anything happen around here without you and Jolie knowing it?" Leigh asked with a curious look at Stephen, wondering at all of the family secrets he must know.

"Well, we sure try not to let that ever happen," he said ruminatively, thinking the young miss was up to something. He'd seen that mischievous look in her eyes far too often not to be concerned now. "Don't know what this household would come to if somebody didn't sleep with one eye open 'round here. But I'm slowin' down, Miss Leigh. Didn't hear you come in just now. Of course, you were walkin' like you didn't want any one to hear yer step."

"I didn't see Mama when I came down," Leigh said, hiding a guilty look as she stared down at her oldest pair of slippers, the soles so thin it was almost as if she were walking in her stockinged feet. Jolie had threatened to throw the slippers out just the day before, declaring that even a scullery maid would have more pride than to be caught wearing such a scuffed pair of shoes. "I've never known Mama to sleep past dawn. Papa's still asleep. I heard his snores coming from the nursery when I came down the hall. She isn't ill, is she? Is that why Papa is sleeping in the nursery? I didn't see Jolie, either."

"Mister Stuart was sittin' up late with Mister Nathan, an' you know how yer papá is when he gets to talkin' an' drinkin', an' he can't hold his liquor like he used to, not that anyone can tell him so, 'specially when he's drinkin' with Mister Nathan, he's such a big gentleman, I don't think there's enough corn whiskey in this county to put him under the table. So Mister Nathan, still steady on his feet, helped me put Mister Stuart, singin' sad songs, in the nursery so he wouldn't disturb Miss Beatrice Amelia. She an' Jolie went out back mighty early. There're some sick who need tendin'. Jolie says she reckons it was that Jassy gettin' sick from eatin' too much catfish an' cracklin' bread last night. She's a giddy-headed goose—" Stephen paused, and censoring himself, he continued, "an' thunder always scares her into a fit an' then she gets everyone's hair standin' on end. Never heard such a commotion with all the wailin' an' moanin' goin' on. Reckon a fox sneakin' into the hen house couldn't have caused more noise."

"Did you know that Jolie predicted the thunder?" Leigh asked, nervously twisting the ribbons of her bonnet as she held it in front of her.

"Always does," Stephen replied, unimpressed by Jolie's omniscience.

"She said it was angry spirits," Leigh added, watching him closely.

Stephen snorted. "More likely she felt it in her big toe. It's been achin' her somethin' fierce of late."

Leigh frowned. "You really think so?" she murmured, breathing easier.

"Now, Miss Leigh, what're you goin' to eat fer breakfast?" Stephen asked, his thoughts returning to more important details as he held out a chair for her at the long mahogany table and patted the green satin seat encouragingly.

"I just want a muffin, or one of these sweet rolls," Leigh

replied, reaching out for one of the flaky caramel pecan pastries piled high in a silver basket in the center of the table. She was more worried about what had happened to the buckskins than what she would eat for breakfast. Jolie had told her last night that she would hang them up in the kitchens, close to the hearth so they would dry faster. She had to retrieve them before anyone else saw them, and then get out to the stables before her mother and Jolie returned to the big house.

"Now, Miss Leigh, you know I'm not goin' to let you leave this house till you've eaten a proper breakfast. What would Miss Beatrice Amelia say? An' my papa? *Mon Dieu!* That's what he'd say if he was alive today, Miss Leigh, an' I don't want to disturb his restin' peaceful. An' I know if I let you sashay out of here with a couple of sweet rolls you'd be feedin' those two beasts of yers instead. An' don't look at me like that with those big blue eyes, Miss Leigh, 'cause I've already seen you swipe two apples from the table when you thought I wasn't lookin'. Took me near an hour to arrange that so pretty like," he mildly rebuked her as he stared at the silver epergne with its lovely arrangement of fruit.

"You've been playin' possum, Stephen, but you're as wily as a fox. And you haven't slowed down that much yet that you can't still catch me," Leigh said with a laugh, for she and Stephen had been playing their sleight of hand game since she'd been a child.

"It's not that I'm fast, Miss Leigh, I'm just experienced where this family is concerned," he said, his eyes crinkling around the corners when he smiled.

Taking the two apples out of her pocket, Leigh shined them on her skirt before she replaced them. Unfortunately, she knocked a couple of cherries onto the fine damask tablecloth when she tried to squeeze the apples into the silver dish already crowded with bright red strawberries. But she quickly caught the errant cherries before they rolled onto the rug and tucked them in beside a clump of dewy grapes artistically draped to dangle just above a grouping of blushing peaches and dark purple plums that were arranged around a pineapple in the center.

Stephen stood silent for a moment, then nodded as he angled the grapes in his masterpiece more to his satisfaction.

"Now, we've got some nice baked eggs, just the way Miss Althea loves them with her buttered toast an' marmalade. I don't know, but I've been thinkin' she doesn't have too much of an appetite in the mornin's anymore, so maybe she's goin' to give Mister Nathan a son this time. Been real worried, her not givin' him more than one child. One of these days real soon they might be movin' back to Royal Bay. Doesn't seem to me that Mister Noble is his ol' self anymore. Came callin' the other day in a carriage, Miss Leigh," he said, shaking his head. "Could just as easily have been a hearse the way Mister Noble was sittin' there all stiff like. Never thought he'd get himself down out of that carriage, what with Miss Effie tryin' to help an' pushin' him first this way an' then the other way an' cluckin' over him like a mother hen. An' I don't see those folks of his gettin' that Mister Adam to do anything proper when the time comes.

"You like yer eggs scrambled nice an' fluffy, Miss Leigh, so we have them that way. An' we've apple fritters, fried potatoes, an' bacon slices for Mister Guy. He'll be hungry 'cause he's been talkin' 'bout ridin' over to the Canbys, though, he just might be walkin' this mornin' so we'd better fill that boy up. Those Canbys, 'specially one in particular, will be pleased to see him even if he is all hot an' dusty," Stephen predicted with a wide grin as he imagined the young gentleman giving his short legs a little stretch down the road.

Leigh shook her head in disgust. "I just hope Guy is smarter than he acts at times. He always manages to worm his way out of trouble. But if he thinks he can sweet-talk one of the Canbys and not get caught, with the rest of the Canbys falling over each other listening outside the parlor door, then he's more of a fool than we all think he is. One of these days he is going to meet his match, and then the lady he's been smiling so sweetly at and making promises to that he has no intention of keeping will have his ring on her finger and one through his nose. Or she might even have the intelligence to have nothing to do with my handsome, insensitive brother. He thinks he can have any girl in the county eating out of the palm of his hand, then slap her away when she becomes too demanding. It would certainly destroy his self-esteem to be spurned by the lady of his affections. But until then, it wouldn't hurt if he had longer legs, then he could outrun Sarette Canby, because she won't lose her chance to catch Guy."

"That Miss Sarette sure is a mighty healthy lookin' young miss. Bet she puts away a real good breakfast each mornin'," Stephen said.

"I just hope you won't have to serve her breakfast each morning, and I won't have to sit across the breakfast table from a sister-in-law I detest, and who detests me even more. She has probably already packed her bags, ready to move into Travers Hill, now that Stuart James has Willow Creek and Papa is hoping Guy will want to run the farm. She'd have poor Mama and Papa off visiting distant relatives in England. And since I am unwed, she would have me working my fingers to the bone doing all of the sewing for her menfolk. And she would probably try to marry poor little Lucy off to that brother of hers. She knows I'll have nothing to do with him. I've never seen anyone sit a horse as poorly as John Roy. And I've never seen Sarette on horseback at all. She sits over there at Evergreens like a fat tabby, just waiting to sink her claws into Guy, and other unsuspecting folk."

"There's no Canbys, nor other folk, 'ceptin' fer the Braedons, good enough fer the Travers family," Stephen said, and they both knew he included Stuart James's wife, Thisbe, among those not so privileged.

"I suspect there aren't enough good folk left who'd dare take on the whole family," Leigh retorted, thinking of the wild stories that went the rounds at every racing meet, barbecue, and fish fry about what Stuart Travers and his family had outraged the county by doing this time.

"I have no worries as long as Jolie is here watchin' out fer this family. Nothin's goin' to happen that shouldn't. Leastways, it's not goin' to be something I'm expectin', since I know this family an' how to keep most of them out of trouble," Stephen said with a warning glint in his eye.

"Now, we've got some fried oysters an' spoon bread here fer Mister Nathan," he said, lifting the lid to another chafing dish. "Said he wanted to ride out with Mister Stuart to the sawmill this mornin'. How about some of this panfried ham an' redeye gravy, just the way yer papa likes it. I'll fix you up a plate of it, Miss Leigh, with a little helpin' of grits, pipin' hot, an' some biscuits fer soppin'. Hmmm, fergot the mint," he said with a startled expression on his face. "I've never done that before," he muttered. "Better get some before Mister Stuart gets up. He does like my juleps, an' if he's got to ride out this mornin' he'll be needin' somethin' coolin'. Sun's hardly shown his ol' face an' it's already hotter 'n yesterday noon. Made up a batch of punch earlier, but I better bring up another couple of bottles of brandy from the cellar, 'cause Mister Nathan said Mister Adam might ride over to escort them back to Royal Bay, an' he might have some of his gentlemen friends with him," Stephen added as an afterthought as he eyed the crystal decanters of wine, Madeira, sack, and stronger spirits that were grouped together at one end of the sideboard. A big silver coffeepot and teapot on a matching silver tray, a hot water jug on a lampstand, a short, stocky porcelain pot for hot chocolate, and stacks of cups and saucers were crowded together at the other end of the sideboard.

"Now, I know you like waffles, just like Miss Lucy. An' I've some maple syrup fer you, 'cause you don't like that sorghum. Colonel Leigh always had sorghum on his biscuits. He was a good man, yer gran'papa. Real glad he let ol' Jolie come out to Travers Hill with me. How 'bout some blueberry batter cakes? Jolie said we have to have them fer Miss Noelle. That sweet little gal does like them so. Jolie was fit to be tied, 'cause yer mama didn't have time to eat any of this omelette. It's plumb full of mushrooms, with plenty of that spicy sauce on it. It was yer Gran'mama Leigh's favorite. She was a fine lady. Never heard her raise her voice even once. Not even when the colonel was shot in that duel. Never seen so much blood comin' out of a body, an' the colonel, he wasn't all that big a man. Thought fer sure the colonel was goin' to meet his maker that night. But Miss Louise tells him he's goin' nowhere till she finds out why he was duelin' with that no-good Creole fella. Made her so mad him duelin' with a fella who wasn't a gentleman. Nearly got himself killed fer no reason. A gentleman doesn't dirty his hands with trash. So she kept the colonel talkin' an' explainin' himself the whole night so he never had time to up an' die.

"An' we've sweet raisin bread an' sausages, just in case Mister Palmer William arrives earlier than expected. Got more in the kitchens if he's brought home some of his friends again. An' we've some yams left over from last night, an' some chicken hash, an'..."

Patiently, Leigh watched Stephen making his way along the sideboard. Dressed in the hunter green livery he wore with such pride, she knew it would be useless to say anything, because he would just continue from the place where he'd been interrupted. "All right, you win, Stephen," she said when he finally paused to catch his breath. Glancing at the clock on the mantel she was surprised at the hour, and if she was delayed any longer, then the rest of the family would be arriving and she would never get away—and certainly not without an explanation.

"Now, you sip this tomato juice while I get you a warm plate an' serve you up something tasty, Miss Leigh. We've got to put a little flesh on those bones," Stephen said with a stern look in his dark eyes as he eyed the pale slenderness of her arm. "Got to fatten you up like Miss Julia. She's a plump little miss. Should be married with a couple of little ones by now," he said, adding another spoonful of egg to the plate he'd taken from the serving table and was now filling with special care.

Leigh was glad Julia wasn't sitting at the table to hear Stephen's opinion, even if a complimentary one in his eyes, for it would have ruined her appetite and then she would have been grumpy until luncheon. Everything had worked out perfectly, Leigh thought, blessing Jassy for eating too much catfish the night before. But she conveniently forgot about the thunder and Jolie's premonitions of disaster, thinking she wouldn't have to worry now about getting away from Jolie, or having to explain her early rising to her mother. And Stephen thought she was going down to the stables to help Sweet John with Rambler—not knowing that she'd been down there the night before—so there would be no questions about her disappearance at breakfast when the rest of her family came down. Now, all she had to do was find the buckskins, and with the leather pouch she'd retrieved from the blanket chest and distastefully tied around her waist when putting on her petticoat, she'd ride back to the pond and return the stranger's property to him—although not in person. She would prefer not having to take a groom with her. She rode faster when alone. But Sweet John would be no problem, Leigh was thinking with a slight smile curving her lips as she formulated her next plan of action.

Lost in her preoccupation, she wasn't aware that she had been served breakfast until she glanced down at the plate Stephen had just placed before her.

Two golden waffles floating in melting butter and thick maple syrup, a mountain of fluffy scrambled eggs, several sausages, browned until tender, a mound of fried potatoes and crisp apple fritters, and a couple of corn muffins, sitting precariously close to the floral-edged rim, filled the plate until she thought the fine porcelain must crack from the weight.

Leigh opened her mouth to complain, but upon meeting Stephen's pleased, expectant smile she put a forkful of egg into her mouth instead. Nodding his grizzled head contentedly, he turned and busied himself at the sideboard, glancing over his shoulder every so often just to make certain the food piled on the plate was disappearing at the speed he thought proper.

A moment later, he placed a cup of steaming, fragrant tea before her. Then he moved a delicate pot of amber honey closer, then the cut-crystal dishes of jams and preserves, before returning to the sideboard and tunelessly whistling his favorite melody as he patiently double-checked the breakfast courses one last time.

"Now, I'm goin' to have to leave you, Miss Leigh," Stephen said regretfully, eyeing the half-eaten waffles with a sigh, but at least she had eaten most of the eggs and a good bit of the fried potatoes. He glanced upward, hearing the squeaking of floorboards upstairs. He had every intention of being back in the dining room by the time the rest of the family appeared for breakfast. It would be scandalous if there was no one here to serve them, and he was the only one he could trust to do it properly. He had hoped to train Sweet John to replace him one day as majordomo at Travers Hill, but Sweet John had always been happier out in the stables with his horses, knowing better how to clean out a stall than set a proper table. If it hadn't been that the master was so pleased with Sweet John, swearing by Sweet John's handling of his prized bloods, then he would have been disappointed in his only son. But

Sweet John had done them proud even if he hadn't become majordomo, or even a valet, Stephen admitted, although he had never admitted as much to Sweet John. "I've got to go into the cellar an' bring up another couple of bottles of brandy, then fetch some more mint from the gardens out back. Now, you goin' to be good an' clean yer plate, honey?" he asked, staring down at the young miss with fatherly concern.

"I will, Stephen," Leigh replied, spearing a juicy piece of sausage and dipping it in syrup just to set his mind at rest, then glancing down in dismay at the big, sticky drop of maple syrup that now stained her bodice.

She was glad she had worn her old calico, Leigh thought as she dabbed ineffectively at the spot with her napkin, and she did have to admit she felt far more capable of completing her task since she had eaten so hearty a breakfast under Stephen's watchful eye. But as she heard the jingling of Stephen's big ring of keys fade down the hall, she pushed back her chair, leaving the rest of her breakfast uneaten. She hurried from the room, leaving two corn bread muffins sitting in place of the shiny apples she had just reclaimed from Stephen's masterpiece.

Leigh found the buckskins where Jolie had promised she would leave them: hanging to dry in front of the great fireplace in the kitchens. Ignoring the curious stares and sly giggles from several of the maids, Leigh, with a nonchalant tilting of her chin, took possession of the disreputable pair of buckskin breeches and fringed shirt as if she had every right to do so. She couldn't quite hide her dismay, however, when she escaped outside and stared down at her prize. The buckskins were half-stiff and half-limp, the wet patches contrasting darkly against the light patches that had dried, making the stranger's clothing look far worse than before. If she tried to fold them into a neat bundle, they would most likely break in two, but she had no choice. Carefully, she took each stiff leg and bent it in two places, wincing at the loud crackling noise before she tucked the long lengths of buckskin beneath the seat of the breeches. Still slightly damp, the shirt was soft and easy to fold.

Determined to waste no more of her precious time, she hurried across the greensward toward the stables. Even at this early hour, the stable block was a hive of activity. The fires in the forge were already glowing with red-hot coals, the blacksmith's hammer sounding a steady beat as he shaped and welded the malleable iron against the anvil. Inside the stables, the stalls were being cleaned out of wet and soiled bedding from the night before and spread with fresh, dry straw. Most of the horses had been watered and fed lightly with hay before being let out for exercise.

The Travers Hill stables were as spotless as the kitchens in the big house, with the heaps of manure stored in a field nearby bearing evidence of that cleanliness. The oldest pile of manure, packed down and well-rotted, and mixed with cow manure, fish fertilizer, and bone and cottonseed meal, was bound for Beatrice Amelia's rose gardens. And any guest to Travers Hill, interested enough to inquire, was given careful instructions on how to blend the manure for the best results. And Beatrice Amelia's roses, famous throughout the county, convinced any doubters to accept the sample bag of manure so graciously offered by the mistress of Travers Hill.

Facing south, the stables were light and airy, with a slightly sloping brick floor and the same green-shuttered windows that marked the big house and all of the outbuildings of Travers Hill. Bales of wheat straw were stacked at one end of the stables, next to a group of pitchforks, shovels, brooms, and dung skeps hanging on hooks high on the wall. A colorful array of woolen rugs and blankets were neatly folded and stored on a shelf near the saddles, bridles, and halters. Leigh inhaled with pleasure the strong, familiar smell of leather, well-worked with neat's-foot oil and saddle soap, as she walked along the row of hayracks and mangers, the brick flooring still wet from having been washed down and cleaned of droppings. Every stall had a fresh bucket of water, and the horses' feed—a mixture of bran and oats and molasses—was being spread into the mangers for the first feeding of the day.

"Morning, Sweet John," Leigh said as she came up to the stall where he was standing by Rambler, his hand gentle as he sponged the roan's muzzle, his words coming soft and low as he spoke close to Rambler's ear.

"I was tellin' Rambler here that Miss Leigh would be first

down to see him. He's real sweet on you, Miss Leigh. Think he only lets Mister Guy ride him so he can gallop alongside you an' that sweet lil' mare of yours," Sweet John said, smiling when Rambler neighed in reply, seeming to nod his agreement with a playful shake of his head. "Now don't you mess up yer mane, fella, I got it all brushed so you'll look pretty fer Miss Leigh."

Tall and broad-shouldered, Sweet John was a handsome man, his skin the color of sweet chocolate—which was what Jolie had nicknamed him when he had been born and she had gazed down at him with such loving pride. She had declared that they'd call him John James, in honor of Jean Jacques and Colonel James Evelyn Leigh—but Sweet John he'd always been called and answered to since he'd taken his first steps. He had inherited some of Jolie's Cherokee ancestry, evident in his high cheekbones and high-bridged nose, but she swore the straight-backed way he carried himself brought back more vivid, and frightening, memories of his grandfather Jean Jacques than of Creeping Fox.

Leigh pressed a kiss against Rambler's velvety cheek, scratching him behind the ears as she stared into his big brown eyes. "He's a charmer, just like his unthinking master," she said, wondering if Guy would ever learn to think before he acted. "How is the sprain?" she asked, glancing down at the roan's foreleg.

"Don't think it's goin' to be too serious, Miss Leigh," Sweet John told her, his sensitive hand caressing Rambler's shoulder. "I put some kaolin paste on it, an' in a couple of days I'll wrap it up in cotton wool pads an' lotion. But we'll have to let him rest up a bit fer the next few days. Reckon Mister Guy'll have to ride Maiden's Blush fer a while. She's a sweet one, but she's not goin' to do any jumpin' of fences."

Leigh could smile now, but she'd felt the same anger she knew Sweet John had yesterday when they'd examined Rambler's sprained tendon. "I think Guy might fare better with Pumpkin, especially if he tries to get him to jump that fence. He would teach Guy the error of his ways, and give him a painful nip for good measure," Leigh predicted as she gently touched the roan's foreleg. "It looks like some of the swelling has already gone down and there doesn't seem to be too much heat in it. Not as much as last night."

"Yer mare an' the lil' cap'n are out in the paddock waitin' fer you, Miss Leigh," Sweet John said, anticipating her request. "I'll get one of the grooms to ride with you."

"No, Sweet John, that's not necessary, truly. I'm just riding down the road a piece. Not far. I'll be back before anyone else is even out of bed."

"I don't know, Miss Leigh," Sweet John said, frowning slightly as he noticed the bundle of buckskin she'd been holding in her arms, but Leigh had already gotten halfway out the stable doors.

Sweet John watched as she ran across the stableyard, her shrill whistle bringing the mare and colt galloping across the paddock to her side. He smiled when he saw them nudge her, then his smile widened as he saw the two shiny apples she held out to them. A moment later, she was balancing on the rail of the gate as it swung open, then she'd climbed on Damascena's back and was riding across the far pasture, Capitaine racing ahead.

Sweet John walked back into the stables, thinking Miss Leigh was like one of his fillies, and he couldn't help but worry about her friskiness getting her into trouble. For a moment he stood with his dark head resting against Rambler's flank, then he laughed softly when he felt the roan's hot breath against his cheek, and whistling the same tuneless song Stephen was fond of, he continued with his task.

Riding alone, Leigh reached the narrow path that mean-dered away from the lane within minutes—or so it seemed to her. She felt a strange sense of excitement—an excitement mixed with both dread and anticipation. And she found herself wondering if she really wanted to discover that the stranger had left. After having been awakened by the thunder just before dawn, she had lain awake, her thoughts filled with the stranger. Every time she had closed her eyes, he had been there before her, haunting her until she couldn't escape the vision of seeing him rising from the water, his muscular body bared and golden.

Lying in the dark and quiet of her bedchamber, safely tucked in the big four-poster with Blythe and Julia as bedmates, she had allowed herself to remember. Her heart had quickened its beat until she thought its pounding would awaken the other occupants of the bed, who were still lost in peaceful innocent slumber. But her thoughts were not innocent, Leigh remembered now with a wild blush staining her cheeks.

She had remembered the stranger's nakedness and remembered her own words to Julia, spoken so casually, about breeding. But it was different when she actually thought of the stranger in an encounter so intimate. She found herself wondering what it would feel like to be held in his arms, to be pressed against his naked chest, with his hands moving over her body and molding her closer. What would it feel like to be kissed by him?

She remembered his features, hawkish and looking as if they'd been cast in bronze because of the darkness of his tanned face. Many would not have even considered him handsome, certainly not like Matthew Wycliffe, or even Guy, whose features were masculine, but delicately molded. The stranger's nose was straight as a blade, and his cheekbones high and his jaw strongly curved. It was a hard face, with no softness, even in the finely chiseled lips. His hair was a dark golden shade even when wet, and he wore it longer than society would have deemed proper. She hadn't been able to see the color of his eyes, narrowed against the glare and shadowed beneath the darkness of his lashes, but somehow she knew they would be pale, reflecting the sun as he gazed at the sky, or the flickering of candlelight at night. He had risen from the water, moving with a slow gracefulness that reminded her of a wild animal stalking its prey; each step deliberate and controlled.

Leigh knew a feeling of growing dismay, not understanding the aching emptiness that suddenly filled her. She had never thought of Matthew Wycliffe this way, so why should she think such unladylike thoughts about the stranger? And especially a stranger who was no gentleman. If Jolie was right, then this stranger was little better than a savage. Why else would he dress in buckskins that bore a similarity to those worn by a wild heathen and carry around a small leather pouch filled with strangely barbaric, although prized, possessions.

What was the fascination? she wondered, glancing down at the buckskins folded across her legs, touching them tentatively, then allowing her fingertips to linger against a spot of soft leather. With her heart pounding nervously, she jerked her hand away as if burned and rode through the woods. Some instinct urged caution, and she circled the meadow rather than cross the open space. Leaving Damascena near where she had left her the day before, Capitaine disappearing into the trees, Leigh hurried through the sun-dappled shadows bordering the meadow, watching for any sign of the stranger. No white-tailed deer bolted from cover as Leigh neared the blackberry brambles where she'd hidden from the stranger yesterday. Overhead, she could hear the low cooing of wood pigeons, undisturbed by her trespass. In the distance, the gentle murmuring of the creek beckoned her into the grove of hemlock as she moved ever closer to the tall sycamore, beneath which she had stolen the stranger's clothes.

It was strangely cool in the shade beneath the tree, and Leigh shivered slightly as she glanced around, but the glade and the grassy bank, even the pool, was empty. The stranger was gone. Without regret, or so she tried to convince herself, she carefully placed the clean buckskins on the ground. Lifting up her skirt and petticoat, she untied the leather pouch from around her waist and placed it on top of the neatly folded clothes. Feeling a sense of relief now that they were no longer in her possession, Leigh turned around and started back toward the meadow, where the sun was shining so brightly and warmly.

She hadn't quite reached the tall grasses when her step faltered and she felt as if she were being watched. Licking her dry lips, Leigh quickened her step, but Damascena, grazing beneath the trees, suddenly seemed so far away. If she crossed the meadow, it would be quicker, but she would reveal herself to anyone watching.

Leigh shook her head in disgust. She was being fanciful. There was no one here. The shrill cry of a bird sounded close by, startling her, but nothing more. The stranger had left, apparently not too distraught about having lost his clothes and the leather pouch—despite Jolie's fears to the contrary. Or, perhaps he was searching for the thief elsewhere, but at least she had accomplished what she had set out to do and had returned the stranger's clothing. Her conscience was clear and she hoped she never saw the stranger again—or his troublesome buckskins.

Leigh was congratulating herself as she hurried across the meadow, when she sensed the shadow before she actually saw it swooping toward her out of the sun. Her eyes momentarily blinded, she raised her hand to shield them so she could see, and that was when she saw the stranger standing before her, blocking her path.

Instinct again prompted her to flight, but wrongly so this time, for there was no chance of escape, and before she had taken more than a step or two she felt the stranger's hands clamp down hard on her shoulders.

"So, *you* are the thief who stole my clothes," Neil Braedon murmured softly, more pleased than he could possibly have believed by the discovery of the thief's identity.

Like the hawk overhead, be quiet and watchful, waiting for the moment to strike, the Comanche warrior Hungry-As-The-Stalking-Wolf had told him day after day when they had hunted the desolate canyons and the high slopes of sparsely wooded timberland. And now his patience had been rewarded. He had camped by the pool last night, contenting himself with a cold meal of dried beef, waiting for either the return of the thief—looking for more valuables—or for dawn when he would search the nearby farms, and if unsuccessful in his attempt to regain his possessions, then he would seek assistance from his uncle and cousins at Royal Bay in tracking down the thief. But his satisfaction when hearing the approaching hoofbeats had turned to surprise when the identity of the thief had been revealed to him, and then the puzzlement had become pleasure as he'd watched the fair creature of the day before carefully replacing his buckskins, and the pouch, back by the pool.

"Let me go! It was a mistake. Please believe me," Leigh entreated, less pleased than she could ever have believed now that she knew the stranger had not left. Meeting him in the flesh was not nearly as enjoyable as in her daydreams, she discovered, trying to free her shoulders from his painful grasp.

"A mistake?" he asked doubtfully, enjoying her ineffective struggles to free herself, for he had waited for this moment of confrontation during a very long night.

"Yes!" Leigh answered emphatically, looking up into his

eyes for the first time, then wishing she hadn't. She suddenly found herself forgetting what she was going to say, for they were as pale as she'd imagined them. "Yes," she repeated, "I thought you were someone else."

He laughed, and it was a deep warm laugh. "Someone else? Am I to understand that it is your usual practice to go around stealing a man's clothes? What happened to the famed Virginian hospitality? Had I not had the good fortune of having other clothing, I could very well have caught my death of cold during the storm."

"It was very warm last night, hot even, and there was only thunder, no rain," Leigh corrected him, unwilling to be blamed for something that wasn't true. "Please, let me go. I am sorry about what happened."

"I suppose you are only sorry because I happened to be the wrong man?"

"No, no, you continue to misunderstand me, and this is all so unnecessary. I mistook you for someone else. Someone who deserved to have his clothes stolen."

"Not very hospitable at all," he said, thoroughly enjoying himself—both the girl and his possessions were within his grasp.

"I thought you were Adam Braedon, but you aren't," Leigh explained reasonably, refusing to give in to her panic, and not seeing the flash of recognition, and amusement, that entered his eyes when she mentioned his cousin's name. "If you knew Adam Braedon then you would understand completely and not hold me responsible."

"Oh, but I do know the gentleman in question, and I do hold you completely responsible. And I intend to hold you accountable for your actions."

"I didn't steal your buckskins, and I did wash them before I returned them, which you should thank me for. And I returned that pouch, which Jolie says is very important to you, and with everything intact, so you should indeed be grateful, and if I hadn't been so startled when you turned around in the pool and I saw that you weren't Adam—"

"You saw me bathing?" he asked, momentarily startled, his gaze penetrating as it moved intently over her blushing face.

Leigh felt her cheeks burning scarlet under his appraising

glance, and realized that trying to explain was getting her into worse trouble.

"I was so startled," she repeated, "that I forgot I had your buckskins. It really is your fault, for you are trespassing on Travers land. And besides, I turned away before you left the water," Leigh lied, her voice muffled as she stared down at his shirt front, realizing for the first time that he was dressed quite fashionably in fawn-colored breeches and riding boots, the oxblood leather having been buffed to a high sheen. His pleated shirt front was neatly pressed and startlingly white against his tanned throat.

"How fortunate for you, and how very fortunate for Adam that you mistook me for him," he said.

"I beg your pardon, but this has nothing to do with you. I've said I am sorry and I demand that you release me this instant," Leigh told him, her voice cool.

"Oh, but it has everything to do with me, since I am the injured party. I could bring charges against you for theft. Good Lord, what a scandal that would cause in the county," he mused, the fine lines fanning out around his eyes crinkling when he smiled.

"Oh, no, please. You mustn't," Leigh pleaded, thinking of the uproar at Travers Hill should her mother and father hear any breath of scandal about this unfortunate meeting. "I have returned your buckskins. No real harm has been done. What more do you want?"

Neil stared down into her heart-shaped face, the slight smile curving his hard mouth widening. "Blue, a dark, deep blue," he murmured, staring into her eyes. Like the night sky just before dawn, he thought, noting how thick her gold-tipped brown lashes were and how they kept fluttering down and shielding her eyes from his. He breathed the same lovely fragrance of lavender and roses that had scented her silk stocking, and the sweet perfume of lilac rose on the heat from her body, but as he leaned closer to her, there was another aroma that tantalized him.

He laughed aloud, startling Leigh from her absorption with the dark gold wave of hair that had fallen across his wide brow. "Lavender and roses, lilac, and maple syrup. A heady combination for a man who has spent over a month on the trail," he said, his gaze lingering on her slightly parted lips. They were beautiful lips, delicately proportioned, not too wide, but generous as they curved upward at the corners, and with an underlip full and soft.

"So, you and Adam are friends? He has always had good taste, but I believe he has outdone himself this time," he remarked, his hand sliding from her shoulder to capture the long mane of chestnut hair. It was like silk shot with golden threads as he allowed his hand to become tangled in the long strands, something he had wanted to do since first seeing her.

"Whatever are you talking about?" Leigh demanded in growing concern as she felt the stranger's hand against the softness of her breast as he gathered her hair in his hand as if he'd every right to do so, claiming the blue ribbon as his prize. Except for the womenfolk of her family, only her father and Guy had ever tugged playfully on her long hair.

"You are Adam Braedon's lady friend, aren't you?"

"What?" Leigh demanded, outraged, and her tone damned such a suggestion.

"You are not his lady friend?" he asked.

"Of course not!"

"Good, that eases my conscience somewhat, although we are blood brothers and therefore must share and share alike. What is his, is mine, and I feel very much like claiming that right. And you do owe me something for the inconvenience you caused by stealing my clothing and something that is very precious to me."

Leigh drew herself up as proudly as she could beneath his hands. "I do not have any money with me now, but I will see that you are paid in full for the inconvenience caused by my actions."

"That isn't exactly the kind of payment I had in mind," the stranger replied quietly. "Even if Adam were your lover, I don't think he would resent my stealing one innocent kiss," he said, and before Leigh knew what he was about, his mouth had found hers.

Leigh remained stiff in his arms, her lips closed and unresponsive against his.

When the stranger released her lips, he was frowning. He

was standing so close, his head and shoulders bent down to her, that she could see the golden stubble of beard covering the firm angle of his jaw and the leanness of his cheeks. His golden lashes were thick and long—too long, in fact, for a man, Leigh thought almost resentfully.

Leigh turned her head away, but the stranger's hand cupped her face and turned it back. Helplessly, Leigh stared up into his narrowed eyes. They were intent upon her face, piercing her deeply whenever she dared to meet them. She was mesmerized by the gray-green depths, gold-flecked and as clear and cool as a mountain stream. But the heat of his body next to hers burned her, making her aware of the soft, vulnerable contours of her own body.

"Unwilling to pay your debt?" he challenged.

Leigh was breathless, but more from the heady experience of receiving her first kiss than from anger at the stranger. Her heart pounding, she parted her lips, trying to draw breath, but before she could, his mouth had closed over hers again, the gentle pressure he exerted parting her lips wider as his mouth moved against hers caressingly. Never before had she been kissed by someone other than her family—and then never on the lips with such familiarity. With a sense of disbelief she felt the softness of his tongue licking against her lips and she cursed herself for ever having wondered what it would feel like to be kissed by this man.

She was so slender in his arms, Neil thought. Although she was taller than her companions of yesterday, the top of her head hardly even came as high as his shoulder. He could crush her willowy length so very easily—or would she bend to his will? he wondered idly as he felt the bones of her shoulder, delicate and small beneath his grasp as he held her captive in his embrace. He molded her closer, moving his hand along the curving line of hip and buttock that had tantalized him so the day before. She arched her back away from him, contracting her stomach muscles against the intimacy of his body pressing against her, but he increased the pressure of his arm behind her waist, forcing her into a closer intimacy. Yesterday, she had escaped him—but not today. Today, he was close enough to see the dark blue of her eyes.

"Kiss me," he whispered against the soft lips quivering beneath his. "Kiss me, and your debt will be paid, and," he added, staring down at the creaminess of her face and the light sprinkling of freckles across the delicate bridge of her small nose, "nothing more will ever be said, or heard by others, of this afternoon."

Whether she hoped to end as quickly as possible the encounter with the stranger, or to experience again the feel of a man's lips touching hers in passion, Leigh found herself reaching up to draw his lips closer, her hands leaving their position of refusal against his chest to curve around his strong neck and touch the curling gold of his hair as she brought his mouth to within inches of her own parted lips.

Neil drew in his breath, surprised by the feeling that raced through his blood as he stared down into her face; her eyes were heavy-lidded and half-closed, their color gleaming like dark sapphires, and her lips were half-parted, waiting for his kiss.

As soft as a butterfly's wings, he touched her lips with his. Gently he moved his mouth against hers, then lifted it to leave a trail of kisses along her jaw and the delicate contour of her flushed cheekbones, before returning to claim her lips again, but this time with purpose as he parted them and sought a more intimate contact with her.

Lowering his arm from her waist, he tightened it around her hips as he held her against him, feeling his own passion rising against her softness. His hand spread out over her buttocks, making her aware of his ardor as he held her closer against his increasing hardness, and he knew that one innocent kiss would not be enough from her. His other hand found her breast, fondling its softness beneath the faded calico. His kiss deepened when he felt the hardness of her nipple beneath his thumb and knew she was aroused by their intimacy.

Leigh was aroused, but it frightened her, and sensing the moment was developing into far more than an innocent kiss, she reacted to save herself. She heard her brother's voice saying, "When in a fight you are losing, the hell with being a gentleman, hit your opponent where it will hurt most—in the most sensitive part of his Inexpressibles." And Guy, even for his slightness of build, had seldom lost a fight.

She laughed uncontrollably at Guy's choice of words then, but now, as she remembered and acted upon his advice, Neil felt an incredible pain, and with a sense of disbelief felt the punishing impact of a raised knee striking him in the groin. Doubling over, he fell to his knees, releasing the woman he'd held so passionately in his arms only seconds before. He sat down, shielding himself from further abuse. Glancing around, however, he saw that his former captive had not suffered the same fate as he, and was running across the meadow with a flash of pure white petticoat. Despite his pain, a slight smile curved his lips when he heard the shrill whistle, and he was not surprised when the chestnut mare came galloping across the meadow.

Like the seductive murmuring of a cool mountain stream, reach out to touch, to capture, but the water remains elusive, slipping through your fingers, his sister had been fond of saying. The girl had mounted the mare and was galloping toward the safety of the trees—each hoofbeat taking her out of his reach.

Neil smiled. "We'll meet again," he spoke softly. Getting to his feet, he made his way back toward the stream and his possessions. Taking the blue silk stocking from his pack, he held it up to the light. It was soft and delicate and fragrant, and it was his possession, along with the blue ribbon he had just won, and soon so would be the young woman who had worn it, he thought, preparing to track her down.

Six

Sensations sweet,
Felt in the blood, and felt along the heart.

William Wordsworth

LEIGH LIGHTLY PLACED HER FINGERTIPS TO HER MOUTH. Still tender from his kiss, her lips were sensitive to the touch. Her very first kiss, Leigh thought in wonderment, and from a stranger.

"Oh, Lord!" Leigh murmured.

Thinking of the stranger, Leigh suddenly remembered what she had done to him. Her last sight of the stranger had been of him bent over double, pain racking his lean body. Guy had taught her well, perhaps too well, she worried, for even if the stranger had deserved so punishing a blow from her raised knee, she hoped she had not crippled him.

Then her mood changed. How dare he kiss her, she fumed, fanning the fires of indignation and outrage that had been strangely slow to burn earlier, but the more she fueled her anger, the more she remembered the rough feel of the stranger's mouth against hers, his hands moving over her body as if he'd the right to touch her so intimately.

Leigh drew in her breath, exhaling on a shudder as she glanced down at her breast and felt again the pressure of his hand against its softness. She blushed wildly as she remembered his thumb and the surprising way her nipple had risen into hardness beneath it.

Shakily, Leigh rubbed her hands over her hips, smoothing the creases from her gown, then wished she hadn't as she remembered yet again the stranger's touch and the manner in which he had held her against him.

Leigh closed her eyes in confusion, wondering what had happened to her. What had the stranger done to her in that instant in the woods when he had kissed her?

How could she ever face her family again? she despaired.

Surely they would all see the guilt written across her face in flaming colors, and know the traitorous way her body had betrayed her to the stranger. That was the most damning remembrance of all—she had responded to his kiss. How could she have? How could she have allowed herself to be fondled by a strange man? How could she have actually felt a strange, sweet pleasure firing her blood, making her heart pound deafeningly when he had touched her, held her close against the hardness of his body? And that had been why she had fled, not because she had disliked being held in his arms.

Why did she now remember so vividly the strange beauty of his eyes? She'd stared up into them, mesmerized, feeling herself pulled deeper into their depths.

But his eyes were deceptive. One moment the pale, gray-green color reflected a golden fire that must come from the heart, warming her in its glow, and in the next instant, they became crystalline, repulsing her with a coldness that numbed to the soul. And it frightened her, for she had been unable to resist either as she'd been drawn relentlessly into his embrace.

Leigh shook her head in denial, feeling the heat burning her scarlet cheeks. But she could not forget her shame. She had been too quick to pay her debt with a kiss, she accused herself, mortified by her actions. She'd never before felt such confusing emotions. Never before had her heart pounded so erratically, not even when she'd stood close to Matthew Wycliffe, or some other handsome, respectable gentleman of her acquaintance. When strolling along the Battery, her gloved hand placed lightly upon Matthew's arm as propriety decreed, she hadn't felt the almost breathless excitement she had when in the stranger's arms. At least it was heartening to know that she did not fall into every man's arms, she comforted herself, salvaging some of her pride and forgetting the pleasure she had felt in those arms.

But it was not supposed to happen this way, Leigh thought, frowning in contemplation of what had happened, unable to comprehend the import of the revelation she had yet to admit to herself. Love was supposed to come gently, nurtured by the customs of courtship, when a deep affection would grow between two people. There was a meeting of gazes, a brief look of recognition, a shy glancing away, then a soft smile of encouragement from the lady, followed by a polite comment from the gentleman concerning the unseasonable warmth of the afternoon, a remark certain to elicit a response in kind from the lady, which would lead into genteel conversation. And should they meet at a soiree, the gentleman would ask the lady to partner him in the next reel, then fetch her a refreshment after he had returned her to her chaperone's care. He would be allowed to sit next to her on the settee as she languidly fanned herself and lingered over her punch with a graciousness of manner. Chaperoned carriage rides in the golden glow of late afternoon. Strolls through the fragrant gardens with aunts and uncles hovering within earshot like busy bees. Delicate nose-gays of violets, ribbons, and lace and sweetly penned poems declaring undying devotion would be delivered to the demure young woman from her ardent admirer. Invitations accepted, and attended together, to a barbecue or fish fry, followed by an invitation from the lady's approving parents to stay over the weekend at the family's home and then attend Church with them on Sunday. The gentleman would accept, and shortly thereafter, he would ask for the young lady's hand in marriage. Soon would come the expected announcement of an engagement, the festive year of parties to fete the happy young couple, and finally, the nuptials that would follow in springtime.

That was the way it was supposed to happen, the way her mother had been courted by her father, and Althea by Nathan, and Thisbe by Stuart James, who had even traveled to Philadelphia during their courtship. And how Matthew Wycliffe had been courting her in Charleston and since her return home to Virginia. It was all very civilized. One had to go about love in the proper manner, Leigh reminded herself, pleased with the thought for a moment, until another, far less comforting realization came to her.

Love....? No, Leigh shook her head vehemently, unable to believe such an incredible notion. No, it could never have happened. Not so suddenly...not so unexpectedly...and not so unacceptable. She was going to marry Matthew Wycliffe. Matthew was the man she loved. He was the man she wanted for her husband, the man she wanted to be the father of her children, the man she wanted to spend the rest of her life with—and the man her parents would approve of. For who was this man, this stranger who had entered her life with such destructive force, causing her to forsake all that she held dear in mind and body when close to him? Since first seeing him she had been unable to forget him, or the vision of his body bathed golden by the sun. She knew nothing about him—not even his name.

And yet, how could he be the half-savage Jolie believed him to be when he wore a gentleman's attire as if well-accustomed to the feel of fine linen against his sun-bronzed skin, and his voice, despite a slight drawl, had been soft and cultured, each word spoken with the eloquence of a well-educated gentleman of leisure. He must be a gentleman, and yet...

"So there you are!"

Leigh drew in her breath sharply and spun around in surprise.

"We thought you'd been kidnapped or even worse!" Blythe said as she ran into their bedchamber, her voice breathless. "You disappeared without a trace. And then Stephen couldn't be found anywhere. You should have heard the ruckus. It woke Julia and me up. And then Nathan, half-dressed, with Althea right behind him, and whiter than her nightdress, came charging out of their room and Guy nearly knocked Julia down when he banged open his door and ran out, waving a pistol in his hand, and that caused Julia to scream. Although, I suspect it was seeing Guy in his nightshirt that really set her reeling. And then Noelle started crying and we had to stop and see to her, and then we were all coming down the stairs, when Mama and Jolie, carrying her big basket of smelly medicines, came in the back. Jolie was so startled she dropped the basket and one of the bottles, that disgusting dark green bottle with the cod-liver oil in it, broke and the most sickening odor started climbing up the stairs. And there was Papa, still dressed in his evening clothes, and barefoot and unshaven, his hair ruffled on end, standing in the middle of the foyer and dripping gravy all over the rug and demanding to know where the devil Stephen was. Papa had been in the dining room, actually trying to serve himself, because there was a sticky trail of gravy all the way back into the room, and every time he demanded where Stephen was, he shook the ladle of gravy all over everyone. I thought Mama was going to faint. And then Althea made a strange gurgling noise and ran back upstairs, only she didn't quite make it because I heard her getting sick on the landing. And you'll never guess what happened to Stephen! He got himself locked up in the cellar by mistake," Blythe said with a laugh as she perched on the foot of the bed, swinging her feet back and forth, almost giddy with excitement. "That was what awakened us all. There had been this awful banging and faint cries for help. While we were standing there, trying to figure out what had happened to you, because Julia had suddenly cried out that you were missing, and that it was a slave uprising and we'd all be murdered in our beds, it all started again. The banging and cries for help, only louder this time. Papa was about to grab Grandpapa Travers's fowling piece, thinking one of Guy's hounds had cornered a rat in the cellar, but Guy said you were probably stuck up a tree, when Jolie stomped past Papa saying the ol' fool had finally gone and done it this time. For an instant, Papa had the funniest look on his face, especially when Jolie grabbed the gravy ladle out of his hand. I think he thought Jolie was talking about him," Blythe said, tears starting to fall from the corners of her eyes as she laughed even harder, her slender shoulders shaking with mirth.

She frowned slightly when Leigh didn't laugh too, as she normally would have. Instead, her sister turned her back on her and resumed rummaging through the high chest of drawers.

"I don't mind, Leigh, but those are my chemises you're wrinkling so thoroughly," she said, watching curiously as Leigh pulled out two different shades of stockings, unaware that they did not match as she tossed them over her arm. "I haven't gotten much of a bosom yet, not like you, so my chemises will probably be a little too tight for you now. And I don't know what Mama will say when she sees you wearing one pink stocking and one blue stocking. Although, after what happened earlier, I doubt it'd seem in the least bit strange, after all, there were even two corn bread muffins in the centerpiece. I couldn't tell if Stephen was laughing or crying, though his eyes were tearing up, when he saw those two corn bread muffins," Blythe added, shaking her long ponytail in dismay for this had turned out to be a most unusual morning, and she wouldn't be at all surprised by what might happen next.

Leigh turned around and stared at Blythe as if she were seeing a stranger in her bedchamber instead of her little sister.

"Your chemise and stockings are on the chair," Blythe reminded her, gesturing toward the lacy underclothing and silk stockings that had been neatly folded and placed on the chair by someone earlier. "And your good muslin, the mauve-striped one, is hanging in the clothes press. I gather that is the one you intended wearing, and you'd better change into it before Mama finds you in that old blue gown that even I couldn't wear now. You've got some explaining to do, because she didn't look in the least bit pleased to learn you'd gone out so early and without your hat, because it was sitting right there on the hall bench beside hers. But Stephen said he'd made you eat a proper breakfast. And then Jolie grabbed hold of me, Leigh, those yellow eyes of hers glowing, truly, they were, and she made me promise to tell her as soon as you returned," Blythe confided. "Why do you think she wanted to know?"

But Leigh didn't hear her.

Blythe frowned, and jumping off the bed, she hurried over to Leigh's side. Pressing the back of her hand against Leigh's cheek in concern, she opened her mouth in surprise. "I think you've got a fever, Leigh. Your cheeks are burning. And your lips look kind of puffy and red. You didn't get stung by a wasp, did you? Do you feel sick? I think you've even got chills. You're shivering slightly. I'd better get Mama. Maybe it was something you ate, like Althea. Mama said it's the morning sickness. I hope we all don't come down with it. Do you think you have it, Leigh? I wonder how you got it. I'll have to ask Mama. But I don't think it is too serious, not like swamp fever, because Mama didn't seem too upset and Jolie was grinning from ear to ear."

"No! Don't get Mama," Leigh said more sharply than she'd intended, but she didn't want her mother and Jolie to find her like this. She wouldn't be able to hide the truth from them, especially Jolie, who already knew too much. They would know she'd been kissed, you couldn't hide something like that, Leigh thought, horrified as she grabbed the hand mirror from the dressing table and stared at her reflection. She did look different.

"I'm all right, Lucy, truly I am. I was out riding," she said.

"Stephen said you'd gone down to the stables, but to go out riding so early?" Blythe demanded, thinking her sister must be feverish. "Of course, Julia does snore, so you probably couldn't sleep anyway. I felt like stuffing a pillow in her mouth last night, and that was before she even fell asleep. I declare, Leigh, I've never heard anyone talk as much as she does, and half the time she doesn't say anything. Thank goodness she's still downstairs eating breakfast."

"I had something to think about, and I wanted to be alone," Leigh said lamely, looking down in amazement at the unmatched pair of stockings she held.

Blythe stared at her sister for a long moment, then patted her hand understandingly, as if she were the older of the two. "It's what happened yesterday afternoon, isn't it?" she asked, nodding her head wisely.

Leigh's eyes widened in dismay. How did Blythe know about the stranger and the stolen buckskins?

"You know," she prompted helpfully when Leigh continued to stare at her dumbly. "Matthew Wycliffe. It's true. You're going to marry him, aren't you? I do like him, but I wish you weren't going to marry so soon. You just came home from Charleston, and now you'll be going back there. I'll never get to see you anymore, and when I do you will have changed. Being married will do that to you. Remember how much fun we used to have with Annie, but now that she's married to Reverend Scunthorpe, she never laughs anymore and wants to be called Cora Anna instead. She's gotten so stuffy and plump, and she's always cooing over little children. She really should not wear gray all of the time. She reminds me of a big pigeon. I wish Matthew Wycliffe lived in Virginia," Blythe added, sighing, for this summer just hadn't been the same as the ones before. Something was happening. It was different, but she didn't know why. It was as if there was something crackling in the air. Like the sound of distant thunder just beyond the hills, or heat lightning flashing in a darkening sky at twilight. You knew the storm was coming, you could feel it, but it wasn't here yet. It just made you jittery. Maybe it was because she was turning sixteen on Friday and she would be attending her first ball, and...

"Do you think anyone will ask me to dance, Leigh?" Blythe asked diffidently, voicing her most worrisome thought. "Mama has such high expectations, and, well...I don't want to disappoint her," Blythe admitted, glancing up from her perusal of her feet, and the depressing revelation that her feet were far too big, not dainty like their mother's or Althea's, or even Leigh's. And suddenly she began to worry that she would grow even taller than Leigh. She'd never catch a husband then. Why, she'd be even taller than Guy, Blythe thought, a horrified expression crossing her young, earnest face as she saw herself towering over everyone, her big feet stepping on the toes of any gentleman foolish enough to have asked her to dance.

Leigh smiled softly, understanding more than her young sister might realize. Blythe was like Capitaine, coltish, all legs and tail, and tripping over her own feet. But one day...one day she'd be lovely, and as graceful of body as she was of spirit now. "Your dance card will be filled and Papa will have to keep a stern eye on you, lest some gentleman tries to take you out into the gardens unescorted."

"Do you really think so?" Blythe asked shyly, a dreamy look crossing her face.

"You're going to be the prettiest and most sought-after girl at your party," Leigh told her honestly, for Blythe, with her dark hair and hazel eyes, which were always brimming with laughter, had a quality about her that drew people to her. Everyone was her friend. "In fact, I wouldn't be at all surprised if Justin Braedon couldn't keep his eyes off you, so beautiful will you be in your new gown," she added, for she hadn't missed her sister's gentle questioning of Julia about Nathan's young cousin from the territories.

Blythe made a comical face, swallowing her surprise with an unladylike gulp, for she hadn't turned sixteen yet, nor had she danced her first dance in the arms of a handsome young gentleman admirer, so she hadn't had time to learn to hide her childishly honest reactions behind the cool mask of a sophisticated belle.

Dancing over to the window as if in the arms of one of

those gentlemen, Blythe stared out across the gardens. Leaning her elbows on the sill of the opened window, she took a deep breath, the heady scent of roses perfuming the air as the heat of a summer's sun chased away any early morning mists that had lingered too long in the vale. She wished she would see Palmer William and Justin Braedon riding up the lane. Maybe he wouldn't even be coming to visit his relatives at Royal Bay. And if he did, maybe he wouldn't even want to come to her birthday party. "I think Justin Braedon is a very pleasant young man, nothing more than that," she said in denial of anything more, unwilling to admit even to Leigh that she cared for Justin Braedon in case he didn't ask her to partner him on Friday for at least one dance—if he even showed up.

"And I am certain he thinks you are very pleasant too," Leigh said, feeling calmer and far more herself now that she was talking with Blythe in the safety of her bedchamber, her family and friends around her. She was back at Travers Hill and the stranger couldn't touch her here. In fact, perhaps she had dreamed everything that had happened, Leigh decided, putting back the stockings and Blythe's chemises with a steadier hand.

"Good Lord! Who is that?" Blythe squealed. "And why does he have the lil' cap'n tied to that big bay of his?" she called out, leaning even farther out of the window as she craned her neck to see more. Hurrying to the side window, she had a better view of the stranger who'd just ridden into the yard, for their bedchamber, a corner room, overlooked both the front of the house and the stables across the greensward toward the back.

"What?" Leigh said faintly, not having to see the big bay her sister mentioned to know who rode it so boldly onto Travers land, but she found herself going toward the window anyway.

"He's got your colt, Leigh!" she repeated, turning around to stare in amazement at her sister.

"Capitaine?" Leigh felt a sinking in her heart as she rather belatedly realized that Capitaine hadn't followed her home from the meadow. So blinded by her own self-absorption, she hadn't even noticed that he was missing.

She'd even rubbed down Damascena, never wondering where he was. How could she have forgotten him? Leigh berated herself. *Never*, never before would she have forgotten about her horses.

"He's riding right into the stables!" Blythe breathed, nearly overbalancing out the opened window as she tried to catch one last glimpse of the stranger. "I wonder who he is," she asked again, glancing at her sister as if expecting an answer.

"Well…don't look at me. How should I know?" Leigh demanded, her dark blue eyes bright with anger and self-disgust. "But I intend to find out," she added bravely. "How dare he come riding onto Travers land as if he'd every right to!"

"Don't worry. Sweet John will take care of him if he's done something wrong," Blythe said reassuringly. "He'll rassle him to the ground if he doesn't have a good explanation of why he has the lil' cap'n in tow."

"Sweet John isn't in the stables. He's down at the track exercising the horses."

"Then you can't go down to the stables alone. He might be a thief, after all, he's got Capitaine. Maybe he's going to steal more of our horses! Of course, he did bring the lil' cap'n back to Travers Hill. Maybe he just found him? But I wonder how he knew where he belonged," she said, puzzled. "I thought at first that it was Adam Braedon. He sure looked like him. And did you see the packhorse he had? He must have come a long way, so how'd he know about Travers Hill?" she demanded, a thousand unanswered questions coming to mind. "I wish Papa hadn't already left, but he and Nathan went to the sawmill. And Guy left for the Canbys just a little while ago. Mama's having a tray in her room, then she's going to take a short nap. Althea's resting. And I don't know where Jolie is. Everything seemed to get back to normal once Stephen was rescued, and then everyone was going to search for you, at least they were until Stephen said you'd gone down to the stables, and then Jolie nodded, and that settled that, because she said you'd said something to her about riding out with Sweet John or one of the grooms," Blythe explained matter-of-factly, for if Jolie knew about it, then everything was all right.

Blythe ran back to the window. "I don't see him yet. I wonder what he's doing in the stables," Blythe whispered.

"I'm going down there," Leigh told her again, determined to deal with the stranger once and for all. She would be able to handle him; after all, she was at Travers Hill now.

"Oh, Leigh, no! You can't go by yourself. I'll come with you," Blythe offered.

"No!" Leigh said, grabbing her arm before she could race from the room. She had no idea what the stranger might say about their previous meeting—and that was something she wanted kept a secret.

"Listen," Leigh said, pulling Blythe back to the window. "You wait here. You'll be able to watch the stables and—"

"And call for help if you don't come back out," Blythe concluded helpfully.

"Yes," Leigh said slowly, "but I don't think there will be any need for that."

"You don't?" Blythe breathed in awe, wondering how her sister planned to deal with the stranger.

"No," Leigh said, a slight smile curving her lips as she thought of how she would greet the stranger. "You wait here, Blythe. Give me time to handle this. Promise?"

Blythe nodded, her cheeks flushed with excitement. "If I hear you scream, then I'll get help."

Leigh nearly halted in the doorway, but gathering up her courage, she hurried from the room, slowing only enough to tiptoe past her mother's bedchamber. Then she was down the stairs in a flash, stopping in the foyer to pull the bench beneath the parlor door so she could reach her grandfather's fowling piece. With the quick efficiency of one who has done a task before, Leigh primed and loaded the flintlock, then she left the big house by the front door. She had taken a chance passing by the dining room where she could hear the chink of silverware against china, and Julia and Noelle arguing. But it had been worth the risk, for she had avoided passing beneath the windows of her mother's bedchamber, where she might have been seen crossing the yard toward the stables.

Blythe nearly fell from her precarious perch on the windowsill when she spied her sister running across the yard carrying their grandfather's fowling piece, as if ready to shoot a turkey flushed from cover by one of Guy's hounds.

Seven

Eyes of unholy blue.

Thomas Moore

WITH ANGER RIDING HIGH NOW, AND A FAR MORE acceptable feeling to deal with than the newfound emotion of love, Leigh reached the stables. Her steps faltered as she shifted the flintlock to a more comfortable position in her arms, then gathering up her courage, she entered the stables.

The stranger's big bay, with the heavily laden packhorse and her little Capitaine tied behind, was blocking her path. Leigh glanced around, but she didn't see the stranger anywhere. Despite her nervousness, and the uneasy feeling she was being watched, Leigh walked along the passage, her hands tightening around the smooth stock of the flintlock musket she held protectively before her.

"Ah, the welcoming party," the stranger murmured, startling Leigh as he appeared behind her without having made a sound. "I suspected if I waited long enough someone would come running from the big house. Especially since my arrival was observed from the upstairs window by the little dark-haired girl. Did she cry the alarm?"

Swinging around, the barrel of the musket pointed threateningly at his chest, which was broad and would have made an easy target for even the poorest of marksmen, Leigh stood her ground.

"You're on Travers land."

"So you told me before," he said, not disappointed by her hostile greeting, and noting that she'd been the only one to enter the stables.

Neil glanced down at his gloved hands, trying to control his grin, for things had gone much easier than he'd anticipated. He'd been prepared for questions upon his arrival at Travers Hill. But the reason for his unannounced arrival would have been obvious: the return of the colt. He had expected more difficulty in discovering the whereabouts of the young woman, without revealing a prior acquaintance with her. But to his amazement, he now found her standing in the middle of the empty stables, slender hands locked around the stock of a musket held steadily in his direction, softly rounded chin tipped aggressively, rich chestnut hair falling in thick shiny waves, and apparently determined to do him bodily harm.

"You are trespassing. How dare you follow me here," Leigh brazened, her voice sounding confident despite the shaking of her knees, especially when she saw the half smile curving his lips.

"Remembering the sweetness of your lips...and your gentle touch," he added mockingly, grimacing slightly as he moved toward her, "I've come to the foolhardy conclusion that I would follow you just about anywhere. Pleasure, followed by pain, makes it all the sweeter. And often, pain is then rewarded by pleasure. It can become an opiate to the senses. Not to be denied, and to be sought after at any cost. And as you can see, I suffered no permanent damage, and have come seeking pleasure. You are very fortunate, my dear. You would never have forgiven yourself," he said, his eyes warm with the humor only he seemed to appreciate.

"*I* would never have forgiven myself?" Leigh responded with an incredulous look that mirrored the innocence in her eyes. "You would do well to get back on your horse and leave. As I warned you before, you are on—"

"Travers land," he finished for her, taking in the cleanliness of the stables and the fine markings of the blooded roan in the stall at his right. "I stand warned. I quake in fear of the awesome Travers name."

Leigh swallowed her panic, for the stranger did not seem in the least bit impressed, or fearful of having trespassed. She couldn't believe the audacity of the man in following her here. Leigh bit her lower lip in growing vexation, wishing Sweet John would hurry back from the track. Surely he would be returning to the stables within minutes, she thought with rising hope as she glanced toward the opened doors to the stables.

"No sign of help on the way?" the stranger murmured pityingly as he closed the distance along the row of stalls. Looping the big bay's reins over a hook, the stranger said quietly, "I believe we still have some unfinished business."

"I finished it, much to your discomfort, if you remember," Leigh reminded him unnecessarily, and refusing to retreat before him.

"Oh, I do remember," he replied, his gaze moving over her with amused speculation, lingering for a moment on the quick rise and fall of her breasts beneath the tight bodice of the faded blue gown she wore so proudly. Then his glance fell to the shapely length of stockinged ankle and calf, the shoes she wore having seen better days. "You truly cannot be as young as you look," he said with a disbelieving shake of his golden head.

"I'm not," she warned. "I am very capable of causing you serious injury again, and unless you truly enjoy pain so much, then I would suggest you get back on your horse, which I suspect must be stolen because I doubt the Braedons would sell you one of their bloods, and leave Travers Hill immediately. But first, you have yet to return my property to me," she reminded him, gesturing with the barrel of the musket in case he had trouble understanding plain talk. "And I can use this, and very accurately too."

The stranger's smile widened, but it wasn't the kind of smile that made Leigh any less uncomfortable. "I have no doubt whatsoever that you speak the truth, for you seem a most accomplished young woman," he said. "In fact, I'm certain you could shoot the tail feather off a robin," he remarked. Thinking she referred to the stocking and ribbon he had taken from her, he said, "I am afraid I cannot part with so tantalizing a reminder of my encounter with you in the woods. They will always be a sweet remembrance of an enchanted afternoon," he said, then, when he saw her worried expression, he belatedly realized that the ribbon and stocking might be the only ones she had and he suddenly wished he could buy her a hundred ribbons of every hue and the finest silk stockings to wear against her soft, scented flesh.

"So, you think you can best me again? I'll take that bet. Should you win, you reclaim what was yours, but when I win, your forfeit this time will be more than a chaste kiss."

A chaste kiss? It had been far more than that to her. "I want my property. You are nothing better than a thief, and a stupid one if you think you can get away with this," Leigh said, raising her voice in anger and fear and the hope that someone might hear.

"I would be very careful about calling names, my little light-fingered one, for you stole from the wrong man this time," he reminded her, and Leigh suddenly found herself retreating before his tall figure. "Don't come any closer. I will shoot."

The stranger shook his head. "I don't think so," he said.

Leigh backed into one of the empty stalls, wondering how Travers Hill could suddenly seem so abandoned. Never before had she realized how far away the big house was from the stables. No one would hear her if she screamed—not even Blythe, who would be listening for just such a sound.

As if reading her mind, the stranger reached her in a stride, startling Leigh from her thoughts, one hand closing around the curly-maple stock of the musket, while the other took possession of the long barrel. Struggling to keep her hold on her grandfather's prized fowling piece, Leigh's fingers moved for a firmer grip, finding and closing over the trigger guard just as his hand reached it. Their hands met, their fingers entwining and somehow moving against the trigger. A deafening roar, accompanied by sulfurous smoke that seemed to Leigh to have been belched from the fires of hell, filled the small stall. Stepping backward too quickly without looking, her attention centered on wrestling the family heirloom and her hand from his grasp, Leigh stumbled over a pitchfork that someone had carelessly left half-concealed in the hay. As her foot pressed down on the curving forked end, the long handle rose suddenly from out of the hay like a dragon's head, ready to strike against the enemy. The stranger managed to jump clear before the end could hit him where her knee had done damage before, but he lost his balance as Leigh suddenly released her hold on the musket. Falling backward, he lay sprawled in the fresh hay spread across the floor of the stall, an incredulous look on his handsome face. Catching the hem of her gown with her heel as she tried to find her own balance, Leigh fell into the hay next to him.

Suddenly Neil heard the low, soft laughter that had drifted to him across the meadow the day before.

Despite her predicament, Leigh couldn't help her laughter. It was irrepressible. Never had she seen such a startled expression cross someone's face as it had the stranger's in that instant when he'd become aware of the danger lurking before him. But it had quickly turned to concern when he'd quickly scissor-stepped the handle of the pitchfork, then comical disbelief when he had fallen into the hay in an undignified sprawl, when only moments before he had so arrogantly thought himself in control of the situation.

"Sauce for the goose is sauce for the gander," Leigh warned, her voice husky with laughter as she risked retribution by challenging him with the moral.

But Leigh was startled by his reaction this time, her laughter fading as she heard the stranger's. Her breath caught as she listened to the rich sound and stared at his face, the harshness banished into boyishness as he laughed. The fine lines etched around his eyes crinkled with humor, and there was no cynicism or malice now in the smile that widened his mouth, showing the gleaming whiteness of his teeth.

Carefully placing the musket in the hay, he held out a gloved hand. Thinking he meant to make peace between them and help her to her feet, Leigh reached out unhesitatingly to accept his assistance, forgetting her previous opinion that he was not a man to be trusted.

Light as a feather, Leigh felt herself pulled to her feet, but then his arms were around her. They felt like iron bands enclosing her as he pulled her against his chest and between his legs as he rolled into the hay, carrying her along with him in his tumble.

"You are far too trusting," he said, his breath warm against her cheek.

Breathless, Leigh stared up into his face, wondering how she had ended up beneath him, one of his long legs wedged between hers.

"A tumble in the hay with a lovely maid—or a rather silly little goose who seems fond of sticking her neck out too far, especially when there are wolves around," he said, reminding her of the moral she had taunted him with moments before, but his grin quickly faded when Leigh's teeth bit into his shoulder. "Damn," he muttered, grasping her chin and forcing her into releasing his flesh.

Stormy blue eyes met and held startled but amused gray-green eyes.

"You obviously haven't the same sentimental feeling for a tumble in the hay that I do," he said, rubbing the painful bite on his shoulder.

"That is because it is always the gentleman who is doing the tumbling, and too often not at the request of the lady," Leigh informed him, her back itching from the scratchiness of the hay beneath her.

"Ah, but a gentleman seldom tumbles a lady in the hay," he corrected her, quite comfortable with their position in the hay.

"*Ah*, but only those beneath them," Leigh couldn't resist adding.

"Witty as well as beautiful. And dangerous," he said, feeling a slight throbbing in his shoulder where her teeth had left their brand on him. "Where did you learn to fight? On the levy?" he inquired silkily, but the pleasure of holding her warm, slender body in his arms had been worth the pain of the wound. He had never met anyone like this young woman and she fascinated him.

"My brother taught me all I need to know about repulsing the unwanted attentions of someone who is not a gentleman," Leigh warned.

"A brother?" the stranger repeated, glancing over his shoulder just in case the fellow was lurking nearby to brain him with a cudgel. Striking from behind a man's back did not seem out of character for this brother of hers, and if he possessed even half the spirit and fight she did, then he was in serious danger. "Remind me never to get in a fight with him. I'm not certain I would survive such chicanery. However, he does seem to possess some intelligence, for beauty such as yours should never be wasted on some common lout of a fellow who could be expected to honor it with only his unimaginative praise and clumsy touch. And certainly not with the expensive trinkets from an eager gentleman admirer that a lovely and ambitious young woman would quite naturally expect as her due. Nor should she be cheated of that gentleman's expertise as a lover.

I wonder how many favors this brother of yours has demanded just to have you smile at an interested gentleman. However, I would question your claim of 'unwanted attentions,' for I remember a pair of soft lips kissing mine most persuasively."

"Sometimes a person will do something distasteful just to avoid something far worse," Leigh told him with brazen honesty, surprised to see a look of cruelty cross his face, but just as quickly it was gone and his gaze remained only slightly narrowed with amused speculation. "I've always been good about taking my medicine."

"My kiss? Like taking medicine? That awful, was it?" he asked with a deep laugh, apparently not offended in the least. "I had no idea I was such an ogre. I would have thought you'd have had to put up with far worse. You've probably had to fight off the attentions of the young gentlemen of the family you work for since you were about thirteen," he told her, his finger sliding through a long strand of her loose hair as if he could not resist the temptation. "Have you always managed to escape?" he asked softly, curious about this vibrant woman he held in his arms.

Leigh stared at him in puzzlement. "The family I work for?"

"Yes, this *is* Travers Hill. And you are either the head groom's daughter or the overseer's, and there are several eligible sons in the Travers family. One of the daughters, the eldest, I recall, is married to Nathan Braedon. Nathan might have married her, but he'd have had to have been blinded by love not to have seen you and sought your favors. Or did he?"

Leigh stared at him in amazement, then realized that her appearance had led him to believe her nothing more than a servant—certainly not a properly brought up young lady. No wonder he had taken liberties with her, daring to touch her and kiss her, knowing she would not expect him to act the gentleman. Indeed, in his mind, he might even have thought she wished for his attentions, hoping he would offer to remove her from her life of drudgery. And even had she not, she could not have stopped him had he wanted her. Nor could she have expected help from anyone, for it was accepted by society that poor serving girls had no virtue to be protected should some disreputable gentleman have seduction on his mind. And had the maid been innocent, then it was a pity, but she had probably enticed the young gentleman into his lustful actions on the unfounded hopes that he might offer her marriage. When attending her young lady's finishing school in Charleston, Leigh had heard many a horrifying tale of unfortunate young women who had been ruined. It was scandalous talk reserved for whispers at night when innocent, well-bred young girls were safely tucked away in the cool darkness of bedchambers as chaste as cells in a convent.

And this stranger thought she was a serving girl, or a lady's maid, or even the groom's hoydenish daughter, Leigh realized in dismay. Her mother would have swooned, Leigh thought, suddenly unable to bridle her sense of humor, for once he discovered her true identity, this arrogant stranger, who seemed at times almost a gentleman but not quite, would be embarrassed and chagrined, humbled and humiliated before her. He might even know a moment's fright, thinking her father or brothers might challenge him to a duel for sullying the family name. Or, if a bachelor, he might even feel it necessary to ask for her hand in marriage to save her from having been dishonored by his ungentlemanly conduct. And that—having *this* gentleman asking for her hand in marriage—would truly cause her mother a fit of the vapors.

Neil wasn't prepared to hear her sudden laughter, the low, warm laugh having a strange effect on him as he held her quivering body close to him. He wanted to be laughing with her again, sharing the humor, but he had the distinct impression that she was now laughing at him, and it stung him to the quick as only a few things could. He felt apart from her, like the outsider he was and always had been.

"The Travers boys, unless there is something dreadfully wrong with them, would be as hot on your scent as their hounds after a fox, my dear. I am surprised you aren't used to being caught and bedded in the hay. I thought I had given you chase enough. Or is this coy, maidenly demeanor of yours part of the game? What price will you now demand?" he challenged in a roughened voice, no longer amused, and wanting to hurt her as she had him.

Leigh opened her mouth, outraged by his remark about

her brothers, and herself, and raising her hand, she slapped the stranger across his lean cheek before he could draw back. The impact left a ruddy mark against his dark skin.

"You've stolen from me, you've nearly unmanned me, you've drawn blood, you've insulted me, and now you've struck me. I've never had the incredible misfortune of meeting such a bloodthirsty young woman before. Not even held captive by the Apache would I be treated with such abuse. Not even by their women. But without a good fight, there is no honor in the victory, and you have proven a most challenging opponent. But you have lost, and I warned you that you would have to pay a far higher penalty," he told her, capturing her hand as she raised it again. He held it bound to the other hand she had raised against his chest in a futile attempt to try to hold him off. Pulling her arms over her head, he stared down at her for a long moment, his gaze lingering again on the seductive curve of breast revealed by the tautness of the pale blue material of her gown. Slowly, he lowered his mouth, prepared to claim more than a kiss as his prize this time.

Neil smiled when he felt her struggling against him, her knee trying to find and strike against his most vulnerable spot again, but she couldn't fool him twice, and her struggles only served to join her hips more intimately with his, which startled her even more when she felt him hardening against her. Her face was flushed, her dark blue eyes full of blazing anger, her golden-brown hair tangled and caught with spiky bits of hay, and he thought he'd never seen such beauty. With a certainty that came of instinct, and which he had learned never to question, Neil knew that this woman and he would become lovers. And even had it only been wishful thinking, he would have believed still, because her eyes could not hide the truth. There had been a look of desire in the dark blue depths when she had looked at him, and although quickly veiled, it had flared briefly, warming him with its fire.

She-With-Eyes-Of-The-Captured-Sky now haunted his thoughts. He could hear once again the softness of her voice in the darkness as she spun wondrous tales until his eyes had grown heavy as the peace of slumber came to his troubled spirit. Her softly spoken words had conjured up the magic of the ancient beliefs...of a destiny one could not change. Of a destiny one had to accept.

It was the destiny of the Morning Star to chase his bride, the Evening Star, through the heavens for eternity. But she would remain just out of his reach, waiting in the dusk of evening, waiting for the warmth of his embrace. As he reached out for her, the darkness would fall and he would flee into it, lost, until she appeared in the heavens to guide him into her arms with her brightness.

Suddenly Neil knew he wanted this woman—perhaps more than he had any other woman—and he intended to have her. He found himself wondering what it would be like to have her by his side always, from dawn until dusk, and in the dark hours between. To return to the territories with her as his woman—his wife—to return home to Riovado. She had no home here at Travers Hill. Except for this brother of hers, whom he suspected would sell her as quickly as a broodmare, she might have no family to call her own. She would welcome his proposal, for a chance to build a home of her own, where she served no one, and could raise a family of strong sons and daughters who would be their own masters.

Yes, she would come with him. There was nothing to keep her here. She would be his—only his.

Leigh stared up into his lean face, her heart quickening its beat as she realized his intent. Her lashes flickered momentarily, for held beneath him, her wrists shackled by the overpowering strength of his grasp, she could do nothing but wait for his touch. But Leigh Travers was not one to give up without a fight, and she opened her eyes, determined not to cower beneath him, but when her gaze met and was held by his she found herself forgetting about her antagonism, for there was a sudden gentleness in his eyes and in the strong hand that touched her cheek, caressing it. He seemed vulnerable as he stared into her eyes, and in that brief moment, she knew that she held the power to hurt him. How? She didn't know, but she knew she possessed it. Slowly he lowered his head, allowing his lips to move against her throat, barely touching her flesh. Leigh felt an uncontrollable shiver quivering through her when she felt his breath warm against the delicate contours of her ear. He spoke softly, his words strange and unintelligible to her, but they were words of love and desire. She waited breathlessly when his lips moved over the hollows of her cheeks, then hovered briefly above her mouth, then they were almost touching her lips.

Her lips parted...

Suddenly a horrible, terrifying, bloodcurdling cry cut through the quietness of the stables. Before the last notes of the savage cry had echoed, the stranger had released her and was crouched above her waiting to spring. Leigh stared in amazement, her eyes wide with disbelief as they caught the flash of the knife blade he held poised in his hand. Any gentleness that had crossed his face had been wiped clean and replaced by a look of such cruelty that Leigh knew he was a man capable of killing.

"Damn it! You son of whoredom! You coyote's hindquarters! You slime on the rock beneath an eagle's aerie. Where the devil are you?" a laughing voice suddenly called from the entrance. "Not playing another one of them Comanche tricks on me? Should I duck in case a stray arrow shoots past my head? Or is someone going to take a pot shot at me?"

Leigh sensed rather than saw, even before the glinting blade of the knife was sheathed, the instinctive relaxing of taut muscles as the stranger sat back on his haunches, a slight smile beginning to curve his lips. Then in one swift movement he had gotten to his feet and pulled her with him.

Leigh tried to restore her dignity, for she, too, had recognized that voice.

It belonged to Adam Braedon.

At first glance, Adam Merton Braedon bore a strong resemblance to his cousin, so it was understandable that Leigh might have momentarily mistaken the stranger for him. But upon closer inspection, the similarity ended, for although Adam Braedon was tall, he wasn't as tall as Neil Braedon. Nor was he as lean and bronzed, although his body was firmly muscled and his face bore the healthy color of a physically active man. His blond hair curled naturally and had more of a reddish tint to it than his cousin's. It was also properly clipped and combed off his forehead, and his long side whiskers, albeit bushy, were neatly trimmed and his mustache fashionably waxed. The color of his eyes was different too; they were a pale gray like his sister Julia's. And there was nothing hawkish about his profile, which was deemed quite without fault by all who were privileged to gaze upon it. Impeccable as always, Adam was arrayed in his finest riding coat and boots, his breeches pressed with a razor-sharp crease, his shirt front starched to perfection.

"Dagger! Good Lord! Appearing out of thin air, you never change, do you, but I'm not surprised since you were spawned of a heathen land and sired by the ol' lone wolf of the pack," Adam Braedon called out when the object of his complimentary greeting stood, revealing himself. "I thought I recognized that bay as one of ours, but when you cut across the meadow, I lost you. I was on the road, my horse doing a gentlemanly trot, my thoughts concerned with the sorry cut of my sleeve, when I spied a heathen rider in the distance. Figured you could only be heading here to Travers Hill, and I knew you weren't lost. Recognized the colt too. How on earth did you come by him? It belongs to Leigh—" Adam Braedon's words halted abruptly as he watched a tousled young woman step from behind Neil's broad back, a dangerous-looking musket held easily in her hands. "What the devil?" he exclaimed, not having missed the rumpled skirt, which she had neglected to brush down, revealing a froth of white petticoat, or her unbound hair, in which several pieces of hay were caught in the chestnut tangles. She looked as if she'd been thrown from her mount—or just been tumbled in the hay by an amorous beau…although, her possession of the musket, and the sound of gunfire he'd heard, would seem to have discouraged any gentleman so foolishly inclined.

However, since he knew Leigh Alexandra Travers would never have been thrown from her horse, the other must be true…but the thought of Leigh Travers being tumbled in the hay by his cousin was just as outrageous an explanation.

Leigh saw the look of disbelief replace the one of surprise on Adam's handsome face and felt herself blushing all the more as she rightly suspected what was going through his mind. And as she stared at his openmouthed expression, she realized yet again that it was all his fault. Her predicament would never have happened if Adam hadn't been up to mischief and planted a garden snake in their picnic basket the day before. She would never have stolen the stranger's buckskins otherwise.

"With that fat head of yours as a target, Adam, I could hardly have missed," the stranger said, apparently on a first-name basis with Adam Braedon.

Leigh glanced at the two men, startled by the resemblance between them, which, as far as her conscience was concerned, relieved her of any blame for her actions of the last twenty-four hours.

"And when I heard the sound of gunfire, I knew Dagger must be involved, for trouble shadows him," Adam retorted, shaking his head, "but that wasn't what had me concerned. 'Twas that Dagger had Leigh Travers's colt. Now, I asked myself, how on earth did Dagger, who just arrived from the territories, manage to get his hands on Leigh's lil' cap'n, when half the county has gone wild trying to?" he demanded, wondering anew as he caught the look of consternation crossing the lady in question's face.

"Leigh Travers? I haven't met the lady of your acquaintance, but it would appear she is not overly careful of her property," Neil responded, thinking of the spoiled blond-haired beauty of the day before.

"You've never met the lady?" Adam repeated, looking at the two in disbelief.

"Mr. Dagger and I have not had the time to become properly introduced," Leigh said, sounding very haughty indeed.

Adam couldn't muffle his laughter, for neither of the two knew who the other was. It was too fine a jest to ignore, he thought. *Mr. Dagger* she had called him, and he, *Dagger*, had not yet met the lady, Leigh Travers. Adam nearly laughed aloud.

"My, my," he said, a look of devilment in his eye. "He has not introduced himself to you, nor have you introduced yourself to him," he questioned.

"No," Leigh said shortly. "We have not had the opportunity to do so."

"I understand completely," Adam murmured. "You saw this unknown man, this stranger, approaching Travers Hill with the cap'n in tow, and thought to confront the man, perhaps believing him to be a thief?" Adam speculated, not realizing that he had just saved Leigh from an embarrassing few minutes by his ready explanation. "And as Miss Leigh's loyal maid, you thought to get back her property," he explained further, turning to face her so only she saw his wink.

Leigh stared at Adam suspiciously, wondering what his game was, but since it served her purpose to not have the stranger, this Dagger, know her true identity just yet, she would go along with his charade. After all, he had been the one who had mistook her for a servant, taking advantage of what he thought to be her lowly station in life. Soon however, soon…he would learn differently.

"Exactly," she said shortly. "But I discovered that Mr. Dagger found Capitaine wandering loose, and very kindly returned him to Travers Hill," she said, not explaining how Mr. Dagger knew the colt belonged at Travers Hill. "He will be rewarded handsomely for his kindness in returning Travers property. There is no need, however, for this incident to be mentioned further, for this is something between Mr. Dagger and myself."

"My pardon, but," Neil interrupted, eyeing his cousin curiously, for although it had been several years since Adam had visited the territories, he knew his cousin too well not to suspect he was up to something. "I am—" he began, intending to correct her concerning his name, and reassure her that he would say nothing about the circumstances of their meeting and her losing the colt. And as the lady had said, it was something between the two of them—and he intended to keep it that way.

But he was quickly interrupted from completing his introduction. "Please allow me to make the proper introductions." Adam spoke first. "Dagger. S. Dagger. He works for my cousin, Neil Braedon. The S stands for Sam, or is it Sonny? Well, we call him Dagger. Nothing more, nothing less. The name speaks for itself, and for the man. Best ranch hand on Riovado, my cousin's ranch. Swears by him, he does," he said with a slight bow and polite gesture between the two, nearly choking as he tried to control his laughter as he saw his cousin's expression. "And this lovely lady is Rose, the ever faithful maid to Miss Leigh. Travers Hill is famous for its lovely roses. Ah, one question, if I might be so bold, but..." Adam said, staring pointedly at the musket in Leigh's hands, "I am rather puzzled, since I do know both parties in question here. And I've never known the lady to miss her shot, nor would I have thought the gentleman could be so careless to get caught in the line of fire. Since I see no blood, and I did hear a gunshot, I assume she missed. Naturally, before explanations and introductions were properly made, of course. Or," he added as if another thought had just struck him, "did it fire by mistake during the struggle for possession of that deadly weapon?"

Adam didn't miss the guilty expression that crossed Leigh's face or the closed one that settled on Neil's, and his lips twitched, for it was very obvious that they had struggled for possession of the musket. He was only sorry he had arrived too late for that match.

"If you will excuse me," Leigh spoke curtly, stepping around the stranger as she saw her chance to escape him now that Adam was here. Halting by her colt, she ran her hand along his velvety muzzle, then pressed her cheek against his as he gently nudged her. Slipping the rope from his neck, she patted his rump and sent him into his stall next to his dam.

Turning around after she had shut his gate, she faced the stranger and said, "I trust you will be coming up to the big house, Mr. Dagger? I'm sure the family will wish to thank you for returning their property. I'm certain Miss Leigh will wish to thank you personally."

"I'll escort him myself," Adam spoke up quickly, slapping his cousin on the back as he caught the glint in his eye. "In fact, I think I hear hoofbeats now, so it must be Neil Braedon arriving. He and Dagger are like this," he claimed, holding up his index and middle fingers and pressing them tightly together. "Almost like brothers. Where one goes, the other is sure to follow. Just like Rose and Miss Leigh. He must have seen you heading this way, same as I did," Adam easily explained, his eyes twinkling with anticipation at that meeting. "My, my, with Nathan and me here, this could develop into quite a family reunion," he predicted. "I'm certain that Miss Leigh is going to want to look her prettiest when meeting Neil Braedon. Why, I might even be able to do a little matchmaking between them. Now I think 'pon it," he said, his grin wide, "they are indeed a well-matched couple."

Walking along the passage to Leigh's side, and taking her hand and tucking it inside his elbow, he urged her toward the door, fearing Neil's temper was near the end of its tether.

"You have a lot to answer for, Adam Braedon," Leigh told him in an angry whisper, glancing back at the stranger for just an instant before they left the stable. Leigh quickly looked ahead, for the stranger was standing by the big bay, his gaze intent on her.

"I?" Adam said in surprise as they stepped out into the sunlight.

"Yes. It is all your fault, and you'll pay soon enou——"

"Good Lord! I thought you were just joking!" Adam's choked exclamation cut her off as he and Leigh came to a standstill just beyond the stable doors. Approaching them at a run, the long blade of a saber glinting dangerously in her hand, was Blythe, a fierce look in her eye as she came to the rescue.

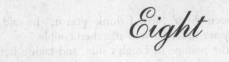

Eight

The little Revenge *ran on sheer into the heart of the foe.*
Alfred, Lord Tennyson

"LEIGH!" BLYTHE CRIED, TRYING TO PULL HER ARM FREE of her sister's grasp. Her feet, which earlier she'd despaired so of being far too large, were now firmly planted on the path, bringing her sister's steps to a halt as she refused to budge until she'd had some answers. "I want to know what happened. Why are we running back to the big house? What happened in the stables? Did you get back the lil' cap'n? Who was that stranger? Did you shoot him? I heard the shot. I couldn't believe Julia was still sitting in the dining room talking when I grabbed Great-Grandpa Travers's saber and ran out. She must have heard the musket fire and my dragging the bench across the foyer. Luckily Mama was asleep and I don't think it woke her. But I don't know about Althea, or Jolie, wherever she is. And what was Adam laughing about when he turned away and went back inside the stables? I could see that grin of his all the way across the green. Did you see his side whiskers? I've never seen any so bushy before. And I don't think there is anything amusing about killing a man. And it's never wise to trust Adam, Leigh. And where did he come from anyway? I didn't see him ride in. I must have already gone downstairs to get the saber. I nearly fell down the stairs, I was running that fast, but there was no one else, Leigh!" Blythe said breathlessly.

"I had to do it myself. I waited for hours and hours, but when you didn't come back out of the stables, I thought you might have been murdered, or even far worse might have happened to you! And when Stephen saw me racing out of the house with the saber, he just shook his head and went back into the dining room. I am surprised, for I really thought he might have come too, but he has slowed down a bit, and I believe he is still upset about locking himself in the cellars. Of course, he probably saw Adam and thought he would handle everything.

And now, if he hears that you've left a dead body in the stables, well, I just don't know what will happen. Jolie will have to fetch the salts for him. He likes everything to be so tidy, even out in the stables. I heard him telling Sweet John so."

Leigh sighed, and leaning against the butt of the musket, the barrel propped haphazardly on the ground, she said, "I did not kill the stranger. And"—she hesitated—"he did not steal Capitaine. He found him running loose along the lane and since Travers Hill was the nearest farm, came here to return him or discover the owner's identity. When I was out riding this morning, Capitaine wandered off," Leigh concluded, thinking her explanation had a definite ring of truth to it. And Blythe seemed to believe it because her expression changed from eager anticipation to crestfallen disappointment at the dull reasonableness of her sister's reply.

"And you believed him?"

"He did bring Capitaine back," Leigh had to admit, although only she knew the real reason for that show of kindness.

"Oh…well, but what about the shot? Why did you shoot at the stranger? Did you wing him?" Blythe asked, hopping from one foot to the other in her growing excitement, and swinging the blade of the saber like a pendulum in front of her.

"No," Leigh said quietly, wishing she had and wondering if any minute Blythe was going to chop off her big toe. "I stumbled, and the musket fired by mistake. And Adam, he saw the stranger riding across the meadow and, recognizing him, followed him here. He was coming here anyway to ride home with Nathan and Althea," Leigh explained. "And I think he came so early hoping he'd get some breakfast. He even told me just now to save him some apple fritters."

Blythe stared at her sister, her mouth dropping open in surprise, but not because of what she had just told her. "You must have fallen into a whole stack of hay, and head first by the look of you. You've got straw stuck all through your hair. You're never going to brush the tangles out. You look worse than a scarecrow. What's his name?" she demanded, finally allowing Leigh to pull her along toward the house again, now that most of her questions had been answered.

"Dagger. Mr. Dagger," Leigh replied, quickening her steps,

for she was determined to reach her bedchamber and change her clothes before Adam brought the stranger up to the house to meet Leigh Alexandra Travers.

"*Dagger?*" Blythe repeated. "What kind of a name is that? What's his first name?"

Leigh frowned, for she hadn't thought his name had been that strange. "Sam, or Sonny, I think."

"*Sonny?*" Blythe said with an unladylike guffaw. "He didn't look like a Sonny to me. Sonny Dagger," she said with a giggle.

Leigh eyed her sister with increasing annoyance. "He thinks my name is Rose," she admitted, a slight sigh escaping her.

"*Rose?*" Blythe was completely bemused, and amused, for this had turned out to be the most exciting morning of her young life. "What does he think your last name is? Garden?" she said, unable now to contain her laughter. Stumbling on the step as they entered the house, she reached out automatically to save herself from falling, the saber slicing upward and sticking into the doorjamb. Struggling, she managed to pull it free, but the blade came loose too quickly, its high arc catching Leigh's skirt and neatly ripping it in two in front.

Leigh stared down in dismay at the ragged tear in the faded blue material.

"It was old, Leigh," Blythe said timidly. "Why does he think your name is Rose?" she asked, hoping to change the subject.

"Because of the way I am dressed," Leigh said, hurrying along the foyer. "He thinks I work for the Travers family," she explained, pulling the bench across the pine planks with a loud scraping noise that left little doubt of the scratches that now marred the glossy, waxed surface of the floor. Replacing their grandfather's fowling piece, Leigh jumped down, helping Blythe pull the bench back across the floor and along the wall so she could replace their great-grandfather's saber, taken from that vanquished British dragoon nearly a century before.

"Didn't Adam say who you were?" Blythe demanded, ever curious.

"Adam? Not likely. He saw a splendid chance to enjoy a laugh at his friend's expense. Which happened to suit my purpose quite nicely."

"They're friends?" Blythe breathed, but then Adam always had been a bit strange. "Why didn't you say anything?" Blythe wanted to know as they began to climb the stairs, neither of them seeing Stephen standing in the opened doorway of the dining room, his widening gaze traveling around the foyer, first from the two figures, and one very disheveled, climbing the stairs, then to the musket, the smell of gunpowder drifting down to him from its long barrel, and finally to the saber, which was hanging at a precariously dangerous angle above the doorway, and an unsuspecting head should someone have entered.

"The man was arrogant and treated me very rudely. His behavior was not at all gentlemanly. He needs to be taught a humiliating lesson, so I want to show him exactly who I am when he comes to the house expecting to be thanked and to collect a reward for returning my property," Leigh said, raising her chin with Travers pride. "For once Adam has given me a chance to have the last laugh. And I will have my little revenge against this stranger," Leigh vowed, disclaiming any feelings she might have momentarily felt for him.

"Oh, Leigh! He will be so surprised when he discovers his mis—" Blythe squealed, nearly missing her step on the stairs in her excitement, then choking back her next words as she and Leigh were about to step on the landing, only to find Althea standing there staring down at them in disapproving silence.

"Whatever have you two been doing? We have had enough excitement this morning without Mama seeing you looking little better than a kitchen maid, Leigh. What have you done to that gown? And your hair?" Althea asked with gentle reproof. And Leigh wondered why Althea could always make her feel so repentant, for she never raised her voice, yet her reprimands were far more chastising than their father's.

"I was out riding."

"So I understand. But it would appear that you, like your brother, tried to jump the fence near the mill. You haven't hurt yourself, have you, dear?"

"No, and I didn't try to jump the fence, and I didn't fall off my horse. I've never fallen off my horse," she added indignantly. "And I was just going to change. Adam is here, and there is a stranger with him."

"Adam? 'Tis quite early yet, how very impolite of him," Althea said of her brother-in-law. "He was not supposed to ride over until noon. I suppose they will wish to be seated for breakfast," Althea mused, eyeing her sisters up and down with a critical shake of her blond head, the chignon, smoothly netted in chenille, resting elegantly at the nape of her slender neck. The lacy collar of her fitted bodice jacket was properly pressed, with a shell cameo nestled amongst the delicate folds and tucks. She was dressed in cream and cinnamon-striped taffeta, with a matching lace trim at the wrists and ribbon niching decorating the full skirt. The fragrance of violets, her favorite scent, drifted around her as she moved gracefully with a rustling whisper of lacy petticoats. Standing by the railing, Althea Louise Braedon was the ideal of young womanhood.

"Stephen, Adam Braedon and another guest have arrived. They will, no doubt, expect breakfast," she called softly down to him, a slightly apologetic expression disturbing the usual serenity of her classical features.

"Yes, Miss Althea, I saw Mister Adam riding into the stables earlier, just before Miss Blythe come runnin' down the stairs like a herd of wild an' woolly buffalo. Figured Mister Adam might want somethin' to eat after all the excitement," Stephen called up to Althea, not explaining further about the excitement he referred to, but his gaze met the two younger Travers daughters' round-eyed gazes with meaningful hesitation. "Figured there might be folks already arrivin' at Travers Hill, so I've been keepin' the dishes warm. Got plenty to last. An' Mister Stuart an' Mister Nathan just might want something else when they return from the mill. Soon enough we're goin' to have carriages pullin' up to the house every few minutes. Yes, ma'am, we're goin' to be busy," he said, apparently not inconvenienced and pleased to be back doing what he knew best—the smooth running of the Travers household. "I've got to set this ol' sword straight first, though. Don't want a guest to Travers Hill to lose his head if it should fall," he said. "Leastways, not any more than some usually do," he said with a chuckle, for there were some who didn't know how to hold their liquor. "Oh, an' Miss Julia an' Miss Noelle are around the side of the house in the rose arbor. Sent them out there with their sewin', figured it'd keep them out of trouble, especially that Miss Julia. She's not her best so early in the mornin'," he remembered to tell Althea, knowing she would be missing her little one now that she was feeling better and was up and about again. "An' you come on down an' eat somethin', Miss Althea. You need to keep up your strength now you've got two mouths to feed," he told her with a wise nodding of his graying head.

Althea looked momentarily startled, her cheeks glowing with a rosy blush of embarrassment as she wondered how he knew already that she was with child. She hadn't even told Nathan yet. Then she sighed with resignation, for there were no secrets at Travers Hill, and certainly not from Stephen and Jolie. "Thank you, Stephen. I do not know how Travers Hill could survive without you," Althea said truthfully, her brown eyes full of warmth as she stared down at the aging black man who was as much a member of the Travers family as any beloved aunt or uncle.

For as long as she could remember Stephen had quietly guided the family through one uproar after another, his calm voice sounding above the commotion long enough to bring order to any situation—and if that didn't succeed, then he always knew where Jolie could be found. Althea exchanged an understanding smile with him, then turning away, she took each of her young sisters by one of their arms, her grip surprisingly strong for one so slender, and escorted them down the hall toward their bedchamber.

"Two mouths to feed!" Blythe said, her thick-lashed hazel eyes full of wonder as she stared at her eldest sister. "Are you really—"

"Yes."

"Oh, Althea, 'tis wonderful news," Leigh said, her dark blue eyes glowing with love and admiration for her beautiful, and very proper, sister.

Althea hid her smile as she glanced between her two wide-eyed sisters. They were both still so young, but one day soon…

"I would, however, appreciate it if you would say naught of this until I have spoken to Nathan. And that means both of you. Nathan does not know, and I would like to tell him of our being so blessed myself. And," Althea added softly, "perhaps this time I will give him a son to bear the Braedon name."

Althea spoke wistfully, for she felt she had not done her duty by her husband or his family. Quite naturally they adored Noelle, and she was the apple of her father's eye, but she was, after all, a female, and one day she would marry and take another's name. Nathan, as the eldest son, had a right to have his son inherit Royal Bay. It was a time-honored tradition from the Old Country, the eldest son inheriting the titles and the estate, the smooth transference of ownership preserving the family's land and possessions for generations to come. From firstborn son to firstborn son, it was a trust given and accepted by each, and she knew that his parents were disappointed that she had not been able to fill their home with grandchildren, especially a grandson who would understand his responsibility as Nathan always had.

"Our lips are sealed!" Blythe promised, holding her finger pressed against her lips. Meeting Leigh's glance, she returned her nod vigorously, her long dark hair flying around her shoulders.

"Thank you, my sweethearts," Althea said. "Now—"

"Althea? Is that you?" a querulous-sounding voice called from their mother's bedchamber.

"Yes, Mama," Althea replied, stopping by the doorway and leaning inside just enough to see around the partially opened door, but never relaxing her grip on either one of her sisters' arms even as they stilled like frightened mice just beyond the door and just out of sight of their mother's view.

"I thought I heard voices and the stomping of feet seems never-ending and is beginning to sound like drumbeats in my aching temples. I do believe I feel a migraine coming on. Where has Jolie gotten to? I thought I heard Blythe's laughter, dear. Is that whom you were talking to? And where is Leigh Alexandra? I must have a talk with that child. I did not have the opportunity yesterday eve. We have so many important details to discuss, and so little time if she is to be wed by spring. And I fear I must have been dreaming, but did I hear a gunshot? Is there anything amiss?"

"No, ma'am, I'm sure you must be mistaken, for who could possibly have fired a gun around Travers Hill?" Althea responded, genuinely surprised by the question, for she had heard nothing. "All the menfolk are away. Although Adam

Braedon and a friend have arrived. I've asked Stephen to lay a place for them at table."

"Thank you, dear, quite thoughtful of you, *at least*," their mother's voice commented, her last words tinged with censure, for apparently she was well aware of the earliness of the hour for callers. "I can always count on you to do what is proper. I truly do not know where Effie went wrong with that boy of hers. Quite different from Nathan. Ah, well, 'tis high time I was up. I did manage to doze off briefly. I really cannot abide napping during the day when there is still so much work to be done. I wake up more tired than before, worrying about idle hands. And I do hope the maids have finished with the laundry. 'Twill be the ruin of this family's good name if we've no clean pressed sheets for the guest rooms. Your Aunt Maribel Lu would never let me hear the end of it, indeed, I seldom hear anything but criticism about the way I manage this house and family. Thinks she still lives here and runs this household, and I know she thinks I haven't done a proper job as mistress of Travers Hill," Beatrice Amelia snitted, touching her trembling lips with a handkerchief that had magically appeared in her hand from some secret place on her person. "As soon as she arrives, you mark my words, she will be hotfootin' over to Royal Bay to gossip with Effie about how I prepare our dishes too much in the French manner. Bossy, interfering woman. I do not know how I have put up with her since I married into this family. There is no pleasing her or telling her anything different than what she already believes to be true. I declare, I'm surprised J. Kirkfield hasn't gone stark raving mad having to live with her these many years. Your father, and he's her own flesh and blood, said it was a godsend when she up and married that scrawny little man and took herself off to Richmond like a battleship under full sail, cannon fire roaring right and left... No, that's not quite right, is it, dear? The sides of a ship are called something quite different, although I'm sure I don't know why. 'Twould be far simpler if they just said right and left. But men do so complicate matters."

Althea tightened her grip around the tender flesh of two soft arms to silence the muffled giggles she could hear behind her back. "You needn't disturb yourself, Mama. I will be returning to the dining room shortly. I am feeling better, so I shall enjoy a cup of tea and perhaps some buttered toast and marmalade. Rest a while longer, please, ma'am," Althea pleaded, for their mother looked rather frail, her complexion startlingly pale as she lay against the piled-up pillows of her bed. She had loosened the customary, tight chignon, allowing her hair to fall in long golden strands that curled naturally over the soft cashmere of her dusky rose dressing gown.

"Shall I have another pot of tea brought up for you, Mama?" she inquired solicitously, for she could see a half-emptied china cup next to her mother's bed, the contents having grown cold.

"No, truly, I will be quite refreshed when Jolie returns with my syllabub. As soon as I make myself decent, I will join you in the dining room and greet our guests. But the mere thought that your Aunt Maribel Lu will be arriving tomorrow causes my temples to pound, and I dare say the milk is already beginning to curdle in anticipation of her visit," she declared, lightly pressing her fingertips against her blue-veined temples. "And no telling what ideas she will have planted in Thisbe's head if she and Stuart James rode up with them. Oh, and where is Leigh Alexandra? Did she return from her ride?" Beatrice Amelia asked again, not having forgotten her middle daughter for a second.

"Yes, ma'am, she's changing," Althea replied, bending the truth slightly.

"Give her a hand, dear, will you? I trust you can help her do something with her hair. It is so thick and unruly. Inherited from the Travers side of the family. And I do believe we will allow Blythe to wear her hair in a more sophisticated style come Friday. I've also decided she may dab on a drop or two of my gardenia *eau de toilette*. It is a lovely, light scent I picked up in Charleston at my perfumers, but only a drop or two, and no perfume for her quite yet. Now, run along, dear, and see that Leigh finds the appropriate morning gown. One never knows who might come to call. And make certain you have plenty of butter on your toast."

"Oh, I'll see that Leigh looks quite proper, Mama," Althea reassured her, backing out of the doorway as her mother settled herself more comfortably against the lace-edged pillows, the lavender and roses fragrance that permeated the fine linen apparently soothing to her nerves because she sighed deeply.

"Oh, Leigh, did you hear?" Blythe whispered, her voice rising as they reached their own bedchamber. "Mama said I could wear scent! I've never worn any before! And it is to be her finest from Charleston," Blythe said in awe, her steps carrying her figure spinning into the room, where she threw herself onto the bed. Arms folded behind her head, she stared up dreamily at the canopy above her head, wondering what hairstyle she would choose. "In another year I'll be able to wear perfume. I want a scent bottle just like you have, Leigh, and filled with jessamine perfume. That is your favorite, isn't it, Leigh?"

Leigh glanced over at Blythe's ingenuous expression. "Yes, that is my favorite, but are you certain you haven't already sampled some of it?" she asked, for her perfume always seemed to be in a different position on their small dressing table.

Blythe blushed guiltily. "Only twice, Leigh," she admitted. "But I do so love the way you smell after you've used some of it. And it is such a pretty bottle. I just love to hold it," she said, glancing over at the tear-shaped flacon of dark sapphire-blue glass, cut and polished and gilded with stars. The ornate mount and top of shining gold.

Leigh smiled understandingly, suddenly feeling as old and wise as Althea, for she could never become truly angry with Blythe. "I love it too."

"I'll have to bring back one for you too, Lucy, only in a deep emerald-green, the next time Nathan takes me to Paris," Althea promised, a smile tugging briefly at the corners of her lips as she thought of the present she would give Blythe on Friday to celebrate her birthday; for she had indeed brought back that scent bottle for her youngest sister with the intention of giving it to her on the special day when she would be considered a young woman.

"Oh, Althea, would you really, truly do that? Promise?" Blythe asked, her dreams soaring as she looked again at Leigh's treasured scent bottle.

"I promise. I've always liked this gown on you, Leigh," Althea commented as she took the mauve-striped muslin down from where it hung on the clothes press. The layers of gauzy muslin floated airily around her figure as she placed it on the bed, carefully spreading out the folds of the full skirt. The many flounces were decorated in a wide-bordered, exotic-patterned print in varying shades of purple and trimmed in lace. The tight-fitting bodice had a row of tiny silk-covered buttons, and the bell sleeves showed the crisp linen of the undersleeves. The high neckline had a wide, turned-down lace collar that was fastened with a colorful trimming of matching silk ribbons; just the gown for a demure young woman.

"Really, Leigh, I do not think I have ever seen you looking quite so…so…" Althea paused, unable to find the proper words to describe her sister's appearance.

"She tripped and fell into a haystack," Blythe said, wondering how Leigh had even managed to get straw stuck in the lace of her pantalettes. Suddenly, she sat up, and as straight as her mother never seemed tired of requesting her to, her expression incredulous.

"*Married by spring?*" She repeated their mother's words of moments before. "Are you really getting married, Leigh? You never told me Matthew Wycliffe had actually asked for your hand in marriage," she said, her eyes full of hurt bewilderment. "I thought it was just wishful thinking. Has he really asked you? When? When did he ask you? I wish you'd told me."

"He hasn't asked me," Leigh said, her voice muffled as she pulled her petticoats over her pantalettes with their lacy, beribboned hems.

"He hasn't?"

"No," Leigh said, puzzled herself now by their mother's statement, and as her head appeared above the petticoats, her curious gaze met Althea's.

"Well, I believe it is rather more than wishful thinking on the part of our mother," Althea said, watching Leigh's expression carefully. "It would seem as if Matthew Wycliffe will ask Papa's permission to ask for your hand in marriage this week. What do you say to that?"

Leigh quickly glanced down, pretending to be lost in the act of tying the strings of her petticoats, but Althea's hands gently replaced her fumbling fingers as she quickly completed the task.

Glancing around Leigh's hunched shoulders, Althea frowned slightly as she noticed Leigh's curiously disturbed expression. Her sister was either being very modest, and was extremely embarrassed by the thought of Matthew Wycliffe's proposal, or she was concerned that he might not ask for her hand as Guy seemed to expect him to, or…Leigh did not welcome such a proposal.

Standing in her freshly laundered chemise and petticoats, the smooth curve of the back of her neck exposed as she tried to pull the tangles from her hair, Leigh suddenly seemed so vulnerable to Althea. She didn't want her sister to feel pressured into accepting Matthew Wycliffe's proposal if she did not wish him for her husband.

How fortunate she had been that Nathan, whom she loved dearly, had asked her to become his wife. Although one did one's duty in life, to be wed to a man one did not love would be unbearable, Althea thought, thinking of the intimacies she shared with Nathan as she gazed at her sister's down-bent head in growing concern.

Taking the silver-backed brush from the dressing table, she patted Leigh's slim shoulder comfortingly. "You do not have to marry anyone unless you wish to. Always remember that, my dear," Althea told her, beginning to brush the long strands of golden-brown hair.

"I am fond of Matthew. Very fond. In fact, I like him better than any other gentleman of my acquaintance. He is a fine man, a man one would be proud to wed," Leigh said softly in praise of him. "And lately, I have come to believe that I am in love with him. I have no objections to anything about him, either in appearance or demeanor. And I suppose I have led him to believe that I would welcome his suit. B-but what is love? How do you know when you are truly in love?" she asked suddenly, staring up worriedly into Althea's eyes.

"Love is a very strange emotion, and it is one that cannot be explained very simply," Althea said, continuing to brush Leigh's hair until the strands were free of tangles and straw and crackled beneath the bristles. "Sometimes it grows gradually, and sometimes, it comes very unexpectedly."

"How did you feel when you fell in love with Nathan?" Leigh asked again, determined to have it explained so she would know exactly when it happened to her—or if perhaps it already had. She needed to know.

Althea stilled for a moment, her thoughts drifting back across the years to Charleston. It had been her last summer there, before returning home to Virginia—and to Nathan. She had fallen in love, but not with the man she was expected to wed. Not with the man she had grown up with, who had been her dearest friend. Althea smiled with contentment, for she did love Nathan with every breath in her body. It was a love she treasured, which was strong and everlasting, which had grown deeper with each year of their marriage, but that summer, when she dreamed of her secret love, it had not been Nathan. She had thought she would die with the pain of her aching heart. For the man had been no gentleman, although he was of an aristocratic family from the Coast. He had been a heartbreakingly handsome rake. A gambling man who smiled with pale eyes and sensuous lips, and played a woman as false as the cards he laid down on the green baize.

"Your heart pounds so wildly that you cannot catch your breath," she said softly, her brown eyes saddened with remembrance of the foolish young girl she had been, dreaming dreams that summer that could never come true. With gentle efficiency, she plaited Leigh's long length of hair. "Your stomach churns with butterflies, you shiver uncontrollably, and your palms feel clammy," she continued. "When you meet his eyes, you feel as if he can see into your soul, and it bares itself to him. You cannot hide your love from him, and, if he is not a good man, he can hurt you," Althea said, her words hardly above a whisper as she remembered the stolen kiss she had foolishly believed had been a declaration of love—at least until she'd seen him in the gardens with another man's wife, their passionate embrace shocking her back into common good sense and the arms of Nathan Braedon.

"Well, I'm never going to fall in love if that's what happens," Blythe declared in amazement, her rapt attention broken by so horrible a description. "It sounds like swamp fever."

Althea laughed, for it had been a long time ago, and she could hardly even remember his face. "One day, little one," she warned, taking the two heavy braids and wrapping and pinning them into a neat coronet atop Leigh's head. Finding a pair of delicately hued silk bows, she pinned them where the two braids met at the crown. "However, do not mistake infatuation for love. There is a difference. And if you confuse the two, you

WHEN THE SPLENDOR FALLS 155

could come to make a tragic decision that could affect the rest of your life, destroy it even, and the people you love."

"How do you know the difference?" Leigh asked, her heart pounding sickeningly as Althea began to button her into her very proper mauve-striped muslin, her hair neatly confined in prim braids and dressed in a manner her mother would have approved of.

Althea sighed. "Sometimes it is difficult to know the difference. That is the danger. Now, a little cologne," she said, picking up a floral-painted porcelain bottle and touching the light scent of jessamine and roses behind Leigh's ears and on the underside of each of her wrists. With a low laugh, she added, "I will give you the truest test of love. Infatuation is like cologne, it will fade after a short time. It is light and airy, never meant to last because it was never as strong to begin with. However, it has its proper time and place to be worn, perchance a dalliance in the afternoon, but love, love is much like perfume, and should be worn for special occasions, a masked ball, or perhaps at a wedding. A perfume is based on essential oils which are rich and long-lasting. When placed on a woman's skin, and at a point where the pulse is warm with her heartbeat, it will blossom into a very heady fragrance, and one that will endure. That is what should happen with love.

"Infatuation never truly touches the heart. Love comes from deep within the heart, and touches it in so many ways. Love goes far beyond mere attraction. Physical appearance changes through the years, and the attraction one might have felt once for a person can fade. That is why love, especially when between two people who marry, should be based on more than that initial attraction. There must be respect and trust between them. They must honor each other. If they are friends, then their faith in each other, their love, will always remain. That can never fade."

"Is that what you and Nathan feel?" Leigh asked, thinking her sister had never looked more beautiful, for her words had been reflected by a warm glow in her brown eyes when she spoke her husband's name.

Althea nodded. "I have been very fortunate that Nathan offered me his love. I cannot imagine a life without him now," she admitted. "So search your heart very carefully before you give it into the possession of someone who is not deserving of so rare a treasure," she warned her sister, for Leigh had a very giving heart, full of warmth and love, and she would despair of seeing the wrong man stealing something so precious from her. "'Tis far too priceless a gift to squander," she said, turning Leigh around and nodding her approval as she smoothed a fold of the mauve-striped muslin.

"Oh, look, Leigh! It's Adam, and his friend, the stranger, they're walking up to the big house. I can hardly wait!" Blythe cried from the window, where she'd run just moments before, hoping she would see their guests.

Leigh hurried over, squeezing beside her as she leaned out over the windowsill, forgetful of ladylike behavior as she tried to catch a glance of them, but they'd already disappeared beneath the veranda roof.

"I'd better meet them," Althea said, pleased with Leigh's appearance as she started to turn away, then glanced back, for her sister was standing in her stockinged feet. "Your shoes, dear, don't forget them," she reminded her as she left the room, intent now upon her hostessing duties.

"Hurry up, Leigh," Blythe called again from the doorway where she was impatiently waiting while Leigh struggled to put on a pair of fine kid slippers.

"Wait! Blythe! I'm coming!" Leigh cried out, lifting her skirts high as she raced after Blythe's long-legged figure disappearing down the hall.

Blythe stopped abruptly at the head of the stairs, and Leigh, hardly a step or two behind her, bumped her slightly, nearly sending her tumbling down the flight of steps.

"Leigh!" Blythe whispered, glancing around warningly. But Leigh needed no cautionary hush, and remained carefully hidden behind Blythe, risking only a quick glance over her shoulder as she sought the stranger's figure below.

He seemed taller than ever in their foyer, his muscular figure dwarfing Althea's as he nodded politely to her, her slender hand engulfed by his as he was introduced to her by a widely grinning Adam Braedon. Leigh frowned as she heard Althea's tinkling laugh, then a low-voiced reply from the stranger, which must have been very complimentary, because her sister inclined her blond head as if graciously accepting a compliment from an admirer.

"Come on," Blythe urged, grabbing hold of Leigh's hand and refusing to let go when Leigh tried to tug her hand loose, suddenly feeling an attack of shyness, or perhaps cowardliness, now that she must come face-to-face with the stranger again.

Taking a deep breath, Leigh began to follow Blythe down the stairs, her eyes downcast as she watched her step, determined not to miss her footing and land in an undignified heap of muslin and petticoat at the stranger's feet. After all, she was Leigh Alexandra Travers of Travers Hill, and she would now show the stranger how mistaken he had been.

She and Blythe had gotten halfway down the stairs when their entrance was ruined by a shrill screaming coming from a small figure running into the house from just behind Adam Braedon and the stranger.

"Mama! Mama!" a tearful Noelle Braedon cried, flinging herself against Althea's figure. "She pinched me and pulled my hair!" Noelle told her mother between watery gulps.

"Well, look what she did to me!" Julia cried indignantly, pushing her way past the two startled men, and holding out a limp hand for all to see, although the drop of blood was hardly more than a pinprick. "She stuck me with her needle! She said she'd sew my fingers together."

"That was only after you pinched me!" Noelle charged, moving quickly behind her mother's comforting figure, which was safely between her and her wicked aunt.

"And that was because you stole my favorite length of pink thread. It is all I have left from Charleston!"

"If you would sew your stitches more neatly, and much closer together, then you would not have so little thread left. You waste half of it, and 'waste not, want not,' I always say," Noelle returned, her comically adult logic causing Adam to raise an impressed eyebrow.

"Pity she's a girl, or we'd have another lawyer in the family. Certainly takes after Nathan," he said, shaking his head in mock despair.

Althea looked properly put out, for Julia was short-tempered and easily provoked, and responded with childish revenge.

Both Leigh and Blythe had suffered their share of bruised flesh over the years from her punishing pinches and bites.

"Welcome to Travers Hill," Adam said, laughing as he grabbed hold of his sister as she would have lunged behind Althea and grabbed another handful of her niece's hair when she saw Noelle sticking her tongue out at her.

"Adam, let loose!"

"You should have been here earlier," Althea said. "This is calm indeed."

"Ouch!" Adam said, jerking loose his hand. "You bit me!"

"Not as hard as I could have," Julia said, smiling sweetly at him, then she blushed as she met the cold, pale-eyed stare of the tall stranger standing next to her brother. He was quite handsome, she thought, wondering who he was as she eyed him from her slightly lowered lashes and practiced her best coquetry on him.

"She should have been turned over to you years ago and taught proper manners," Adam said, rubbing the reddened spot on his hand that showed the perfect imprint of where her teeth had clamped down on him.

"Having the raw flesh scraped from that pretty blond hair before it was hung on a scalp pole might be lesson enough," the stranger murmured thoughtfully.

Julia paled. Never had she been spoken to in so rude a manner, but even more disturbing, the man hadn't seemed in the least enamored of her beauty. "Well, really, how dare you speak to me, sir," she said, raising a haughty shoulder as she turned up her nose at him and took a delicate step away from his offensive proximity.

"We have not been properly introduced, nor do I intend to be," she added witheringly.

Althea couldn't control her smile, thinking it was a pity that Neil Braedon hadn't had a hand in raising his spoiled cousin. Noelle, peering from behind her mother, stared up at the stranger in fascination, wondering who he was. He seemed a god in her impressionable eyes, for no one had ever treated her aunt so cavalierly before. Her brown eyes met his, and opened even wider when he smiled down at her. Young as she was, her heart was captured by its masculine charm.

Althea pulled her around in front of her and gently pushed her forward. "This is Nathan's and my daughter, Noelle."

Neil's smile widened with genuine pleasure. "Hello, little one," he greeted her, bending down from his great height to take her tiny hand, which she held out unhesitatingly to him.

"Hello. Who are you?"

"I'm—" he began, then glanced up as he caught a slight movement on the stairs, his gaze pinning the two figures and halting their descent as they became aware of his perusal.

"Please! Allow *me* to make the introductions now that we are all here," Adam said as he caught sight of the two Travers sisters standing in the middle of the stairway, staring down at them.

"First, we have my dear little sister, Julia, but then you have already had the pleasure of her acquaintance," Adam began, laughing softly as she glared at the stranger, her expression very odious indeed. But her pride was somewhat soothed by the fact that the stranger seemed quite dismayed to discover her identity.

"And this," Adam said, walking over to take Blythe's hand as she reached the bottom step, "is Blythe Travers, and the youngest of the family," he added unnecessarily as she hopped down the last step, her expression looking as if she were holding her breath in anticipation of some surprise that was to follow. "And, last, but hardly least," Adam said, managing to capture Leigh's hand as she glided gracefully down the last few steps, "is one of the fairest *roses* of Travers Hill, dearest little Leigh, the spoiled owner of the colt you found wandering along the lane."

Leigh met the stranger's start of surprise with a satisfied smile lurking at the corners of her lips, turning them up slightly as Adam brought her close to him. Her smile faded, however, when he held out her hand for the stranger to take as he concluded his introductions with a dramatic intoning of his voice.

"Leigh Alexandra Travers, meet Neil Darcy Braedon. My onetime, long-lost cousin from the territories, who is also known to a select few as Sun Dagger, once a feared Comanche brave."

Nine

That most knowing of persons—gossip.

Seneca

ROYAL BAY, BIRTHPLACE OF HIS FATHER, AND HIS FATHER before him. Neil glanced around the elegant library with its fine eighteenth-century furnishings that had been brought upriver by ship, the precious cargos unloaded at Royal Bay's Landing. There, wharves and warehouses had been built by Royal Bay's first master a century earlier to handle the docking of ships arriving from as far away as Europe and the West Indies with the luxuries only the Old Country and exotic lands could provide in the colonial wilderness. The mahogany of the silk-upholstered settees and chairs, rubbed to a rich patina over the years by constant use and care, glowed warmly beneath a sixteen-light crystal chandelier that had been imported from England by his grandmother. One of a matched set, the other chandelier graced the dining room and hung from a plaster rosette above the great banqueting table, which on special occasions was still set with his grandmother's finest English porcelain dinner service. A pair of globes, one terrestrial, the other celestial, sat at either end of the wall of floor-to-ceiling bookshelves. The Aubusson carpet showed remarkably little wear, and the ornate plasterwork ceiling rising high above his head was as startling white as the first time he'd seen it years earlier. Gilded girandoles, each surmounted by rising phoenix birds, reflected the wealth and old world charm of Royal Bay in the jewel-toned hues of a Chinese export hunt bowl, the glint of sterling silver in a teapot and a candelabra, the warmth of gold-leaf framed family portraits, and the carved ivory of chessmen positioned on a board near the fireplace, where the blue and white of delftware filled the mantelpiece.

Euphemia Braedon was sitting on the settee, engaged in conversation with Althea, while Noelle occupied the place of honor between mother and grandmother. Euphemia's hair, more gray than brown now, was confined and neatly netted at the nape of her neck. A gold locket, suspended from a gold chain, was the only jewelry adorning her plain day dress of sprig muslin. She had never been an acclaimed beauty, but as an heiress in her own right, with the house and lands inherited from her father, she had come to Royal Bay a strong-willed, independent woman who spoke her mind. Some less kind than others had said Effie Merton had been lucky not to have been left on the shelf, being over twenty years of age, sharp-tongued, and homely, and the only reason the handsome and eligible Noble Braedon had taken her hand in marriage had been because of the Merton lands she would bring with her as part of her dowry. Paralleling Royal Bay on the far side of the river, River Oaks Farm, now a part of Royal Bay, had made the Braedons the most influential family in the county.

In an upholstered wingback chair near one of the opened French windows, Noble Braedon sat, the faded gold of his hair liberally streaked with silver. Every so often, his proud head fell slightly forward as he nodded off, oblivious to the conversation around him as the warm afternoon air wafted in from the terraced gardens and lulled him into drowsiness.

"Oh, Grandmama, I want to pour the tea today! Let me do it! I can! Truly I can!" Noelle cried out, sliding off the settee and, in her haste, bumping the tea table set up in front of her grandmother. The sound of china clattering noisily together startled her grandfather from his peaceful doze, his head jerking up as he awakened. He choked slightly as he cleared his throat, the cigar he'd been chewing rather than smoking, out of deference to the ladies present, dropping from his fingers as he tried to catch his breath.

Adam, who had been pouring brandy from a crystal decanter on the sideboard, moved quickly to his father's side, slapping him gently yet firmly between his shoulder blades, his other hand patting the old gentleman's shoulder comfortingly.

"There you are, sir," Adam said softly, showing a gentleness that few people knew he possessed beneath the careless facade of the devil-may-care gentleman he enjoyed playing with such finesse.

"Swallowed a piece of cigar! Don't make these cigars

like they used to. Not like ol' James Palmer, now he knew how to grow tobacco, yes sir," Noble said gruffly, glaring over at Althea as if she were somehow at fault. "Your great-grandpappy knew how to grow tobacco, yes, sirree, not like these young upstarts just out of short pants. Hope Stuart James has at least a drop or two of good planter's blood in his veins, or he'll be losing Willow Creek Landing before harvestin' enough leaf for even one cigar. His great-grandpappy, God rest him, would turn over in his grave knowing strangers were planting on Palmer land if that brother of yours ain' sharper than the auctioneer come sale time."

"Well, I think it was a fine thing indeed, Althea Louise, your grandmother leaving Willow Creek to Stuart James. He and that wife of his need a place of their own. I declare, but I've never heard such arguing when your papa and Stuart James get together. Both so hardheaded, I'm afraid they'll come to blows one of these days. Can't tell them anything. And Stuart James's wife doesn't help matters any with her brusque Northern ways, well, I just never have taken a liking to her. I am sorry, and I know it's not Christian of me, but I can't change the way I feel, Althea," Euphemia told her. "Always feel she's looking down her nose at me. And you know your own mama feels much the same way, and Beatrice Amelia is quite citified coming from Charleston. There has to be something wrong with someone who doesn't like grits, I declare, child, I've never seen such a pained look on a body's face when that Thisbe Anne was served boiled hominy grits the first time she came visiting at Travers Hill. You'd have thought from the way she was carrying on that your poor mama was serving up something rotting out of the cornfields to her. Not that I don't still believe your mama uses far too much cayenne pepper in her cooking," Euphemia added. "I'll give her my new recipe for ham when I go visitin' midweek. You make several deep cuts in the ham and stuff them with sweet pickles, corn bread, and brown sugar. Maribel Lu should be at Travers Hill by now, and you know how we do like to sit a spell together and catch up on all the goings-on. I told your mama I wanted them all here for supper tomorrow evening, especially if young Palmer William has arrived home. We're expecting Justin tomorrow too. She's got enough to do preparing for Lucy's birthday celebration and the weekend festivities. Now, I am not being unkind, Althea, but I declare, she did look haggard the last time I saw her. You talk sense to your mama, and get them to sup with us tomorrow. You'll be riding over with me, won't you, dear?"

Althea smiled and nodded, but inwardly she sighed, knowing it would be far more tiring and vexing for her mother trying to gather together the whole family, and the newly arrived guests, for a carriage ride to Royal Bay.

"Naturally, we will take the carriage now that you are with child. Oh, Althea, I am so pleased. When Nathan told us the good news yesterday eve, well, I could have cried," Euphemia said huskily, patting Althea's hand affectionately while searching with her other hand for her handkerchief to dab at the sheen of tears misting her eyes.

"That disdainful look you spoke of earlier, ma'am, is Thisbe Travers's usual expression of most things Southern," Adam said, returning to the sideboard and the half-filled snifters of brandy.

"She just takes a little getting used to," Althea said in defense of her brother's wife, but her comment had little effect on the others, since everyone knew Althea could get along with anyone, even the devil—or a Northerner.

"Now mind you, only a quarter full for your father, Adam," Euphemia told him, sending a frowning Noble a speaking glance that kept him muttering quietly beneath his breath. "Well, I don't know why she married Stuart James then, if that's her opinion of Southern hospitality."

"Just of Southern cooking, ma'am. I believe she takes to our refined way of life like a duck to water, or a duchess to a title," Adam claimed, handing his father his measured amount of brandy and receiving a snort in response, before he handed a snifter to Neil, who was standing in silence by the French windows.

"Such a pity. Stuart James could have married any girl of his choosing hereabouts. Why, I'm sure Sarette Canby was heartbroken. She figures on catching that sweet-talkin' brother of yours, Althea. Already tried to catch Adam here. Why do you think he went to the Coast, except to escape her?"

"Made it aboard ship just in time, ma'am, and, fortunately for me, the lady in question cannot swim," Adam said with a grin. "I have never made the mistake of underestimating a lady when she has her little heart set on something."

"Can I pour the tea? Can I?" Noelle pleaded, stamping her foot impatiently.

"Hush, child! When you learn to act like a lady, showing the proper decorum, then, and only then *may* you serve tea as a lady of this house would to her guests," Euphemia told her granddaughter, and Noelle, looking properly chastised, nodded apologetically, her downbent head hiding her sudden rush of tears.

"I do have my heart set on it, Grandmama," she added softly, peeping through a dark curl that had fallen across her cheek.

Euphemia glared at her son as Adam's laughter filled the room, but for now Noelle was, after all, Euphemia's only grandchild, and incorrigible as she was, she could not deny the child her pleasures. "Now, if you will watch me very carefully while I prepare this cup for your mama, then I will allow you to pour this other cup for your grandmama, then, if done properly, you may prepare one for your aunt."

"Mama!" Julia cried, becoming impatient herself as she eyed the steaming teapot.

Noelle looked up, her eyes glowing, the tears already drying on her rosy cheeks as she watched her grandmother's every move, then imitated her to perfection as she prepared a cup of fragrant tea. Her smiling mother watched proudly as her daughter placed a wedge of lemon on the rim before handing it to her, then attended to Julia's cup, adding the proper amount, but not too generous, of sugar and cream.

"You spoil that child, Mama," Julia complained, eyeing with growing annoyance the brimming teacup Noelle was carefully bringing her way with a sloshing of its contents. "It had better be sweet enough, and as far as I'm concerned Noelle is still in disgrace for her behavior at Travers Hill yesterday morning. She was very unladylike and she should've been sent to bed without her supper. I'll never go visiting with her again. No child of mine would act so rudely while with company, even if they are kinfolk. And look at this," Julia complained, holding up a soggy and brown, tea-soaked cake.

"That is what is known as a tea cake, and if I recall,

dearest Julia," Adam said, winking at Noelle, "the first time you served tea you missed the cup and poured scalding tea, Souchong, I believe, all over Reverend Culpepper's lap. Poor man had to give his sermon the following Sunday in a falsetto, while you and Leigh giggled in the front pew. And just the Sunday before, he'd read his sermon almost doubled over with stomach cramps, having been gentlemanly enough to drink a goodly quantity of the tea Leigh had brewed when he'd called at Travers Hill. What did she use again? Mixed some of Jolie's special purgative herbs? Senna leaves and slippery elm? No wonder the man could barely walk. A deadly combination."

"Leigh made a little mistake, and you tripped me, if you will recall further," Julia reminded him. "Your feet are almost as big as your mouth."

"Now, children," Euphemia said, repeating the reprimand spoken far too often over the years to carry any weight now.

"I do recall the incident," Adam said with a chuckle of appreciation.

"Oh, Mama! I am so excited. You will never guess the news!" Julia said, turning a dismissive shoulder on her grinning brother.

"What, dear?"

"I will be returning to Charleston!"

"Yes, dear, I know. We will all be staying there, and as guests of the Benjamin Leighs. I received their most cordial invitation today. Your mama, Althea Louise, insisted upon writing to them when she heard of our plans to tour England in the spring. We will have a nice visit with them while waiting for our ship to sail," Euphemia told her, pleased at the prospect of visiting Europe again. "A pity they won't be visiting this week, but Mr. Leigh has been under the weather."

"Oh, Mama! I know that. I was speaking of something altogether different. 'Twill be after we return from England, unless of course I have wed a duke or a count, and then I shall never return to Virginia, except to visit of course," Julia said, sighing as her head filled with dreams.

"Whatever are you talking about, dear?"

"Mama, Leigh Alexandra Travers will announce her engagement this very weekend to Matthew Wycliffe, who only happens to be one of the wealthiest and most handsome gentlemen in all the Carolinas!" Julia cried out for all the room to hear, and still irritated with her cousin from the territories, she didn't even glance his way, so she did not see the slight start of surprise that crossed his lean face at her news.

But Adam had been watching his cousin, having glanced over curiously when Julia had mentioned Leigh's name. He frowned now when he saw the startled expression quickly masked by one of apparent boredom as Neil listened to gossip that held little or no interest to him—or perhaps it did?

"Really, Julia?" Euphemia asked, looking over at Althea for confirmation of such an exciting revelation, although she had hoped Julia would marry first. However, she was quite fond of Leigh Travers.

Althea frowned slightly, wondering how Julia had heard the news, for even Leigh was not certain of the proposal and had been reluctant even to admit to her feelings for Matthew Wycliffe. She wished Julia had kept her silence until it could have been announced by her own family, if there was to be an announcement, but at least she had not blurted out the news before any strangers.

"Althea?" Euphemia questioned, glancing back at Julia with a doubtful expression.

"It is true! It is, Althea, isn't it?" Julia demanded. "Leigh herself told me how much in love she is with Matthew Wycliffe. She talked of nothing else at our picnic day before yesterday. It's the truth! And he could not keep his eyes from her when in Charleston. He was calling every single day, and as a suitor he is completely acceptable to your mama and papa. The Benjamin Leighs think most highly of him, and they could not do enough for him when he came to call on Leigh. It was quite an honor. Half of Charleston was drooling, for he is quite particular about his acquaintances. You cannot deny that he is without fault."

Althea shook her head. "No, I cannot. And I believe Leigh does indeed care for Matthew, more than for any other gentleman of her acquaintance. She told me that herself just yesterday. And apparently Matthew Wycliffe is very much in love with Leigh, which does not surprise me in the least, for she is very lovely and sweet. And, yes, he would be perfectly acceptable to my parents as a son-in-law, they have already said as much. But whether he will ask for Leigh's hand in marriage this weekend or not, we shall just have to wait and see, Julia, and I would not speak further of this until then, lest you look foolish should the announcement not be made," Althea advised, not willing to admit all of what she knew. But if Guy were correct in his information, then Matthew Wycliffe would indeed ask Leigh to marry him, and she suspected Leigh would say yes.

"There! I told you so!" Julia claimed, dismissing the last of Althea's statement with a careless shrug, for she had heard what she wanted to hear. "And Leigh has promised me, as her dearest friend—why, we are almost like sisters—that I can come to stay with her and Matthew in Charleston. Matthew has a town house there, and an estate overlooking the Ashley River, and, of course, his plantation is supposed to be magnificent. The house sits on a cliff overlooking the sea, and he owns half the coastline. I dare say it will be the wedding of the Season, perhaps of the century. Leigh will make such a beautiful bride. She'll be dressed in ivory taffeta with layers and layers of lace and a long train held in place with a wreath of orange blossoms. Oh, I can see it all now. They'll probably be wed in Charleston, with dignitaries coming all the way from Europe to attend. And we will be so beautiful walking down the aisle, because as one of her bridesmaids, I will be gowned in robin's egg blue. 'Tis one of my favorite shades and most becoming to me."

Adam looked skyward, wishing a robin would fly over his sister's silly head.

"If you have indeed been privy to Leigh's confidences concerning Matthew Wycliffe, I would suggest you keep her secret until she announces the news. 'Tis her right," Althea suggested gently, not wishing to have Leigh's day spoiled by Julia's indiscreet comments.

"Of course I am in her confidence. We always tell each other our deepest secrets. Neither one of us would dare to fall in love with someone without telling the other one first. But this is no secret, after all, everyone will know this weekend. I suspect they will announce it at little Lucy's party, or at the barbecue on Sunday. What a celebration we shall have.

Anyway, we're all family here," Julia said, defending herself.
"Well, almost," she added, glancing over at the tall man
standing alone. Even if he was her cousin, a fact she seriously
doubted, then he was still a stranger in their home. Not at
all like his half brother Justin, who was a gentleman and had
been accepted as one of the family. And he at least had never
threatened to scalp her, she thought, touching one of her fair
curls lovingly.

"Well, this is indeed wonderful news. The Wycliffe name is
highly thought of in the Carolinas, and we have had dealings
with the Wycliffes in the past. My father bought a number
of mares from the Wycliffe stables when Carlton Wycliffe,
Matthew's grandfather, was alive."

"That was long before your father and I came to an agreement," Noble reminded her. "Any of the River Oaks horses
that won the honors were out of the Royal Bay stables. But I
will allow that they raise good Thoroughbreds in the Wycliffe
stables now. This Sea Racer of Wycliffe's may give Royal
Blood a run for the money come Sunday," the master of Royal
Bay admitted with reluctance, staring down gravely into his
empty brandy snifter. "Might even beat Travers's Tuscany,"
he predicted gloomily.

"Not really, sir?" Adam questioned, surprised to hear such
an admission from his father.

"No one's beaten Royal Blood yet, but...there's always a
first time. Yes, sir, might be the beginning of the end of Royal
Bay to have that little filly, the chestnut-haired girl, the one
who can ride so well, marry into the Wycliffe family. Pretty
little thing. Has a slender, long neck and trim flanks. Like the
way she walks, nice and light on her feet. What's that child's
name?" Noble demanded irritably, thinking Stuart Travers had
sired far too many children, and he never could keep them
all straight, just like all the hounds that always seemed to be
underfoot at Travers Hill.

"Leigh Alexandra," Althea said patiently.

"That's right. The high-spirited little one with the colt.
Wycliffe will have his hands full with her. Reckon he's marrying her just to get his hands on that lil' cap'n of hers? Could start
a whole new stable. One way of keeping the colt from stealing

any races from you one day. Heard tell from her papa that she won't sell him to anyone. Turned down that swine Canby. Remembered his name, same way I do most any horse's as—ah, name," Noble said with a wheezing chuckle. "Never forget, no, sir! But I'd rather be beat by one of Wycliffe's bloods than one bred in Kentucky. Gettin' too high-handed, them folks, thinking their bluegrass is sweet as their corn whiskey and better than ours. Did I tell you about the time I went North, back in '23, it was, and all the way up to New York to see the race between Eclipse and Virginia's Henry? We should never have lost that race, but them Northerners…"

Neil turned his back on the room and its occupants. He stared out across the covered veranda, past the white columns entwined with wisteria and crape myrtle, toward the sweeping view of the river beyond. It flowed quietly and lazily by, with nothing more than an occasional sandbar to disrupt its flow. Indeed, nothing seemed to interrupt the genteel quality of life that flowed around Royal Bay, or their nearest neighbors at Travers Hill.

Leigh Alexandra Travers. Neil silently spoke the name, and would have cursed it beneath his breath except he liked the sound of it too much. What an incredible fool he had been, he remembered now, seeing again the breathtaking beauty of the young woman descending the staircase at Travers Hill. There had been no mistaking her this time for a lowly groom's daughter or a lady's maid. From the neatly braided chestnut hair atop her proudly held head, to the fine kid slippers on her high-arched feet, to the triumphant glint in her dark blue eyes, she had been every inch the beloved and cosseted daughter of the manse.

And with each step she had taken, drawing closer to him as he stood waiting at the bottom of the stairs, she had moved farther out of his reach. He hadn't even won her yet, and already he had lost her. She was a part of this life, as much as the pampered, blooded mares grazing in fields of sweet bluegrass.

Nothing ever changed, he mused, listening for a moment to his uncle's reminiscences now about a horse race he'd lost nearly a quarter of a century ago, and yet it could have been yesterday for all that had changed during those years in between. Just like the river beyond the green willows, flowing gently and peacefully—never-ending, never altering its course toward the sea.

That was the way of life in Virginia, in all of the South, and he knew a sudden resentment of it, of these families of gentle blood, of their almost courtly existence while living off the sweat of others less fortunate, of their patrician airs and graces, of their exalted positions that discouraged trespass by interlopers. They seldom stepped from that elite circle of family and friends that surrounded them, the intermarrying of families creating a larger circle, a continuity that would never be broken. It had become a heritage, handed down from generation to generation, of pride and honor, of graceful manners and gallantries, of duty and dignity, and of ladies fair and gentlemen brave, their affability tinged with condescension.

And that was her heritage too. Not his, he reflected as he thought of Riovado, and the cabin he lived in. The wind was not a gentle, soft breeze, sweet-scented from the gardens, but a cold, gusting wind from the High Plains that wailed plaintively outside the cabin walls, then found its way through chinks in the mud between the rough-hewn logs. The small windows covered by animal skins were practical, not decorative like these delicate, multipaned French windows with their silken hangings. Riovado's fireplace of rock kept the one-room interior warm, and the single black pot hanging over the fire served up a hearty, simple meal to the hungry. But there were no collectibles gracing its mantelpiece, no family portraits, except for one, hanging from the bare walls. The floor with its random planking of heart pine had no brilliant sheen of wax, nor finely woven carpet, but it was dry, and the bear rug before the hearth was soft underfoot, and the heavy door, with its sturdy iron hinges, was barred at night, keeping intruders from trespass.

But Riovado, like Royal Bay and River Oaks, and Travers Hill, was more than a crudely built cabin or an elegant mansion overlooking the river. Riovado was a way of life that was a part of him now. Riovado was the mountains and the sky that surrounded it. It could embrace you, taking you into its heart; but, if you feared it, or made a careless mistake, it could just as easily destroy you.

Neil glanced across the room at Adam, raising his brandy in

a silent toast to his cousin, who nodded in polite acceptance of the honor due him. The slight curl to Neil's lips and the patient expression in the pale eyes warned Adam that he had not yet been forgiven and should be on his guard. Adam sighed, for he knew Neil too well, and his cousin would not easily forgive and forget his coup of yesterday.

Had Neil not been so surprised himself at discovering Leigh Travers's true identity, then he might have enjoyed a moment's pleasure at the start of surprise that had crossed her lovely face when she'd been apprised of *his* true identity.

But even Adam did not realize how complete his cousin's defeat had been yesterday. And Neil, remembering anew, felt again the desolateness that had surged through him as Leigh Alexandra Travers had been surrounded by her loving family. Invited to stay for breakfast and polite conversation in the parlor afterward, he'd remained apart, as he did now, watching and listening to the gentle banter between family members who were so close to one another that a remark tinged slightly with ridicule or sarcasm was greeted with nothing more than good-natured laughter, and seldom did an offhand comment need to be explained further, for there were no secrets, no surprises amongst these family members.

Well…almost none, he thought now, as he remembered the feel of Leigh Travers's body against his and the taste of her lips pressed to his.

He'd watched almost jealously as her brother Guy, a handsome, rather arrogant young gentleman of fashion, sat on the arm of her chair, his hand resting on her slender shoulder now and again with the ease of one who was held in great affection and knew his touch would not be spurned. Time and time again she'd glanced up at him in response, her dark blue eyes full of laughter, but their warmth had turned cool whenever she'd happened to glance his way, and, by chance, their eyes had met.

The young dark-haired girl, now known to him as Blythe Travers, had stared at him from wide hazel eyes brimming with curiosity, her lips quivering uncontrollably too often for her to muffle completely the giggles that escaped into the room whenever she met her sister's warning glance. Perched on a low footstool in front of her sister, at least when she managed to still herself long enough to remain seated on the embroidered seat, she had barraged him tirelessly with questions about his home in the New Mexico Territory and his life with the Comanche. Neil had answered patiently, for it had given him the chance to stare at her sister sitting so quietly behind her and listening with polite interest to their conversation.

Her father had been a genial fellow, quick to laughter and just as quick to anger as the conversation had veered from horse racing to politics, from religion to the best recipe for mint juleps, but with his cheeks flushed from a steady flow of bourbon, his brown eyes twinkling with mischief, he had an easy charm about him that had been passed down to several of his offspring.

Beatrice Amelia, the matriarch of the family, and, Neil suspicioned, the person who held the tightest reins on all the family members, including Stuart Travers, was a soft-spoken, gracious woman of unfading beauty. Glancing between the mistress of Travers Hill and her three daughters, Neil could see the graceful airs and classical features they had inherited from their mother.

Althea Travers Braedon was truly more beautiful today than she had been when on her honeymoon over six years ago, Neil had thought. And he had not lied when he'd complimented her when meeting her in the foyer earlier. She was a very self-possessed woman, her slender hands at rest in her lap, her smile indulgent, her expression contented as she listened to those around her. And he suspected she had never been as daring and high-spirited as her two younger sisters, not because she was so very proper, but because it was not her nature. Noelle, her daughter, and his cousin Nathan's only child, was as quick-witted as her father, and would one day have the beauty her mother possessed.

What had initially amused him, then troubled him, however, had been the strange look the mulatto maid had given him when he'd seen her passing by the door, craning her long neck to see inside the parlor, her slanting yellow eyes piercing as they settled on him as if in recognition, and he would have sworn she'd mumbled an incantation beneath her breath as she hurried from his sight, bumping into the grizzle-haired butler and nearly overbalancing the tray of juleps he carried.

"There you are, Nathan." Euphemia greeted her eldest son as he entered the library, her words drawing Neil from his thoughts of Travers Hill.

"Papa! Papa! I poured the tea, just like a proper lady, Gran'mama said," Noelle cried out proudly, her flying feet carrying her into her father's outstretched arms with unlady-like speed.

"What an armful you've become," he complained with a deep laugh, thinking his daughter was growing up far too fast for his peace of mind. His gaze traveled across her dark head to meet his wife's, and the warmth exchanged between them was as declarative as if they'd spoken aloud of their love.

Neil moved uncomfortably as he witnessed the gentle meeting of glances, and he looked out the window again, his restless gaze seeking something unknown in the peaceful landscape beyond.

"I fear becoming a representative has brought me rather more work than I suspected. Never realized there were quite so many people who wanted attention," Nathan said, accepting the brandy Adam had poured for him.

"Or favors," Adam said. "I warned you against becoming successful," he reminded him. "Brings you nothing but trouble. You will never be able to please everyone."

"You've finished your correspondence for the day, then?" Althea asked, thinking Nathan had time for little else nowadays, even his practice. "Come here, dear," she said, holding out her hand to Noelle. "One of your ribbons has come untied."

"Completely, at least for now. I fear I shall have to hire a secretary by year's end, though," Nathan said, joining Neil by the French windows. "Ah," he sighed, taking a deep swallow of his brandy. "Never knew a fellow could work up such a thirst at so quiet a task, nor that I would look longingly at dusty law books. It's good to see you looking so well, Neil."

"And you," Neil returned, a smile of genuine warmth momentarily softening the hardness of his mouth as he raised his glass.

"I did not have a chance to tell you yesterday how very sorry we were to hear of your wife's death."

"Thank you."

"It must have been very difficult for you, and for your wife's family. Something so tragic, well—"

"Yes," Neil interrupted, his almost rude abruptness usually discouraging further questions or offers of sympathy, but Nathan was his cousin, and a lawyer used to getting information out of difficult witnesses or defendants on the stand. Nathan ran a hand through his hair, leaving it standing on end, which was a sure sign to those who knew him that he was troubled. And he was, for he was suddenly thinking of his own cousin as if he were a criminal he was trying to get a confession from. And yet his lawyer's instinct told him that Neil was hiding something from him. But what?

Neil swirled the brandy around in the crystal globe of the glass, warming it against his palm, then he emptied the contents. "I did not murder Serena, if that is what is troubling you so."

"Good Lord! Certainly not," Nathan said, wondering whether he should feel more offended or guilty by his cousin's offhand remark. Either way, it made him all the more uneasy. "I did not think anything of the kind, Neil."

"Then I apologize," he said, inclining his golden head slightly in deference. "But there were many who thought as much. It is no secret that I came close to being lynched by an angry mob of my wife's bereaved relations, and others who saw a chance to rid themselves of my presence."

"So I gathered."

"Yes, of course, your mother and my stepmother have few secrets and their will to correspond is without equal. But as you can see, I survived, as I always seem to."

Nathan wanted to reach out and comfort his cousin, and his friend, but he knew his gesture would seem pitying, and Neil was not a man to be pitied; feared, yes, but never pitied, even though Nathan could sense the deep wound that Neil carried within and allowed no one to heal.

"It would seem as if I timed my arrival perfectly. I understand that there will be quite a celebration this weekend when one of the Travers daughters announces her engagement on Friday. Perhaps Stuart Travers will know a generosity of spirit, and prove his hospitality to a stranger by not trying to rob me when selling his bloods," he commented dryly, wishing to change the subject.

And Nathan, this time, was willing to allow him to do so. Looking surprised, he said, "That news, which has yet to be announced, certainly traveled fast. I would not be in the least bit surprised to learn you heard about it in the territories," he declared, then following Neil's glance, he nodded good-naturedly. "I should have realized that Julayne would not be able to hold her tongue concerning so momentous an occasion about to occur in the county."

"Then it is true?" Neil asked casually, as if amused by the whole affair.

"Yes," Nathan confirmed, and having glanced away to watch his daughter pirouetting across the carpet, he didn't notice the tightening of Neil's mouth. "Althea told me last night that Matthew Wycliffe will ask permission of her father this weekend for Leigh's hand in marriage. And from what Althea confided in me concerning her sister's feelings, I would say Leigh will accept without hesitation. If anyone knew the truth of the matter, or of Leigh's heart, then it would be Althea. They are quite close, even for sisters."

"A love match?" Neil murmured.

Nathan looked at his cousin thoughtfully, for he had not missed the edge of sarcasm in his voice.

"Yes, I believe so. Although, even were it not, they would be well suited to one another, and it could prove most providential for Travers Hill."

"Really? In what way? Travers Hill looked quite prosperous when I rode in yesterday. And I was in the stables. One can usually tell the state of affairs from the condition of the stables, and I've seldom seen any finer."

Nathan laughed. "That is because Stuart Travers loves his horses almost as much as he does his family, and to Sweet John, his handler, those horses *are* his children. This is in confidence, and I would not speak of it outside of our family, but Stuart Travers is dangerously in debt. He has even mortgaged Travers Hill to pay off his most outstanding debts, and were not the man who held the mortgage a gentleman, and soon to become his future son-in-law, then, well..."

Nathan shook his head, amazed anew at how quickly a man's fortunes could change.

"How very convenient, and farsighted of this Wycliffe fellow. Having met Leigh Travers, I can understand the man's determination, despite the cost, to make her his wife. She is exquisite, and quite extraordinary," he added.

"Yes, Leigh is a lovely young woman, and much sought after. She has countless beaus, and would be welcomed as a daughter-in-law in any family in the county, despite the Travers family's reputation for being slightly unconventional. But since they are so well liked, and have one of the best stables in the South, and Beatrice Amelia Travers is so very proper, they are forgiven their little eccentricities."

"Then this Wycliffe is even smarter than I suspected. For how better to ensure his position of favor than to have the daughter of the family, whom he hopes to wed, feel indebted to him for saving the family home and fortunes," Neil said, his eyes narrowed in thought, an unpleasant twist to his lips as he speculated upon Matthew Wycliffe.

"True, but you're mistaken about Matthew Wycliffe, Neil. Were it any other man, I might be inclined to agree with you, for it is not unknown for a man to take advantage of a situation in order to strengthen his suit with a lady. But Wycliffe is no scoundrel. In truth, he is the most honorable gentleman of my acquaintance," he admitted, and Nathan was an excellent judge of character, and his approbation and respect were not given unless well deserved. "I've never met so high-principled a man. In all of his business and personal dealings, with those of his own station, and even with those who do the most menial work for him, he is evenhanded, generous, in fact, to a fault. I have never heard even a breath of scandal attached to his name."

"Obviously a paragon," Neil said.

"Some have said as much. You might think, and with every reason, that a man like Wycliffe, with his family name, which is highly respected, his fortune, which is vast, and his appearance, which has made him the most eligible bachelor in the South, would be supercilious, and yet he is one of the most unpretentious people I know. He and Guy Travers, one of Leigh's brothers, have been friends for years. And he has most kindly recommended, without expecting anything in return, my law practice to friends of his who have need of legal advice here in Virginia. Mrs. Travers is from Charleston, and they visit relatives there quite often, and Leigh attended finishing school in Charleston, so when Leigh moves to South Carolina with Matthew, she will not be without her family and friends. I can honestly state that I cannot think of anyone I would rather see Leigh marry than Wycliffe. I'm very fond of her. She's quite a young woman."

"Yes, so it would seem," Neil said softly. "She is very beautiful. In fact, the whole family would seem to have been so blessed."

Nathan smiled, glancing over at his wife as he nodded his agreement. "Unfortunately, that is also the biggest cause of Guy Travers's problems. Things, and people, come too easily to him. He doesn't have to work hard enough to get what he wants," Nathan said, voicing his first criticism of the Travers family.

Neil smiled. "I had the distinct impression that he took an instant dislike to me."

Nathan frowned. "I had hoped you would not have noticed."

"It was rather hard not to when everything Adam said about my years with the Comanche, the stories of which even I admit have become highly exaggerated over the years and many a retelling, was questioned and dismissed by Travers as lies."

"I'd hoped you wouldn't take offense, either. Guy can't stand to be bested. For a good bit of his life he has heard Adam's and my tales of you. I'm afraid you've become a bit of a legend around here, Neil. Guy is competitive. And he can ride as well as anyone I've ever seen, except for you, and one other," he said, laughing as if at a private jest. "He knows that, and he's jealous of you. Don't be surprised if he challenges you to a race to prove who is the better rider, because unless you beat him, he'll never accept it, and even then he'll probably find a good excuse to explain his loss. Guy also loves to bet, too much for his own good. It is a pity, because, if given the right opportunity, Guy could become a fine man one day," Nathan added, wondering what on earth could change the course of that young man's life. "But Leigh, now Leigh is different. You've never seen her ride," Nathan said with a wide grin of pleasure, "but the wind couldn't catch her."

"No, but it would seem as if Matthew Wycliffe has," Neil said, smiling slightly as Nathan laughed at his remark and turned the conversation to other, far more important subjects, but try as he may, Neil could not banish quite so easily the image of Leigh Travers from his mind—or his heart.

Ten

The wicked are wicked, no doubt, and they go astray and they fall, and they come by their deserts; but who can tell the mischief which the very virtuous do?

William Makepeace Thackeray

FRIDAY. IT WAS THE DAY OF BLYTHE LUCINDA TRAVERS'S sixteenth birthday party. Leigh glanced up at the house. She could see the veranda, crowded with people milling about. Some gentlemen were lounging on the steps, while others sat more decorously on benches and chairs close to the ladies, and the refreshments were being served by the green-clad majordomo and his elite troop of footmen, who seemed to be at every elbow at just the right moment with another tall julep or pale lemonade. The droning sound of voices, raised in chatter and laughter, drifted to Leigh across the gardens. The household was in a turmoil, with her mother and Jolie meeting themselves coming and going as they tried to stay a step ahead of the countless, last-minute details that suddenly popped up. Since midweek, carriages had been pulling up every few minutes and unloading family and friends to be settled in the guest wings, the unattached gentlemen placed in the rambling, genteel quarters between the house and the stables. Even Guy and Palmer William had given up their rooms to take up temporary residence with the other bachelors, where their late-night hours, filled with drinking and gambling and, perchance, vulgar jesting, might not disturb the more refined of the guests and their families visiting Travers Hill.

But this afternoon, Leigh had escaped it all to wander down to the paddock, where the only disturbing sounds were those of softly neighing mares and the gentle thudding of hooves as their foals galloped playfully around the meadow, perhaps sensing, with a quick sniff in the air, the last days of summer were approaching all too quickly. In the cool shade of an oak, Leigh stood leaning against the split-railed fence.

Neil Darcy Braedon. That was the stranger's name—not

Dagger, as Adam had been so quick to tell her. His cousin. And no stranger, as she had mistakenly thought, nor a common ranch hand, as Adam had claimed. And not a man easily dismissed by anyone. But then, she hadn't been Rose, the servant, either. And had the tables not been turned so suddenly and surprisingly on her, she might have enjoyed the discomfiture that had momentarily flickered across his hard face when she'd descended the stairs and been introduced to him as one of the Travers family. Adam, however, had certainly enjoyed his little jest, and she'd hoped he would choke on his laughter all the way home to Royal Bay.

That had been four days ago, but her anger flared briefly again as she remembered Adam's grinning face and the endlessness of that day, at least until Nathan and Althea, accompanied by Adam and their cousin, had left for Royal Bay. Neil Braedon had held an adoring Noelle in his arms as he'd made his polite farewells. Far too young and innocent to realize the danger of the man, Noelle had grinned down at everyone from her superior position above their heads. Holding out her arms to each of them, she'd demanded her customary hug and kiss, which Neil Braedon had generously allowed her by bending slightly to each person so she could wrap her short arms around their necks. Leigh had received her tight hug and smacking kiss from her niece, but it had seemed to her heightened senses as if Neil Braedon's face had come far closer to hers when he bent down, bringing their lips embarrassingly close for just a moment, their eyes locking above Noelle's dark head, before she was released and could step away, her heart pounding. She hadn't seen any of them since, except for Althea when she'd come calling with Euphemia Braedon two days later.

She didn't care that he hadn't come back to Travers Hill, that he had obviously found far more interesting things to do with his time, Leigh told herself for not the first time that week, wondering why she felt insulted by his actions. She suspected she felt exactly the way the serving girl he'd mistook her for would have when her gentleman lover had failed to return after enjoying her favors. How differently he had acted toward her before discovering she was a Travers, pursuing her ruthlessly, tracking her down, and trying to seduce her. But as soon as he'd learned she was no serving wench to be bedded and abandoned, his ardor had cooled considerably. Obviously, Neil Braedon was a man who took his pleasures without wishing to be held accountable for them. She would no longer be of interest to him now, she thought, wondering why that made her feel so angry, and so humiliated. Neil Braedon was nothing to her—nothing. So why should it trouble her, hurt her so, that he hadn't come near her since that day. He'd wanted only a dalliance with her, a quick tumble in the hay, those had been his own casually spoken words. To have sought her out, to have offered her an apology for his actions, to have learned more about Leigh Travers, to have befriended her, had not interested him. No, once he had realized that she would say nothing of their embarrassing encounter, he must have heaved a great sigh of relief. Yes, that was the manner of man this Neil Braedon, this Sun Dagger, was.

Of course, she had heard all about the Braedons' cousin from the territories that first day when he'd sat in the parlor of Travers Hill, his gentlemanly demeanor almost proving false the colorful stories Adam had entertained them with concerning his cousin's unusual childhood. And despite herself, and pretending polite interest, she'd listened avidly to Adam's talk of his cousin's kidnapping by the Comanche, and the never-ending pursuit by Neil's father to rescue him and his sister Shannon. And even if Guy's questions had bordered on rudeness, his guffaws of skepticism becoming embarrassing after a while, he'd managed to elicit a great deal of information. But Blythe had more than made up for her brother's lack of hospitality by her enthusiastic insistence on knowing every detail of Neil's life. And he had been very patient in his good-natured answers to Blythe, even when she'd asked the awkward question about his dead wife, demanding to know if it had been the Comanche who had left her stranded in the canyon. Even Adam had had the grace to look slightly apologetic for ever having brought the subject up. But Leigh hadn't been able to forget the expression that had crossed Neil's face when he'd been reminded of his dead wife. It had been one of pained remembrance, and Leigh had known then that he must have loved her deeply, still loved her, and no other woman would ever be able to replace her in his heart.

And for the last few days, even though she'd not seen the man, her curiosity about him had been satisfied again as Guy had regaled her with stories about the legendary Braedon cousin from the territories. Guy had ridden to hounds at Royal Bay and Evergreens. He was one of the best huntsmen in the county and he and his prized hounds were sought after for every hunt. He'd joined the shoot at River Oaks Farm, and after each day's sport, he'd enjoyed a night of gambling and drinking with his gentlemen friends and their guests, among them Neil. Unfortunately, at least as far as Guy had been concerned, he'd held the losing hand far too often and lost heavily, and most often to Neil, which had angered him all the more, and Guy was as quick-tempered as their father. Leigh suspected had it not been for the calming influence of Adam, and a restraining hand gently yet firmly placed, her brother would have been guilty of accusing Neil of cheating, for he claimed no gentleman's luck could hold for so long. *If* he played fair, that was.

"Hello, little sister," a voice spoke behind her, startling Leigh from her thoughts. "Escaped the madness?"

"Stuart James," Leigh said, smiling as he approached her from the stables.

"I thought I'd find you either with the horses in the stables or out here watching them. Your position keeps you rather well hidden from view. Which, I suspect, was your intention when coming this way."

"I confess, 'tis true," Leigh said, laughing with him as they both stared at the crowd on the veranda, neither in a hurry to return there.

"I can scarcely believe that little Lucy is sixteen. She has grown a foot or more since I moved to Willow Creek. She seems all leg."

"I think she fears she will grow even taller than I am," Leigh said a trifle self-consciously, for although Stuart James was taller than Guy, he wasn't all that much taller than she was.

"You needn't worry, little chestnut-top," he said, using his old nickname for her, "for you've grown into one of the most beautiful and charming women I know, and," he added, a twinkle in his brown eyes, "quite a bit shorter than Matthew Wycliffe."

Leigh glanced up, startled.

"You cannot keep such news a secret for long. I heard nothing but talk of your upcoming nuptials when in Richmond. I was quite offended to hear the news while walking along the street, and minding my own business, and from some strange woman who was wearing the most amazing bonnet. I could neither confirm nor deny her claim since I'd not been informed of the glad tidings by my own family. She was quite indignant about the whole affair. I thought her husband was going to call me out and demand satisfaction."

"Richmond? A woman on the street?"

Stuart James nodded. "I suspect Aunt Maribel Lu's fine hand. There is nothing she cannot ferret out once she gets the scent. She has a great many friends in Charleston, including several of Matthew Wycliffe's aunts."

"But there is nothing to announce yet."

"A small matter as far as everyone else is concerned."

"Well, it is very important as far as I am concerned. It will be the most important decision of my life, and yet I am beginning to feel as if I have nothing to say in the matter at all," Leigh pondered aloud, wondering why she felt as if it were someone else who was contemplating marriage to Matthew and not herself. Suddenly life seemed so much more complicated than it had just a week ago.

"How very embarrassing for everyone, especially those who have already planned on attending the wedding and spent too much on their gowns, if Matthew doesn't ask for my hand in marriage," Leigh said, forcing herself to laugh.

Stuart James shook his head. "He will ask."

Leigh eyed him thoughtfully. He was thinner than he had been when last she'd seen him, and the lines were deeper around his mouth, but Stuart James had always been serious and reserved, not carefree and quick to laugh like Guy.

"You seem very certain."

"I am. I hope you will not be offended by what I am about to say, and please do not be angry with him, but Matthew could not hide his feelings for you when he accompanied us from Richmond. In fact, every other word he spoke was either your name or something about you, and 'twas quite obvious he is very much in love with you. And the only time I saw him actually become impatient was when there was a delay in our leaving Richmond. I really thought he was going to raise his voice when Aunt Maribel Lu couldn't get all of those hat boxes in the carriage. So I thought, as your elder brother, that I should find out his intentions, which were indeed honorable, since he told me he would be asking Father for your hand in marriage this weekend. And although he did seem hopeful that you would accept," he added quickly, lest his sister misunderstand, "he was not in the least boastful, in fact, he was quite diffident about it all. I do like him, Leigh, and would be pleased to see you wed him, but only if it is what will make you happy."

Leigh kissed his thin cheek. "I happen to like him too, and if he can indeed keep his patience with Aunt Maribel Lu, then he is a man of uncommon goodness."

"Good," Stuart James said, sounding almost relieved. "I'm glad you said that rather than that you thought yourself head over heels in love with him."

"Why?" Leigh demanded, puzzled. "Is that not the way it should be?" she questioned, wondering why she had not said "love" when speaking of Matthew, and yet…when she remembered a pair of pale gray-green eyes, she felt her heartbeat quicken, the way everyone said it would when you were in love. But then she found herself remembering Althea's words of warning about knowing the difference between infatuation and true love.

"One day, you might suddenly find yourself not in love with that person you thought you could not live without, and you begin to wonder if you ever were truly in love with them. Then, much to your disbelief, you discover that you do not even like that person, that you have nothing to discuss, hardly any civility to exchange, and that is when your life can become rather a nightmare," he said, running a nervous hand through his hair. "That is why I am so pleased that you and Matthew are such good friends, and you have so much in common— your backgrounds, your love of horses, your sense of honor and duty. Believe me, dear, when I say that will become the cornerstone of your marriage. And I suspect, that if you do not love him now, you will come to love him, and if you should never come to love him, then you will still be on friendly terms. You will have a splendid marriage, just like Althea and Nathan. She was fortunate. Love *and* friendship in her marriage. Of course, I've never known Althea to do anything that wasn't right and proper. Nathan's a fine man. But then I've always thought the womenfolk of the Travers family are the brightest of the lot of us."

"Is everything all right, Stuart?" Leigh asked, knowing that all was not well between him and Thisbe. She glanced up at the veranda, where she knew Thisbe was sitting, surrounded by the usual group of gossiping women and admiring gentlemen.

"Of course; what could be amiss?" Stuart James replied, since he was not one to confide, even with family, for although he bore little physical resemblance to their father, and acted even less like a Travers, he had inherited one very important characteristic from their father, and that was the Travers pride.

"My wife is one of the most beautiful women in the Tidewater. We are never without invitations to one party or another. I've two charming children. Our home is much admired by all who visit, and there has never been a more gracious hostess than Thisbe, loving wife and mother, and mistress of Willow Creek Landing. And after this harvest, I should be a very successful planter, and more than able to keep my wife in the manner in which she has all too quickly become accustomed," he added, and Leigh had never heard such a cold hollowness in her brother's voice before.

"A good crop this year? That is wonderful news, Stuart."

"Yes, I think Father will be quite pleased, and surprised."

"Not all that surprised."

"You were just now. After the last couple of disastrous years, and having lost all of the money he has poured into Willow Creek, I will now be able to pay him back in full. And I will see that he has a tidy profit to show for his investment, and for his faith in me."

"He will be so proud of you," Leigh told him quickly, hoping their father would be.

Stuart James shrugged. "That would be nice for a change. I'm afraid I've seldom given him reason. It was Guy who managed to become the lawyer, not me, and I studied far harder. And I've never been good with horses, not like you and Guy.

And that is how Father judges a man's merit, how good his seat is. Horses are his life. For me, a horse is in my stable so I may ride from here to there, and be pulled along in my carriage in complete comfort with my family around me. Is that too wrong of me?"

"Of course not."

Stuart James grinned. "You never think ill of anyone, especially family, and we take advantage of you, I fear. Do you know, I've often believed Father thinks more of Sweet John than of me, and he is more of a son to him than I am," he said. "But this is my chance, Leigh, to prove to him that I can succeed at something. That I'm not a complete fool."

"You don't have to prove anything of the kind," Leigh told him, seeing for the first time some of the despair that Stuart James had hidden behind his quiet demeanor all of these years. "I love life down there in the Tidewater. It is so peaceful. I take my boat out and just drift on the tide sometimes, especially at sunset when the sky looks like it is on fire. I've even set up an easel on the bank and tried to paint it once or twice," he confessed with a sheepish look. "Our secret," he admonished. "Well, it'll be getting dark soon," Stuart James said, sighing as he glanced toward the veranda for a moment, knowing they must rejoin the others. "When Matthew stayed over, while waiting to accompany us here, he spoke quite knowledgeably of tobacco. In fact, Leigh, he has bidded most handsomely, generously, in fact, for Willow Creek's biggest crop yet. He has a warehouse in the Carolinas, and he ships to England through his own company. He has sent down one of his finest managers to advise us on the next planting. Naturally he wants the best if we are to become partners," Stuart James confided, his brown eyes showing some of the old warmth and enthusiasm that used to brighten them. "He is a brilliant businessman in his own right, not just living off what he inherited, so I believe I shall profit greatly from our arrangement. And what better, Leigh, than to be in business with your brother-in-law?"

"Yes, what better," Leigh murmured.

"You and Matthew will be able to visit us at Willow Creek quite a lot in future, and I'll even take you drifting down the river."

"Promise?"

"Promise. Now, hadn't I better get you back up to the house so you can start your preparations for the big party?" he asked, tucking her hand in his as they turned and began to walk along the lane. "Jolie will be on the warpath looking for you."

"Blythe was thrilled with the green velvet cloak Thisbe gave her as a present. Mama was certainly impressed by its quality. It is quite expensive with the fur lining. Is it really ermine?"

"Yes, our Thisbe never buys anything but the best." Stuart James smiled just slightly, for only he knew Thisbe had ordered the cloak for herself but, upon delivery, had decided the dark green color too unbecoming. Never worn, it had been folded away in the box it'd come in, and left forgotten for nearly two years, until Thisbe had declared it the perfect gift for Blythe.

"Blythe was happiest with your gift to her. It was very thoughtful of you to give her Grandmama Palmer's garnet ring," she added, remembering Blythe's excitement that morning when she'd slipped it on her finger when the family had gathered together privately for their gift-giving.

"I wanted her to have something very special for her sixteenth birthday. When I inherited Willow Creek, I also received many of the family heirlooms. Although not one of the more expensive pieces, Thisbe has those, I understand that ring was one of Grandmama Palmer's favorites. That reminds me, I had a nice long talk with Palmer William last night."

"He is looking well, isn't he," Leigh said.

"Yes, he was well named, since he inherited Grandpapa Palmer's height. There is a portrait of him at Willow Creek, and Palmer has a look of the old gentleman about him. Did you know he is definitely planning a career in the army?"

"No, I didn't. Oh, dear, I don't think that will please Mama at all," Leigh said, seeing again her mother's tearful cries when Palmer, standing taller and broader than she remembered, had swept their mother up into his arms, her feet lifted clear off the floor when he'd greeted her with a suffocating bear hug. The rest of the evening their mother had fussed over him, complaining that he wasn't eating enough and that he was spending far too much time out in the sun, and reminding him how delicate his skin was. But Palmer had laughed away her concerns with masculine disdain, and with a new deepness to his voice had claimed he ate far too much, having had to have all of his uniforms let out in the shoulders and waist, and that precision drills on horseback had him tanned darker than a pecan and feeling fit as a fiddle.

They reached the veranda, and Leigh stood for several minutes with Stuart James, politely returning greetings and casual remarks, her gaze resting momentarily on Thisbe's silvery head bent close to another's in private conversation, her tinkling laughter sounding slightly malicious to Leigh's sensitive ear. Which, the night before, had burned from overhearing the abusive language that had flowed between Stuart James and his wife when in the privacy of their room next door to hers and Blythe's.

Burying her head beneath her pillow, she had cringed to think such words could be exchanged between two people who loved one another, who were man and wife, for although her own parents often argued, their arguments never had the vicious edge she'd heard in Thisbe's and Stuart James's conversation.

Glancing between them now, Leigh remembered Stuart James's words of advice, and she realized he'd spoken of his own marriage, and had been warning her not to make the same mistake he had. He and Thisbe were no longer in love, and it was painfully obvious that they disliked one another. As Leigh watched, Thisbe glanced up into the handsome face of one of her gentlemen admirers, the intimate look they exchanged causing Leigh to look away in embarrassment, and to hope Stuart hadn't seen it.

Excusing herself, Leigh made her way indoors. It was nearly an hour later when she finally reached the quiet haven of her bedchamber, having been stopped numerous times and held in conversation by friendly, well-meaning gossips, by neighbors hungry for the latest news, by second and third cousins eager to share theirs, and by gentlemen too eager to impress, most having heard the disturbing rumor that Leigh Travers was to wed Matthew Wycliffe. Closing the door firmly behind her, she leaned against it and glanced around the empty room. Spread out across half the bed was Blythe's pale green silk gown with its rows of ruffles trimmed with Brussels lace cascading down the skirt. A deep fall of matching lace adorned the puffed sleeves and a delicate frill tucked along the bodice raised the décolletage enough to maintain a young woman's modesty. A pair of pale green silk slippers with satin rosettes and ribbons was waiting to be slipped onto her dancing feet. In fact, Blythe's feet had hardly touched the ground since morning, when she'd opened the gift left for her by Althea, the emerald-green perfume bottle with its etched stars, causing her to squeal with delight and dance around the room. Her treasure was now sitting on the dressing table next to the sapphire-blue perfume bottle and the set of a silver-backed brush, comb, and hand mirror entwined with her initials, which had been the gift from their parents. And Leigh's own gift, a pair of pearl drop earrings, to match the pearl necklace given to Blythe by their Aunt Maribel Lu, would adorn her small ears this eve.

Smiling with pleasure, Leigh admired the voluminous skirts of her own ball gown, which were spread out over the other half of the bed. She touched the diaphanous tarlatan that was flounced over a slightly darker shade of apricot silk. The scalloped edges of each flounce had been intricately woven with golden threads and tiny beads that would shimmer and sparkle with each step she took around the dance floor in matching silk slippers, and a feather fan dyed in gradually darkening shades of apricot and sprinkled with gold dust would dangle by a velvet ribbon from her wrist. Layers and layers of stiffened, ruffled petticoats were piled high on the pillows, and balanced precariously on top, the fine lawn chemisettes and pantalettes, silk-spun stockings, lacy, beribboned garters, and elbow-length gloves that she and Blythe would soon be dressed in.

Picking up Blythe's new mirror, Leigh stared at her reflection critically, wondering at Jolie's decision to braid her hair into a double-rowed coronet, and weaving it with fragrant, star-shaped blossoms of white jessamine, apricot-hued rosebuds tinged with gold, and a spray of dark blue forget-me-nots over each ear. She hoped it would not be too severe a coiffure, but Jolie had been adamant. Julia had boasted that she was having her golden curls styled in the latest Parisian fashion, while Blythe was to have her dark hair pulled into a sophisticated chignon arranged high on her head, with several curls dangling over each ear and graced by a white camellia, and across the crown, a delicate tiara of a single, pale green velvet ribbon sewn with pearls.

Blythe would look like a princess tonight, Leigh thought, hoping her dreams would come true and Justin Braedon would ask her to partner him in more than one dance. She would be able to flirt with him from behind the ivory *brisé* fan that had been Palmer William's gift to her, and if she stepped outside for a breath of fresh air, Justin Braedon could place across her slender, bare shoulders the muslin evening shawl edged in Chantilly lace that Guy had given her for her birthday. When Justin had arrived with Palmer, staying only long enough to have luncheon with them, Blythe's wide-eyed gaze had seldom left him, although apparently her ability to speak had, for Leigh had never seen her so tongue-tied and shy, bobbing her head up and down in answer to every question. At the thought of Justin, who looked remarkably like his half brother, although in temperament he was nothing like him, being a complete gentleman, Leigh felt her breath catch slightly. Tonight she would see Neil Braedon. He was one of the invited guests to Blythe's birthday party, and he would be accompanying the other Braedons when they arrived from Royal Bay.

Leigh walked over to the window and gazed down on the gardens below, not seeing the deepening shadows, or feeling the cooling breeze that played in the light folds of the curtains as she fiddled nervously with the delicate gold ring in her earlobe. Neil might even ask her to partner him tonight in a dance. And if he did, then she would very politely decline the honor, proving to him, and to herself, how little she cared about him.

Shivering slightly, Leigh hid her face in her hands, ashamed of the rush of heat that had burned into her cheeks just at the thought of Neil. Would she ever be able to forget his touch, the feel of his lips against hers? Why did he have to come swaggering into her life? A week ago she would have gladly accepted Matthew's proposal of marriage. Never doubting that she was in love with him, never doubting she would happily spend the rest of her life with him. But now…now she was no longer certain of her feelings for Matthew.

What did she feel for him? When he had arrived at Travers Hill she had been glad to see him, but her heart hadn't quickened its beat, thumping uncomfortably because she was near him. He was still one of the most handsome men she knew, with his black hair and soft brown eyes, so full of gentle humor and compassion, and love when they met hers. Tall and broad-shouldered, he stood above every other man in a crowd, but not just because of his greater physical attributes. Matthew had a presence about him, a quality of honor and integrity that came from within. He was all that she'd ever dreamed about in a man, and he wanted to marry her.

Leigh drew a deep breath, thinking of Althea, of her gentle words of wisdom, of the love she shared with Nathan. In fact, Matthew reminded her quite a bit of Nathan with his quiet strength. Then she thought of Stuart James, and the sadness of the broken dreams he could not hide, of his hopes that now, because of Matthew, he might see fulfilled.

What was she to do? Why should she even be questioning her feelings? Leigh asked herself. After all, Neil was a stranger, and he'd never been part of her life at Travers Hill, nor did he wish to be. He had made that very clear by his absence. And from what Guy had told her, he apparently had been enjoying himself at Evergreens, and in the company of Sarette Canby the last few days.

Continuing to stand before the opened window, lost in her thoughts, Leigh became aware of the sunset, reflected by a rosy glow shimmering on the river in the distance. Above the dark silhouette of the trees along the bank, the sky was losing its golden light, the streaks of mauve and lavender fading into violet. Leigh shivered slightly as she felt the coolness of twilight touch her, then her laughter sounded softly. She was being foolish. Everything would work out the way it was meant to. She needn't worry, for she had all the time in the world to discover her true feelings—and Neil's. No one was forcing her to do anything against her will. She touched her throat, easing the restriction that had momentarily tightened it. Feeling the bareness of skin beneath her fingertips, she suddenly remembered her cameo brooch, left in her mother's bedchamber yesterday. Her mother was going to attach a new velvet ribbon to it so it could be worn this evening. She had to retrieve it, before their mother began the lengthy preparations of her toilette—and no one dared disturb her then.

Leigh hurried from her bedchamber, stopping briefly to close the half-opened door to Guy's room, which was now being used by their Aunt Maribel Lu and Uncle Jay. She knocked first, peeking around the door, just in case her aunt and uncle were inside, but on seeing the empty room, she started to close the door, her gaze lingering in disbelief on the jumble within. Trunks were stacked almost to the ceiling against one wall. Round, striped hat boxes were piled high on the bed, with a couple of the exotic bonnets having escaped to perch on top of the bed posts, while stockings of every shade were tied like big bows around the girth of each fluted post. Dainty parasols, some fringed, some spangled, some lace-edged, and one that looked like a small red pagoda, were propped against the foot of the bed. Several headless dress forms, garbed in Aunt Maribel Lu's finest gowns, stood at attention near the windows, and were surrounded by a small army of shoes, slippers, and boots.

Shaking her head, Leigh backed out of the bedchamber, wondering if there had been room left in the trunks for Uncle Jay to bring a change of clothes. She had almost reached her mother's bedchamber when Leigh paused, a puzzled expression on her face as she wondered about the empty spaces on Guy's bedchamber wall. Many of his valued pistols were missing from his collection. Odd that he would take those with him, when he'd cleaned out his chest of drawers for his short stay in the bachelors' quarters, Leigh thought. She was starting to take a step closer to her mother's door when she heard voices coming from within and she stopped, not wishing to intrude. The voices, however, which she recognized as her parents', were clearly audible.

"...and you've put far too much money into Willow Creek to help Stuart James make that plantation pay, and so far there has been little enough to show for it, except for Thisbe Anne's efforts. I will say that much for her, she, at least, has been putting her time, and our money, to use. I only wish I could say the same thing about your son. Did I not already know the answer, I would demand an accounting of exactly what those funds are being spent on. But I can tell you exactly what that money has been spent for. Thisbe has been spending all that we send down there just to make that house look like some kind of palace," Beatrice Amelia said. "And I doubt very seriously it will ever be another Monticello. Do you know what she is talking about doing now? She is actually thinking about renaming Willow Creek. The name is not dignified enough for our Thisbe, oh, no, she has to have something fancy in French. Asked me, she did indeed, since I attended Madame Talvande's, and, if I do say so myself, can speak French as well as my ancestors in France did, if I had any ideas? Your grandmother, and a fine woman she was, must be turning in her grave, and I said as much to Stuart James. But he just shook his head. Never have known what that boy is thinking.

"Well, I can tell you, I gave Thisbe an idea or two to think about. I declare, but she must have thought when she up and married Stuart James that she'd be living like a queen, being waited on hand and foot. If we all sat around fanning ourselves nothing would get done around here. She didn't even know how to mix up a decent batch of medicine, and claimed she wouldn't set foot inside one of those dirty cabins out back. Well, I ask you, if the house servants get sick and die, who's going to do all the cooking, scrubbing, and cleaning she expects to be done every day so she can lie in bed until noon? Yes, doesn't stir herself until then, and then she's off calling on the neighbors in her carriage. You cannot leave your home and the servants unsupervised, it's asking for trouble. And I tell you, Stuart, I don't like her attitude toward her servants at all. I'm not surprised they're sullen and surly to her. Treats them like animals, and mistreated ones at that. I declare, I heard she even took the whip to some of them herself. Scandalous behavior! And can you imagine, she didn't even know how to salt pork, Stuart. And the linens at Willow Creek the last time we visited weren't fit for decent folk to sleep on. She doesn't know anything about washing. Some neighborhood woman always came in and did it for her family in Philadelphia. I don't really blame Thisbe Anne for that, because it was her mother's place to prepare her for marriage. She hasn't got an excuse now, but she won't raise a finger to do anything around that place. Thinks she can just sashay out and buy whatever she needs.

"Not that I don't think Stuart James and his family ought to have a proper place to live, but really, Stuart, do they need a twelve-columned portico and eight chimneys? And the furniture she has special ordered, have you heard about that? Took three hours to show me all of the swatches, and I've never seen the like. Striped satins in the brightest colors I've ever seen and funny-looking doodads stuck all over everything. She went up to Philadelphia to order her furnishings. You'd think Richmond, or certainly Charleston, would be good enough. Well, apparently not for the likes of Thisbe, I'm thinking. Has all of her gowns made by some outrageously expensive dressmaker, and in New York of all places. What do they know about fashion up North? Except for the fact that Thisbe doesn't even blink an eye about owning slaves, she is about as Yankee as they come," Beatrice Amelia said, sniffing with disapproval. "I never did think Thisbe would make our Stuart James a good wife. He has gotten so thin and nervous since last we saw him. I'm sure you remember my very words, and spoken in this room not more than six years past," Beatrice Amelia reminded her husband. "Nothing good will come of that marriage, I said. Not that I'm displeased with young Leslie and Cynthia, for they do us proud. Cynthia Amelia is already blossoming into a beauty, and how she does love her Grandmama Travers's sugar cookies," Beatrice Amelia said with a pleased chuckle.

"Needs a hickory stick taken to her more than another sweet," Stuart mumbled.

"She's a bit high-spirited, that's all," Beatrice Amelia said, defending her granddaughter.

"Noelle is a bit high-spirited. Cynthia is spoiled rotten," Stuart corrected, ignoring the irritated glance he knew was being leveled at him from a pair of narrowed, dark blue eyes beneath finely arched eyebrows. "And if a man hasn't enough gumption to remain master in his own house, then he should be gelded and sent out to pasture. If Stuart James was master of Willow Creek, he'd sit that Thisbe Anne down and give her a good talking to. Have you seen the way that young woman's been flirting with any man who can fill up a pair of breeches?"

"It seems to me that Stuart James isn't the only one who can't seem to stand firm when Thisbe Anne starts her wheedling ways. I'm surprised you haven't busted a button so puffed up you've become," Beatrice Amelia returned, not seeing the startled look her husband sent her from under hastily lowered bushy brows, but her remark had been innocently spoken.

"And here you stand before me now, telling me that we can't even paint our own house, when Thisbe, the young Mrs. Travers, has painted and repapered that mausoleum of hers inside and out, and with our money! And off to Newport for a month to recover from the redecorating, then on to Philadelphia to spend the holidays with her family, when we haven't even been to Charlottesville once this month, and, I dare say, we won't be able to visit Warm Springs this year. The waters would do me such good. Well, I just don't know what to say," Beatrice Amelia said with a tearful catch in her voice.

"I'm certain you will find something, my dear," Stuart said patiently.

"Are you being impertinent, Mr. Travers?"

"Not at all, Mrs. Travers. Just confident of your ability to find the appropriate words to express yourself."

"Well, I always have prided myself on saying what was on my mind. I'm not one to suffer in silence, as well you know," Beatrice Amelia declared. "I do so wish Stuart James had taken my advice and married that Bartley girl. An only child, Stuart, and an heiress now. They say she has had several offers from European royalty. Even Sarette Canby would have been better."

"No son, or daughter, of mine will ever marry a Canby."

"That's just because you think none of them has any horse sense. Well, at least Althea Louise made a splendid match, and Leigh Alexandra will even outdo Althea. I wonder how wealthy Matthew Wycliffe really is. I'll have to get a letter off to my cousin Benjamin and find out. Oh, Stuart, I declare, this truly is the best news I've heard in some time. I feel quite refreshed by it all, despite everything else. Indeed, dear, I feel all of our worries are past. You mark my words."

"I will not borrow money from my children, or their spouses, Mrs. Travers," he said, more sternly this time.

"Now, now, *Mr. Travers*, dear," Beatrice Amelia responded with a conciliatory note in her voice. "I wasn't suggesting anything of the kind, and well you know. However, it certainly would be to our advantage having Matthew as our son-in-law.

He would hardly foreclose on Travers Hill and evict us from our home like others might if we failed to make our mortgage payments on time. Out in the snow, the lot of us! Lucky you are, Mr. Travers, he is indeed to become our son-in-law."

"I am no fool, *Mrs. Travers*, despite what you may believe, and I only dealt with Matthew in the first place because he is so honorable a gentleman. There would never be any cause for concern should I default on my payments. He'd never call in the mortgage, even if his suit were rejected by our daughter, and he remained outside of this family."

"Hmmmph, you know nothing about an *affaire de coeur*, Mr. Travers, if you believe that," Beatrice Amelia warned her husband, thinking men were indeed fools at times. "We cannot afford to take any chances, or make any mistakes now. Things are not as rosy as you would paint them. I know you're planning to sell off that bottom land on the south side of the river."

"The Braedons have wanted that land ever since they got River Oaks Farm, and before that old Merton himself tried to buy it off my papa. Reckon it just might be the time to sell it to them. We don't have much use for it anymore," he explained, his reasoning sounding well even in his own ears, Stuart Travers thought, wondering if he'd fooled Beatrice Amelia.

"I heard you talking to J. Kirkfield Samuelson not more than two hours ago about getting a loan from his bank. I could see he was reluctant to agree to that. Never seen a man who can wiggle and squirm more than he does and never move an inch. Then I heard you tell him you were thinking about selling off those city lots you own in Richmond. Saw him perk up at that. You mark my words, Stuart Travers, J. Kirkfield is a banker first, and a brother-in-law second, and he's the first to remind you of that. Many a time I've heard him say he must think of the bank's investors and answer to the board of directors for every penny spent. And I might add those very same directors he claims he has to be so subservient to are all friends of his. But he is fond of assuring you that if it were up to him alone, then the bank's vault would be open to you. Cold comfort indeed, the tightfisted miser. I've yet to see a penny squeezed out of his bank that he doesn't get back a dime."

"Now, now, Bea. We will do just fine. I don't want you

worrying about this. The memory of the ol' colonel, and that sword he was fond of wearing strapped to his waist, is still too vivid in my mind to ever do anything to disturb his resting in peace. His daughter will never be destitute, promised him that when I asked for your hand in marriage. But good Lord, woman, no one is ever going to foreclose on Travers Hill. This is our home. I'd die before I'd ever let that happen. I'm a Travers! Don't I always manage to find the money we need? Persiana is in foal, and she gave us Tuscany, don't forget that. And when he wins the race on Sunday, well, you just wait and see, we'll be sitting pretty again, and I'll take you to Charleston to get yourself some fancy new gowns and gewgaws, then we'll go to Newport, and enjoy ourselves promenading. And, this is in confidence, don't want to tip our hand to any of our neighbors, but Matthew has been talking, just hints, of course, about leaving Sea Racer here. Put that beautiful stallion in the paddock with Blanchefleur, or perhaps even Damascena. And Matthew will pay plenty for that privilege. Of course, it will be Leigh's decision. Figure we might even be able to get one of the foals as part of the deal the next time, if she, and Matthew, agree, of course."

"I am certain she will. Why wouldn't she, after all, she will be Mrs. Matthew Wycliffe. Naturally, however, since this will occur before their marriage, we will handle it in a completely business-like manner, as if he were not family. We can have Guy draw up the papers. But I declare, it will be quite wonderful once Leigh is married to Matthew. Blythe will be able to go to Charleston now and attend school there. She can stay with Leigh on the weekends. Leigh will be such a success, and that will improve little Lucy's chances of catching herself a husband. She's a sweet child, but rather awkward at times. I could scarcely believe my eyes watching her around that young Justin Braedon. I was quite beside myself with nerves for fear she would spill something. He's a nice young man, but not at all suitable. Good Lord, if she were to marry him, well, he'd probably want her to return with him to the territories. It would be unthinkable. I would never agree to one of my daughters going out to that savage land. I would never recover, I'd be so heart stricken, never!"

"You worry far too much, my dear. None of our daughters, except for Leigh who'll be moving to Charleston, which grieves me, will ever leave Virginia, and then she'll come visitin' half the time. She's got bluegrass in her blood. Life will continue as it always has, with our sons and daughters and grandchildren around us. I've only friends and family, and no enemies that I am aware of who will cause us any harm here at Travers Hill. You work yourself up into a lather needlessly, but then you always have been a worrier. It is a beautiful summer's eve. How about a little stroll into the gardens before we greet our guests. I can remember a time not too long ago, when you and I…"

"Yes, yes, that is a very good idea. I want to check the Chinese lanterns and make certain they've all been lit properly. And I'm not certain we've enough napkins by the punch bowl despite what Stephen says, and last time there was far too much whiskey in the punch for the gentlemen. I declare, it was the dirtiest brown color. I nearly fainted, thinking some…some…" Beatrice Amelia frowned, searching for the right description.

"Yahoo?" Mr. Travers supplied helpfully.

"Exactly, Mr. Travers, that some Yahoo had spat tobacco juice in the punch bowl, and I told Stephen as much, and to be on the lookout for so uncouth an individual, for you'll remember we had a number of those unruly, crude frontiersmen visiting from Tennessee last month, and I still say it was a mistake to invite them to stay up at the house, and you were up all night drinking and telling tall tales. I've never seen so many spittoons so close to overflowing."

"Them Tennessee boys are the best marksmen around. You have to admit, *Mrs. Travers*, their aim was without fault. You can have no complaints on that score, for there wasn't a stain to be found on your waxed floor," Mr. Travers said, grinning, for he had never had such a night.

"Indeed, *Mr. Travers*, I only wish I could say the same for their marksmanship where the chamber pots were con—" she began, not seeing her husband's shaking shoulders as he followed her figure, stiff-backed with ladylike dignity, from the room.

Eleven

No one is so accursed by fate,
No one so utterly desolate,
But some heart, though unknown,
Responds unto his own.

Henry Wadsworth Longfellow

BRIGHTLY COLORED CHINESE LANTERNS SPILLED AN EERIE, amber glow into luminous pools of light that appeared suspended between heaven and earth like small captive moons. The air was heady with an exotic perfume that overpowered the senses. The scent of roses and jessamine, blending with the smoke rising from the flickering candles of bayberry wax, created an incense that drifted along the shadowy paths of the darkened garden as if lost in an Arabian night. Flashes of light, like sparks of fire, appeared mysteriously and, just as quickly, disappeared, before flashing magically again high in a treetop or deep within a spiny hawthorn hedge as fireflies flitted to and fro on fairy wings and enticed strolling couples deeper into the gardens.

Inside Travers Hill, the setting was no less magical. The long banqueting tables were lit by many-branched silver candelabras and decorated with a profusion of fresh flowers arranged in tall cut-crystal vases that sparkled with prisms of dazzling light. Garlands of evergreens were draped around the moldings of the ceiling, the windows, and the double doors, and potted palms and miniature orange and lemon trees were grouped together in the corners of the room where chairs had been placed for those wishing to sit and converse quietly while catching their breath from the more arduous demands of dancing.

The damask-covered tables were heavy with the bountiful feast offered in celebration of a young girl's sixteenth birthday and coming of marriageable age. The tables were crowded with diners progressing from course to course while they inched along a slowly moving line and were offered ample time to choose from a variety of tempting delectables. Silver dishes full of pecans, walnuts, and almonds; molded jellies, pâtés, crepes, and turnovers; consommé clear soups, chilled ones, bisques, and gumbos; shrimp, melon balls, salmagundi, salads, chicken and marinated; oysters on the half shell, crabmeat, and lobster; garnishes and stuffings and relishes; French peas, snow peas, black-eyed peas; asparagus spears, okra and stewed tomatoes, ratatouille; mounds of steamed rice and wild rice, or potatoes, rissole, creamed, fried, and sweet; casseroles and souffles, puddings and puffs; ham and joints of meats, tender veal or lamb, roasted fowl and stuffed game; salmon, trout, and flounder; stacks of muffins, biscuits, hard rolls, and fritters; sauces, Madeira, sweet and sour, tarragon, and apple brandy; pyramids of fruit, fresh, dried, and sugared; cheeses; mousses, cakes, tarts, and charlottes; frozen creams and ices, custards, cookies, and dumplings. And centered in a place of honor, in a great crystal bowl, a mountain of ambrosia, the slices of oranges, grapefruit, and pineapple, blended with strawberries and blueberries, and sprinkled with shredded coconut, ripened overnight in sherry, orange juice, and corn syrup, then chilled, was sweet enticement for those who wished to taste the food of the gods.

A steaming coffee urn, and several decanters and carafes full of assorted spirits, and sparkling silver and crystal occupied the last table.

People drifted from room to room, some choosing to sit and partake of the feast, while others, hearing the soft strains of music from the small grouping of musicians in the corner of the ballroom, chose to dance a reel or two, or if having already consumed a goodly portion from the buffet or punch bowl, a slow-stepping waltz would serve as exertion enough.

"Enjoying yourself?" Adam Braedon asked his young cousin. "Saw you dancing a couple of waltzes with the red-headed Misses O'Farrell."

"They're very charming, and their father is a professor of mine at VMI," Justin Braedon remarked, nodding in polite acknowledgment of several people walking by.

"Well, I'd say the most charming young woman in the room tonight is our young hostess," Adam commented, his light gray eyes following the pale green figure of Blythe Travers as she moved among the guests attending her party, laughter following in her footsteps as she entertained them with a quick-witted, humorous retort and a ready smile.

"Who? Oh, Palmer William's little sister. Yes, quite nice."

"Nice? I hardly recognized her tonight. She's blossomed into a beautiful young woman," Adam said, his gaze searching out her figure again. And he was not speaking in exaggeration, for he had been almost speechless when greeting her this evening at the entrance to Travers Hill. Dressed in her pale green ball gown of ruffles and lace, she had been a startling vision of loveliness. Her dark hair was swept up to reveal the swan-like arch of her neck and the lovely contours of her bare shoulders, and the lacy décolletage of her bodice had revealed a tantalizing curve of soft breast, and Adam had forced himself not to stare like a country bumpkin standing dumbfounded before a queen. Why had he never noticed before what a lovely shade of hazel her wide long-lashed eyes were, and how they sparkled with humor? Her soft skin was creamy and touched with a blushing pink, her lips beautifully shaped and full above her delicately rounded chin, and when she smiled her left cheek dimpled just slightly, and the more he had watched her, the more he could guess by the dimple when she was about to smile. And it was indeed odd that he'd never realized what a perfect height she was. He had come to find it quite tiresome to hang his head low while bending down from the waist to converse with some of the smaller women of his acquaintance. But now Blythe, yes, Blythe was...

"...yes, well I suppose some might consider her pretty, but she is rather quiet. Doesn't say much, although I suppose she is bright enough," Justin remarked, his eyes lingering on a petite blond who was chatting easily with friends nearby.

"Quiet? Little Lucy?" Adam demanded, wondering if they were speaking of the same young woman. He laughed softly as he remembered her charging across the green with a saber in her hand. "Quiet?" he repeated.

"Actually, I rather prefer fair-haired women. A pity only Althea inherited the fair hair from Mrs. Travers," Justin remarked as Althea danced past, held close in the arms of her husband. Dressed in a ball gown of Lyons silk, with deep falls of lace trimmed with dark rose satin ribbons, she was, in Justin's adoring eyes, the most beautiful woman he'd ever seen, and she was married to his cousin. "Although not fair-haired like her sister, Leigh Travers is certainly beautiful, in fact," he allowed as she waltzed by in the arms of a handsome gentleman, "I've never seen her looking quite so lovely. She does have fine eyes, doesn't she, and a very small waist," he added, noting how easily the gentleman's arm fitted about it while they danced. "And she certainly dances well," he said with a look of admiration in his eye as she swung by again, showing a flash of lacy petticoat and slender length of silken calf above apricot-tinted silk slippers.

"Well, I happen to like dark-haired women," Adam said, feeling oddly irritated by his cousin's cavalier dismissal of Blythe, "and admiration is all you are allowed as far as Leigh is concerned. She's engaged, or have you already forgotten?"

"I could hardly forget. My ears are still ringing from the tumultuous cheers that greeted the news. It would seem to be a match made in heaven. Leigh Travers and Matthew Wycliffe. An acclaimed beauty, and a handsome, wealthy gentleman, and a well-respected one at that. And both from good families, and from what I've heard, Matthew Wycliffe is the wealthiest man in the Carolinas. Do you know, I don't believe I have heard a word spoken against the man's name this whole evening? Quite remarkable. You'd think he'd have at least one enemy, would have slighted at least one fellow. Someone must bear a grudge against him. And everyone seems exceptionally pleased by the announcement," Justin stated. "You'd think they were all about to marry the man."

"Yes, so it would seem."

"Except perhaps for that auburn-haired young woman in yellow," Justin said, nodding in the direction of the woman of whom he spoke.

"Sarette Canby. Once she gets over her envy, she will be quite pleased to have Leigh out of the county, and beyond her brother's ear, for I suspect she thinks Leigh has influenced Guy against her. But Guy, when he is thinking clearly, is not stupid, despite the way he acts at times. His temper will get the best of him one day, I fear."

"Wasn't she after you last summer, at least till you took to your heels?"

"Yes, I could introduce you again, but I don't think she'd like army life, and that is what you intend, isn't it?"

"Seems a respectable career. I'm not like my father, or Neil. I am not content to spend the rest of my life in the territories, at least, not as a rancher. Both he and Neil like roaming the hills by themselves, and riding into the high country to hunt. Neither of them answers to anyone. They are lords unto themselves. A pity they don't get along better. Now, I happen to like army life, and having my days regimented. I like order. And, I imagine, I'll be back out in the territories soon enough when I get my commission, but I'll be going back there with the power of authority of the United States government on my side. And I will use it against anyone who breaks the law, whether he be a white man, or a red man. And a Comanche is the worst, for he answers to no man," Justin said, glancing across the room momentarily before emptying his punch glass. "Well, I must say, this has certainly turned into quite a celebration. It was a surprise, of course, to me, about the engagement. However, half the gathering seemed to be holding its breath in anticipation of the betrothal," Justin said with a wide grin, winking at the petite blond who managed to move slightly closer to where he stood in conversation.

"Yes, quite a surprise for some," Adam agreed, his glance finding that same familiar, dark-clad figure across the room that Justin had been staring so intently at only moments ago.

Justin was right. What an evening it was turning out to be, he thought, wondering about all of the undercurrents swirling about the room and promising himself he'd find Blythe and ask her to dance before the evening was over.

"You danced with Blythe earlier, didn't you?" he asked Justin, casually flicking a nonexistent piece of lint from his cuff as if more concerned by that than the answer to his question.

"Yes, as a courtesy to Palmer and the family. It is her party, after all. Stepped on my foot too. Palmer does dote on her, though. And since I'm the same way about my little sister, Lys Helene, I can understand and take pity on both of them. Don't want the wrong sort dancing with your sister. Knows she is safe with me. I'm like a brother to her. Wish I'd been with Lys Helene in Charleston. Had a rotten time, poor child. She's much too shy and came hotfootin' back to the territories after a year. Wasn't good enough for her snooty classmates."

"I liked her when I met her," Adam said, surprised. "Ah, is Blythe's card filled?"

"Believe so, although I feel I should warn the gentlemen to watch their step, but being a gentleman, I'll hold my tongue. Are you interested?"

"I've known Blythe her whole life," Adam said, looking at his cousin as if he'd become a lout before his eyes. But he spoke nonchalantly enough. "As you said, courtesy demands I should ask her to dance."

"Well, since I happen to be on her card for another two dances, I'll allow you to have the honor in my stead," Justin offered, an amorous glint in his light blue eyes as he looked down at the golden head of the young woman now standing at his elbow.

"Your generosity has become my good fortune," Adam murmured, hiding his pleased grin.

"And mine," Justin returned, asking the lovely young woman beside him to partner him in the next waltz that had been promised to Blythe.

With a loud laugh that jarred Adam's nerves, the fair-haired miss walked away with a flirtatious swing of her colorful skirts, Justin's name now on her dance card. Adam eyed his cousin up and down and grinned. "I believe it must be the uniform. I don't believe she even saw me standing here. Or else she thought I was a potted palm. But then the ladies do like men in uniform."

"Now I know why you invested in that ship of yours, so you can strut along the quay in a blue coat."

"I'm only the owner, not the captain, and I never strut," Adam disclaimed. "And you'll not catch me in uniform. I haven't a heroic bone in my body. Hate the sound of gunfire. Lord help me if there's a war, I'll be branded a coward. But despite the advantage you have over me, I'd say I was by far the more fortunate, since I do possess a natural charm, so I never had to resort to wearing a uniform like you lads. A beautifully tailored blue frock coat and a Panama hat was all I needed to attend university. Scarcely managed to graduate even at that. Never would have had I been in uniform, what with all the ladies flirting with me. I would have been far too handsome and charming for my own good. And I would have been worried sick. Damned embarrassing, and uncomfortable, don't you think, if you should sit on your sword by mistake?" Adam commented.

"Ah, there speaks the civilian. You see, the very first training a cadet receives has to do with his sword," Justin declared, his expression very serious. "Lesson One in the manual, 'How to sit down without emasculating oneself.' Every cadet learns that one by heart," he proclaimed, placing his hand over his heart as if swearing to the truth.

Adam laughed. "A little lower, lad," he advised.

"I've never yet heard of any officer to make his promotions who had a high voice," Palmer contributed, overhearing the jesting comments as he came to stand by his classmate.

"Then he's been fortunate never to have met our Julia," Adam added, much to the laughter of the group that had formed around them, for many had been in church that Sunday for services when the Reverend Culpepper had delivered his sermon in a high pitched, squeaky voice, his step that day rather mincing, as if he still suffered some tenderness from the scalding.

"I've come on a mission of the gravest urgency," Palmer said, glancing back toward the door, where a slender figure in pale green silk stood waiting nervously. "I believe you have a waltz to dance," he said conspiratorially, placing a hand around Justin's elbow to guide him forward.

"Actually," Adam intervened, stepping forward quickly, "I have the great pleasure of the next waltz with Blythe."

"Oh?" Palmer questioned, glancing between the two cousins expectantly.

"Yes, I discovered, much to my dismay, that Blythe's card was filled, and I'd not yet had the pleasure of her company. So, since Justin had already danced with her, he very generously offered me the opportunity to dance with the loveliest young woman in this room," Adam said, bowing slightly to them. "And as long as it is a Braedon your sister is dancing with, what difference does it make? We're all cut from the same cloth," he chided as he walked off, stopping momentarily by a vase to pluck a flower from the bouquet.

Palmer stared after him suspiciously, for he knew Adam Braedon too well to take what he said very seriously, and he wasn't going to have Blythe's birthday ruined by one of his jests. But as he watched, Blythe's momentary look of disappointment fled and was replaced by a shy smile as she looked up into Adam's handsome face, then accepted the single rose he offered, then, with her gloved hand held firmly beneath his on his arm, he led her into the group positioning themselves as they waited for the first steps of the waltz to begin. Hurrying into a place next to them were Justin and the golden-haired woman he'd been eyeing, her giggles almost drowning out the first notes as the musicians began to play. And next to them, Julia, dressed in her yards and yards of blond lace, her shining golden hair a mass of curls à la Grecian and stuck with a long feather that kept flicking her partner's nose every time she moved her head. And on the other side of Julia, who was smiling from ear to ear as she nodded at her dearest friend, were Leigh and Matthew, their figures gliding away in time to the music as if they'd danced together their whole lives.

"If I may say so, this county has the most beautiful women in Virginia," commented one of Palmer's classmates as he watched the assemblage of colorful skirts, and the flowerlike faces with their petal-smooth complexions.

"If I may correct you, sir, all of Virginia has the most beautiful women, and in all of the country. I'm from Rappahannock County."

"My apologies. A toast, then! To the lovely ladies of Virginia!"

"I'll drink to that, since I married the prettiest little gal in Appomattox County."

"Another toast, if I may? To all Virginians."

"Here, here!"

"I've never enjoyed such hospitality," offered a young cadet from Alabama, who had been invited by Palmer, along with several of his classmates, to stay at Travers Hill. "To the Travers family, and their home, Travers Hill," he said, holding up his glass to Palmer.

"To the Old Dominion. Seat of liberty, heart of the Republic."

"Despite the fact that a Bostonian, or perhaps a Philadelphian, might dispute that, I'll drink to our honored heritage."

"You've obviously never been to Texas," another gentleman drawled.

"Figure Texas hospitality is kissin' kin to fightin'. I was there just long enough to get snakebit, catch a Comanche arrow in my leg, and learn to hate the sight of mesquite," an older gentleman remarked, rubbing his thigh for emphasis. "Was down there at the border, defendin' the Rio Grande in '46."

"You saw action, then, sir?" asked an eager-eyed young cadet, the gold buttons on his uniform bright and shiny, and untarnished by time or battle.

"Rode down there with Brigadier General Zachary Taylor himself. Old Rough and Ready. Now, there was a feller who knew how to fight Injuns, but then he was a Virginian, and come out of the cradle fightin' on the frontier in Kentucky. I was part of Sam Ringgold's flying artillery. Was just like bein' back at the Point, being trained by him. Saw half of my ol' classmates. Kirby Smith, Sam Grant, William Henry. Lost a good man when the major fell, yes, sir. But my luck was holdin' strong, 'cause I dodged that Mexican cannon fire to cross the border without a scratch. Got all the way down to Mexico City and those pretty *señoritas* in time to see the Stars and Stripes raised high. Landed with Major General Winfield Scott right there beneath their noses on the Gulf Coast, then went climbing into the mountains with nothing more than I could carry on my back, didn't know when I'd eat my next meal. Fought in the battle at Cerro Gordo, then rode with another good Virginian and West Point man, Robert E. Lee, when he and Kearny attacked Chapultepec, an old castle outside the gates of Mexico City, and then we broke through to take the enemy. Reckon that settled the score for what they did to us at the Alamo."

"Sir, did you know a Thomas Jackson? I understand he was in that engagement. He also graduated from West Point. He is a professor now at VMI."

"In that engagement? Son, if it hadn't been for Major Jackson, I wouldn't be alive today to be tellin' you this tale. He and his men laid down a barrage of fire that gave cover to our cavalry. Received a commendation and a promotion for that."

One of the young men in uniform hooted incredulously. "Ol' Fool Tom!"

The older gentleman drew in his breath with an indignant puffing up of his chest. "I don't believe I heard you correctly?"

"My apologies, sir. A slip of the tongue," the young man apologized quickly, for he didn't want his indiscretion getting back to that particular professor.

"No offense meant, sir, but we all feel that we've been in battle when in Professor Jackson's class. Never seen such a stiff-necked, straight-backed, sour-faced man. Don't know how many times I've been skinned by him."

"Heard tell his sour disposition is caused by dyspepsia."

"More likely from sucking lemons."

"And buttermilk. Never seen a man with such a likin' for it."

"Was told it'd settle his stomach."

"Follows the regulations as if he'd written them himself. Preaching them to us like he was quoting from the Bible. Always vowing that we're going to bring down the wrath of God on our irreverent heads."

"Professor Jackson isn't one to forget and forgive, either. Placed one student on report because he was talking in class. Ended up in a court-martial, sir, and Old Jack had him expelled just months before his graduation."

"Reckon, boys, that you've had life too easy. Reckon if you intend on soldiering for the rest of your lives, unless you want them to be real short ones, then you'd better learn about discipline and proper military conduct," the older gentleman, who apparently practiced what he preached, and had lived to reach his age of great wisdom, advised them unsympathetically. "Hard work and dedication, and following orders, that's what makes a man strong, and keeps him alive in battle. I'll tell you this much about 'Fool Tom' as you call him. I never saw a man work harder, show more dedication than he did. Just an orphan boy from the hill country when he came to West Point. He was at the bottom of his class. Didn't know hardly a thing. When he graduated, he was almost at the top. Some of you might remember that. If lucky, you'll get to serve under him one day."

"I'd almost wish that, sir, just to get in a good fight. Wish we were still at war with Mexico. Sometimes I wonder why

I'm going to VMI, except that my brothers and uncles did. Waste of time. Don't know how much good this kind of learning will do when it comes to fighting Indians."

"Reckon you might be right glad of that training in the next fight, 'cause I figure it won't be quite so easy to separate the two sides. Easy enough to take aim on an Indian with a head feather, or on one of Santa Anna's troops, one of them *caballeros* in fancy uniform, but reckon it'd be a damned sight harder to tell a store clerk from New York and a farmer from Georgia apart, seein' how they'd probably be on different sides, but both wearin' blue wool. Reckon we'd have to be changin' our colors if it comes to a fight. Don't know about that? Blue's a mighty fine color, but you got to be able to tell one side from the other, especially when you got a lot of civilians fighting."

"You can't actually believe there truly will be a war between the states, sir?" a serious young cadet demanded.

"More 'n think it, boy. Too much talk now to stop it."

"I would have said there hasn't been enough talk."

"Now when has a slow-talkin', hotheaded Southerner ever listened to a fast-talkin', coldhearted Northerner? Don't talk the same language. I want to talk about tobacco and horses over a lil' corn liquor, and all he talks about are factories and railroads, and tells me he's joined a temperance league and helpin' runaway slaves. No, sir, I say let's have our own republic."

"I doubt we will be able to form one peacefully. You can expect opposition from those who have plans for the South. They won't hold to havin' us mindin' our own business down here. It'll stick in their craw."

"Could be. But no state has seceded yet," young John Drayton said.

"Give 'em time. They will. We're not afraid of a little shooting."

"Virginia won't," John Drayton said, thinking of his sister in Maryland.

"Want to bet on that?"

"I'm a Virginian, and I believe in the Union. I don't want to see it torn apart. I got kinfolks just across the mountains in Pennsylvania and Ohio. If Virginia seceded, and there's war, then they'd be the enemy. I was talking to my father last month when I was home, and he can't believe Virginia will leave the Union. At least the people up around Romney don't want to secede, despite what John Brown did at Harper's Ferry."

"Well, that's surprising, considering that's all we ever hear from you folks the other side of the Shenandoah. Always talking about separating from Virginia and setting up your own state government. Might just be getting your chance sooner than you thought. But as a state in the Union, or…"

"I figure we'll do just fine on our own if we secede. Better even. Tired of them interfering Northerners," John's brother, Talbot, declared.

"Exactly. Can't tell a man how to go about his business. And that's what it comes down to. Stickin' your nose in another man's business. Best way to start up a fight. Reckon I'm not too old to lend a hand to you young bucks should it come to it," the older man chuckled.

"Don't figure it'll last very long, sir. Probably promote you to general, sir, they'll need experienced officers."

"Won't your leg trouble you?"

"Nope. Can still ride, and I ain't plannin' on doin' any walkin', son. I'm cavalry."

"How'd you get that wound, sir? A Comanche arrow, you say?"

"Yup, but should've been my scalp," he claimed, running a loving hand through his fine, gray-streaked hair.

"How did you escape, sir?"

"The fact that I wasn't Texan. Come face-to-face with this Comanche brave. Figured he was going to murder and scalp me right then and there, mean-eyed critter that he was."

"What happened to stop him? Did you shoot him?"

"Nope, didn't have time. As soon as that Comanche caught sight of the man standing beside me, he shoots me in the leg and leaves me to hobble around, that arrow sticking out of both sides of my leg, and believin' I couldn't reach my gun."

"Why did he do that? Why didn't he kill you?"

"'Cause I figure this Comanche wasn't stupid. He knew the difference between a Virginian and a Texan, and as soon as he caught sight of that poor feller from the Brazos, he decided which of us he was goin' to scalp. Speared him with his lance. Got him right through the heart, stickin' him to the ground, then with a yippee yowlin', he scalps him and hightails it into the rocks faster 'n a fox raidin' the hen coop, and with both our horses in tow and wavin' that lance he'd pulled back out of that feller, who was still squirmin'. Never seen anything happen so fast in my life. Just like lightning that Comanche rode in, took aim on us, jumped off his horse, scalped that feller, then was back up on his horse and ridin' away and his moccasins had hardly touched ground once. Got off a couple of shots myself, but he'd dropped low on the other side of his horse, and I couldn't even see him. Besides, don't like shootin' horses. And he was ridin' a real purty lil' pony."

Someone coughed politely, as if doubtful of such a tall tale.

"Don't believe me, eh?"

"I do," Palmer said. "I've heard some hair-raising tales from Justin Braedon. He's from the territories."

"Ought to ask him, he'd know," someone suggested, gesturing across the room.

"Him? He wasn't there," the storyteller said, eyeing with some disgust a tall man dressed in a black frock coat and trousers, the broadcloth of the finest quality, the cut and fit without fault, his waistcoat of black satin, the finely pleated linen of his shirt front and neat neckcloth of the purest white, the bow tied to perfection. "*That* fancy gent! He'd run scared if he caught sight of an Injun! Though they'd have been after him fast enough with that purty golden hair of his," he chuckled.

"Could well have been him doing the scalping, sir. That's Neil Braedon, Adam Braedon's cousin and Justin's half brother. You remember Nathaniel Braedon? That's his eldest son. Nathaniel Braedon was the one who left Royal Bay and went out to the territories," Palmer explained. "A number of years ago Neil Braedon was visiting here, stayed at Royal Bay and traveled up North to school. He and Nathan are still good friends."

"Remember him, I do. Hmmm, got the look of his pa about him," he said grudgingly as he looked closer at the man who could have been any well-dressed gentleman of fashion enjoying a party.

"Neil and his sister were kidnapped by the Comanche. He

was raised as a Comanche brave until his father rescued him. His sister died in captivity. He spent half his life with the savages."

"Sure he isn't the one who scalped that Texan?"

"Why'd that Comanche kill the Texan and not you?"

"'Cause, I reckon a Comanche hates a Texan almost as much as he does an Apache."

"Why is that? I thought the Indian just fought the white man."

"Figure they got their likes and dislikes same as us. The Comanche, now, they're real friendly like with the Kiowa, and the Kiowa, they used to hate the Cheyenne and the Arapaho, leastways till they came to an understanding. A real pity, that, 'cause even though they still don't like each other much, they ain't fightin' anymore, just causin' trouble for the white man. Would have killed each other off, otherwise. But with the Apache, now, that's an old enemy of the Comanche and they're still fightin'. Lords of the plains, that's what them Comanche think of themselves. Long time ago, the Comanche fought the Mexicans and the French, but they didn't give them much trouble, and ended up tradin' together in liquor, guns, and slaves. But now in come these pale faces, pushing their settlements into Comanche territory. These Texans, lovingly called *soldados god dammes* by their good neighbors south of the border, can be just as mean and ornery, and now they're moving west across the Staked Plain, buffalo lands, where the most feared of the Comanche live. The Kwahadies. Best raiders you've ever seen. Once they get on a horse, no one can ride like them, or shoot as sharp. Can't kill what you can't catch hold of. And the Texans are finding that out. Surprise attacks, that's the way of the Comanche. Them Comanche come striking into camp, stealing your horses, and your women, torturin', mutilatin', and murderin' others that ain't worth stealin', burning you out, then just like that they've disappeared across them treeless plains and back into the mountains. Can't catch them, I tell you. Like scorpions, they crawl around that terrain. They think ahead too. Set up another camp nearby, stocked with fast horses, then, after they've raided, they hop on their fresh mounts and ride for hundreds of miles without stopping for nothin'. Don't leave no tracks neither. Some folk say that's because they ride faster than the wind. But the Texans, now that they got themselves a state, they ain't plannin' on leavin', especially seein' how they won it from the Mexicans. So the fightin' is gettin' purty fierce. Don't know how much longer them Rangers can handle things, and so far they only got infantrymen at them forts out on the frontier. Goin' to need the cavalry if they're goin' to win."

"You think this Neil Braedon would give us a demonstration of how a Comanche brave rides and shoots?" someone asked.

"I know he could demonstrate the war cry," Palmer said, glancing around at the assembled guests and wondering how fast he could clear the room if he cut loose with the blood-curdling cry he'd heard Nathan and Adam scream on many an occasion. He, and many a confused and cursing cadet, had been brought up out of bed like a bolt of lightning the first night he had been at school, when Justin, laughing himself off his bed at the reaction of his classmate, had given vent to his war hoop.

"How about a contest? One of our best, like Guy Travers, going against Braedon?" came the suggestion.

"No contest. Guy can ride better and shoot sharper than anyone in Virginia. He's a Virginian."

"Well, boys, now I know Guy is mighty fine, none better in the state, however, if this Neil Braedon really was raised by the Comanche, then I'd have to bet on him."

"He's also half-Virginian," someone remembered.

"Sir! You can't be serious!"

"So serious, young'un, that here's my money. Are you that certain?"

"I'll take that bet."

"And I'll double it!"

"We've got to get the participants first," someone reminded them.

"What do you think, Palmer? Do you think Guy would race against Neil Braedon?"

Palmer rubbed his jaw, a thoughtful look in his soft blue eyes as he remembered his older brother's angry, insulting remarks about Neil Braedon. He also knew his brother had lost a lot of money to the other man and would be more than anxious to win it back and even the score. For some reason, he had taken an intense dislike to Neil Braedon.

"What do you think, Justin?" Palmer asked as his friend rejoined him, his fair-haired partner not straying too far from his side.

"About what?"

"About a race between brothers. Mine and yours. Guy and Neil. To see which is the fastest?"

"We were talking about the Comanche, and Major Smythe, who saw action down in Texas, said that a Comanche was the best rider he'd ever seen, and if there were a race then the Comanche would be sure to win. Well, since the closest thing we got to a Comanche is Neil, and the best rider Virginia has to offer is Guy, we thought we could put it to the test."

Justin shook his head. "I don't think you'll get Neil to race."

"Why?"

"Isn't he good enough?"

"Maybe not." Guy Travers spoke, having come up to join them and overhearing the last of the conversation. "I'm willing to put my reputation on the line, but it seems to me all I've heard this week is how fine a rider Neil Braedon is, how accurate he is with a rifle, and how he can even throw a knife faster than another man can shoot. I feel like I should be down on bended knee before him," Guy said, snorting slightly as he glanced around. "Well, seems to me that's all it has been, talk. I haven't seen any of this great skill we've heard so much about," he challenged.

Justin frowned, wondering what had gotten into Guy, he'd never seen him so argumentative. He was usually a splendid fellow. A gentleman born and bred, charming and amusing, and always a pleasure to be around.

"In fact, seems to me, that all I've ever heard about, for years and years now, is the legendary Neil Braedon, Comanche brave. I've never seen proof of it. Have any of you?"

"I'd let it drop, Guy," Justin said softly. "He is my brother. And although a Braedon, he is also Comanche in spirit, if not in blood. And if he ever agreed to a race, then I would bet on him, because I am afraid you would lose."

Guy glanced at the younger man who had surprised him by his quick defense of his brother, for he had not thought they were especially close. Then he glanced at his own brother, ignoring the warning in Justin's words. "How about you,

Palmer? Would you be as stouthearted in support of your brother's abilities?"

Palmer took his elder brother's arm, and leaning close, and smelling the brandy on his breath, said, "This really isn't necessary. You do not have to prove anything to anybody, Guy. Everyone knows how fine a rider you are. And no one can shoot better."

"I think we do have something to prove, and I'm proposing a little cross-country race, which should test each man's mettle," Guy said. "So, how would you bet, little brother?"

"On you, of course. As I've said, I've never seen anyone ride as well, except, perhaps, Leigh," he added, hoping to add humor to the situation, but he had miscalculated badly, because the laughter that followed his remark seemed to mock Guy's abilities even more.

"Would the gentlemen have to ride sidesaddle or the lady, clad in breeches, astride?" someone joked.

"Now, that would be a race," someone suggested. "Leigh Travers against this Neil Braedon. Would still bet on a Travers, though," he admitted, because everyone knew Leigh Travers, even if just a female, could ride as well, if not better, than her brother Guy.

"The stakes could prove interesting in that race, especially if Neil Braedon won. I wonder what he would demand of the lady," an uncouth individual remarked, his voice trailing away when he caught the glares sent his way by the Travers brothers and their friends.

"Guy, you already owe Neil more than you can pay now. I don't care how good you are, if luck isn't riding with you, then you'll lose. And your luck has been bad all week. Besides, what could you wager?" Palmer tried to talk sense to his older brother.

"And even more to the point," Adam said, having joined the group, but having remained quiet as he listened to the talk, "what would you ride? Rambler came up lame, didn't he?"

"He's almost mended, but I'll ride Apothecary Rose," Guy surprised them by stating, not seeing the look of surprise Palmer gave him.

"Apothecary! Lord, what a race that'd be. He's Travers Hill's best hunter. I thought only your father rode him?"

"I've ridden him before," Guy said.

"Braedon rides one of Royal Bay's bloods doesn't he, Adam?"

"One of our best-bred quarter horses. That's why Neil is here, to purchase more for his ranch, Riovado, and for Royal Rivers, my uncle's spread. They're the best mount you can ride in that rough country. He's already bought up most of our stock. Won't have much money to spend tomorrow at the auction. And Capitaine's the only one he's interested in."

"And we all know he's not for sale. Maybe your father would let him ride Crimson Royal. I'd bet handsomely to see that race. Head-to-head, two men, two horses, and the roughest terrain around. Better than the one on Sunday, I'll wager. When the field gets too crowded, and you're just racing around a track, the fastest will win, if he can break out of the pack, but this, now this riding cross-country takes skill, speed, and cunning."

"How about you, Adam? Who'll you bet on?"

Adam sighed, not liking what was happening, for he was well aware of the enmity between Guy and Neil, although it seemed mostly on Guy's part.

"Well?" Guy demanded, a truculent look on his handsome face, his heavy-lidded, bleary eyes full of defiance, his hand slightly unsteady as he lifted his glass, and more often than he should have that evening.

"*If* there were a race, which I seriously doubt, then I would have to bet on Neil. You're a damned fine rider, Guy, but Neil, well..."

"Neil is better? Is that what you think?" Guy answered for him, his temper flaring, for when it came to riding he'd never been second to anyone, and now this Neil Braedon was being touted above him. And never before had his luck been so bad. He'd always been lucky before Neil Braedon came to Travers Hill. And he'd always had his pick of the ladies. And yet, even Sarette Canby, who'd made it very clear she would accept his proposal of marriage should he have asked, could scarcely keep her admiring gaze from Neil Braedon's tall figure. "Are you certain you still want to back me since you believe my luck is so bad?" he demanded of his brother. "You can always change your mind if you've lost your nerve."

Palmer and Adam exchanged glances, for when Guy Travers set his jaw at that stubborn angle, there was no changing his mind either. "Of course I believe you'll win. And I'll bet on it. But are you certain you'll be able to ride Apothecary? Father loves him like he was his own flesh and blood. Treats him like a child. I don't know what he'll say, or Sweet John," Palmer advised his brother. "And if anything were to happen to him, I don't know what he'd do. Take his whip to you, probably."

"He will say yes. Have you ever known him to let a challenge go unmet? The Travers name is at stake. We can't have our pride ridden into the dust beneath Crimson Royal's hooves, now can we?" he said, grinning, his good humor restored as he thought of Neil Braedon riding in his dust and choking on it as he recouped his losses from the man. "Well?"

"Well what?"

"Are you going to ask him, Justin? Or you, Adam?" Guy asked, glancing between the two Braedon cousins. "Or would you prefer that I do it?"

"I would prefer no one having to, and certainly not you in this mood. However, I will, although I don't have any influence," Adam said with a grimace as he sought Neil's figure across the room. "Neil does as he wants, and he could care less what someone thinks of him."

"Why don't we both go? I'll be right behind you," Justin suggested, grinning, and hoping he wouldn't have to be the one to confront his brother with the suggestion, for he already suspected what his answer would be.

"Good idea," Adam said, "only watch that sword of yours, I don't want to end up riding it if you follow me too close behind. Of course, we could always get Nathan to ask him. But, alas, being of a saner mind, he'd be against it and do our cause more harm than good. For once I'd welcome his opinion and hope it would prevail," Adam added beneath his breath as he suddenly caught Neil's eye and signaled him over.

Neil could feel the tense excitement and anticipation, barely held in check, that pervaded the group as he walked across the room, every eye watching him with more than casual interest as he came to stand beside them.

"Adam, Justin," he said, nodding politely to Palmer, then

to Guy, who gazed at him for a long, assessing moment, then nodded almost insultingly.

"Mr. Braedon, why does a Comanche hate an Apache so much?" someone couldn't resist asking.

Neil smiled, and it raised the hair on the back of the young man's neck as he remembered that this man had been raised by the Comanche and might even have scalped someone— perhaps even that unfortunate Texan.

"For many reasons. And the new feuds keep the old hatreds alive. They have always been the enemy. Although perhaps the most damning reason comes from contempt, because an Apache would eat a horse as soon as ride him, and the horse is sacred to the Comanche."

"Guess a Comanche and a Virginian aren't too different after all," a laughing voice declared.

"To the Comanche, the horse is a god dog. And since the Apache also eat dog, that makes them even less than buffalo dung in the eyes of the Comanche."

"Reckon an Apache and a Northerner have more in common than I thought too," the same gentleman remarked much to the appreciation of his listeners.

"What is a god dog?" one of the serious-minded cadets asked, for if he were posted out in the territories, it would serve him well to learn a bit about the savages he would be fighting.

"Until the horse came to our land, by the good grace of the Spaniards, the dog was the beast of burden for *The People*. He was very valuable to them, for he carried all their possessions on his back and could pull a heavily loaded travois. But the horse brought magic to the tribe. As a packhorse, it could carry far more than the dog and travel greater distances. And when ridden, the tribe could attack its enemies. And it could escape from them. The god dog is powerful medicine. For the brave who can catch him and master him, he will know the glory of victory by defeating the enemy. And he will bring prosperity to the tribe by hunting the buffalo," he explained, his own thoughts echoing with the softly spoken words of She-With-Eyes-Of-The-Captured-Sky when she told him of the great warriors and how *they were no longer bound to the earth, but could soar above the clouds like the eagle, the thunder in the sky, the pounding of hooves against the wind.*

"A brave's life isn't worth anything unless he has a fast mount beneath him. To become a fierce warrior and master of the plains," Neil continued, a strange light in his pale eyes, "is the dream of all young men of the tribe. The horse made that possible, and the Comanche's skill and bravery made it happen. There is a saying that the Comanche lives by, 'A brave man dies young.'"

"Good Lord," an impressionable young man muttered, eyeing Neil Braedon as if he'd suddenly sprouted head feathers.

"How about proving how fast the bold Comanche brave rides?" Guy asked, the tone of his voice doubtful.

"Someone suggested," Adam said hurriedly almost apologetically, for things were getting out of hand, "that it might be interesting to see who was best. We thought a little cross-country race. Crimson Royal is yours for the race. Guy will ride Apothecary."

"You've my hand as a gentleman that I'll make good my debt to you, but I thought you might be more interested in a fine pair of eighteenth-century holster pistols by Barbar of London I wanted to show you. Had offers for them many times, but never sold them. Part of my collection. Also got a pair by Brunn of Charing Cross, and they were used by the Prince Regent himself. I've a pair of dueling pistols made by Wogdon & Barton. Best English made around. I've even got a pair of short-barreled wheel-lock pistols. Sixteenth century. You'll not find many of them around, and not in such good condition. The collection is worth more than what I owe you. I thought we might come to an arrangement, but now, now I'm going to bet them," Guy offered easily, sure of himself as he heard the murmurs of approval from his gentlemen friends, many of whom knew the value of those prized dueling pistols.

"I don't need a pair of sixteenth-century pistols to mount over my fireplace. And I have no use for dueling pistols at Riovado, since I seldom indulge in dueling, or pleasure shooting. I need a gun that will bring down a wolf savaging my cattle, or a puma raiding my corralled horses, and it has to be accurate whether at close range or across a distance of three hundred yards. I carry a Remington and a Sharps. I need nothing more, *unless* you have a Henry .44 rifle you want to pay your debt with, then we might be able to talk. But I've no need of a gentleman's toy I'm not really interested in—"

"Losing? Not surprising, Braedon, that you don't want to destroy your image, since all we've heard from you is only talk," Guy interrupted, stung by the other man's contemptuous rejection of his offer. "Not man enough to prove me wrong?"

But Neil wouldn't rise to the hotheaded, younger man's jibing challenge, his pitying smile as he glanced down at him answering for him as he started to turn away. Insulted, and unable to exercise his better judgment, Guy grabbed his arm, and said angrily, "You ride better, shoot better, probably even whore better than the rest of us, and apparently, you boast better. Bet you'd turn out to be the biggest coward of the lot too."

Even Guy, befuddled from too much drink and allowing his tongue to become indiscreet, sensed the danger and released his grip, taking a cautionary step back when he met Neil Braedon's cold-eyed stare.

"You, Mr. Travers, cannot afford to lose any more than you already have, and since you have nothing I want, this time I will save you the ignominy of being in my debt further," was all Neil said before turning to walk away from the now quiet group.

His face flushed from whiskey and humiliation, Guy pushed his way clear of his silent friends, none of whom would meet his eye, and hurried from the room.

Adam looked heavenward, wondering how he let himself get involved in such harebrained schemes, and the resulting embarrassing scenes. Glancing around, he sought again the pale green figure that he couldn't forget, but she was nowhere to be seen. He smiled. He had claimed that other waltz with her, and although he was impatient to hold her in his arms again, he was not worried, for he had the rest of the summer to pursue Blythe Travers. Adam frowned as he smoothed his mustache a trifle nervously, wondering if she liked him and pondering anew how strange life was. Yesterday he'd been flirting with the ladies, enjoying his bachelorhood, and taking pride in having beautiful mistresses in Charleston and Richmond, but now all he could think about was Blythe, the long-legged, coltish girl with the laughing eyes, who'd grown up right beneath his nose. And he'd never even noticed until tonight what a beautiful woman she'd become. But now, his main concern was that other gentlemen might have taken notice of the blossoming of Blythe Travers. In fact, one of them might have dared to take her into the gardens for a moonlit stroll, he realized, alarmed. Cursing beneath his breath, he thought of her in another man's arms, listening to another man's seductive talk, and he quickened his step as he left the ballroom in search of his newfound love.

Neil stood alone, also searching for one particular figure as the dancers glided by the double doors to the ballroom. He'd watched Leigh Travers all evening, feeling both pain and pleasure as he felt the flame of desire flickering through his blood, quickening it, yet knew that she belonged to another man and would never be his. He'd found himself recalling his first impression of her, when watching her in the golden sunshine of the meadow, and knew again that he would never be satisfied to gaze upon her beauty from afar. He hadn't seen her since that first morning when he'd arrived at Travers Hill, purposely staying away after discovering her true identity, and after listening to the talk at Royal Bay and learning she was to marry a man named Matthew Wycliffe.

She was beyond his reach. She always had been if he had but known it.

But he hadn't forgotten her—he couldn't—or how much he still wanted her. It had been almost self-torture to stay away from her, knowing she was nearby, hearing about her from others, from the friends and family who had every right to speak her name. But to gaze upon her, without being able to touch her, to claim her, would have been far worse. Disgusted, he'd almost convinced himself that he'd been mistaken about the tantalizing allurement of Leigh Alexandra Travers, but he'd deluded himself into believing he was not susceptible to the seduction of her smile, of the graceful way she moved when she entered a room. And so he had not been prepared for the raw emotions that had raged through him upon seeing her again when arriving at Travers Hill for the party held in honor of her sister's birthday.

He had even been deprived of having the satisfaction of

disliking Matthew Wycliffe. When he'd met the man he'd found him to be the perfect gentleman, and, under different circumstances, a very likable one. Intelligent, warm, and friendly, not in the least pompous or pretentious despite his family name and wealth, he was the man a woman like Leigh should marry. Neil had found himself coming to believe that as he'd watched them together. They belonged, and their happiness had been destined long ago. At least, he had believed that until, by chance, his eyes had met and locked with Leigh's dark blue eyes; her gaze, burning with intensity, in that brief, unguarded moment, had revealed more to him than she could possibly have realized. In that instant, her soul had become his, the look in her eyes one of tender yearning, of unfulfilled desire. He had felt strangely triumphant in the revelation, yet at the same time, he felt as if he had suffered an incredible loss.

Taking a snifter from a silver tray being carried around by the majordomo, and offered only to the gentlemen, he moved to stand near a grouping of tropical palms and citrus trees, content to sip his brandy, knowing he would catch sight of her soon enough, and he would somehow manage to be alone with her. He glanced around curiously when he heard voices coming from the far side of the palm, which effectively hid the two people in conversation, allowing them a false sense of privacy. He didn't need to see them to know the names of the two: Maribel Lu Samuelson and her husband, J. Kirkfield.

He remained still, not revealing his presence, not that he wished to overhear their private conversation, but rather because he did not wish to join them in it. One such encounter was enough, he thought, remembering his previous conversation with Maribel Lu Samuelson earlier in the evening. An overbearing, tightly laced busybody who could scarcely catch her breath was the impression he had come away with after being held in her grasp for over half an hour. But out of respect for his stepmother, who was one of her longtime friends and would wish to hear all about this evening in the greatest detail, he had remained, showing polite interest in all that she said. But now, since he couldn't help but listen, he knew a genuine interest in her conversation.

"What a party this has become. Not that I'm surprised.

Beatrice Amelia does know how to entertain. It's in her French blood. Can't fault her there, although I would have set the buffet tables over against that wall instead. And I would have been so disappointed if your gout had kept us from attending. To think that the announcement of Leigh's engagement came tonight! Well, it has been an exciting evening."

"Well, I'm damned relieved. Best thing that has happened to this family, Maribel Lu. Stuart is a fine man, I've no criticism there, but when it comes to finance, he doesn't have a head for business. And unfortunately, Beatrice Amelia's father lost most of the Leigh fortune in bad investments. So there was no looking there for assistance. I'm surprised the Benjamin Leighs are living as well as they are. I have done the best I can, because I'm family, but there is only so much I could have done to keep Travers Hill out of the hands of the creditors. Stuart, with his damned Travers pride, hasn't helped matters any by refusing to be reasonable. Acts as if things were like they were thirty years ago. Well, they're not! I was amazed, Maribel, absolutely astounded, to learn that your brother owes just about everyone in Virginia. Advised him to sell that bottom land to the Braedons, and that property in Richmond. I'll handle that for him, of course. I just hope Matthew Wycliffe knew what he was taking on when he asked Leigh to marry him. From what I understand, however, he knew exactly the position the family was in, because he now holds the mortgage on Travers Hill. But with his money, and being a breeder himself, this will prove to have been a good investment. Can't lose. Can't fault Stuart's head for horses, either. Still has the best stables in the South. Well, Wycliffe has pretty much got himself Travers Hill, debts and all, but I just hope he can manage this family. Don't think Stuart will take kindly if he tries to give advice. Know Guy won't, even if he and Wycliffe are friends. None of the Traverses do. Hardheaded bunch of Scotch-Irish, only wish they were as tightfisted with their money too."

"Do remember, J. Kirkfield Samuelson, *I* am a Travers too."

"I've never forgotten that, Maribel Lu. Indeed I have not, for the Travers name is still much respected and known throughout Virginia. We've gotten a lot of business because of it."

"Well, I am most pleased by the announcement of Leigh's engagement to Matthew."

"Wonder about that," J. Kirkfield muttered.

"Wonder about what?"

"About this engagement. Do you know, Maribel, that young Leigh sought me out in the library earlier today and asked me to tell her exactly what the financial situation was at Travers Hill. I tried to tell her, and most politely, but firmly, that she needn't concern that pretty little head of hers about such things. I was in the middle of an important business deal at the time, but I have never seen such a determined young lady. Said she would wait, then, and stood by my shoulder until I finally got up and accompanied her into the gardens. Made me so nervous, you know how I cannot abide someone standing over my shoulder while I'm trying to think. Well, I must say she looked worried. In fact, I thought she'd been crying, but when I suggested she was worrying needlessly, and she should retire for a nap before the party, and didn't she want to look her prettiest this evening, she actually glared at me and told me she had far more important worries and would I please treat her as if she had a brain in her head. It was not filled with bows and bonbons, and she had a right to know about her family's situation," he said, snorting again with the same sense of surprise he'd felt then, when being accosted by a young female relative demanding to know things she had no business knowing about.

"Well, I hope you told her, J. Kirkfield," Maribel Lu told him, coming to her niece's defense.

"I had very little choice in the matter. I was deathly afraid she was going to make a scene otherwise, and you know how I do dislike scenes. I didn't need a fainting female on my hands. Apparently, she'd no idea how in debt they were. She seemed quite stricken by the whole affair."

"It can't harm, her knowing. Actually, it will be the best thing all around, because you know how proud Stuart is, too proud for his own good. He'd never ask for a penny from her, or from any of his children, so they could starve to death here at Travers Hill without Leigh Alexandra ever knowing a thing about it in Charleston. Not that Beatrice Amelia wouldn't be above it, but then, I don't think there is anything wrong in that at all. I would myself. What are families for? I ask you."

J. Kirkfield snorted. Maribel Lu had never *asked* him a thing in her life. "Well, it did make me wonder, what she said."

"What? What did she say?" Maribel Lu demanded.

"She said something about the sun and a dagger. And there wasn't any time, there never had been, only this summer, and she would do what she had to do, what she was meant to do all along. Thought she was thinking of stabbing herself. Much too scandalous an act. Just foolish talk."

"Well, of course she'll do what she has to do. Must have gotten too much sun this afternoon. I saw her out there near the paddock talking to Stuart James. Now that Leigh has announced her engagement to Matthew, and will be married to him by this time next summer, and now knows exactly how precarious the Travers family finances are, she will be able to help them. It is her duty. I'm sure Stuart James was relieved too, since Matthew is thinking about becoming a partner with him in selling Willow Creek's tobacco crop."

"I think Leigh already knew how bad things were before I told her. That's why she asked me in the first place, so I really didn't tell her anything she didn't already suspect. It was almost as if what I told her, confirming what she knew, had helped her to make up her mind about marrying Wycliffe. If it weren't that he was such a fine young gentleman, I would indeed suspect that was the reason for her marrying him."

"Nonsense. It's a love match. Pure and simple. Why, I've never seen such a handsome couple. He adores her. I've known they would wed since last winter. She probably only wanted to hurry up the wedding in order to help her family. Never a doubt in my mind it would happen. Just when."

"Indeed?" J. Kirkfield said, eyeing his wife in amazement.

"Certainly. Cissy Wycliffe Meegram, Matthew's aunt, is one of my dearest friends. And she told me Christmas last, that Matthew was in love with Leigh Travers. And our Leigh Alexandra is no fool. She's always been a bright girl. Naturally, if Matthew asked for her hand in marriage, she would say yes. And if she were fool enough even to think about saying no, then having discovered how destitute her family is, would have convinced her to change her mind fast enough. Leigh loves her family and Travers Hill. She knows her responsibilities. This is, after all, her heritage too. She is making the right choice. And I ask you, who else would she have married? There is no one finer than Matthew Wycliffe. And, I must say, this whole affair has been weighing heavy on my mind of late. Lost my appetite, and I've tossed and turned every night, J. Kirkfield. I truly do not think I've gotten a night's rest since I started hearing the rumors about how deep in debt the Travers family was. Rumors! The way people will talk, and when it is none of their business. I'll certainly sleep better now, knowing that everything will be fine at Travers Hill."

"Yes, so will I," J. Kirkfield said, sighing with relief as he thought of getting a good night's sleep himself for a change. Hearing a rustling in the palm fronds behind him, J. Kirkfield glanced around, but there was no one standing on the other side, and he returned a thoughtful eye to what Maribel Lu was now telling him about the color of the drapes in the ballroom.

❧

Leigh took a deep breath, filling her lungs with the sweetly scented fresh air of the gardens. It had been hot inside, hot and stuffy, she thought, feeling slightly faint. Tipping her head slightly, she listened for a moment to the cricket's song somewhere in the cool darkness beyond the garden walks.

"Blythe?" Leigh called out softly. "Are you out here?" she called again, thinking she had seen Blythe's figure crossing toward the garden doors earlier.

"Over here," came the answer.

"What are you doing?" Leigh demanded, moving toward the sound of the voice coming from the edge of the terrace.

"My stocking was unrolling, and I didn't want it to fly off during a reel," Blythe explained, her laughter coming easily at the thought. "There! I am once more decent. Mama would have fainted had my silk stocking landed in the punch bowl," she said, stepping out of the darkness, where she'd been making her repairs, her pale green figure looking fairylike as she moved into the lantern's light, a firefly momentarily caught in her hair. "It's a wonderful party, isn't it, Leigh?" she asked a trifle diffidently.

"Yes, it is. Are you enjoying yourself?" Leigh asked. "I've

heard such lovely comments about you tonight. I've been so very proud of you."

"You have?" Blythe said, pleased by the compliment as she hooked her arm through her sister's and they strolled back toward the house.

"Yes, I have, and so have Mama and Papa. He is about to bust a button showing you off to everyone. And Mama said you reminded her of Grandmama Palmer, so gracious were you, and with your dark hair, the same color as hers, swept up so becomingly."

"Grandmama Palmer?" Blythe repeated in awe.

"I saw you dancing with Justin Braedon," Leigh said casually. "He seemed to be enjoying himself very much."

Blythe made a comical face. "Just one dance. He was supposed to dance two more dances with me, but I don't think he will now. He is very much the gentleman, and did not say a word, but I stepped all over his feet while dancing with him. It was so embarrassing. I felt so clumsy and stupid," Blythe admitted, then laughed, surprising Leigh by her lightheartedness over what could have been a devastating occurrence. "Adam came to the rescue. I think Justin must have asked him, begged him probably, but do you know, Leigh, I enjoyed dancing with Adam far more than I did with Justin. I've never realized how nice Adam can be," she said, holding a single rose to her lips as she breathed its fragrance. "I've always thought he was rather wicked, but he really isn't. He's quite charming and amusing, and he is a wonderful mimic. I thought for a moment I was dancing with the Reverend Culpepper. And do you know, I didn't step on his feet even once. I was afraid that I couldn't dance at all until I danced with Adam. And I forgot to count my steps and felt like I was ice-skating. He's quite handsome, don't you think so?" Blythe asked, trying to see her sister's expression in the darkness.

Leigh couldn't believe what she was hearing. Adam Merton Braedon? Charming? Kind? Amusing? Leigh had always thought Adam as amusing as a bee sting.

"He said he thought I was the most beautiful, entrancing woman he'd ever met," Blythe said in almost a whisper. "Do you think he was telling the truth, or just flattering me because it is my birthday?" she asked worriedly.

Leigh swallowed the quick retort that trembled on her lips. "I'm certain he must have been telling the truth," she said quite honestly, for Blythe was indeed beautiful, and anyone who did not think so was just a boorish clodhopper in her eyes. Apparently Adam wasn't as outlandish as she'd always believed if he could be so nice to Blythe. Far nicer, in fact, than Justin had been, Leigh realized, vowing to have a word with him before the night was over.

"Even Julia was saying how pretty you looked," Leigh said, laughing as she remembered the startled look on Julia's face when she'd seen Blythe dancing with her favorite beau.

Blythe laughed. "Did you see poor John Drayton? He went into a fit of sneezing when he danced with her and that feather kept tickling him under the nose. Adam and I started laughing so hard we could scarcely finish our dance," Blythe said. "And Adam said it took half the day to get all of those curls set atop her head, and that Bella threw up her hands in disgust and stomped out in a fit of the sulks when Julia demanded one more, teeny, weeny curl to just touch her lovely, magnolia-tinted shoulder. Guess what Adam calls his sidewhiskers? Piccadilly Weepers! That's what they call them in London. Oh, Leigh, this truly has been the most wonderful night of my life. And I'm so happy you announced your engagement to Matthew tonight. It made everything all that much more special. I don't think I've ever seen Mama and Papa quite so happy. Did you see the way they danced together? It was almost indecent the way Mama was kicking up her heels and showing her ankles. And Papa, he seemed as happy as he was years ago. Not that he isn't happy now, but…I don't know, he just seemed so very happy, almost relieved. You won't be leaving right away, will you?"

"No, not right away. But Mama and I'll travel to Charleston before next month for the announcement there with Matthew's family," Leigh said, thinking about what Blythe had just told her about how happy her mother and father were.

"Matthew is handsome, Leigh. And so nice. He danced with me twice!"

"He is a very nice man, Blythe. I am very fortunate," Leigh said, thinking again about Matthew's tender declaration of love when he'd asked for her hand in marriage, then his happiness when she had said yes.

She had done the right thing by agreeing to marry Matthew. She would come to love him. She already respected him and liked him. And although he had expected nothing in return, never saying a word to her, he had saved her family from dishonor, from the shame of being evicted from their home. Her father would not have been able to live with the disgrace.

Yes, she had done the right thing, Leigh told herself, pushing the vision of Neil Braedon far from her mind. If only she could banish him from her heart as well, she despaired, remembering again the look in those pale gray-green eyes when their glances had met earlier. She'd been watching him, thinking herself unobserved, unable to look away from him, then he had turned, and his glance had captured hers. She had felt so vulnerable before him, as if he could somehow sense what was deep within her heart. A foolish notion, he did not know of her feelings for him. She had glanced away, refusing to look his way again. Righteously ignoring him for the rest of the evening. But she felt damned. She felt as if she were somehow being unfaithful to Matthew. He was the man she was going to marry, the man who would become her lover, the father of her children. He was the man who loved her, cared about her. Not Neil Braedon. Why, then, could she imagine herself only with Neil Braedon?

It was so wrong. It was not meant to be. She had made her decision.

"So, there you are. I've been searching for you. I thought some rakish scoundrel had made off with my only true love," Adam declared, sounding as if he yet again jested as he took possession of Blythe's hand, tucking it safely away inside his bended elbow, his hand holding it there, lest she think of escaping him.

"I have averted social ostracism. It was my stocking, Adam," Blythe returned, her eyes brimming with humor as she stared up into his laughing face. "I was desperately concerned it might end up in the punch bowl when next we waltzed. Can you imagine the scandal? It would have been acceptable if it'd been pink, but 'tis green," she told him with a low chuckle, then catching her breath as he pressed a kiss, as if well accustomed to taking such liberties, against her cheek in response, the possessive arm around her shoulders holding her close against him.

"What an incorrigible miss. I swear, she's won my heart," he said, not quite realizing the import of his own statement, but later he would remember and waste no time acting upon it.

"Aren't you coming in too, Leigh?" Blythe asked as her sister hesitated at the door to the ballroom.

"I saw Matthew a few moments ago. Can't remember who he was with," Adam contributed.

"A business acquaintance," Leigh said. "Someone cornered him earlier and was most insistent about discussing some business deal they were involved in. Matthew couldn't say no to the man, so...I will not be missed if I remain a few minutes longer out here. I've a bit of a headache," Leigh lied, only wishing for the peace and quiet of the garden for a few minutes longer by herself before she had to rejoin the crowd inside, with their well-meant congratulations, their questions coming politely, yet intrusively.

"Our dance, Lucy," Adam reminded her, pulling Blythe after him into the ballroom in time to join the dancers gathering together for the next waltz, the one promised to him.

"Bye, Leigh!" Blythe called out to her sister as she disappeared into the colorful swirl of dancers.

Leigh remained where she was for a moment longer, watching Blythe's beautiful, laughing face as she danced in Adam's arms. Blythe had been right, she danced well, without a misstep, when in his arms, the single red rose tucked in the lacy edge of her bodice. Leigh's eyes widened slightly as she watched Adam incline his head, as if breathing of the rose-scented sweetness of Blythe's warm flesh. Leigh closed her eyes in disbelief, a sudden thought striking her. Then shaking her head, she turned away and wandered out into the gardens, determined to steal a few more minutes of quiet by herself.

Leigh shivered. Odd, she should suddenly feel cold on as pleasant an evening as this. Leigh heard a step behind her and turned around, thinking Matthew had concluded his business and come to find her.

"Matt, did you—" she began, her words faltering as she recognized the tall figure approaching her with the almost catlike tread. He had moved quickly and quietly along the path behind her, never making a sound until he had wanted her to hear him.

Before she could even take a backward step, Neil Braedon was beside her, towering over her as his body blocked out the cheerful, comforting lights shining from the windows of the ballroom.

"You're not in love with him," he said bluntly, his hands reaching out and caressing her shoulders when she would have turned away.

"Whatever do you mean? Let me go, Mr. Braedon. You have no right to say such a thing to me. How dare you!" Leigh finally found her voice, desperate to get away from him, from the look in his eyes, from the touch of his hands, from the isolating darkness that had enveloped them.

"I dare."

"Leave me alone. I have nothing to say to you, Mr. Braedon," Leigh said, turning her face away, but he moved, dragging her along with him until they stood in the lantern's revealing glow.

"Tell me you are in love with Matthew Wycliffe; then, and only then will I leave you alone."

Leigh looked up at him in surprise, wondering at his demand, and opening her mouth to assure him that she was in love with Matthew, but when her eyes met his, she couldn't seem to find the words proclaiming her love for Matthew, words that, if spoken, would mock the feelings she knew she felt deep within her heart for Neil Braedon.

"I am going to marry Matthew," she said slowly, pronouncing each word carefully. "I have pledged myself to him. He is the man I am going to marry. He is an honorable man, a kind man, and he loves me."

Neil smiled, but it was a cruel smile. "You can't say them, can you? Don't look away," he said, releasing her shoulder to capture her chin and hold it tilted up to his gaze as he searched her face for any sign of her true feelings. "You don't love him. Your eyes can't lie, even if your lips might. Do you mold yourself against him, Leigh Alexandra, when he holds you, touches you, kisses you? Do you burn where he touches you? Has he ever kissed you, touched you like I have? I don't think he has, he's too much the gentleman, isn't he?"

"Something you're not."

"No, I'm not. And that is why I stole that kiss from you. Your first kiss, wasn't it? And yet," he reminded her, unfairly, "you kissed me back, as if we had been lovers for a long time."

Leigh lifted her hand to hit him, to stop him from revealing any more of the truth, but he caught her hand before she could strike him, and held it pinned behind her back instead, bringing her breasts against his chest, her thighs pressed to his.

"Have you missed me this week?" he asked, taunting her, wanting to anger her so she would respond to him, forget herself long enough to admit the truth. He hadn't intended this to happen, but when seeing her standing alone in the garden, he hadn't been able to control himself any longer. He knew why she was marrying Wycliffe, but now, he also knew that she was not in love with the man she had promised herself to.

"Missed you? You have an incredible opinion of yourself, Mr. Braedon. One kiss, and a stolen one. A case of mistaken identities. A tumble in the hay, that is what you said you were interested in, wasn't it? And then when you discovered I was more than a wench to be bedded and forgotten, you took to your heels. You wanted a dalliance, nothing more. After all, you'll be returning to the territories very soon, won't you?" she asked, making her tone of voice sound hopeful that there would be no delay in his departure. "You should be quite relieved that I'm to marry Matthew."

"You've sold yourself to him to save your family."

"No! That is a lie. I've known and liked him for years. I've thought of marrying him for some time."

"Thought? Admit it, you only now have decided to marry him because of your family debts."

"You don't know anything about me. About my family. You're nothing in my life. Nothing!"

"Nothing?" he repeated, a challenging glint in his eye. "Your family is in debt. You've agreed to marry Wycliffe in order to keep them from losing Travers Hill."

"My family is everything to me," Leigh whispered.

"And I am nothing."

"You have nothing to do with this. Just go back to the territories. Back to the memory of your beloved wife. And leave me alone. I don't understand why you're saying these things to me. What does it matter to you?" she challenged.

"Maybe I'm not just interested in a dalliance as you claim."

Leigh pressed her hand against his chest, trying to push free from his embrace, to gather her strength against him, against the seduction of his words.

"Am I to feel honored by such a declaration? Whether you are interested in a dalliance, or more than a dalliance, is of no concern to me."

"Isn't it?"

"No."

"For once be truthful. Admit that there is an attraction between us. Or am I to assume that you kiss every stranger like you kissed me?" he asked insultingly.

"If you think that, then—"

"No, Leigh. I don't believe that. And that is why I'm here. And I think you know that too."

Leigh swallowed the fear rising inside of her. "If I felt a momentary attraction to you, then that was all it was," she said, trying to laugh. "Infatuation, Mr. Braedon. That was all it was," Leigh said bravely, almost convincing herself that it was true.

"Prove it to me."

"I don't have to prove anything to you."

"Scared? No? Then prove that you're in love with Wycliffe. If you can, then I'll leave you alone, and agree with you that we were briefly infatuated with one another, and I'll trouble you no longer," he said, but he didn't give her a chance to answer him, and his mouth closed over her slightly parted lips as he kissed her deeply, moving so she had to lean against him or fall.

Leigh shuddered uncontrollably at his touch. His mouth was hard against hers. His lips were rough and demanding, then soft and persuasive, barely touching hers. They lifted for a tantalizing second before they returned to claim possession again, the pressure even deeper until her mouth parted wider, allowing a more intimate contact between them as his tongue touched her lips, sliding along them and feeling their shape, then moving between to touch and taste the moist softness of her tongue.

His arms held her against him, until each breath she struggled to draw into her lungs became his. His hands followed the smooth, tapering contours of her back, then settled possessively around her waist for a moment, holding the slender roundness clasped between, and held so easily by his greater strength, before moving to caress her arms, one of his hands sliding the thin gauze of her sleeve from her shoulder to leave it bare beneath his hand. He slid his hand down, to touch the soft rise of breast, the heat from her flesh sweetly scented as his fingers slipped underneath the edge of her loosened bodice and found the delicate nipple that had budded beneath. To feel it taut and hardened was proof enough for him.

He released her lips, his mouth moving along her flushed cheek to her ear, where he nibbled gently, the heady perfume of jessamine and roses from the garden entwined in the thick braid of chestnut hair crowning her head forever to bring memories of Leigh Travers to his mind.

"Deny me. Deny what is between us, Leigh, and you damn us both," he told her harshly, then becoming still, hope filling him, when he felt her touching him, her breasts pressed against him as she caressed his neck as her hands moved to cradle his head, her fingers sliding into the curls of golden hair that just barely touched his collar, her lips opening beneath his, no longer denying him as she sought his kiss.

"There you are, Braedon!" Guy's slurred voice sounded out of the darkness. "I thought I saw you come out here. Want to finish that business once and for all."

Leigh heard her brother's voice and stiffened in Neil's arms, then she tried to move free of his embrace, but he would not release her. "Please, let me go," she begged, trying to pull up her sleeve with an unsteady hand, suddenly feeling the coolness of the evening air against her bared breast.

For what seemed an eternity, he stared down into her face, memorizing each feature, her lips soft and full from his kiss, her eyes heavy with the passion they had shared. His hands tightened unconsciously on the delicate bones of her shoulders for a second, then he released her and turned to face Guy, a dangerous glint in his pale eyes.

"Guy?" Leigh questioned worriedly as she moved from behind Neil and watched her brother stagger forward drunkenly. But despite his condition, she had never been so happy to see someone in her life. His timely arrival had saved her from betraying her family—and of betraying her own honor. She had promised to marry another man and she would not dishonor him. A moment of stolen passion, with a stranger, in a darkened garden, could not answer for a lifetime of shame.

"Leigh? What are you doing out here with this swine? Trying to take liberties with you, has he? Not surprising. He's no gentleman, Leigh. Could've told you that."

"No, Guy. He was…was just offering me his congratulations on my betrothal," Leigh said, not looking at Neil, even though she felt his piercing stare when she made her explanation. "And…and he wanted to know if I was interested in selling Capitaine," Leigh added, remembering her conversation earlier in the evening with a man who, despite her refusals, was determined to buy the colt.

"The fool. You'll never sell him. Capitaine is not for sale, Braedon, and never to you even if he was. Go inside, Leigh. Braedon and I have some unfinished business to take care of. I won't be but just a minute," he said arrogantly, thinking to deal quickly with Braedon.

"What is this about, Guy?"

"Won't race me. Knows I'll beat him. Says I don't have anything he wants. Doesn't think I'll pay my debt to him. Well, I'm a gentleman, and I always pay my debts, even to riffraff like him. But I've a far better way of paying this one," he said, stepping closer, and into the light.

"No, Guy. Please. Put it down!" Leigh cried when she caught sight of the pistol in his hand.

"Went and got my dueling pistols. My gentleman's toys, as you called them, *Mister* Braedon. We'll see who's the best shot since you're too much the coward to race me, to give me the chance to win back what I lost to you, like a real gentleman would have. Well, I challenge you, sir, to a duel," he said, stepping forward unsteadily and slapping Neil across the face with one of his gloves. "Turned me down in front of my friends, made me look the fool, well, try to turn me down this time, sir, and you'll be branded the coward I already know you to be."

"Guy, stop it!"

"Stay out of this, Leigh. This is between Braedon and me. We'll finish it here and now. We'll see how accurate my pistols are at twenty paces, eh, Braedon?" he said, holding out the other pistol he carried for Neil to accept, which he did.

"Oh, Guy, no, don't!" Leigh cried, too late, for Guy had already walked across the garden to take a stand before an old cedar, his pistol held out before him, and remarkably steady considering all that he had consumed. He took aim on his opponent.

But neither Leigh nor especially Guy could believe what happened next. A knife had embedded itself in the tree beside his head. And there was no doubt in anyone's mind that it landed where it had been carefully aimed. Limply, Guy dropped his arm, stunned by how close to death he had come.

"I will not duel with you, Mr. Travers," Neil told him.

But Guy, drunk as he was, or perhaps because of it, felt a surge of pride and courage quickening in his Travers blood. "I insist, sir," he responded, raising his arm and the pistol again.

"Very well, sir, but this is hardly a fair match. You have been warned."

"I insist, sir! 'Tis a matter of honor."

"Unfortunately, yes."

"Please, you can't do this!" Leigh pleaded, rushing between them. "He's drunk. He doesn't know what he is doing."

"Ah, but I do, sister dear. Will ten paces serve, sir, rather than twenty?"

"Quite acceptable."

"On the count, sir?"

"At your discretion, Mr. Travers," Neil responded cordially. "Please, Leigh, get out of the line of fire."

"No, no, I won't move! Stop this! This is madness. You don't hate each other. You are not enemies. No real harm has been done. Your damned pride. That is what it is all about, Guy."

"I would advise you to move, Miss Travers," Neil advised, playing with the gun as if testing its weight and probable accuracy. "Very nice."

"I did tell you so, sir."

"Yes, you did."

"No, no, please," Leigh cried again, glancing between the two men as if they were crazed. But Guy, with a casualness that bespoke his drunken state, had stepped slightly to her right, and had taken aim again on Neil's tall form.

Neither man spoke. Suddenly there was a flash of fire, then smoke, the roaring of the pistol deafening.

Leigh stared at Guy in disbelief, but he continued to stand upright, his eyes never leaving Neil.

Leigh followed his gaze, dread filling her, but Neil had not fallen. He still stood.

"My shot, I believe."

Even through his drunken haze, Guy, upon meeting Neil's eyes, knew that death awaited him. But he stayed where he was, facing it with the pride he had been born with. "I hope your aim is as good as you have claimed, sir. I do not wish to linger. And 'twould be even worse to be maimed."

"I'll do my best," Neil said, his lips twitching slightly.

"Thank you."

"You can't shoot him!"

"Leigh," was all Guy said, shaking his head.

"I wonder. What is your brother's life worth?" Neil asked, his pistol aimed at Guy's heart.

Leigh stared at Neil, wondering what kind of man he was to bargain with another man's life. But Neil had no intention of killing Guy Travers, despite the fact that Guy had not missed his shot. His aim had been almost on target, and a wound now bled in Neal's shoulder.

"What do you want?"

"Your brother has nothing I want, but you, Miss Travers, do."

Leigh glanced around, wondering why no one had heard the shot, but as she looked toward the house, she heard the sound of music and voices. No one would have heard anything unusual, and certainly not a gunshot they were not expecting to hear.

"Go on, Braedon! Get it over with!" Guy said, his nerves finally beginning to tighten under the strain. "Pull the trigger!"

"What do you want for my brother's life?" Leigh asked him.

Neil wanted to hurt her, wanted to take something dear from her. "I'll take your colt, Miss Travers. Give me the colt, and your brother lives," he said, hating himself in that instant for what he did, but he had lost her, and he wanted her to suffer some of the pain he was feeling. When he left Virginia, she would not soon forget him. He would take something dear to her heart with him. And she would remember him.

Leigh stared at him in disbelief.

"You claim to love this family of yours so much that you'd even marry to save them, so won't you give up this prized colt of yours for your brother's life, Miss Travers? Too great a sacrifice?"

"You can't be serious?" Guy scoffed, feeling as if he'd already been shot. "Leigh loves that colt," he said, glancing over at his sister in dismay, and finally feeling some of the guilt for his actions.

"I'm very serious, Mr. Travers. I can use that colt. Far more than I can your death on my conscience. And remember this, when you die, your debts would become your family's. I would, however, consider your debt paid, *if* I received your sister's colt as payment. Surely your life is worth that much? I came to Virginia to buy horses. This colt would suit my needs admirably. And since I will, no doubt, not be welcomed tomorrow at the auction, I'll make my bid now. I want the colt."

"You bastard!" Guy said, slumping against the tree.

"It's a deal, Mr. Braedon," Leigh told him, feeling as if she were truly seeing him for the first time, and he was once again a stranger to her.

Neil lowered the pistol, uncocking it. "Your debt is paid in full, Mr. Travers," he told Guy.

"Don't ever show your face on Travers property again," Guy warned, "or next time, you won't walk away."

"You needn't fear, for I will not be returning."

"We'll send Capitaine over to Royal Bay. Don't bother coming by to collect your winnings," Guy told him. "I'll shoot you for trespassing if you show your devil's face around here again."

"Believe me, you'll be in hell when you see my face again," he told him.

"What's going on here?" a voice demanded, and recognizing it, Leigh turned to see Matthew coming toward them.

Neil glanced back only once. He saw Leigh running across the garden and into the outstretched arms of Matthew Wycliffe.

Part Two

Virginia—Winter 1864

In the winter wild.

John Milton

Twelve

THE DENSE WOODLAND WAS QUIET. THE TREES, BARREN of leaf, stood like sentinels against the gathering dusk, the ashen sky above darkening with clouds that were sullen and heavy with the approaching storm.

A low rumbling of thunder sounded beyond the hills in the distance. Echoing closer was another, far more ominous sound that became discordant as it grew louder. It was the sound of marching feet as foot soldiers trudged along the muddy road, packs weighing them down, their muskets and rifles held at the ready in case of ambush. The sound of horses' hooves and the creaking of harness and ringing of spurs followed as the cavalry came next, outriders racing ahead to reconnoiter. Then came the artillery, with a rumbling of wheels as cannons and guns were pulled along behind, followed by the cracking of the teamsters' whips as mules strained against the heavy weight of wagons loaded with supplies and baggage, and ambulances crowded with the wounded and dying. It was an army on the move. But with darkness falling, the commander would soon call a halt to his troops' march, setting up picket lines as they made camp. The warm glow of fires would appear in the darkness as they settled in for the long night, the lonely outposts keeping guard against surprise attack.

"Who do you think they are?" came a disembodied voice from a tangle of bushes in a thicket nearby.

"Where the hell did they come from?"

"Reckon it could be a ghost column? Marchin' through the night with ol' Stonewall Jackson himself leadin' them into battle, chargin' the front line on that ol' sorrel of his?" someone asked, his imagination heightened by the surrounding gloom. Another soldier, tired and cold, and scared, glanced around, almost expecting to see a ghost rider in gray, saber drawn, come charging up behind him, his mount snorting fire and damnation.

"That Stonewall Brigade of his sure fought hard when retaking Romney," another man remembered.

"I was there at the first, at Bull Run, when he stood there like a stone wall orderin' the charge. Still got a scar on my shoulder from the bayonet wound given me by one of them damned Virginians. Thought a devil was comin' at me the way that fella was screamin' fer my blood."

"Heard tell some of his men called him Old Blue Light, so God-fearin' and pious was he."

"Holy as that, eh? Reckon he could still be out there ridin' right now. Man like that don't die easy nor rest when he does."

"And to think he was shot down at Chancellorsville by one of his own men mistakin' him fer the enemy."

"Hush!" a throaty whisper cautioned. "You want *him* to hear, and he ain't dead. Leastways, not yet."

"Shucks, hear anything over that ruckus? Besides, he disappeared across the meadow. 'Course even o'er there he could hear you break wind. Seems as if he can see in the dark better 'n most can in the daylight, so reckon he can hear better too. Betcha it's a column of butternuts. Ain't goin' to be any bluecoats, 'ceptin' fer us, this deep behind enemy lines."

"Unless you want him after you, Bucktail," someone advised the Pennsylvanian, "I'd be as quiet as a mouse within spittin' distance of a cat's whisker."

"Faith, but ye'd better be listenin' to him now, don't want to end up way down in Georgia, stuck in Andersonville like a flea-bitten rat, d'ye? Nothin' comes out of there alive, even the plague. And I'm thinkin' I wouldn't want to be buried in red clay without receivin' the last rites, some Baptist preacher standin' over me instead. Aye, me poor soul would be damned then, and me mother, bless her, would turn in her grave to think a Protestant was prayin' over her only son."

"If anyone gets us caught, then it'll be you, you bigmouthed mick, and your mother is still alive. You had a letter from her just last month, read it to you myself."

"All the way from Ireland? Thought yer mam couldn't read nor write?"

"Well now, she'd heard about the fightin' over here, and she got the fine and fancy lady she does washin' fer to write it down fer her. That worried she was, that she sent me her own cross, and blessed by the same priest who was there fer me christenin'."

"He's got a lot to answer for."

"Well, I'm wearin' it now, around me neck, and it's kept me safe, and against me heart I've me dear mother's lovin' words, and written by a beautiful, kindhearted lady, so 'tis double-blessed, I am. Besides, I fear *him* more than I do a whole regiment of graybacks."

"Keep rememberin' that, Hay Foot, and the cap'n'll get us out of these damned woods alive," the Bucktail suggested.

"I know me left foot from me right better 'n yerself, Straw Foot."

"If you both don't shut up, neither of you'll have any feet to worry about 'cause they're goin' to be shot off," someone told them, looking over his shoulder, then giving a reassuring pat to the pocket-sized Bible he carried in his jacket. A ragged hole torn through the middle of it from a bullet that had lodged in the New Testament instead of his heart bore silent witness to his continued faith.

"Probably end up gittin' shot by an ol' backwoodsman who don't even know there's a war goin' on, jus' out shootin' squirrels and drinkin' corn whiskey, and sees this here feller with the deer tail stuck on his cap, and mistakin' him fer a buck's ass 'cause he's so ugly, or even a scrawny tom turkey if his eyesight wasn't good, wings him with his fowling piece."

"Seem to recall you joined up carryin' an old flintlock musket yourself."

"Right you are, but got me a Spencer repeatin' rifle now. Only have to load it once a week, dependin' that is on how many rebs I bring down."

"D'ye know," the Irishman said, pulling the sleeve of his heavy wool overcoat free of a bramble, "I bet these woods are full of blackberries come summertime, sweet and juicy, and this creek here, the trout would be that fat and fine, they would. Used to dream about layin' meself down in sweet bluegrass and ridin' easy a soft-skinned saucy lass when I was workin' the rails."

"The only thing risin' is goin' to be flowers over yer bleached bones come spring, navvy, and the only grinnin' will be on your skeleton head, all the fat rotted away, if you don't hold your tongue."

"Better that than goin' back to the coalfields like you, boyo. Ye Welshmen never learn, not like the Irish, now. Hear tell there ain't no place on a coal miner's body that damned soot don't get in."

"Hey, an eight hooter, listen to that," the Bucktail said, stilling as the *whoo, whoo, whoo, whoo—whoo, whoo, whoo, whoo-ah* sounded from the branches of a big sycamore overhead.

"Better be careful, lad, 'cause that means he might be out huntin' skunk this time of year. This is when skunks come out to mate."

"Lucky devils!"

"Hell, from the smell of ye, bet the skunk comes courtin', and he won't have any trouble findin' ye," someone said with a low hoot of laughter.

"Well, pardon me, but I didn't have time for my ablutions this mornin', seein' how my valet let me oversleep and I hardly had time for more than a bite or two of my apple dumplings and sausages, and the fool didn't press my trousers worth a damn."

"Just as well he didn't, I think we're squattin' beneath where that owl's been roostin' anyways," someone murmured with distaste, wiping his hand on the side of his muddy trousers.

"Reckon there's one thing these Virginians know how to do, and that's smoke ham. Best I've ever eaten. 'Twas especially sweet when we stole it right out from under the nose of Jeb Stuart himself. Remember that day with all of us sneakin' 'round Fredricksburg, didn't know who was wearin' blue and who was wearin' gray? In one of the first skirmishes I was in, up 'round Falling Waters, before I joined up with you lads, nearly rode back into Richmond with Stuart himself. He was still wearin' his ol' blue army uniform. Hell, I thought he was one of us, after all, they say he was a West Point man same as half the reb officers. Heard later he captured fifty or more prisoners when they threw down their weapons 'cause he rode right up to them without them firin' a shot, thinkin' he was their commander. Heard tell now he's taken to wearin' a tasseled yellow sash and a foot-long ostrich feather stuck in his hat, and when he rides into battle his scarlet-lined cape billows out behind him and makes the enemy madder 'n bulls bein' baited. Makes a fine target. Should've kept wearin' his ol' blue and kept everyone more confused than they already are."

"That's one way of smokin' out the enemy. Oughta try that kind of switch more often."

"McGuire here, now he knows how to smoke a ham. Blew up a depot full of salt beef and pork barrels last week."

"How was I to know that's what was in them. Faith, I only wish you hadn't run away so fast like you was buckshot. We could've had quite a feast that mornin'."

"Yeah, ham stuck full of rusty nails instead of clove buds."

"I took some hardtack off a dead reb. Foulest tastin' stuff I ever ate. A piece of sheet iron would've had more taste. Figured he died from eatin' it and not from my bullet."

"Speakin' of sweet things to be dreamin' about. I'd turn traitor for some roast goose with apple stuffin', plump noodles, and sauerbraten."

"You ain't Dutch, thought you'd want stew," someone reminded the Irishman.

"No, but the widow who used to cook me supper was. Never quite got to finish me sauerbraten, but she always gave me some of them tasty crullers to take with me when I left the next mornin'. Called them tangled britches, she did, laughin' as she tried to straighten mine out of knots, but then she was an eager wench. A fine, lusty woman, she was. Buried two husbands in three years."

"Lucky you volunteered. You've a better chance of survivin' facin' a twelve-pounder, McGuire."

"Well, I'd turn the whole lot of you in just for some griddle cakes," said one of the younger soldiers with a sigh, the memory of his mother's griddle cakes still strong in his mind, not having met anyone like the Dutch woman.

"Wonder where the cap'n is. It's startin' to drizzle. Might even snow before dawn. It's goin' to be a cold night. Reckon this creek will ice up," one of the men grumbled, rubbing his stiff hands together.

Hunkered down on the bottom of a creek bed, the men waited, listening nervously to the rumble in the distance, the cloud of vaporized breath from their mounts creating an eerie fog around them.

"How you reckon the cap'n knows this land so good?"

"Don't know, but I ain't questionin' nothin'. Been ridin' with the cap'n fer three years now. Ain't many lucky enough to still be around to claim that, and 'specially after all the action we seen. Figure by now I know Virginia as well as any man born and bred right here, even General Robert E. Lee himself."

"'Ceptin' fer makin' sure that yer gun is shootin' clean, an' he's real mean about that, the cap'n don't care if yer boots ain't blacked, or ye're missin' buttons, an' yer hair ain't been trimmed in a month of Sundays, or even that ye ain't got no extra pair of drawers. He's more concerned about how ye packed yer cartridges than how ye packed yer knapsack."

"Figures that ain't important if ye ain't alive."

"Yep, best thing that happened to me was gettin' transferred into the cap'n's outfit. He's never left a man behind yet to die or to be buried deep in an unmarked grave, forgotten by his kin."

"Well, he didn't pick you 'cause of yer good looks."

"Best sharpshooter here, that's why," the man boasted proudly.

"You got the fastest mouth here, and that's the truth too."

"It'll be Henderson this time that gets sent out."

"Me?" a small, slender-built young man squeaked, his boyish voice hardly having had time to change before he'd volunteered to do a man's fighting.

"Yep, my horse threw a shoe this mornin'. And next to my mare, and, of course, the cap'n's mount, you got the fastest horse here. If he gets the information he wants about this troop movement, then he'll be sendin' back a courier to Headquarters. Better get yourself ready, son. Only hope we can get out of here before the fightin' starts. Usually does when we're around, and we end up sittin' right in the middle. Figure one of these days our luck ain't goin' to hold and we're goin' to get caught without no way of escapin' the rebs tightenin' a noose around our necks."

"What the hell was that?" someone demanded, his hands tightening around the butt of his rifle.

"Jus' McGuire, lettin' out a little hot air from the other end this time," someone groaned.

"Well, now, would ye rather I blew up like a balloon and floated out over the enemy lines, then?"

"Would ease some of the sufferin' in our lives."

"Figure that's the best way of doin' some reconnoiterin', way up high in the clouds where no bullets can reach you," a voice sounded wistfully from the muddy bank.

"Think ol' Thaddeus Lowe has missed out on a real good man here for his Balloon Corps by not signin' up McGuire. Don't need no fancy gas generators with him around."

"Remember when we come face-to-face with two regiments of mounted infantry? Jus' mindin' our own business after settin' them charges, waitin' fer the bridge to blow sky-high, when up they ride bold as brass and grayer than a grave digger's face on a stormy night."

"Yeah, lucky for us the bridge blew just then, catchin' them by surprise and we had a chance to ride while they were still calmin' down their horses and tryin' to figure out where we'd skedaddled to, not knowin' like we did that there was another hollow with a real nice dry creek bed just beyond the road that we could race up unseen. 'Course, since we'd blown the bridge, there wasn't no way for them to get across that river real quick even if they had seen us. Smart the cap'n is, 'cause he'd already scouted ahead and knew where we could ford it and we were across and scootin' into the hills before them rebs could give the cry."

"Reckon the cap'n's got another bridge fer us to blow?"

"If he don't then I've been carryin' around this pack of black powder fer nothin'. Don't like sittin' on top of it."

"Good thing fer us ye're carryin' it and not McGuire, ye know how tetchy that powder can get, one spark and varrooom!" someone said, ribald laughter following the comment, but the jesting did little to relieve the tension, for they all knew the danger. No one had forgotten the charge that had exploded prematurely and blown off the arm of the man setting it. He'd died before they could get him back to camp.

"Hope the lieutenant don't trip over his own big feet again like he done last time, his pistol firin' wild like it did, shouldn't' a had it cocked. Nearly got us all killed that day, warnin' that picket on duty. Still nursin' that raw spot on my backside where his shot grazed me, and it wasn't from the reb's gun, either. Hell, the lieutenant's s'posed to be on our side, ain't he?"

"Well, let's just hope his spectacles don't fog up like they did the last time he was out scoutin' with the cap'n. He can't even see his own two feet in front of him without them specs."

"Figure the best way of savin' ourselves, is fer each of us to git a pair jus' like his and carry 'round in our pockets jus' in case he loses his like he did las' week. Had the camp in an uproar till we found them, an' they was pushed up on top of his head the whole time."

"Always bent over double makin' them little drawings of his. Can't make head nor tail of them, myself, but the cap'n says they're worth more 'n gold. Heard the cap'n wasn't too pleased at first, havin' the lieutenant along, seein' how he ain't a very good fightin' man, an' you remember, he could hardly even sit a horse. Reckon he'd always ridden around in a carriage?"

"Hasn't fallen off in over a year now," someone added.

"Yeah, but he still can't shoot straight. I was outside the cap'n's quarters the day the colonel told the cap'n that since we was goin' behind lines, deep into enemy territory, that we might as well have someone along to map it, so when the rest of the army comes chargin' in they don't end up bogged down in a swamp or with their backs up against a steep river gorge. Fought him hard, he did, the cap'n, sayin' how he didn't have no time fer some feller who couldn't ride and shoot and get the hell out when the bullets come flyin'. Said he was a raider, not a sucklin' nurse fer some babe."

"Figure the little mapmaker is doin' all right. Bein' so quiet, and soft-spoken, and gentlemanly, not like some I could mention, he ain't never given away our position, 'ceptin' fer that one time, and after that the cap'n told him to keep his pistol in his holster in future or he'd take it away from him. Don't think he's ever had it out or fired it since."

"We can all rest easy."

"Yeah, well let's hope nothin' happens to them," someone said, squirting tobacco juice across the creek with a fine aim, a brown stain appearing on a large flat rock, "'cause I don't know how we'd get back out of here without the cap'n, and the lieutenant's the only one with a compass. Don't forget that."

The lieutenant in question was following his captain's steps unerringly, carefully placing each foot squarely down in the exact footprints where his captain had stepped only moments before, and so quickly that there hadn't even been time for the prints to fill with the rain now falling heavily.

The captain's dark figure moved without hesitation, as if he'd skirted this meadow before, in a more peaceful time, weaving in and out of the trees along the perimeter, only pausing once to survey the field, which bore traces of battle, before ducking beneath the brushwood and disappearing into the dense woods that sloped toward the narrow road below.

Lieutenant Chatham pulled his low-crowned kepi down lower over his eyes as he peered up at the sky. Cursing the inclement weather beneath his fogging breath as he shivered down deeper into his caped overcoat, he nearly bumped into the captain, who had stopped suddenly and crouched down low, never making a sound.

The lieutenant seized the opportunity to pull off his metal-rimmed spectacles, quickly cleaning and polishing the round little lenses with his fine linen handkerchief as he glanced around at the blurred, inhospitable world that surrounded him. Putting back on his spectacles, he peeped owlishly at the woods now brought back into sharp focus, but no less frightening to his timid soul. His gaze, however, had not missed the distance to the river, or its width and probable depth and speed of current, or the ridge rising to the east, his mind instantly memorizing every detail; the degree of slope, the spacing of large trees, the ease with which heavily laden wagons and cannon might surmount it.

Dropping down on his hands and knees in a most undignified position for a member of the Chatham family of Boston, he followed the captain through the tangled underbrush, feeling the sting of scratches from thorny branches slapping his face. The full beard he wore provided some protection, but it did little to mask his youthfulness. He breathed a sigh of relief as he knelt beside the captain, who had now trained a spyglass on the long gray column trooping past on the road below. It was strange, but he never felt afraid when in the captain's company. Even though the captain's course always led them behind enemy lines, and, sometimes, right into the enemy's camp, he had complete faith and trust in the man, as did all of the men who followed him.

He'd learned just last week that the captain had a rank of brevet colonel, but everyone still thought of him as the captain.

After all, his nom de guerre was Captain Dagger.

Unlike his Confederate counterpart John Mosby, who with his Rangers were the best band of guerrilla fighters in Virginia, no one seemed to know Captain Dagger's real name. Probably better that way, Lieutenant Chatham thought, for retribution against the captain's family would be difficult to accomplish. And he suspected the captain's family lived in these parts, or somewhere along the frontier, or in Texas, or even the territories. Some misinformed people, many frightened by the rumors that spread like wildfire through the civilian populace, were beginning to believe Captain Dagger was another Quantrill, the murdering bushwhacker who raided and looted along the Kansas-Missouri border. It would be far safer for all concerned if Captain Dagger's identity remained a mystery. Lieutenant Chatham shook his head in disgust, for the captain had never pillaged during one of his raids, although some of the men jokingly claimed they struck too fast to loot. Like lightning striking a tree, leaving nothing more than smoke curling into the sky to show they'd been there, the lieutenant thought proudly. Nor had they ever murdered innocent civilians, or harmed them in any way. The captain had warned each of them that he'd rip the genitals off any man found guilty of such an offense, then string him up and use him for target practice. Cruel punishment indeed, the lieutenant thought nervously. And just as well *that* had never been one of Captain Dagger's actions reported and printed in glaring headlines in Confederate papers. But every daring raid, every blown-up munitions depot, every derailed train, every crime and heinous act, from rape, murder, and mayhem, committed against the Confederacy seemed to be blamed on Captain Dagger and his Bloodriders.

Lieutenant Chatham couldn't help but smile. His mother and father up in Boston thought he was with the Second Massachusetts, a regiment that could count a good many Harvard men in its ranks, and that he was serving in the engineering corps. Instead, he was one of the notorious Bloodriders. Men to be feared, the mild-mannered Lieutenant Chatham chuckled, wondering what the taunting upperclassmen at Harvard would have thought could they have seen their studious, bespectacled classmate now. Little had he known taking degrees in geology and engineering at the university would earn him a place in Captain Dagger's select company of men.

And since he rode with Captain Dagger, he knew that only the most daring of those offenses attributed to the Bloodriders were true, and they happened to be the escapades with the least casualties suffered, on both sides. But in a war, people needed their fears and hatreds to burn hot and not smoulder away into cooling ashes if they were to keep fighting, to keep their cause strong and united, and believing Captain Dagger little better than a bloodthirsty outlaw served the purpose far better than discovering that he was a conscientious man fighting for the cause he believed in. If people only knew what a fine man Captain Dagger was, he thought worriedly. Although he was indeed a man to be feared, and he was a ruthless, dangerous opponent, he wasn't a cold-blooded murderer, the admiring lieutenant thought, and if he lived to see the end of this rebellion against the Union, and if he lived to return home to Boston, then he would write and publish his memoirs about his experiences during the war. He had every raid and scouting mission documented. He would set the record straight concerning Captain Dagger. *Memoirs of a Daredevil Bloodrider. The Daring Escapades of Captain Dagger's Bloodriders*, yes, he liked the sound of that title, he thought, hunching down in his coat as he felt a trickle of cold rain sneak beneath his collar.

Lieutenant Chatham came out of his daydreaming to find himself staring into the cold, pale-eyed stare of his captain. "*Sir?*" he said nervously, wondering if the captain had spoken to him. "I-I thought I'd start taking my measurements, sir."

"By all means, Lieutenant, it'll be dark very soon. But I would suggest you take shelter beneath that tree," Captain Dagger said, pointing toward a large, sheltering oak, the thick canopy of branches creating a fairly dry spot beneath.

"Yes, sir!" the lieutenant mumbled, crawling over to the tree, where he quickly pulled his compasses, altimeter, sketchbook, pen, and ink from the second haversack he carried, wasting little time now in making his readings for his topographical survey of the area.

He glanced up once from his busy scratchings across the page to see the captain maneuvering farther down the bank. The long, black spyglass was raised, pointing at the road below as he continued his surveillance, and soon several pages of the small black notebook he carried would be filled with carefully detailed notations written in code about the strength of the enemy.

The next time Lieutenant Chatham glanced up, the captain was beside him, startling the young man from his sketching. "Come," he said, waiting for a moment while the lieutenant hastily repacked the tools of his trade; then, with the lieutenant stumbling to his feet, he moved off into the trees.

To the young lieutenant, struggling through the underbrush and trying to move as quietly as the captain, and knowing with each noisy step he took that a regiment of rebels could come swarming over the ridge, it seemed an eternity before they finally halted.

He followed his captain's gaze, watching curiously as the rebel troops began feverishly assembling a pontoon bridge across the river, the long column coming to a temporary halt as they waited to cross, determined to put the river between themselves and the federal troops before nightfall.

The black notebook came out, and the captain quickly made his entry.

Resting on his haunches for a moment, as if he had all of the time in the world, and not a single care to worry him, the lieutenant thought almost resentfully as he muffled a sneeze, the captain remained where he was. Then suddenly he moved, signaling the lieutenant to follow.

They began to climb a hill, no more than a gentle knoll, meandering their way to the top, stopping now and again to listen. But no sound grew closer or louder, following their footsteps. In the distance, the sound of the rebel army could still be heard, but becoming fainter now.

Unquestioning, Lieutenant Chatham continued to follow where his captain led. He nearly cannoned into his captain again, when the man halted abruptly. Staying just within the last grouping of trees, he stood staring at a house and outbuildings in the distance. Even in the fading twilight, with a downpour of silvery rain falling between, Lieutenant Chatham could see that the building had once been a fine, graceful home of mellowed brick. And despite its rather decrepit appearance—several of the green shutters were missing from the row of windows that flanked the covered veranda in front, and the garden was overgrown with weeds that infringed upon the lane—it still bore evidence of a more gracious era as it sat proudly atop the knoll. The house was like a beautiful woman grown old, or a rose faded with time; nothing could steal the inner beauty from the woman, or the sweet perfume from the withered petals. Beauty like that could not fade, he thought sadly, even if sometimes it lingered on only in memory.

The lieutenant leaned against a peeling, whitewashed post that still stood upright. What was left of the split-railed fence bordering an open stretch of pasture had fallen into disrepair, and he found himself wondering about the family that used to live in this house. Once, it had been a gentleman's estate. It appeared abandoned now, as if the family had gone, or, perhaps, was no more, its sons gone off to war, its daughters married or widowed and far from the fighting. One of the wings looked as if it had been blown away by an errant shell, and several of the outbuildings had burned to the ground. But one long, low building, recognizable as the stables, remained. As he stood staring, lost in his thoughts, a light suddenly appeared from one of the windows of the main house, its warm glow spreading beyond the casement and out into the descending darkness.

John Chatham swallowed a tightness forming in his throat as the light seemed to reach out to him, touching a tenderness deep within him. The house wasn't abandoned, someone still lived there after all, he thought almost joyfully. He blinked, for the captain had disappeared. Panic rising, his heart pounding, the lieutenant glanced around, sighing in relief when he saw a shadowy figure and recognized it as the captain's. But his momentary relief vanished when he realized the captain was moving steadily closer to the house, as if drawn by the light too.

Taking a deep breath, the lieutenant followed, part of him wishing to curl up in the underbrush and hide, and another part of him wanting to have a glance inside that house. Of course, it could be occupied by rebs, the frightening thought came, and looking around nervously as he crossed the open meadow, he prayed a sharpshooter's rifle wasn't trained on his hurrying form. Cold rain hit him full in the face and cooled some of his fears as he neared where the captain stood waiting, having safely traversed the same field only moments before.

The lieutenant's nostrils twitched slightly as the pungent odor of wood smoke from cedar logs drifted down with the rain and floated around him as he skulked around the house. With night coming on, they must have just lit the fire, he thought wistfully, not having seen smoke rising from any of the chimneys when approaching the house. He bit his lip, forcing himself not to cry out when his trouser leg caught and held on a thorn that cut deep into his flesh. Freeing himself, he stared in amazement at the rosebush he had gotten tangled up in. Forgotten from summer. A pity the lady of the house hadn't pruned it this year, and he wondered if it would survive the cold winter months. He remembered how his mother had always seen to her roses herself, not allowing the gardener to touch them. They were her special pride and brought her such joy when she picked a fragrant bouquet from her garden.

Lieutenant Chatham moved very quietly to stand beside his captain, who had come to a halt beside one of the windows along the far side of the house. He glanced at the captain for a moment, as if to ask permission, but the captain's attention was centered on the scene revealed to him on the other side of the windowpanes. As he stood concealed just within the shadows, the captain's hawkish profile was outlined against the pale light filtering through the window, his hard face looking as if it had been cast in bronze, and giving it the appearance of a stranger's. The lieutenant shivered with uneasiness, puzzled anew by this man who led them in and out of danger so easily.

But the lieutenant couldn't resist the temptation to look inside, and moved closer, almost holding his breath as he angled his head so he could take a quick peek. John Chatham felt his throat muscles constricting painfully, and he was glad now it was raining. The salty warmth of his own tears was quickly washed away, leaving no trace of the sudden rush of emotion he hadn't been able to control as he'd stared at the family gathered together within the sanctity of their home.

He felt ashamed of himself for spying on them; but he couldn't seem to look away and he continued to stare through the window, his gaze hungrily memorizing every detail of the room, and its occupants.

He'd thought at first the room was a parlor, but on closer inspection he could see that it was too small. It was more of a gentleman's reception room or a study. And the lieutenant was certain that the dark wood of the paneled walls was far too masculine in appearance to suit the refined tastes of the lady of this house. Her parlor would be papered in a delicate floral print. And the Oriental carpet was too large for the room, as if it really didn't belong, but it made the room seem snug and cozy against the cold. A couple of comfortable looking high-backed chairs were positioned near the fireplace, where a cheerful blaze was adding its warmth to the chamber. Strange, the lieutenant found himself noticing, that the chairs didn't match; one was more delicate of style and upholstered in a rose damask, while the other was a deeper-winged chair of dark green velvet, and another chair across the room, a gilt-framed chair with a delicate silk tapestry cushion, looked as if it should have been in a ballroom. It was as if the furnishings of this room had been collected together from different rooms of the house. And the pale blue striped cushions of the sofa looked well worn, threadbare, even. The lieutenant frowned. Odd, there were hardly any paintings on the walls, or vases or china bric-a-brac one might have expected to see in a home such as this. Looking more closely, however, the lieutenant could see the faint outlines on the walls where paintings must have hung once. They would have been family portraits, or hunting prints, he guessed, trying to envision the study as it once had been furnished.

His gaze settled on the man who was sitting in the green velvet chair before the fireplace. The lieutenant couldn't see his face, because of the angle and high back of the chair, but he could see the man's gray trouser leg and the highly polished black leather of one of his riding boots, and the yellow cuff on the gray sleeve of his jacket. He was a cavalry officer in the Confederate army.

On the rug in front of the brass fender, a dark-haired little girl sat cross-legged, her small fingers moving steadily as she worked her embroidery. Every so often, she reached out and pressed down gently on one of the wide rockers of a cradle set close to the warmth of the fire. A boy, who couldn't have been older than three or four years of age, his hair dark and curly above his laughing face, was riding a wooden rocking horse back and forth in the corner, his short arm waving an imaginary sword in the air. Lying on the sofa, a floral-patterned quilt arranged across her legs, a frail-looking woman was propped up against several pillows. She was exceptionally lovely, in an ethereal way, and he suspected that she'd recently suffered an illness, or a great loss. There was a haunted look on her face that still showed the signs of suffering in the dark circles beneath her eyes and the tightness of her lips, as if she struggled to keep from crying. Her thin hands trembled as she smoothed a blond strand of her long unbound hair away from her face. She pressed her fingertips against her temple, perhaps easing some pain as she closed her eyes.

The door opened as the fascinated lieutenant continued to watch, admitting a black man dressed in green livery, apparently a butler or majordomo, his steps slow as he moved across the room to say something to the man in the wingback chair before the fireplace. Shaking his head, as if displeased with the answer he had received, he turned, glancing over at the disinterested woman on the sofa for a moment before he left the room, shaking his head again.

Hardly a minute passed before the door opened again, this time to admit two women. One was a tall, thin black woman. The lieutenant's eyes widened slightly, for he'd never seen a mulattress before. This woman's skin was coppery in tint and with her strange eyes and high cheekbones she made him think of some of the paintings of wild Indians he had seen in books published by artists who had traveled across the Great Plains. But rather than wearing fringed buckskin, she was wearing a neat woolen gown, a crisp white apron tied about her narrow waist, and rather than carrying a feathered spear, she was holding a tray loaded down with crockery, which she began to set out on the scarred top of a sofa table in the center of the room, her hands moving efficiently as she set the table for supper.

The woman who had accompanied the mulattress was slender, almost to the point of being too thin, the thick chestnut hair netted in a chignon at her nape seeming far too heavy for the slender column of her neck. Although dressed in the somber black of mourning, her beauty seemed enhanced rather than diminished, for there was a purity of bone structure revealed in the contours of her cheeks and the line of her jaw that bright colors and fancy trimmings would have detracted from. But what drew his eye the most was the graceful way she walked, the few petticoats she wore allowing her to move freely, naturally, her feet hardly seeming to touch the ground as she went to the cradle and lifted into her arms the small bundle wrapped in a soft woolen blanket. As he watched, the young woman pressed a loving kiss against the baby's pink-cheeked face, then rested her own pale cheek against the fine dark hair that covered the little head, her finger caught by the tiny fist that reached out to claim her as she cuddled it against her breast.

The young woman smiled down at the baby as she carefully placed it back in the cradle, and although he couldn't hear her soft laughter, he knew it would be warm and loving. Silently, he sighed, wishing he knew this family, but, most especially, this beautiful young woman. Something stirred deep down inside of him, and he wondered if he'd live to sire a son or daughter, or have a wife like this woman bending down to kiss his brow as she did the soldier in gray, his hand reaching out to clasp hers for a brief moment of sharing. There was something about this woman that drew him the same way the fire flickering in the hearth did, and he suddenly felt an almost painful sadness engulfing him and he wanted to turn away.

Lieutenant Chatham glanced over at the captain, thinking

he'd heard him say something, but he must have been mistaken, for the captain hadn't moved a muscle and stood as if turned to stone.

Of course, he couldn't blame the captain if he had damned Lee, for that was what it had sounded like he had said. They wouldn't be standing in the cold rain outside of someone else's home like strangers if the South hadn't seceded from the Union. In another, far saner time, they would have been shot as trespassers, the lieutenant thought glumly, glancing around just in case someone else had been of a similar opinion about their status. Or in another time, they might have been invited in, offered hospitality by this family.

Glancing back, Lieutenant Chatham saw the young woman kneel down when the girl, who must have been about ten years of age, proudly held up her embroidery. The young woman examined it carefully, then said something to her, which must have been words of high praise, because the little girl's solemn expression suddenly turned to one of pleasure as she smiled shyly. Pulling on one of the girl's dark curls playfully, the young woman stood, stretching her shoulders slightly, as if they ached, then she was hurrying across the room to scoop up the little boy who'd ridden too hard and been thrown from his wooden mount, his cries of pain and hurt pride sounding loud even in the lieutenant's ears. But the young woman had a deft touch with the youngster, and soon she had his tears dried and his sturdy little legs back in the stirrups as he proudly sat his hobby horse again like the finest, bravest officer of the cavalry. And he even managed to wheedle a kiss from his lady—proving even at this young age the lad possessed officer caliber.

The young woman made her way to the sofa, where the other woman had dozed off, even the sound of the boy's bawling not having awakened her, and pulling the quilt up closer over her shoulders, she pressed the back of her hand against the woman's brow. The lieutenant frowned, hoping the convalescent woman wasn't feverish.

He caught his breath as the young woman in black walked toward the window, and he steeled himself not to move, to remain in the dark where he knew she wouldn't be able to see him even should she have glanced out into the darkness. She was so close. He could even see the color of her eyes. And they were beautiful eyes. The color a dark blue that seemed to reflect the warmth of the firelit room inside.

As he watched, she pulled free the sash that held one of the heavy velvet hangings to the side, allowing the curtain to fall over half of the window. He could barely see her now as she moved to the other side, closer to where the captain stood.

For a brief moment, she stood at the window, gazing out at the rain, her slender back to the room, and believing her expression hidden from prying eyes, she allowed her true feelings to show.

Lieutenant Chatham looked away, unable to intrude upon this young woman any longer, the naked pain and anguish revealed in her dark eyes in that moment too heartbreaking for him to bear.

Then she was gone, the velvet hangings closing out the night and the two men who stood outside the window.

He glanced over at the captain, but he was already moving away. Lieutenant Chatham hurried after him. He glanced back only once at the house as they left, following a path alongside the stables. A streak of lightning flashed across the sky, and for the first time he noticed the weather vane atop the small cupola; it was a running horse, spinning wildly as the wind buffeted it.

Thirteen

There is a Reaper whose name is Death,
And, with his sickle keen,
He reaps the bearded grain at a breath,
And the flowers that grow between.

Henry Wadsworth Longfellow

THE YOUNG WOMAN REMAINED FOR A MOMENT LONGER before the window, staring out at the darkness and watching the rain blowing against the windowpanes in splattering gusts. She shivered and let the green velvet hangings fall together, closing out the inhospitable night. Straightening her shoulders, she turned back to the enveloping warmth of the room behind her. Stephen had lifted the glass chimney to the oil lamp and was lighting the wick, the flame flickering momentarily, then glowing bright as it caught and began to feed greedily on the small amount of kerosene that remained in the base.

Shaking his head of snowy white hair, he sighed, muttering beneath his breath as he set the lamp on the table.

"Now you hush yer grumblin'," Jolie told him, placing a stack of china dishes in front of one of the place settings. "Miss Leigh an' I made up a whole batch of beeswax candles the other day. I like the sweet smell of them better anyway. Reminds me of summertime. Knew she'd find that hive an' steal some sweet honey an' a honeycomb from those bees. Creepin' Fox would have been that proud, he would. An' we still have some bayberry candles too, so we're goin' to do fine. Nothin's goin' to happen to us. I've this feelin', Steban," she confided, affectionately using the nickname only she was permitted to call him. "You heard the thunder this afternoon. Been feelin' like my skin's been crawlin' all day. Somethin' cracklin' in the air, I can feel it."

"Your big toe's been botherin' you again, that's all, an' I'm hopin' the only thing cracklin' 'round here is bread for supper, 'cause the last time I heard cracklin' in the air, the outhouse got struck by lightnin'," Stephen said, still unconvinced after all these years. "An' you probably picked up some lice in the ballroom, where those soldiers were. Told you we didn't get it scrubbed clean enough. Didn't have enough lye. Mister Stuart, now, he wouldn't have stabled even a mangy field mule in there, so poorly did it look after those Yankees up an' left," he told her, his voice beginning to tremble, his hand shaking slightly as he pulled down the frayed cuff of his green jacket as he tidied himself, as if expecting Stuart Travers's short, bandy-legged figure to appear at the door to the reception room any second, a tall julep in one hand, a fine cigar in the other, and a score of his gentlemen friends a step behind.

Jolie patted the back of his hand comfortingly as they exchanged glances, no words necessary between them as they both remembered.

"Horses! Horses! Hubby rides fast! Hubby horse rides fastest! Just like my papa!"

"Ummm, ummm, that does smell good, doesn't it, honey boy?" Jolie said, picking up the little boy and settling him on her hip. The tantalizing aroma from the tureen had drawn him from his hobby horse and the mock battle he'd been fighting, and winning. His dismount had not quite been up to cavalry standards, but he'd picked himself up with admirable speed, not a tear shed over his scraped knee as he'd hurried to Jolie's side.

"Pretty Jolie. Hungry. Eat now! Mama. Mama, eat now. Mama eat too," the little boy said, his brown eyes round with expectation as he watched Leigh dishing out the steaming yams onto each plate.

Jolie chuckled, smoothing his dark brown curls as she popped a pinch of corn bread into his mouth. "That oughta keep you quiet for a second or two. Squealing like that, you're goin' to wake the dead, honey boy," she said, glancing over worriedly at the woman who had fallen into fitful slumber on the sofa.

"Sick. Hush, honey boy. Honey boy, hush," he said understandingly, his mouth full of crumbling corn bread.

"That's right, she's been real sick," Jolie said. "An' you've been real good, like when I hush a puppy," she said, laughing, then becoming serious as she looked again at the sleeping woman. "Got to get somethin' hot inside her, somethin' that'll stick to her ribs an' put meat on those skinny bones of hers. Don't know how much longer she's goin' to last if we don't," Jolie said, ladling up a plate full of the stewed meat, the gravy thick and looking like it would stick like glue once inside a person's stomach. She handed the dish to Leigh, who'd been cutting the corn bread into thick squares. Walking over to the sofa to sit on a low stool next to the sleeping woman, Leigh touched her lightly on the arm.

"Althea?" she said softly.

Althea Louise Braedon opened her eyes, trying to sit up. "Nathan?" she said, glancing around frantically, a look of hope briefly brightening the dullness in her brown eyes.

"No, no we haven't had any word, Althea," Leigh told her almost apologetically, still hating herself for having had to break the news to Althea just before Thanksgiving that Nathan had been reported missing in action.

"Nothing?" Althea said, shaking her head in despair. "I don't understand. If only I were still in Richmond. I could find out something there. Has Aunt Maribel written? Surely she has heard something. Uncle Jay has so many important contacts in the army. They must have heard about Nathan's whereabouts by now."

"Don't you remember, Althea, Aunt Maribel and Uncle Jay are in Europe? They left Richmond right after they brought you here. That's why you came back to Travers Hill. With them leaving, there was no one for you to stay with in Richmond. You were deathly ill, remember? Aunt Maribel knew we could care for you here," Leigh explained, as if talking to a child.

"I remember now. We had to leave. I was so sick," she said, closing her eyes for a moment as if reliving the pain. "You haven't heard anything from anyone else, then? Adam? Adam would know. Surely he has heard something?" she asked hopefully, opening her eyes. "Royal Bay? They must have heard something there. I should be over there, not here. No one would know to contact me here. I must go to Royal Bay."

"There is no news, Althea," Leigh told her sister for the thousandth time, but Althea never tired of asking, refusing to give up hope that Nathan was still alive.

Staring at her, Leigh thought her sister looked like a ghost with her shadowed eyes and pale hair flowing about her shoulders like a shroud. She could still remember her horror when Althea had arrived from Richmond. She had looked as if she were indeed dead, her skin a strange waxy color as she lay on a stretcher in the back of a wagon. Maribel Lu had accompanied her, along with J. Kirkfield. As an important member of the Confederate government in Richmond, now the capital of the Confederate States of America, he'd managed to find space for his niece and her family in the back of one of the supply wagons heading to the front. Maribel Lu and J. Kirkfield had stayed only long enough to catch the same wagon, now filled with wounded, on its return journey to Richmond. Leigh would never forget the comical incongruity of Aunt Maribel Lu sitting in the back of the wagon, wrapped in a voluminous gray cloak trimmed with yellow braid, her bonnet a stunning tribute to the Confederacy with the Stars and Bars emblazoned on the brim and the crown, and stuck with three small red, white, and blue feathers, and one large gray ostrich plume that waved defiantly as they disappeared from sight, her parasol decorated like a battle flag. *General* Maribel Lu, the soldiers had quipped, would see them safely back to Richmond, because no Yankee was fool enough to get in her way. Leigh hadn't seen them since that day when she'd stood on the lane by the river and waved to them. Immediately upon their arrival back to Richmond, they'd left for Europe aboard a blockade runner. J. Kirkfield, with his banking and business acumen, had been sent by the Confederate government to solicit loans and valuable materiel for the war effort from various sympathetic European sources, as well as try to influence European policy toward the Confederate cause.

Until last summer, Althea had lived in Richmond with Aunt Maribel Lu and Uncle Jay, moving in with them when the city had become overcrowded as the war progressed; as politicians, men in uniform, government workers, and profiteers, and the multitude of hangers-on, seeking power in a struggling, divisive government, had poured into the city. But most of the crowding came of the continuous flow of refugees straggling along the roads, wagons piled high with what was left of their worldly possessions, as the runaway slaves and the homeless families flooded into the city to escape the battles raging across the countryside as the Union soldiers fought deeper into the heart of the Confederacy.

Althea's own home, the one she had shared with Nathan in a happier time, had been taken over by the government for officers' housing. As so many others had before her, Althea volunteered to work at one of the many hospitals, reading correspondence from home to convalescent soldiers, writing letters to loved ones for those who were illiterate, or too weak from their wounds to lift a pen. She'd even written to strangers, informing them of the death of a husband, a father, a brother, or a son. For two years she had worked untiringly, until she had caught typhoid and nearly died as the disease swept through a city already stricken with famine and death.

"Althea, you must eat something."

"I can't, Leigh. I couldn't keep it down. I wish you didn't have to wear black. It's a hateful color," Althea whispered, turning her face away from the somber reminder of what life seemed to hold for most of them, her strength leaving her as she fell back against the pillows.

"Yes, you can eat this, and you will," Leigh said, ignoring her, her voice sounding harsh even in her own ears, but she would not stand idly by while her sister slipped away from her. "Have you forgotten? You have a son and a daughter to care for. Who do you think will be here to care for them, if you aren't? I love them, but I'm not their mother. Have you forgotten I have another child to care for?" Leigh told her with brutal frankness, hoping to anger her into some kind of response. "And," Leigh added, steeling herself to speak the words she had trouble believing, "how do you think Nathan would feel to return here and find that you have died because you didn't have the courage to keep on living, to care for his children, to wait for him to come home?"

"*Miss Leigh!*" Jolie said, shocked by such talk. Opening her mouth, she found she could say nothing, and she closed it tightly. When Leigh had glanced over at her warningly, Jolie had thought of Beatrice Amelia, for there had been the look of her mama in her eye in that instant, and she kept her silence.

"Leigh," Althea said, her eyes full of hurt bewilderment. "How could you say such horrible things to me?" she demanded, a blotch of angry red color appearing on each sunken cheek. "How dare you speak so disrespectfully to me?"

"I dare, because I don't want you to die, Althea. I've seen too many people I love leave me, and I couldn't do anything to help them. But I can help you. And if you don't eat this, then I'm going to pour it down your throat, and if you die, then it will be because you choked to death on this leathery ol' possum," she warned, her eyes blazing with anger and frustration. "Oh, Althea, I don't think I could go on if you leave me too," she admitted, her momentary rage dying. Shamefaced, she looked at her sister. "I'm sorry. I shouldn't have said that. I'm just so tired. And not only is the roof leaking, but I think we've got rats in the attic," she said trying to shrug off her worries with a halfhearted laugh.

Althea stared at her younger sister, truly seeing her for perhaps the first time in several years.

Leigh had grown up.

"No, I am the one who is sorry," Althea said, taking Leigh's thin hand in hers, and feeling the chafed and callused skin from the work she did every day without ever complaining. Leigh ran Travers Hill, now, just the way their mother always had, but Althea knew Leigh wouldn't be able to keep going on forever. She had to get well and start helping her, she told herself. After all, as Leigh had said, what would Nathan think when he returned to find she had given up, had not done her duty by his family, by his son? Althea glanced over at her son, her eyes full of love as she noticed again the dark brown hair he'd inherited from his father. Nathan had been so proud of him. They'd named him for both of their fathers, Steward, after his, and Russell, after hers. And Noble Braedon had lived long enough to attend the baptism of his grandson. He'd died in peace, before Virginia had seceded from the Union, before war had been declared, and before...

"Yes, that does smell delicious," Althea said, her voice holding some of the old pride and determination in it as she struggled to sit up. Pushing her limp hair away from her face, she grimaced. "Tomorrow I will wash it. I don't want

Nathan seeing me looking like death," she said, trying to smile. "You've heard nothing?" she questioned again, watching Leigh's face carefully for some sign that she was hiding something from her.

"No, nothing," Leigh said truthfully.

"He must have been wounded, and is probably in a hospital. If only he hadn't left Virginia. I could have gone to Richmond. He'd be where I could care for him," she said, her eyes clouding as her thoughts ran on to an even less pleasant thought. "Or, God help us, Leigh," she added shakily, "he is a prisoner. And he is in some Yankee prison up north."

Leigh avoided meeting Althea's tortured gaze. "Nathan would do just fine even in a federal prison. He's probably handling the legal affairs for half the Yankee prison staff, or maybe Lincoln himself."

"Yes," Althea said, her worried expression lifting as she thought of that possibility, never realizing its improbability, but it gave her hope. "Possum?" she said, frowning slightly as she forced herself to eat, at first slowly, then with the appetite of a person determined to get well. "It's quite good. Very good, in fact. I might even have a little piece of that corn bread. It smells delicious."

"Good," Leigh said, standing up, a satisfied smile on her face as she saw the contents of the plate disappearing.

"Where is Noelle?" Althea asked with motherly concern, and the first she had shown in several months.

"By the fireplace. She is embroidering a handkerchief for you," Leigh told her, pleased to see her showing some interest in her children again. "She's becoming as fine a needlewoman as Mama was. She asks about you constantly. She misses you," Leigh said gently.

Althea nodded. "Would you have her come over here after she has eaten? It has been far too long since I've been with her. I've neglected her badly. I haven't read to her in so long."

"You've been ill."

"No, even before that. I am surprised she does not resent Steward. I have spoiled him so. But I was so pleased to give Nathan a son."

"She is very loving to him. I've heard her tell him that

while you are ill she will be his mama and take care of him, and she does, Althea. She is very good with him. In fact, she reads to him from the same book of fairy tales that you read to her. You and Nathan can be very proud of her. She is a great help to me. I always know Steward and Lucinda are being watched when I'm not here."

"Yes, I am proud of her, Leigh," Althea told her. "Sometimes she reminds me so much of Nathan. She is such a serious little girl." Glancing around the room, her gaze lingered on the rose damask chair near the fireplace. "Mama's chair."

"When the Yankees came, taking over the house for a field hospital, we moved what furniture we could in here. We thought it best to stay well out of their way. Fortunately, we'd already hidden all the silver and other valuables, and the family heirlooms," she said, her gaze lingering on the empty spaces on the walls, where once family portraits had hung. "Our heritage is safe, thanks to Adam," she added, a mischievous glint in her eye as she remembered Adam showing up at Travers Hill one afternoon and proudly displaying a ramshackle wagon pulled by a team of ancient mules—somehow overlooked by the troops requisitioning anything that wasn't nailed to the ground. He had just emptied the wagon, and for the fourth time, of all of Royal Bay's finest furnishings and objets d'art. They were safely hidden away from the Yankees, he'd claimed, and now he, rather than the bluebellies, would loot Travers Hill. Far easier, he'd laughed, to reclaim one's possessions from him than a federal trooper who intended to become a rich man after the war on the booty he'd stolen. Adam, her father, and Sweet John had loaded up everything of value, even piling high with prized possessions the little cart hitched to Pumpkin, and delivered it safely to some secret hiding place only Adam had known about. Her father had been in a very boisterous mood when they'd returned home, and she suspected they'd been enjoying a jug of corn whiskey to ease their thirst, but her father had shaken his head, saying that he finally knew where the wild Braedon boys had hidden all those years ago, as if they'd dropped off the face of the earth.

"Actually, though, when the Yankees came, the officers were very civil to us, and the wounded soldiers, so many of them hardly more than boys, were very polite and grateful."

"How do you know that?" Althea demanded, staring at Leigh in amazement.

"I helped the surgeons with them, Althea. I couldn't just stand by and watch them die," she admitted almost defensively, her eyes shadowed still by the memory of the amputations and the agonized screaming. "Some of them were from West Virginia and Maryland. They were almost like neighbors. They didn't seem any different from Palmer William, Guy, or Stuart James. I kept thinking about their families, worrying about them the same way we were worrying. I only did what I could, which wasn't very much," Leigh said, wishing she could have done more for the young men who lay dying, knowing that they would never see home again. "Actually, we ought to be grateful to the Yankees."

"Grateful? Now you go too far," Althea said, shocked by such a treasonous thought. "I've heard horrifying tales about thievin' Yankees. My dear friend, Mary Helen, down in Baton Rouge, has written to me about the Yankees breaking into her home, searching for silver, threatening her and her family with violence when they couldn't find anything. When her servants tried to clean up the mess, the soldiers told them to leave, that they no longer had to serve her family, and if they didn't leave, then they'd shoot them."

"Well, if the Yankees hadn't been here, then Travers Hill might have been shelled worse than it was, like Royal Bay, Althea, and then we wouldn't have even a leaking roof over our heads."

"Poor Euphemia," Althea murmured. "If only she had come over to Travers Hill. She'd be here with us today."

"We asked her to, begged her even, but she said she wasn't leaving her home. She was there by herself, except for a couple of house servants. She'd even sent old Bella to Richmond with Julia. She was so proud and stubborn," Leigh said, the scene of Royal Bay in flames still vivid in her mind, as if it had happened yesterday instead of a year ago. "Why would anyone want to destroy such a lovely place?"

"Plain meanness," Althea said.

"At least with the Yankees camped around the house, we were safe for a while from the deserters, especially the ones deserting from our own army. They're the vilest ones, preying on their own people," Leigh said quietly, unable to forget the afternoon when five deserters, dressed in ragged, dusty gray uniforms, had come to Travers Hill to loot; four were now buried in the manure field back of the stables.

"There was little we could do to refuse the Yankees' request, out of fear of being shot because we didn't open our homes and hearts to the Yankee invaders. A General Pope decreed that any Virginian caught aiding the enemy would be executed. His troops would live off the land, meaning they could steal whatever they wanted from us, leaving us to starve, and if there was any guerrilla activity nearby, we would be held responsible and dealt with accordingly. We could, however, to save ourselves, sign an oath of allegiance to the Union."

"Yes, I heard about that madman in Richmond. It caused quite an outrage." Althea sighed, thinking not for the first time that they found themselves in a never-ending nightmare. It was madness. Nothing made sense any longer. And what used to seem important, no longer did.

She smiled sadly. "I wonder what Mama would say to see us eating in here. She was always so very proper. Even now, I fear she'd have us sitting down to dine in our Sunday best, and ever cordial and the perfect hostess, she would've invited those Yankees to dine. I can just hear her asking Stephen to bring in the tea service. No one, not even a Yankee, would ever accuse her of being inhospitable, she was always declaring. And somehow, she'd have had a clean, pressed damask tablecloth spread beneath our finest china, even with cannon fire in the distance, and she'd sit there serving chicken curry and rice. Remember how we used to have it every Sunday? Odd, isn't it, the little things like that you remember, and you miss."

Leigh glanced down at her work-roughened hands for a moment, realizing that their mother had never been able to accept the war that had taken her loved ones from her one by one, destroying the genteel way of life at Travers Hill. She'd tried to carry on as if nothing had happened, as if nothing had changed. And, eventually, she had begun to believe that nothing had, that it was the summer of '60 again, not 1863, and Travers Hill was filled with family and friends. There were so many things for her to do, she would say, looking dazed as she hurried from one empty room to another, dragging Jolie after her, never seeing the change, always calling out for a member of the family who'd never appear before her again. There would be a fish fry beneath the willows on the riverbank, and the barbecue on Sunday, then the routs and races, and she had to see to the preparations for Blythe's sixteenth birthday party. Her daughters would do her proud, she had said with the old gleam in her dark blue eyes.

That had been in summer, when she could walk in her garden, the fragrance of her beloved roses surrounding her, and lose herself in long-forgotten dreams of days that were no more. But winter had come all too soon. And one cold morning, the frozen ground covered with the first snowfall of the season, they had found Beatrice Amelia in her garden. Barefoot, the cashmere of her dusky rose dressing gown no protection against the cold, she had wandered out in the night to prune her roses. A week later, she had died. Leigh's only consolation had been that her mother had, in death, finally found the peace she had been searching for.

Leigh looked around the room, and saw only too clearly the changes that'd had to be made if they were to survive. "It's the warmest room in the house," she told Althea. "We keep most of the other rooms closed, and we don't have a fire in here until evening. We light one in your room, and in the kitchen before dawn, bank it so it burns low and lasts, then light it after dusk again. It's better not to draw too much attention to Travers Hill," she added, thinking again of the gangs of deserters that drifted around the countryside looting abandoned homes, or those protected only by women. "And at night, we use only a couple of the bedchambers. I don't like to waste our wood. I'm not very good at chopping it up into kindling. I'm afraid Stephen is even worse. He never had to chop wood before," she explained, remembering his look of offended dignity when she'd suggested they needed wood and would have to chop it themselves. "We try to use what is close at hand, I don't like anyone to go far from the house. There are so many strangers around, and you don't know your enemy. You can't trust the color of a uniform any longer."

"I think you are being very wise," Althea said nervously, noticing for the first time the rifle next to the door, and hanging just out of reach of small hands. "Where do Noelle and Steward, and the baby, sleep?"

"They've been sleeping in the trundle bed in my room. Jolie has been staying with you at night in case you needed anything."

"Now that I'm feeling better, I'll move them in with me. You need your rest, my dear, and it will be comforting for me to have my children with me again. I'd be happy to have Lucinda too," she offered, worrying about the dark circles beneath her sister's eyes that bore proof of the long hours she worked and the restless nights, her sleep disturbed as she tended to the children.

"No!" Leigh answered abruptly. Then she said more quietly as she glanced over at the sleeping child in the cradle, "I'll keep Lucinda with me. Noelle and Steward can start sleeping with you, but you mustn't let them tire you. You are still very weak, Althea, and it will take you a while to recover your strength," Leigh reminded her, taking the empty dish. "Would you like a little more?"

Althea nodded. "Yes, I would. I'm being a pig. But I've discovered I have a ravenous appetite for possum all of a sudden."

"Possum," Stephen muttered, watching unhappily as Leigh dished up another plate for Althea. "Not fit food even for peckerwoods. An' last night you served this family peanut soup."

"An' we're goin' to have it tomorrow night too, with mashed yams fried into cakes from what's left over tonight," Jolie told him, the look in her eye brooking no opposition.

"I don't know what the colonel would say if he could see us, woman," Stephen fretted, eyeing the steaming contents of the tureen with a despairing shake of his head, amazed at how fast it was disappearing right before his eyes.

"An' day after, if I can get my hands on that sneaky hen's eggs, she's been hidin' them from me, then we're goin' to have squirrel pie, 'cause I've been watchin' him like a fox."

"If little Mister Steward's Gran'papa Noble knew his only gran'son was eatin' possum an' hog fodder, well, I couldn't look him straight in the eye. It's just not right."

"Now you listen to me, ol' man," Jolie said, a glint in her

yellowish eyes as she glared at him. "The colonel might jus' be turnin' in his grave to know we've been servin' his kin what poor white trash wouldn't even throw to their hogs, but he'd be spinnin' if we let his grandchildren, an' one named in honor of him, an' his great-grandchildren, starve to death. Same with Mister Noble. You jus' think about that, you fussbudget. An' I'll tell you this, I'd serve this to the colonel himself, an' he'd eat it too, it's that good. Went out an' got myself all the herbs I needed an' been storin' them away since fall like that fat-cheeked squirrel. I know those woods good as my papa would have. Creepin' Fox didn't sire no fools. There's nothin' Jolie can't find if she wants to. Simmered this possum in thyme, laurel, cloves, parsley, an' celery, dash of red pepper an' a bud of garlic, then found some yams growing wild, baked them nice an' tender an' plumb full of nutmeg, an' made up a pan of corn bread, crisp an' hot. We've got ourselves a mighty fine supper here. So you quit'cher complainin'. I've got enough to do. Still can't believe that Rosamundi and those fool maids runnin' off with those Yankees. Goin' to cook and wash for them, she tells me. Thinks they'll be safer with them. Hmmmph!"

"Well, I'm not complainin' any," the gray-uniformed man in the chair said, the aroma having drifted to him. "And you really can't blame the Yankees, after all, you taught Rosamundi how to cook. They'd have been fools not to have wanted her fixing them up some good Southern cooking. You're truly a jewel, Jolie. I don't know what the Travers family would do without you and Stephen. Thanks to Stephen, I'd wager Travers Hill still has the best corn whiskey in all of the Old Dominion. Don't know where he hid that still when the Yanks came callin'. Glad I had some with me to pour on my wound until I could get here, probably kept me alive, or at least pickled nicely, and combined with that horrible smelling salve you keep putting on me, Jolie, I'm surprised you don't have me bunking out in the stables. I have detected a hint of garlic in it," he said. "I'm glad you stayed," he added softly, feeling that same sense of gratitude he had when arriving at Travers Hill to find Jolie and Stephen still running the house and what was left of the Travers family, despite Lincoln's Emancipation Proclamation, and, before that, the Confederacy's order demanding half of all the able-bodied male slaves on every farm or plantation to report to work camps.

Jolie snorted, hastily wiping away a tear as she gave the mixture a brisk stir. "Got nowhere else to go, Mister Guy. Travers Hill is home, an' this is our family. Miss Leigh read that proclamation to us herself, an' she told us that we were free to do as we liked. Got it folded up right here in my pocket, so I can tell anybody who asks that I know I'm free. Heard tell them Canbys didn't tell their slaves they'd been freed. 'Course, weren't many left there anyway. First chance they got they run off. Well, I told Miss Leigh that I got things to do in the kitchens, so if she wouldn't mind, I'd just get on with my chores. For me an' Steban, it's no different today than was yesterday. Your mama, Miss Beatrice Amelia, was a real fine lady. Never raised her voice nor a hand against me nor any of my kin. An' she worked just as hard as I did. Same with Mister Stuart. He treated Sweet John like he was his own flesh an' blood. He was real proud of that boy, same as he was of you, Mister Guy. Your papa died tryin' to save my Sweet John from those deserters that come lootin' here at Travers Hill, an' they were wearin' gray, Mister Guy. Wearin' gray. Mister Stuart didn't have to do that. He could've shot at them from the house. But he was cussin' somethin' terrible, tears rolling down his face when he sees them takin' my Sweet John to that oak. Sweet John had already knocked one of them against the side of the stables, split his head wide open. Then Mister Stuart, he shot one of them dead, but they'd already beat an' hanged my Sweet John by then. Sweet John didn't want them stealin' that sweet mare of Miss Leigh's. She was the only horse we had left outa all the fine horses we once had at Travers Hill. Everything else, includin' Mister Stuart's favorite, Apothecary Rose, from pigs an' hens an' cattle, to them fat milk cows an' plump geese was taken by the soldiers long ago, along with all the oats an' corn. Hardly anything left," she said, sniffing loudly.

"Then the other man, he got off a shot, an' poor Mister Stuart, he fell dead. Never suffered none, he didn't. Miss Leigh, she come runnin' from the house 'bout then, totin' that gun of yer grandpapa's, a bunch of your hounds barking at her heels. Those river rats didn't think she knew how to shoot, not knowin' she was Mister Stuart's lil' gal, that she was a Travers. She shot him dead, Mister Guy, blew away that *C* that'd been branded on his face for bein' a coward. Figure he should've been shot then. An' the other two, they figured to jump her when she'd fired off that gun, knowin' she couldn't shoot them too, but she up an' pulls out a pistol she'd been carryin' in her apron an' shoots the varmit between the eyes. Scared the other one yellow, seein' her shoot like that, 'cause he took to his heels, squealin' like a stuck pig when she winged him, an' runs back down to the riverbank and this barge they'd come floatin' down the river on like a pack of rats. Last we seen of him, but I doubt he lasted very long, 'cause we found a mighty deep pool of blood down there in the sand before the current got him an' he got carried downriver."

Guy's trembling hands balled into fists on the arms of the chair as he felt the rage filling him that he couldn't control, and couldn't do anything to vent, when thinking of his father's and Sweet John's deaths, and the danger that Leigh and the rest of his family had been in that day. And they were still in danger. Nothing had changed. In fact, it had gotten worse, with deserters almost outnumbering those willing to serve, or so it seemed to those on the front lines. And the next time deserters came to Travers Hill his family might not escape them. And he wouldn't be any good to them.

"An' since I raised your mama from the cradle, an' helped bring each of you Traverses into this world, I'm not leavin' this family to those Yankees, or yellow-bellied deserters. Where'd me an' Steban go anyway?" she asked him, her eyes becoming watery as she stared at Guy, but she didn't bother to hide her tears this time.

The light from the fire couldn't soften the thin, cruel-looking scar that cut across his face from brow to cheek, the black patch he wore over his sightless, scarred eye a vivid reminder of the fierce fighting on the battlefield the day he had been wounded. His right eye, still a bright shade of green, unclouded and unmarred, stared at them from behind a fringe of thick lashes, but he could not see them. The concussion he'd suffered from the shell that had exploded beneath his horse during a charge had cost him his sight in the other eye as well, even though there had been no physical damage to it. But whether or not he'd ever see again, the doctors had been unable to reassure him. Time, they had said. Only time would bring him the answer.

Restlessly, he moved his shoulder, easing the stiffness. The wound was almost completely healed, giving him only an occasional twinge as the flesh tightened along the puckered scar from the saber's blade that had sliced across his shoulder. "Poor ol' Rambler," he murmured to himself. He would never forget the roan hunter that had carried him safely through so many battles, easily jumping the open trenches and earthworks the enemy had sought to trap them with, never faltering, never panicking even as cannon fire roared deafeningly and smoke obscured the field. Rambler had proven himself a great warhorse. As great as General Lee's Lucy Long, Guy thought, smiling as he thought of his own sister, little long-legged Lucy. And Rambler had been as fast as Jeb Stuart's Thoroughbred mare, Virginia. And even that damned bluebelly Grant had a horse he could be proud of; Kangaroo, left by a Confederate officer on the battlefield at Shiloh, they said. Guy's smile turned bitter as he thought of the ironies of war.

But Rambler had held his ground, carrying his rider like a knight of old into the fray, leading the charge time and time again. And he had died on the field of battle, protecting his rider from being mortally wounded. Guy's hands relaxed, as if he were still lightly holding Rambler's reins, only this time they were riding across a field of rolling bluegrass, his hounds racing ahead, their barking sounding soft and sweet to the ear, and disturbed only by the melodic notes of his hunting horn, not the bugler's frenzied warning cry.

Guy dropped his hand down beside his leg, gently tugging at the soft ear of one of the two hounds that still remained at Travers Hill. The others had either died or run off, frightened into running wild by the sound of cannon fire. He felt the roughness of a tongue licking his hand, and patted the dog on top of his head, comforted by the familiar feel.

"Here you are, Guy." Leigh spoke softly beside him, startling him, so lost in his thoughts had he become that he hadn't heard her approach.

"Careful," she warned, stepping back to avoid his jerky movement of surprise.

"Shouldn't sneak up on a person like that. Especially a blind man," he joked.

"Sorry," Leigh said, placing the tray across his lap, then guiding his hand to the spoon next to the plate.

"Did I hear Althea's voice?" he asked, beginning to eat, his spoon moving slowly and carefully between his mouth and the plate. "Damn!" he muttered, feeling the hot gravy seeping through his pants leg where he'd spilled a drop. "Clumsy oaf."

Leigh looked away, still finding it hard to watch Guy in his helplessness, to see his frustration day after day. "Yes, I think she is going to get better. She actually ate some supper, and she asked about Noelle and Steward. She wants them back in her room at night."

"That's a good sign. No word about Nathan?" he asked, slipping a piece of corn bread to his hounds, and hoping Leigh hadn't seen him do it.

"No, no word," Leigh said, watching as Noelle helped Steward into his chair at the table, the stack of books beneath his chubby rear end putting him close enough to his plate for him to eat.

"Miss Leigh, you get over here an' eat before your supper gets cold," Jolie warned.

"Can I get you anything else, Guy?" she asked solicitously, thinking he'd eaten his corn bread rather fast, but then that was easier for him to eat than the possum in gravy. "More corn bread?"

"No, nothing more, Leigh," Guy said, sounding slightly impatient. "I've got to learn to feed myself. You go eat. You need it more than I do," he said without self-pity, for even though he knew great frustration, he had learned to live with his blindness, even if others hadn't.

Leigh continued to stand beside Guy for a moment, staring down at him and thinking he was no less handsome even with the black patch across one eye, and she found herself remembering his words, spoken so carelessly when he'd arrived at Travers Hill. "Makes me look quite piratical, doesn't it? I'll have the ladies swooning when in my presence." Neither of them had spoken aloud the memory of Sarette Canby breaking off the engagement when hearing of his disfigurement. They'd heard rumors that she was to marry a general from Georgia this spring.

Good riddance, Leigh thought, smiling as she watched Guy sneak a piece of corn bread to one of his beloved hounds. Unaware that she sighed, her expression turned to one of pity as he dropped his napkin onto the carpet.

Leigh reached out automatically to help him, then drew back her hand as he fumbled for it.

As if he could sense her feelings, even if he could not see her expression, Guy suddenly said, "Go on, Leigh. I'll be all right," he told her, managing to find and pick up his napkin.

"Miss Leigh!" Jolie called again, her hands on her hips as she waited for Leigh to take her place at the head of the table, then sitting down to take her place next to Stephen, and across from the two children, who were chattering. Hushing them, they quieted as Leigh said grace, then the ordinary sounds of a family dining together filled the room.

"You don't eat enough, honey," Jolie told Leigh as she cleared the empty plates from the table. For a moment she watched Leigh cradling the baby in her lap as she fed it, handing Leigh a cloth when the baby gurgled and laughed, dribbling gravy down its dimpled chin, its small hand pushing away the spoon. "She's close to bustin', you got her so full of milk and honey and gravy. An' sure am pleased to see Miss Althea eatin' somethin' more than she has," Jolie said, glancing over at Althea, who was sitting up, Noelle and Steward on either side of her as she read to them.

Stephen was putting another log on the fire, but soon he and Jolie would help Althea to her room. He'd already brought in a couple of mattresses and blankets, which he'd place close to the hearth later, and where he and Guy preferred to sleep each night. Guy claimed it was far easier for him to remain in the study than to stumble upstairs, but his real concern was the safety of the house. Although they'd never said anything, both he and Stephen felt better being downstairs where they could be easily alerted if anyone prowled around Travers Hill at night; Guy's hounds growling at the least little noise.

"I'm going to take her upstairs and tuck her in," Leigh said, holding the warm bundle close against her breast for a moment, then across her shoulder as she patted her gently, the resulting burp causing Steward to giggle and mimic her noisily until Althea surprised him by admonishing him into quietness, for he'd never received a reprimand from his mother before.

"Are you quite certain you want that little rascal in your bedchamber tonight?" Leigh questioned, holding out her hand for him to kiss with gentlemanly dignity and giggles, which was their usual ritual every evening.

"I'm a gentl'mon, Steban says," he told everyone proudly. "Jus' like my papa."

Althea stared at her son in surprise, never having heard him put more than two words together. "You certainly are," she told him.

"Alwuz kiss Auntie's hand," he said, and Leigh suspected it was only a matter of time before he'd be winking at her.

"Me too, Mama?" Noelle asked, staring at her mother hopefully.

"Yes, indeed, both of my babies are going to be with me tonight," she promised, pressing a warm kiss against her daughter's cheek.

"We'll have to get that little fellow on Pumpkin's back one of these days soon, never heard of a Braedon, and certainly not a Travers, who couldn't sit a horse, or at least a pony, properly," Leigh heard Guy say as she walked to the door, taking the lighted candle from Stephen. She turned at the door, watching them gathered together; all that was left of the Travers family of Virginia.

The rest of them were gone now.

The foyer was cold, the darkness hiding the bloodstains on the pine planking of the floor where wounded soldiers had lain dying. The flickering candlelight guiding her, Leigh made her way up the stairs and along the darkened hallway.

Reaching her bedchamber, she placed the candle on the windowsill, then carefully put the baby down in another, far more elaborate cradle next to the big four-poster. The canopied cradle, draped with delicate damask hangings to keep out the drafts, had rocked several generations of the Travers family into peaceful slumber. Lovingly, Leigh covered the baby with a thick quilt, tucking it in securely around the already sleeping child.

Leigh stood for a moment, resting her shoulder against the bedpost, remembering the sound of voices and the pale images of familiar faces.

Palmer William. Almost a year to the day, July 21, 1861, after that summer four years ago, Palmer William had died in the Battle of First Manassas. The Yanks called it Bull Run. Riding with his onetime professor from the Virginia Military Institute, it had been the battle where General Jackson had won the name "Stonewall." Palmer William had fallen in the afternoon, at Henry House Hill. The Confederate troops had made a valiant defense, driving the federal soldiers back. It had been a costly defeat for the Union; and an even costlier one for their family.

Leigh walked over to the blanket chest that had been pushed against the wall beneath the window to make room for the trundle bed. She opened the lid, moving the candle closer to reveal the contents. Her hand found the fringed officer's sash and she held it tightly for a moment before carefully placing it back in the trunk, next to the pair of gauntlet gloves and the jaunty slouch hat with the ostrich plume Palmer William had favored as being far more dashing than a kepi. His sword lay on top, next to the pistol he had carried into battle, and which she had used that day to kill the looters. His possessions had been returned to them by the family that had buried him in their own family plot, Justin Braedon having carried his friend's body from the battlefield to a nearby farm to be buried with dignity.

Justin Braedon. It hadn't been long after that, just after Christmas, in the first month of a new year, that they'd heard from Nathan that Justin had been killed in a skirmish in the Shenandoah Valley. It was during the Romney Campaign, and his troop had been trying to destroy the tracks of the Baltimore and Ohio Railroad. He'd still been with Stonewall Jackson, riding proudly into battle to the stirring music from the Stonewall Brigade Band, the brass band of the Fifth Virginia Infantry. Palmer William had written to her about them, claiming he had taught his horse, Bourbon, to prance in time to "The Bonnie Blue Flag," but he'd charge whenever he heard the first notes of "The Star Spangled Banner," sensing there were Yankees around.

Leigh reached deeper into the trunk, lifting out a large leather-bound book that had been placed against the side. Carefully, she opened it, staring curiously at the watercolor scenes of Confederate troops camped in the woods, of a young, unidentified cavalry officer, of gunboats patrolling a peaceful stretch of the James River, and various landscapes she'd never seen before.

Stuart James. He had left his artist's portfolio with her the last time he had visited, before he had been wounded at Gettysburg last summer. Somehow it seemed almost appropriate now that Stuart James had been wounded while attacking a place called Cemetery Hill. He'd lingered for six months. He was buried now next to other members of the Travers family who'd died before him, but most of them peacefully, and not before their time.

Thisbe Anne. A bitter smile curved Leigh's lips as she thought of her former sister-in-law. Thisbe Anne had spent most of the war in Philadelphia. She'd run back up to the North as soon as she'd discovered all the fighting was in Virginia and the rest of the South. The only time they'd heard from her was six months after Stuart James had died. She wanted information about Willow Creek Landing, as well as Travers Hill, for as the widow of Stuart James, the eldest son, she wanted to know if she now owned the Travers house and land. She was also now Mrs. Stanway Billingsley. She had married a prosperous Philadelphia businessman. With pleasure, Leigh had written to her informing her that Guy Travers was still alive, and as the only surviving son, was heir to Travers Hill. To assure his wishes were followed, when his eldest son had inherited Willow Creek from the Palmer estate, Stuart Travers had made a will naming Guy as sole beneficiary of Travers Hill, and had he died without issue, then Palmer William inherited. Stuart James's widow had no claim to Travers Hill. They would hear no more from Thisbe Anne. Leigh's only regret was that they'd never see Stuart James's children. And if they heard again from Thisbe, then Nathan would know how to deal with her.

Nathan. They'd received word from him in the fall that he was in Tennessee. He'd gone with General Longstreet to reinforce the Confederate troops fighting at Chattanooga. They'd joined the battle at a place called Chickamauga Creek. Jolie had told them that Chickamauga was a Cherokee word. It meant "River of Death." None of them had slept easy after that, and when word had come that Nathan was missing in action, Jolie hadn't seemed surprised.

He'd know what to do about this too, Leigh thought, taking the piece of stiff paper from her skirt pocket, where she'd been hiding it from the others. She stared down in dismay at the tax assessment she'd received, wondering how they could possibly pay it. They didn't have any hogs to slaughter, or horses to sell, or fattened cattle to send to market, the government taking the share it believed it was entitled to in bacon, cavalry horses, or beef to feed its troops, courtesy of a generous tax assessor. They certainly weren't fools, Leigh mused, since they wouldn't accept the inflated Confederate currency, which bought so little, as payment of taxes.

What was she going to do? Angrily, she wadded up the offending piece of paper, stuffing it deep into the trunk. Then she smiled, pulling out the thick packet of letters she had received from Blythe.

Opening a couple she scanned them quickly. Remembering, without even seeing the words in the dim light from the candle, Blythe's descriptions of Richmond, written with such incredulity and humor.

...April 17, Leigh, we've just about, or so Adam tells me, seceded from the Union. By May we will have. You wouldn't believe the excitement. They pulled down the old flag, the Stars and Stripes. I have to admit, Leigh, it made me feel odd, sad even, because that is our flag, but they pulled it down. Bells rang, cannons fired, and the cheering was deafening. All week long, the celebrations continued. There were torchlight processions through the streets of Richmond. Rockets! Roman candles! Music from countless bands. Down Main Street, past Church Hills, past the State Court House, beyond even the Exchange Hotel, speeches and cheering, all the way down Franklin Street. The speakers say we'll capture Washington within days.

...such incredible people you see on the street, now, Leigh. No one can be certain if one is talking to a spy, a pickpocket, a counterfeiter, a lady of ill-repute, or a government worker. Adam says there is little difference between the latter two.

...Leigh, I don't quite know how to tell you this, but Julia has done something quite scandalous. She has run off with a married man. He is a gentleman, or so they say, and an Englishman with a title. Adam is outraged, since he introduced Julia to the man. He was in America, supposedly on behalf of the British government, to buy cotton. I fear, Julia is ruined. Adam received a letter from her from Paris, and she says she has never been happier. She hasn't heard about her mother. I don't think Adam is going to tell her. I would.

...there was a riot today. Aunt Maribel Lu and I were out trying to find lamb chops, when, suddenly, all of these angry women swarmed onto the street, led by this woman brandishing a pistol, a six-shooter, Leigh, and marching on Capitol Square. It was frightening! Aunt Maribel Lu and I got caught up in the crowd, and I thought I had lost her, until I caught sight of the Stars and Bars and recognized her bonnet. We managed to escape, but we never got our lamb chops.

...$9 a pound, Leigh, for bacon! $275 for a barrel of flour! Potatoes, $25 a bushel. Everyone barters now. Two bushels of salt for a pair of shoes. Five scrawny turkeys for a bonnet. Fortunately, we had five of Aunt Maribel Lu's bonnets to trade for one fat turkey.

...and tell Papa that the cavalry has been quartered at the racecourse, and, for once, appropriate quarters for them and their horses. The federal prisoners have been quartered in a smelly tobacco warehouse on the James River. Papa would be quite pleased with the arrangements.

Blythe Lucinda. Little Lucy. It had been Blythe who had married her beloved Adam that following summer when she had turned seventeen. They had honeymooned in New Orleans, sailing there aboard Adam's ship, *The Blithe Spirit,* a coincidence of names which he very seriously believed, almost superstitiously, was a good omen for the future. They'd stayed at Royal Bay until the war had started, then moved to Richmond, living with Nathan and Althea, Blythe helping Althea with her newborn son and Noelle. And, later, they'd comforted each other when their husbands left to fight.

Leigh thought about her own wedding. It should have

been in April of 1861, but had been postponed because of the death of Matthew Wycliffe's mother. She and Matthew had waited, watching the events unfolding around them. South Carolina had long since seceded, along with state after state across the rebellious South. A Confederacy, made up of states that had seceded from the Union, had been proudly established. Matthew had visited them very little that winter after the announcement of their engagement. He'd hardly stayed more than a day or two at Travers Hill during his many trips between Charleston and Montgomery, Alabama, where a Confederate cabinet had been formed, with secretaries of state, the treasury, and war, meeting to discuss strategy.

But she had never been forgotten by him, and had always been in his thoughts. Even in this time of emergency, she'd received letters and gifts—special little reminders of his love—from Matthew almost every day.

That April, when she and Matthew were to have been wed, the Virginia State Convention passed an ordinance of secession, and Richmond was offered as the new capital of the Confederacy. Fort Sumter was fired upon by Confederate forces demanding the removal of federal troops from Confederate soil. And Matthew returned to Charleston immediately, fearing that, finally, the secession of the united states of the South from the Union had finally led to armed conflict.

Matthew had been right, and by fall they were at war with the North.

Matthew. Dear Matthew. He'd died somewhere in North Carolina, before he could return to Virginia, before they could marry. She'd never seen him again, and she had loved him. His aunt had written a very formal letter to her informing her of Matthew's death. She had addressed her letter from Wycliffe Hall, where she and her son now lived. But it had been from the Benjamin Leighs that they'd learned how Matthew had died. Such a tragic waste, they had written. He'd been killed by a sharpshooter lying in wait as the column of rebel troops had passed along the road. He had never even seen the man in hiding who had cold-bloodedly taken aim on him and shot him.

Leigh replaced the packet of letters, feeling the coldness of Blythe's fan, the one of ivory *brisé* that had been Palmer

William's gift to her on her sixteenth birthday. Next to it Leigh
felt the softness of the muslin shawl, Guy's gift. Disturbing it
slightly, a sweet fragrance with just a touch of something spicy
drifted to Leigh. Her hand touched the dark green perfume
bottle with its etched stars so like her own. Blythe had found
her own special perfume, not jessamine like hers, or violet like
Althea's, or lavender and roses like their mother's. Blythe's
scent was of orange blossoms, with just a hint of cinnamon.

Leigh closed the chest, still unable to accept that Blythe
was gone. Weakened from complications that had followed a
difficult childbirth, she hadn't been able to fight the typhoid
fever that had infected her, and a month later she had died.
Walking over to the cradle, she stared down at Blythe's daughter, Lucinda. Adam had insisted they call her that in memory
of her. So young, both mother and daughter.

Leigh touched the baby, sleeping so quietly, then turned
and walked back to the window. Staring out at the night, she
remembered all of the other times, especially when troubled,
she'd stood at this window.

The last time had been when the Yankees had bivouacked
at Travers Hill. She'd stood alone, looking out at the campfires
glowing in the darkness as the soldiers began to cook their
evening meal. She'd continued to stand before the window,
until twilight had fallen. Suddenly, she'd heard the melancholy
notes of a bugler, and the campfires and candles had slowly
been extinguished. Never had she heard such a mournful
sound, as if it were a cry from the heart.

Fourteen

Even in laughter the heart is sorrowful.

Proverbs 14:13

THE FIRST LIGHT OF DAY REVEALED THE STORM CLOUDS that had threatened the night before still hanging heavy and low on the eastern horizon, blocking out the pale light of the winter sun. Too cowardly to show its face for long, the sun disappeared behind a blanket of clouds, hoarding its warmth to itself as the day dawned cold and bleak.

But it wasn't thunder that rumbled in the distance. A roiling black cloud of smoke climbed high into the gray sky and fiery comets spewed forth from its glowing underbelly, where tongues of flames licked hungrily around the charred and broken skeleton of the railroad trestle that had just been blown sky-high.

The siege gun, with its long, rifled barrel that resembled a vicious snout and wreaked such devastating destruction with its thirty-two-pound shells, would roar no more. But the man-made beast was not silenced yet. The flatbed railroad car it had been mounted on, protected by iron plate shielding, hung precariously for an instant over the edge of the collapsing bridge and bellowed its rage. A hideous screeching and groaning, as metal was rent apart, filled the air like a death cry. Then the flatbed car, dragging the black engine still coupled to it, fell into the inferno, the artillery shells shooting like rockets into the sky as crates of ammunition continued to feed the voracious flames.

In a thicket below the crest of the ridge, and just downstream of the destroyed trestle bridge that had stretched across the ravine, a group of men huddled, their faces glowing like brass masks in the light of the flames.

"Damn!" someone muttered, wiping the back of his hand across his cheek and licking it curiously. "Whiskey!" he crowed, the whites of his eyes looking startling against his soot-smudged face as he stared up at the barrel that had just blown past his head. "Must've had a whole flatbed full of whiskey barrels on that train too!" he muttered in disbelief. "Should've joined up with the artillery, 'stead of the cavalry. They know how to travel. 'Specially them gentlemen rebs!"

"*Now* ye tell me," McGuire said, watching sadly as the exploding whiskey barrel disappeared over the top of the ridge in a shower of corn liquor.

"Would've tasted mighty fine right now," the Bucktail said, licking his dry, cracked lips. "Got one hell of a thirst."

"Well, at least that fire-breather won't be eatin' up any more bluebellies for breakfast."

"Killed the steely beast, we have," someone said with satisfaction as he mounted his horse, pulling sharply on the reins as the horse shied nervously when a thunderous roar sounded as another flatbed car loaded with shells and supplies fell into the ravine below.

"Come on, McGuire. Better ride as fast as you talk, now, 'cause the cap'n has already cleared the ridge. Know how he don't like to dally none," someone warned, seeing the reddish-brown rump of the captain's big bay disappearing through the trees.

"Ain't the time to be sittin' here enjoyin' yer handiwork, boyo," someone else advised, glancing around to see a troop of soldiers making their way along the ridgeline, ducking automatically when he saw a flash of gunfire, then heard the thud of impact as a bullet hit and embedded itself in the bark of a tree trunk beside his head, flying splinters of oak scratching his cheek.

"Don't understand it. Half the bridge is still standin'. Didn't get it all this time, an' I used plenty of powder."

"Don't worry, it'll burn to the ground soon enough, or if it don't, you can come back tomorrow and finish it. Get a reb to light the fuse for you, be real gentlemanly of him. Figure, though, with this side gone, ain't nothin' goin' to get across to the other side fer some time."

"Git movin'!" someone cried, urging his mount up the slope, his spurs jingling the alarm.

"Don't need to convince me none!"

"What the hell?"

"Lord help us! Where'd they come from?" the Bucktail

croaked, his eyes widening in dismay as he reached the narrow road atop the ravine and saw the riders approaching at a fast gallop along the road from the opposite direction, their gray uniforms, glinting sabers, and fierce rebel yells leaving little doubt that a whole regiment of cavalry must be close behind. "Hell, no one knows we're even here, leastways till now they didn't. We been as quiet as mice tiptoein' 'round a sleepin' mouser."

"Got us caught between them! Ain't s'posed to be no cavalry behind us! Saw them cross the river yesterday!" a voice cried out unnecessarily, because the sound of gunfire sounded all around them as bullets whizzed past their heads from seemingly every direction except from above.

Then, as if to mock them, a troop of graybacks suddenly appeared over the crest of the hill above the road, bayonets fixed as they charged down the slope, copses of proud old oaks and cedars affording adequate cover for their attack.

If he lived to tell the tale, this would be one of the best adventures yet, Lieutenant Chatham thought excitedly as Captain Dagger and his Bloodriders returned fire, but they were outnumbered, the patrol of foot soldiers having taken up defensive positions in the underbrush as they fired on the federal troops. Caught like sitting ducks in the middle of the road, the lieutenant mused unhappily, wondering if, perhaps, it was to be their last daring raid and his memoirs would be published posthumously.

McGuire felt a burning sensation in his shoulder and slumped forward, but still managed to keep his seat, determined no reb was going to capture him without a fight. It seemed to be the captain's opinion too, because he yelled a bloodcurdling cry, which never failed to raise the fine hairs on the back of McGuire's neck, and raced back toward them, right toward the line of infantrymen who'd now moved into the road to block their escape—never a retreat—signaling to his men to ride back down into the ravine while he drew the enemy fire. With a look of mingled pain and anger, McGuire saw the young, bespectacled Lieutenant Chatham, who always seemed to be just a step behind the captain, unseated and begin to fall as his frightened horse reared suddenly as a barrage of bullets caught the dappled gray in the chest. The lieutenant's

boot caught and held in the stirrup, and for several frightening
seconds he was dragged beneath the horse's hooves before
he finally tumbled onto the road. McGuire couldn't believe
it when he saw the little lieutenant struggling bravely to his
knees, trying to pull his sword free to defend himself as he
stood his ground alone against the onslaught of the rebel
cavalry charging down the road toward him.

McGuire's eyes widened with incredulity as the captain
wheeled the big bay around and, hanging low on one side of
the saddle, swooped the lieutenant up into his arms right in front
of the enemy. Throwing him across his saddle horn, he spun
back around and charged the rebel line of infantrymen that was
advancing steadily down the middle of the road under cover of
fire from the underbrush. The captain jumped the big bay over
several rebels who were too slow, or startled, to move or shoot,
while scattering the rest like a basket of overturned butternuts
before he turned and disappeared into the thicket with the young
lieutenant looking like a side of beef, his sandy brown head, hat-
less now, bobbing up and down on one side of the saddle, while
his feet, one boot missing, stuck out on the other side.

Captain Dagger's men had claimed they'd follow their
captain into the burning fires of hell if they had to. Some of
them must have thought that boast had come true as Captain
Dagger, the big bay's coat turned bloodred, disappeared into
the black, swirling smoke as he raced into the flames that were
spreading to the trestle that still stood, leading his men either
toward certain death or freedom as they followed.

"So much smoke," Leigh murmured, staring out at the gray
clouds, her gaze lingering on the black smoke that rose high
into the sky just the far side of the low hills in the distance.
She pulled the window shut on the cold, acrid-smelling air.
"No one is likely to notice the trail of smoke coming from
Travers Hill today," she said, turning away from the big
kitchen window and picking up the load of linens she'd pulled
from the beds and dumped on the brick floor by one of the big
wooden tubs. "Guy said it wasn't thunder, and he was right.
I wonder what blew up." She spoke more out of habit than

interest as she began to sort through the pile, dropping the pillowcases into the steaming, soapy water, then pushing them down with a long stick.

"Now, Miss Leigh," Jolie said, hands on her narrow hips, "I told you I'd do this washin'."

"And I told you, Jolie," Leigh said, mimicking her with a grin, her hands placed on her hips as she faced her, "that you cannot do all of the washing yourself, and cook, and care for all of us, and since no bed at Travers Hill, no matter how darned the linens are, will be made with dirty sheets, I intend to help you. We owe it to Mama," she added, glancing down at her chafed hands as if they belonged to someone else. "Remember what that Yankee major said about never having slept so well in such sweet-scented sheets?"

"Hmmmph! Sweet-talkin', an' sweet-dreamin', that's what he was doin'. Kept my eye on that good-lookin', honey-tongued Yankee after that, 'cause I figured he had himself a wife an' children back home, an' if he didn't, then he was hopin' to take you back home with him, only figure he wasn't plannin' on waitin' till he got home to start that family. Saw the way he was eyein' you, missy. Wasn't decent. Those Yankees got no manners. Shouldn't be 'round decent folk. He was jus' waitin' for a chance to get you alone. An' you didn't help none bein' so sweet to him like butter wouldn't melt in your mouth. Should never have smiled at him, missy. You can't smile at a gentleman like that, especially when he's no gentleman. An' the look in your eye jus' dared him to do something no gentleman should with a lady. Lost a week's sleep worryin' 'bout you. One of these days, Miss Leigh, you're goin' to smile like that at the wrong man, an' you're goin' to look like that from those big blue eyes, darin' a man, an' he's goin' to do something 'bout it."

"That Yankee did leave us some flour and beans, enough for two weeks' cooking. Those biscuits were mighty good."

"Hmmmph. Probably stolen from some other poor family up the road a piece, an' probably left a red-eyed, swollen-bellied miss back somewhere too, grinnin' devil that he was. Jus' lucky, we are, that we don't have a bluebelly's baby layin' in that cradle next to Miss Lucinda right now."

Leigh's cheeks flushed brightly. "I'll do what I have to do to keep this family from starving, or being turned out of our home. I'll do just about anything to keep us all alive, *except* get into bed with a Yankee," Leigh told her, pleased to see Jolie's startled expression at her plain talk for a change. "Smile and sweet-talk a Yankee, yes, even shoot one, or a bushwhacker, whatever the color of his uniform is, yes, I'll do that, and that's the truth. But I've still got my Travers pride, and that is one thing I'll never lose, or shame," she said, pushing a long strand of hair out of her face, and even though her shoulders ached, and her back felt like it was going to break in two sometimes, she never felt ashamed of herself and how they lived at Travers Hill—at least it was still here, and theirs.

"Figure you wouldn't have much to say if some Yankee, and no gentleman, is smart enough where you're concerned, decides he wants you in his bed. Figure you couldn't sweet-talk yourself outa that, missy, 'cause was sweet-talkin' that got you in his bed in the first place. 'Course, you keep workin' yourself like some field hand, there won't be no Yankee, nor reb, gentleman or not, who'll want you, so we won't have to worry none, an' I'll be sleepin' easy again," Jolie muttered with a disapproving glance, still unable to accept Miss Leigh bending over a tub scrubbing soiled linens, although she had to admit she did a better job than Jassy ever had. Jassy, hmmmph, Jolie thought, a glint in her yellow eyes as she remembered how quickly she'd run off with some upstart that'd come onto Travers land trying to lord it over the Travers family. Jolie looked heavenward, remembering the sight of Jassy sashaying off barefoot, and wearing the fanciest bonnet Jolie had ever seen, her nose held up in the air as proudly as if she were gentry, Jolie thought, still worrying about the little maid and wringing out a sheet as if it were Jassy's fool neck between her hands instead.

Dressed in a plain gown of somber, dove-gray wool, the sleeves of the bodice jacket rolled up around her elbows, the prim collar opened and unbuttoned to the top of her chemise beneath, her hair woven into a thick braid that hung down her back, Leigh bent to her work. She felt the muscles tightening across her shoulders and down to the small of her back as she stirred the soapy water, then scrubbed the linen back and forth between her hands with more determination than strength.

"Runnin' out of soap," Jolie said, careful of the amount she had used in the tub she was loading with another batch of linens. "Don't know how we're supposed to wash when we don't have any hogs an' cattle to slaughter to get the fat. It's mighty lucky I know where to find soapwort out in the woods. Not too much lather, but it cleans nice."

"And we'll rinse everything twice in sweet water," Leigh said, glancing over at the tub where the fragrance of lemon balm was strong.

"Just hope there aren't more Yankees 'round," Jolie said. "We're never goin' to get them outa bed."

Leigh smiled bitterly, thinking it might just be the best way to win the war. For the next two hours she and Jolie washed and wrung out the linens, hanging them up to dry on the flaxen lines they'd strung across the kitchen.

Blowing a stray strand of hair out of her face, Leigh dropped the last diaper onto the pile she'd just finished washing, flexing her leaden shoulder muscles as she straightened away from the edge of the tub. Easing the pain that nestled in the small of her back like a grumpy animal curled up for a long winter's hibernation, she found herself wondering if spring would ever come.

She stared at the sleet blowing against the windows and rubbed her chilled arms, hugging her own warmth close for a moment. Picking up the pile of dripping linen squares, once a fine bedsheet, now very serviceable diapers for Lucinda, Leigh glanced around the kitchen as she began to hang the diapers. At first glance, the room seemed little changed from before the war, with clay pots of aromatic cooking and medicinal herbs filling the windowsills, bunches of drying herbs hanging from the raftered ceiling, along with woven baskets, a corner cupboard displaying a shelf full of dusty recipe books and crockery, and in the hearth, a large copper pot bubbling perhaps with chicken and dumplings or corn chowder. But upon closer inspection, one would have found the copper pot was filled with a thin broth that would do little to satisfy one's hunger; the crockery was chipped from constant use; there was no smoked ham, succulent and pink, the pride of Travers Hill's smokehouse, sitting on a fine china platter to be served for Sunday supper; no beaten biscuits or flaky rolls were browning in the ovens along with cinnamon squares and brownies; nor was her father's bourbon pecan cake sitting in sweet splendor, a candied cherry crowning it.

Bowls full of creamy butter, large brown eggs, snowy white sugar and finely ground flour, pitchers of sweet milk and buttermilk, and chunks of chocolate would once have crowded the tabletop. Instead, several jars of preserves and pickled vegetables sat on the table, and were all that was left of the summer crop from the orchard and vegetable garden. Over half of the orchard had been burned, along with the fields of wheat and corn, and the kitchen gardens, full of ripening tomatoes, squash, peas, beans, and other vegetables almost ready to be harvested, had been trampled when troops from both armies had fought near Travers Hill last summer.

Leigh ignored the rumbling in her stomach as she remembered how, at first, her father had felt it his duty and honor to send his share, 10 percent, of all the crops harvested at Travers Hill to support the war effort. And later, with tears in his eyes, he'd sent some of Travers Hill's finest hunters and racing horses, knowing he'd never see his prized Thoroughbreds again, but at least another Confederate officer would ride proudly into battle defending the Confederacy.

But soon, squads of Confederate soldiers had come onto Travers land uninvited, arrogantly requisitioning whatever they saw fit to take. Then federal troops came foraging, living off the land, stealing, it mattered little what they called it—it was still theft, whether by one army or the other. The few remaining stable and field hands, were forcibly taken away. Overnight, it seemed, Travers Hill was emptied of its teams of farm horses, mules, and oxen; cattle, sheep, cows, goats, geese, chickens, and hogs disappeared from the corrals and pens. The wagons and carriages, harnesses and blankets, the tools—plows, hoes, and scythes—for planting and harvesting, were gone, and there was no metal for the blacksmith to forge into new tools, so the furnace remained cold and silent, the bellows stilled, and the fields fallow, and the next year, barren.

And finally, the remaining Thoroughbreds, the special ones so beloved by her father—the lifeblood of Travers Hill—were stolen from them too. Nothing was left. Nothing except their pride.

Pride, yes, Leigh thought, forgetting for a moment the dull ache in her back and the stinging redness of her hands as she glanced around proudly at the rows of dripping laundry. A satisfied smile lurking in the corners of her lips, Leigh turned and began to fill a bucket with steaming water from the big kettle over the fire.

"What're you doin' now?" Jolie demanded, looking up from the pair of drawers she was washing.

"I promised Althea I would help her bathe and wash her hair today."

"You sit down an' rest a spell. You don't know if you're comin' or goin', missy, an' I heard you up last night with lil' Miss Lucinda, singin' an' croonin' her back to sleep while she suckled on a sugar teat," Jolie told her, frowning as Leigh never hesitated, continuing toward the far side of the kitchen, where the big, slipper-shaped metal tub had been pushed against the wall. A loud scraping noise sounded as Leigh pulled it across the brick flooring by one of its handles.

"I'm not tired, truly I'm not. I felt wonderful this morning watching Althea eat more than a biteful of food for a change. She seems so improved since just yesterday eve, don't you think? You know how she has always hated anything dirty or soiled, and how particular she has always been about her toilette. She'll feel much better with her hair clean. I don't want to disappoint her. It will keep her spirits up, and she was talking about taking on the darning and mending chores. She can do that without tiring herself."

"Just like her mama. Miss Beatrice Amelia was ever so tidy about herself an' her fine linen chemises an' petticoats. Such pretty things, she had, an' always kept them so nice," Jolie said, glancing down quickly. "Got soap in my eye," she murmured, her eyes burning. "An' you get that Steban to get that fire goin' if it's died down. Don't want Miss Althea catchin' her death of cold now that she's on the mend," Jolie warned. "It'd help us a lot, her doin' the mendin' too, after all, she's a real fine needlewoman. An' she can watch young Mister Steward an' Miss Noelle, not that Miss Noelle ever causes us any trouble.

Real sweet an' quiet, she is," Jolie said approvingly. "Not like some I could mention when they was that age," she added, truly getting soap in her eye this time as she rubbed away the threatening tears when she thought of Guy Travers's blindness. "You bring her down here. Wish Mister Guy would let us help him more, why, you would think I'd never seen his bare bottom before," she said. "Only lets Steban help him with his bath," she said, shaking her head disapprovingly, because in her eyes Guy Travers would always be the same little baby boy she had wet-nursed when the mistress hadn't been able to feed him, not having enough milk of her own. Jolie's look was tender as she remembered having plenty of milk for both Sweet John and the little chestnut-haired baby who'd been so demanding at her breast—a bond that could never be broken had been formed between them. It had been the same with Miss Leigh. She had suckled at her breast too, only that time, her own little girl baby had died, and she'd had too much milk to give to Beatrice Amelia's little daughter, who had also received all of the love that Jolie had been unable to lavish on her own stillborn child.

"Nothin' goin' to happen to my little ones," she muttered, plunging her arms deep into the water as she scrubbed the linens as if scouring the world of sin, and feeling her purpose in life, her dedication to Beatrice Amelia and the Travers family, stronger than it ever had been, and held inviolable by her love for them.

Leigh made her way upstairs, pausing midway to rest and catch her breath, then continued the rest of the way to Althea's bedchamber. The room was warm, a fire burning brightly in the hearth.

Althea was sitting up in bed, Noelle next to her as she showed her several new stitches to try.

"Ready?" Leigh asked. "Haven't forgotten, it's washing day, for both people and linens."

Althea smiled, pointing at the neat pile of underclothing she'd placed on the foot of the bed. "Yes, I'm ready," she said, getting slowly to her feet, and leaning heavily against Leigh when she placed a supporting arm around her shoulders. "I was looking through my trunk, and I found a bar of soap. I'd forgotten I had it," she said, her pale cheeks flushed with anticipation.

"Violet too," Leigh said, recognizing the lavender paper

sprigged with dark purple violets wrapped around the soap. "Your favorite."

"Yes," Althea said, remembering it had been Nathan's favorite too.

Seeing the stricken look that had suddenly crossed Althea's face, Leigh asked, "Where is Steward?"

"He's with Guy in the study. I fear he is more interested in riding his noble steed than watching Noelle and me sew stitches. Already, the impatient little man," she said, laughing softly, hoarsely, and it sounded strange to Leigh, startling her. She hadn't heard her sister laugh in a long time.

"Better bundle up, we've got to go out to the kitchens," Leigh reminded her, pulling a blanket from the chest at the foot of the bed and wrapping it around Althea, who was dressed in her nightdress and dressing gown.

Althea looked at her sister in dismay. "The kitchens? Whatever for?" she demanded, shocked by the thought as she glanced down at her dishabille.

"Without anyone to carry the buckets of water into the house, Jolie and I found it far easier to set up the tub in the kitchens," Leigh explained, gently reminding Althea that Travers Hill was no longer a hive of activity.

"Oh," Althea murmured, ashamed of her momentary forgetfulness.

But Leigh only laughed. "You should have seen Jolie and Stephen and me trying to get the tub downstairs and through the door. Stephen slipped, and the tub fell to the bottom, thumping like thunder all the way down, with Stephen trying to get out of the way in front of it, but he couldn't, and it caught up to his flying feet on the last step and bumped him, knocking him into the tub. I've never heard Jolie laugh so hard," Leigh said, seeing again Jolie's thin shoulders shaking uncontrollably as she stood at the top of the stairs.

"It must have been amusing. But poor Stephen, he is so very dignified," Althea said.

"He wouldn't even talk to her for a week."

Althea looked at her sister's gown, and said, more sharply this time, "You're not even wearing a shawl over your shoulders."

"Strong as a horse," her sister answered, guiding her toward the door. "But I don't linger long between the kitchens and the big house."

"Bye, Mama," Noelle called out, returning the kiss her mother had blown to her as her aunt led her frail-looking mother from the room, her large brown eyes bright as she returned her attention to the beautiful stitching her mother had demonstrated for her earlier that morning. Glancing back up for a moment, she giggled, thinking of the handkerchief she was embroidering in secret for her aunt, hoping she would be pleased with the square of linen, and the delicate bluebells she was embroidering in the lace-edged corners.

"Mama would be horrified to think of us bathing in the kitchens," Althea said as they walked along the hall and she saw the closed door of their mother's bedchamber. "Papa, however," Althea continued, a mischievous look in her eye, "would have enjoyed it. Within arm's reach of the still," she added, laughing.

"And he did end up out there on many an occasion," Leigh said, "*because* he had been too close to the still. Remember when Mama wouldn't let him in the house, because he could hardly stand up, having been sampling the latest batch from the still, and on his way down to the stables for a ride, he'd fallen into the manure field and had come back up to the house to change. She had him washed down in the laundry room like that grinning hound of Guy's that liked to roll in cow dung. Papa was madder than an angry hornet and stood outside her window cursing. I thought she was going to make him stay out there all night long. I can still remember him, about an hour later, standing outside and calling up to her, and looking so forlorn as he stood there holding a bouquet of roses," Leigh said, hurrying Althea across the covered walkway between the big house and the kitchens, their laughter trailing after them as they disappeared into the kitchens.

An hour later, Althea sat before the hearth, her golden hair bright and shining as she dried it before the fire. She sipped a cup of tea gratefully, and thirstily, even if it was made from willow and sage leaves, and other mysterious herbs Jolie gathered from the woodlands, rather than the fancy imported Chinese tea she was so fond of.

She sighed, and although still weak, she felt better than she had in a long time.

She glanced around the room, shaking her head in disbelief as her gaze lingered on the long rows of washing. She still couldn't believe that Leigh and Jolie had washed all of the linens by themselves.

"Let me put a lil' more honey in that tea, Miss Althea," Jolie said, coming to stand beside her.

"Thank you, Jolie," Althea murmured, wondering what life would have been like if Jolie and Stephen had left Travers Hill.

"Ah, such pretty hair. Jus' like your mama's. You want me to brush it till it crackles?" Jolie said, not waiting for Althea's answer as she took the brush from Althea's lap and began to brush the long strands, the same way she had Beatrice Amelia's, and Althea's, before she had married and moved to Richmond.

"Where is Leigh?" Althea asked drowsily, her head nodding back slightly.

"Now where you think, Miss Althea?" Jolie said, thinning her lips with disapproval. "With those animals of hers, that's where. So tired, she is, she can hardly stand on her feet without falling, an' now she's back there in the laundry with those critters. Figure she'd have brought them into the parlor if I'd let her. But I told her it was either them, or me," Jolie said, nodding her head emphatically. "Warned her I wasn't a field hand to be sleepin' with farm animals, much less cleanin' up after them."

"What animals?"

"The ones she's got hidden away in the laundry. Turned it into a stable, she did, after the stables got broken into. Figured she could guard her animals better up here at the big house than down in the stables. 'Specially since she had to stay up night an' day with that mare. Surprised it didn't up an' die, so poorly did it look."

"What mare? We have lots of mares at Travers Hill," Althea said, remembering another time.

"Nothin' but rats out in the stables now, Miss Althea. Everything was taken, or stolen, till there was nothin' left."

"Nothing left," Althea repeated, thinking now of Royal Bay.

"That's why, honey, when that lil' mare come home last month, Miss Leigh just 'bout fainted. A bag of bloodied bones, it was, draggin' itself up the lane to the big house. Remembered, it did, that this was home. Thought Miss Leigh was goin' to go wild, she was so happy. Then, she saw that wound on the mare's back, an' the deep spur marks on her side, an' she was so angry she could've spat. Figured if that reb had been standin' there she would've killed him with her bare hands. I've never seen such a look in her eye before, 'ceptin' when she killed those looters."

"Damascena?" Althea asked in amazement. "Someone stole her?"

"That's the one. You know Miss Leigh has always been sweet on that mare, 'specially when she lost the lil' cap'n to that no good Braedon fella. Thought her heart was goin' to break that summer. An' then again, when them rebs was nearby an' they come onto Travers land an' break into the stables. This one, an' he was an officer, only he was no gentleman," Jolie said with a sniff. "He takes Miss Leigh's mare to ride into battle, only horse we got left at Travers Hill. This reb's horse was shot out from under him. I didn't know what we was goin' to do, 'cause I knew Miss Leigh would be heartbroken, 'specially after all that's happened 'round here. That mare was all she had left, an' she loved it so."

"Oh, no, poor Leigh," Althea said quietly. "What happened?"

Jolie frowned. "Thought at first she was goin' to shoot the man right out of the saddle, 'cause she had that gun with her, then, I don't know what happened, 'cause she just stood there watchin' them ride off. Never said a word 'bout it after that. Then, a month later, the mare shows up here," Jolie said, giving a hoot of laughter. "Reckon someone else took a dislikin' to that reb. 'Cause someone, or something, blew him outa his boots, cause they was still in the stirrups, along with his left big toe."

Althea's brown eyes opened wide for a moment in shock, then she closed them against the image as she wondered what her sister and the others had been through here at Travers Hill while she'd been delirious with fever, unaware of the war raging around them, unable to help.

"An', of course, that nasty-faced pony is still here—"

"Pumpkin?" Althea said, smiling.

"That's the one, an' a meaner, an' ornerier beast, I've never met. Figure that's why no one bothered stealin' him, more trouble than good he'd be. Didn't know those critters lived so long. It's because they're so mean. But we got him doin' his share. Miss Leigh an' Steban hitch him up to the cart an' take him with them when they go to fetch logs from the woods. An', Miss Althea, you're goin' to be surprised, but we even got ourselves a cow," Jolie said with a wide grin.

"A cow?" Althea said weakly, thinking of the herd that used to graze the meadowlands of Travers Hill.

"She's not much to look at, an' we don't know where she came from, but she gives us good, sweet milk. Don't know what we'd do if it wasn't for her, 'cause lil' Miss Lucinda has to have milk with no mama to suckle," Jolie said with another sniff. "An' Mister Steward does love his puddin'," Jolie added, as if that was explanation enough.

And Althea, not knowing whether to cry or to laugh, began to laugh until the tears finally did fall.

"'Course, he only gets puddin' when I can get my hands on that sneaky hen's eggs. She's goin' to end up in the stew pot one of these days soon," Jolie promised, smiling her approval as she refilled Althea's cup of tea, thinking it was good to hear her laughter again.

Leigh was thinking the same thing as she heard Althea's laughter coming through the narrow passageway that led from the pantry and scullery into the laundry, where she'd stabled her menagerie. And it made a very snug stable, indeed, Leigh thought as she looked around at the straw she'd spread across the brick flooring and the trough she'd filled with hay, and, occasionally, oats, when she could buy or barter them. Right now, the trough was woefully low, and the woebegone expressions she was receiving from the three pairs of big brown eyes were hard to ignore.

"All right, no need to stare at me like I was a Yankee raider," Leigh said, pressing a kiss to Damascena's velvety muzzle, feeling the mare's hot breath against her cheek as Damascena snorted her recognition and neighed softly. Leigh's hands touched her tenderly, calming the slight shivers she could feel shaking the mare beneath her thick winter coat, but the shivering came of nervousness, not cold, for Damascena still shied easily, rolling her beautiful oval-shaped eyes around and flattening her pointed ears whenever she heard a strange noise, or saw a sudden movement.

Leigh smoothed the rug across Damascena's back, patting her comfortingly, not having to see the ragged scar etched deep from flank to buttock. She could feel it through the woolen rug, and she cursed anew the rebel officer who had stolen Damascena from Travers Hill.

Leigh spoke softly to her for a few minutes, but it took longer to calm her today than usual, and Leigh remembered the thunder at dawn—no, the explosion—and realized that Damascena would have been terrified by the sound, distant though it had been.

"There, there, girl, no one will hurt you ever again. I won't let them," she said, her voice familiar, and as gentle and soothing as if she spoke to a frightened child. "You're all I have left, Damascena," she whispered, resting her cheek against the chestnut coat, welcoming the slight roughness of it. "I'm not going to lose you too."

Leigh jerked in surprise, feeling a painful nip against her hip. "Not jealous, are you?" she asked, turning around and running her hand through the Shetland pony's shaggy mane as she stepped away from the mare. "Good thing you like hay and grass more than oats," she said, her laughter soft and husky when she felt his muzzle pressing into her hip again as he searched for the apple that he still, in some hazy corner of his mind, seemed to remember as his treat. Not as fat as he once had been, Pumpkin was still a plump pony, and a good stall mate for Damascena, as was the cow that had never stopped chewing her cud, her large bovine eyes watching everything with contented detachment as she remained undisturbed by the war that had almost destroyed life at Travers Hill.

Leigh walked over to the small window and glanced out. There was a brisk wind blowing, but it didn't seem to be raining as heavily. Now would be a good chance to get another bale of hay for their feed before the storm gathered force and broke over their heads again. Pulling a rough woolen blanket over her head and shoulders, Leigh let herself out of the laundry room, stopping for the wheelbarrow, left beside the door, then pushing it across the greensward toward the stables, the mud coating the wheel and slowing its movement through the rain-soaked field with each step she took.

Leigh glanced back at the familiar shape of the big house, the warmth of its mellow brick walls always beckoning. She stared up at the windows. Most of them were shuttered against the storm, the others were dark, except for the study window on the side of the house where Guy was, and the big kitchen windows. The trail of gray smoke rising from the chimneys seemed welcoming, and was certainly comforting, Leigh thought as she dug in her toes to keep from slipping, pushing harder, her slight weight straining against the wheelbarrow as she rolled it closer to the stables, anxious to return to the warmth of the great hearth in the kitchens.

Her hands were clumsy with numbness as she fumbled with the bar across the stable doors, then one of the heavy doors swung wide and she wheeled the barrow into the stables, hurrying to get out of the cold, gusting wind that had found its way under the blanket she huddled beneath, lifting it from her head and baring it to the light rain that continued to fall steadily.

Leigh stopped midway through the door and stared in disbelief.

She stood frozen, meeting the equally shocked gazes of the Yankee soldiers she had walked in on. Some were sitting propped against the stalls, a couple were stretched full length on the brick flooring, while others were leaning tiredly against the posts, but all had turned to watch the stable doors opening, and apparently had not been surprised until they'd seen her bundled-up figure. Because only now were some of them quickly drawing their pistols, others sabers, and one man was beginning to move threateningly toward her along the crowded passageway between the stalls.

"Sure as hell ain't the cap'n."

"Not with them pretty blue eyes, it ain't, so reckon I've died and gone to heaven. Only thing that bothers me, is what the hell the rest of you cutthroats are doin' here? Didn't figure none of you'd see heaven," someone laughed, then began to cough.

Leigh took one look at the bloodied and blackened inhuman faces, catching sight of the hellish grin on the one coming toward her, his eyes feeding on her face hungrily, and shoved the wheelbarrow in front of him. She dragged the door back, slamming the bar down with a strength she hadn't known she possessed.

"Stop her, Buck! Don't let her git away! Probably a troop of rebs comin' up the road right now!" someone warned. "That sweet lil' reb gal will bring them down on our heads."

"Don't worry, 'cause she's not goin' far," a voice called out from the far end of the stable near one of the side doors where the man had been standing guard.

Leigh turned away from the barred doors and ran, but not before she heard the incredible sound of laughter coming from inside, as if they were unconcerned about her having seen them, or of her alerting that rebel patrol they were so worried about discovering them holed up in her stables.

Leigh didn't wait to learn the reason for their jesting as she sought the safety of the big house—where she had foolishly left the pistol and the rifle. Her feet slipped in the field that was little better than a mire as she struggled across the greensward, cursing herself for her slowness, expecting to hear the soldiers behind her any second, for they could easily have opened the stable doors from inside and given chase.

She was about to glance back over her shoulder when she felt a painful tug on the long braid that dangled down her back, then an iron band clamped around her waist, tightening as it lifted her feet from the ground. She tried to scream, but a rough hand, her chestnut braid of hair wrapped around it, closed over her mouth, muffling her cries for help.

She fought like a wild creature, her feet kicking at her attacker's legs as she tried to free her arms, tangled in the folds of the blanket caught between their bodies. But the man held her easily, his great strength terrifying her as he carried her back toward the stables and the men waiting there.

No, not like this, Leigh thought, hot tears scalding her cold cheeks, her heart pounding sickeningly as she remembered the laughing men, the one with the lustful glint in his eye, and realized what her fate would be once inside the stables where no one would hear her screams. Desperation lent her renewed strength, and Leigh swung her leg between her attacker's, risking breaking hers as she wedged it behind his knee, halting his long stride and causing him to lose his footing in the slippery mud. Suddenly they were falling. Her arms were freed as the blanket loosened, but she didn't have time to catch herself and roll away as she hit the ground, because the man came down hard on top of her, trapping her beneath his heavy body.

Her chest heaving beneath his, Leigh struggled to draw breath into her lungs as she stared up into the man's face, raising her arm to fend off his attack, but her small fist was caught and held, his steely fingers closing around her hand, holding their hands clasped together.

Leigh closed her eyes, feeling a strange lethargy seeping through her limbs and she knew she must be dreaming. Then she opened her eyes, thinking the vision that had haunted her for so many years would have disappeared—as it always did in her dreams. But, instead, she saw again the hawkish-featured face, sun-darkened, the carved angle of the jaw, hard and unforgiving, the gray-green eyes, so cold in their crystalline depths. The dark gold hair was even longer than she remembered, and it had been woven into a heathenish-looking braid that just touched his shoulder, while around the strong column of his neck, a leather pouch, which she knew the contents of, hung suspended by a rawhide thong.

It was a face she'd thought never to see again.

Fifteen

In many ways doth the full heart reveal
The presence of the love it would conceal.

Samuel Taylor Coleridge

LEIGH STARED UP INTO THE FACE OF NEIL BRAEDON.

"Neil." Silently, she mouthed the word, unable to speak aloud his name, a name she had cursed silently for so long, a name branded deep by her own heart's betrayal.

She closed her eyes again, shaking her head in disbelief and denial. She had been so frightened…but to discover the Yankee who'd attacked her was Neil Braedon was a cruel jest indeed. Neil Darcy Braedon. No friend to her, or to her family, she realized, remembering the violence of their last farewell. How many times since that night had she been haunted by his face in her dreams, his mocking voice sounding in her ears, longing to see him again yet hating herself for not being able to forget him?

"Leigh." He spoke her name softly now, a gleam of amusement, or perhaps malice, in those pale eyes looking so deeply into hers, his breath warm against her cold cheek. She felt his body tensing above hers, then watched as he glanced over her head at the house and the green-shuttered windows peering down on them. Then his gaze traveled across the greensward toward the woodlands and the river beyond, his eyes narrowing intently as if searching for something. With catlike agility he was on his feet, easily pulling her up with him.

"Not frightened of me, are you?" he chided, not having missed her worried glance back at the big house. "We are, after all, old friends."

"You had better let me go," Leigh warned in a low, furious tone as she found her voice and began to struggle against him as he headed toward the stables. "You're trespassing. This is Travers land—or have you forgotten?"

Neil laughed. It was a rough sound, as if he had seldom

found reason to laugh during the last few years. "No, I haven't forgotten," he said in a hardened voice. "Some things never change, do they? I seem to remember being warned about trespassing on Travers land the last time you and I met so unexpectedly. We seem destined to meet under the most amazing circumstances," he said, ignoring her struggles as he kept walking, roughly pulling her behind him, her stubbornly dug-in feet sliding through the mud and hindering him little.

"A tumble in the hay, now a tumble in the mud," he said mockingly as she lost a shoe and he stopped just long enough for her to slip it back on her mud-soaked, stockinged foot.

"Damn you," Leigh said, not trying to hide her animosity as she glared at his broad back and tried to pry loose his ironhanded grip, but she was far angrier with herself than him. She had known a momentary gladness in her heart when seeing him, having wondered if he still lived, for Adam had told her his cousin had joined the Union army to fight. And now, her heart was pounding with its traitorous beat even though she hated him for the man he was, and for the blue uniform he had chosen to wear.

"Is that any way to greet an old friend? I thought you'd be pleased to see me after all these years. You haven't missed me then? No sweet peck on the cheek to welcome me back to Travers Hill? Where is that famed Travers hospitality?" he taunted her cruelly, unable to contain his own anger as he saw the intense dislike in her beautiful blue eyes, and suspected she would without the slightest remorse turn him and his men over to the rebel patrols searching for them.

And he hadn't given her much reason to feel otherwise. They had not been the best of friends when last they met. And she had little reason now to befriend him, he thought, recalling the empty shabbiness of her home and the poor condition of the stables—once the pride and glory of Travers Hill. He saw again the six brick chimneys rising so forlornly from the ashes; all that remained of Royal Bay. He still couldn't believe Royal Bay, his father's home, was gone. They'd ridden first to Royal Bay, where he'd thought he and his men could rest, and the wounded could have been treated, but he'd been stunned to find the grand old house in ruins, the outbuildings tumbled down. He remembered seeing Althea Braedon, Nathan's wife, lying ill on the sofa at Travers Hill, and he couldn't help but wonder what had happened to the rest of the Braedon family. Where were they now? Did any of them still live? And the Travers family. What of them? He could understand now Leigh's hatred of Yankees—especially one particular Yankee.

Damn, he thought to himself. Why couldn't he and his men have remained safely hidden in the stables until nightfall, when, rested, they could have made their escape under cover of darkness, no one at Travers Hill ever having been the wiser? Instead, they had been discovered, and now he found himself in a devil of a predicament.

What was he to do with Leigh Travers? No, Mrs. Matthew Wycliffe, he reminded himself. She certainly had a knack for being in the wrong place at the wrong time. But there was nothing he could do about it; his men were in no condition to move. They were cold and tired, and half of them were seriously wounded. And their wounds, especially McGuire's and young Chatham's, needed to be tended before they moved to another, safer hiding place. They had just barely made Travers Hill before McGuire had fallen from the saddle, weak from loss of blood. The lieutenant had been unconscious when they'd hauled him down from his ignominious perch—but at least he still breathed.

Dragging Leigh behind him, they reached the stable doors. The doors opened almost magically, but Leigh knew someone had been waiting and watching, and then she found herself once again inside and facing the hostile looks of a score or more of federal soldiers.

"See you caught the lil' reb spy, Cap'n," someone said.

Captain, one of the soldiers had addressed him. Leigh was not surprised to learn that Neil Braedon was the leader of this scruffy band of Yankees.

"But not without a fight," another gruff voice commented, reminding Leigh of her own muddied gown, and drawing her attention to Neil Braedon's odd appearance. No Yankee she'd ever seen had worn a uniform quite like his, and she wondered how he managed to do so without having been reprimanded by his superiors. But then, Neil was the kind of man who did as he damned well pleased. Beneath his caped overcoat, she could see the dark blue belted jacket of a

Union officer, but his trousers were hardly standard military issue, and were only too familiar to her. Buckskins. And on his feet he wore moccasins and buckskin leggings, which looked far more water-resistant than the shoes and boots his men were wearing. All of the men had long and shaggy, almost shoulder-length hair, which meant they seldom stayed at Headquarters for long, and had apparently been living a rough-and-ready existence behind enemy lines for some time. But none wore their hair woven into a braid as did their captain, and none were clean-shaven, as was Neil, and Leigh could suddenly envision the Comanche brave he once had been. No one would hear him prowling or sneaking up behind, Leigh found herself speculating, a suspicious thought entering her mind as she wondered just what Neil Braedon and his men were doing behind enemy lines.

"Wouldn't mind rasslin' that sweet reb to the ground, but s'pose rank has its privileges."

"All clear, ain't no Johnny reb hotfootin' it after her, Cap'n," the guard at the door said, shutting it firmly.

"Always suspected them rebs were fools, leavin' a pretty lil' thing like this one all by her lonesome."

"What we goin' to do, Cap'n? Can't let her go, can we?"

"Reckon she'd turn us in, eh?"

"With them pretty *Yankee* blue eyes?"

"She's wearin' *rebel* gray, Billy Yank, don't ever be forget-tin' that."

"The way we was ambushed, somebody already ratted on us."

"Can't understand it, Cap'n. Where'd them rebs come from? How'd they know we was there? Almost like they was sittin' in wait fer us, like they was already riled up about something. Never happened like that before. We come close to gettin' caught, sure, but we've always managed to slip out of the noose them rebs been tryin' to tighten around our necks."

"And we'll escape the noose this time, Johnson," his captain replied matter-of-factly and apparently setting his men's minds at rest because Leigh heard the sighs of relief and saw the exchange of glances that followed his easy statement.

"Hell, all we did was blow up that little railroad trestle," someone said with a grin.

"And the gun, don't forget that," another chuckling voice reminded proudly.

"Yeah, but that shouldn't have gotten them that mad. Made 'em madder last month blowin' up that depot full o' pork barrels. We been real good little boys since then."

"Reckon them rebs been lookin' fer us that long, an' they're just now findin' us!" the man called Johnson said with a guffaw that had his friends laughing, and the tension in the stables easing almost visibly as a number of them started grinning and trading jokes.

Raiders, Leigh thought, eyeing them as if they'd suddenly sprouted horns, especially Neil Braedon.

He stood just inside the stable doors, his relaxed attitude giving the impression he'd just come down from the big house and was awaiting the saddling of his hunter for a leisurely morning ride across country to enjoy a bit of gentlemanly shooting of pheasant. He stood so tall, so arrogant, so self-assured, that Leigh wasn't surprised his men had confidence in him, but Leigh had been the only one who had felt the momentary tightening of his hard fingers around her hand when he'd reassured his men about the prospective ease of their escape.

Leigh was breathing a little easier herself, for even if Neil was the enemy, and he held her captive, she was not as frightened as before, after all, as he himself had said, they were old friends. And even if there were some old scores left to be settled between them, she could not believe he would allow his men to harm her. And as some of her fears left her, she gradually became aware of the men grouped around her. Their faces were soot-blackened and bloodied, and some, she now realized, were badly wounded, unable to stand or even sit as they huddled together miserably in the stables.

"Beals, you're on watch," Neil ordered brusquely, moving along the passageway, and pulling Leigh along with him, but as his men closed in around their figures, she suddenly found she didn't mind being under his protection, at least for the moment. "Hendricks, stay sharp," he called to the man on duty at the far end of the stables.

"Yo, Cap'n," the man said, his hand resting easy on his rifle as he leaned a shoulder against the stable wall, the door cracked just enough for him to see the lane disappearing down toward the river.

"Patterson, keep an eye out that window. Watch for anything moving in the woods to the southeast. If they've managed to track us this far, they'll be coming from that direction. I want us out of here before that happens," Neil said, glancing around at the stables as if sizing it up as a possible stronghold.

"Reckon if they stumble across us, it'll be just that. Dumb luck," someone grumbled.

"Yeah, 'cause we didn't leave no tracks, 'specially comin' through the woods single file the way we did."

"Best way of keepin' 'em guessin' 'bout how many of us there is. They'll come in real slow like, worryin' so. Wouldn't want to be trackin' the cap'n, I wouldn't, or even tracked *by* the cap'n," he said, thinking of all the tricks the captain had up his sleeve. They said the captain had Indian blood in him, and even if he didn't look it, half of them believed the tale.

"How are you doing, McGuire?" Neil asked, releasing Leigh's hand as he squatted down beside a man whose pallor and bloodstained overcoat left little doubt that he was suffering.

"No fancy jigs, Cap'n, reckon they got the fiddler," he said, trying to grin, but his mouth wobbled and a spot of blood appeared where he'd bitten into his lower lip trying to control its trembling.

"Wishes he had that Dutchwoman here to keep him warm, I bet."

"Aye, now that she could, with plenty of warmth left over fer the rest of ye lads, if I was in a mind to share," McGuire said, grimacing when he moved his shoulder trying to laugh. "But it takes an Irishman to handle the reins when ridin' her. 'Course, reckon I might not be man enough fer her right now," he said faintly, falling back as he tried to sit up.

"We'll fix you up just fine, McGuire."

"Ain't goin' to leave me to rot away in some reb hospital, are ye, Cap'n?" he asked worriedly. "Figure ye might as well put me out of my misery now. Don't want no one hackin' away at me piece by piece," he said, shivering uncontrollably as he thought of gangrene spreading through his body.

"No one gets left behind."

McGuire nodded. "Faith, but I've been wantin' to ask you this, Cap'n. Don't know much about ye, sir, not even yer given name, but I was bettin' the lads that ye had a wee spot of Irish in ye. Ye would, now, wouldn't ye? 'Cause I been figurin' that 'twas only an Irishman I'd have followed grinnin' into hell an' back like that, an' singeing off me eyebrows to boot."

"My mother was Irish," Neil told him quietly.

"There, ye can't be foolin' an' Irishman. 'Tis in the blood, 'tis. That does me heart good. Reckon 'twas meant to be, after all. But what I wouldn't give now, to be back in Ireland," he murmured, grimacing. "An' what is her name, Cap'n? Something lyrical, to be sure?"

"Fionnuala," Neil said, frowning as the Irishman closed his eyes against the pain.

"Like music in me ears," he said, slurring his words slightly. "Is she still livin'?"

"No."

"A real pity that. Bet she was a fine woman. All Irish women are. Best mothers in the world, they are. An' d'ye have any other family, then?"

"A father."

"But not Irish, I'm thinkin', 'cause ye got a hard, mean streak in ye, Cap'n, an' that's got to be English blood."

"No, he's not Irish," his captain answered, wanting to keep the Irishman talking so he wouldn't lapse into unconsciousness.

"Any brothers or sisters?"

"A young sister, and two brothers. One too young to fight, the other lost in the war. And, once, I had an older sister. Her name was Shannon," Neil said, speaking her name aloud for the first time in years, and it sounded strange on his tongue.

"Shannon. 'Tis the loveliest name in all of Ireland, I'm thinkin'." McGuire sighed. "Did ye know, Cap'n, I was born on the green banks of the River Shannon. 'Tis a fine, ancient river flowin' through the heart of Ireland. When a wee lad, I used to sit on the bank, watchin' the waters flowin' by. They gently touched the land, leavin' it green an' fertile before flowin' on into the sea, flowin' on forever, I was thinkin', an' I wanted to reach out an' stop them from leavin' me, an' when I couldn't, then I wanted to follow wherever the river flowed, but again I couldn't. I could never quite catch it, an' the river disappeared, to be embraced by its true love, the sea. Ah, I was jealous, that I was. Felt betrayed, I did. But the next mornin', the river, my Shannon, was still there, flowin' by, and I knew then that it remained a part of the people, of the heart always," he mumbled drowsily.

Shannon Malveen. Yes, his sister Shannon was like McGuire's beloved river, Neil thought sadly. Flowing on forever, disappearing from sight, but always a part of the heart. If only he had understood like McGuire had. So much had been lost because he hadn't. She-With-Eyes-Of-The-Captured-Sky had tried to tell him she would always be with him in spirit, and in the heart...but he hadn't listened, hadn't believed.

"He'll die if we don't stop the bleeding," Leigh said softly, jolting Neil from his memories. She was staring down at the Irishman, a pitying look in her eyes.

"*We?*" Neil said doubtfully, glancing up at her, but she was already kneeling beside the young, sandy-haired lieutenant, his soft blue eyes behind his round-rimmed spectacles suddenly reminding her of Palmer William.

Gently, Leigh touched the lock of hair that fell across the young lieutenant's brow, feeling the clamminess of his skin beneath her fingertips, his breathing labored as he struggled to draw breath into his lungs. "I think you've cracked a couple of ribs."

"I have?" he whispered, apparently unconcerned as his lips curved into a smile as he stared up at her, his hand reaching out to grasp hers. Leigh frowned slightly, for there had been a definite look of recognition in his glance.

"My father was always breaking a rib or two. He loved to ride, but sometimes he couldn't keep his seat, especially when he'd been into the corn liquor," she said, smiling down at the wide-eyed lieutenant, trying to reassure him. "In fact, one night, he'd enjoyed himself rather too much at the punch bowl, and the next morning, still not quite himself, he went out and saddled the fence instead of Apothecary Rose, his favorite hunter," Leigh said, hearing a snorting laugh from one of the men close enough to have heard her story.

"I'm afraid I'm not even that much of a horseman. Not like the cap'n," he said, gazing up at Neil as if he were some kind of a god. "He didn't leave me to them rebs, miss. Could've though. But he came swooping down on me and carried me off just like the wind," the lieutenant said.

"Ain' never seen nothin' like it."

"Left them rebs openmouthed an' lookin' stupid," someone recalled.

"There're goin' to be even more wild stories told before this night's over about the devil cap'n an' his death-defyin' men."

"Hey, Lieutenant. You're still goin' to write it all down, ain't ye? Figure it'd make me and my folks mighty proud to read 'bout it after the war. Ain't no one who'd believe it otherwise. Think I'm shammin' them. Somebody back in Springfield I'd kinda like to impress. Be the proudest day of my life when people find out I rode with the cap'n. Jus' be sure to spell my name right."

"I will, Schneickerberger," Lieutenant Chatham promised weakly.

Leigh glanced up at Neil, the captain these men seemed to idolize, and, apparently, were willing to die for.

"Do you have anything to treat these wounds?" she demanded, getting stiffly to her feet, her knees threatening to buckle, especially when the young lieutenant refused to release her hand, but Neil's hand was there, steadying her.

"Enough," he answered shortly, wondering why she should be interested.

"I have clean linens up at the big house. They make fine bandages. And Jolie has special medicinal salves that can keep the infection from these wounds setting in. She's a healer, and half-Cherokee," she reminded him. "Otherwise, your men won't last long enough to leave Travers Hill. We also have a big pot of broth simmering on the hearth. I think that would do better than anything to help your men regain their strength."

"Don't have some of yer pappy's corn liquor 'round?" someone asked hopefully.

"Can't trust her, Cap'n. Probably put poison in it," a suspicious-sounding voice commented.

"Have you wondered why, although shabby, our home still stands?" Leigh asked. "It was used as a field hospital by federal troops. I helped the surgeons. I do know how to treat your men's wounds, and if that ball is still in that man's shoulder, then it will have to come out. Will you let me help?"

"Why should you want to? You haven't any love for bluebellies, do you?" Neil asked coldly, but it was the raider Captain Dagger who stared into Leigh's eyes, searching for the truth. There was too much at stake to make a mistake now because he trusted the wrong person.

Leigh glanced down at Lieutenant Chatham, who still held onto her hand, at the Irishman, who was watching her with feverishly bright eyes, then at the other wounded men, some beginning to shiver from the cold. "I don't care what color their uniforms are, Captain. The men who murdered my father were wearing gray," she said quietly. "I shot them and buried them out back. I don't want to have to bury these two. They, at least, deserve better," she said, not seeing the looks of amazement, and grudging admiration, that crossed several Yankee faces.

"I can help your men," she repeated.

"Travers word of honor?" Neil asked.

Leigh met his searching gaze steadily, knowing his question had been meant sarcastically. "Yes, on my word of honor as a Travers," she said simply, holding out her other hand to him. "Other things may have changed at Travers Hill, but not that. And if you doubt me, then think of this as one way of getting you off Travers land," she added.

"Sure we can trust her, Cap'n?" someone asked doubtfully, remembering another sweet-faced Southern woman who'd held a long-barreled musket on them, threatening to blow them to kingdom come before she'd missed her aim and blown off the top of the weather vane by mistake.

Neil stared down at the small hand he'd grasped in his. He turned it over curiously, having felt the hard calluses on the palm. It was a work-roughened, capable hand he held, and as he met her steady gaze, he knew that her word was good.

"Cap'n!" the man who'd been standing guard at the far door cried out suddenly. "We got company! Reb patrol, comin' up the road on foot."

Captain Dagger was beside him before anyone could move.

"Got more, Cap'n, comin' out of the woods. Looks like a troop of cavalry."

Their captain glanced around, cursing himself for getting them trapped in the stables. As long as they could ride, they'd always been out of reach of any foolhardy rebels seeking vengeance. But now there was no way out. They would have to stand and fight.

He saw Leigh standing with his men and signaled to them to let her go.

"You'd better get back to the big house."

Leigh glanced around at Neil's men as they checked their weapons, several affixing bayonets to their rifles, others, bloodied from the earlier skirmish, pulling out their cartridge boxes while struggling to their feet, their expressions hopeless.

"I came out here for a bale of hay. Could you oblige me by loading it into the wheelbarrow?"

Neil stared at her as if she'd gone insane.

"Oughta be a general, such brass has this lil' reb."

"Can't let her go, Cap'n! She'll tell the rebs we're in here. Catch us like a bunch of treed 'coons."

"They'll find us soon enough when they search the stables," was their captain's curt response.

"I might be able to stop them from searching the stables," Leigh's voice came softly, but it carried enough to cause a nervous silence to descend on the men taking their positions in the various stalls as they prepared to fight.

Neil stared at her intently, and as Leigh held his gaze, she felt as if she stared into a stranger's eyes, so impersonally assessing were they.

"If they don't believe you, and search the stables, you and your family could be burned out," he told her.

"I'll just say the Yankee swine held a gun pointed at my back and threatened to murder me and my family if I didn't lie to the rebels," Leigh countered, quelling her fears, for she was well aware of the price she and her family would have to pay if she failed.

"Reckon we gotta trust her now," someone breathed.

"Ain' no way I'm fer trustin' a damn reb!" someone else spat contemptuously, cocking his rifle.

Neil continued to stare into Leigh's face.

"You do not have the time, Captain, *not* to trust me."

He nodded. "Very well. You see, gentlemen," he said, glancing around at his assembled men, "the lady and I are old friends. One might even say we have family ties that bind us together."

The only man among them who wasn't too surprised to do more than stare, chuckled wheezingly. "Damnation! Which one of us got himself a guardian angel?" he asked, slapping his knee with ill-contained glee. "'Cause one of us has been blessed, either that, or the cap'n sure as hell is the devil himself to git us outa this mess!"

"Whooptee!" someone said beneath his breath, another one whistling softly as he eyed the captain and the lady curiously, because, from the look of them, they didn't seem like friends.

Within a blink of an eye, a small bale of hay had been carefully placed on the wheelbarrow, one of the men even going so far as to assist Leigh with guiding it through the door, ever careful, however, not to show himself.

Leigh glanced back once, meeting the pale-eyed stare of Neil Braedon for a brief instant before she turned and left the barn, then the door closed behind her.

The men stood silent, some unable to draw a breath as they watched her push the wheelbarrow across the muddy field. Leigh's feet kept slipping, slowing down her progress, her slender back bent low over the barrow as she strained against the load's greater weight, but, finally, she made her way into sight of the rebels.

They rode toward her, their horses prancing, raised hooves sending mud flying, yellow sashes waving. They encircled her small figure, closing in around her, but she stood her ground, the wheelbarrow looking as deadly as a cannon aimed at their heads as she stared up at them with the pride and arrogance of a Travers.

As still as stone statues, the Bloodriders watched as the young woman pointed back toward the stables, one of them cursing beneath his breath, thinking she'd betrayed them. And why shouldn't she, a couple even had the temerity to think. They were, after all, the enemy. They might even have killed members of her family on the battlefield. What right did they have to expect this woman to protect them?

But to their amazement, they saw the rebel officer take off his hat with gentlemanly courtesy and laugh, then he signaled to one of his men, who quickly dismounted and came to her aid, taking hold of the wheelbarrow with a fine show of manly strength.

"What she tellin' them?" someone finally had to ask, unable to bear the suspense any longer, his finger fidgeting on the trigger as he took aim on the rebel major who looked a bit like a portly pigeon sitting astride a long-legged Thoroughbred.

"Don't know fer sure. Something about havin' been in the stables. No Yanks there or she would've had them shoveling manure," another voice contributed, sounding slightly offended at the notion. "Got 'em believin' she hates Yanks."

"Easy enough to do. She probably does," another voice rasped, watching with amusement as the rebel troop moved smartly away, trotting behind the lone figure like a group of eager-to-please swains.

"Think the one, the major, knows her, or knew her brother. Seems real impressed, an' not likely to question her word of honor. Now she's tellin' him something about his horse. Don't seem quite so pleased with himself now. I think she's givin' him hell 'bout somethin'. Pointin' to his horse's hindquarters."

"That reb major reminds me a bit of that fat-assed General Pope, talkin' so big an' sayin' his headquarters were in the saddle an' how he'd have ridden right through to Richmond, then on through the South to New Orleans had he been in command 'stead of McClellan. He wasn't there in the Shenandoah. But reckon he'd blow right down there into Cajun country fast enough havin' so much hot air in him. Figure they was right sayin' he don't know his headquarters from his hindquarters, 'cause he's been sittin' on 'em too long," someone said, spitting.

"Let's jus' hope this reb major is as windy."

"Lord love her, gettin' that one to push the wheelbarrow for her an' now even to unload it, an' him such a scrawny-lookin' lad," one of the Bloodriders breathed in awe.

Neil smiled humorlessly as he watched Leigh flirting with the rebel captain who'd been so quick to come to her aid, her long braid of hair swinging provocatively around her hips as she walked alongside him, her face turned up to his as if she waited breathlessly on his every utterance, yet ever careful not to forget the pompous major riding beside her.

"It's them bonnie blue eyes," someone said. "Go right to a man's heart, they do," he added, thinking of his own blue-eyed sweetheart back home in Ohio.

"Don't s'pose she's asked them to stay fer supper, d'ye?" a worried voice asked, his growling stomach remembering her earlier offer of hot broth. "We was here first," he added with a resentful look at the gray-uniformed soldiers riding up to the house so boldly, as if certain of their welcome within.

To his great satisfaction, however, the rebels, after a moment's conversation, turned their mounts around and rode back toward the road, where the soldiers on foot had waited for them.

Someone sighed audibly, for the rebels were riding away to continue their search elsewhere, and at least for now they were safe.

"Think she'll come back?" Someone voiced aloud the thought most were worrying about silently.

"She gave her word," was all their captain said as he stood by the partly opened door, waiting for her to return.

❧

"Yankees! Yankees! Out in the stables!" Jolie choked, sucking in her breath. "What were them rebs doin' leavin'? Everybody's gotten crazy as coots 'round here, 'ceptin' for me," she added as Stephen entered the kitchens, looking as if he hadn't a care in the world as he picked a piece of lint from his faded sleeve. "An' what were you doin' saunterin' 'cross that yard like you were out with your beau for a Sunday stroll?" she asked, startling Stephen from his preoccupation with his sleeve.

"Who're you talkin' 'bout? I never left the house after seein' Miss Althea back to the study," Stephen said, looking properly shocked.

"I'm not talkin' to you, ol' man. Knew where you were all the time, or at least where you'd better have been," Jolie told him dismissingly, returning to eye Leigh now that she had dealt with Stephen. "Saw you flirtin' with that officer who was pushin' the wheelbarrow. Betcha turned all mealymouthed on him, just the way I know you can, lil' honey. What're you up to? You tell Jolie," she demanded, hands on hips as she planted her feet in a battle-ready stance.

But Leigh wasn't listening. She was staring across the yard toward the stables, where *Captain Dagger* and his men, the notorious *Bloodriders*, were waiting for her return.

Leigh shook her head in disbelief, wondering anew what madness had seized her. If the rebels ever found out she had hidden Captain Dagger and his Bloodriders in the stables, and had lied to them, they would ride back to Travers Hill and burn the house down with a vengeance.

"What're you shakin' for, lil' honey?" Jolie demanded, peering into Leigh's pale face. "I don't like this at all. I got a feelin' 'bout this."

"Saw you limpin', figure it's that big toe again," Stephen said softly, avoiding Jolie's eye as he got the tureen down from the cupboard.

She'd never made the connection between the infamous raider Captain Dagger and Neil Braedon—at least not until the rebel major had damned the name of the murderous Yankee raider they were searching for, and had given her a very colorful description of him and his parentage. She should have remembered.

Sun Dagger.

What had she done? Leigh asked herself, for Neil and his men were not just ordinary Yankees hiding out at Travers Hill. Then she remembered the wounded men in the stables, and thought of the shooting, and the dying, that would have been the outcome had she given away their hiding place. And then she saw the image of Neil lying dead and bloodied, those rebel officers standing over his body and gloating, and she suddenly knew she could never have betrayed him.

"Jolie, I—"

"Don't like that tone, missy," Jolie said, watching Leigh like a fox.

"Jolie," Leigh began again, "it is too late now not to help those Yankees out in the stables. And do you know why?"

Stephen's eyes widened slightly. "Yankees? In the stables?" he muttered beneath his breath, shaking his head.

"I'm sure you're goin' to tell, an' I'm sure I'm not goin' to like it."

"Because, if we help them they'll leave Travers Hill sooner than if we didn't, an—"

"I like that."

"—and since I did lie to those rebels, we have to help those Yankees now so they'll go, or they'll get angry, an—"

"Don't like that," Jolie declared.

"—and, one of those Yankees out in the stables is Neil Braedon."

Jolie looked as if she'd swallowed her tongue, and poor Stephen splashed some of the broth he'd been ladling into the tureen onto his shoe.

"And those rebels, if they ever discovered Neil Braedon was Nathan's cousin, might think we, and certainly Althea, who bears the Braedon name, had been helping them all along," Leigh hurriedly told them.

Jolie finally managed to find her tongue. "I've never, an' I mean never, known a body who could talk herself in an' out of trouble like you do. Oughta be one of them no-good, fancy po-lu-ti-cians!"

"I just hope the rebels don't come back before I can treat those wounds," Leigh said worriedly, but perhaps looking a little too innocent as she pulled down a large gathering basket from a hook and began to fill it with various bottles.

"What wounds?" Jolie asked, watching her every move.

"I didn't tell you?" Leigh said, her back to Jolie as she selected one of the clean sheets that had dried and began to tear it into strips.

"You know you didn't," Jolie said, staring in amazement as she watched Leigh's actions.

"Bandages," Leigh said. "The Yankees were in a skirmish, and several have bullet wounds, and one has several broken ribs. I'll have to bind him up tight before he can move again. I don't think he has a punctured lung yet. And we should feed them. They're shivering with cold."

"You're touchin' no man, an' no Yankee like that, Miss Leigh. Not fittin' for a daughter of Miss Beatrice Amelia's. Never liked it much before, you bloodying up yer hands, but at least you were here in the big house, an' under my eye, an' jus' helpin' them doctors," Jolie said, sniffing her disapproval even as she gathered several more bottles of her cures from the shelf and added them to the basket.

"Are you coming with me?"

Jolie snorted. "You know I am, missy. You haven't fooled me with that sweet talk since you was that lil'," she said, holding her hand about knee-high.

"An' once you serve Miss Althea and the children luncheon, an' Mister Guy, an' don't you say a word to him 'bout anything, Steban," Jolie warned, "you get yourself right back over here an' bring that pot down to the stables. We're goin' to get them fed an' out of here before them rebels return," she said, selecting a worn sheet she had been meaning to mend, easily tearing it in two.

"Yes, ma'am," Stephen said, his tone causing Jolie to stop what she was doing and give him a suspicious stare. "I'll be doin' jus' dat, *Miz* Jolie, an' I'll jus' bring down dat shootin' rifle o' Mist' Guy's. Jus' to make certain dem Yankees doan 'cause no trouble fer Miss Leigh, 'cause dis ol' man ain' as dumb as some folks been thinkin' all dese years," he said, casually tidying his green jacket before picking up the heavy tureen and walking with great dignity from the kitchens.

Jolie opened her lips, then closed them tight. Adding a pair of scissors and a butchering knife to the basket, she said indignantly while trying to take the basket from Leigh's grasp, "Well, I've never heard such tomfoolery in my life. Where'd he learn to talk like a chawbacon? My Steban's fine as any gentleman. Let me have that basket, Miss Leigh!"

Keeping a firm hold on the handle, Leigh bent over it and kissed Jolie's coppery cheek. "And you've always said Stephen didn't have a sense of humor," she teased.

Jolie drew in her breath, puffing out her thin chest, then a slow, reluctant grin started to cross her face, followed by a laugh that started out silently, then gradually grew in tone until her shoulders were shaking and tears were streaming down her cheeks.

"Isn't he somethin', that Steban of mine," she said, wiping her cheeks with the back of her hand, while she held onto the basket with the other, but Leigh wasn't going to give up and jerked even harder, pulling the basket free from Jolie's grasp.

Swinging it around behind her back, Leigh pointed to the

flat, wooden box that had been wedged next to the recipe books in the corner cupboard. "Don't forget that, Jolie, and you might bring along that jug of corn liquor," she said, hurrying from the kitchens before Jolie could protest.

The Bloodriders, watching from the stables, must have experienced a few mixed feelings at the sight that met their eyes a few minutes later. Certainly there were a few sighs of relief as they saw the young woman returning, and carrying a large basket loaded with bottles and bandages over her arm. And there were even a couple of surprised gasps when a tall, thin mulattress came running after her with a corked jug under one arm and a narrow box tucked beneath the other, her scolding voice causing a couple to cringe and wish they were facing the rebels again. But when the next figure appeared, a green-liveried black man with snowy white hair, his feet slipping and sliding across the muddy field, the suspenseful silence that had hung so ominously low over the group gave way to sidesplitting laughter. The comical antics of the dignified old man trying to keep his balance, ever careful of where he stepped, while carrying a large, black iron pot, mouthwatering steam rising from it, and a rifle dangling haphazardly from beneath his crooked arm, the barrel tipping up and down dangerously with each step he took, had been too much for them.

It was certainly almost too much for Leigh, who'd already entered the stables and was unloading her basket by the Irishman, when she heard the muffled, tittering laughter around her.

Neil had opened McGuire's overcoat, cutting away the sleeve, then part of the jacket and shirt beneath, and baring the ugly, bruised and bloodied flesh around the wound. Leigh threw off the blanket she'd worn like a shawl and unbuttoning the neat cuffs of her gown, she rolled up her sleeves as professionally as any field surgeon might have while eyeing the work to be done on the wounded soldier lying before him.

Jolie shouldered her way in, managing to insinuate herself between Leigh and the tall Yankee captain, her eyes meeting his for a long, sizing-up moment that told him clearly enough that *she*, at least, remembered him and hadn't forgiven him. Then she turned a damning shoulder to him and began to select her potions.

Within an instant, she'd mixed a sweet-smelling brew, the fumes almost overpowering as she held it to the astonished Irishman's lips and ordered him to drink up, then, when he hesitated, looking to his captain for salvation, she bribed him with the promise she'd let him wash it down with a swallow of corn liquor. Neil grinned as McGuire quickly emptied the cup, looking up expectantly, but to Jolie this time, and Neil knew the woman had practiced her wily ways on the Travers family for far too long not to know how to handle McGuire now.

Neil couldn't hide his surprise when Leigh opened the long, flat box the mulattress had brought in and placed beside her.

"Good Lord! Where did you get that?" he asked in amazement as Leigh's delicately feminine hand began to hover over the deadly looking tools of a surgeon's field kit, where all manner and size of knives and saws fitted neatly into the proper compartments, alongside scalpels, forceps, probes, a tourniquet, and silk thread; every conceivable device needed for amputating some unfortunate soldier's limbs.

"One of the surgeons left it at Travers Hill by mistake," Leigh answered without bothering to look up as she carefully selected a small knife. "We don't have any chloroform or ether, but Jolie's mixture will have the same numbing effect," Leigh explained. "I must probe for the ball and any broken bone fragments. I think, however, we are lucky, because he seems to be bleeding from the back as well."

"That comforts me to know, miss," McGuire said with a sickly grin, his eyelids already beginning to droop from the drugging effects of Jolie's secret ingredients.

"The ball most likely passed right through the fleshy part of his shoulder, missing the lung because he isn't having trouble breathing. And except for his bloodied lip, he's not bleeding internally," Leigh said, her expression fixed with grim determination as she began to clean the wound of dried blood.

"Ain' rightly fair to git so shot up fer jus' blowin' that trestle," one of the soldiers commented from somewhere close behind Leigh's back as he kept a watchful eye on the young woman and the knife she was poking into his friend's shoulder.

Leigh frowned as she heard his words, but she never looked up as she said, "That's only part of the reason they're so determined to hunt you down. Two days ago, a supply train riding the Orange and Alexandria railroad was attacked. It was blown up except for the engine and two boxcars; the first car and one in the middle of the train. Inside the car midway in the train was a well-guarded shipment of gold bullion. The raiders knew exactly which car the gold had been loaded inside, and which one not to blow up. The guards were butchered in cold blood *after* they had surrendered. Only one survived to inform the authorities the train had been attacked by the Bloodriders. The major called it one of the bloodiest massacres he'd seen. The gold was loaded into the first car and the raiders made their escape using the train. It was found toppled into a ravine just south of Gordonsville. The raiders, and the gold bullion, gone. And to make matters worse for you gentlemen, federal raiders tried to attack Richmond, but failed, although they burned and destroyed property along the James River. The major just received orders to stop the federal soldiers, who, when last seen, were retreating north, with Confederate forces in pursuit. That's why there are so many rebels searching the countryside around here," Leigh told them, glancing up when she heard the angry curses and shocked denials.

"Now, miss, we didn't have nuthin' to do with no gold shipment bein' stolen. Shoot, it ain' fair, gittin' blamed fer it an' I ain' even got a gold piece to my name. Ain' been paid nuthin' in I don't know how long."

"We ain' no butchers neither!"

"Did your major mention the names of the raiders who attacked Richmond?" Neil asked curiously.

"A General Kilpatrick, and a Colonel Dahlgren. Friends of yours?"

Neil smiled. "No. My men are telling you the truth. We didn't blow up *that* particular train, nor did we steal any gold bullion," Neil told her, and strangely enough, Leigh believed him, or maybe it had been the outraged indignation of his men that had convinced her, for they had not been hesitant to take the honors for the destruction of the railroad trestle, so why not this other, even more daring raid, unless they hadn't been involved and were telling the truth.

For the next hour, Neil stood silently by, while Leigh and the mulattress treated and dressed his men's wounds with an efficiency and care to cleanliness that would have done any field hospital proud. With hands that ministered gently, but firmly, Leigh had Lieutenant Chatham sitting straight, his breathing coming easier now that his ribs had been tightly wrapped, molded together, and moved back into place, where they would have a chance to mend properly. His ankle had been similarly dealt with, the beads of perspiration that broke out on his brow wiped away by a cooling cloth that smelled like mint and soothed his nerves. And the young lieutenant, drowsy with Jolie's potions, and far from home, fell hopelessly in love with the young woman who cared for him with such kindness.

Neil glanced around the stables at his men, and although still on guard, and ready for a fight, they stood easily, their bellies full, their wounds treated, with a good chance now to heal without further complications, which was a wounded man's greatest fear. It helped to ease a man's mind, since death came more easily, and agonizingly, from wounds and disease than from a bullet on the battlefield. He sensed a return of their spirit, and no longer could he smell the fear seeping out of his men and tainting their sweat.

His hardened gaze came to rest admiringly on the young woman washing her hands of blood. *Leigh.* He said the name silently, caressingly, so many images of her drifting through his mind. He saw once again the long-legged, slender girl with flowing chestnut hair, riding her mare with such daring across a summer meadow, her carefree, innocent laughter beckoning him closer. *Leigh Alexandra.* He remembered a soft, balmy night in a magical garden, the scent of jessamine and roses filling his senses, and a beautiful woman in a gown that shimmered dancing into his heart and out of his reach. He realized now that she had been a girl then, a cool, pale image of the warm, vibrant woman she had become—a stranger to him now.

She was like the willow on the riverbank. She bent to the winds that swept across Travers Hill. She had adapted gracefully to the changes that had come so tragically into her life. She hadn't broken trying to resist, to fight against a far greater force that would have destroyed her. Nor had she been weakened by the struggle, she had become stronger, finding a strength within that she might never have known otherwise.

Neil stared down at her bent head, at the vulnerable, soft curve of neck, and felt a fiery-hot flame of desire to possess her, in both mind and body, begin to flicker and burn deep inside of him. It would become a consuming flame, feeding off every emotion that his love for her would bring him...*if she were his*, he reminded himself. But she wasn't. She belonged to Matthew Wycliffe. She had chosen another man that night, not him, Neil thought savagely, feeling his jealousy like an ache inside as he thought of her in Wycliffe's bed, thought of her in another man's arms, thought of her as another man's lover, bearing another man's children, sharing her warmth with them, never with him.

"No ring?" he commented harshly, unable to speak the words of gratitude he had intended as he eyed her ringless hands, or ask the many questions about his family's whereabouts.

"It's washing day at Travers Hill," Leigh said, thinking of the cameo ring she'd taken off and left on the mantelpiece in the kitchens. "And I don't think your Irishman would like to have my ring sewn up inside his shoulder," Leigh said, rubbing the back of her neck tiredly as she stood up, perhaps not seeing the helping hand he held out to her, which was ignored.

"But soon you'll have the good Matthew's ring back on your finger. Where is he? Fighting in the Carolinas?" Neil asked, wanting to see her expression when she spoke of her beloved husband.

Leigh glanced up at him in surprise, realizing he believed she was still engaged to Matthew.

Leigh looked back down, seeing her ringless third finger. "Matthew is dead," she said, hardly able to remember what her engagement ring had looked like. It had been his mother's and in the Wycliffe family for generations. She had returned it to his family upon hearing of his death. That summer seemed so long ago, now, another lifetime when Matthew had placed his ring on her finger and pressed her hand to his lips, his dark eyes glowing with such promise for their future together.

Neil couldn't hide the start of surprise when hearing her quietly spoken words.

"Widowed so young," he murmured, "and left with two small, fatherless children," he said, thinking of the little

dark-haired boy and the baby lifted from the cradle and held
with such motherly devotion by Leigh the day before. Her
children. And both had inherited Wycliffe's dark hair. He
might have died, but those two children Wycliffe had sired
would always be a reminder to Leigh of him. A child of hers
should have soft chestnut curls, Neil found himself thinking, wanting to reach out and caress the long golden brown
strand of hair that fell across her cheek. "Not very obliging of
Matthew, but unless the Wycliffes have already lost everything
during this war, you will be well cared for. But I imagine a
smart man like Wycliffe would have made investments in the
North, perhaps even in Europe. I am surprised to find you sitting here in the heart of the battlefield. There are safer places,"
he commented, still disbelieving that she was a widow—that
she was free.

"My family is here," Leigh said simply. "What kind of a
person do you believe I could be that I would leave my family
in danger while I ran to safety?"

"My mistake, I had forgotten how very close-knit the
Travers family is, and how you would do anything to keep
them from the road to ruin. Always so self-sacrificing, aren't
you? So, you now find yourself a very wealthy young widow,"
he said as if musingly, but inside he knew an anger against
this family of hers that always seemed to come first, and he
wondered what it would feel like to come first with her. "And
Travers Hill will soon be restored to its old glory, courtesy
of your late husband's fortune? I suppose the war has been
something of a mixed blessing for you, hasn't it?"

He had forgotten how proud she was, and how easily her
temper flared, and he wasn't fast enough to stop her, the sound
of her hand striking his lean, tanned cheek drawing the startled
attention of the mulattress and most of his men. Neil saw the
accusing glances leveled at him, knowing they rightly blamed
him for her actions, and knowing they all thought themselves
in love with her. But he couldn't blame them. Leigh had that
effect on a man.

Leigh started to correct him, but then decided it was none
of his business, and she didn't want his pity, or his hurtful
sarcasms if he discovered that Matthew had died before they

could marry. *All for naught,* he would have said, smiling that cynical smile. Let him believe she had been happily married to Matthew, and borne his children; she would never see Neil Braedon again. It was none of his business.

"Your men have been tended to, Captain," she said coldly, hurriedly gathering up her doctoring tools and healing salves, stuffing blood-soaked compresses into the basket. "I would appreciate it if you left Travers Hill with no further delay. I might find it difficult to lie so easily and convincingly next time," she told him, and a haughtier, more condescending mistress of the manor it would have been hard to find.

"I stand warned, madam," Captain Dagger replied courteously, his smile unnerving as he added, "but since I wouldn't wish to cause you any more inconvenience than I already have, you will agree that leaving after dark would be far safer, attracting less attention. You may sleep easy this eve, for no one will see us leaving Travers Hill. Far safer for you and your family, ma'am, as well as for my men."

"Miss?" Lieutenant Chatham called out, saving Leigh from saying anything further in response to Neil's stinging rebuke which had made her feel the fool.

"Yes, Lieutenant?" Leigh said, kneeling down beside him again and touching her hand to his forehead in growing concern. "Are you having any trouble breathing? I must have wrapped your ribs too tight," she said, glancing over worriedly at Jolie for reassurance, for Jolie had wrapped Stuart Travers's bruised and broken ribs on more than one occasion.

"Oh, no, I'm feeling much better, Miss Leigh. I just wanted to thank you for your kindness. You're an angel, Miss Leigh," he said, his eyes full of adoration, and Leigh didn't dare glance up into Neil's face, for she'd heard the imprecation uttered softly beneath his breath. "And that is why I would ask you not to think too ill of the captain," he begged. "He's a fine gentleman. I've never met anyone quite as brave, and he has risked his life time and time again for us. He saved mine today. I wanted you to know what kind of man he is."

Neil's mouth tightened into an ominous line as he heard the lieutenant begging forgiveness for him.

"You needn't worry, Lieutenant," Leigh reassured the

young man, patting his hand comfortingly, "because I do know exactly what kind of man your captain is."

Lieutenant Chatham managed a smile. "Thank you, Miss Leigh," he said, speaking her name as lovingly as the mulattress had while helping her tend the wounded, and because he thought so highly of his captain, he never realized the meaning of her words, but Neil had been in no doubt when meeting her glance as she began to rise, unable this time to avoid the hand that closed around her elbow with such strength of purpose, easily lifting her to her feet.

"Miss Leigh? I'll never forget you," Lieutenant Chatham declared, blushing with embarrassment after his outburst.

"And I'll never forget you, Lieutenant," Leigh told him fondly, smiling down at him before she walked toward the doors of the stables, returning the friendly smiles and grateful farewells from the men, Jolie a step behind, Stephen already waiting at the door, holding it open to speed their escape.

"A real lady, her," someone remarked.

"Sweet lil' reb. Reminds me a bit of my sister back in Tennessee. Wish I knew how she was doin'. Married to a reb, although he's a fine man despite that," another man said, worrying about her welfare should federal soldiers have hidden out on her farm.

The next couple hours seemed endless to the men as they waited for darkness to fall, when they could make their escape, and although many might have wondered, no one had the courage to ask their captain exactly where they'd escape to. They wouldn't be able to get very far with all of the wounded, and as they sat, waiting, they tried to amuse themselves. Some told tall tales, others played poker, holding the different suits of their Miss Liberty playing cards up to the fading light to determine the winning hand that might display a pair of shields, a straight flush of five-pointed stars, or a straight with patriotic eagles and flags.

Others dug deep inside their haversacks, pulling out treasured daguerreotypes in fancy frames or dog-eared photographs of loved ones they might never see again. Several pulled out pipes and tobacco pouches, carefully packing their hoarded tobacco into the bowls, a match lit and shared among many until burning itself out. The pungent smoke drifted around the stables, mingling with the tallow smoke from a stub of candle stuck in a spiked candleholder someone had had the presence of mind to pack with his belongings, the scratchings of his pen on a piece of paper spread across a writing kit propped on his knee, perhaps the last letter to be written home. Another close by peered at the comforting verses in the Bible he was reading, while another leaned closer to the candlelight to thumb through his New England Almanac, wondering if he'd ever return home, if he'd ever know again the joy of planting and harvesting his crops.

McGuire's friend had unrolled his sewing kit and was sewing back on McGuire's sleeve, certain his friend would have need of it in future, even if he seemed dead to the world right now. Lieutenant Chatham stared down sleepily at the theater tickets for a performance he would never see, while another lonely soldier fingered the bawdy pictures he'd traded his Jew's harp and a pair of socks for when last in camp.

"Wish that lil' lady had left her papa's corn liquor with us." A disembodied voice spoke suddenly out of the darkness that now enshrouded the small confines of the stables where they felt holed up in like rats.

"Best I've ever drunk. Always heard these Virginians made a brew fine enough to blow yer boots off while slidin' down as smooth as molasses."

"Beats swallowin' Ol' Red Eye," someone said, taking a deep swig of water from his canteen as he remembered the cheap whiskey that made the rounds of the camps, the foul taste of turpentine hard to get off your tongue.

"When we leavin', Cap'n?" Someone finally voiced what was on all of their minds. "Reckon we'll be the only ones ridin' tonight with this storm comin' on, 'cause the wind's pickin' up. Figure it'll be pouring down rain soon."

Neil straightened, pushing himself away from the door, where he'd stood for over an hour staring at the big house through the fine mist that had begun to fall. In another twenty minutes, it would be dark. He glanced back at his men, most were ready to ride, and the odds were more in their favor now, thanks to their respite at Travers Hill, that they would survive. They might not be able to reach their own lines, but for now, he knew a safe place for them to hide; a place no reb, except for two, would know to look for them.

The horses had been fed and watered, and were well rested. There was no reason to delay any longer once dusk fell, Neil thought, damning himself for not having found out what had happened at Royal Bay and to his cousins. But it was too late now, too late even to thank her for all she had done today to help them, he thought as he walked along the passageway eyeing his men, his hard-eyed expression causing a few of the men to look away uneasily. "We'll leave within half an hour. Start gathering up your kits, and I don't want anything, and that means so much as a burnt match, left in this stable. We don't want to cause trouble for the lady," he warned them, his voice as cutting as a knife's edge as he bent down to pick up a playing card that had somehow strayed from the deck, the owner looking sheepish as he quickly tucked it in his haversack and wondered how the lady would have explained that playing card, emblazoned so prettily with the emblems of the Union.

"Whoa, Cap'n! Lookee here. Guess they was in a hurry to leave, 'cause they fergot this stack here. Didn't even notice it pushed back here in the corner."

Neil stopped beside the man who'd called out, staring down in dismay at the neat pile of linens, torn into bandage-sized strips, on top, a pair of scissors, two bottles of medicinal lotions, and a wad of blood-soaked blue uniform. "Damn," he bit out as he picked up the incriminating evidence that, if found by a rebel patrol, could have had tragic consequences for the Travers family—for Leigh.

"Get ready to ride immediately upon my return," he ordered, turning back toward the door. "I'll signal you. Otherwise, don't make a sound, gentlemen, and don't open the door for anyone else. In this gray mist, you might let in a whole troop of rebs before you even knew the difference."

"Where you goin', Cap'n?"

"To return these items to the lady," he answered abruptly as he anticipated another meeting with the lady in question. "And to reconnoiter the area. I don't intend to ride out of here blind. After shaking them off our scent, I have no intention of riding into a reb camp by mistake."

"Want me to bury that bit of uniform, Cap'n?"

"No, we'll let them burn it up at the house, that way no trace will be left to be found by someone sniffing around," Neil said, slowly opening the door, then slipping through and disappearing into the twilight.

⁂

Sitting on a small three-legged milking stool before the open hearth in the kitchens, Leigh slowly drew a brush through the long strands of her hair until it hung in thick, shining waves over one shoulder, nearly touching the floor.

Dropping the brush on top of her damp towel, she poured a couple of drops of the roses and lavender lotion that would always remind her of her mother into her palm, smoothing the creamy liquid into the chafed skin of her hands. Standing up, she allowed the quilt she'd wrapped around her shoulders to drop to the brick flooring. The warmth of the hearth lightly touched her naked body, bathing it in golden firelight as she poured more of the fragrant lotion into her hand and began to spread it on her arms and shoulders, then lower, onto her breasts and hips, then down the length of thighs and calves, trying to blot out the memory of her bloodied hands and the torn flesh of those men in the stables.

Surely they, and Neil Braedon, must have left by now, Leigh thought, glancing at the windows, and the darkening sky beyond.

Earlier, and without a backward glance, she, Jolie, and Stephen had made their way back to the kitchens from the stables. No one had spoken and it had been a silent vow between them that nothing would ever be spoken of their afternoon's activities. The less said the better. And soon, it might be forgotten.

She'd had time only to scrub her hands and face, brushing her hair free of tangles and drying mud before confining it in a chignon and hastily joining Althea and Guy in the study, her excuse of having eaten in the kitchens accepted and not questioned as she fed Lucinda and talked with Guy, reading to him from the three-month-old newspapers Adam had brought with him on his last visit to Travers Hill. She'd caught Althea's puzzled gaze on her more than once, but Althea had said nothing, and she hadn't enlightened her. After that, household duties had required her attention and she and Jolie had made the beds with fresh linens, then she'd helped Jolie replenish her stock of potions, then, leaving Jolie in the kitchens preparing the evening meal, she and Stephen had gone out and collected kindling, staying well away from the stables in their search of the woods, and forcing herself not to think about the men hiding there.

Only now, had she found the chance to bathe. She'd filled the tub with steaming water and scented it with a few drops of jessamine oil, the flowering vine having grown wild and plentiful over the years in the woods and on the fences that still marked Travers land. Sinking down deep into the healing waters, she'd felt her body relax. Drinking a cup of Jolie's specially brewed tea had left her feeling drowsy and docile beneath Jolie's soothing hands as she'd massaged her neck and shoulders, releasing the tensions. She'd suspected Jolie had brewed it especially strong. Her hair had been lathered with chamomile blended with one of Jolie's fragrant soaping lotions, then rinsed until once again it felt clean.

Jolie had returned to the big house, a preoccupied look on her coppery face when she'd pushed Leigh down on the stool before the fireplace. Leigh remembered something about conjurin', a full moon, and thunder as Jolie had scurried away, mumbling beneath her breath, her eyes wild.

Shivering now, Leigh pulled the quilt over her shoulders, wrapping it snugly around her body as she added another log to the fire, careful not to disturb the glowing coals beneath the big pot at the far end of the hearth, where a tantalizing odor drifted from it. Huddling closer, she watched as the log was engulfed by flames. Her body warmed by the fire, she allowed her eyes to close, and her thoughts to linger on Neil Braedon. Somewhere in the distance, Leigh heard Damascena whinny, but she was too tired to do more than open a heavy-lidded eye in lazy curiosity.

Suddenly, both eyes opened wide, for standing in the doorway was the disturbing object of her thoughts. How long had he been there? she wondered, glancing down at the soft-soled moccasins that allowed him to move so silently, and catch people off-guard, she thought crossly.

Leigh got quickly to her feet, almost losing her balance

as her head spun. Trying to pull the quilt closer around her shaking body, her foot caught in a fold as she turned to face him.

"I came to tell you we are leaving, and to return these items to you. In your haste, you left them in the stables. The circumstances of their having been there would have been hard to explain," he told her, holding out the stack of linen strips he carried, the scissors and bottles balanced on top. "I would suggest you burn this," he added, holding up the bloodstained blue material as he placed the linens on the table.

Leigh continued to watch him as he came toward her, his eyes never leaving her as he moved quietly across the room. Then he was standing before her, staring down into her face as he dropped the piece of blue cloth in the hearth, where the flames climbed the highest and would consume the quickest, leaving nothing but ashes.

"As usual, our parting was not as I would have wished." He spoke in a low voice, startling Leigh by the unexpected gentleness in it. "I wanted to thank you. I thank you not for myself but for the lives of the men your tender ministrations might very well have saved today."

"I only did what had to be done," Leigh murmured, glancing down uncomfortably at her bare feet.

"You did far more than most," Neil contradicted her, reaching out a hand to touch the softness of her unbound hair, the back of his hand grazing her fiery cheek.

Leigh jerked away as if burnt, and he dropped his hand, his expression suddenly hardening. "I did not have the opportunity to ask you earlier, nor did I wish to reveal too much to my men, but what happened at Royal Bay?"

"You've seen it?"

"Yes."

"There was a battle. I'm sorry I can't remember when," she said with a frown of concentration, swaying slightly on her feet. "I don't even know if the house was hit by rebel or Yankee cannon fire. It doesn't really matter. It's gone. Your aunt, Euphemia, died that night. She was the only one left at Royal Bay and a shell hit the house directly. She wouldn't come here and stay with us. She was a proud woman," Leigh remembered. "Your uncle died before the war, before Royal Bay was destroyed."

"Yes, I know. Nathan?" Neil asked, and seeing the expression that crossed her face, he wasn't certain he wanted to hear the answer.

"They sent him to Tennessee to fight. We heard this fall that he was missing in action. It's been too long, hasn't it?" she asked, not really expecting a response as she looked up at him. He couldn't conceal the despair that momentarily flickered in his eyes, and she knew the answer. "Althea still believes he is alive. She has to have some hope, or I think she would give up and die."

"She's been ill?"

"Typhoid. She was in Richmond, waiting for Nathan, when the epidemic struck. Blythe was living with her."

"Your sister. The dark-haired girl who was always laughing?" Neil remembered. "She married Adam, didn't she? Just before the war."

"Yes," Leigh said, liking his description of Blythe, for it had captured the essence of her, like the perfume she'd worn.

"What happened?" he asked, frowning as he saw a single teardrop fall from her lashes.

"She died. She wasn't strong enough to fight the typhoid fever she caught."

"Adam?"

"We saw him a few months ago. He was badly wounded, and he's been on leave recuperating. He won't talk about how ill he was, but I think he nearly died. He tries hard, but he just hasn't been the same since losing Blythe, he adored her so. We had a letter from him just last week, telling us he would be here any day," Leigh said, hoping it was true.

"Julia?"

"Julia is where she always said she would be, in Europe. Only I fear she left quite a scandal in her wake. She ran off with a married man. Adam has never forgiven himself for introducing her to the Englishman. Adam says the scoundrel will never marry her, even if he could, and now that she has ruined her reputation, she'll never have any hopes of marrying a gentleman. Nor will she ever again be able to show her face in Virginia," Leigh said, sighing as she remembered Julia's dreams of becoming a duchess.

"That is the only news that doesn't shock me," Neil said unsympathetically.

Leigh's eyes suddenly blazed with anger. "You have no right to criticize Julia. You don't know what might have happened to her to cause her to do what she did," Leigh defended her friend.

"Oh, but I do know. She didn't have the courage to stay. She was a selfish, spoiled young woman who thought of nothing but herself. I'm sure her situation was intolerable. No more balls to be the belle of, nor picnics to be pampered at. No more beaus for her to flirt with and tease into harmless indiscretion, and certainly not if they returned to her side maimed. And even had there been a ball to attend, what would she have worn? There would be no more beautiful ball gowns for her to dance in, only faded woolens to wear because the rest had gone to clothe the armies."

"How dare you say such horrid things about her? She's your cousin. I don't blame her for leaving. Her home was burned to the ground. Her mother and father are gone. There was nothing left for her here."

"But you stayed, Leigh. You're here at Travers Hill, half-starved, scared, and at the mercy of both rebels and Yankees. Your land a battlefield, your home filled with the dying. Your father? You said he was killed by rebels?" Neil questioned relentlessly, determined to know everything.

"Looters."

"Your mother? Dead?"

"Yes, but she died inside long before she left us. She just couldn't accept what had happened to her family, to our way of life. To her beloved roses," Leigh added, smiling to herself.

"Your brothers?" he asked, but Leigh remained silent, still lost in her thoughts.

"Your brothers?" he repeated harshly, reaching out and grasping her arm, gently shaking her until she met his eyes.

"Only Guy is left now, and he…well, he's where you wished him. I can still hear your words, Neil Braedon, spoken so damningly that night. You told Guy that you would both be in hell before he ever saw your face again," she threw the words back at him. "You'll be pleased to know that he's in hell, but he will never see your gloating face. He's blind. And Palmer William and Stuart James, they're both gone. Your brother was with Palmer William when he died. He carried him from the battlefield and saw that he was buried properly. You know about Justin?"

Neil nodded, remembering the letter from home informing him of his brother's death.

"I wanted to ask you something about that night," Leigh said, her eyes so bright with unshed tears that Neil felt as if he were drowning in the deep blue color.

"That night?" he questioned, but he knew what night she spoke of.

"Yes. Guy didn't miss, did he?"

Neil smiled. "No, his shot, considering how drunk he was, was quite accurate, although not enough to cost me my life. And?" he inquired.

"My colt?" she demanded, and he knew what it must have cost her pride to have asked him that.

"When I left Riovado, Capitaine had already shown promise of becoming a magnificent stallion."

"*Capitaine?*" Leigh repeated the name in surprise. "You kept the name."

"No other name seemed to fit as well."

"Fast as the wind?"

"Faster."

Leigh surprised Neil by her soft, unexpected laughter. "I never thought to be grateful to you for taking him from me, but I am thankful."

Neil's eyes narrowed thoughtfully. "Grateful to me? I thought you would still be cursing my name."

"Oh, I still do," she said, smiling up at him, her blue eyes glinting now with wicked amusement. "Every night with my prayers."

Neil moved closer. Leigh tried to step back, but his hand tightened its grip around her upper arm, holding her just within inches of his body. Raising her chin, she stared up at him defiantly.

"Why should you wish to thank me? I hurt you that night,"

he reminded her, wanting to see if he could still hurt her, if she still cared enough to give him that power.

"You saw his dam when you came into the kitchens, didn't you?"

Neil's eyes widened with revelation, remembering now the sad-looking menagerie in the first room he'd entered before finding the passage into the kitchens. A sick nag, a grizzled pony, and a cud-chewing cow had eyed him when he'd entered.

"Your mare, the chestnut?" he asked, incredulous.

"Yes, a fine, upstanding member of the Confederate cavalry stole, no, forgive me, requisitioned her, from our stables one day. She returned a month later, looking far worse than she does now, but she was luckier than her rider, for all that was left of him were his boots, still in the stirrups. As you may have noticed, we no longer have Thoroughbreds at Travers Hill. If you hadn't taken—"

"Don't you mean received? The terms were agreed upon. No one forced you to make the decision you did. You, apparently, valued quite highly your brother's profligate life," Neil interrupted, reminding her of the circumstances, despite the fact that he wasn't proud of what he had done that night.

"My mistake," she said silkily. "I was trying to spare you the embarrassment of reminding you of your threat to murder my brother if I didn't give you Capitaine," Leigh said, trying to free her arm and step away from him, but she was drawn even closer against him.

"I seem to recall it was my shot, and since your brother had already wounded me, I believe I was being extremely lenient with him. He needed to be taught a lesson."

"Yes, he learned his lesson well, and he may have forgiven you, but I haven't."

"Forgiven me, your brother, the hotheaded Guy Travers?"

"He's changed. He says you had every right to do what you did. He blames himself for the loss of my colt, not you."

"Amazing," Neil murmured, genuinely surprised. "But you, of course, have not forgiven me?"

The half smile tantalized Neil as he watched it slowly appear, a challenging look in her eye. "Yes, I have forgiven you," she surprised him even further by declaring. "If you hadn't stolen

Capitaine from me, he would probably have met an agonizing death on the battlefield. I would rather see him belong even to the likes of you than have him die so horribly," she told him, the quietness of her voice adding to its angry intensity. "So, I owe you a debt of gratitude," she taunted. "You thought to hurt me that night, to steal something precious from me, but, you see, you actually did me a favor. Now let me go, and take your men and leave us in peace," she told him, struggling to get away from him and the blazing anger that had flared in his pale eyes.

Suddenly, she was free, and she stepped away triumphantly, too late realizing he now held possession of the quilt, and he pulled it from her, letting it drop to the floor as he bared her nakedness to him.

Standing so close to her, he had breathed the sweet scent of lavender and roses, mingling with the heady fragrance of jessamine, rising from her warm bare flesh, the velvety smoothness of her pale shoulders curving enticingly above the scalloped edge of the quilt. Her unbound, silken hair, bronzed with firelight dancing in it, moved sensuously around her, one golden-brown strand veiling part of her heart-shaped face, outlining the delicate line of cheek and jaw, and drawing his gaze to her eyes, darkened into indigo with her anger, and never more mysterious to him than now behind their thick fringe of long, golden-tipped dark brown lashes.

For just an instant, Leigh stood as if rooted to the floor, stunned with embarrassment, especially when she glanced up to see his gaze moving over her lingeringly, caressingly. Indignation and anger warred with her initial embarrassment as she took a step to retrieve the quilt, but before she could reach it, Neil Braedon's hands had closed over her shoulders, then his arm was like a vise around her waist, his other arm sliding behind her shoulders, his hand resting lightly against her ribs, just touching the curve of her breast.

She stood so slender and pliant in his arms. He bent her back over his arm, staring down into her face for a long moment before he lowered his mouth to hers, finding it even as she turned her head away, easily claiming her slightly parted lips as she tried to catch her breath. They molded to his as his kiss deepened, his tongue finding hers and touching it, feeling and tasting its softness. Lifting his mouth from hers, her lips seemed to cling to his for an instant, then he pressed her even further over his arm, holding her so her hips and thighs were pressed against him and the aching hardness in his loins. He stared down at her soft breasts, the rose-tinted nipples hardened and erect with desire. He lowered his lips and touched one of her nipples, his lips brushing against the taut bud, teasing it, his tongue licking it and the paler pink areola surrounding it. He could feel her heart pounding beneath her ribs, the slender cage that stood guard over her heart outlined delicately beneath her flesh.

She seemed so defenseless in his arms, he thought, his hand moving from her waist and over the soft roundness of her buttocks, pressing the smooth flesh against him, feeling the roughness of his buckskins rubbing against her bare skin, and heightening his awareness of her nakedness.

He found her mouth again, tasting of its sweetness, his breath becoming hers as the kiss deepened while his hand fondled her hip. Moving intimately lower, sliding into the curling hair between her thighs, his fingers were gentle against the vulnerable curve of soft warm flesh hidden there.

He felt her body briefly stiffen at his intrusion, her hand on his, trying to protect herself as if she were still a virgin unused to a man's sexual intimacies with her body. Then she surrendered, her fragrant warmth melting against him. The throbbing hardness of his manhood pressed against his breeches, seeking the exquisite release that only spilling his seed deep inside of her would bring. He wanted to feel himself embedded within her soft body, to hear her cry out as he took her to the heights of passion, knowing that he had made her forget the touch of any man but himself. And he would make her forget. He had not imagined the softness of her lips quivering beneath his, returning his caress. He knew not what game of seduction she played, but she had responded and she would again, he promised, pulling her closer...

"Captain! Captain! You in there, sir?"

As if through a haze, Neil heard the voice he recognized as one of his men's calling his name from the far end of the narrow hallway. He shook his head, clearing it.

Releasing Leigh, he bent down and picked up the quilt, wrapping it around her quivering body. For a brief second he stared down into her lovely face, her lips reddened from his kisses, her dark blue eyes drowsy with passion, and he knew that there would be another time for them.

He would find a way to come back for her, to make her his. He wasn't going to lose her again, he vowed as he walked away from her for the second time in his life.

Sixteen

Oft in the stilly night,
Ere Slumber's chain has bound me,
Fond memory brings the light
Of other days around me;
The smiles, the tears,
Of boyhood's years,
The words of love then spoken;
The eyes that shone
Now dimmed and gone,
The cheerful hearts now broken.

Thomas Moore

"STILL CAN'T BELIEVE YOU GOIN' AFTER THE CAP'N LIKE that. Got the nerve, you do, when he told everyone to stay put."

"He was gone too long," the man in question defended himself. "Figured that lil' reb could've stuck them scissors in him and buried him out back with them rebs if she was of a mind to. Never know 'bout a woman, 'specially one as pretty as her. Be as sweet as an' angel one minute, then spittin' an' scratchin' like a wildcat the next. Get you when you least expect it. Reckon the cap'n fell fer them blue eyes of hers, 'cause the way the cap'n was watchin' her he wouldn't have been thinkin' straight. Never seen the cap'n so hot fer a woman before. Could almost see the sparks flyin' between them. Thought he was goin' to catch fire and take her right there in the stables. Reckon they had some unfinished business between them, the cap'n sayin' they was old friends. Wouldn't mind bein' that kind of friend myself. Wonder how they met in the first place. Figure the cap'n's got family 'round these parts? Sure knows the land, so he must, though he don't talk like no Virginian I ever heard. Besides, thought I'd better find him, 'cause swear I heard hounds barkin'."

"'Twas from inside the house, I tell ya."

"Nope, comin' from back towards the woods. Figure they

got hounds trackin' us. Know it's the only way they're goin' to catch us. Thought the cap'n oughta know, an' might not even have heard, him still bein' in the house, his mind on other things. 'Cause I saw him go in, an' he hadn't come back out."

"Damn 'em, bringin' in bloodhounds to sniff out the Bloodriders," someone spat and cursed in the same breath.

"Good thing the cap'n didn't try to ford the river upstream a-ways. They got gunboats patrolling it, and they would've caught us, and I've already seen two patrols walkin' the banks both sides the river. Never seen so many folks millin' 'bout like they knew what they was doin'. We sure stumbled into a hornets' nest this time," the Bucktail said worriedly, wondering if it wouldn't have been wiser to have stayed in the streambed they'd ridden through to throw off the scent of their trail.

But his captain didn't slow his pace any as he led his men straight for the bend in the river. The gentle rise of hill it wended around, crowned by a steep cliff overlooking the black waters below, and the thick stand of woods surrounding the base, seemed the ideal place to set a trap for unsuspecting riders.

"Where the hell is the captain takin' us?"

"My horse ain't goin' to hold McGuire and me for much longer. Don't want him comin' up lame. Never will get out of this damned reb territory. Never seen so many graybacks in my life. Figure that whole column we saw yesterday come back across the river and camped just upstream."

"An' wouldn't you know the moon would show its round, sickly face 'bout now. What happened to them clouds when we need some cover? Feel as naked as if I was sittin' in a room full of people without my breeches on."

"No one's goin' to get too excited, reckon they ain't goin' to see much," someone snickered.

"Don't worry. The cap'n knows what he's doin'."

"Looks to me like we're headed right toward the river. We goin' to be seen, an' if we find ourselves on the bank, or in the woods between, or atop that hill, then we'll git caught fer sure, Jimmy," someone fretted, beginning to believe he heard the lapping of water against the sides of a gunboat lying in wait midstream, or the cocking of a rifle hammer as a reb sharpshooter took aim on them from the summit of the hill.

"Like I said, the cap'n's been playin' the devil with them rebs. Ain' nothin' to worry about."

"Yeah, well I jus' hope we don't find ourselves caught between the devil and the deep this time, 'cause I can't swim."

"Well, if we do, then I still ain't worried, 'cause if the devil's own captain don't save us, figure someone up there is watchin' over the little lieutenant. Ever since he joined up with us, we been havin' mighty good luck. Reckon we got folks high an' low watchin' over us."

"We're the Bloodriders! Luck's ridin' with us!" came the cry that was answered by several low, savage howls that had stiffened their spines with courage on many a raid.

"Wouldn't exactly call this *good* luck," someone less willing to believe reminded them, his teeth chattering, his bones aching, and his spine like quivering jelly.

"S'pose 'tis all in the way you look at it. Figure we could already be dead," someone said, finding it a heartening thought as he rode through a tangle of undergrowth and overhanging vines that threatened to unseat him.

Those words of fortitude had hardly been uttered before the speaker found himself wondering if his time had indeed come as his captain, the lieutenant holding on for dear life, disappeared underground. His horse, sensing his nervousness, and fearing the black void that loomed ahead, shied, whinnying as he threatened to balk. Another rider before him rode into the chasm, disappearing, perhaps into Hades, the frightened raider thought, remembering his many sins of the past. But nevertheless, he spurred his horse onward, knowing that certain death waited with bated breath behind.

And to the rebels searching the countryside, Captain Dagger and the Bloodriders might very well have had the hounds of hell on their heels, because they seemed to have disappeared off the face of the earth.

But no hell awaited the Bloodriders that night. The cave they entered was more like the treasure cave from the *Forty Thieves* in the *Arabian Nights* stories, and their captain was Ali Baba, leading them into safety with the magically spoken words, "Open, Sesame!"

The first surprise, however, had been when entering the

darkness, for it had only lasted an instant. Suddenly moonlight had spilled down on them, bathing a large clearing on the other side of the natural stone bridge they'd passed beneath. The stone arch was overgrown with Virginia creeper, and the thick curtain of vines had fallen back into place behind them, looking undisturbed, as if the lush foliage clung tenaciously to the hillside. The Bloodriders dismounted, leading their horses into the broad, curving mouth of a shallow cave behind. The overhang was deep enough to shelter the horses from the storm that was approaching as a low rumbling of thunder sounded across the distance; the moon having shown its face only long enough to guide them to safety.

One of the riders glanced up, his face eerie in the silvery light as he stared at the moon's face, thinking it had looked down kindly upon them this time.

Lieutenant Chatham found himself leaning against the cool rock, his chest tight as he struggled to fill his lungs, his heart pounding deafeningly in his ears, his knees wobbly as he tried to stand on one foot. Riding through the blackness of night with the captain was an experience he would not soon forget, he thought, surprised he was still alive to be scared to death. But never before had he felt such raw power emanating from man and beast, and holding onto the captain's waist, he'd sat frozen, half expecting to tumble from the big bay's rump as they'd flown along the streambed, the cooling spray of water that hit him in the face the only thing that had kept him from fainting from the sheer exhilaration of their wild flight.

He glanced up curiously as the captain walked past him, holding a lighted match cupped protectively in his hand as he went deeper into the cave, entering through a slightly narrowing passageway, and the lieutenant was curious how the captain had known this cave existed. Rather fortuitous, he thought, wondering how long their luck would hold, but he didn't worry for long as he followed the captain into the cave, feeling foolish as he rode between Johnson and Jimmy, balanced on their crossed arms as they hurried to stay within sight of the flickering light ahead. Lieutenant Chatham glanced down trying to see where they stepped, but he couldn't even see his own feet in the Stygian darkness. Suddenly he blinked, blinded by the brilliance that flooded into the passageway, revealing the stone-walled interior. An even greater illumination came from the end of the tunnel, where the captain had disappeared.

Lieutenant Chatham's mouth dropped wide open, and he was thankful now he was being carried, because he could have been knocked over with a feather as they entered the chamber and beheld a magnificence that took the breath away.

"Lordee! Would ya lookee here!" Jimmy crowed, his eyes reflecting the glowing light from a crystal chandelier that hung suspended from the stone roof of the cave.

"Must have a dozen or more lights in it!" he said, awed.

"Sixteen, Jimmy," Captain Dagger said quietly, surprising his men that he could have counted that fast.

"Now I know I've died an' gone to heaven," McGuire sighed groggily, staring up at the sixteen-light crystal chandelier with tears in his bleary eyes. "Never thought I'd make it."

Neil Braedon had been just as surprised as his men when entering the chamber, the shrouded forms taking shape as he'd lit the candles in the chandelier that had once hung in the dining room of Royal Bay and brought his grandmother such joy.

Neil glanced around the cave where he, Nathan, and Adam used to hide when boys, expecting the worst consequences to befall them at the hands of their elders because of their rowdiness. Then, it had been empty, except for a cache of boyhood treasures, collected on their many forays across the countryside.

Now, now it held the cherished possessions of generations of a family; the legacy to those who might survive. Rolled up and propped against the stone walls were the fine carpets that for so many years Braedon feet had walked across. A wall of crates, carefully marked on the outside of each, held fine china and crystal, the porcelain figurines and objets d'art, the rare books and maps so lovingly collected through the years. A pair of globes, spun by boyish hands dreaming of faraway places as of yet unvisited, were cradled in two wingback chairs. Filling the cavern were most of the furnishings, the family heirlooms, from Royal Bay, only the essentials for everyday living having remained in the big house.

"Reckon we could place the lieutenant down on this fancy settee here, Cap'n?" the Bucktail asked, eyeing the blue-and-gold-striped silk cushions revealed beneath a linen sheet Johnson had pulled from the sofa.

"Put the sheet back on, please, if I'm to be placed there," the lieutenant pleaded, knowing his mother would have been outraged had he put his muddy boots on so lovely a piece of furniture. "*Louis XV*," the lieutenant murmured with admiration, his eyes caressing the delicately curved lines of the rococo styling.

"Well, I don't know who the devil this Louie Cans fella is, an' why you should know him, but he ain't here now to complain none," Johnson said, but as his captain gestured at the sheet, he pulled the protective covering back across the cushions before they set the lieutenant down.

McGuire found himself stretched out on another covered settee, feeling as if he were dreaming as the springtime fragrance of lavender and roses drifted to him and he closed his eyes, content to die right where he was.

"What the hell d'ya suppose all of this stuff is doin' in here?"

"Looks like someone's settin' up housekeepin'," one of the raiders said as they all crowded inside, staring around in amazement at their luxurious surroundings. One of the men, who'd just entered the cave, and was standing behind the others, bumped into a small mahogany chest of drawers. Curious, he tried to open the lidded top, but a small brass lock kept it closed against him. Pulling out his jackknife, he easily sprung the lock, opening the lid to reveal a velvet-lined interior glinting with silverware. Glancing around, and seeing no one watching him, he quickly picked up several elaborately scrolled spoons, the solid silver feeling cold and heavy as he slipped the pieces inside his haversack.

"Well, if it ain't my own face lookin' back at me," someone said, staring at his grinning reflection in one of the gilded girandoles hanging on the wall. "Gave me a start, it did, seein' how ugly it was, thought fer a minute there it was Johnson," he continued, laughter echoing around the cave as the men began to wander around aimlessly, as if lost in another world, and feeling safe for the first time in several days.

"Did you ever see such fancy ladies and gents?" the Bucktail asked, almost doffing his cap as he stared down at the gold-leaf framed painting he'd accidentally kicked with his boot.

Overcome with curiosity about what manner of gentlefolk had hidden their valuables in a cave, he pulled another of the paintings into view.

"Hey, if I ain't a duck in thunder, this is the house we saw burned to ashes downriver a piece. Recognize them six chimneys. Ah, what a pity. Mighty fine-lookin' place, it was. Like them columns, I do," he said. "Reckon all this stuff come from there? Must've hid it when things started lookin' bad fer the rebs, our troops fightin' so deep into Virginia."

Sliding another, slightly smaller painting from the stack on top of a tapestry-covered sofa table, he was standing there gazing at it, when suddenly he sucked in his breath, choking so that his eyes bulged and someone standing close by slapped him hard between the shoulder blades.

Gulping, he looked up, his startled gaze meeting his captain's pale-eyed stare in disbelief.

"*Cap'n?*" he questioned, glancing between the hawk-featured face of the young, golden-haired gentleman dressed for riding in the painting, and his hawk-featured, golden-haired captain, dressed as a Yankee raider and standing in the flesh not five feet away.

Silence descended on the cave as the men stilled, all eyes turning to stare at the painting the Bucktail had held up to the light.

Someone whistled softly beneath his breath. Sure enough, it was the spitting image of the captain. Only the man in the portrait, standing indolently in the door of a blacksmith's shop, was dressed in shiny black Hessians up to his knees, his tight breeches of the finest buff-colored buckskin, his blue coat long-tailed with brass buttons and cut away in front to show the flowered silk of his vest, and his lacy cravat elaborately tied beneath his strong, square chin. His hair was styled in elegant curls of a fashion worn over a quarter of a century ago. Quite the dandy, standing there with the blooded bay, which, some-one else decided, bore the distinct markings of the captain's own big bay, Thunder Dancer.

"Gives me the shivers," Johnson mumbled, risking a glance at the captain, almost believing he might be staring at a ghost. "Figure that's why we been so lucky? We been ridin' with the dead? Maybe the captain can't be kilt," someone of a similar frame of mind voiced nervously, pinching the man next to him to make certain he was real, the responding yelp of pain comforting to him.

"My father, gentlemen," Neil said, coming to stand close enough to the painted face in the portrait for a number of the men to shake their heads in dismay at the resemblance between father and son.

"This cave is filled with the possessions from Royal Bay, that white-columned house," he said, glancing briefly at the painting of the house the Bucktail had spoken of as being the same they'd ridden past earlier in the day. "My father's family has lived at Royal Bay since before the Revolution. My father chose another way of life, and traveled west to the territories. That is where I come from, but this," he said, his raised hand encompassing the contents of the cave, "is my heritage. These treasured possessions were hidden here by my cousins so that something belonging to our family might survive this war. I shall take full responsibility for the safety and care of these items. I know I need not remind you men of my policy concerning looting," their captain said, slowly glancing around the gathering, meeting and holding each man's gaze.

No one noticed when the man standing hunched over at the back of the group returned the stolen silver to its rightful place in the velvet-lined chest, his hand shaking so he fumbled with the pieces, the clinking together of the silver sounding like thunder in his guilt-sensitive ears. Instinctively he placed a cupped hand over his groin, almost expecting to feel the lightning-fast flash of the captain's knife slashing down on his own most treasured possession.

Lieutenant Chatham, who'd nearly fallen from his perch on the settee while trying to see the portrait around the captain's broad back, and who'd been preoccupied with how he'd work this revelation into his tale of the Bloodriders, suddenly blurted out, "No one would ever betray you, Captain! You've our word, word of a Bloodrider, that nothing will ever be said of this cave, and its contents. We all took the blood oath when we signed up with you. Damnation, sir!" the lieutenant bellowed, surprising everyone, including himself, with the profanity and the loudness of his voice, for no one had ever heard the mild-mannered, soft-spoken lieutenant curse. "Hell, you're our captain, and you've saved all of our lives too many times to count, never leaving any of us behind to rot in some reb prison. No one," the lieutenant repeated again, his soft blue eyes hardening as he gazed at the others, "would betray you, and let it be known right now that they would have the rest of us to answer to if they did."

"The lieutenant's right, Cap'n," the Bucktail said, glancing around at the others, some of whom were nodding in agreement—and especially vehement, one of the riders at the back.

"Ain't none of us who'd betray ye," McGuire vowed. And for two reasons, he thought silently. One, because he respected the captain. The lieutenant was right, the captain had saved all of their lives more than once. And two, he'd have to be a fool to want the captain out searching for him and seeking revenge. He wouldn't bet on anyone so inclined to live long enough to enjoy his ill-gotten fortune.

For a moment, Neil said nothing, then he nodded. "We'll camp in here tonight, men. Unsaddle your horses. And no fires. Jimmy, you're on duty first, then I'll stand the watch."

"No problem, Cap'n," someone said, "that soup is still warmin' my innards, thanks to that lil' reb, and at least we're dry. Don't know what was in that broth, 'cause it sure looked thin, but it's been stickin' to my ribs since it went down."

"Cap'n, sir, look at this crate. It's marked in green with the name 'Travers.' Reckon some of the stuff in here is from the place we were at? Travers Hill, wasn't that the name of the farm?"

Neil glanced around, seeing now that another group of crates, set slightly apart from those from Royal Bay, had been marked with the Travers name.

"Reckon them bein' neighbors, they hid their belongings together, this bein' the best place around."

"My cousins married two of the Travers daughters," Neil said, knowing Nathan and Adam would have suggested to Stuart Travers the perfect hiding place for Travers Hill's cache of valuables.

"One of them marry that pretty little miss who helped us, Cap'n?"

"No," his captain answered abruptly, "she married someone else." The man didn't ask another question.

The Bucktail, trying to replace the portrait, knocked over a painting from another stack leaning against the wall. Ever curious, he looked at it as he was replacing it, a smile of recognition crossing his weathered face.

"Cap'n, speakin' of the little lady," he said, lifting the painting so it was in the golden glow from the chandelier. "Betcha this is the whole family, here. What happened to them, d'ya s'pose?" he wondered aloud as he stared down at the Travers family portrait.

This time, Lieutenant Chatham did fall from the settee, so determined was he to see the portrait of the family that had once lived at Travers Hill, and that had so captured his imagination.

Helping hands tried to assist him back onto the settee, but he insisted, and somewhat testily, that he be carried closer to view the portrait.

Taking off his round-rimmed spectacles, Lieutenant Chatham quickly cleaned them, then carefully resettled them back on the bridge of his short nose, his blue eyes widening with wonder as the painting, with the people posed so naturally in the scene, seemed to come to life before him.

The Travers family was enjoying a lazy, summer's afternoon. It was a peaceful, somnolent setting. The house as comfortable as an old friend with its rosy-bricked facade and green-shuttered windows thrown open to catch the cooling breeze. On the veranda, a lovely, gracious woman stood with a woven basket full of roses over her arm. Apparently she'd just plucked a bouquet of the summer blooms from her garden. The lieutenant sighed; he'd been in that garden. Standing next to her was a woman the lieutenant recognized—the mulattress. She was laying a damask-covered table with all manner of appetizing fare. And just behind her, stepping from the house with a tray of tall glasses, was a green-liveried black man; the same man the lieutenant had met that morning, only his hair had turned as white as snow. On the first step, a serious young man with dark hair stood, offering one of the red roses to a young woman with the same golden hair and delicate features as the older woman. The lieutenant recognized her too. It was the same woman he'd seen lying so ill in the study at Travers Hill a couple of days ago.

The lieutenant glanced over at the captain, who'd also been staring intently at the portrait. As if feeling his gaze, the captain glanced at him.

The lieutenant placed a hesitant finger on the young woman's figure.

Seeing the question in the young man's eyes, Neil said, "Althea. And that is her elder brother, Stuart James, I believe that was his name. He died sometime during the last four years. The other woman is Mrs. Travers. She's gone too. And you met Jolie and Stephen."

The lieutenant nodded sadly, then moved his finger to the little dark-haired girl sitting on the knee of a boy with a shock of thick golden curls, her grinning face staring out at them as she tried to grab the pup the boy was holding just out of her reach.

"Blythe and Palmer William," Neil answered. "They are both gone now."

The lieutenant's hand hovered over the figure of a handsome young man with chestnut hair, surrounded by a pack of hounds as he walked across the yard, and even stilled in time by the artist's brush, there was a definite look of devil-may-care arrogance in the man's stride.

"Guy Travers," Neil said, his tone causing the lieutenant to frown slightly, for he'd heard that harsh note in the captain's voice too often not to take notice; it usually boded ill for someone. "He still lives."

Out in the yard near a stately oak, fluffy white clouds floating across the blue sky above green hills in the distance, a short-legged, stocky gentleman stood beside a beautiful roan Thoroughbred, his hand stroking the satiny coat, while the reins were held by a tall, smiling black man. Sitting on the horse's back was a small, chestnut-haired girl, not more than nine or ten.

"Stuart Travers, master of Travers Hill, and Sweet John. They're dead. Sweet John was the best trainer of Thoroughbreds in Virginia. Another breeder wanted Sweet John, but Stuart Travers damned the man, saying his trade was raising and selling horses not humans."

"Slave owners," someone said in disgust and spat on the floor of the cave.

"Them two we met this mornin' is free enough now. Heard the man tell Johnson that when he was servin' us that broth. Seemed sort of a lordly fella to have been a slave, and sure surprised me how fancy he spoke. Felt almost as if he was lookin' down his nose at me, and wouldn't have let me in the big house, 'ceptin' through the back door. Got the feelin' he kinda resented me even bein' out in his stables."

Lieutenant Chatham didn't need his captain to tell him the name of the little girl sitting astride the Thoroughbred in her sky-blue dress, a lacy froth of pantalettes leg showing above a white-stockinged foot that dangled high above the ground, yet no fear showed on her young face, despite the precariousness of her perch, as she stared out at them. Her rounded chin was raised proudly, her blue eyes wide with the wonder of her vaulted position.

One small hand was holding onto the roan's long mane, the other the blue ribbons of a wide-brimmed straw bonnet, which she'd pulled from her chestnut curls.

Neil stared at the child's face painted there, then remembered the warmth of the woman he'd held in his arms not an hour past, the woman this little girl had become, and he knew a sudden despair. She was just as far out of his reach today as she had been four years ago, as she was in this painting.

He had lost Leigh when she had chosen to marry another, and now, when he could have taken her, made her his, made her forget Matthew Wycliffe, he had to walk away and leave her.

Always just beyond his reach, he thought savagely, turning away from the painting, and issuing his orders in a harsh tone of voice that had his men jumping.

❧

"I can't reach it," Leigh said, standing on tiptoe as she tried to knock down a cobweb.

"Here, let me." A voice spoke behind her, then a masculine hand had taken the feather duster from her and with a clean swipe had freed the corner of the unsightly cobweb.

Leigh cried out in surprise, spinning around and nearly tumbling from the footstool.

Strong arms reached out and caught her, swinging her down.

"Adam," Leigh breathed in relief.

"Who else?" he demanded with a laugh.

In truth, Leigh had caught her breath when seeing him, thinking it was Neil Braedon behind her, forgetting about Adam for the moment when she heard the deep voice and saw the gold of his hair. Still shaken from her last encounter with Neil, even the thought of him brought a wild blush of color to her cheeks, for she could not forget his fiery kiss, or the intimacy of his touch, or her own shameful response.

Adam smiled as her arms embraced him, holding him close for a moment, then she placed a sisterly kiss against his cheek, and he responded, placing a brotherly kiss against her brow.

"You are worse than Noelle holding up her face for her expected farewell kiss," he complained, pleased nevertheless to be included amongst those so privileged. "You're working too hard," he said, frowning as he noted her flushed cheeks and wondered about the shadowed expression that had entered her eyes for an instant, then, just as quickly, had vanished, as if she'd banished an unwelcome thought, or image, from her mind.

Leigh laughed, hugging him with surprising strength for a moment before she looked up at him. "I'm so happy you've come," she said, trying to hide her dismay at how ill he looked, far worse since last she'd seen him.

"Lucinda?" he asked eagerly of his daughter.

"More beautiful and precious every day," Leigh told her, and reaching out, she smoothed a golden curl from his brow, feeling the light beading of perspiration beneath.

Adam jerked away from her soothing hand, then managed to smile apologetically when he saw her bewildered look. Holding her away from him for a moment, an almost pained expression in his light gray eyes, he stared at her. Sometimes, he thought shakily, the way she tipped her head, the twinkle in her eye, her lips curving so readily into a smile, the way she moved reminded him so much of Blythe, as if she were still here with him.

"Blythe was always doing that," he said quietly. "I threatened to have the curl cut, but she threatened to leave me if I did," he said gruffly, then turned away quickly, gesturing to a large woven basket he'd set on the bench in the foyer.

"Good thing I've brought supplies, you're getting too thin. I would have gotten here yesterday afternoon, but the storm opened up and rained buckets down on me. I had to stay over at the Draytons. I was relieved to see Meadowbrook still standing. Reverend Culpepper is staying with them. His church was burned. Wonder if it had anything to do with one of his pompous sermons. I must say, he wasn't too friendly. Forgive and forget, I was always taught," Adam chuckled, then sobered. "Poor Jasper looked like death. They lost two of their grandsons at Sharpsburg. One at Dunkard Church, the other in the fighting at Bloody Lane. Even more tragic for them, one of their nephews crossed Antietam Creek during the battle, only he was with the Union forces. Ruth Canby was born in Maryland, and one of the Drayton girls is married to a lawyer in Baltimore. That must be hell for them, wondering if…"

"Did you hear about John Roy Canby?" Leigh asked, unwilling to think about one cousin wearing gray, the other blue, and meeting on the battlefield. "He joined the cavalry. They only let him in because he had a horse of his own, even if he couldn't stay in the saddle."

"Sounds intriguing already," Adam said, grinning with anticipation.

"He managed to get a command and was leading his men into battle during a charge at Chancellorsville when he lost control of his horse and went galloping off in the opposite direction. His men followed, thinking he meant to flank the enemy, and apparently it worked, because the enemy retreated. He's a colonel now, but they've assigned him to desk duty at Headquarters. His commanding general, and a friend of the Canby family, said riding a chair was the only way John Roy could keep his seat and the Confederacy safe."

"Uncle Adam! Uncle Adam!" Noelle cried out, racing from the study and throwing herself into Adam's arms. "What's wrong with you?" she demanded, gazing up at his face. "Do you have a tummy ache?"

"Hello, sweetheart," he said, meeting Leigh's amused gaze as Noelle placed kisses all over his face. "I'm not sick, just bent over double laughing at something wicked your aunt told me. My, my, you're growing as fast and as tall as a sapling hoping to be brought into the house in time for Christmas and the dressing of the tree," he declared.

"*Joyeux Noel!*" Noelle said, "*Je m'appelle Noelle Rose Braedon, et puis-je vous presenter Mademoiselle Travers?*" she said, holding out her hand and lifting her chin with the haughty and graceful airs of a grand dame.

"*Enchanté,*" Adam murmured, his eyes full of laughter as he bent and kissed her hand with gentlemanly courtesy.

"Aunt Leigh is teaching me to speak French," she confided. "*Je voudrais des haricots verts,*" she requested, giggling.

"Green beans?" Adam said, reaching into his coat pocket. "I'm sorry but all I've got is this," he said, holding up a length of red velvet ribbon. "Do you suppose it will do instead?" he asked, worried. "I do believe it will look far more attractive tied around your head than a green bean."

"Oh, Uncle Adam! For me? Truly?" Noelle asked, almost breathless.

"Yes, for you, my Christmas rose," he said, letting it drop into her outstretched hands.

"Oh, thank you," she squealed, her brown eyes glowing as bright as her red velvet ribbon.

"You're spoiling her," Leigh said good-naturedly as Adam was soundly kissed again.

"I learned early how to please the ladies. This is the surest way I know to receive kisses. And admit it, you're only jealous because I didn't bring a bonny blue ribbon for your hair," he said, a twinkle in his eye. "However, I do have plenty of treats in the basket, and maybe even a blue ribbon. Felt like a scoundrel, or a sutler, coming through the lines with my booty. Took my life in my hands, but I wasn't going to give my little cache here up to anyone, even General Lee himself, since I'd already sold my pride and was down to my last gold tooth to get most of these things."

"What's a sutler, Uncle Adam?" Noelle demanded, eyeing the basket suspiciously. "Is it some kind of an animal?"

"Something like that," Adam agreed. "Some remind me of rats, come to think of it. They're the lowest creatures, the duty they perform, the dirtiest. They're scavengers, and they travel behind an army like a pack of vultures. They stockpile what every soldier needs; boots, gloves, tobacco, even food and tents, and then they charge the poor fellows five to ten times too much for the goods, knowing they have to pay or they go without. Ought to shoot them, but they have government approval to set up their tents right at Headquarters. So sure of themselves, the rascals cheat even the generals," Adam said in disgust.

"Can I peek inside, Uncle Adam?" Noelle asked.

"*May* I?" Leigh corrected.

"You too, then," Adam said, winking at Leigh as he lifted the lid and held out his arm dramatically. "I bring you oranges and lemons, pickles and nuts, sugar and flour, fancy English soap and chocolates, and for more practical uses, woolens. If not the most fashionable, at least guaranteed to keep you snug on cold winter nights," he proclaimed.

"Oh, I must tell Mama and show her my ribbon!" Noelle cried, dashing back into the study.

"How is Althea?" Adam asked, closing the lid on their treasure chest.

Leigh smiled, tucking her hand in Adam's as they walked more sedately than their niece into the study. "Better, Adam. She is still weak, and it will take some time for her to recover completely her strength, but in the last couple of days she seems like a different person, as if she has found something to live for. She reminds me of the way she used to be, before the war."

"That's the best news I've heard in some time, and—excuse me," he interrupted himself, hurrying back to the chest to withdraw several folded newspapers and a couple of books. "Promised Guy I'd bring him the latest news, such as it is," he said with a grimace.

"We heard about the attack on Richmond," Leigh said.

"Oh? News travels fast, I must say. Heard anything else?" he asked eyeing her closely.

Leigh hesitated, knowing she should tell Adam about Neil. He had a right to know, they were cousins, and yet it would be difficult to admit to him that she had helped him and his men. Even if they were cousins, he might not understand her having helped Yankees, especially the notorious Captain Dagger and the Bloodriders. And she wondered if he even realized that Neil Braedon and Captain Dagger were one and the same. Nor did she wish to have Adam prying too closely into what had happened during that encounter. He had a way of ferreting out information.

"A troop of rebels came through yesterday looking for—" Leigh began, pausing for a moment, then decided to tell him of his cousin.

"—for Kilpatrick and Dahlgren, the Yankees who tried to raid Richmond. They won't catch Dahlgren," Adam concluded, a note of satisfaction in his voice. "He was killed near Queen and King Court House. Caught him in an ambush," he said, stopping and pulling Leigh around to face him. "They found papers on his body, Leigh. He intended to murder Jeff Davis and his cabinet, then burn Richmond," Adam told her.

Leigh's face paled. How many innocent civilian lives would have been lost in the panic that would have swept over Richmond with the flames? And what a severe blow to the Confederacy that act, and the cold-blooded murder of its president, would have been.

"I've been afraid of just something like this happening. This time they failed, but what of the next time? Both sides are becoming desperate to win this war, and, Leigh, I don't think it's going to be the Confederacy," Adam admitted, and it wasn't just his pessimistic belief as he remembered a recent editorial in the Richmond *Examiner*. "Leigh, listen to me, please," Adam said, his hand tightening around her arm, which he could already feel tensing with resistance to what he had to say, and his voice became almost pleading. "We've spoken of this before. Travers Hill sits in the heart of the war, right in the center of a path of destruction the Union is going to march down. Look what you've lost already. And you saw what happened to Royal Bay? Ashes! Ashes, Leigh, that is all that is left. My God, Leigh, just over a month ago our own army took all of the food you had left at Travers Hill to feed the troops, leaving you to starve. What happens when another army, the enemy this time, comes marching down the Shenandoah? What they can't take, in food for themselves and fodder for their horses, what livestock they don't need, they will destroy. They will burn everything, Leigh, the barns, the mills, the fields, because they can't let us retake the Valley. The Shenandoah means food for our troops, for our people. It means survival. It is what will keep the Confederacy going. They won't let us. But I think what frightens me even more is afterwards, after the war is over. If we lose, we will be the defeated. The Yankees will be *our* masters. Life for us will not be easy. Do you understand, Leigh?"

"I'm not leaving Travers Hill, Adam," Leigh told him, meeting his earnest gaze with a determined one of her own. "Besides," Leigh said bitterly, "where would we go? This is our home, and I intend to stay here. I'm not going to become a refugee on the road, with no place to call our own. At least here we have a roof over our heads, and we, like our army, can forage something from the land. When summer comes, the woods will be thick with blackberries, and the streams with trout, and—"

"Damn you, Leigh. I've never known such a hard-headed, stubborn—"

"Talking about my little sister, Adam?" an amused voice asked from just within the study.

"Guy!" Adam said, holding out his hand, then remembering his friend was blind, he let it drop until Guy held up his, then he took it firmly. "Yes, and maybe you can talk some sense into her, Guy," Adam said, and suddenly coming to a decision, he added, "and I think it about time you know exactly what your situation is here at Travers Hill."

"Adam!" Leigh said, glancing at him warningly.

"I suspect I already do," Guy said. "I have come to place great value on my hearing, which has become rather acute of late, and I could not but help overhear your rather heated argument."

"Then you heard what I told him," she said, placing her hand on Guy's arm as they stood together against Adam.

Adam shook his head, believing they would stand against him with their damned Travers pride riding high.

"Yes, I did, and, unfortunately, I have to agree with you."

"Unfortunately?" Leigh repeated, giving him a puzzled look, and thinking not for the first time that Guy had changed. It wasn't the black patch across his eye that made him seem different which, as he himself had jested, actually made him look rather daring and piratical, it was his seriousness, a thoughtfulness and deliberateness of manner that he'd never possessed before.

"Yes, Leigh, because I happen to agree with Adam."

"Guy!" Leigh said, her tone accusing, her glance between the two suspicious, as if they conspired against her.

"We can't go on living here much longer, Leigh," he said, grasping her hand and holding it in his. "God, you're nothing more than skin and bones. I could break your wrist in two so easily. Althea is ill. You've three young children to care for. Stephen and Jolie are working themselves to the bone and can only do so much to help you. And you've got a blind man and his two hounds to help you if you need protection. And, as Adam says, what happens to us *after* the war?"

"I can protect us now, and later. I have before."

"Leigh Travers standing alone against the combined forces of Grant and Lee," Guy mocked, unable to see the hot tears in his sister's eyes, but Adam could and he regretted having to fight her, but he was determined to make her face the truth.

"Listen, I've got a pass to get you all to Richmond. There, you will board my ship, *The Blithe Spirit*, from there you'll sail to Nassau, in the Bahamas, and from there you'll take a British ship to England. You'll be safe there."

"The Bahamas!" Leigh said incredulously. "England! And how do we live there? I've a trunk full of hundred-dollar notes, the only problem is that they're stamped 'Confederate States of America,' which won't buy us more than daydreams even here in Virginia. Dreams, Adam, is all this idea of yours is."

Adam's face flushed uncomfortably, even though he had expected her argument, but he would not be ridiculed out of his decision. "No, not dreams, Leigh. I'm a blockade runner. This is my business. I can get you there safely. Once you're there, *The Blithe Spirit* will bring you enough to live on. You'll sell her in the Bahamas. She's a good coastal schooner. She'll bring you enough."

"No, I won't even consider it," Leigh said, turning away.

"I'll let it rest for now, Leigh, but this is not settled. You may turn your back, pretending not to listen, but in the end you will, because you love this family of yours too much to risk their lives because of your pride."

"Adam, that was uncalled for," Guy rebuked him.

Adam sighed. "I'm sorry, Leigh. I didn't mean that. But I

did mean everything else. And if I cannot make you see reason, then I will take Lucinda with me when I leave." Adam's voice came harshly.

Leigh stopped in the middle of the study, her back rigid. Then she turned around and faced him, her blue eyes blazing.

"Oh," she said in too quiet a voice. "And who will care for her, Adam?"

"I'll get a woman, a nanny, to care for her."

"And will she love her like I do? Can you buy that kind of caring?"

"Leigh," Guy warned, knowing his sister was treading on dangerous ground now.

"No, but then that would be your decision, wouldn't it, Leigh?" Adam countered, his gray eyes glinting with anger and frustration, knowing she was right.

"I gave Blythe my promise that I would always care for her daughter. You would have me break that promise?"

"And I promised Blythe that I would never let anything happen to my daughter, to *her* daughter. Or have you forgotten that I am her father? I have the right to make the decisions concerning her safety, as, indeed," he added, hesitating for a moment before he spoke, then braving her anger as he said, "I have the right, as Nathan's only brother, to assume the responsibility for his wife, and his son and daughter. I am their legal guardian."

Adam steeled himself to face Leigh, and had he slapped her in the face he could not have shocked her more. "I'm sorry, Leigh, but you had better consider that too."

"Don't I have anything to say in this?" Althea's voice came softly from the sofa, where she and Noelle, and a napping Steward, had been sitting in horrified silence listening to the argument.

"Of course you do, Althea, but I know what Nathan would have wished, and I intend to honor my promise to him," Adam said.

"I have handled everything so far to everyone's satisfaction, and I believe I can go on doing so, if some people would not interfere," Leigh responded.

"Interfere! Good Lord, I have the ri—"

"So do I!"

"I do not think this arguing will settle anything, especially since you are both right and you are both wrong, and since you both mean well and have done so much for us, I cannot be angry with you, and neither of you should be angry with the other. This will achieve nothing. I do not think I need remind you of the truth of the Gospel, 'If a house be divided against itself, that house cannot stand.' Now, I insist you both come in here and sit down, and later, after Adam has rested, and we've all had a chance to say our piece, then, and only then will we be able to consider our situation and what we will do about it," Althea said in so reasonable a voice that both Leigh and Adam glanced at each other slightly shamefaced.

Although he could not see them, Guy could imagine the surprise on both Adam's and Leigh's faces as they received a scolding from Althea, whom they'd both been bossing around for far too long. "Well spoken, Althea," Guy said with a deep chuckle. "At least you quoted Mark and not Lincoln. Help me back to my chair, will you, Leigh? I'm befuddled."

"I apologize. I had no right to speak the way I did. I shall always be grateful to you, Leigh, for your care of Lucinda. I know you love her as if she were your own daughter, and I can never repay the debt I owe you for the sacrifices you make every day for her," Adam said, holding out his hand to her as she returned from helping Guy into his chair.

"You owe me, us, nothing, Adam. I love Lucinda because I loved Blythe, and because I love you," Leigh said, taking his hand in hers, their earlier, angry words forgiven, but not forgotten, because nothing was settled yet, and they both knew that.

"Damn you, Leigh," Adam said again, only this time it wasn't in anger and frustration, but affectionate exasperation as he went and knelt beside the cradle where his daughter slept so peacefully.

"You certainly know how to cut the ground out from under a man, little sister," Guy said.

"I don't understand what you mean."

"Exactly. If it had been calculated, it would not have worked. But you spoke so sincerely, so sweetly, with such genuine love and affection for poor Adam, that he could hardly continue to argue with you without seeming incredibly boorish," he said, patting one of his hounds, the bitch looking up at him with adoring eyes. "Now, now, don't give me that look. She is, isn't she, Adam?" he asked, staring blindly at Leigh.

Adam laughed. "I should have been prepared, for Mrs. Travers was always rather accomplished at putting one on the defensive," he said. "I don't believe your father ever did win an argument with her. And Leigh did inherit her blue eyes. I wonder what color Lucinda's eyes will become. Her hair is already as dark and thick as Blythe's. I hope her eyes are hazel," he murmured, touching the soft fringe of lashes. "She is more beautiful than ever," he said with a father's pride as he gazed down at his only daughter. "But she'll be prettier with hazel eyes, not my gray ones."

"They probably will become hazel," Leigh told him.

"Most babies have grayish-colored eyes when they're born," Althea told him reassuringly.

"Did I, Mama?" Noelle demanded.

"No, you had just as big brown eyes as you do now."

"Am I in my usual room?" Adam asked.

"Yes. We were expecting you so we made up the bed."

"By any chance, did you bring us any news, Adam?"

"Newspapers," Adam said, remembering the papers he'd placed on the table.

"Adam said they caught the Yankee who tried to attack Richmond," Leigh told them quickly, before Adam could speak further, and not mentioning the papers they'd found on the man's body detailing his plans to burn Richmond and murder Davis.

"Fewer papers than before, I'll wager. How many have gone out of business, now? And what color is the paper this time?"

Leigh giggled. "I do believe it's a lovely shade of pink."

"Lord help us! Pink?"

"And the print seems to be black, but I'm not certain. It could be a very dark purple. It's very pretty," Leigh couldn't resist adding. "They are most apologetic, but the editor says he is having a very difficult time finding paper and ink, their allocations being so unreliable, not to mention compositors and printers, all of whom have been so unconscionable as to march off to fight, and after this issue, the paper will even have to find a new editor. He says he has no other choice but to quit, his honor is at stake, since the next issue is going to be on lavender paper."

"Well, I should hope so. The man ought to be horse-whipped. Do you have time to read to me? At least I will be spared the indignity of having to look at it," Guy said.

"I'll read to you, Guy," Althea said before Leigh could offer. "I think Leigh will be busy unpacking that wonderful treasure chest I've been hearing about from Noelle."

"Good, because I suspect Leigh doesn't always read everything to me, only what she believes I should hear."

"Guy!" Leigh protested, but not as vehemently as she might otherwise have, since Guy spoke the truth.

"Can't deny it, can you?"

"I don't see any reason to read name by name the casualties of the latest battle, nor will I read one of those horrible editorials criticizing President Davis. The very same people crying the loudest now, blaming Davis for all our woes, are the very same who were crying the loudest for secession before the war."

"Well, if they continue to print all of our troop movements and the locations of what industries we have, and when our blockade runners are sailing, then the war will be over quick enough. I was astounded the last time you read to me, I thought you'd gotten your hands on a secret military cipher."

"Mister Adam, good to see you, sir," Stephen spoke from the doorway. "See you didn't forget us," he said, gesturing back at the chest. "See you even remembered to bring us that flour. We might be havin' some biscuits for supper this evenin'," he said.

"A feast, Stephen, because I even managed to get my conniving' hands on a small smoked ham, not up to Travers Hill's standards, mind you now, but I don't suppose anyone will mind," he said, getting slowly to his feet, and with a last glance at his sleeping daughter, he started toward the door.

"Ah, that'll please Jolie somethin' fierce. Always makes her feel better when she can cook somethin' special. Been mopin' 'round like one of Mister Guy's hounds since yesterday when the cap'n an' his soldiers come, 'cause she always gets this bad feelin' when he's 'round, with nothin' good coming of it like four years ago. An' there was thunder last night too," Stephen was saying somewhat grudgingly, when he suddenly remembered that no one was supposed to know about the captain, and he cut himself off abruptly, drawing even more attention to himself.

"The captain and his men?" Adam asked, his gaze intent as Stephen stared guiltily at Leigh, as if they shared a secret, and had something to hide.

"Yes, the rebels I told you about. They were looking for the Yankees who attacked Richmond," Leigh said quickly, rather too quickly, Adam thought, noticing the nervous way her gaze wouldn't meet his.

"I thought he was a major. Demoted him rather fast, haven't you?" Guy asked with an amused laugh.

"*Pouvez-vous prendre la boîte, s'il vous plaît?*" Adam called to Noelle, who opened her mouth in surprise, jumping to her feet as she understood his question and ran after him and Stephen to unload the box of smuggled-in goods.

"Let's see, now," Althea murmured, opening up the newspaper Leigh had handed her. "It's all right, Leigh, I do have the strength to hold the paper," Althea said, glancing up in surprise when Leigh continued to hover nearby, but Leigh had been watching the door nervously, wondering what Adam might be asking Stephen.

"The headlines, first, Althea," Guy said. "Then some of those amusing vignettes. I read some real sidesplitters in Richmond years ago. They were reprinted from a Georgia newspaper. They were supposedly letters sent to a 'Mr. Abe Linkhorn' from a bumpkin called 'Bill Arp.' Lampooned everything and everyone."

"All right. Hmmmm, what do you want to hear about first?" Althea asked, perusing the headlines quickly. "Deserters? There seem to be more than ever, and the government is offering amnesty and pardons to those who will return immediately to the ranks. Otherwise, they will be dealt with harshly; by courts-martial. How about the current price of meal? Good Lord! Four dollars a peck for turnip greens. Oh, my, whatever is this world coming to? A Baptist preacher was actually attacked for selling a barrel of flour for five hundred dollars. I wonder if any of his attackers were from his congregation," she said worriedly. "My goodness, over a hundred escaped last month from Libby Prison. The federal prisoners dug a tunnel and walked right out onto the streets of Richmond. A couple of escaped prisoners drowned trying to swim to safety, others were caught in the homes of Unionists in the city, or on the outskirts hiding out in abandoned farms, but almost half made it back to the federal lines.

"And listen to this! Just a couple of days ago a train full of gold bullion was robbed. They stole the engine, then ran it off the tracks near Gordonsville. They blew up the rest of the train and murdered the soldiers guarding the gold shipment. A Major Montgomery Stanfield was their commanding officer. Shot them down in cold blood after they'd disarmed them, leaving only one survivor. Later, after they'd destroyed the engine, the engineer and the train's crew were killed. How horrible," Althea said, shaking her head in disbelief at the viciousness of the act.

"Stanfield?" Guy questioned. "I knew a Major Stanfield. Met him at Headquarters a couple of times. A real gentleman. What a shame," Guy said sadly, wondering if anyone was going to live through this war.

"That stirred up the countryside," Adam said as he reentered the study, carrying an armful of woolens and other items. "And, of course, when Dahlgren tried to raid Richmond every regiment was alerted and went in pursuit, or so it seemed. I've never seen so much activity."

"They say here that the raiders who stole the gold were led by the murderous Captain Dagger. What a frightening name. I don't believe I remember you reading to us recently about this raider, Leigh. I think I remember hearing about him in Richmond. Something Blythe said. She was always so curious about everything. But I do know about Major Mosby, and... oh, look, it says here that he was promoted to lieutenant colonel, and I know about Jeb Stuart, of course, and even that awful Quantrill."

Leigh's hand suddenly shook as she took the bar of soap from Adam. Dropping it, she bent down quickly to retrieve it, not seeing Adam's eyes narrowing thoughtfully on her.

"That's because this one is a Yankee. The others are rebel raiders," she explained offhandedly.

"And which side you happen to be on makes it either right

or wrong, and how his exploits are reported and perceived by the public," Guy said with a laugh. "Well, whether it's Dagger, or Quantrill, whether wearing blue or gray, there isn't much difference. Bushwhackers, the lot of them."

"They call his men the Bloodriders. I can see why. I hope they catch them and hang them all," Althea said, sounding bloodthirsty herself.

"I think, sometimes, what we hear about certain raiders, certain skirmishes, must surely be exaggerated, perhaps even false. I'm sure this Captain Dagger cannot be the outlaw he has been reported to be," Leigh heard herself saying, and glancing up, she caught Adam's eye. For a long moment they stared at each other.

"I'll be glad to see the 'sun' again," Adam said, sounding casual enough as he changed the subject, except to Leigh, and she knew then he knew the truth of Captain Dagger's identity. He had not forgotten his cousin's Comanche name either.

"Summer," Althea said softly, as if already breathing the warm, softly scented breezes drifting in from the gardens.

"I wonder if this Captain Dagger is anywhere close," Guy suddenly demanded.

"I certainly hope not!" Althea said, a frightened expression crossing her face.

"With all of the soldiers scouring the countryside, searching for this raider, I doubt we are in any danger. But Gordonsville, where the train was robbed, isn't too far distant, and I heard that a railroad trestle, quite nearby, in fact, was blown just yesterday. They caught this Captain Dagger in a crossfire on the road not far from here. I ran into a number of patrols, and they had quite a tale to tell. Seem to think this Captain Dagger is indestructible. He rides a big bay, with wings, one of the soldiers said, because he seemed to fly out of danger with a thundering of hooves, and out of range of their barrage of bullets. They cannot understand how he escaped their ambush, riding away unscathed, although some of his men weren't so lucky," Adam said, staring intently at Leigh's face, but she was avoiding meeting his eye this time and he found himself wondering why, especially when remembering Stephen's strange comments earlier.

"I knew I heard an explosion yesterday," Guy said, slapping his thigh and startling his hounds. "Are you sure it was this Dahlgren the troop of soldiers that came through here yesterday were looking for, and not this Captain Dagger?" Guy questioned.

Leigh cleared her throat of huskiness. "I really don't remember. Is it important? A Yankee is a Yankee."

"Women," Guy snorted in masculine disgust. "No, not really, just curious, that's all."

"Well, you don't have to worry about Dahlgren. They caught him," Adam said.

"Leaves Captain Dagger, then."

"Yes, that leaves Captain Dagger, doesn't it," Adam murmured. "Our troops seem to think they've got him trapped hereabouts," Adam speculated, seeing a flash of dismay cross Leigh's face before she could hide her true feelings this time.

"Maybe I should offer my services. Could send out my two hounds, here, hunt him down," Guy joked. "If he can't get out, if they've actually managed for once to tighten the noose around this raider, then he's probably holed up just like a fox," Guy mused. "Wish I did have my pack of hounds. If this Dagger fella tried to double back on his trail, or tried to cross the river or ride the streambeds to lose his scent, then we'd find where he came out, we wouldn't lose him. We'd catch him. Track him right to his hiding place, just like a fox thinking he's safe in his den in some hollowed-out log or a cave up in the rocks."

Adam stood for a moment as if struck by lightning as he stared at Guy Travers, then he suddenly laughed softly.

"Come on, Stephen," he said, "I'll help you carry the chest out to the kitchens."

"Oh, Mister Adam, it's not heavy now. I can manage just fine," Stephen said as he followed Adam from the room, glancing back at Leigh worriedly, because the young gentleman had already been asking far too many questions about the goings-on at Travers Hill.

"Fine, I'll stable my horse," Adam said, surprised by the sudden look of fear that crossed Stephen's face as he picked up the lightened chest.

"Miss Leigh doesn't put the animals in the stables anymore. Don't you remember, Mister Adam? We got them stabled in the back kitchens now. You don't want to go down to the stables. They're not real clean anymore," he said quickly.

"My cousin, Neil Braedon, Captain Dagger, isn't still down there, is he?" Adam suddenly asked, his question catching Stephen off guard, as Adam intended it should.

"Oh, no, the cap'n an' his men left yesterday after dark—"

"So, I was right, Neil has been here, hasn't he, Stephen?"

"Mister Adam, I can't say anything more. Don't you ask me now, 'cause I'm not sayin'. Don't know who'll be the madder, Miss Leigh, or Jolie," he said fretfully.

"Don't worry, Stephen. I already suspected as much," Adam told him.

"You suspected what?"

Adam turned to see Leigh standing in the doorway.

"That you have aided and abetted the enemy," he said slowly, but when seeing the stricken look on her face, he relented. "I would have done the same, Leigh. He is my cousin."

Softly, yet firmly, Leigh shut the study door behind her and hurried to his side. "You know?"

"That Captain Dagger is my cousin? Yes. That Captain Dagger and his men, these murderous Bloodriders, came to Travers Hill and found shelter in your stables? Yes."

"I didn't have much choice."

"Oh?"

"No, he didn't give any."

"Sounds like Neil."

"He and his men were already in the stables when I went down there to get a bale of hay. He attacked me, Adam, out in the field and carried me back into the stables."

Adam couldn't help but laugh. "I seem to remember you accosted him, and with your grandpapa's fowling piece, the last time you met," he reminded her. "How was he?" he asked, suddenly serious.

"Unhurt. But some of his men were badly wounded. We did the best we could for them," Leigh admitted.

"You helped them?" Adam said, shaking his head in amazement.

"They were hurt. I didn't do any more than I did when our home was used as a Yankee field hospital," Leigh told him.

"There is a slight difference in the circumstances. And weren't they still in the stables when our soldiers came through? Stephen says they didn't leave until after dark," he said, asking the question Leigh had hoped he would not.

"Yes. I lied to them," she said, staring up at Adam almost defiantly.

"You could have betrayed them."

"I didn't want fighting on Travers land. There are children in the house, as well as Althea and Guy," she explained readily enough.

"Of course," Adam said, as if it was all very plain to him. "Nor did you wish to see Neil and his men massacred, did you, Leigh?" he added softly. "That is what would have happened with them trapped in the stables, his men wounded."

Leigh shrugged. "It doesn't matter now. He's gone, Adam. And I don't know where he is, and I don't care."

"Don't you?" Adam persisted.

"No!" she cried, her cheeks flushed. "Guy and Althea don't know he was here. I thought it best to keep it a secret," she said, glancing at a guilty-looking Stephen.

"Don't blame Stephen. You forget, I knew the identity of Captain Dagger, and that he'd been seen in these parts. He knows this countryside. If he needed a place to hide, I think I know where he would go. I'm surprised he came by Travers Hill, but if he had wounded, it would have served his purpose."

"He and his men didn't steal that gold," Leigh told him, for some reason wanting Adam not to believe his cousin was a cold-blooded murderer.

"How do you know?"

"He told me so."

"And you believed him?" Adam asked. "Why should you believe anything good of Neil Braedon? I know about that evening, Leigh, the evening you announced your engagement to Matthew Wycliffe. I know what happened in the gardens."

"Neil told you?"

"No, Guy did. When he sobered, he was quite ashamed of himself, and what he'd cost you. Of course, we were all surprised about Neil's sudden departure from Royal Bay, and that when he left he took Capitaine, the colt you would sell to no one. I understand he drove a hard bargain that night. Your colt, or your brother's life. So why should you believe Neil Braedon innocent of this latest brutality?"

Leigh had her answer ready. "Because they didn't know about the gold bullion having been stolen. They, his men, were shocked. They weren't lying, either. I would have known. They were very indignant. Angry, even, that they were being blamed. They admitted they'd blown up the railroad and that was why they were here; not to steal and murder. I believed them," Leigh said.

Adam smiled, touching her hot cheek with the tip of his finger. "I always knew what Blythe was thinking. She couldn't hide anything from me. Her eyes, and the wild blush that stained her cheeks, always gave her away," Adam said.

Leigh opened her mouth to protest, but Adam had turned away.

"I'm going to stable my horse, then unpack my things," he said tiredly. "But after that, we're going to have that talk, Leigh," he reminded her, his expression determined.

"I'll see to your horse, Adam. No, no arguments. You know I do a better job," she said, noting worriedly the bluish tinge around his lips.

"I cannot argue, at least with that," he added, picking up the small bag he'd brought in with the woven chest and climbing the stairs.

For a moment, Leigh watched him, but when Adam stopped on the landing and looked back, she was gone.

Adam stood there for a moment, out of breath, a bleakness in his eyes as so many memories came flooding back to him. He walked past the closed doors to the silent rooms. He paused for a moment before the door to Leigh's bedchamber, once Blythe's too—before he had taken her as his bride.

On impulse, he entered the cold room, shutting the door behind him. He stared at the big four-poster, the quilt folded neatly, the blanket chest at the foot, where the trundle bed used to be, the cradle placed close where an arm could readily reach out to rock it gently during the long night. On the soft pillow was the silver baby rattle with the coral handle that he and Blythe had selected together when she'd discovered she was with child.

Dropping his bag, he knelt down beside the chest and opened the lid. Drawing a deep breath, he reached inside, removing the sword that had belonged to Palmer William. He pulled the glinting blade partly from its scabbard, staring at it for a moment, a faraway look in his eye. Then he shoved it back in, moving it aside and forgetting about it when his hand came into contact with the softness of Blythe's cloak. How many times had he seen her wearing it, the emerald green reflected in her hazel eyes, shining with such love of life, her laughing face hidden in the dark fur?

Why Blythe? he wondered for the thousandth time. Why had she been taken from him? His blithe spirit, the light of his life. Why her? Why a lovely young creature of such sweetness and innocence, who had never hurt anyone or anything in her life? Why? he asked, hot tears falling onto the velvety folds of the cloak.

He touched the moist spot and saw the ivory fan. He remembered the night of her sixteenth birthday party, when he'd first realized she had become a beautiful woman, the woman he had fallen in love with. She'd flirted innocently with him that night, peeking at him from behind the delicately carved ivory, teasing him, and never realizing she'd captured his heart. Folded on top of the cloak was the shawl. He ran his finger along the lacy edge, remembering draping it across her pale shoulders, and placing a kiss against her throat, where her pulse had been beating wildly, and he had known then she was not averse to his touch.

Adam's hand closed around the dark green perfume bottle. How she had loved it, he thought, and removing the stopper, he caught his breath as the sweetly spiced fragrance floated around him, reminding him of when they had lain together as lovers. Carefully, he replaced it, his hand touching the silver brush and comb that had graced her dressing table. He felt the flatness of the delicate, floral-painted embroidery work box that held her sewing materials: mother-of-pearl thimble, needle cases, scissors, and tape measure. He had given it to her, thinking it merely a pretty box, but she'd seemed to take great pleasure in actually using it, especially when mending his clothes, although she'd despaired of ever having enough gray thread. He'd gotten her the cut brass and red tortoiseshell desk set when in the Bahamas. She'd used it to write letters home, and to him. Long, loving letters that had been such a joy to receive, lifting his spirits as he thought of returning to her. A stack of neatly tied letters had been placed next to the desk set in the chest.

Her letters to Leigh, he was thinking, when he noticed a wadded-up piece of paper tucked down deep on the side. He pulled it out and smoothed it open.

"Damn!" he cursed softly beneath his breath as he read the tax assessment and knew the reason now why the offending piece of paper had been crumpled into a ball and stuffed deep in the chest.

He had one just like it in his own coat pocket.

Replacing Palmer William's sword, he lowered the lid of the chest, closing out the memories of happier times, of other days, of those who had died. He thought of the family cemetery on the high ground overlooking the peaceful river, where he had stopped and knelt beside his wife's grave, the rest of the Travers family at rest around her. He couldn't help them any longer, but his daughter, and these people at Travers Hill, who were his family now, he could help, he decided as he walked over to the window and stared out across the barren trees toward the bend in the river—remembering a secret place where he, Nathan, and Neil had hidden when boys.

And he wondered if Sun Dagger—Captain Dagger—had remembered it.

Seventeen

Thou hast given him his heart's desire.

Psalm 21:2

"WISH WE HAD SOME MORE OF THAT HOT BROTH RIGHT now. Would taste mighty good," the Bucktail said wistfully.

"Wish we did too, Bucky, just to keep your stomach from rumbling so loud," the sentinel about to relieve himself agreed as he heard the loud grumbling from behind his turned back. "Sure to give us away to any reb patrols nearby," he commented, selecting a couple of green leaves and thinking they would do nicely.

"Reckon they'll jus' think it's thunder."

"What was that?" his friend asked, jerking up his breeches. "Wouldn't you know, after all the battles I been in, the rebs would finally catch me, and me with my breeches down 'round my ankles," he said, humiliated.

"Didn't hear nothin'," the Bucktail said, gazing into the darkness beneath the stone bridge. "Gettin' light," he said, glancing at the gray clouds, tinged with pink, overhead.

"Wonder how long the cap'n's goin' to stay holed up here."

"Reckon till some of them reb patrols get tired of bumpin' into themselves comin' and goin' and findin' nothin' of the Bloodriders. Besides, McGuire and the lieutenant wouldn't be able to get far, 'specially if we had to make a run for it. McGuire's been feverish the last two nights. Never heard such babblin'. Lil' reb knew what she was doin', though, 'cause the cap'n says McGuire's wound ain't festerin' none. Wish Jimmy was doin' as well. Too bad, him havin' that attack of swamp fever. Thought he was lookin' a bit peaked. Kept gettin' the shivers yesterday. Came down with it last summer. Remember when we were in White Oak Swamp? Didn't think we'd ever get out of there to Seven Pines, then, couldn't believe all that marshland north of Fair Oaks Station. Never thought we'd make it to the banks of the Chickahominy, and Jimmy comin' down sick with that fever and rebs swarmin' all over the place. I sure thought he was over it. Would've brought along a tin of quinine if I'd known."

"Wish we had a fire. It'd help poor ol' Jimmy stop shakin'. Don't think he's goin' to have any teeth left. Say, you remember them ash cakes we had a while back?" the other one asked, thinking of the cornmeal they'd mixed with water and salt and some beef drippings. Patting the mixture into cakes, then wrapping them up tight in wet cloth, they'd buried them under hot ashes. "Nice an' crunchy, remember? Now that'd make a tasty breakfast this mornin'. Figure we'll be chewin' on beef jerky. Least it ain't rainin'."

"Ought to have wars just in summertime. Figure the best time for fightin', and bein' out in the countryside, is in late summer or early autumn, 'cause there's plenty to eat. You remember that cornfield? We took them ears of corn and roasted them right in the shuck. Best tastin' I've ever had."

"Only wish we'd had some butter."

"Yup, would've too, 'ceptin' for you makin' eyes at that farmer's wife. Shouldn't have done that, Bucky. 'Specially after they gave us that buttermilk, and him standin' there with that bucket of hog slop," his friend complained, wandering around the small clearing as if searching for something.

"Didn't want to disappoint her, her bein' so glad to see a good-lookin' man for a change," the Bucktail said. "Never seen such an ugly fella as that jug-headed jackass she was hitched to."

"Yeah, well he missed his aim and it took me a week to get that slop out of my clothes," he remembered.

"Gotta learn to move faster, Davy," the Bucktail warned. "Figure you stood there lookin' like a fool for about a minute."

"Yup, had me cold, he did. Me standin' there jus' to the left of you. Missed you by 'bout a foot didn't he?"

"You was about a foot back of me and to the right a bit. Wish you'd keep still now. What're you looking for anyhow?"

"Some more green leaves."

"Ain't you finished yet?" the Bucktail demanded with a sigh. "Here, I'll help you. Thought I saw some big, soft green leaves over this way," he was murmuring thoughtfully as he moved toward the stone bridge where the entwining vines dangled thickly like a concealing curtain. "How many you goin' to need?"

"Reckon 'bout three."

"That many, eh?"

"Yup. Say, do you remember when we got our hands on that whiskey and tried to sneak it back into camp?"

"Sure do."

"Hid one barrel in Schneickerberger's breeches. Tied the legs off and stuffed them full of corncobs. Put the other barrel in his coat, then stuck that lil' pumpkin on top, with Schneickerberger's slouch hat pulled down low. That picket let us walk right by, though I saw him eyein' Schneickerberger's breeches mighty close like, 'specially seein' how that corncob was stickin' out where it shouldn't have been. Would've done all right, 'cept that dogrobber of a cook found the barrels and started to do a little double-shot drinkin' out of them every time he was in our tent. Still wonder what he started puttin' in the one to keep it filled. Kept gettin' more sour by the day. Thought he was goin' to faint when we forced him to drink from it."

"Ah, here's one," the Bucktail said, pulling on a green leaf from the vine, "and...two...and...THREE!"

Suddenly he ducked beneath, his friend doing the same at precisely the same instant. There was a scuffling sound and some cursing, then they reappeared from behind the curtain of vines, dragging their struggling captive with them into the revealing light.

"Works every time," the Bucktail said with a grin, before making a sound like a whippoorwill, then glancing down at the man held trussed like a turkey between them. The knife held pressed against the man's throat suddenly wavered, however, as he stared into the man's pale eyes.

"Cap'n?" he said in disbelief, shaking his head as if to clear it of grogginess, the knife falling from his hand.

"Cap'n, sir!" Davy said, releasing the man's arm as he took a step back, thinking they were in trouble now. He would have sworn no one had gotten past him. "Didn't fall asleep, sir! I swear on my mother's honor."

"I'm sure you didn't," the man spoke softly, his amused Southern drawl startling them.

Davy glanced over at the Bucktail, who'd also rather quickly released his hold on the captive, but who'd also been eyeing the captain up and down, a frown gathering on his brow as he took note of the gray trousers beneath the long gray cape.

"Always thought the cap'n was taller, didn't you, Davy?" he asked now, his troubled gaze meeting his friend's bewildered one as he stepped back and raised his rifle. "Jus' knew we wouldn't catch the captain sleeping. Hands up, reb!"

"You sure he ain't the cap'n?"

"The cap'n don't have no mustache. And he ain't this skinny!"

"Shoot, ye're right, Bucky. But then who the devil is he, if he ain't?" he asked, still not quite convinced.

"Hello, Adam." Their captain's voice spoke behind them.

"Neil." Adam Braedon returned the greeting cordially.

The Bucktail and Davy spun around, then glanced quickly between the two. "One of your kin, Cap'n," the Bucktail stated, spitting just short of Adam's shiny boot.

"My cousin."

"Thank you," Adam said, relieved to be identified.

"Reckon I just about slit his throat. Figure him lookin' so much like you, saved his reb neck."

Adam laughed. "Ah, one of the Bloodriders. And as bloodthirsty as I've been led to believe. This is truly an honor. I was afraid I'd never have the opportunity of making your acquaintance," he said. "Your exploits are becoming legendary. You'll forgive me for not holding out my hand, but I suspect any sudden moves would end in my demise."

"Real smooth-tongued talker, ain't he?" the Bucktail said, eyeing this supposed kin of the captain's suspiciously.

"He was spyin' on us, Cap'n. Caught him skulkin' behind the vines," Davy said, quick to explain himself.

"*Skulking?* Good Lord, I've never skulked in my life," Adam said, sounding insulted. "You've trained your men well, Neil. They did indeed catch me woolgathering. I was about to announce my presence, when my attention wandered momentarily. I am curious, though, did you really sneak those two barrels of whiskey into camp, or was that just for my benefit?" he demanded.

The Bucktail laughed. "Yes, sir, it really happened, though Davy and me exaggerated a bit now and then just to keep the tale interesting, and sweetly baited. Never know what kind of fish we're goin' to catch on our hook," he said, then glanced over at his captain. He'd come up quietly behind them, having heard the signal that they had trouble. The rest of the men were gathered at the mouth of the cave, alerted and ready to fight.

"Sir?" he asked now, wondering what they were supposed to do with the gentleman reb they'd caught. "He's the enemy, Cap'n," he reminded him unnecessarily. "He might be of a mind to give us away, 'specially if you got any feudin' in your family. Reckon these folks might not look kindly on you wearin' blue."

"Had I been of such a knavish disposition, I already would have alerted the countryside. The whole Confederate army seems to be hot on your trail," Adam told them. "I had the devil of a time avoiding the many patrols, but since they caught Dahlgren, and southeast of here, they've loosened the noose somewhat. Although, Captain Dagger and the Bloodriders would be quite a catch for some troop hungry for glory."

"Has a way with words, he does," the Bucktail muttered.

"Thank you," Adam said, a slow grin spreading across his face as he met Neil's glance.

"Hey, how'd he know who we was, and where to find us?" the Bucktail suddenly demanded.

His captain held out his hand, Adam grasping it unhesitatingly and warmly. "My cousins and I used to hide out in this cave when we were boys. And I was known to them then as Dagger. He's always been very good at putting two and two together. We can trust him. I'll stand the watch now," he said, ordering his men back into the cave, while he remained, standing alone with Adam in the clearing that was now lightened by daybreak.

They stood in silence, each taking the other's measure, their hands still clasped for a moment in friendship.

"I had wondered if I'd ever see you again, Adam," Neil said.

"And I you, although I did have the advantage of being able to follow your daring exploits in the newspapers," he said.

Neil frowned slightly. "You should not believe all that you read."

"I never have, but I've also had the advantage over most Southerners who do. I know Neil Braedon, and Sun Dagger, they don't."

"Thank you," Neil said, eyeing his cousin curiously, and worriedly, for Adam did not look well. His once healthy complexion was sallow, his cheeks sunken, his eyes almost feverishly bright, and although always of a slender build, he was gaunt-looking now. "How did you know I was here?"

"I arrived at Travers Hill yesterday."

Neil nodded understandingly.

Adam laughed. "No, Leigh didn't tell me, at least not until I'd already tricked the information out of Stephen. Then, and most reluctantly, she confessed her sins of having helped you and your men, and then stated most emphatically that she had no idea where you had gone—although, I suspect she hoped it might be to the devil," Adam added, being purposefully provocative as he watched his cousin's face.

"Naturally," Neil said shortly, his pale gray-green eyes glinting with a strange expression.

"You certainly have a way of rubbing her the wrong way."

Neil looked momentarily startled, and Adam smiled, an interested gleam in his eyes as he wondered about what had happened between them. "Coming from Richmond, I heard about the gold bullion being stolen."

"That is one of the stories about the Bloodriders that you shouldn't believe," Neil reminded him.

"So I understand. Apparently Leigh believed you when you told her you hadn't massacred those guards. However, I understand you can claim as your handiwork the blowing up of the railroad trestle. I also understand that you were caught in an ambush. Hear you've quite a few wounded, so I suspected, if you were still around here, this was the only safe place you could hide. I hadn't realized you would go to Travers Hill first—but then, perhaps, that shouldn't surprise me," he stated oddly.

"I hadn't planned on it, but after seeing Royal Bay—I am sorry, Adam," Neil said abruptly, remembering the haunting sight of the solitary chimneys rising from the ashes of the once great house.

"Leigh told you what happened?"

"Yes. And she told me about your family. She says Nathan is missing in action in Tennessee."

"Good ol' Nathan. What a waste," Adam said bitterly. "Althea thinks he'll come back one day, and I haven't the heart to tell her that he's probably dead." He hesitated, then said, "Leigh told you about Blythe?"

"Yes."

Adam nodded, unable to say anything for a moment. "I still cannot believe she is gone, Neil. We had so short a time together, but it was the happiest time of my life. I look around, and I cannot believe any of this has happened. Sometimes I feel as if I'm going to wake up, and find that I've had a horrible nightmare. Royal Bay gone. Mother. Nathan. Even Julia is lost to us. I heard about Justin."

Neil said something beneath his breath that Adam couldn't understand, the tongue unintelligible to him. "He was a fine young man. Years ago, when our father wasn't around to overhear, Justin would talk me into telling him stories of the great Comanche warriors. He always seemed fascinated that a warrior's destiny should be to die honorably on the field of battle."

"Seems like yesterday, Blythe's birthday party. I can still see Justin and Palmer William in their uniforms, both so young, and now both gone. How is Aunt Camilla?"

"I had a letter a couple of months ago from Lys Helene. She says her mother collapsed when she was informed of Justin's death. Did you know she was planning a trip to Virginia? She wanted to attend his graduation from VMI."

"Your father?" Adam questioned.

"He never says much. He was always proud of Justin, and they got along well enough, but Justin was closer to Camilla. At least she still has Lys Helene and Gil, who is too young to fight in this war. And what fighting there was in the territory is over now that it is under federal jurisdiction again."

"We...ah, the Confederacy, claimed the territory early in the war, I believe," Adam said, frowning, for he hadn't paid much attention to the battles in the west.

"Yes, some Texans under Sibley, but they were driven out during the fighting in Apache Canyon and Glorieta Pass.

Lys Helene said my father would have fought them whether they'd been wearing blue or gray, more concerned that they were Texans."

"There hasn't been much fighting out there, since?"

"No. At least not between the Union forces and the Confederacy."

Adam coughed, choking slightly. Tapping his fingertips together as if lost in thought, he asked, "Royal Rivers is safe from Indian attack, isn't it?"

"No place is safe from attack, especially if you get careless," Neil said.

"Have there been many attacks, or massacres, recently?"

"When I left the territory, Kit Carson, who was the Indian agent for the Pueblo Indians, the Apache, and the Utes, and is now in command of the First New Mexico Cavalry, was handling any uprising that threatened. Lys Helene wrote that he led an expedition against the Navajos, and defeated them at Canyon de Chelly and on the Little Colorado. Why?"

"It just seems to me that Royal Rivers hasn't been bothered by the Indians in some time."

"It hasn't, probably because my father takes every precaution he can to protect his family, and the servants and workers who live at Royal Rivers. And we get protection from Fort Union."

"Aunt Camilla? She's been content living in the territory? She seemed very happy when I visited there."

"You saw Royal Rivers. Aunt Camilla lives like a queen. Royal Rivers is a kingdom unto itself. As you know, my father inherited a handsome sum from our grandfather, and he's made a fortune selling his beef and wool, especially since the war. The house has been furnished like a palace. My father has never begrudged Camilla, and the others, anything, except perhaps his love, but I've never heard Camilla complain. Of course, she has her family around her, and her widowed sister and two maiden aunts are now living at Royal Rivers. They keep her company. She has countless friends in Taos and Santa Fe, Las Vegas and Cimarron. The ranch always has overnight visitors."

"You still have rooms there, don't you?"

"Yes."

"And Riovado?" Adam asked.

"Someday," Neil answered, thinking of his cabin in the high country. "Why all the questions, Adam?" he suddenly demanded.

"You saw Travers Hill," Adam returned, avoiding his cousin's question for the moment, curious to hear Neil's opinion.

"Yes, I didn't need to see the condition of the house to know that things had changed drastically for the Travers family. The stables told the tale. Once the pride of Travers Hill. Leigh said her father and Sweet John were murdered by looters."

Adam smiled grimly. "Did she also mention what she did to the looters? At least there wasn't much left to steal, which reminds me, what do you think of our cave?"

"I was quite surprised to find it so comfortably furnished. You may rest assured that my men will not touch anything. This cave, and its contents, will remain a secret."

"I'm not worried. Your men seem to have a healthy respect for you, or perhaps it is fear. Whatever, I doubt they'd care to cross you. And I know you'll never say a word about the cave. We took a blood oath, remember? Well, I did break it, just once," Adam admitted, "but since he was my father-in-law, I thought it acceptable under the circumstances to let him in on the secret," Adam explained.

"I've seen the crates inside marked 'Travers.'"

"You should have seen Stuart Travers, Neil, when I brought him here. He was as excited as a child. He couldn't believe this cave had been here his whole life and he'd never known about it. He was quite pleased with himself. Mrs. Travers, however, wasn't as pleased. In fact, she wouldn't even hear of it at first. While we were packing and crating up everything at Royal Bay, Stuart kept trying to make her see reason, finally, he just threw up his hands and told her he was emptying the house, and he did, although later he said he'd never been so frightened. I showed up with a wagon and a team of mules, somehow overlooked by our respective armies, and Stuart, Sweet John, and I loaded all of the valuables from Travers Hill. Took us several trips. Even hitched up that nasty-dispositioned pony to the cart and had him hauling household goods. Nipped me when I tried to hurry him. And

Mrs. Travers wasn't of any better a disposition, either. Wouldn't talk to us for about a month. I've never received such reproachful glances, and never felt quite so guilty in my life. Then one day she just started acting like everything was still there, that nothing had changed. Talked about picnics and fish fries, and lived in her own world after that. If it hadn't been for Leigh, I don't think any of them would still be alive today," Adam said. "And that is part of the reason I'm here. I did want to see you, but I've an ulterior motive for seeking you out," he admitted. Looking directly at Neil, he added, "I don't know how much longer they can continue to live at Travers Hill."

"I agree with you. They should leave Virginia."

"Easy enough said. I've been trying, but unsuccessfully, to persuade Leigh to do that for almost over a year now."

"You are not seriously suggesting that I should have a word with the lady?" Neil asked, incredulous. "She and I did not part friends, and nothing has changed. She and I, as usual, had few kind words to say to one another."

"Yes, I understand you attacked her outside the stables. Not very gentlemanly of you, Neil."

"I've learned, with that particular lady, gentlemanly actions don't always work," Neil said.

"You may be right," Adam surprised him by saying. "She needs to be given little choice in the matter," Adam said, quoting Leigh's own words about her meeting with Neil.

"I was surprised to find her at Travers Hill."

"You were?"

"Yes, I asked her why she hadn't gone to a safe place, but as always, her family comes first. She won't leave them. She feels responsible for Althea and Noelle now that Nathan is gone. Althea has been quite ill, I understand. And Guy Travers is blind. She could hardly abandon him, but what of her own two children?"

"Two children? Leigh doesn't have any children," Adam told him, wondering where his cousin had gotten that idea.

"I saw her with the young, dark-haired boy, and with the baby," Neil told him. "It was dark-haired too, and she was rocking it in a cradle."

"The young, dark-haired boy? That is Steward Russell,

Nathan's and Althea's son. The baby is named Lucinda, and she is my daughter, Neil."

"I see," Neil said slowly. "I just assumed, seeing Leigh with them, that they were hers. But that doesn't change anything. Even though Wycliffe has died, I would have thought he had enough wealth to assure her and her family a safe place to live."

"Wycliffe?" Adam repeated in surprise. "What has he to do with this?"

"She married Matthew Wycliffe," Neil reminded him, unable to mask the bitterness in his voice.

"Leigh and Wycliffe were never married." Adam spoke softly, watching Neil's face closely, wondering how much that information mattered to him.

If Neil was surprised, he didn't show it. His hard face remained expressionless.

"They announced their engagement, but his mother died that spring, and they postponed their wedding, then the war started, and there was another postponement, and then Wycliffe was killed. Leigh is still Leigh Travers, her home is still Travers Hill, and that is why she is there. She's never married."

Neil laughed softly, but Adam didn't care for the sound of it. "Well, well…" Neil murmured thoughtfully. "So Leigh Travers never married."

"She didn't tell you?" Adam asked, puzzled.

"No," he said abruptly.

"She's had her chances. I understand one of the Yankee surgeons was determined to marry her, and there have been others, but…"

"…but she wouldn't abandon her family, would she?" Neil concluded for him.

"No. And she's even less likely to now than she was four years ago. She wouldn't then, would she, Neil?"

"What do you mean?"

"You were in love with her."

"Love?" Neil questioned doubtfully.

"Well, maybe not love. You didn't have time to fall in love, but you wanted her, didn't you? No, don't deny it, I saw the way you watched her. I was there that night, I felt the tension between you whenever you were close."

Neil smiled unpleasantly. "I don't deny it. She's a beautiful woman. I found her quite fascinating, and quite a challenge. I wouldn't mind having her in my bed," he said bluntly, wanting to destroy any notions Adam had that he was in love with Leigh Travers.

"Maybe you can, if you're still interested," Adam said, hoping Leigh would forgive him for speaking this way, although he wondered if he would live to apologize to her, because Neil's pale eyes narrowed dangerously.

"I've never needed help to get a woman before," Neil said quietly, but there was a savage undertone to it.

"You will now, cousin, if you want Leigh."

"I hadn't realized you were in procurement."

"I'm no whoremaster, Neil, but I am a very desperate man. And now that I've beheld the answer to my prayers, I'll do anything to get what I want."

"So it would seem," Neil said lazily. "And, just out of curiosity, how would you manage to get Leigh Travers for me? *If* I wanted her, that is? And what am I to have her for? One night? I'm hardly in a position to take the lady to bed. And what price are you asking? What do I pay for that pleasure?"

"You can have Leigh for a night, or, if you want, for a lifetime. It's up to you. Of course, you've got to survive the war to claim the latter," Adam reminded him.

"Of course."

"I'm not worried. You've always been good at surviving, Neil."

"And the lady, of course, is agreeable to this. I must say, she has hidden her feelings well."

Adam smiled grimly. "She doesn't know yet. But I do not foresee any difficulties, because I hold the winning hand this time."

"You amaze me. Leigh Travers is not a woman who does anything unless she wants to. And I don't quite see her wishing to climb into my bed. Or has she led you to believe otherwise?" Neil asked softly, but there was an intentness about him now as he watched his cousin.

"No, and I'll leave that part of the arrangement to you, but she'll do what I want."

"You sound very certain. You'll forgive me if I have my doubts," Neil said.

"If she wants to keep my daughter, she has no choice. She loves Lucinda as if she were her own. She promised Blythe she'd always care for her. I've threatened to take Lucinda away from her, to take her to a place of safety."

"Blackmail, Adam?"

"I'll do anything to save my daughter. To give her a chance to live. I don't need to tell you what the next few years will be like. We're losing the war, Neil. The Union forces, followed by the federal government, with all of the politicians and profiteers flocking into the South, will be hard taskmasters when they occupy the disbanded Confederacy."

Neil didn't try to argue.

"We will be the vanquished. Our pride, our heritage, ground into the dust beneath a Yankee heel. No, it's the truth. The war may end, but it won't be over for a lot of people. Until now, Leigh has always managed to call my bluff. She knew I'd never take Lucinda away from her and give her to strangers to care for. I am also guardian of Noelle and Steward, by Nathan's request, and I have the responsibility of Althea's welfare to think about. If Althea had not become ill, if Nathan were still alive, I would have given Lucinda to them. Leigh would have agreed to that, but I don't have that choice.

"I want them out of Virginia, Neil. I had thought to send them to the Bahamas, then to England. I am not without contacts, and aboard my ship I could see them safely to Nassau, then, with the proceeds from selling her, I'd get them to England. I'd thought to contact Maribel Lu and J. Kirkfield, but I'm not even certain where they are. They are constantly on the move, traveling from one European capital to another, still trying to drum up support for the Confederacy. Until now, I'd never considered sending my daughter, and Althea and her children, to Uncle Nathaniel and Aunt Camilla. It wasn't possible. I knew I couldn't get them out to the New Mexico Territory. And even if I had, they'd just have been homeless relatives to house and feed, and I couldn't be certain that Leigh and Guy would agree to go out there. And I knew if they would not, then Althea wouldn't. But now that you're here, I've suddenly realized that there is another way that I can ensure a family, and a home, for my daughter. My first thought was that you, with your Yankee connections, could make certain that Lucinda, and Althea and her family, got safely to the New Mexico Territory. You could, couldn't you?"

"So that is what I do? Get your daughter and Althea and her children out of Virginia. And in return, I get Leigh Travers? Would you mind showing me your cards, Adam, because I don't quite see how you intend to win the hand."

"Very well, but could you?" he persisted.

"If you chose that course of action, then I would telegraph a message to Santa Fe, letting my father know of your plans. He would, most likely, meet Althea and the children in Westport or Council Grove and escort them the rest of the way into the territories. He wouldn't trust anyone else with their safety. He trusts the teamsters less than the Indians. But I would have some difficulty getting them out of Virginia."

"No problem. I have a pass to get them to Richmond. From there they'll sail to New York. Then you take over and see that they get to New Mexico."

"But, Adam, you know that Royal Rivers would always be a home for you and your family, for Althea and hers. You're Braedons. This business with Leigh is unnecessary. I'm certain, if she chose to come, and she will if you take your daughter from her, that she, and even Guy, would be welcome in my father's house. Royal Rivers is always full of guests, and two more people wouldn't make any difference. Besides, as you say, the war can't last much longer. Then you can claim your daughter. I'll see that she gets to New Mexico, to Royal Rivers. She'll be safe there until the war is over."

"It won't matter, Neil, whether the war ends tomorrow, or two years, or three years from now. I'm dying, Neil," Adam said quietly.

This time Neil couldn't hide the expression that crossed his face.

Adam shook his head. "No, don't look like that, cousin. I had almost four years of happiness, and I was blessed with a beautiful daughter. My Blythe is gone, and once I see that our daughter is cared for, I can die contented."

"Adam."

"There is no hope for me, Neil. Three months, four, I don't know. I'm becoming weaker by the day. I've consumptive lungs. I've been coughing up blood for some time. Bed rest, the doctors said. To prolong the agony?" Adam laughed harshly. "I'm not going to waste away. I suspect I caught the damned disease when I was wounded and had to stay in the hospital. I'm afraid I wasn't strong enough to fight off the infection. I'd had pneumonia, complicating my recovery. The only plague I didn't seem to catch was typhoid fever. I suppose it had infected too many Braedons already."

"Damn," Neil said beneath his breath, staring at Adam's thin face, and realizing now the reason for his shortness of breath.

Adam could feel his despair and was touched. "That is why I must be certain my daughter will have a home, will have a family to care for her. Leigh loves her. She is Lucinda's mother now. I doubt Leigh will ever marry, because she'll put Lucinda's needs before her own, and most men would be reluctant to take on another man's child, especially one that's not even his wife's by a former marriage. A niece? And what of Althea and her children? Leigh seems to think she is the only one who can care for them, and I do not see a prospective bridegroom looking forward to that responsibility. None of their futures holds much hope. Royal Bay is gone. Travers Hill may not survive, and afterward, how will Leigh and Guy be able to keep it? I saw the tax assessment Leigh received, and it's hopeless. They will become homeless, and that is why I want you to marry Leigh."

"*Marry?*"

"Yes, together, you and Leigh will become my daughter's family. That is my deal. Leigh will marry you in order to keep Lucinda. And I'm hoping that you desire Leigh enough that you'd marry her, or if you have no feelings for her then because you cared enough about my daughter and Nathan's family that you would agree to my terms to ensure that they get out of Virginia. You see, I've also thought that it would be far easier for you to assure their safe passage if Leigh were your wife. Right now, if they were to leave Virginia, they would be spat upon as rebs, perhaps even accosted and denied transportation. But as the wife of a Yankee officer, Leigh and the others would have safe passage. But if that were not reason enough, then I've one other card to play. And it's one you cannot beat. What is the price of your men's lives?"

Neil's eyes narrowed on Adam's flushed face.

"You have wounded men. One has a shoulder wound? Another has several broken ribs? I've just overheard that another is suffering delirium from malaria? And the countryside is crawling with Johnny Rebs out for your blood. Your chances aren't very good, Neil. But what if they saw the infamous Captain Dagger riding hell for leather toward Charlottesville, then spied him near Richmond. Then on the docks, maybe planning his escape by sea? You, and your men, could take a nice, leisurely ride in the opposite direction, no rebel troops in pursuit, and what a wild-goose chase I'll lead them on. Yes, me. I do look like the infamous Yankee raider, don't you think? We do bear a remarkable resemblance to one another. Your men just proved it. Even they mistook me for Captain Dagger. It's your chance, Neil. Take it, and take what else I offer you."

"Leigh Travers?"

"Yes, you get Leigh. You've always wanted her. And you get your men out safely. You may never get another chance. What do you say to that?"

"I'd say I couldn't lose. You've given me everything. Except that I don't want the lady under those conditions. I don't want her marrying me to save her family, to keep your daughter. I'll see that your daughter gets to New Mexico, and I'll always be responsible for her, and I'll take care of Althea and her children, but I won't marry Leigh. All you have to do is call her bluff. She'll come out to the territories, because she won't want to lose Lucinda. But I am not going to be blackmailed into marriage. Believe me, Adam, it is not an auspicious beginning for a life together. I learned that when I found out that Serena had only married me because her father had forced her to. And my motives weren't much better. Although I found her beautiful, I wasn't in love with her. But it seemed a good arrangement. I thought it time I took a wife, and I wanted the land her father was thinking of selling to an outsider. It was a parcel of grazing land with a year-round stream, and bordering Royal Rivers and Riovado. Alfonso Jacobs made it his wedding gift."

"You and Serena were never happy? You never came to love one another?"

"No. Serena was in love with another man when she married me. He was a man unacceptable to her father. They eloped and secretly married, but were caught, and Alfonso almost beat the man to death. But Alfonso knew that dead, the man would no longer be of use to him. Alive, he could threaten Serena with her lover's death unless she did as he wished. He had the marriage annulled, then planned her marriage to me. I had openly pursued her, and my intentions were honorable. Serena finally agreed out of fear for her lover. We married, but Serena was a very devout woman, and in her heart she was still married to another," Neil told him. "I pity her now, but I was in a rage at the time, believing I'd been cheated, and we became bitter enemies. I sometimes wonder if she wasn't going to meet him that day when she became lost. Another rider had been there. I saw the tracks, but the trail was washed away before I could follow it."

"I never knew. I'm sorry, Neil, but I won't change my mind," Adam said with quiet determination. "Either you marry Leigh, or the deal is off. You will have to find your own way out of Virginia, which won't be easy. And what of Nathan's family? You are my only hope. And what of Leigh? Will you walk away from her again?" Adam asked, little realizing how deep a wound he probed with his words.

Neil remained silent, no sign of the emotions warring within showing on his face. Love never seemed to be given without some sacrifice having been made, he thought broodingly. First it had been his mother, followed by She-With-Eyes-Of-The-Captured-Sky. Then Serena. And, finally, Leigh. No love had ever been given freely to him. That was how he wanted Leigh—not as a sacrifice.

And what of his own sacrifice? Would he sacrifice his men, Nathan's family, and his own chance for a brief happiness because of his pride? Because that was all it was that was keeping him from agreeing to Adam's offer. Why shouldn't he take what he had wanted for so long? He might not even live to see the end of the war, to worry about why she'd married him. But at least he'd be able to call her his now. And if he survived, then she would be his when he returned to Riovado. She would never escape him there.

Yes, it was his chance. Leigh Travers would finally be his, but not because she loved him, but because she would do anything, even marry him, to save her family.

Adam stared at his cousin, searching his face for some sign of capitulation, but Neil's face was as expressionless as a bronzed mask. Adam held out his hands in supplication. "There are no two people alive I trust more than you and Leigh. If Leigh were to marry someone other than you, I would never know what manner of man she had wed. But I do know you, Neil. And I know you'd never betray my trust. My daughter, my little Lucinda, all that I have left of Blythe, and the love we shared, would always be safe. She is my most precious possession. My God, Neil, let me die believing she will have a life of happiness ahead of her. Don't make me beg. Remember our blood oath? We pledged to one another as brothers. Did it mean nothing, Sun Dagger?"

Neil's gray-green eyes rested on Adam's tortured face, then he placed his hand on Adam's shoulder and nodded.

"I'll marry Leigh Travers."

❧

"*Marry?*"

Leigh stared at Adam as if he'd lost his mind.

"Marry Neil Braedon? I do not think that is very amusing, Adam," she said, her heart beating so wildly that she felt almost faint as the blood roared in her ears.

"Nor do I, although it has the makings of one of my finer jests," he said, a strange smile flickering across his face for an instant, then it was gone. "I am serious, Leigh."

"Adam?" Leigh said worriedly. "Adam, sit down, please. I think Stephen still has a jug of corn whiskey hidden away somewhere. You're not well," she entreated him, although she had to admit he looked better than he had yesterday. There was a briskness about him now, a lightness to his step, as if he were full of energetic purpose, and his eyes were bright, as if lit from some inner fire.

"I feel better than I have in months. We have spoken of this before, yesterday, in fact, and I told you then that this matter was not settled between us."

"And I thought it was," Leigh responded coldly, trying to calm herself.

"No, you correctly assumed you'd called my bluff. And until this morning, it was settled. I had no alternative. You knew I'd never take Lucinda from you. You knew, perhaps better than I, that I couldn't take her from the only family she had, and from you. Give her to a stranger? No, you were right, and I would never have done that. And even had you agreed to leave Virginia, along with Althea and the children, to have lived in Europe as expatriated Americans would never have been acceptable. You would have run out of funds eventually, and I don't intend to have my daughter raised in a foreign country," Adam vowed, then smiled triumphantly. "But you see, my dearest Leigh, our situation has changed since yesterday. I now have an alternative."

"Neil Braedon." Leigh said the name softly.

"Yes, Neil. I met with him at dawn."

Leigh stared at him almost resentfully. "I didn't even know you'd left the house. I thought you were still upstairs asleep. I didn't want to disturb you. I was just about to bring you a cup of tea and a couple of these biscuits Jolie made yesterday," she told him, glancing down at the tray she'd prepared.

"I'm sorry, but I couldn't tell you where I was going. I wasn't certain I would even find Neil, or what I was going to say to him if I did, but I did know where to look and I took a chance he'd be there. We made a deal, Leigh. Because he is a Braedon, and we are his family, he will help us. And in return for seeing that you arrive safely in the New Mexico Territory, I'll help him and his men escape from behind Confederate lines."

Leigh returned his smile, but humorlessly. "And what exactly can you do to help Neil Braedon and his men?"

"That is between Neil and me. But what I do will allow him and his men, many of whom are wounded, as you well know, the opportunity to escape."

"Some would brand you a traitor, Adam, for helping a Yankee raider."

"Yes, I know, but a man, or a woman," he said, reminding Leigh that she had helped that same Yankee raider, "must answer to his own conscience. And if I don't help him, then the rest of my plan is worth nothing."

"I see, then am I to understand that I and my family are to ride with the Bloodriders? I can imagine the ease of it now for three young children, a sick woman, and a blind man—of course, Jolie, Stephen, and I are well enough to travel. And what will we ride? Travers Hill's finest? A broken down mare, an old pony, and a cow," Leigh said, trying to ridicule Adam into common sense again. "You must indeed be feverish, Adam."

"You are an unrelenting adversary, Leigh, but I have made my decision. As I told you before, I have a pass to see you safely to Richmond. There you will board my ship, and from there we will sail to New York. Neil will assume the responsibility of your journey after that. As his wife, wife of a Union officer, you will be able to travel through the North. If you did not wed Neil, then, if something happened to him, if he couldn't get out of Virginia, then you would not have the protection of his name and position. This way, whatever happens, you will be Mrs. Neil Braedon, not Leigh Travers, daughter of the Confederacy," he explained, thinking that alone was reason enough for her marriage to Neil. And there was no cause to tell her the real necessity for the marriage. She need not know he was dying—he knew Leigh too well, and she would never agree to his plan if she discovered the truth. "Neil will have wired the news of your coming to his father, who will meet you in Missouri and see you the rest of the way into the territories. Once in New Mexico, at Royal Rivers, you will be safe. You will be living with my family, with your family, Leigh, because you will be a Braedon. And you and Lucinda, as Neil's family, will never have to worry about being homeless."

Leigh stared at Adam in amazement. He had everything worked out to the minutest detail. "What about you? You are Lucinda's father. What happens when you come to claim her?"

"The war isn't over for me. Nor do I have a home to take my daughter to. Neil does. He can offer her, and you, more than I can at this time. What you and Neil decide to do *after* that, is between the two of you. You could always get the marriage annulled, or you might even have fallen in love, and would wish to remain together," Adam said casually, but his eyes never left her face.

"And if I don't agree to your plan?" Leigh finally found the courage to ask, thinking to call his bluff yet again.

"That would be very foolish, my dear, but it would be your privilege. I have no authority over you. Naturally, I would wish for your cooperation in this, for you to accompany Lucinda, and Althea and the children, but your decision would change nothing. I am taking Lucinda when I leave Travers Hill. I am going to see that she reaches Royal Rivers safely. I am making Neil her legal guardian. Althea will also be leaving with us. She has seen the wisdom of my decision. And if you come with us, then Guy is in agreement too," he added, laying all of his cards on the table, certain to win the hand because he'd stacked the deck in his favor, determined not to lose the game to Leigh.

Adam glanced away from the stricken look on Leigh's face. "What? You've already spoken to them? How could you have? How dare you go behind my back."

"Damn it, Leigh, I dare! I knew you'd be stubborn. I knew you'd fight me. But I don't give a damn about fairness. Yes, I'm cheating, Leigh, but the stakes are too high, and I'm going to win," Adam warned her. "I returned to the house over an hour ago. I have explained everything to Althea and Guy."

"Without me? You spoke to them without me?"

"Yes. And I convinced both of them that this was the only solution to our predicament. They are both in full agreement with me."

"I don't believe you. You're lying! What lies did you tell them? They'd never agree to leave Virginia, to leave Travers Hill. They know how I feel," Leigh demanded, coming to stand before Adam accusingly.

"I told them the truth," he said, grasping her arms when she would have turned away, forcing her to listen. "I told Althea that Nathan made me guardian of his children. He left me, not you, Leigh, responsible for his family's safety. I promised him, the same way you promised Blythe, to care for his wife and children. And I intend to keep that promise. I told her Nathan would want her to do what I decided. I also told her that if she didn't, if she decided to remain here in Virginia, then you would all face an uncertain future, a future full of suffering and further unhappiness even after the war is over. I asked her if that was what she wanted for her children, for you, Leigh. Althea knows that if she leaves Virginia, then you will come too."

"And Guy?"

"Guy isn't a fool, Leigh. He may be blind, but I suspect he can see things far more clearly than you right now. I didn't need to convince him. He knows he is helpless. He depends on you for everything, as Althea has. He knows you would all be safer elsewhere. And he knows the only place where you would be welcomed as family, would be at Royal Rivers," Adam said, not telling her more of the private conversation he'd had with Guy and Althea. They both knew the truth. He'd taken a chance, telling them that he was dying, but he needed their support if he was to win over Leigh's objections. They knew now exactly how serious their situation was. Adam frowned as he remembered Guy sitting there so silently, staring blindly at him. Guy Travers, once so proud and arrogant, now humbled. And yet, Adam found he respected and liked Guy more today than he had when they'd ridden to hounds together or gambled late into the night.

Adam had watched as Guy's trembling hand had gently rubbed his hound's ears, as if drawing some comfort from that familiar feel. But he had not been completely certain that Guy, because of his old antagonism toward Neil, would agree to traveling to Royal Rivers, or having his sister wed to the man he'd once dueled with, his Travers pride still guiding his actions, so he played on that pride, on Guy's love for Travers Hill, his birthright—he told him about the tax assessment Leigh had received, and that it had not been the first, nor would it be the last.

That threatened Travers Hill as much as the armies crossing its land, fighting in its fields. But he could pay the taxes on Travers Hill, as he intended to on Royal Bay, Adam had told Guy. With the sale of his ship, he'd have enough money. He had originally intended the money to provide for them in Europe, but now he could use it to save their land—to keep it out of Yankee hands. And, someday, he'd told him, sounding convincing even in his own ears, they might be able to return to Travers Hill.

"And what of you, Leigh? Do you really care about your family?" Adam now heard himself demanding of an ashen-faced Leigh. "If you did, then you would do anything to make certain they survive. What happens to them if you become ill? Aren't you being selfish, thinking only of your pride? Who will take care of them? Answer me that. No, you can't. Prove to me how much you care. Marry Neil."

Leigh pulled free from him, turning away. When she turned back to face him, her lips were trembling.

"Marry Neil Braedon. It was your idea, wasn't it?" Leigh asked.

"Yes," Adam answered reluctantly, sensing what her next question would be.

But Leigh knew, without having to ask, what Neil Braedon's initial response had been to Adam's request.

"He wasn't pleased, was he," Leigh stated, then, when Adam remained silent, she held out her hands to him pleadingly. "Please, don't lie to me now, Adam. Do me the courtesy of telling me exactly how reluctant Neil Braedon was. I have a right to know."

"He refused, at first," Adam admitted uncomfortably, his cheeks flushed with growing embarrassment.

"He was just as unwilling to agree to this mockery of a marriage as I was?"

"Yes," Adam confirmed, unhappily.

"He is still in love with his wife. Her memory is still too dear to him for him to want—" Leigh began to say, but Adam interrupted.

"No, that's not it at all. Neil and his wife, Serena, were never in love; in fact, from what he told me, I do not believe they were even lovers. She was in love with another man when she was forced into marrying him and she was a wife to him in name only," Adam confided, believing it would help Leigh to know the truth about Neil's first marriage.

"Neil never loved her," Leigh murmured softly, then her gaze hardened as she met Adam's curious glance. "Then how he must hate being forced to wed me."

"Well, no man wants to be blackmailed into marriage. Forgive me, Leigh, that's not what I meant to say," he added quickly, seeing the shocked expression on her face.

"No, I think you said it very well, Adam. *That* is the truth. And you cannot deny it. You have also blackmailed me. I do not wish this marriage, and neither does Neil Braedon."

"Leigh, I—"

"No, it is best that neither of us be under any illusions about this marriage we are about to enter into. It is a marriage of convenience. Nothing more than that."

Adam closed his eyes, feeling an awful dread creeping over him as he remembered his own words spoken so casually about giving Leigh to Neil, and Neil's own words, spoken so arrogantly, about the pleasures he was to receive in payment for agreeing to marry Leigh. It was to be no marriage of convenience as far as Neil was concerned, and he was worried what Neil's reaction would be if Leigh threw that idea in his face—as had his first wife.

Suddenly, Adam was startled from his thoughts by the soft sound of Leigh's laughter.

"You lose, Adam," she said.

"What do you mean? I don't understand. I thought you'd just agreed to my plan," he demanded.

"I did, but it really doesn't matter whether I agreed to marry Neil Braedon or not. You see, you've forgotten one, very important person in these machinations of yours. Who is to marry us?" Leigh asked, believing even Adam incapable of pulling a preacher from his hat.

The Reverend Culpepper had never been so outraged in his life. Rudely awakened from peaceful slumber, pulled out of a warm bed, forced into his clothes by ungentlemanly hands, and soundly cursed when he hesitated to venture out into the cold darkness of night, he had been speechless with indignation, which had been a blessing had he realized it. And soon enough he had, when he'd felt a pistol barrel pointed at his head to persuade him to keep his silence as they'd descended the stairs of the house, the Draytons continuing to sleep undisturbed as he was manhandled through the hallway to the back door.

Stopping by the door, the scoundrel set down the oil lamp he'd carried to guide his thieving steps through the house. In the flickering light, the frightened cleric met the glittering eyes that stared at him from behind the mask that covered half the man's face. Snuffing out the light, the man, with inelegant haste, pushed him through the door and out into the frigid night air of the gardens of Meadowbrook, where, to Reverend Culpepper's amazement, his very own horse was saddled and waiting.

He thought the ride through the night would never end, and he almost wished it would not, for he knew not what awaited him at journey's end. But he felt somewhat comforted by the knowledge that his Bible rode with him; although why the blackguard had insisted he bring his robe and surplice, as well as the parish register, remained a puzzling mystery to him. One would have assumed he was about to perform church services, clad in his vestments, the parish register at hand and opened to record the joyful baptism of the newest member of the congregation, or the sacred joining of two of his flock in holy matrimony—or, he thought, on a far more blood-chilling thought, the death of a beloved member of the community—himself!

Dear God, this miscreant who had abducted him was obviously bedeviled and deranged—or he was one of the Devil's own. A hell-rider, the panicked man of the cloth thought as he heard the frightening sound of baying hounds close by.

But the Reverend Culpepper felt his heart slow its irregular beat when he saw a golden light shining from a window somewhere in the darkness ahead. They rode up a curving lane, drawing ever closer to the light, until finally his kidnapper halted before the darker shape of a house that loomed up before them.

Dismounting, the reverend found the rascal's hands upon him again, guiding him none-too-gently up the steps of the house. Illuminating light suddenly spread across the porch, as if some unseen visage stared out upon them, and had been lying in wait in the shadows. In the golden glow, Reverend Culpepper recognized the perpetrator of such a shocking attack as the thief pulled the green-checked gingham neckerchief from his face, and he nearly choked on the name that came sputtering off his tongue.

"Adam Braedon!" the good reverend croaked. "This is

scandalous behavior indeed, even from you," he said in his deepest stentorious, pulpit-voice, but the words of censure were hardly more than an indignant squeak as they stuck in his dry throat like dust as he tried to straighten his collar, but one of the ends kept popping up and poking him beneath the chin.

"Now, now, Reverend Culpepper, don't be so persnickety, I'll have you tucked back safe in your bed before dawn, with no one being any the wiser to your midnight ride," Adam promised, grabbing the reverend's hat as it slipped from his head, and placing it firmly back on, never realizing it was a tasseled nightcap.

"I demand you unhand me this instant, sir!"

"It could be worse, Reverend," Adam said, keeping a firm grip on the struggling cleric as he escorted him into the house as the door opened.

"Indeed?"

"I might have been a complete stranger to you, or a Yankee raider," Adam said, to comfort him with the cheering thought, which did have the reverend momentarily grateful until he realized that he had still been kidnapped and was now being forced to enter a strange house. Although, there was something vaguely familiar about the pineapple-shaped brass door knocker, which Adam Braedon had not even had the courtesy to use before he barged through the door, dragging the poor reverend behind him.

Later the Reverend Culpepper would calmly accept what had happened as being nothing out of the unusual, considering the people involved in the night's bizarre activities. The names Braedon and Travers explained only too well the madness that had threatened him. However, knowing the identity of his kidnapper had made him none the less uneasy about his midnight assignation, for had he not been plagued by the two families since first coming to the county nearly fifteen years earlier? Mischief makers, the lot of them.

The wrathful reverend was in no mood to be placated, had that been on Adam's mind, which apparently it had not, for it didn't help matters any when he handed him his wrinkled robe and surplice and started to chuckle as he stared in amazement at the reverend.

The man had never shown him the proper respect, Reverend Culpepper fumed as he glanced frantically around, his eyes opening wide as he caught sight of his own ruffled reflection in a looking glass hanging in the foyer. Jerking off his tasseled nightcap, he glared at Adam's grinning face.

"Sir, I demand an explanation! You will not hear the end of this ungentlemanly act of yours, let me assure you, Adam Braedon!"

"Reverend Culpepper," a cultured voice said softly and graciously from the opened doorway leading off the foyer, "I do hope you will forgive us, but we were in desperate need of your services. Had it not been of the utmost urgency, a matter of life and death, we would have invited you for tea, and we could have discussed the matter in a most civilized atmosphere. I do hope you will accept my apologies, and on behalf of all of us, for the inconvenience you have suffered."

Travers Hill, he sighed thankfully, realizing now where he was. Reverend Culpepper felt some of his anger deserting him as he recognized the woman standing there, her slender hand held out to him so welcomingly, and he thought for not the first time in many years that never had he met a young woman with so pleasant and genteel a manner. "Mrs. Braedon, I am indeed pleased to see you," he began, and he was indeed, for she, at least, was sane, "but I must say I am surprised to find you involved in such a craven act. Do you realize that your brother-in-law kidnapped me from my bed?"

"I had hoped Adam would show a certain amount of discretion for once, considering the delicacy of the matter," Althea said reproachfully, much to the reverend's satisfaction, but her gaze was understanding when it met an unrepentant Adam's.

"I didn't have the time to convince the good reverend that his services were needed without delay. And I felt Reverend Culpepper would come more willingly, and quietly, if he did not realize that no harm would befall him at my hands."

"Hmmmph!" the reverend huffed, not in the least reassured, for hadn't harm befallen him at the hands of Julia Braedon? He had nearly been emasculated by that scalding tea—and she had giggled! Not surprising, then, that she'd turned into a harlot, he thought with self-righteous superiority.

Althea sighed, leaning against the door tiredly. "You will forgive me, Reverend, if I do not linger here, but I have been ill, and it has been a rather long day for me. I must sit down for a moment or I fear I will faint."

"Of course, my dear, dear woman," the reverend said quickly, for Althea Travers...Braedon, he mentally corrected himself, had always been his favorite of the Travers family, along with the late Mrs. Travers, who'd been such a fine lady. Ah, what a pity, he thought, folding his hands together complacently, momentarily forgetting the unusual circumstances of his arrival as he smiled benevolently at the recently widowed Althea Braedon.

"Allow me to assist you," he offered, hurriedly stepping forward before Adam could lend her a supportive arm, and Adam suspected had he reached Althea first, he would have been callously elbowed out of the way. "Indeed, madam, I would suggest you retire immediately. You look quite pale," he said, always his best when being conversationally solicitous, although he had to admit Althea Braedon did not look at all well. In fact, she looked as if she'd been crying, her eyes red-rimmed and shadowed as if by some recent sadness. "I dare say your physician would be most displeased to find you up at so late an hour...ah, which one cannot help but wonder about. But, naturally, I am at your service now, to provide whatever words of comfort and wisdom that may be required in this hour of need," he offered politely, his voice having resumed its rich basso tones, his manner at its most punctilious.

"Thank you, Reverend Culpepper," Althea murmured faintly, truly thankful for a strong arm to lean on, even if it was Reverend Culpepper's, his voice droning in her ears like the annoying buzz of a fat bumble bee. It had taken all of what little strength she had to prepare for the evening's ceremonies, Leigh being less than helpful in her own preparations for her hastily arranged marriage, and had it not been for Jolie's bullying they would never have been ready in time.

It had been Jolie who had remembered which trunk the wedding gown had been carefully stored in for safekeeping years ago. Her wedding gown, Althea remembered, seeing so clearly Nathan standing next to her as she said her vows and became his wife. If only she could hope that Leigh's marriage to Neil Braedon would be as happy, she fretted, but she had to believe that someday they would, that Adam's faith hadn't been misguided.

Althea glanced over at Adam, still unable to believe what he had confided to her and Guy. They were sworn not to reveal the truth to Leigh, but it was hard not to show the heartbreak she felt so deep within. Drawing a deep breath, she said, "The Reverend Culpepper is here. Shall we begin?"

The Reverend Culpepper, however, was anything but ready. The scene that had met his startled gaze when he stepped into the study nearly caused him to falter, and forgetful of the frail woman whose arm he'd held so protectively only moments before, he would have turned and fled without so much as a by-your-leave.

Leigh Travers, dressed in an ivory-tinted gown of silk brocade and cobweb-fine blond lace, her chestnut hair partly concealed beneath a short veil of fairy-spun Brussels lace, the scalloped edges floating around her shoulders ethereally and held in place by a coronet of delicate silk rosettes, was standing next to the infamous Yankee raider, Captain Dagger.

And in the apprehensive mind of the already overwrought reverend, as if to mock him further, the scene became even more macabre as he met the slanting yellow eyes of Jolie, her coppery face looking heathenish as the firelight flickered over it, casting strange shadows that melted into the ebony face of Stephen, the sound of ancient, impious chants whispering against his Christian soul as he heard a soft muttering coming from the mulattress.

Reverend Culpepper nearly fainted from fear, and had it not been for Althea's supportive arm now, he would have fallen, the stiffness having left his knees as fast as his courage.

And yet, perhaps, it was all some terrifying nightmare, brought on by indigestion, for he had overindulged earlier that evening at supper, but it had been such a long time since he'd enjoyed a well-prepared, generous-proportioned meal. And Mrs. Drayton had served the most delicious pork chops and fried potatoes, and she'd been so pleased to see him cleaning his plate of a third portion. The reverend blinked his eyes, hoping he'd been seeing double, but, no, Adam Braedon still stood beside him, and across the room stood Captain Dagger, for there was no mistaking the heathenish braid he wore, marking him as the notorious Yankee raider depicted in the newspapers.

"Wha—what is the meaning of this?" he demanded, gulping nervously as he met the cold-eyed stare of a man thought to be little better than a demon from hell. "Is this some sort of hoax?"

"Hardly that. We need you to perform a marriage for us, Reverend Culpepper," Adam said good-naturedly as he hustled the now stiff-legged reverend closer to the pair standing before the hearth. "Not quite the wedding I had imagined, but nonetheless binding. Never forget, Guy Travers was a lawyer in peacetime, and has acquainted me with all of the legal niceties concerning our hasty marriage, so it will indeed be quite legal," Adam warned, grinning as he placed the parish register on Althea's lap where she now sat in a chair close by.

"The witnesses, the brother and sister of the bride, Althea also serving as matron-of-honor, and myself, also serving as best man. Quite a family gathering. Now, if you would be so obliging."

"Ma-marriage! Certainly not!" the reverend exclaimed, staring in disbelief at the bride. "You would marry this…this…"

"Oh, did I neglect to make the proper introductions, Reverend Culpepper?" Adam interrupted before Neil could say anything. "I gather, by your expression, that you've recognized Captain Dagger. But perhaps you didn't realize that he is also Neil Braedon. My cousin. Now, if the Union wins the war, and my cousin here survives to come back to Virginia, then you can expect to have your neck wrung if you don't perform this ceremony right now. If you live to see that day, because, if I were you, I wouldn't want to cross Captain Dagger here. The Bloodriders aren't far away, and a lot depends on this marriage," he said, shaking his head as if sorry for what was about to happen to the good reverend.

Reverend Culpepper opened his mouth to speak, then thought better of it as he met Captain Dagger's eyes.

"Also, I would advise the utmost discretion concerning the events of this evening. Indeed, were I you, I would forget I'd ever come to Travers Hill at midnight for the nefarious purpose of presiding over the marriage of Captain Dagger, well…I just don't know, but I'm certain there would be quite an outcry should the good citizens of the county learn that the Reverend Culpepper had been involved. They would not look kindly upon the man who had given Leigh Travers into the hands of Captain Dagger."

Although bloated with pride, the reverend was no fool.

"Excellent," Adam said, sounding for all the world the cordial host. "I am so pleased you've decided to cooperate," he said as the reverend began to hurriedly pull on his gown, which Adam had very kindly held up for him. "Yes, you look quite splendid. Now the surplice. Yes, yes, very nice indeed," Adam murmured approvingly as he straightened the white linen garment with its long, full sleeves. "Here is your Bible. Are we ready, then? You may proceed, Reverend Culpepper, in uniting Leigh Travers and Neil Braedon in holy matrimony."

The vows had been made, the solemn promises to love and to honor until death do them part dutifully recited. A ring, hastily taken from Althea's own hand, the ring Nathan had lovingly slipped on her finger, had been slipped on the third finger of Leigh's left hand, Neil's strong, tanned hand closing around her slender, pale one for the briefest of instants, then her hand had been released. The church register had been duly signed and witnessed, the recording of their names and the date of their marriage appearing on the same page as Blythe's and Adam's four years ago.

Although he'd not been at his best, the Reverend Culpepper had always prided himself on having mastered the ceremonial part of his calling, and weddings and burials were among the finest of the services he performed, next to his Sunday sermons, of course. And except for the hound that had constantly been underfoot, and sniffing him at the most inopportune time, and in the most private of places, he could take pride in his performance this night.

And he had to admit he'd seldom tasted better cake, and the ratafia had been quite exceptional. He'd been quite surprised when the majordomo and the mulattress, having left the room, had reentered with refreshments. The reverend, after a second glass, had begun to reassess his original impression of this marriage, for it was beginning to appear quite civilized and he had even joined in a toast to the couple's continued good health and future happiness together.

"Now, Reverend Culpepper, I think I should, and with all due haste, return you to your bed," Adam suggested, offering the reverend his coat when he would have lingered in conversation with Althea, whose blond head was already beginning to droop from fatigue.

"We wouldn't wish to have your activities questioned, should someone happen to see you and wonder what the Reverend Culpepper was doing riding around the countryside in the black of night."

"No…ah, quite right, although I would certainly leave them in little doubt that it was none of their business. I am a servant of God, and as such, in order to serve my flock, I must find myself out in the cold at all hours of the day and night, and called upon to perform all manner of service unquestioningly, and without complaint or care to my own safety," the reverend told them with such affronted dignity that anyone might dare to question his actions that Adam had no fears that anything would be said of this evening, and the service Reverend Culpepper had performed. And should anyone have noticed the most recent marriage recorded in the church register, then all they would note as odd was that yet another Braedon had wed a Travers.

Neil glanced over at his wife. Her slender back was turned to him almost disdainfully, as if she distanced herself from him, and the marriage that had just taken place between them. She'd been as warm and loving as one of the icicles hanging from the eaves of the house. And her hand had felt even colder when he'd taken it in his and placed the borrowed ring upon her finger, claiming her as his wife. Her lips, when he'd kissed her, sealing the ceremony, had been as soft and yielding as carved marble.

"I'll accompany you, Adam," Neil said, picking up his coat, but Adam shook his head, turning at the door as he tried to escort the reverend from the room, the reverend having stopped to empty his third glass of ratafia.

Leigh glanced over at them. Standing before the fire, trying to warm herself, she watched Neil with a cool-eyed stare. He could hardly wait to leave, she thought, remembering the brusqueness of his greeting when he'd arrived at Travers Hill.

Beyond that, and his curt demand to know if she agreed to Adam's plan, he'd hardly spoken two words to her, spending most of his time in conversation with Althea, who'd seemed pleased by his gentlemanly attentions.

"No, I wouldn't want to give away our game too soon. Can't take the risk of being seen together, or your being put in unnecessary danger, Neil," Adam joked. "At least no more than usual. Can't tempt fate too much. I should be back in an hour and a half, or two, or three. Going to stay off the roads. Don't want to attract attention. I also remember seeing a wagon at Meadowbrook when I was there a couple of days ago. I'm going to see if I can borrow it. The Draytons are good friends. There shouldn't be any trouble. We'll talk further about the details for the journey when I return. When do your men expect you back?" he asked.

"When they see me."

"Good," Adam said, pushing the reluctant reverend through the door ahead of him.

Neil stood for a moment, hearing Adam's cough from the foyer, followed by the door slamming shut, then there was silence.

Turning around, he caught Leigh's glance on him. For a long moment, their eyes held, but neither knew what the other was thinking, and with an abruptness that bordered on rudeness, Leigh excused herself, professing a need to change from her wedding gown before preparing a bottle for the baby.

"Braedon?"

Neil looked over at Guy Travers, where he sat near the fire, his hounds sitting at his feet.

"Braedon? You still here?" he demanded.

"Yes."

"Want to have a word with you," he said shortly.

Neil frowned, thinking Guy Travers still bore a grudge against him despite what Leigh had claimed.

"What is it?" Neil asked, coming to stand closer.

But Guy remained silent, his expression almost diffident. "I hoped you would accept my deep apologies for what happened between us four years ago."

Neil was startled, for he hadn't expected an apology from the man. "There's no need," he began.

Guy laughed harshly. "Please, allow me to offer, and you would be within your rights not to accept it. My behavior that night, the whole week of your visit, in fact, was unforgivable. I regret it deeply. I could try to excuse myself as having been young, and arrogant, but I will not, because I suspect that I would still be that way today had certain events not taken place to alter drastically the way I perceive the world. I have seen too many fine young men die, some by my own hand, others standing beside me, to have anything but disgust for my actions that night when I would have taken your life for no other reason than that I was jealous of you, that I was arrogant and selfish, too accustomed to having everything I wanted in life, without ever realizing the value of what I took, what I accepted as my due. I've lost my mother and my father, my two brothers, and a little sister, and countless friends. I will never again accept the taking of a life as anything but tragic and senseless. It is no gentleman's sport, entered into to save honor, to salve wounded pride, to boast about having taken another's life as if tallying the flushed pheasant bagged in a shoot. Death is agony, and it is final, and I see it in my mind every hour of the day."

Neil stared at Guy and saw a stranger. He was a changed man, a man who had found honor on the battlefield, not because he sought glory in another's death, but because he regretted the taking of that life.

"I offer you my hand," Guy said, gazing up at Neil blindly.

Neil took the hand being offered, holding it firmly in his grasp before he released it.

"I was surprised when Jolie offered me that cake. Haven't had any in ages. Where on earth did she find it? Or do I really want to know that?" Guy said, smiling slightly, and feeling a weight had been lifted from him.

Althea laughed softly. "It was an inspired, if conniving, act." Althea surprised the two men by her answer. "Jolie knows the Reverend Culpepper only too well, and remembers his healthy appetite. She thought refreshments might put him in a better frame of mind, and I do believe he left here quite pleased with himself. Foolish man," Althea murmured with uncharacteristic harshness.

"And the ratafia? Where did she unearth that?"

"Exactly. She has a small cache buried in a corner of the cellars. Whenever she's had the herbs, and the brandy, she's brewed up a batch. This was made from the brandy Adam brought last spring, and Leigh said this was sitting on the kitchen windowsill all summer. It is quite heady, and I believe it is becoming more and more potent. I feel quite light-headed, and I only sipped mine. We shouldn't have had so many toasts."

"We don't get to celebrate often, Althea," Guy said, still enjoying the warming glow in his blood.

"You and Leigh both had too much. And I do hope the reverend will be able to stay on his horse, he did imbibe rather freely," she said, sighing as she rested her head against the back of the chair.

"Stephen should be back in a few minutes, Althea," Guy said, hearing the tired sigh. "It has been a long day. You should be in bed," he advised, pulling his tobacco pouch from his coat pocket and with little fumbling managing to fill the bowl with tobacco. He was about to light it, when he remembered Althea and stopped.

"Please, go ahead, Guy. It won't bother me," she told him, but he continued to sit with his unlit pipe, patiently rubbing one of his hound's heads.

"No, no hurry. Where is Stephen, anyway?" he asked.

"He's with Jolie in the kitchens. She had him fetching some wicker baskets. They're already beginning to pack up the items she told him she would need."

"But it's probably dark in the kitchens, except for a little bit of firelight," Guy said.

"You know Jolie can see in the dark," Althea reminded him.

"May I help you to your room, Althea?" Neil asked, not waiting for her acquiescence as he came to her side.

"Yes, thank you, if you wouldn't mind. I'll just lean on your arm, please." Althea said, getting slowly to her feet, but before she could take a step, Neil had easily picked her up in his arms.

"Thank you. Good night, Guy," Althea called back. "You may light your pipe now."

"'Night, dear, sleep well," Guy called to her.

"My candle," Althea said, stopping Neil by the door as she

reached down and selected a taper, lighting it from the oil lamp, then carefully shielding it as they moved into the drafty foyer.

"Which room is yours, Althea?" Neil asked when he reached the top of the stairs, carrying Althea with little effort.

"First door on the right, yes, this one," she said, unable to hide her yawn.

Neil opened the door and entered, the candlelight casting flickering shadows over the room. Sleeping peacefully in a trundle bed near the big canopied bed were two children tucked snugly beneath a down comforter. Neil stopped for a moment and stared down at them. Noelle, her dark brown hair spread out around her angelic face, her lips curved upward with a smile, was dreaming sweet dreams. Her brother, Steward, his dark curls tumbled into disorder, a thumb stuck in his mouth, had obviously dreamed of wilder things, because the comforter on his side of the bed was tangled, with a short, chubby leg dangling above the floor, where his pillow had landed during the fight.

Neil smiled. "He's a fine-looking lad. Nathan would be proud of him," he told the boy's mother as he set her down by the bed.

"I hope someday he'll hear his father tell him that. Thank you, Neil," Althea said huskily.

"Good night, Althea. I wish you a safe journey."

"We won't see you again?" she asked, looking up from her loving glance at her sleeping children.

"No, I'll be leaving with Adam later. Then we go our separate ways. I trust we'll meet again at Royal Rivers," he said, his tone casual, as if he'd every reason to believe they would.

"I hope so too, with all my heart," Althea said, staring at him curiously. "And thank you for what you're doing for us."

Neil eyed her thoughtfully. "There's no need to thank me. I'm getting just as much in return."

Althea shook her head in disagreement. "I prefer to thank you anyway, and I will continue to think kindly of you."

"As you wish. Where is Leigh?" he asked abruptly, and seeing Althea's startled glance, he smiled. "I want her to have these letters of introduction I've written to friends of mine in New York, and I've made a list of names of people who could help should you have any difficulties once you've started your journey. I've also prepared detailed instructions for her to follow. And you needn't worry about the cost. I'll make certain that you will be well provided for. You will have ample funds to see you comfortably during your journey. I'll wire my bank, and the money will be deposited in a New York bank."

"I don't believe I will worry, now that you and Leigh are married," she said, her glance resting for a moment on the ring of gold Leigh had returned to her shortly after the ceremony.

"Which room is Leigh's?" he asked again, turning toward the door.

"The last door; it's the corner bedchamber on this side," she said, sounding almost reluctant to furnish the information. "I-I could…ummm, should you…I mean, is she ex—"

"You needn't be concerned, Althea," Neil said, opening the door and looking back at her. "After all, she is my wife."

With that, he closed the door behind him and walked down the dark hall, treading lightly on the pine flooring. He stopped before the last door on the right, hesitating, momentarily unsure. He raised his hand to knock, but the door hadn't been completely shut and swung open.

Leigh was sound asleep, half lying against the pillows propped up against the headboard of the bed, the crackling fire in the hearth creating a warm, golden glow around the room. She was still dressed in her wedding gown, the baby cradled in her arms. She'd pulled off the gauzy veil, and her hair had been freed from whatever style she'd worn it in. Noticing the veil had floated to the floor, he suspected she'd hastily removed it, and the pins from her hair as well, for they lay scattered across the small rag rug by the bed, a hairbrush dropped haphazardly next to them, along with a pair of silk slippers, the ribbons tangled.

Neil entered, closing the door behind him, and locking it.

He walked over to stand by the bed and stared down at her—his wife. She was asleep with such sweet innocence, unaware of the man, the husband, who gazed down at her, a tightening in his loins as passion stirred deep inside him. He started to reach out to capture a long strand of hair, but as he stretched out his hand, the baby reached out, the tiny hand grasping his finger with surprising strength for one so small. Big eyes watched him curiously, trustingly.

With a gentleness of expression that would have surprised anyone who knew Neil Braedon, he bent over and lifted the soft bundle from the curve of Leigh's arm. He picked up the half-emptied bottle of milk and placed it on the night table. Holding the child with a tenderness of hand that he had seldom showed, Neil placed the baby in the cradle and covered her with the quilt, carefully tucking it around her. Then he rocked the cradle for a moment until the baby's eyes began to flutter, finally closing with sleep.

Moving back to the bed, he sat down beside Leigh's sleeping form. His hands still gentle, he pulled her into his arms. Lifting the thick tresses of golden brown hair from her back, allowing the long, silken length to drape over his arm, he began to unfasten the gown, slipping the heavy silk from her shoulders when he'd completed his task.

Drowsily, Leigh murmured something, her heavy-lidded eyes remaining closed as she shrugged her arms from the gown, helping him to undress her. "Couldn't unfasten them myself," she said, the curtain of hair falling across her face as she bent over, facilitating the removal of the gown over her petticoats. The froth of petticoats followed, then she breathed deeply as the laces were loosened on her corset and the garment removed.

Leigh stretched indolently, then smiled as she felt the tension leaving her as her hair was brushed, beginning to crackle as the brush was drawn slowly through the long strands again and again with untiring strokes.

Neil felt her head nodding forward, her shoulders falling back against him and he eased her over into the center of the bed, then stretched out beside her as he took her yielding body into his arms, content for the moment just to hold her against him, the scent of jessamine rising from her warm, perfumed flesh an opiate to his senses, and unable to resist, he pressed his lips to the curve of her shoulder, pushing aside the lacy sleeve of her chemise and baring the soft skin to his burning touch. His mouth moved along the lovely arch of throat, feeling the steady pulse that beat there.

"'Night, Jolie," she said huskily, welcoming the dream sleep that was engulfing her. "No, not Jolie. Neil," she murmured, smiling enchantingly.

His mouth lightly touched her slightly parted lips, her breath warm as it mingled with his. One of his hands slid into the thick, silken hair that spread out around them, while his other hand moved lower, sliding beneath the chemise, his fingers finding and touching her nipple, his thumb moving over the rosy crest until he felt it hardening and rising into a tight bud.

Her breasts were beautiful, he thought as he cupped one, feeling the warm firmness as it swelled in his hand. Lowering his head, he moved his lips along the gentle curve, his tongue feeling the nipple, licking it hungrily. He pulled the chemise lower, until her breasts were bared to him, and he buried his face against them, hearing her heart pounding beneath, his fingers touching the delicate outline of her ribs. His hands drifted lower, stilled momentarily by the waistline of her pantalettes, but he found the tapes that held them tied against him, and slid them lower over her hips, his fingers sliding down further to touch the soft curling hair between her legs and the womanly contours it covered, lingering intimately a moment inside, feeling the moistness against his fingertips. Reluctantly, he removed his hand to pull the pantalettes completely off, then the chemise and her silken stockings.

He gazed at her body, bathed golden in the firelight, and thought he'd never seen a woman look so beautiful. And she was just the way he'd always imagined she would look: perfectly proportioned, from the joining of the slender column of her neck to her shoulders, the breastbone revealing the delicateness beneath, to the roundness of her breasts, the firm undercurve holding them high and proud, the nipples a delicate rose pink, to her narrow waist above the gentle curving of slender hips, the slightly darker triangle of hair curling between her thighs, her legs long and lean, tapering from smoothly muscled thighs to elegantly shaped calves and feet.

He looked at his tanned hand against the magnolia-softness of her flat belly, her hipbones jutting out slightly, and caressed the creamy flesh between, his hand touching her navel, then slipping lower to find again that intimate joining of thigh and hip, his lips lightly touching her slightly parted mouth, kissing her as he had dreamed a thousand times of kissing her.

Leigh was lost in the eroticism of her dream, experiencing

feelings she'd never known, her body responding with a treacherous will of its own, the well-aged brandy she'd consumed burning like fire in her blood. The hidden desires she would never have allowed herself to explore in the dark recesses of her soul were now revealed to the fiery light of the passion that spread like wildfire through her.

How often had she dreamt this? she wondered in growing confusion as she felt Neil's hands on her body, touching her, his mouth against her lips, kissing the breath from her, his body burning hers wherever it touched. She felt an incredible sensation suddenly snake through her wildly, vibrating with a tingling awareness of something deep within her. There was a feeling of fullness between her thighs as she felt a strange warmth, a moisture as the pressure continued to build, spiraling higher inside her belly and she arched her hips sensuously against the gentle, yet insistent probing that had entered the most intimate part of her body, the rhythmic movement steadily going deeper, without lessening its throbbing beat. Suddenly she gasped, unable to control the blossoming of feeling that filled her, as if petal after petal of a flower were opening to the life-giving warmth of the sun.

A voice spoke roughly in her ear, tickling her. Leigh drew a ragged breath, feeling vaguely uneasy, then shivered as she felt a coldness touch her. She groaned slightly, opening her heavy-lidded eyes, slumberous with passion.

Her heart started to pound even faster as she tried to rub the sleep from her eyes, and the vision of Neil Braedon standing naked before her like a pagan god. The flames from the fire surrounded him, dancing over the sinewy muscles that rippled like molten gold, his golden hair hanging loose around his neck and shoulders.

Her startled gaze lingered for a moment on the hard length of manhood that rose challengingly from the matting of hair at the base of his taut belly, then she glanced up at his face, meeting his intent stare, his gray-green eyes glittering as they caressed her.

Leigh opened her mouth to speak, unable to believe what had happened. She started to rise, then became aware of her own nakedness and knew it wasn't a dream, but before she could cover herself, Neil had joined her in the bed, his arms sliding around her shaking body, molding her close against him.

"Let me go," she whispered hoarsely.

"Never," Neil answered thickly, his voice roughened with passion, his mouth silencing her protests, the hardness of his manhood pressing against her thigh.

His hands moved slowly over her, seducing her with their touch as they fondled her, learning the secrets of her body, stealing her resolve from her as she felt his hand resume its play between her legs, the sensations she'd thought only part of a dream responding to him, not to her as she felt the intrusion of his fingers inside her, rubbing the soft flesh until she felt a strange quivering that left her trembling.

Her lips had parted from the increasing pressure of his mouth, his tongue tasting of hers, seeking the softness of touching, his kiss deepening until she was breathless.

Suddenly, his mouth left hers, and he drew away from her, allowing their bodies to part. Taking her chin in his hand, Neil stared down into Leigh's flushed face, feeling as if he were lost forever in the dark blue depths of the eyes staring at him with such confusion.

"One night, Leigh. That is all we may ever have together. Forget the reasons why we married, why we are together, *except* that we want each other. Infatuation? I believe it much more, but whatever this is between us, will you let me love you tonight?" he asked simply, the chiseled lines of his hard mouth softened with passion, his pride forgotten as he waited for her response.

Suddenly, the aching loneliness, the heartache of the last four years overcame any false pride that would have kept her from becoming his lover. The cold, barren years that would stretch ahead if she denied him now, the thought that she might never have another chance to say yes to him, to give him the love she'd hidden in her heart for so long made her catch her breath painfully. She was his wife, and now she wanted to be his lover.

A marriage in name only was not what she wanted, despite what she had told Adam. She knew now that he had not been in love with his first wife, that he held no cherished memories that would fight against her love, there were no ghosts she had to fight to win his love. She no longer cared why Neil had married her. Infatuation? It no longer mattered. She did know that he wanted her, that he had desired her for years, and now, that was enough, Leigh thought, and in that moment of discovery, truly becoming a woman—the woman who would love Neil Braedon forever.

The gray-green eyes that had been watching her so closely widened imperceptibly, his breath catching when he felt the tentative touch of Leigh's hands moving over his chest, her palms rubbing across his hardened nipples, then down to his belly, sliding over the tautness of muscle, her hand finding the thick matting of golden hair and sliding through it roughly to close over him, holding him with a gentle touch now, her fingers leaving a circle of fire with their play on the shaft of his manhood, hard and throbbing between their bodies.

"Yes, tonight is ours, Neil, and for no one else," Leigh promised.

His arms wrapped around her, pulling her beneath him as her arms wound around the strong column of his neck, the fingers of one hand threading through his hair, while the others entwined themselves around the rawhide thong that held the leather pouch around his neck.

He stared into her eyes, searching for something elusive in the deepening indigo as he parted her thighs with his, feeling the softness of her flesh slide along the outside of his. Raising slightly, he kneeled over her, then he entered her, slowly moving deeper inside. Sensing the shield of her virginity, he tensed, almost unable to control the bunching of muscle in his loins as he poised above her, then cupping her buttocks, and widening the spread of her legs, he thrust himself deep, tearing the fine membrane, the blood that flowed his prized proof of possession.

Leigh felt the momentary, searing pain, and met his gaze in wounded surprise, but then his mouth closed over hers, caressing her lips, his tongue seeking hers, moving against it caressingly, his hands beginning to fondle her buttocks, and she felt herself opening wider inside to hold him as he filled her with a warmth that sent waves of feeling washing over her leaving her panting for breath. He stilled, giving her time to grow accustomed to the feel of him inside of her, and he kissed her, his mouth returning again and again to her lips, until they were swollen and tender from his.

Then she felt the hard, throbbing length of him sliding inside her with an undulating movement, driving deeper and deeper with each slow thrust of his hips against hers and she moved in response, feeling a sense of excitement sweeping over her as she rode with him, holding on tighter to the rawhide strap around his neck, racing the storm that threatened to overtake them, his heart sounding like thunder, lightning flashing behind her eyes as she felt him touch the center of her being and she cried out with the joy of it, knowing that nothing would ever be the same in her life.

With a sense of triumph, he heard her cries of pleasure as she moved beneath him, and he felt himself drawn deeper into her, sheathed by her warmth, the moist, tingling flesh enfolding him gently, caressing his manhood, holding him inside of her. They were one, and never again would she be apart from him, even when they were separated physically, she would be his. He knew her now as a lover. They had shared the intimacy that made a man and a woman one. She was his—and he belonged to her, *if* she ever chose to claim him.

He could bear no more as he took her, and never had a woman pleased him as much as she. He plunged deep inside her, the tightness that closed around him heightening his pleasure as he felt the throbbing of her womanly flesh around him. Holding her buttocks he pulled her closer and closer, until the flatness of his belly pressed against hers, their hips locked together as his rhythm increased, her slender thighs wrapped around his hips and reminding him of the way he first had seen her, riding her horse with such gracefulness of movement, and he filled her womb with his seed as he climaxed, exploding inside her, hoping he would leave something of himself deep within, where it would be nurtured, and flower, for he would have her, and only her, bear his children.

❧

She was asleep when he left the warmth of her bed and dressed. He stood staring down at her, wishing he could remain by her side forever, but once again he had to walk away...then he smiled, for he would carry the memory of her lovemaking with him this time. He pulled the quilt over her bare shoulders, his hand lingering against the softness of her breast, then he pressed a tender kiss against her lips and was gone.

Shivering slightly as she felt a cold draft touch her shoulders, Leigh opened drowsy eyes, then closed them as she snuggled deeper beneath the quilt, falling into a contented sleep. Her hand closed more tightly around the rough leather pouch that held the only memories of a Comanche brave once known as Sun Dagger. Now he was only a memory to the people who had once called him theirs. The barbaric charms had always protected him from harm, but now they belonged to another, as did his heart.

Part Three

Territory of New Mexico—Spring 1865

For winter's rains and ruins are over,
And all the season of snows and sins;
The days dividing lover and lover,
The light that loses, the night that wins;
The time remembered is grief forgotten,
And frosts are slain and flowers begotten,
And in green underwood and cover
Blossom by blossom the spring begins.

Algernon Charles Swinburne

Eighteen

The hills,
Rock-ribbed, and ancient as the sun.

William Cullen Bryant

THE *CONQUISTADORES* HAD CHRISTENED IT *DESPOBLADO*. They had seen only the emptiness, the desolateness of a land stretching from desert to mountain, never the beauty of a solitary, snowcapped peak rising toward the heavens, or a slender-leafed yucca blooming in the stillness.

They had not found a land rich in treasures of gold and silver. The wondrous stories of *Quivira, The Seven Cities of Gold*, and *El Dorado* had proven false—fabulous legends that would remain forever elusive.

But there were other treasures to be found—and far more precious—if one knew where to look.

The glint of silver as a mountain stream tumbled through the red rocks of a steep-walled canyon. The emerald green of meadow grasses unfurling tender shoots in spring. The reflection of the sun on a white-winged dove rising into the deep sapphire blue sky. A field of wildflowers, with the gold of sunflowers and poppies burning brightest.

The fiery sun, momentarily impaled on a jagged peak, fell into the cool shadows waiting beyond the western horizon. Thunder rumbled across the distance as storm-swept clouds climbed high, their towering heights rimmed with sungold. For a suspended moment in time, the sun-dried bricks of the ancient ruins glowed golden, as if *The People* still lived; the winds echoing through the stones sounding like forgotten voices; the paintings on the rock walls unfaded as a child is born, a maiden continues to dance for rain, a man plants corn, and, finally, a human sacrifice is offered to appease the gods. And the sacred beasts, the feathered bird figure and the bear striking with lightning, the creatures that soared between earthbound man and the spirits above, are captured forever in the darkness of a cave painted with the stars and the clouds.

There was magic between earth and sun.

It was timeless.

Day into night into day. And a new moon would begin its journey across the starlit heavens; a harbinger of birth, life, and death—the circle never-ending.

Nineteen

I arise from dreams of thee
In the first sweet sleep of night,
When the winds are breathing low,
And the stars are shining bright.

Percy Bysshe Shelley

ROYAL RIVERS. THE FIRST LIGHT OF DAWN BATHED THE adobe walls of the *rancho* with a rosy blush that faded to primrose as the sun began its climb above the high, snow-covered peaks of the Sangre de Cristo Mountains. Magically, as if caught in the spell of an enchantress, the walls turned golden beneath a noonday sun, then were burnished into bronze as the westering sun descended toward the Rio Grande and the Jemez Mountains, until Royal Rivers glowed crimson as the fiery sun fell into the desert sands beyond.

The icy mountain streams, more priceless than a river of silver flowing past the door, created a fertile valley where sheep and cattle grazed the grasslands and the corn grew tall, sheltered from the storm-driven winds by the dense forests of evergreens climbing high toward the timberline.

It was a peaceful valley, golden beneath the sun.

Nathaniel Reynolds Braedon had wisely chosen to build his home of adobe, the bricks, earth-harvested, sun-dried, and smoothed with mud plaster, keeping the inhabitants comfortable under a blazing summer sun and snug during a winter's howling blizzard. The architecture of the ranch house bore a distinct Spanish influence. A covered gallery stretched along the front of the rambling, one-storied, flat-roofed structure built around a central courtyard, and a low-walled *plaza* enclosed the immediate grounds, which had been cultivated with gardens and orchards and possessed a deep well of sweet water. On the back acreage, still within the safety of the walls, were a stable block and corrals, and a number of outbuildings, including a smokehouse, tannery, chandlery, smithy, barns, workshops, and living quarters for the house servants, ranch hands, and *vaqueros*. The remaining outbuildings, paddocks, and corrals were grouped close by.

Nathaniel Braedon had seen the practicality rather than the beauty of the plan when building his home; for Royal Rivers was almost a fort with its self-contained settlement behind heavily shuttered windows and thick walls. And the bell tower of the chapel served more to warn the occupants of an Indian attack than to call them to worship. Fortunately, the bell seldom sounded an alarm, ringing with a pure and peaceful clarity each morning, every noon, and again in the evening when the workers came in from the fields.

Despite its fortified appearance, the atmosphere of Royal Rivers was welcoming. Drying in the sun, *ristras* of bright red chile peppers and ears of colorful corn hung from the carved posts outside the kitchens, and the aroma of bread baking in the beehive ovens in the yard blended with the spicy steam drifting from the big pots of *puchero*, the hearty stew simmering for hours on the hearth. Generously ladled into deep pottery dishes and served with *tortillas de maíz* beaten to a thin roundness and baked on a hot griddle, no one, from the master to the lowliest hand, ever went hungry at Royal Rivers. Nathaniel Braedon, the *patrón*, had a strict rule. Anyone who worked hard could expect to eat well, whether he be a High Plains drifter helping in a roundup, and who might have ridden on by morning, a Mexican *pastor*, a shepherd spending most of his time in the hills watching his flock, or an Indian, planting and harvesting the green fields—all were treated fairly. If they had families they lived in safety on the *rancho*, the women working in the main house cleaning and cooking, grinding the corn into meal, weaving baskets or carefully shaping clay, coil upon coil, into pottery. Their children were taught to read and write in a one-room schoolhouse and, later, useful trades, as well as the traditions of their forefathers.

Past the heavy oaken doors of the entrance, the main house was light and airy with its whitewashed adobe walls and tall, deep-silled, and arch-crowned windows. The floors were of random-planked pine and brick and covered with *jergas*, the coarse woolen cloth woven at the *rancho*. The ceilings were formed of pine logs, the rough-hewn *vigas* creating a warm, secure atmosphere. On an evening chilled by cool mountain air, firelight from the raised hearth in the great hall would reflect on the silver plate and fine china set out on the long banqueting table lit by many-branched silver candelabras. Nathaniel Braedon's family and guests were served their meals in royal splendor, with fine crystal filled with the finest European wines and the best wine from El Paso, or Kentucky sipping bourbon and the local whiskey, Taos Lightning, so named by the American traders who'd first sampled the fiery brew. And any one evening, gracing a plate of English bone china, one might dine on the elegant cuisine of stuffed game hen and rice seasoned with wild herbs, or crown roast of lamb with a blanc-mange to follow, or more hearty fare of panfried beefsteak and corn dumplings. One might even find a spicy dish of *enchiladas*, *frijoles colorado*, or *chorizo picante*, hot sausage with red chile sauce, Nathaniel Braedon having many Spanish friends who were honored when served their native dishes in his home.

A *banco* built into the thick adobe wall, and piled with woven pillows and blankets, allowed for extra seating and convivial conversation. Colorful calico cloth covered the lower portion of the walls, serving as wainscoting to protect the whitewash from rubbing off. Heavy chests and straight-backed, leather-seated chairs of New Mexico yellow pine, the soft wood carved with flower-and-leaf and geometric designs, blended well with the groupings of finer and more fashionable furnishings—a mahogany pianoforte from Baltimore, a rose-wood étagère from New York, a marble-topped serving board from Boston, a cherry buffet from Missouri, a curly maple sugar chest and walnut cellarette from Tennessee, a couple of mulberry ladder-back armchairs from Louisiana, a tall clock that faithfully struck each hour, its face proudly inscribed with the name of its Philadelphia maker, and all freighted at great expense across the plains by enterprising Yankee traders.

Long passageways with inviting pine benches, and lit by tin wall sconces when night fell, opened onto the courtyard and led to the adjoining wings that housed the kitchens, a study for the master of Royal Rivers, a morning room for the mistress, a family parlor, and the bedchambers, guest rooms, and storerooms that abounded. There were always guests arriving from great distances to spend several days or a week or more enjoying Nathaniel Braedon's hospitality, or lost travelers straying into the valley and finding shelter against a sudden dust storm or early snowfall, or perhaps seeking protection from the Comanche or Apache marauders on the trail.

No one was denied sanctuary.

This was the Royal Rivers that Leigh Braedon, formerly Leigh Alexandra Travers of Travers Hill, Virginia, had first seen. It was also a place she had come to call home, and had come to love with the same fierce passion she had the mellow-bricked, green-shuttered home she'd been born in.

Leigh awakened each morning in the shadow of the mountains, her sleep no longer disturbed by a wolf's lonely howl echoing down from a high canyon, her heart beating wildly when she stood at the darkened window, staring out at the engulfing blackness of the night sky, the stars shimmering as tears fell, the loneliness of the memories of loved ones who were no more still haunting her dreams. And during those long wakeful hours before dawn, Leigh found herself wondering about the fate of the husband she barely knew and if she would ever have the chance to come to know him, to offer her love to him.

And those were the most unsettling moments, when Leigh was most vulnerable, when her self-doubts, heightened by the uncertainties of her relationship with Neil, overwhelmed the romantic daydreams of living happily ever after. Theirs was no ordinary marriage. And although they had shared a bed and become man and wife in more than name only, that had been only one night, and over a year ago. What would happen when Neil returned? Would he still want her? Leigh had worried night after night when lying alone in his bed. They both knew why they had married—and it had not been for love of one another.

At least, Neil had not taken her to wife out of love, and she would never reveal her love to him, not now that she knew about *Señora* Alvarado. Diosa Marina, the beautiful Spanish woman who had been Neil's mistress, and who had made it very plain during their first encounter at the *rancho* that she was the woman Neil Braedon loved, and had when he'd been married to his first wife. And nothing had changed, *Señora* Alvarado had warned her—except the lovely *señora* was now widowed.

Leigh sat down on the brick sill of the deep window embrasure and stared out dejectedly, not seeing the sun on the mountains as dawn broke, the light no more than a glimmer as it slowly spread across the green slopes covered in wildflowers. The pale light touched her as she sat deep in thought, her arms resting on her drawn-up knees, her bare feet tucked beneath the warmth of her nightdress.

Diosa Marina Alvarado. The Widow Alvarado. A black widow, Althea had with unusual acerbity, albeit accuracy, pronounced with a delicate shiver of repulsion after meeting her for the first time. She and her brother, Luis Angel Cristobal de la Cruz Martinez y Sandovares de Jaramijos—or lil' Louie Angel, as Guy called him—were frequent visitors to Alfonso Jacobs's ranch, Royal Rivers' nearest neighbor. Alfonso and Mercedes Jacobs were their aunt and uncle, and also Neil Braedon's former in-laws. *Señora* Alvarado, who was a very wealthy woman with many profitable sources of income, including a partnership with Nathaniel Braedon in a freight business, had a home in Santa Fe, and also enjoyed visiting the family *rancho*, which she shared with her brother, and was conveniently close for visits to Royal Rivers.

Diosa, Leigh thought uneasily. The raven-haired, sloe-eyed beauty, whose curving smile had been one of contempt, the assessing glance from her jaded eyes scornful, seemed to derive malicious pleasure in her taunts. Since that first meeting, Leigh had looked over her shoulder often, half expecting a stiletto of fine-tempered Toledo steel to strike deep between her shoulder blades, for the lovely Castilian-accented Diosa had made no secret of her dislike. Leigh wound a long chestnut curl around her fingers, wondering how she could fight Diosa. Especially when Diosa knew Neil better than she did, and was so arrogantly assured of his continuing affections. Before she had met the woman, Leigh had been so certain, if given the chance, she could win Neil's love. She hadn't had the memory of a beloved first wife to fight, to conquer, as had Camilla, Neil's stepmother. Camilla had apparently failed in her efforts to win Nathaniel's love, and had gracefully accepted her defeat, and all of the wealth generously offered her by a husband who could not give of his heart, for there were no affectionate and tender glances exchanged between them, only the courteous civilities expected of a married couple by polite society. Leigh knew she could never live as Camilla did. She could never live with Neil without his love—nor would she share him with another woman.

But was Diosa the love of Neil's life? Was Diosa the woman who possessed Neil's heart? Was that why he hadn't wanted to marry her in Virginia? Had he hoped to return to Royal Rivers and ask his widowed mistress to become his wife? Had Adam, out of a tragically misguided belief that his sacrifice would save them, give them a future, actually ruined their chances for happiness?

Suspicious as she had come to be of Diosa's motives, she'd had to believe her when the Spanish woman had confided to her that Neil had never been happily married to Serena. Leigh remembered only too clearly Adam's words spoken the day she had married Neil, and how, later, they had gladdened her heart when she had lain with him, but now they only caused her pain, for they confirmed Diosa's claim and the hurtful words she'd spoken to her in the courtyard.

"You know the truth, don't you?" Diosa challenged her, her dark eyes searching for any sign of vulnerability. "Neil was unhappily married to a woman who was in love with another man, a man Serena had secretly wed against her father's wishes, and whom she still believed herself married to despite an annulment. And poor, foolish Serena was a true daughter of the Church, and even when forced to wed Neil, she held true to the sanctity of those first vows. And Neil? Such a pity. He found himself married, but with no wife to warm his bed," Diosa told her with calculated bluntness, her black eyes glowing warmly as she spoke Neil's name possessively, her lips softening into a sweet curve, her slender hands with their long, thin fingers suddenly stilled from their usual restlessness as she caressed the golden bracelet enclosing her wrist, and perhaps a gift from a lover. "Neil is a very virile man, not one to become celibate just because his wife chooses to live the life of one martyred. *El Dorado*. The golden man. He burns like molten gold touching the flame, *sí*, or perhaps you are like Serena and have not shared his bed? It would not surprise me, for you do not have the fire that Neil desires. You mask your eyes, your thoughts. There is too much innocence in your eyes. Although wed to him, you are cold, as if untouched, just like Serena. What was he to do, married to a woman who could give him no love?" Diosa asked almost conversationally.

Then Diosa smiled that slow, secretive smile of hers, her glance self-pitying as she spoke of her own arranged marriage to a very distinguished and fine man, but a man nearly thirty years older than she, and a man who was an invalid. Neil had been alone, she had been alone, and they had sought solace with one another, their passion becoming an all-consuming love. And they had been content to meet secretly, knowing that it was enough to be together, if only for a short time.

"Then, Serena died. It was such a tragedy. I truly was shocked, for I wished her no ill. She had always known that I was Neil's mistress, and at first, she was quite content with the arrangement. Neil stayed away from her bed, and I believe they actually came to an understanding about their life together, and more and more often they spoke cordially to one another. And I had my own home and a husband who, although ill, made certain that I wanted for nothing. He was very wealthy, and well thought of in Santa Fe and Mexico. My own family comes of the true blood of Spain. I am a daughter of the *conquistadores*. I was most contented. What more could I wish for?"

Leigh had bitten her tongue, sensing that Diosa Marina would never be satisfied with what she had—she would always want more.

"Unfortunately, when Serena began to know Neil better, she made the tragic mistake of falling in love with him. Poor *Tío* Alfonso, seeing the love in his daughter's eyes when she looked upon Neil, thought the marriage was happy and that one day he would have many grandchildren. But Serena made another mistake. She had asked her father what had happened to her former *esposo*, and *Tío* Alfonso lied to her, telling her the man had died, because he thought this would finally convince

Serena to accept Neil as her husband. When Neil tells me this, and that is why Serena wishes for a true marriage between them, I know it is not true! *Tío* Alfonso sent the man money to keep him away from Serena. My brother, Luis, used to handle this for *Tío* Alfonso so Serena would never discover. So, because of this, Serena now felt free to pursue Neil. They had such a horrible disagreement, because Neil spurned her advances. Neil was in love with me, and he wanted nothing to do with her. Well, they say she rode off in a wild rage, and that was when she became lost and died so tragically. *Tío* Alfonso has never forgiven Neil. I, of course, was married, and I was no threat to Serena when she decided she wanted her husband. It was Neil's decision, not mine. *Tío* Alfonso never blamed me. I am not even certain he knew that Neil and I had been lovers. We were very discreet."

Diosa sighed, as if in great pain. "I fear, in a way, I am to blame for what happened that day. And I must share in the guilt. I told Neil that I would never see him again. Serena came to me and told me that *she* was Neil's wife, and intended to perform all of her wifely duties. She begged me to leave Neil alone. It broke my heart, but I told her I would abide by her wishes. Ah, but Neil, *sí*, was not so understanding. And we were so in love. You must understand this. Always the same argument between us. Neil wanted us to be together all of the time, not just during stolen moments. He knew that soon my husband would die, and then...if something happened to Serena...well, Neil was always so impatient.

"Sometimes, and I tell you this, but only to warn you, my dear, so you do not make the same mistake that Serena did, I think perhaps Neil knows far more than he has said about what happened to Serena. Perhaps he was there? Who can say? He could have followed Serena into the canyon. Perhaps you should ask him where he was that day. Others have. But he will not say. It would have been an opportunity to rid himself of an unwanted wife. Sometimes I believe he might have murdered Serena, knowing it was the only way we could be together. There are some who thought as much, even though most have accepted Serena's death as an accident, holding no one at fault. But *Tío* Alfonso never has. He holds Neil responsible for Serena's death. He stopped her the day she left the *rancho*.

She was in tears. Very upset. She would not stop to speak with him, but she said that everything was ruined, that she had been betrayed. What was she to do? She despaired so. And Alfonso knew that Neil was the cause of Serena's unhappiness. Even if Neil did not kill her, then he drove her to her madness."

Leigh knew that at least some of Diosa's story was true. She had heard about Alfonso Jacobs, Serena's father, leading a group of vigilantes against Neil, and it had only been because Nathaniel Braedon had stopped them at gunpoint that Neil had not been hanged. No charges had ever been brought against him in the death of his wife.

"Of course, nothing was ever proved, but to ease the tension, Neil left the territory to visit these relatives of his in this place called Virginia. While he was away my husband died from one of the many illnesses he suffered. When Neil returned, I was in mourning, and although he begged me to wed him, despite what people might say, I could not. And then, these foolish gringos have to start a war, and Neil and I are separated yet again. We would have wed then had he not left to fight in this war that has nothing to do with him. I still love Neil, even more so knowing what he might do for me…and," she said quietly, pausing for a long moment before adding in almost a whisper, "what he might already *have* done so we could be together. He still loves me, this I know. Always remember that. Serena could not come between us, could not have Neil's love, and neither shall you."

Leigh shivered, even though she sat in the warmth of the early morning sun that had risen slightly above the mountains now. Diosa's black eyes had been so full of hatred when she had stared at her, and Leigh knew what a shock discovering Neil had married another had been to her. But Diosa was no fool, and if she truly had been as close to Neil as she claimed, then she must indeed wonder about his sudden marriage—doubt it, even.

As far as Neil Braedon's family was concerned, however, she and Neil had fallen in love and he had quite naturally wanted to send his wife and her family, who were also his cousins' family, far from the ravages of the war.

And Leigh had made everyone believe that lie. She had

her Travers pride, she'd told Althea and Guy, knowing they would keep the secret of that night to themselves. But would Neil? Leigh drew a shaky breath, wondering what the truth really was. Althea and Stuart James had been right. Infatuation. That was all it had been that summer so many years ago. Neil, believing his mistress still wed to her husband, had wanted a brief affair. He hadn't really wanted anything permanent. He knew that one day Diosa's aged husband would die, leaving them free to wed. And later, when they met again, he had no choice but to wed her if he wanted to save his men, and help Adam save his family.

What did she really know about Neil? He was a ruthless man, but could he actually have wanted his first wife out of the way so desperately that he could have left her to die alone, lost in a forgotten canyon somewhere? Or was he so cruel a man he could have purposely driven her into madness? No. No, she would never believe that, despite what Diosa would have her believe.

Leigh glanced around the bedchamber she called her own—but it was also her husband's—or it would be when he returned to Royal Rivers, *if* he returned from the war. When she had first seen the room, it had been simply furnished, almost stark, which seemed a reflection of Neil. Leigh smiled slightly, for it seemed more her room now than his. Her gaze lingered on the daybed that served as a napping couch with its striped woolen coverlet, coarsely twilled and handwoven on the *rancho*, but it was cheerful and she'd folded across the foot of the narrow bed one of Travers Hill's quilts, its flower garden pattern bringing back so many memories of days gone by. The slant-top desk she'd placed near the window to catch the light was a constant reminder of her mother. She'd sat at her slant-top desk day after day, Jolie by her side, and together they'd run Travers Hill as ironfisted as any general commanding his troops in the field. A dressing chest, a manufactured piece of cottage furniture that would never have seen the light of day at Travers Hill, stood proudly now beside the great wardrobe that held her clothing, and what remained of Neil's, which she had pushed aside to make room for her own. Not finding the side chair with its rawhide seat very comfortable, she had also unearthed from the dusty storeroom a rocking chair, in which she rocked Lucinda to sleep every night. Her cradle had been placed close to the high-post bed, and often during the night Leigh reached out to rock the cradle and lull Blythe's and Adam's daughter back into peaceful slumber.

Sadly, Leigh gazed at the sleeping child.

What had seemed such madness, a hushed wedding ceremony at midnight with the Reverend Culpepper, kidnapped from his bed, performing the service with a fine show of ill humor, now made sense. Adam had understood only too well the need for such outlandish tactics, and yet, knowing Adam, Leigh knew he had thoroughly enjoyed himself that evening—especially since he had never been overly fond of the Reverend Culpepper.

Adam. Dear, sweet, noble Adam. Adam was gone. A few months ago they'd received a letter from the Draytons. After Adam had gotten them safely out of Virginia, he had gone back. He had been staying with the Draytons when he died. As he had wished, they had seen that he'd been buried next to Blythe at Travers Hill. Leigh closed her eyes for a moment, still finding it hard to believe, wishing she could banish all that had happened during the last five years—the heartbreaking years since that lazy summer so long ago.

But Adam had accepted the truth, the harsh reality of what the future held. He had known he was dying. And now she understood why he had been so determined to see Neil and her married, why he had wanted a family for Lucinda. Why he had wanted them out of Virginia, safe at Royal Rivers, with his relatives. He had known all along he would never see his daughter again, that he would not be here for her, or for Althea and her family. And he had not been blinded by tarnished glory and misplaced honor, like so many others who refused to believe; he had known they were losing the war and had dreaded the day when the South must accept its defeat, and its surrender—and its loss of pride.

They would have to accept that there would never be another summer, not like the last one—the war had changed all of that forever.

Leigh could still remember, as if yesterday, her last glance of

Travers Hill. It had looked so forlorn with its windows shuttered against the storm and trespass, the white split-railed fences fallen into disrepair, the paint faded and peeled, the pastures empty, the fields lying fallow, the woods barren and sere, the family cemetery so full of freshly turned earth and unweathered headstones. She had almost envied Guy his sightlessness as he'd sat stiffly upright in the wagon, his shoulders squared proudly as he'd stared down the road as if he still had his sight, and perhaps he had. But it had been the sight of memory, and as they left Travers Hill, he saw it the way it once had been—the mares grazing peacefully in the green fields of sweet bluegrass; the roses in full bloom, their heavy perfume scenting a warm afternoon; voices raised in laughter carried on the gentle breeze drifting up from the slow-rolling river; the family gathered together on the veranda, their mother with her ever-present needlework, peering up every now and then to make a practical comment concerning something their father had said, and their father with his tall mint julep, pausing just long enough to take a hefty swig to ease his thirst, then continuing to talk up a storm as if never interrupted.

Like refugees of the road, they had packed all of their worldly goods and most cherished possessions into the wagon borrowed from the Draytons. Adam had somehow managed to get his hands on several canvas sheets, and when sewn tightly together and stretched across the high sides of the wagon they had created a shelter to protect them from the inclement weather. They had huddled within the small confines, their trunks stacked snugly around them, the piles of blankets and quilts keeping them warm, while the team of grizzled field horses had pulled them steadily along the deep-rutted, muddy road toward Richmond. With Guy and Stephen taking turns sitting beside her on the wagon seat, Leigh had held the reins firmly in her gloved hands, the rifle propped against her knee, and close enough should they have been accosted by rebel deserters or Yankees. Adam had ridden alongside, his pistol always handy, the cow, the pony, and the mare tied to the wagon and trailing along behind. Guy's two hounds had raced ahead every so often, before jumping back inside the wagon with muddy paws and trying to sneak beneath the warmth of the quilts, their wet tails shaken in excited greeting giving them away as a roar of protest sounded from within the shelter.

They'd spent several nights on the road, sleeping one night beneath the sheltering arms of a great oak, icy rain tapping against the canvas cover, acrid smoke from their campfire floating eerily through the leafless branches overhead, while another night they'd slept in an abandoned barn, the sounds of scampering mice keeping the hounds growling warningly in the darkness, but it had been a comforting sound, and another two nights had been spent in greater comfort in small inns along the road, where other weary travelers sought shelter and human contact. It was during one of their nights at an inn that they'd heard about the most recent and terrifying escapades of Captain Dagger. He must have had a horse with wings, because he'd been seen all across Virginia, even down into Georgia, some had declared, their voices hushed, their eyes wide, as if expecting the feared raider to show his face any moment.

Leigh could remember hearing a hastily muffled snort from Adam, who'd been sitting by the fire warming his hands around a tankard full of hot buttered rum, a delicacy he'd claimed it had been far too long since he'd enjoyed. After that comment he had been far too quiet, and glancing over at him, Leigh had been reminded of the old irrepressible Adam, the Adam so full of mischief. As she'd watched him, he'd begun to fiddle with a lock of his hair, as if accustomed to it being longer, his lips twitching almost uncontrollably as he'd listened to the far-fetched stories—especially the incredulous incidents that had happened fairly recently when Captain Dagger was seen riding backward on his horse through the streets of Gordonsville, twitching that heathen braid at people, then had awakened the sleepy residents of Yanceyville at dawn when he'd raced through the town with a bloodcurdling howl that would have raised the dead, and then at Thompson's Cross Roads and Columbia, with a troop of rebels on his heels, the devil rider had actually greeted several of the town's most upstanding citizens by name, and first name at that, saying he'd see them in Church on Sunday.

Managing to catch Adam's twinkling eye, Leigh had suddenly realized exactly what he'd been chuckling about with such devilish satisfaction—especially when she remembered the resemblance between the real Captain Dagger and his cousin. She had even made that error, of mistaking one cousin for the other, years before, which had caused her no end of trouble. It had been her first introduction to Neil Braedon.

It had all come back to her; Althea's shocked discovery that a long golden curl of her hair had been mysteriously cut, and her accusing gaze at an openmouthed, indignant Jolie, who'd denied knowing anything about it and had turned an affronted back to the assembled group for suspecting her of witchcraft—which she'd given up when she'd left Charleston, she'd said huffily. Adam had found the situation extremely amusing, going into a fit of laughter, which had brought on a paroxysm of coughing. Leigh knew now where he'd gone when he'd disappeared from Travers Hill for several days after he'd arranged her hasty marriage to Neil. When he had returned, his horse lathered, his gray eyes had been feverishly bright, and his spirits had been as high as the fever Leigh suspected he was burning up with. He had shrugged off her ministrations, saying all he needed was to rest. But the very next day, he'd disappeared again, but for less than an hour this time, and when he'd returned to the house, he'd been smiling widely, as if at some private jest, which he would not share with them—except to say that Captain Dagger and his men had made their safe escape from Virginia. *And* they could now pack their trunks and be on their way, because they could be assured of safe passage through the North, because Neil Braedon would see that all of the arrangements were made for his wife and family.

They had reached Richmond without anything more troublesome befalling them than a wheel becoming stuck in the mud, the pass Adam carried never questioned, especially with Guy sitting on the seat in his gray cavalry uniform. Unable to find accommodations in the crowded capital, they had immediately boarded Adam's ship, *The Blithe Spirit*, where they had waited in relative comfort and safety to sail.

Althea, who'd suffered a slight relapse, had spent most of the time in her narrow bunk, Noelle and Steward keeping warm with her as she read to them for hours at a time from the fairy tale books she'd managed to tuck into her trunk, along with a silver-framed daguerreotype of Nathan, and a number of Steward's toys, including his wooden sword. Althea hadn't had to find precious space for Noelle's two dolls, one an old, beloved rag doll, given to her by her Grandmother Braedon, the other a far fancier bisque-headed doll dressed in a satin and lace gown beautifully stitched by her Grandmother Travers. Noelle held the two dolls tightly in her arms at all times, and sometimes was heard talking to them as if they were at a tea party.

When not in his cabin, Guy had stood for hours on the deck. One of the sailors remained close by, lest the blind gentleman lose his balance and fall overboard, but his presence was never intruding as the onetime soldier stood alone, staring out across the gray, choppy water as if steering a course only he could follow.

Jolie had taken over the galley, shoving aside a thin, nervous little man who decided it wiser to let the yellow-eyed mulattress have her own way, for she seemed dangerously short-tempered, but the crew hadn't complained, and with the first meal served them, they'd started singing sea chanties in honor of copper-skinned Jolie. Stephen's highly prized dignity, however, hadn't fared as well when lampooned in verse, especially when his green-clad livery and gentlemanly ways made him such an easy target for uncouth sailors.

They had stayed in port for little over a week, only long enough to properly fit out the schooner and load her with bales of cotton. Adam had been in good spirits, claiming that he was putting to sea with the most valuable cargo *The Blithe Spirit* had ever carried: his family. Laughing, he'd claimed that at the beginning of the war, when he'd set sail with a cargo of cotton filling her hold, all he could contract for and sell when he returned to the South were luxury goods, such as corset stays and Cockle pills. Couldn't have the ladies dressed improperly, or the gentlemen suffering liver ailments, now could he? But as the days had lengthened into years, he'd found more profit, even if regulated by the government, in shipping munitions, iron, and coal; Cockle pills somehow not quite as important as they once had been.

Leigh had questioned him about their route, and what

would happen to both the cargo and the ship when they reached the North? She knew that Confederate blockade runners, when captured by the federal authorities, were thrown into prison, their cargoes confiscated and auctioned, their ships taken into port and sold, the Stars and Bars replaced with the Stars and Stripes on the mainmast.

Adam had just grinned, saying that only happened if a runner got caught. He knew the coast too well, the U.S. Navy was easily duped, their tactics known to every captain who knew North from South on his compass, and who time and time again ran the blockade with no more than a seagull being any the wiser, and besides, *The Blithe Spirit* was too swift a lady to get caught by federal guns.

He was going to put them ashore in New Jersey. He had often made port in a sheltered cove up around Toms River, waiting for either a storm to blow itself out, or a federal frigate or sloop to disappear over the horizon. Where better to hide than in the enemy's camp? He'd told Neil about the place, and Neil had promised someone would be there to meet them. Then, and only then, would he put them ashore and set sail. He would be in Nassau, selling his cotton, and *The Blithe Spirit*, before they reached New York, he bet Leigh, holding her close for a moment. He had quickly looked away, claiming the salt spray was already beginning to sting his eyes, even if they were still in port.

The money from that sale would, for now at least, pay the taxes on Royal Bay and Travers Hill. He didn't think Blythe would mind, even if she had loved to sail aboard *The Blithe Spirit*, calling the ship her third sister.

And Adam had been right. He and his captain had known the Atlantic coastline, with its maze of uncharted coves and inlets, and late one moonless night, they had dropped anchor in a secluded cove. Adam hadn't seemed nervous until then, perhaps fearing that Neil hadn't gotten in contact with his friends, or that they hadn't agreed to help his reb cousin and his family. Leigh had watched him pacing back and forth on the deck, then he'd glanced over at her almost assessingly, and Leigh knew that he was counting on the fact that she was now Neil Braedon's wife—that would assure their safety.

He'd signaled twice, then waited. Then he'd signaled again,

but only once, and he had waited again. Then he'd signaled twice again, pausing, then signaling three times. He'd waited for what seemed an eternity, before an answering sequence of lights had flashed from the shore.

Before she could hardly voice her farewells, she, Althea, Guy, and his hounds, Noelle, Steward, Lucinda, Jolie, and Stephen had been lowered into a boat and rowed ashore. Then their menagerie, accompanying the boat when it returned to shore with their trunks, had been lowered rather unceremoniously into the cold waters; but so close to shore had Adam anchored *The Blithe Spirit* that even the short-legged, disgruntled Pumpkin, who had now been nicknamed "poop off" by the crew, which meant "small cannon," or so they swore, Damascena, her long Thoroughbred legs treading the water easily, and the cow, showing some interest for once, had made it safely to shore.

Leigh still shook her head in amazement at what had followed next. A very soft-spoken, elderly gentleman had introduced himself to her as a friend of Neil Braedon's, then he had made his introductions to the rest of her family, remaining in conversation with Adam Braedon for some minutes, then he'd quickly escorted them into several carriages. They had waited for a few moments while Adam had remained by one of the carriages, holding his daughter close for one last time before handing her through the window of the carriage. Leigh had touched his hand briefly, meeting his eyes, then he had smiled and waved the coachman on. Leigh had glanced back once, but Adam had already disappeared from sight.

After that, it had all seemed like a dream. Through the night they had journeyed, until eventually they'd arrived in New York. Their trip across the North had been as smoothly run as any military campaign, for not once had they been harassed, hindered, or detained in their journey to Kansas, where they would begin the last part of their trip to New Mexico following the Sante Fe Trail.

She'd always thought Virginia had too many railroads, but she'd been amazed at the countless and seemingly endless lines of track crisscrossing Pennsylvania, Ohio, Indiana, and Illinois. Traveling on railroads with names like Pennsylvania Central,

Cincinnati & Zanesville, and Ohio and Mississippi until finally reaching St. Louis and the Pacific railroad that carried them into Missouri.

Throughout their exodus, they had been met with civility, and kindness; by the men who'd seen them, including their menagerie, aboard each train as they'd made their way across the states of the Union; and by the families who had taken them into their homes and offered them hospitality, and friendship, when the trains had been delayed, or they'd been kept from boarding because of a troop train commandeering the rails as they sped toward yet another battle, or they'd been sidetracked because of a train bringing the wounded and dying home.

Leigh had felt some of the pain and anger draining out of her. She had come to accept these people as being no different than her own. They were families who had suffered painful losses of loved ones, whose sons, husbands, brothers, and friends had died. Their lives had been altered forever, the same as hers, yet they could open their homes and hearts to her and her family, who were Southerners.

Leigh rested her head on her bent knees, staring out on the sunny slopes, the wildflowers a rainbow of color that dazzled the eye, and suddenly the horrors of the war seemed far away, like a fading memory.

"Miss Leigh! What're you doin' up so early? You been sittin' there long, honey? Why, you must be half-frozen. You haven't even got your slippers on an' that girl hasn't lit the fire in here yet, an' I thought that Jassy was slow-footed. What're you doin' up before the sun? Now you get back in bed an' drink some of this sweet chocolate I brought you," Jolie said, setting the tray down on the bedside table.

"Just remembering, Jolie, and dreaming a little. That's all," Leigh told her, turning away from the bright sunshine beyond the windows.

Twenty

Wild Spirit, which art moving everywhere;
Destroyer and preserver; hear, oh, hear!

Percy Bysshe Shelley

"NEVER KNEW THIS WORLD COULD BE SO BIG," JOLIE SAID, shaking her neatly braided head in disbelief as she plumped up the pillows on the bed. "I don't like them mountains none. Feel like I'm bein' watched all the time," she added. "It's not natural, honey. There's strong spirits 'round here. An' they've been 'round a long time. I'm not sayin' they be good, not sayin' they be bad, but they be mighty powerful. Most people don't know 'bout them, but I've got this feelin'."

"Your big toe hurting you again? Sit down and have a cup of chocolate with me," Leigh said, patting the bed invitingly, for Jolie's big toe had been hurting her more and more of late.

"Been talkin' to that woman out back, always shuckin' corn. Never seen anybody as old as her. One of the *Ancient Ones*," Jolie said reverently. "She's got the feelin'. Says the harmony's gone. A wicked magician's disturbed the balance. Points that gnarled finger of hers to the sun, then to the mountains, the sacred ground, then makes these strange drawings in the sand. Like stars that's been scattered into the dust and broken apart. It's a bad omen. The stars, where they're the milkiest in the night sky, they're the backbone of the world. She knows, missy. An' the maize harvest wasn't good this year, she said. When you haven't corn fer the table, it's a bad day."

Curling up beneath the warmth of the blanket and coverlet, Leigh stared through the window at the mountains, which never failed to beckon her, then back to Jolie's figure. There was something comforting about Jolie with her warm coppery skin, which was faintly scented with an aromatic mixture of her favorite herb oils. Although Jolie claimed it wasn't her place to smell fancy, Leigh was always tantalized by a hint of something sweet rising from her flesh, as if she'd blended a drop or two of fragrant rose oil into the lotion. Sometimes… Jolie and Travers Hill—they just seemed inseparable. To think of one brought memories of the other. And there was nothing more familiar to Leigh than the printed calico gowns Jolie wore with the starched and pressed collars and cuffs, and tied around her narrow waist an enveloping apron of snowy white linen, which had been very handy for drying away a tear or wiping fingers stickied from the sweets she had tucked into one of the voluminous pockets; and there always had been a treasure or two hidden deep inside when Leigh had been growing up.

Jolie drew a deep breath. "Now what would your mama think if she could see me perched on this bed like I was gentry? Shame on you, missy," she scolded, but one of her hands tugged on a long strand of Leigh's chestnut hair affectionately. "You've been talkin' to Steban? That ol' man doesn't ever believe me till it's almost too late, then he moves those old bones of his fast enough to set them rattlin' up a storm. An' even he says he's never heard thunder so loud in his life, 'course, it's made him deaf, since he doesn't listen to me, *if* he ever did, an' it's goin' to take some cracklin' lightnin' strikin' him dead before he does," Jolie said, placing the tray over Leigh's lap and clucking her tongue as she ran her bony finger along the top of the table, leaving a winding trail through the fine red dust.

"Hmmmph! Jus' wiped this clean yesterday. Miss Beatrice Amelia would be fit to be tied with all this dust. Wouldn't stand for her house not bein' tidy. Your mama was that proud. Never know who's comin' callin', she always said. What're you doin' up so early anyways?" she repeated softly, eyeing Leigh closely as she poured her a cup of the thick chocolate. "Isn't that fancy fella comin' 'round, is it? I don't care for him none," she said, pronouncing harsh sentence on the unfortunate gentleman in question.

"Luis? No. Gil and I are going to ride up to the north slopes," Leigh confided, her voice full of anticipation. "The snows are melting and one of the shepherds is out of food. He can't leave his flock, so we're taking the supplies to him. I haven't been that far up the slopes yet…not into the high country," Leigh said, her gaze drawn again to the mountains.

"I don't like it. It's not safe with them savages sneakin' 'round. Reckon that lil' Luis will be mighty upset if he thinks he's goin' to find you here. But he's not the one I was thinkin' 'bout. Was thinkin' 'bout that no-good Mister Boyce. Don't care for the look in his eye none at all. Shifty, that's what it is. Like a coon that's been treed by hounds an' is tryin' to get himself outa a tight spot without losin' any of his striped tail. Reckon he hasn't seen all those stub-tailed coons I have, or he'd watch his step real careful like. Never seen a body strut like that Mister Boyce. You'd think he thought he had somethin' other men don't, an' it's not proper wearin' breeches as tight as he does. 'Spite them airs he tries to put on, trash is trash, you can't hide it, same as them Canbys. Well, he's no gentleman, an' I'll tell you this, he's no Coast aristocrat neither, even if he *says* he's from Charleston. Only way he come to Charleston was by sneakin' off a ship like a rat. Reckon he's kinfolk to that no-good Creole fella your Gran'pappy Leigh shot in that duel? Hasn't fooled me none with his honey-tongued ways, an' if he calls me mammy one more time, I'm goin' to forget I've a Christian soul an' let him have a dose of one of my potions like you did the good reverend that day."

"I didn't do it on purpose, Jolie," Leigh reminded her... although, now that she thought about it...

"Hmmmph! Figure that'll keep Mister Fancy Pants busy mindin' his own business so he'll stay outa ours. So you just keep away from him, y'hear me now, Miss Leigh."

Leigh nodded obediently, thinking no one had ever fooled Jolie. She'd always been as keen-eyed in sizing up a person as Sweet John had a horse. "It's trying to keep a proper distance from his hands that is the problem," Leigh said, remembering the way Courtney Boyce's hands always lingered a little too long when grasping her hand in greeting, or when placing her shawl across her shoulders, his fingertips just managing to touch bare skin.

"He's been takin' liberties with you, honey? You remind him you're married, an' even if you weren't, he wouldn't be good enough for you. I declare, thinkin' he could put his hands on a Travers! Wouldn't even let him set foot on Travers property. Your papa would've shown that vermin off his land fast enough, an' with his whip crackin' close behind. But if he keeps troublin' you, honey, you tell me or Mister Nathaniel."

Leigh hid her smile, wondering which of the two Courtney Boyce would prefer having to face, and she suspected it was not Jolie. "I think our Mr. Boyce is more interested in *Señora* Alvarado. She seemed flushed when they came in from the courtyard the other night. He can't seem to keep his eyes, or his hands, off her."

"Hmmmph! I don't think she's been slappin' them away none either. I saw her straightenin' that bodice of hers."

"He seems harmless enough, if a bit annoying," Leigh said, and somewhat generously, for she was almost thankful Courtney Boyce was around to interest Diosa. "He reminds me of some of Guy's old friends, they used to flirt as easily and as frequently as they emptied their juleps. Courtney Boyce is no different, he thinks every woman expects such attentions from him. It's just his way," Leigh said of the South Carolinian gentleman who was staying at Alfonso Jacobs's ranch, having arrived in New Mexico less than a year ago. Claiming that a debilitating wound suffered in battle kept him from the fighting, he had left the South and gone into partnership with Alfonso Jacobs, whom he'd met during the war. There were times when they saw very little of him, for he often traveled into Texas and Mexico on business. Odd, however, that he never seemed to suffer from the wound; his riding and shooting, dancing and swaggering unhindered by it.

"Hmmmph. Hate to see that sweet Miss Camilla taken in by the likes of him, but s'pose he reminds her of Charleston, an' her still grievin' for Mister Justin she needs to laugh, an' Mister Nathaniel, good man that he is, isn't one for small talk. Not like your papa was. An' you should see the way that lil' Miss Lys Helene takes to her heels when that Mister Boyce comes into the room. An' he won't have nothing to do with me, missy. Figure he deserves that fancy woman, an' all the trouble that's goin' to come with her," Jolie declared. "Steban says she's always watchin' him real strange like. First time she set eyes on him I thought she was goin' to up an' faint. Makes him uneasy, it sure does, 'specially her knowin' Steban's name before anybody ever said it, an' sayin' it in that funny way of talkin' that she has. Steban's scared that she's put the evil eye on him. But when she turns those eyes on me, I jus' stare her down like a fox after a chicken, an' it shames her, it does, into actin' proper. Though, how a woman who smokes like a gentleman can be considered proper, I don't know. I've never heard of such a thing 'cept in places where ladies an' decent folk don't go, an' I heard rumors 'bout them places, but never been myself," she added quickly, still scandalized by the scene of *Señora* Alvarado sitting so ladylike in the parlor while she deftly rolled the *cigarrillo* she was fond of smoking, holding the cigarette to her lips with a delicate pair of golden pincers so she wouldn't get tobacco stains on her pale hands.

"Reckon ol' Jolie knows what's goin' on behind those dark eyes of hers. Can't fool me. She's a bad one. Now, Mister Gil, he sure is a nice young man. Real polite. Miss Camilla's done a fine job raisin' that boy of hers. Doesn't remind me any of that brother of his," she said with a sniff.

No, Gil was nothing like his brother, Leigh agreed. Gilbert Rene Braedon; Gil to anyone who wished to remain friends with the lanky sixteen-year-old who was determined to prove himself a man in as short a time as possible.

"What's this?" Leigh asked, picking up a sprig of pine, its pungent scent drawing her attention to where it lay beside her napkin.

"Ever…green, missy. It'll bring you a long, healthy life, so you wear it. Tuck it in yer waistband," Jolie said matter-of-factly, as if it were something most people did everyday without question. "S'pose though, that brother of his isn't all that bad, after all, he did help us get out here," she added, but somewhat grudgingly. "An' these folks of his be real good people, even if they're not from Travers Hill. Sometimes I still can't believe we're here, Miss Leigh, wherever here is," Jolie muttered, avoiding glancing out the window as she walked to the dressing chest and began to sort through Leigh's underclothing.

"I'll show you the map in Nathaniel Braedon's study so you'll know exactly where we are and how far we traveled from Virginia," Leigh offered, and not for the first time.

But Jolie, as she usually did, just shook her head, and vehemently. "Don't want to see any map! Don't want to know how far we've come," Jolie said over her shoulder as she pulled out a fresh chemise. "Sure you couldn't have found a better dressing chest than this thing? Not near as fine as that furniture in Miss Althea's room," she complained, throwing a pair of pantalettes over her arm.

Leigh glanced around the bedchamber, pleased with what met her eye. She was very comfortable in here, and it offered the best view of the mountains rising in the distance, and at least Neil had never shared this room with his first wife. Althea and her children were sleeping in Serena's room—the room next to this one—and the room Serena had slept in alone. It was a larger room, and Camilla had thought Althea and her children would be more comfortable in there than in one of the smaller rooms. She'd graciously offered to move some of the finer furnishings into this room, but Leigh had politely declined, wanting nothing that had belonged to Serena. Camilla had sighed, glancing around the room, then shrugged her shoulders in despair and declared that Neil had never been particular about the room, having spent so much time at Riovado.

"An' I need to talk to that girl who does the washin', 'cause she's not gettin' it clean enough to suit me," Jolie grumbled, searching through the linen underclothing stacked neatly in the drawer.

Leigh sipped the steaming chocolate with its spicy aroma of cinnamon and vanilla. Sometimes, she silently echoed Jolie's earlier thought as she leaned back against the pillows, it felt as if they'd always lived here, so settled into the household routine had they become. But they hadn't, and the long journey it had taken to reach Royal Rivers would always be vivid in her memory.

Reaching St. Louis, they'd continued to travel by train to Jefferson City, where they caught a riverboat up the Missouri, their pilot and crew keeping a watchful eye for guerrillas lying in wait along the banks, their rifles trained on any traffic moving on the river. Without incident they made it to Independence, but had not tarried long, taking another boat upstream to Westport, a bustling town on the border between Missouri and Kansas, and leaving behind the familiar and comforting sight of the steepled courthouse and tree-lined square of Independence. Once, the town had been the last outpost before crossing the plains and the dangers that awaited toward sundown, but as the settlements followed the river, moving ever westward, the town was left behind to face a more dangerous threat that had arisen from the east, where Border Ruffians and Free Staters had fought in bloody skirmishes across the territory ten years earlier over the question of slavery. The violence had been only a prelude to the lawlessness that followed as bushwhackers, led by Quantrill, spread terror across the plains as they raided, burned, and looted the towns and isolated farms, while the battles fought between the Union and the Confederacy scarred the lands of Missouri and Kansas as each side sought control of the Mississippi.

They had remained in Westport several days, resting from their journey across the heartland of the Union. They expected to travel next to Council Grove, where they were to have been met by Nathaniel Braedon, but he had surprised them and was already waiting for them in Westport.

Leigh would never forget her first sight of Nathaniel Braedon. She had needed no introduction to the man to know the stranger was her husband's father. He was a tall, sinewy man with thick silvery hair, his narrowed eyes only a slightly warmer shade of greenish-brown-flecked gray, the fine lines deeply etched and fanning out around them telling their own tale of a man whose gaze continually searched the horizon. But it had been when he'd turned his sun-bronzed face that she'd seen the true resemblance between father and son, for both possessed the same hawkish profiles. She'd had the distinct impression that he'd watched them for some time before walking over to introduce himself, and she wondered what his impression of them had been. A taciturn man, he'd said little after speaking his name, but she'd felt his piercing gaze resting on her more than once. Nettled by it, she sought his, holding his stare with a slightly defiant glance for a long moment before he looked away—but she would have sworn she saw a glint of amusement lurking in his cold gray eyes.

Nathaniel Braedon had wasted little time in his preparations for their trek across the plains. He had many friends and business acquaintances in Missouri and Kansas, and despite the shortages that war had brought, and that it was spring, when so many wagon trains set out to beat the prairie blizzards and the early snows that would close the mountain passes come fall, he had little difficulty in purchasing the wagons and supplies they would need. Too often for them to discount it as just talk, they'd heard from the townspeople how lucky they were to have Nathaniel Braedon guiding them. He was an old hand at making the trip, they were assured time and again, having first come to the territories from his adventuring in Texas in the twenties, and trapping and hunting high in the Rockies, then trading and fighting with the Indians and Spanish along the border, before finally settling in his newfound land.

And now it had become their land, Leigh thought.

Fortunately, they'd had more room in their wagons than most wayfarers facing the uncertainties of crossing the plains and, eventually, the new life that lured them with the promise of a golden future. There had been no need to take up valuable space for the furnishings and household goods necessary to set up housekeeping when they arrived, or rope to their wagons' sides the building materials and farming implements that would be indispensable to survival when the settlers reached trail's end.

Their wagons had ridden light, an easy load for the six-yoke team of oxen, and although the wagons weren't even five feet wide and a little over ten feet long, there was ample room inside, with a frame of hickory bows covered in canvas rising protectively overhead. They managed to store within the wagons' narrow sides most of the comforts of home. Cooking utensils that gladdened Jolie's heart were piled in the back along with their trunks. There were big ladling spoons and butchering knives, a great pot, a kettle, and a skillet, a dutch oven, a teapot and coffeepot, coffee grinder, butter churn, and tableware, all the basics for preparing a feast—even a white tablecloth to spread over the crates and barrels for the evening meal by lantern light.

And the supplies had indeed seemed bountiful to them, when for the last four years in Virginia, sugar and flour, rice and beans, salt and baking powder, eggs, bacon, molasses, coffee, tea, and dried fruit had been at times impossible to come by.

A mound of quilts and blankets and pillows made the night's

rest come more easily on the feather beds that often were set up beneath tents, which had been folded and packed with poles, stakes, and rope inside the wagons. Lashed to the sides and wedged into whatever space could be found were barrels of water, and the tools and equipment that might be needed on the trail to make repairs: extra oxbows and ox shoes, spokes, axles, linchpins, and other necessary parts for the wagons.

Leigh had shared one of the wagons with Althea, Jolie, and the children; the baby's cradle rocking gently as the big-spoked, ironbound wheels creaked day after day, rolling steadily westward, the grease from the bucket hanging from the back axle silencing the groaning for only a few hours at a time.

The little pony, the cow, and Guy's two hounds had survived to cross the plains. The pony, already too ornery and stubborn to be inconvenienced, the cow, too disinterested to be concerned, and the hounds, too loyal to their master to complain, had fared better than Leigh thought they would. First they'd been in the hold of a ship during a storm-driven voyage off the Atlantic coast, then they'd traveled through the North alongside some of the Union's finest cavalry horses, having joined the other animals stabled in the back of railroad cars.

But once on the plains, Leigh watched in amazement as Pumpkin grew fat on sweet buffalo grass, his short legs never seeming to tire as he stomped alongside the wagon. His bosom companion, the fawn-colored Guernsey, had never shown such contentment, nor given quite so much milk; the cream rising thickly to the top of every pitcher, the rich butterfat keeping them busy churning it into frothy, sweet-tasting golden-hued butter. And Guy's two hounds had raced around the wagons, barking excitedly as they chased long-earred jackrabbits and curious prairie dogs back into their burrows; but the litter of brown and white pups, born after two months on the trail, kept the two dogs closer to the wagons at night, and growling when a coyote's howl sounded too close.

It had been the mare that had worried Leigh the most. Although she had always been a gentle creature, she was still a high-strung, easily excitable Thoroughbred. The terrors of the battlefield, where death had surrounded her, had scarred her spirit as permanently as the spur marks that had bloodied her flanks. Leigh had spent hours in the hold trying to calm her when Damascena's terrified screams threatened to drown out the roar of the sea as the storm raged around them, tossing the ship like so much driftwood. And the journey across the North had been no easier for the panicked mare, stabled in the back of a drafty, noisy baggage car.

The cacophony of the rails had driven her into wildness, with the piston-turned wheels clattering against steel and the clash of metal striking metal shuddering through the length of the train with the coupling and uncoupling of cars. Leigh placed a blindfold over the mare's eyes as the black, soot-filled smoke lit by fiery sparks billowed past the train in great clouds from the heaving smokestacks as the engine's boiler was kept fueled and the train kept rolling through the night; but the shrill whistle had pierced the darkness. It was a constant reminder to all aboard of how far from home they were—the sights and sounds assailing them no less strange and fearful to her than they'd been to the frightened mare, Leigh recalled.

But when they left Westport, Leigh began to notice a difference in the mare. She'd calmed down, her eyes no longer rolling wildly at an unexpected sound, her coat no longer lathered from the fear that covered her trembling body in sweat. Grazing each day on prairie grass with its nutty taste, and a plentiful supply of oats, her sides began to fill out and her coat once again bore its healthy sheen.

Leigh watched her stretch her long, sleek neck, raising her small, proud head, her nostrils flaring as she sniffed the air, her deep chest expanding as she filled her lungs with breath untainted by fire and smoke, and death, her delicately pointed ears twitching slightly as she listened to the breeze murmuring softly through the tall grasses of the peaceful prairie.

Leigh knew she wanted to run, to stretch her long legs, to feel the wind in her mane. They began to ride, slowly at first, and for only a short while at a time. They started out walking, Leigh's softly spoken words soothing when the mare turned skittish, but when she felt the muscles quivering beneath her, and not from fear but eagerness, they began to canter, then, finally, when Damascena fought the hand holding her reins, her hooves prancing impatiently, Leigh let her have her head, and they raced the wind across the wide land before them.

It had been a healing time for both of them. Each day Leigh watched the sun's course across the skies, feeling her blood quicken as the shadows were left behind and she lifted her face to the warmth shining down. She felt as if she could ride forever across the open plains, racing the sun until she rode it down. But, always, Nathaniel, or one of his *vaqueros* had been close behind. Leigh sometimes wondered if he'd known that if she wished, they would never have caught her. Ever aware, however, of the dangers that lurked in the tall grasses, whether an Indian, or a snake, or a prairie dog hole—that if stepped in could snap a horse's leg like so much kindling wood—Leigh bided her time, content just to feel the wind caressing her.

More circumspectly, Guy and Stephen had ridden in the wagon behind, followed by a small train of wagons loaded down with freight being shipped to Santa Fe. Nathaniel, sitting straight-backed and ever-vigilant in the saddle whether it was early morning or close to sundown, led them. A number of his *vaqueros*, attired in their short, silver-buttoned jackets and *calzoneras*—the fitted, flare-bottomed trousers—and sitting their horses straight-legged, their roweled-spurred, booted feet thrust forward in the stirrups, had ridden back and forth along the line of wagons to keep any stragglers from falling too far behind.

Leigh had wished Guy, who'd sat patiently day after day in the wagon, could have seen them, for the *vaqueros* were splendid horsemen. Their saddles had high pommels and cantles, and were richly carved, with colorful blankets rolled up behind, and their horses' bridles gleamed with silver. Their mounts were sure-footed and fast, showing their Spanish ancestry, the Arab and Barb bloodlines, in stamina and sturdiness, and their Thoroughbred lineage in speed. It was a tough-bred quarter horse they rode, intelligent and even-tempered, with its stocky, firmly muscled hindquarters giving it the ability to respond instantly to its rider's slightest weight shift, and its iron-hard hooves allowing it to carry its rider across the roughest terrain without mishap. Although Royal Bay had bred some of the finest quarter horses in the South, Leigh had never really seen one proving itself.

She'd been watching in admiration one day as one of the *vaqueros* walked his horse alongside the train, when suddenly horse and rider shot forward, the stocky horse's strides carrying his flying hooves into a full gallop within seconds. Then the rider pulled up on the reins, halting his mount and turning him on his haunches quickly, then covered the same short distance at a fast gallop; safely returning a stray steer back into the herd of cattle being driven along with the train.

After leaving the wooded banks of the Neosho River and the little town of Council Grove, which had been their last sight of civilization, the wide expanse of rolling plain had stretched before them, broken only by straggly cottonwoods climbing up from rocky-bottomed creeks. Halfway between Council Grove and the Arkansas River, they forded Cottonwood Creek, which was always a difficult crossing, but especially so when the waters were flooding after a violent rainstorm. Waiting for the waters to run off, they camped overnight above the creek's high sloping banks, the cattle and oxen herded into the shelter provided by the curving streambed. Reaching the Arkansas at the big bend in the river, they followed its course southwestward, toward the plains rising across the hazy distance, and staying within easy reach of the plentiful water supply for themselves and their livestock.

They reached the safety of Fort Larned, the dangers of Pawnee Rock left behind without even catching sight of an Indian, and crossed the tributary of the Arkansas easier than they had the countless creeks and rivers that cut through the three hundred miles of wilderness prairie between Pawnee Fork and Westport.

Leaving Fort Larned, instead of taking the northerly route along the Arkansas toward the western plains, and the numerous forts that offered protection on the trail from Indians and lawless raiders, then following the rock-strewn trail into New Mexico through the high Raton Pass, Nathaniel led them south at the Cimarron crossing of the Arkansas. Years before, on the sweep of desolate plain between the two rivers, the Pawnee, Kiowa, Ute, and Comanche had warred, and later turned their fury against the white-skinned interlopers, with the Apache striking deeper into the valley of the Canadian.

But Nathaniel knew the land; it was his land, and he rode

across it as if he dared anyone to stop him. He wasn't a man of foolhardy courage and too little caution, and with plenty of food and water, and healthy oxen to pull the wagons, and every man armed as if going into battle, he had carefully planned for any mischance.

They crossed the heat and dust of the Cimarron, the searing sweep of land and sky seeming to stretch beyond the horizon. To the southeast lay the *Llano Estacado*, the Staked Plain of west Texas, where once the great herds of buffalo had sounded like thunder rolling across the land, and to the east rose the snowy peaks of the Sangre de Cristo Mountains, which turned bloodred at sunset. Between the mountains and the high plains, the Comanche were still feared, their raids leaving a bloodstained path through the land where once they had been lords but now had become outcasts, to be driven from the land like the buffalo.

Leigh shuddered, remembering the desolateness that had surrounded them, unable to forget the lonely, forgotten crosses stabbed into the unforgiving earth, and marking another, less fortunate traveler's crossing of the Cimarron. Despite his wishes, she had accompanied Nathaniel when he'd climbed a barren, cone-shaped peak, the dead volcano giving a vantage point where he could spy out the trail ahead. Breathless, she'd stared in disbelief at the empty vastness that reached to the southern slopes of the Rocky Mountains. For as far as the eye could see, there had been nothing but a sunbaked land full of silence.

But even this inhospitable land possessed a beauty, and dawn and twilight had been her favorite times, the peaceful times when the desert air was cool from the night's caress and a delicate shade of lavender washed the eastern sky, or the blaze of a fiery sunset lingered in streaks of scarlet and purple, the earth bathed in a warm, coppery glow as the first stars of night began to appear in the darkening skies.

Only a hundred miles or so from Santa Fe, a mesa that resembled a wagon had risen from the wasteland, looking as if it were guiding the weary the last desperate miles.

Past Wagon Mound, they came under the protection of Fort Union, where two years earlier the federal troops stationed there had defeated the Confederate forces in a decisive battle in Apache Canyon. It was also where the Cimarron cutoff they had followed across the desert joined with the mountainous route wending down from Raton Pass. It was here that an Overland Mail & Express coach, pulled by a team of six lathering horses, the crack of the driver's nine-foot-long whip sounding like a gunshot, careened past, disappearing out of sight long before the dust settled from their abrupt passage. Nathaniel had shaken his silvered head, saying something in Spanish to one of his *vaqueros*, who laughed, then shot forward on his horse and scooped from the dust a gentleman's fashionably dapper, black felt hat that had blown from the stage. Leigh had seen the round-brimmed hat moments earlier adorning the bobbing head of one of the passengers as he'd leaned precariously from the window, waving to them as the stage flew past. Baggage had been piled high on top, almost hiding the man riding shotgun next to the corduroy-uniformed driver wearing a wide-brimmed *sombrero*.

Fifteen days, traveling night and day, it took, from Westport to Santa Fe, Nathaniel had told her, eyeing her curiously; they'd been on the trail for over three months.

Leigh remembered holding his gaze for a long moment, then smiling at him, and he had smiled back at her for the first time. No words had been necessary between them. They both remembered the glorious dawn that had broken that morning, and the embers of the campfire that had glowed late into the night a month earlier on the prairie, when one of the *vaqueros* had sung softly, quieting the cattle as a storm threatened with a low, distant thunder, and flashes of lightning lit the underbelly of the clouds hanging low over the plains.

And as each day passed, Leigh had seen the change in her family. It had been especially evident with Althea, who had slowly, but steadily, recovered her health. Day after day, she had rested in the warmth of the wagon, lying on the feather bed, regaining her strength until she began to sit on the wagon seat beside the driver, talking to him and tending to her sewing and mending, or watching her children, telling stories and reading to them. Before they'd reached the desert, she had even started walking with them beside the wagon for an hour each day, her appetite for each meal returning, her sleep undisturbed each night as she began to accept her loss, her grieving overshadowed by the everyday needs of her children.

But Leigh had been most surprised when Nathaniel had taken an excited Steward up in front of him on the big bay he rode. He'd ridden ahead for a short distance with his talkative, squirming grandnephew, his brother's and Stuart Travers's grandson, held protectively in his arms—the next generation of two families whose way of life was no more. And perhaps he, too, realized that. Leigh, watching them together, had worried about Nathaniel's gruffness, but he had shown an incredible amount of patience and tenderness with the little boy who had a thousand questions to ask and couldn't keep still for an instant.

Across Rio Mora, and nearly seven hundred miles from the beginning of the trail, they rumbled past sleepy settlements, Las Vegas, San Miguel, and Tecolote, the adobe ruins of the old mission church and pueblo in Pecos, then wound through the Glorieta Pass where, at the foot of the towering mountains, with a rolling plateau stretching to the valley of the Rio Grande and the distant peaks west of the river, was Santa Fe.

From the low-lying, pine-darkened hills, the adobe-walled town, with its narrow, rambling streets and central *plaza*, had seemed golden. Most of the buildings were flat-roofed and square, many, as Leigh came to learn later, built around central courtyards. The governor's *palacio*, with its porticoed front overlooking the square, and the *presidio*, a high-walled compound with barracks, prison, and parade ground, and part of the governmental complex, were the most important buildings in the town. And the cottonwoods growing along the *acequias*, the ditches that irrigated the *plaza*, seemed the only shade to be found. Just off the *plaza* the spires of the Chapel of Our Lady of Guadalupe were bathed in sunlight above the surrounding neighborhood of government offices, small businesses, parish churches, and the homes of the wealthiest citizens. Farther from the *plaza*, and across the Santa Fe River, which was little more than a creek, was the *barrio de Analco*. Most of the Indian residents of Santa Fe lived there in more humble abodes, with hard-packed earth floors and ladders propped up against the walls of their homes, the only access to the rooftop entrances.

Down the *calle de San Francisco*, just off the *plaza*, they passed a noisy old inn, *La Fonda*, that welcomed many a weary traveler who had reached the end of the trail. But they had not stopped there; instead they stayed overnight in the quiet, elegantly furnished home of one of Nathaniel's Spanish friends, where every hospitality was offered them, and where the following morning she first tasted cinnamon-flavored chocolate accompanied by *bunuelos*, sweetened fritters, Leigh remembered as she finished her chocolate and handed Jolie the last *bunuelo* on the plate.

"Have to admit, that Lupe can cook," Jolie said, dusting her hands of sugar. "Taught her a few things too, 'bout cookin' an' proper seasonin'," she said with a superior sniff and tilt of her nose. "My, my, what that Miss Effie an' your Aunt Maribel Lu would've thought of those red chile peppers we've been eatin'. Always thought your mama used too much cayenne pepper, they did. Bet Lupe's sauces could lift one of those fancy bonnets right off Miss Maribel Lu's head. Never felt better myself," Jolie declared, and glancing over her shoulder as Leigh got out of bed, she added, "an' I'm pleased to see you got some flesh on those bones, honey. Was awful worried you were goin' to blow away, you got so skinny, those bones stickin' out at every angle. 'Course, figure that's why you took to wearin' these baggy high-water breeches. Don't know what your mama would've said if she could see you dressin' yourself in these clothes. It's not ladylike, missy, showin' your ankles. Should never have let you sweet-talk Althea an' me into makin' them for you. Never thought you'd wear them. Thought I was goin' to have to fetch the salts for the Misses Simone an' Clarice, so upset were those sweet ladies, when you come sashayin' into the parlor wearin' those breeches an' that lil' short jacket," Jolie said as she held up the offending articles of clothing she'd pulled from the big wardrobe.

"It's a skirt, Jolie. And my *chaqueta* is quite proper," Leigh said in defense of the chamois leather jacket that was a feminine version of those worn by the *vaqueros*; but the only adornment was the delicate gold braid on the collar and cuffs.

"I've never seen a skirt split up the center. Baggy breeches, missy. An' mighty short ones at that."

"But very practical for riding," Leigh said, her voice muffled as she pulled her boots from the wardrobe. "Besides, who is there to see, or care?"

"Not practical if you're ridin' proper, missy," Jolie reminded her. "Surprised you haven't split yourself in two ridin' like a man does. Not decent. An' I don't like those boots any better. Never seen a lady wearin' boots up to her knees. You look like a real pretty little man, that's what Mister Nathaniel says. An' I heard him chuckle when he said it."

"Jolie…" Leigh began, her hand smoothing the soft leather of the buckskin riding boots one of the *vaqueros* had fashioned for her, and similar in style to the *botas*, the fancily embroidered, embossed leather leggings most of them wore. The boots had sturdy, slightly curved heels, and gold-tasseled garters enclosed the tops at the knee and matched the gold thread delicately stitched along the seams.

"An' I'll tell you just who there is here to care—me! I know what's right, an' what's wrong, missy. Just 'cause we're out here in this wilderness doesn't mean you can forget proper upbringin', 'cause I'm goin' to keep remindin' you. Owe it to Miss Beatrice Amelia. An' you're never goin' outside this room wearin' hardly more than a chemise and petticoat, an' no pantalettes nor corset beneath. I've seen those women. Figure that husband of yours would set you straight fast enough if he was here," Jolie had to admit, remembering how Neil Braedon always seemed to get what he wanted, even where Miss Leigh was concerned.

"It was Althea who made the pattern for my skirt. She was very clever. I can open this fold of leather and button it across the front, and another fold in the back, and no one would even know I'm wearing breeches when I'm walking. It's almost like having on an apron. Solange thought I looked quite fashionable," Leigh said, reminding her of Camilla's widowed sister's opinion.

But Jolie wasn't impressed. "Hmmmph, that one! She's tetched in the head. That's what comes of marryin' one of those foreign fellas."

"He was French. My mother had French blood."

"Not the same, honey child, 'cause he wasn't from Charleston nor New Orleans."

"He was a Parisian."

"Don't know about that. Sounds fishy to me, but Miss Solange's got a bee in her bonnet. Figure she's been out in the sun too long. Always holed up in that shed paintin', or standin' starin' at the mountains, or walkin' out an' pickin' wildflowers. Smells of turpentine half the time. An' wears that plain ol' gown stained with paint. Not natural. Can't even sew a straight stitch."

Leigh glanced at the painting over the bed, the name "Solange" signed in the bottom corner. Jolie didn't like it, nor did Althea, but Leigh was drawn to the stark landscape with its shadings of blue fading across the canvas, paling into gold above a lone butte silhouetted against the twilight sky. When she'd selected the furnishings for her bedchamber, Solange had offered her a wide choice of the paintings she'd stored in the shed. Leigh could still see Solange's surprised, pleased expression when she'd chosen this particular painting.

"No, she can't sew very well at all," Leigh said, admiring the painting. "Solange is an artist, Jolie."

"Never heard of a woman bein' an artist. A lil' sketching with watercolors is just fine. Miss Althea had a nice little book full of them when she was young. But you can't be a lady an' have paint-stained, work-roughened hands. An' if you're goin' out ridin', then you better take your hat," she said, tossing the wide-brimmed, low-crowned hat onto the bed. "An' this. It'll protect you, honey," she told Leigh as she pulled open one of the drawers in the wardrobe. "Just got this feelin'. The spirits are restless. Reckon you was meant to have it, although, I'm wonderin' what kind of luck Mister Neil's havin' now. He must sure love you, honey, to give this to you. It's mighty important to him. Keeps him safe from evildoin'," Jolie said, carefully picking up the leather pouch that they both had seen at Travers Hill that summer so long ago, and which had worried Jolie so when Leigh had opened it.

Dropping it back in the drawer as if it'd stung her, Jolie continued gravely, "Reckon that's why we be here now. I warned you, missy. Told you, I did, not to mock the spirits. They're always watchin' an' listenin'. Just waitin' to catch you. An' they've got you just where they want you now. Only wish I knew if us bein' here was good or bad," she said, risking a glance at the mountains, then turned her shiver into a shrug when another thought struck her. "But what I still don't understand is how that blue stocking showed up in this drawer with Mister Neil's clothes," Jolie muttered, not happy when things weren't in their proper place; whether it be mysterious spirits, recalcitrant people, or blue stockings.

"It must have been placed in there by mistake when we first came," Leigh lied, for she knew the truth, even if Jolie just suspected it. She remembered only too well where she'd lost that stocking—and who had apparently found it. "Things were such a jumble in here, with clothing all over the place."

"Hmmmph, still say this is the very same stocking I couldn't find nearly five years ago. Can't figure out where it's been all this time. Never yet, missy, have I lost a piece of clothing that belonged to this family. Why'd you think I had Miss Beatrice Amelia teach me those letters? So I could sew into every piece of clothing each person's mark. Always that careful with my countin' so I've always known where every stocking, chemise, an' hankie was, an' what mendin' chores needed to be done. First, I thought it must have been Mister Neil's first wife's stocking, but then I just happened to check it, an' what did I see, but your mark embroidered so sweet-like on it. Just knew that one day, your stockin' might end up in Miss Althea's drawer, or little Miss Blythe's, but I never thought I'd find it in a gentleman's drawer. Now, I asked myself, how did Miss Leigh's stockin' get in this drawer? Didn't like the answer none at all, no, sirree, even if he is your husband now, 'cause he wasn't then. I seem to remember a certain lil' honey who came sneakin' up to the big house with that same gentleman's breeches. An' I also remember you tellin' me you'd been swimmin' in the stream, that's why you were barefootin' it into the house, your pantalettes soakin' wet. Did you tell me everything that happened that day, missy?" she demanded with an accusatory huff, glancing slyly at a silent Leigh. "'Cause I want to know how he got his hands on your stocking."

But Leigh was remembering her own surprise when coming across the stocking tucked beneath a couple of clean shirts in Neil's wardrobe. She, too, had thought at first it had been Serena's stocking, but then, her curiosity forcing her to examine it more closely, she had seen the unmistakable mark of identification; the neatly embroidered *L.* Her stocking, Leigh had realized, her heart beating too fast. Neil had found her stocking by the stream that summer's afternoon, and he had kept it these many years. But why? Unless he really did care for her...

"It doesn't really matter, because he *is* my husband now," Leigh said. "And I did tell you everything that happened that day," Leigh said truthfully, for Jolie had known about the buckskins, and why she'd had them in her possession, but she'd never explained about the next day when Neil had come to Travers Hill.

"Well, if you're still plannin' on ridin' this mornin', then I'm goin' to bring you some more breakfast, an' get that slowpoke girl to fetch the bath water," Jolie said, her lower lip jutting out with displeasure as her questions went unanswered when she knew something was going on that she didn't know about—but Miss Leigh did.

When the door closed behind Jolie's stiff-backed figure, Leigh went to the wardrobe and pulled open the drawer. For a moment she stared down at the leather pouch, then picked it up. The warm, rough feel of the leather was familiar to her now, for it had been in her possession since the morning after her wedding night, when she had awakened to find Neil had left—and that he'd also left the pouch filled with his good-luck charms and mementos. It had been grasped tightly in her hand, which had been tucked beneath her cheek as she slept.

Leigh walked over to the window and stared up at the mountain peaks, tinted golden now as the sun spread its warmth across the skies. Was Jolie right? Had Neil left the pouch with her on purpose—or had he forgotten it? And if he truly believed in its protective powers, then what had been his fate now that he no longer possessed it?

Perhaps he had been wounded, or had died during one of his raids behind enemy lines? No one at Royal Rivers had heard from him in over six months.

Leigh sighed, resting her cheek against the coolness of the adobe wall, her eyes closed against the brightness as she wondered if she would ever see Neil again. And *if* he was still alive, when?

Because the war was over.

Twenty-one

Thy way is long to the sun and the south;
But I, fulfilled of my heart's desire...
Feed the heart of the night with fire.

Algernon Charles Swinburne

LEIGH HURRIED ALONG THE NARROW CORRIDOR THAT opened onto the courtyard, her steps quickening as she heard the last echoing notes of the chapel bell ringing across the *rancho* grounds. She'd promised to meet Gil in the stables by now. He'd warned her they would have to start early if they were to reach the high country and return to Royal Rivers by sundown. Through one of the low windows she glanced out on the sunny courtyard, where a profusion of colorful blooms in carefully tended beds, terra-cotta pots, and stone planters, exotic flowering vines creeping along the veranda roof, and citrus trees created a lush, almost tropical garden within the confines of the *rancho*. It was a beautiful garden, where solitude could be found on a bench hidden in a rose bower, or the family could gather on a warm afternoon in the cool shade of a wisteria-covered, trellised arbor. On those afternoons, when the air was heavy with the fragrance of orange blossoms—and memories were carried on the gentle breeze whispering through the leaves— Leigh remembered the Carolina yellow jessamine growing wild along the white, split-railed fence bordering the green meadows of Travers Hill. And she couldn't keep her thoughts from lingering there as she wondered if the daylilies had blossomed across the blue-green pasturelands, and if the old damask rose in her mother's garden had survived to bloom again. But the memories always faded into sadness, because there would be no one at Travers Hill to breathe of the sweet, clove-scented air wafting in through the opened windows.

Leigh's step slowed as she passed the French doors that led to the courtyard. They were standing open, and her gaze searched the garden for the familiar sight of a slight figure bent over a freshly potted plant, or disappearing into a tangle of shrubbery, or almost hidden behind an armful of flowers. The garden was where one could usually find Lys Helene tending to her beloved plants and flowers. The garden was Lys Helene's domain. Leigh was surprised she couldn't find her. Lys Helene preferred to work in the cool morning hours, and her gloves, pruning shears, and the big woven basket—always at hand to hold the bounty from her garden—were sitting on one of the benches in the arbor.

Suddenly the cloying scent of an exotic bloom that had opened its petals at first light floated to Leigh across the garden. It was overpowering even this early in the morning, and it reminded her of Diosa—and Leigh suspected Diosa was well aware of that. Leigh stared at the odd-shaped tree with its branches raised to the heavens as if in prayer to the ancient gods. And perhaps there was some truth to that imagery. The tree was from Mexico, and according to Diosa, who'd given it as a gift to Serena, it had been sacred to the Aztecs. They had called the tree *yoloxochitl*. Diosa, plucking a fragrant blossom and placing it caressingly against the warmth of her breasts, brazenly revealed by the low-cut bodice of her gown, called it the heartflower.

Leigh slapped her leather riding gloves against her thigh in vexation as she remembered Diosa's dark eyes becoming slumberous with remembered pleasure as she spoke of the passion the flower could induce. One delicate petal, placed beneath a pillow while lovers were lost in an embrace, could cast a spell they would never be free of—the lovers would be bound forever by that night. Touching the flower, Diosa had smiled pityingly at her, as if Diosa and her lover had shared a night such as that—and would again.

Leigh wrinkled her nose with distaste. Stepping outside the door, she broke a small sprig of orange blossom from a low-hanging bough, the light fragrance banishing the unpleasant thoughts of Diosa from her mind. Unable to resist, as if drawn by its magic, Leigh touched the small leather bag hanging from the rawhide strap around her neck—Jolie's superstitious exhortations ringing now in her ears as she thought of the talismans and wondered if they would protect her. But that wasn't why she was comforted by its feel against her breast—it reminded her of Neil. And sometimes when she wore it, she found herself hoping Jolie was right, and its magic was powerful enough to protect Neil—wherever he was.

She straightened the neckerchief of India cotton she'd tied around her throat, the wide, folded square of cloth easily hiding the pouch beneath. Putting on her hat and tipping it at a low angle over her forehead, Leigh wondered if the good luck charms the little leather pouch possessed were strong enough to protect her from witchcraft.

Leigh had almost reached the end of the corridor, and was pulling on her gloves, when she stopped abruptly. She'd just passed Guy's room when a sound startled her.

"Guy?" Leigh called to her brother from outside his closed door. "May I come in, please?" she asked worriedly, knocking sharply.

"Yes, come in," his voice came faintly to her.

"Are you ill? I was passing by your door and I heard you cry out," Leigh explained as she entered his room. "Have you had an accident? I thought I heard something crash to the floor and break."

"I'm all right, Leigh. Don't worry. It was just my usual clumsiness," Guy said with ill-contained impatience.

"You've had another attack, haven't you? It was that sharp pain behind your eyes again?" Leigh asked in growing concern as she walked over to where he lay in bed, the covers tumbled into disorder, as if he'd spent a restless night.

As she stepped closer to straighten the coverlet, she heard a crunching noise beneath her boot and glanced down to see shards of broken china scattered across the floor.

"Leave it, Leigh. Don't cut yourself," he warned brusquely.

"Guy? What have you done? Your hand is bleeding."

"Yes, *dear*, I cut myself," he commented in far too patient a voice. "Careless me. Have I dripped blood all over the coverlet? Ruined it for good this time? Spilled soup on it yesterday, and eggs the morning before. Why should today be any different? I'm just another child the maids have to clean up after," he added in self-disgust, his hand shaking as he tried to stanch the flow of blood.

Unconsciously, Leigh sighed, for Guy had been doing so

well since they'd arrived at Royal Rivers. He had seemed almost his old self. But even had he not lost his sight, he would never be the same Guy Patrick Travers. And she was glad, because she liked the thoughtful, conscientious man he'd become much better than the indolent young gentleman who'd cared more for his own needs than those of others. It wasn't that Guy had ever been truly selfish, just thoughtless and accustomed to having everything he wanted because he was handsome and amiable, and possessed the Travers name. She'd first seen the change in him when in Virginia, when he'd returned to Travers Hill from the war. And even had he not been sightless, Leigh suspected he would still have sat for hours staring blindly, a disbelieving expression on his face as he searched the darkness for an answer. But his face had contorted in anguish when he found no comfort in the reason for what had happened to him, to his family and friends, to the life they had known at Travers Hill. Gradually, though, as his wounds had healed, she'd sensed that Guy had in some way found a peace within, and he began to accept his blindness, making a valiant effort to live a normal life again.

He had seemed especially content since reaching Royal Rivers, and Leigh suspected Lys Helene had something to do with that, for she and Guy were always together, laughing, talking, walking in the courtyard or across the grounds of the *rancho*, her small hand, with a gentle firmness that might have surprised some, guiding his steps. But all of that had changed since he'd had the accident. He'd stumbled over a stool carelessly left in the center of his room and fallen and struck his head.

"I'm sorry, Leigh. Forgive me? I'm being an ass, aren't I?"

"No, just a bit of a grumpy bear of late. But you suffered a serious blow to your head, and we all understand you haven't been well. You're being too hard on yourself. No one else blames you, or expects you to be norm—" Leigh began, letting her words trail off as she touched his hand almost apologetically.

"To be normal?" he concluded for her, less sensitive to the truth than she. "Just an invalid to be cared for day and night?" he asked, grasping her hand tightly. "I won't have it, Leigh, I won't live this way, not any more, not now that I…to think that now I might—oh, what the hell, it's just another foolish dream," he swore, a note of exasperation in his voice, but Leigh caught another note.

"What is it? Is there something you're not telling me, Guy? Are you in pain anywhere else? If you've suffered some injury other than the blow to your head, then I should tell Nathaniel. He'll find a doctor," she told him, starting to pull away.

But Guy's grasp on her hand tightened more painfully as he held her by the bed. "I didn't want to say anything yet because I'm not certain. But, Leigh, for just an instant, I thought I could see again!"

Leigh tried to speak, but couldn't seem to find the proper words to say, or even if she had, should they even be words of encouragement? She didn't want him to hope for a miracle that would never happen.

Guy laughed harshly. "Oh, I know. I don't need to see your face to know what you're thinking. It is in my mind, isn't it? Wishful thinking? Maybe. I don't know. I feel so confused. But Leigh, I shouldn't still be suffering such damnable headaches. I know our mother suffered from her famous migraines, but this is quite different. My headaches do not come at my beck and call as I once suspected our mother's did. I never had a headache in my life until that concussion and wound to my head. I still have the occasional one, but not like I did at first. I swear, when I was first wounded I heard bells ringing in my ears for months. I thought I would go mad. I'm hearing that ringing again, Leigh," he confided.

Leigh didn't have the heart to tell him that the chapel bell had been ringing a few minutes earlier.

"And I'm not mad. But why am I still dizzy? I've no balance at all, and I can hardly sit up in bed without falling flat."

"Don't you remember how hard you hit your head on the corner of the chest? The chest was slammed against the wall, making a hole in it and knocking down one of the wall sconces. We actually found a small sliver of metal protruding from your scalp. We thought you were dead, Guy, you were so still and ashen. And there was so much blood. It's unfortunate you reinjured the old wound. That sliver of metal must have sliced right along the scar, making a very deep cut. Although, Nathaniel is still puzzled, since there was so much blood on the corner of the chest, and he can't see where the metal chipped off the sconce."

"I thought you told me all of my hair had grown back over that scar," Guy accused her good-naturedly as he ran his fingers through the chestnut hair that grew thickly over the tender scar slashing above his forehead. "Makes for good padding."

"Chestnut-top," Leigh said, echoing Stuart James's words of endearment spoken to her years ago. "That's probably why you weren't killed. You can't even get a comb through it without tangling it into knots. Maybe I should have one of the sheep shearers come in and cut it for you, and we'll weave the strands into a cap you can wear to protect that head of yours."

"Don't need it. The Travers family is a hardheaded lot."

"Well your head isn't that hard. It was rather difficult not to see the bump pushing up from your bloodied scalp, and right on the scar. It was awful. And that was not very amusing."

"Stephen said it was bigger than a sweet, sun-ripened plum, and just as purple."

"If you felt as bad as it looked, I'm not surprised you had a headache. And it is not unusual to have dizziness after such a blow. Or," she added slowly, "to think you were seeing bright lights inside your head."

"The last stars I saw were in the cross on the battle flag waving in front of me as I went down," he said wryly. "Listen, after I fell last week, I do admit I was delirious, and I did mumble about being able to see again. That, I know, was a dream. I never saw light then. But just a few minutes ago, when I awoke, and I opened my eyes, I felt the worst pain strike me between the eyes. The pain has never been so severe before. I felt nausea, that's why I was reaching for the bowl and knocked it off the table. Then the pain became more intense, and that incredible light seemed to brighten with each throbbing jab behind my temples. It was blinding, and it burned right through my head. Thought for a moment we were having a storm and I'd been struck by lightning, and in my own bed," he said, trying to jest about what he was afraid to admit might just be false hope, his hand reaching to touch the black patch over his left eye. "But, Leigh, when the light faded, so did some of the pain. And now, I'm seeing light and dark. I can distinguish between the two. There's a grayness, like a drifting fog obscuring my vision, but I'm no longer in complete darkness," he finally found the courage to tell her, his voice hoarse.

"Guy!" Leigh whispered excitedly, the pain of his grasp no longer hurting her. "Guy, remember what the doctors told you. They said you might regain your sight in the one eye. They really didn't know. But they did not believe there was any physical damage to the eye. They said it might take time. It could be happening. Oh, Guy, what if it is true, and you are regaining your sight," Leigh said, a low laugh of exultation escaping her as she began to believe that Guy's vision might be returning.

"Maybe that knock on the head put things back in place. Father always said he could hear my brain rattle at times," Guy joked.

"Oh, just wait until I tell Althea and everyone. They're going to be so excited. This is wonder—"

"No!"

"Of course, I'm sorry, Guy," Leigh said quickly. "You want to share the good news with them yourself."

"No, Leigh, I don't want anyone, except you, to know."

Leigh frowned. "But why? I don't understand, Guy. Everyone will be so happy."

"Even though I am not in total darkness any longer, I am still blind, Leigh. What if my sight doesn't improve beyond this?" he asked without bitterness, and hearing the sigh of unhappiness she couldn't control, he smiled. "It wouldn't be fair to get everyone's hopes up too high. I want to wait to tell them when I can see their expression, and *only* then, Leigh."

"I wish you'd tell Lys Helene. She should know before anyone else, even me," Leigh told him.

"Why?"

"Well…I thought…I mean, aren't you—"

"In love with Lys Helene?" Guy scoffed. "Why should I be? She's a very nice young woman. She has been very kind to me. She's like a…a sister to me," he hastened to say, and even though he couldn't see Leigh's expression, or meet the questioning glance in her eyes, he looked away guiltily.

"Kind? She's in love with you, Guy," Leigh told him

bluntly, wanting to reach out and pinch him to bring him to his senses.

"Is she? I think she pities me. She's even more softhearted than you. I'm like one of her sickly plants that needs a little more attention. That's all. Nothing more than that. How could there be? I'm blind. Why should she think herself in love with me? Good Lord, can't the woman get a whole man? What's wrong with her, Leigh, that she should want to spend all of her time with a helpless cripple who can't even see what she looks like?" Guy demanded angrily.

"She is in love with you," Leigh told him quietly. "You may not be able to see the expression in her eyes, but I can."

"That's just it, Leigh. I cannot see. And if I do regain my sight, then maybe I wouldn't like what I saw. And when I'm able to feed myself, and dress myself, and walk around without a guide, then there will be no reason any longer for her to hang around me," he spoke harshly, pressing his hand over his eyes as if suffering another attack. Then he glanced up, staring blindly toward the door. "What was that? I thought I heard something in the hall."

"Probably just one of your hounds trying to get in. They sneak in whenever a door is left open, especially in the kitchens. And even though Lupe yells at them, they always seem to have a soup bone or a tortilla in their mouths when they come racing out," Leigh said, glancing back at the door. It was partly opened, but she didn't see any of the pack trying to nose their way inside. "It was just the breeze moving the door," she said, turning back to Guy and staring at him in puzzlement. "I truly do not understand you, Guy," Leigh said in exasperation.

"Don't you?"

"No, you sound like the old Guy, who was very careless about the feelings of others. I seem to remember you once prided yourself on all the hearts you'd broken."

"'The old Guy,'" he repeated softly, as if that man were a stranger to him. "The old Guy Travers, although not an especially nice man at times, which I deeply regret, did have three advantages over this Guy Travers. He had his sight. He had his wealth, whether it was from an inheritance, or from the money he would earn in his law practice one day, which meant he could support himself in very fine style. And he had his home. A very treasured home. The home he was born in. Travers Hill was where I'd hoped to take my bride, and raise my future family. I no longer possess any of those advantages, my dear, and so I have no future. Or had you forgotten that?"

"Guy."

"No, it is the truth. Apparently, I can see that more clearly than you. I live here at Royal Rivers on charity because I am your brother. You are a Braedon now, not a Travers any longer, and you are a part of this family. I am still a Travers, even if I have nothing. And unless I regain my sight, I will always be an invalid. And even were I to become sighted again, what could I possibly offer a woman, especially Lys Helene? My prospects are rather limited. We lost everything. And even if Adam paid the taxes on Travers Hill, what about next time? Where will I get the money when we've no horses to sell, and the fields are lying fallow or were burned? There is nothing. I doubt I would ever be able to keep Lys Helene in the style she is accustomed to, *and not as I once would have were she to become my wife*," he said beneath his breath. "I will not embarrass either of us by asking her to marry me. And I dare say Nathaniel would be less than pleased to give me permission to marry his daughter. Probably think I'm a fortune hunter, and throw me out of his house and into the dust as fast as that fancy hat sailing off that fellow on the stage you told me about."

"And what happens if you don't regain your sight?" Leigh asked him, wanting him to face reality now. "You cannot deny that you had begun to accept that, and that you have been thinking about—"

"About marrying?" Guy concluded for her, unable to conceal the bitterness in his voice.

"Yes! You're a young man. You've a whole life ahead of you. Do you want to spend it alone?"

"Oh, Leigh, of course not. I have dreams. I may have lost my sight, but not my masculinity. I still have a man's needs. Lys Helene is a woman. Her body is fragrant and soft. Her hair, when a curl touched my cheek, was silken. Of course I've desired her, but that doesn't mean I've ever thought about marriage. I will not ask her, or any woman, to marry me," he said, his jaw set in that familiar line of stubbornness that reminded Leigh of their father when he'd set his mind to something.

"Travers pride," she said.

"Still got that, have I?" he asked, smiling slightly.

"Yes, and you may come to regret it."

"Oh? And you, have you thought about your Travers pride?" he countered.

"I thought you said I was now a Braedon?" she returned, the old sparring coming easily between them.

"In name, my dear, but you'll always have your Travers pride. It's in the blood. But what happens when your husband returns?"

Leigh glanced away this time.

"You are married, whatever the reason for that marriage. You were our sacrificial lamb, and now you must accept that fate. There's no going back for you, Leigh. You do realize that, don't you?"

"Maybe I don't wish to go back."

"To being Leigh Travers? Or to Virginia?"

"To both, maybe," Leigh said, standing and walking over to the window to stare out at the mountains.

"You love it here, don't you?" he asked suddenly, not sounding surprised.

"I'm not certain why, but I do. I loved Virginia, and I miss Travers Hill, sometimes so much I ache. And yet, I don't think I could bear to go back, to see the destruction, to know that everyone I loved is gone. At the same time though, I'm not unhappy here. I don't feel as if I'm in exile. In fact, I've never felt quite so…so, ah, I don't know," Leigh said, shrugging.

"I do. You feel free out here. You always were the rebel. You've never been like Althea, who has always been happy sitting on the veranda doing embroidery or sketching, visiting friends and gossiping, or comparing recipes and the latest fashions, or when the conversation lulled, discussing politics and literature. She's quite bright, even if she pretends to have no interest beyond her home and family. I don't think she ever felt restless. And little Lucy, although she was more like you, and she managed to get herself into trouble too many times to count, she was just high-spirited, like a long-legged colt, and she was usually following in your footsteps. She always seemed to find the fullest enjoyment in whatever she was doing, or wherever she was. Always so full of life, our Lucy. She would have been happy anywhere. And she accepted who she was. She was never searching for something else. But you, Leigh, you never seemed contented. I'm not saying you were not happy, just that you were not fulfilled. And, sometimes, I wonder if you would have found your happiness with Matthew Wycliffe. You would have been mistress of your own home in Charleston, had all your heart could possibly have desired, including a loving husband and, eventually, a family, but I think you would still have been searching for something elusive. I can't see you having tea and gossiping with your pampered lady friends everyday, or standing for hours being stuck with pins while you were fitted for the countless gowns Matthew would have bought you. Half the time at Travers Hill you walked around in that old, faded muslin of yours. I've never seen anyone so careless of fashion, and yet you always looked so lovely. You said I enjoyed breaking hearts, well, I think you enjoyed scandalizing people in the county. I can remember our mother saying how she hoped your few years at finishing school would turn you into a proper young lady—declaring it was your only salvation if you were to make a brilliant match. But whenever she'd receive those numerous reports from this Madame Something-or-other, she would begin to fan herself in growing agitation, as if about to swoon, then, with Jolie in tow, retire to her bedchamber with a migraine. Father threatened to call the woman out for upsetting his household so, muttering about the excitable French, and somehow never finding your behavior at fault. He was always proud of you. He loved your spirit, just like one of his little fillies, he used to say. But I'm not certain Matthew, much as he would have loved you, would have understood your flaunting of convention. And you're no different now. I've heard about your riding astride, and wearing those 'baggy breeches she's worn in public' an' causin' the Misses Simone an' Clarice to swoon," he mimicked.

"You've been talking to Jolie," Leigh said, but her

expression was solemn as she thought about what Guy had said. She'd never realized how perceptive he was. She'd misjudged him, even during the long, lazy days of summer at Travers Hill, when she'd thought he never noticed anything other than his own pleasures.

"Jolie's been talking, I've been listening. Which I happen to do very well nowadays."

Leigh smiled, but her lips were stiff. "Sometimes, I used to feel like the mares in the pasture. Fenced in, grazing on sweet grass while I waited for my time to foal. I had no choice, and I would have done what was expected of me. But I was tempted one morning to set those fat, lazy mares free. That wouldn't have been fair, though, because that was the only life they knew, and it wasn't a bad one. They were well fed and treated kindly, and beloved by Papa. The only thing they didn't have was their freedom. That's the way I felt sometimes. It wasn't that I didn't like my life, it was wonderful. And I would have married Matthew, and I would have been happy with him. And I promised myself that I'd make life for my family at Wycliffe Hall as happy as mine had been at Travers Hill. Those were wonderful days. And I vowed I would never become a society matron, forgetful of everything but what was considered proper. When I was little, I can remember climbing the tallest tree in the apple orchard and looking toward the Shenandoah. The mountains were so blue in the distance, shrouded in that veil of mist that drifted down into the valleys early in the mornings, and I used to wonder what lay beyond. Was that wrong of me, Guy?"

"No," he said, his words hardly more than a whisper, for he now knew the frustration she must have felt.

"I don't know how many times I've stood here at Royal Rivers, just watching the thunderclouds building over the highest peaks. And I can ride across the lower slopes, into the forests where the pines tower above the spruce and mountain mahogany. The air is so fresh and pure, especially after an afternoon shower, when everything has been washed clean. And I can ride for miles, Guy, without ever meeting another soul, without being questioned about my activities. In Virginia, I'd always meet someone, or be seen riding across a pasture by a nosy neighbor, and I'd know that before I reached home, they would already have visited and told Mama that one of her daughters had been seen riding bareback or wading barefoot along the riverbank. I can do what I want to here, Guy. You may not be able to understand, because you've always done as you pleased because you're a man. Things are different for a woman. Propriety says I must ride sidesaddle, even though I ride astride far easier, and far more safely, especially in this rough terrain. So astride is the way I have chosen to ride. I value my neck more than I do adhering to outmoded customs that might get me killed. Survival dictates in this land, not fashion. And after their initial shock at my appearance, even the Misses Simone and Clarice have come to accept that life is different out here—even for women. There is a freedom here I've never known. And yet, I've never done anything I cannot be proud of. I've not tarnished the Travers name, nor the name of Braedon. And just because I'm a woman doesn't mean I don't have any pride or common sense."

"I'm not certain I would have understood once, but now—now that I can't do as I would like—I think I can understand how you might have felt," Guy said, remembering the many times he'd ridden across the fields, forgetful of everything but his hunter clearing the hedge, and never giving a thought to Leigh, who would have been sitting back at the house, occupied in womanly pursuits. "And what happens when Neil returns?" he asked again. "He is used to doing things his way too. And he is a hard man. He's different from Matthew, or some of your other beaus, whom you could have wrapped around your little finger. You are Mrs. Neil Braedon. He may wish, and I truly cannot blame him, for a real marriage. Don't forget that. He has his pride too, my dear, and he may not be as indulgent of your newfound freedom."

"I haven't forgotten that we are man and wife, but maybe someone else has. And maybe Neil will also wish to forget," Leigh murmured, forgetting how sharp Guy's hearing had become.

"Diosa?"

"She may have more of a claim to Neil than I do, Guy."

"There is one advantage to being blind, and that is that you have to listen very carefully to what people are saying. You cannot know by their expressions if they are smiling, frowning, teasing, or lying. I sit and I listen, and I hear nuances in people's voices that they are completely unaware of. And I have heard a note of fear in Diosa's. She isn't as sure of herself where Neil is concerned as she would have you believe, Leigh. I believe your marriage came as a very unpleasant shock to her. And since I know how beautiful a woman my sister is, and Diosa is not blind, she too must suspect that as the reason why Neil married you. Don't let her jealous lies, or her own wistful memories, ruin the chance you and Neil may have to make this marriage of yours work."

"She hasn't lied, Guy. I know Neil wasn't happy with his first wife, and it's only natural he would have turned to another woman, and one as beautiful as Diosa. I cannot blame him for that."

"Well, then make certain he is happy with you, if that is what you want, so he won't have the need to turn to another woman again."

"Oh, Guy, it isn't that simple. You and I both know why Neil married me. He would have married Diosa, except that she was recently widowed and still in mourning when he left to fight in the war. If he hadn't had to marry me in order to save his men and help Adam, then, when he returned to Royal Rivers, he would have married Diosa. She expects Neil to come back to her, not to me."

"I wouldn't make any judgments about what Neil wants or doesn't want until he returns and makes that decision for himself," Guy warned her, thinking Leigh didn't know Neil Braedon as well as she thought she did if she truly believed he would ever do anything he didn't want to do. And even Adam, with his dying wish, hadn't forced him into marrying Leigh unless he had intended that all along. That much Guy knew about the man he'd once hated—and had because of that very trait of ruthless determination.

"Maybe it won't matter," Leigh said, turning away from the window.

"What do you mean?"

"Neil may never return."

"If he survived till now, he will, and probably soon. The South surrendered," Guy reminded her, still unable to believe the war between the states was over—or the chain of events that led up to General Lee's surrender of the Confederate Army of Northern Virginia to General Ulysses S. Grant, General in Chief of the Armies of the United States, three months ago at Appomattox Court House, Virginia. The date—and he would never forget it—April 9, 1865. A week earlier, the once proud Confederate capital had fallen to the Union, and once again the Stars and Stripes had been seen flying atop the domed Capitol building. But there had been no glory for the federal troops who'd laid siege to the city for so long, for the city they marched victorious into had been gutted by fire. Few of the residents, and most of those were freed slaves, remained to welcome the victors into the charred and smoking ruins of Richmond.

Unwilling to leave the factories and arsenals to the federal troops, the retreating Confederate soldiers had burned sections of the city, with blocks of warehouses going up in flames, the inferno spreading out of control through the city as Jefferson Davis and his cabinet escaped by train, leaving mobs of drunken looters and deserters running wild through the abandoned streets as panicked citizens fled to the south bank of the James River, until the main bridge was burned, cutting off their escape, then they streamed along the north bank, flooding onto the roads crowded with troops moving westward to regroup into an army and fight again.

And the fighting had continued sporadically, with many Southerners refusing to surrender and continuing to offer resistance, but it was a lost cause, and only the most fanatical Secessionists continued to fight a guerrilla war against their conquerors. Even John Mosby, the famed guerrilla fighter known as the *Gray Ghost*, had disbanded his men, refusing to fight any longer, and successfully avoiding ever having to surrender to the enemy. Quantrill, however, had been killed while looting somewhere in Kentucky, his bushwhacking days of terrorizing the countryside over.

Jefferson Davis and his fellow fugitives, having fled from Virginia into the Carolinas, were finally caught by federal troops in Georgia. Their desperate flight to Texas was over. Seeking protection in the Confederate lands west of the

Mississippi, which had still been officially at war, they had never reached the Confederate stronghold they sought, and from where they would have continued the fight with partisan warfare. Or that having failed, they would have fled farther south into Mexico, as other bands of rebels were reported doing. They were hopeful of aid from Emperor Maximilian, the Austrian archduke who was trying to bring French rule to Mexico by overthrowing Benito Juarez, president of Mexico, and at a time when the United States, because of its Civil War, would be unable to send troops to defend its doctrine forbidding European intervention in the Americas. But Jefferson Davis, under armed guard, was sent instead to Nashville, then returned to Richmond, where federal troops had restored order. The onetime president of the Confederacy reentered his capital in chains, bound for a prison cell for his crimes against the sovereignty of the Union.

It was over. The fighting at least. Now, the talk was of reconstruction. Guy sighed, wondering if there was anything left of the South to reconstruct. Certainly life would be different for many, since slavery had been abolished, and a thirteenth amendment had even been added to the Constitution assuring the freedoms first granted with the Emancipation Proclamation. The war had truly become more than a battle to save the disbanding of the Union by a Southern rebellion against Northern interference; the whole social and economic structure of the South had been changed. Guy allowed his thoughts to move deeper into his soul, and he knew that no man, whether of a black-skinned race or a white-skinned, should be the slave of another. If only enough others had felt that way, and if they'd had the time, they might have abolished slavery without the shedding of blood, without the dividing of their nation.

Guy smiled bitterly, for, oddly enough, President Lincoln had been criticized for being too lenient on the South by those who would have sought a harsher punishment for traitorous followers of the rebellion against the Union. But the man's sincerity, and true wish for a healing between the two divided peoples, had been proved to Guy when Grant, on Lincoln's authority, had offered Lee generous terms of surrender. Robert E. Lee had not been put in chains. The defeated general had been allowed to return proudly to his troops and send them home, with the promise that those who threw down their arms and fought no longer, who asked for pardon and from that day forward obeyed the laws of the Union, would suffer no retribution for the stand they had taken.

Guy shook his head in disbelief, still shocked by the singular act of violence that repelled him more than any of the other tragedies that had befallen so many during the war. The assassination of Abraham Lincoln. During the first years of the fighting, he'd hated the man who'd come to symbolize the differences between the Union and the Confederacy as much as any Southerner, but no man deserved to be shot down by an assassin's bullet. Strange to think that the assassin, that madman Booth, may have caused more harm and grief to befall the defeated South by his actions than if Lincoln had lived to see his policies carried out. Guy suspected that those who would now dictate Lincoln's plans for reconstruction, and seeking either vengeance or profit, might not be as sympathetic to the South and its people, forgetting the words spoken by Lincoln in his second inaugural address. The text had been read to him from an Illinois newspaper Althea had found spread across a seat of the train during their journey across the North. But Guy remembered as if the words had been burned into his mind. *"...With malice toward none, with charity for all, with firmness in the right as God gives us to see the right, let us strive on to finish the work we are in, to bind up the nation's wounds, to care for him who shall have borne their battle and for his widow and his orphan, to do all which may achieve and cherish a just and lasting peace among ourselves and with all nations."*

"Guy?"

"What?" he said automatically, still lost in his thoughts.

"I was saying that I have to go."

"What are you doing up so early?" he demanded, wondering for the first time what she'd been doing outside his door.

"Actually, I'm late. I was supposed to meet Gil ten minutes ago. We're riding up into the high country. We're taking supplies to one of the shepherds. Guy, are you going to be all right? I really think I should tell someone about your sight beginning to come back," Leigh said, pressing a kiss to his pale, perspiration-beaded forehead.

"It's not back yet, and until then, Leigh..." he warned.

"All right, my lips are sealed."

"Be careful," he called to her as he heard her walk toward the door.

"I will, oh, and I'll send one of the maids to clean this up."

"A good idea; Stephen would be outraged to find my room in such a mess, and I don't think I can stand having him mother-henning me any more than he already does," Guy said with a grin of amused disgust. "He's been grumbling more than ever of late, and especially about Jolie and her voodoo scaring him out of a good night's sleep, and every night."

"Don't forget to tell him about your hand so he can tend to it," Leigh called back to him as she left the room, closing the door behind her, then turning quickly, and that was when she nearly stepped on the glove that someone had dropped in the corridor.

At first she'd thought it was her own, but when she picked it up, feeling the fine grains of dirt clinging to the slightly dirtied cotton of the fingertips she knew whose glove it was. Lys Helene had been standing in the corridor, and the door to Guy's room had been ajar, just enough for her to have overheard the conversation within, and now Leigh knew what, or rather whom, Guy had heard in the corridor.

Leigh frowned slightly, wondering if Lys Helene had overheard Guy's churlish remarks concerning her hanging around him after he regained his sight. She hoped not, because Leigh did not believe Guy had meant that harsh denunciation of Lys Helene. He might have been serious about never marrying, but then that was pride speaking; the other had been fear. He might never admit it to himself, but Leigh knew he was frightened that *if* he did regain his sight, he might lose Lys Helene. What would he discover when he searched her face, a face Leigh knew he would find lovely, but would Guy see love in her eyes, or pity?

Leigh glanced out into the shadowy coolness of the gardens, searching again for the slight figure, but the garden still seemed empty, and she didn't have time now to find Lys Helene. "Well...they will just have to work this out for themselves when Guy can see the truth for himself," Leigh said to herself, dropping the glove on the windowsill, then walking toward the door at the end of the corridor, intending to let herself out into the courtyard, then through the kitchens at the far end.

"Oops!" a startled voice said apologetically as a door suddenly swung open and nearly caught Leigh on the shoulder as she passed by. "I'm sorry, Leigh. Did I hit you?" Althea asked, softly closing the door behind her with her shoulder, her arms full of bundled up papers and books. "I don't want to wake the children," she said. "It's still early."

Leigh stared at her in surprise. "Yes, it *is* early," she agreed, eyeing her sister questioningly.

"I know!" Althea laughed, her brown eyes glowing with mischievous excitement as she started down the corridor, Leigh having to hurry to catch up to her.

"Where are you going?" she asked carefully, thinking Althea must be delirious, perhaps suffering a relapse of her fever.

"To teach school," Althea replied matter-of-factly, her lips twitching as she watched the incredulous expression crossing her sister's face.

"School?" Leigh repeated.

"Yes. I can read and write, my dear, in fact I'm often complimented on my lovely penmanship, and I've some knowledge of geography, arithmetic, and history. And since I still know some of my schoolgirl's French I do not think I'll have too much difficulty with Spanish, since Lupe and the maids have been tutoring me. My qualifications seem quite acceptable to the *patrón*."

"Qualifications for what?" Leigh demanded, wondering how Nathaniel would allow such a thing.

"For teaching the children here on the *rancho*," Althea told her, squaring her shoulders as if prepared to do battle.

"But you can't—"

"Why not? Solange has been doing that for the past two years."

"But Solange is dif—"

"Different?" Althea supplied helpfully. "If being different is doing something useful, then I intend to be. And do not say I am not well," she told her when Leigh opened her mouth to object, "I have seldom felt better. I may not have proven another Florence Nightingale with my nursing skills when in

Richmond, but I think I can survive teaching children their letters. Solange wanted to paint today, especially this morning when the light bathed the mountains in a certain golden hue she said, but the children have school at that hour. I offered to teach the children for her, and if she will agree, and if I think I can do an admirable job, then I will offer to do so again."

"Well, I—"

"You what?" Althea inquired patiently, a twinkle in her eye as she saw Leigh's hesitancy.

"Nothing," Leigh said, for there was nothing improper about Althea. Dressed in a plain gown of gray silk with a lacy-edged collar, her blond hair pulled back in its usual neat chignon, she looked most respectable, even down to her sensible gaiter boots and the bonnet of gray velvet trimmed with white silk roses slung over her arm, and to be worn to protect her delicate complexion when crossing the sunny grounds of the *rancho*.

"You are worried about the propriety of it? It may not be Madame Talvande's, or our finishing school with Madame St. Juste's proper deportment classes, but it is learning, Leigh, and I want to do something for a change rather than just sit around doing needlepoint. To see those children lettering their names across a page would give me a sense of accomplishment. I've been teaching Noelle and Steward each day, so I see no difference in this. I want to repay the hospitality and kindness my family and I have been shown while we've been guests here at Royal Rivers."

"No one expects you to do that," Leigh said quickly, beginning to frown slightly as she thought about what Althea had just said.

"I know it is not expected, and that is why I wish to," Althea said with such a note of finality in her voice that Leigh was reminded of their mother when she wished to end further discussion. "Thank you, dear," Althea added as Leigh held the door for her to pass through, her steps determined as she crossed the courtyard.

Leigh continued to stand alone for a moment staring after her very proper sister before she followed Althea into the kitchens, wondering what their mother would have thought of Althea teaching school. It couldn't have been more scandalous had she started taking in sewing, Leigh thought, unable to imagine Althea doing anything that wasn't quite proper.

Gil was pacing back and forth impatiently when Leigh reached the stables, but upon seeing her slender figure hurrying across the grounds, a wide grin split his frown in two until it disappeared. He was quick to take the blame when she offered her apologies for her tardiness, explaining that he'd arrived far too early—conveniently forgetting his pacing as the chapel bell had sounded its long-drawn-out notes.

Gil seemed all leg, which he managed to find all too often as he tripped over his own feet in his hurry not to miss anything going on around him.

"Lupe packed us a lunch, and some burros to eat on our way up to the high slopes," he said, chuckling as he remembered Leigh looking around for the burros the first time he'd told her that, knowing she had no idea he was talking about rolled sandwiches made from tortillas and stuffed with meat filling. But she'd gotten even with him by putting an onion beneath his pillow one night, he thought with appreciation, although at the time he'd been highly indignant.

Gil's admiring gaze never left Leigh as she walked toward the corral, where he'd left her mount tied to the railing. She was the most beautiful woman he'd ever seen, and yet she could ride better than anyone he'd ever met—except Neil—he corrected himself, and as he remembered his older brother, the light in his blue-gray eyes faded and he ran a nervous hand through his rust-colored hair, confused by the feelings of jealousy he felt toward the brother he'd always adored until his brother's wife had come to Royal Rivers.

Kicking the toe of his boot through the dust in frustration, he pulled his hat down low over his eyes, hunching his thin shoulders in dejection as he whistled softly, his horse, Jicama, trotting over before the last notes had left Gil's pursed lips. Gil rubbed the dark bay gelding's reddish-brown muzzle. Jicama had been named after an unsightly, tuberous root that, despite its ugliness, tasted crisp and sweet as an apple on the inside.

His Jicama was like that. His dark brown coat blended oddly with the reddish-brown hair on his flanks and face, and his body was stocky, his gait stiff-legged, but he was smart and loyal, and he could climb like a mountain goat, cut any cow out of the herd, and no cougar's cry in the night had ever scared him, Gil thought, scratching the gelding's ears, and receiving a warm snort of affection against his shoulder in response.

No, he wasn't a Thoroughbred, but he was just as good, Gil thought proudly as he glanced over at Leigh's mount, feeling no envy as he admired the stallion.

Capitaine.

He could still remember when Neil had returned from Virginia early that fall over five years ago, the colt trailing behind Thunder Dancer like a pet puppy, a herd of quarter horses, roped together, following close behind the two packhorses.

Over the past five years he'd watched the colt mature into a stallion that was king of the herd. No one challenged him, and no one rode him except for Neil—and then, he'd only broken him to saddle, never riding him again. If anyone thought that odd, especially their father, they had little reason to complain, because Capitaine sired the healthiest, strongest foals to stretch their wobbly legs right after birth at Royal Rivers.

Capitaine—with his well-proportioned frame, deep chest, short back, and long, flat legs, his haunches firmly muscled, his head small, his forehead wide with intelligence—was a champion born and bred. Not a horse to be given away. He was a Thoroughbred. His bloodlines were too pure for him to be anything other than a highly prized racing horse, or a hunter for wealthy gentlemen of leisure, the rich turf of the green fields of Virginia or South Carolina flying up beneath his hooves, never the red dust of New Mexico. So how, and why, he'd ended up at Royal Rivers was still a mystery to Gil, for he was not of the quarter horse stock his brother had gone in search of in Virginia.

And Neil had never offered an explanation of why he'd bought the colt.

Gil stared at the stallion, following Leigh's hand as she caressed its long satiny neck. He still found it hard to believe what had happened that day, remembering his disbelief when Leigh, and only her second day at Royal Rivers, had suddenly broken into a run across the grounds, her flying feet carrying her to the pasture where a number of horses grazed. He'd heard an unfamiliar whistle, and not realizing where it'd come from, he'd panicked when he'd seen the big stallion suddenly gallop across the pasture, sending the mares of his harem scattering as he raced toward the fence, jumping it with an easy grace that mocked their efforts to keep him corralled.

Gil had felt his heart miss a beat when he'd seen the stallion check his stride, then change direction toward where Leigh stood, too frightened to move. But he'd been wrong. She stood unafraid. He'd called out a warning to her, his expression horrified as he imagined her being trampled to death beneath the stallion's pounding hooves, but she hadn't heard him and continued to stand there, even raising her arms to the wild stallion, as if to embrace the beast. He'd thought she'd gone mad, and he'd wondered how they would ever explain what had happened to Neil. If anything had happened to Leigh, they would have had to shoot the horse.

But it all made sense now, like a puzzle that had been solved.

Neil had never said anything about the colt, except that it was from Travers Hill, a stud farm close to Royal Bay. But the name had meant little to him, Gil remembered, until he'd met Leigh, the former Leigh Travers of Travers Hill. Now he understood. Now, he remembered the way Neil had stroked the colt, a gentleness of expression that Gil had never seen before crossing his hardened face as he spoke soothingly to the high-spirited colt. Neil had sat for hours, watching the colt, loving the colt. And yet there had been a strange sadness about Neil when he gazed at the colt, named Capitaine by its previous owners, Gil remembered thinking at the time.

Gil knew now that Travers Hill, that summer five years ago, was when Neil had met Leigh, and when he'd fallen in love with her. And he could understand that, for no man could meet Leigh without falling in love with her. For some reason, however, they had not wed, but he knew Neil, and he knew his brother had the patience to wait once he'd made up his mind he wanted something—and Neil never failed to get what he wanted. He shouldn't be surprised Neil had taken Leigh for his wife—even if he'd had to wait five years.

"Capitaine," Leigh breathed, pressing her cheek against

his muzzle as she always did when greeting her beloved colt. Although, only in her eyes was he still a colt. "Didn't think I'd forgotten you?" she asked softly as she held out the apple, his strong, high-crowned teeth closing over the treat without touching her palm except for the velvety softness of his lips.

Gently, she tugged on his sorrel forelock. "You never forgot me, did you, my love?" she murmured, still savoring the joy of their reunion, when Capitaine had come racing across the field to her whistle—and for a moment, nothing had changed, and the long years between had disappeared and been forgotten.

Although some might claim that horses have little memory, and even less loyalty—either to their own kind or to their human masters—Leigh knew they were mistaken. Capitaine had known her. And he had known his dam. Leigh had led Damascena to stand just outside the corral. The mare had nervously surveyed the field, where the strange mares and their foals were grazing peacefully. She'd neighed softly, inquiringly, but for a long moment there had been no responding neigh to welcome her. Then one of the older mares with a dun-colored coat, and a jealous disposition, had moved slowly closer at the sight of a mare unknown to the herd. Without warning, she'd charged the fence, baring her teeth to bite, her ears flattened angrily. Suddenly Capitaine had appeared and chased the disgruntled mare back into the herd, nipping her neck and flank warningly. Then he'd pranced back up to the fence, his long tail arched high, his nostrils flared as he sniffed the air for the scent that had disturbed one of his mares. It was an unfamiliar scent, and yet…one, two, three steps closer, he came, then he stopped, his beautiful brown eyes watching curiously.

Leigh had smiled when they'd touched muzzles, the bold stallion standing docile as the mare gently nudged him, receiving no punishing bite for taking such a liberty. Then Capitaine had raced away, showing his independence as he'd circled the corral with flying hooves. A minute later, though, he'd returned, walking back to stand beside his dam in companionable silence.

"Ready, Leigh?" Gil called to her, dust flying up beneath Jicama's hooves as he rode the dark bay toward the gates, a packhorse loaded down with supplies tied to a lead behind.

Gil glanced back, hearing the thundering of hooves behind him as Leigh easily caught up to Jicama. Although at first he'd been doubtful when she'd asked to ride Capitaine, he knew now there had never been any danger. And even had his father wished otherwise, which he hadn't, she was Neil's wife and had a right to his property—and Capitaine belonged to Neil.

Usually Leigh rode the mare when she went out riding around the *rancho*, and she had come to know the lands surrounding Royal Rivers as well as anyone, but when they journeyed further afield, she rode the stallion, who was far less skittish than his dam. Although Virginia-born, he was New Mexico–bred, and could climb sure-footed from any loose-banked arroyo or cross any rocky creek bed almost as well as Jicama.

They raced across the grasslands sloping away from Royal Rivers, their horses splashing through the wide stream that meandered across the fertile plain and brought life to the valley. Their destination was the northwestern end of the valley, where a canyon cut through the low foothills, climbing to a pass through the mountains.

They followed a narrow trail through the densely forested slopes of evergreens. The dark green foliage of the tall fir and spruce trees, the lower branches sweeping the ground and dusting the trail before them, blended with the paler green of delicate-leafed aspens. Stopping to share a handful of *pinnon* nuts, sweet and nutty to the taste, they startled a mule deer higher on the trail. Midmorning they rested and watered their horses by a crystalline stream. The water, icy from the melting snowpack, tumbled down from the high mountain peaks in foaming white water as it cascaded around large, smooth boulders. Sitting on the soft bank, the sunshine filtering down through shadowy branches rising high above her head, Leigh stretched out lazily, the warmth soaking into her body chilled from the coolness that lingered early in the mornings. Staring over the bank, Leigh watched the brown trout swimming in the sun-dappled waters of the deep pool formed by a natural dam, while noisy blue jays and squirrels scolded from the safety of their treetop nests.

The sweet fragrance of fir and the pungency of pine resin scented the glade, the lace-edged moss hanging from the branches creating a veil that floated around the forest clearing, shrouding it in timeless mystery; as if it had always existed, and always would.

Leaving the cool evergreen forest, the canyon veered sharply, descending down steeply toward a silvery ribbon wending through the canyon floor. The wild mountain stream was hidden behind groves of cottonwoods until it fell in a torrent of rushing water, a fine diamond-sprinkled spray rising mistily from the base of the sheer cliff. On either side, green fields of wildflowers grew in glorious profusion; primroses, sunflowers, blue lupine, asters, and countless other blooms dazzling the eye with color.

Leigh followed Gil, who followed the stream's course along the canyon floor, the terrain changing dramatically as they neared the desert floor, where the exotic blooms of the honey mesquite and the tall, slender yucca, Spanish bayonet, according to Gil, drew the eye, and thickets of prickly pear cactus kept them from straying from the trail.

An isolated butte rose forlornly in the distance, past the silvery gray sage of the plain, and, far beyond, a faint, jagged tracing of dark blue mountain range could be seen staining the pale turquoise of the sky. They crossed the stream, now no more than a dry creek bed and followed the trail across the canyon, past a sleepy adobe village that seemed lost as it barely clung to existence on the steep hillside, terraced green fields of corn and chile, and orchards of cherry and apple the only evidence of life. Gil told her, as they passed by, about the Comanche raiders who'd stormed out of the mountain passes, swooping down on the peaceful Indian settlements like wolves after sheep, and later attacking the Spanish, who hadn't fared much better even though they'd had the weapons to fight back, the same way his father had defending Riovado, then Royal Rivers. But the Comanche were like a pack of hungry wolves trailing a herd, patiently waiting for one careless mistake, a tired old buck to falter in his step, or a yearling to fall behind, and they would show no mercy, savagely attacking the helpless.

The sun was still climbing high toward noon when they reached the stand of ponderosa pine, and the highland camp of the *pastor*, one of the shepherd's dogs, a black-and-white collie, growling and barking a warning and circling closer as they rode toward the herd of sheep grazing on the summer grass covering the wide plateau.

As they rode into camp, Leigh realized why Gil had seemed to have little trouble in finding the *pastor*, for an almost overpowering odor, like damp, dirty woolens, assailed her senses, and the continual braying of the herd sounded like air caught in a broken-down pipe organ.

"Damn, Pedro, you'd think we were a couple of coyotes sneaking around your herd the way your dogs were eyeing us," Gil complained with a wide grin of greeting for the herder who was approaching. "And what's gotten into ol' Soldado? He knows me. I might expect not being recognized by the other two, they're younger, but this old guy should remember."

"Mr. Gil!" the grizzled old *pastor* called out, waving a gnarled hand in welcome. "Never do they forget Pedro at the *rancho*. *Mi patrón*, he always remembers. A good man, him. Always I know someone will come," he said, throwing the wide flap of his *sarape* across his shoulder as he approached.

"Always, Pedro!" Gil promised, for the old Mexican had been herding sheep for his father since Nathaniel Braedon had herded fifteen thousand head of sheep to the gold fields of California back in 1850. He'd invested almost ten thousand dollars in a herd of the little *churros*, first brought to the territory by the *conquistadores*, then another couple of thousand for provisions, mules, and herders. They'd headed west, toward the San Juan Mountains of the Colorado Territory, and Ute country. After some bartering, with payment made in full to the Utes for trespass on their lands, the caravan had continued without mishap the rest of the over fifteen hundred miles to the High Sierra and the wealth of the mining camps, where mutton and wool brought premium prices.

Gil grinned at the old *pastor*, for his father had made a profit of over a hundred thousand dollars on the transaction. Pedro, however, despite the money he'd pocketed, which had provided handsomely for his family in Santa Fe, had soon returned to the high country and his sheep, his only companions his trusted dogs, and where none of the everyday, petty problems could reach him, including too much tequila and a nagging wife.

Gil glanced over at the herd, some of the older sheep showing their *churro* ancestry. They were smaller and had less wool, and it was coarser. They'd been nicknamed "Mexican bare-bellies" because of that, but they were hardy and could survive the harshest winters and the hottest, driest summers, and that was why his father had bred them with European sheep, paying a high price for prize Spanish Merino rams, the crossbreed developed yielding soft, silky wool.

Gil suddenly became aware of Pedro staring at Leigh in amazement, and he quickly made the introductions. "This is Leigh Braedon, Pedro. She's Neil's wife."

Pedro pulled off his *sombrero* with no hesitation. "*Señora* Braedon? Mr. Neil's wife? Ah," he murmured, nodding his graying head as if in approval, his dark eyes unreadable in a wizened face as wrinkled as a walnut. "*¿Cómo estamos?*" he responded to Leigh's greeting, his face crinkling into even more creases when he grinned. "Is good, I think. But the *caciques demonios* will not be pleased."

"Who?" Gil demanded, dismounting.

"The old ones," he said, shaking his head sadly. "The evil chiefs. *She* calls on them," he said in oblique reference, his lips tightening into a thin line that told Gil he'd get nothing more out of the old *pastor* as he crossed himself, then held his hands up to the heavens in supplication, lest there be other gods listening.

"Well, I don't know who the devil they are, but I figure they don't have much to say about what goes on at Royal Rivers. And Neil does as he damn well pleases," Gil said, beginning to unload the bundles piled high on the packhorse. "The usual, Pedro. Beans and flour, and plenty of coffee. Lupe also sent plenty of *salsa*, and hot the way you like. Said it was the only way you could eat your own cooking. And she even prepared lunch for you," he said, glancing down in surprise at the collie, thinking he'd growled, then he laughed, for it had been his own stomach.

"That Lupe," Pedro said with a wheezing laugh as he gratefully accepted the tightly wrapped packet Leigh handed to him from her saddlebag.

"We'll get ours later, Leigh," Gil called over his shoulder, knowing Pedro would be embarrassed he might cause offense if he ate in the company of Neil's beautiful, patrician wife, and an *inglesa*, even though he knew Leigh wouldn't mind. Handing several packs to Pedro, and taking the bulk of the load onto his own young shoulders, he started toward the crudely built hut that had somehow managed to survive countless winter blizzards.

"Everything all right up here, Pedro?" Gil asked, glancing around the shepherd's campsite, where he stayed only occasionally, having to follow his herd cross-country as they grazed fresh pastureland each day until they returned to their settled range or bed-ground each night. "Soldado and the other dogs seem a bit nervous," Gil remarked as he noticed the collie circling the herd again, pausing now and again beside a couple of slightly larger black-and-brown shepherds, as if they were listening for marauding coyotes or wolves.

"Oh, *sí*, but last night, we have the big trouble with the wolves. They come down from high on the mountain, 'cause they know we got the little ones now and they like to make Soldado awfully angry, 'specially when they steal one of his little lambs," he explained. "But I shot one of them thievin' devils," he added with his almost toothless grin as he pointed toward his rifle propped against the side of the hut, and the gray carcass of a wolf lying nearby. "They don't come back too quickly. It's the coyote Soldado don't like, 'cause they too much the coward to get caught like the brave wolf."

"Did you lose any lambs?" Gil asked, setting down the bundles by the door to the hut.

"*Sí*," Pedro said sadly. "And they got two ewes that wandered off to graze. *Muy loco!* It was midnight. They eat all day long—now they're eaten. And the little ones have no *madre*. One followed his *madre* into the brush and..." Pedro said, throwing up his hands in helplessness to explain more succinctly what had been the fate of the poor lamb.

"Think the wolves are still around?" Gil asked, eyeing the silver gray carcass worriedly, his gaze moving to search the copse of pine, where too many shadows seemed to deepen before his very eyes. "Soldado acts like he knows they're out there."

"*Sí*, but we be ready for them this time. Ol' Soldado, I think he's been eating chile peppers, or...there're Apache around. Never seen him so jumpy, 'ceptin' when they been sneakin' around in the rocks. Soldado hates the Apache. They eat dog," Pedro said, frowning as he decided to keep his rifle closer at hand.

Gil looked over at Leigh, whose eyes had widened in growing dismay. Meeting her worried glance, Gil winked, for no one believed half of what Pedro said anymore. He remembered mostly the old days. Although, Gil thought, the beginnings of a frown forming on his brow, the Apache were always raiding isolated mines and ranches, Cochise never having given up seeking vengeance for his overwhelming defeat at Apache Pass. But he was hiding out in the Chiricahua Mountains most of the time, and the old Apache warrior chief Mangas Coloradas had been killed a couple of years earlier, Gil thought with a return of confidence. And last year Colonel Kit Carson and his troops had fought the Kiowas at Adobe Walls, but now that the Civil War was over, there would be more troops stationed in the territories, and the way Gil figured it, the Comanche were a problem for the Texans since they seemed to do most of their raiding across the High Plains, their war trail cutting across the heart of Texas from the Pecos River to the Red.

It was shortly after noon when they bade farewell to the old *pastor*, who stood waving to them, Soldado by his side, watching until they disappeared from view. Their path carried them along a narrow trail winding down the far side of the highland meadow, and in the opposite direction from Royal Rivers.

Gil was taking her to Riovado.

"I don't know if I ought to do this, Leigh," Gil said over his shoulder an hour later, the fringe on his buckskin jacket stirring slightly in the breeze. "It's later than I thought, and I've only been along this trail a couple of times. I haven't even been up to Riovado since Neil left. Father doesn't like any of us to come here—except Neil, of course, but it's his land."

"Why doesn't Nathaniel want you to come here?"

"Well, actually, he's forbidden it, now that Neil's away," Gil admitted a trifle sheepishly.

Leigh was indignant, urging Capitaine closer as she followed Gil and Jicama single file along the trail. "You should have told me, Gil! I wouldn't have asked you to bring me here otherwise. I knew Nathaniel would refuse to bring me. And I understand why. This is where he lived when his first wife died, and where Neil and his sister were kidnapped. But I didn't think he'd mind you bringing me."

Gil shrugged. "He thinks it's a bad place. He thinks it should be called Malvado instead of Riovado because it is an evil place. But I don't care," Gil added defiantly. "I'm almost a man now, and I can make up my own mind. You have a right to see Riovado," he said, lightly touching his heels to Jicama's sides and sending the dark bay more quickly along the narrow, rocky path.

Leigh glanced around nervously, noticing for the first time how low the sun had dropped toward the distant mountains, and how much deeper a gold the lengthening shadows were, and the air was no longer as warm.

"How far is Riovado, Gil?" Leigh asked, glancing around at the forested slopes that rose around them, the gilded crest of a cloud beginning to form above the hills in the distance and as she watched the cotton-like mounds grew higher, darkening ominously. She wasn't surprised when she heard the thunder.

Gil squinted at the sun. "Too far, I think, for us to make it there and back by sundown, Leigh. I'm sorry," he said, risking a glance back at her, his own disappointment greatest because he'd wanted to please her. But when she nodded her agreement, her smile coming easily, his spirits lifted and he squared his shoulders, glad he hadn't had to find the canyon that led to Riovado, because he wasn't certain he remembered exactly where it was, and he'd have hated to have gotten lost up there with nightfall coming, and then he'd have to explain to his father where they'd spent the night. Not that he was too worried about that, because if they'd reached Riovado, they could always have stayed in the cabin.

"I promise we'll come another day, all right, Leigh?" he asked as they turned their horses around and headed back along the trail.

"That's a promise then," Leigh agreed, glancing up as a hawk's shadow passed overhead. Shivering slightly, she decided she was just as glad they'd turned back.

"We'll stop and water our horses just the other side of this grove of cottonwoods, where we had lunch earlier. We're almost back on the trail now. Pedro's meadow is atop that ridge, but we're going to head across the clearing toward those trees and come out on the trail lower down," Gil told her as they entered the shade of the thicket, slowing their mounts down to a walk as they threaded their way through the tall, waving grasses and tangled undergrowth, the gentle murmuring of a meadow brook coming from just beyond.

"What was that?" Leigh asked, pulling up on the reins just as she reached the edge of the woods.

"What?"

"That! Didn't you hear it?" she asked, turning around slightly as she looked around, her saddle creaking beneath her.

"Probably a prairie dog or ground squirrel."

"No, it sounded like a lamb," Leigh said, climbing down and looping Capitaine's reins over a branch.

"Better be careful, Leigh. It could be a skunk, or a bear cub, and if it is, then its mother isn't far away," Gil warned as he watched Leigh walk carefully toward the nearest tree, and the thick brambles at its base.

Suddenly she knelt down, peering through the leafy growth. "Oh, look, Gil! It's a newborn lamb. Poor thing," Leigh crooned, reaching in to pick up the tiny, frightened creature, its baaing growing louder out of fear of the unknown.

"It's caught on a thorn and can't get loose," Leigh called back to him.

Gil sighed in resignation as he dismounted, not bothering to tie Jicama, who was trained to stay in place. Gil squatted down beside her, looking through the leaves at the big-eyed lamb. "Never known critters that can get themselves into so much trouble," Gil muttered beneath his breath as he pulled out his knife, nonetheless glad that Leigh had heard the pitiful thing.

"One of the ewes that wandered off from camp is probably this little fellow's mother. It would have just stood here waiting, and either died or been killed by wolves or coyotes. We'll have to take it back to Royal Rivers with us. We don't have time to go back up the mountain, and even if we did I doubt we could find another ewe to feed it," Gil said, his knife having sliced through the thorn that held the lamb captive, and lifting the shaking creature in his arms, he placed it well away from the brambles.

Before either Leigh or Gil knew what had happened, the lamb had hopped off, just escaping the arms that reached out to stop its flight.

"Damn!" Gil said in exasperation as Leigh hurried after it, unable to corner it as it shot out into the clearing, its spindly legs carrying it right toward the babbling water of the brook, obviously mistaking it for its lost mother. "Probably drown," Gil said, Leigh's laughter drifting to him as he joined in the merry chase along the grassy bank of the brook.

They'd chased the animal some distance from the grove before they finally caught it, and only because it slipped and fell into the icy water, its blathering drawing no sympathy from either Gil or Leigh as they pulled it, drenched and dripping, from the stream.

"Probably catch its death of cold now."

"No it won't," Leigh said, holding the trembling lamb close against her breast. "I've a *sarape* rolled up behind my saddle. We'll wrap it in that. This little lamb is—" Leigh was saying when she was suddenly interrupted by Gil's hoarse voice.

"Damn," he said. He stood completely still, his blue-gray eyes wide and unblinking as he stared at the grove of cotton woods where they'd left their horses.

Leigh followed his stare, her arms tightening around the lamb convulsively.

"Damn!" Gil said again, his face paling into a sickly pallor as he stared at the group of mounted Indians who'd formed a half circle in their path.

"Apache?" Leigh managed to find her voice and ask.

Gil was silent. Then he shook his head, his shoulders drooping in defeat as he thought of his rifle still in its halter on Jicama. "Comanche," he said, cursing himself for his careless-ness, and for his stupidity in ever bringing Leigh so far off the main trail without a proper escort of armed riders. His father would whip the skin from his hide for this.

He looked over at her standing there, her long chestnut hair woven with gold as the sunlight touched her, and for a moment he thought about pulling out his knife and stabbing her through the heart so she wouldn't know the terror of being taken captive, the rape and torture she would have to endure, but then he realized that he'd dropped his knife by the brambles after freeing the lamb.

Gil felt like crying, and he deserved the death that would shortly follow, but he didn't have the time for further self-flagellation, for the six or seven Comanche, who until now had been sitting patiently on their piebald and shaggy roan ponies while watching them so intently, suddenly surged forward with a bloodcurdling, wild howling that had his scalp tingling with more than fear as he felt the sweat trickling down his back in anticipation of feeling the coldness of a knife slicing along his scalp and lifting his rust-colored hair from his head.

"Come on, Leigh!" he cried, grabbing her by the arm and jerking her, and the lamb that was still locked in her arms, toward the trees, thinking they might be able to lose the Comanche just long enough to circle around to their horses—and his gun.

Gil even found himself laughing as he thought of the bastards' surprise if Leigh had been on Capitaine—they would never have caught her then.

But their escape was cut off abruptly as one of the Comanche braves, apparently the leader of the little band of raiders, ran his horse in their path, his dark thigh bared naked, rippling with smooth muscle above the deerskin leggings with their tinkling brass cones.

Gil glared up at the Comanche and tried to grab hold of the leather strap looped over the Indian pony's lower jaw, and serving as a bridle, but a feathered shield was shoved in his face, splitting his bottom lip and bloodying his nose. Gil staggered back, somehow losing hold of Leigh's arm as he fell to his knees. But he hadn't given up yet—he was a Braedon—and he yelled a foul-sounding word in the Comanche's own tongue, which Neil had taught him, and which had them momentarily startled, at least long enough for him to grab hold of the surcingle beneath one of the Comanche's saddle and give it a vicious tug, which caused the Comanche, feathers, saddle, and all, to slide to the ground, where he landed with a painful yelp, his friends laughing loudly at his misfortune.

Gil ducked, but not fast enough to completely avoid the butt end of the heavy wooden handle of one of the Comanche's quirts as it struck him on the back of the head, leaving him stunned and vulnerable to the rawhide tails slapping stingingly against his face as he tried to cover his head from further abuse.

He was surrounded now by three of the Comanche ponies, penning him in and herding him like a cow toward slaughter, he thought in growing despair as he tried to catch a glimpse of Leigh, wondering what had happened to her, and then wishing he hadn't found out when he heard her cry out in fear.

Leigh had almost reached the trees when she'd been caught. While Gil had kept the Comanche amused, she had tried to make it back to their horses, and the gun Gil had forgotten. Leigh felt a painful jerk to her head before she was spun around by her long braid of hair. The first Comanche, the one who seemed to be the leader, was holding onto it, winding it tighter around his fist.

Leigh glanced over at Gil, who was now being prodded by the Comanche with their feathered lances, the sharp saber points stabbing him whenever he stumbled. Leigh knew a fury growing inside as she thought of Gil's pain, and she dropped the lamb and grabbed hold of her braid of hair, jerking back on it and nearly causing the Comanche to tumble from his mount.

But he wasn't easily unbalanced, this young Comanche brave, and he quickly hopped to the ground, moving with a panther-like stride to stand in front of her, while his companions, still mounted, followed close behind.

Leigh stared up into his eyes bravely, her own widening in disbelief as she met and held the pale-eyed stare of her captor; for his eyes were a brilliant sky blue.

He was tall and slender, his body sinewy with corded muscle, and he couldn't have been much older than she. His features startled almost as much as his eyes had, for they were delicate, his lips full and sensuous, his nose straight but slightly hawkish. His black hair hung in long braids wrapped in deerskin, and several hawk feathers fanned his forehead from his proud scalplock, while long earrings dangled from one of his ears. A bow was slung over his strong shoulder, and a number of eagle-feathered arrows stood up dangerously from a buckskin quiver strapped behind. From his lance several scalps dangled, the long hair of varying shades, the scalps still bloodied.

Slowly, the young Comanche moved closer, drawing a broad-bladed knife from his leggings. Leigh swallowed against the fear rising from her belly, her eyes moving almost hypnotically to the pale blue eyes again, which were intent upon her as he closed the distance between them.

Leigh raised her hand to shield herself from the blow as he raised his knife, but he grabbed her wrists, holding them bound with his hand as he raised the knife in an arc and sliced down through her scarf and blouse, the knife blade a hair's breadth away from her flesh, but the cold steel never touched it, never drew one drop of blood from her bared breast.

Leigh closed her eyes as she felt the warrior's eyes on her, then she sucked in her breath when she felt his hand touch the softness of her flesh, his thumb lightly stroking the hardened nipple, then cupping the firm, pale roundness.

She heard Gil's scream and opened her eyes in time to see him struggle forward, briefly breaking free from the Comanche who'd had him surrounded while they tormented him. Gil had only managed to take a couple of steps before one of the Comanche knocked him a glancing blow with his horse's shoulder, then another had thrown his lance, striking Gil in the shoulder and pinning him to the ground.

Leigh smelled the sweat and leather, and the odor of horse, and there was another odor that came from the grease smeared over the Comanche's bare chest and arms. Leigh could bear it no more and lowered her head, trying to draw breath into her lungs. She jumped when she felt her chin lifted, her throat muscles taut as she stared into the pale blue eyes fringed with thick black lashes.

He grinned, his finger tracing along the soft contours of her cheek and jaw. He glanced back at his friends when one of them, sounding impatient, called something to him. Another had already dismounted and was fumbling with his breechcloth, his erected organ easily outlined beneath the light material that bared his tight buttocks.

Turning back to her, the Comanche warrior with the startling blue eyes, who seemed to have the right to claim her first, allowed his eyes to travel down over her full breasts. Leigh looked heavenward, but there was no comfort to be found, for the sky was a reflection of this savage's eyes, and Leigh began to struggle frantically as she felt him press intimately against her.

Suddenly she felt his body become tense. She felt the knife against her throat, and waited for the warmth of her lifeblood flowing from her throat. She waited, but she felt no pain, except for a stinging at the back of her neck. She'd heard that sometimes, when a person was mortally wounded, they died so quickly that it was often painless. But she could still feel his warm breath against her, and hear his breathing so close to hers.

A voice spoke softly.

Leigh kept her eyes tightly shut. She felt a hand touch her shoulder, shaking her slightly.

Opening her eyes, she met the blue-eyed Comanche's puzzled stare. He held the leather pouch in his palm. He was staring at the contents he'd emptied from it. Leigh suddenly felt more than just fear. She was furious. He had no right to open the pouch. It belonged to Neil. The Comanche just barely touched the single feather, the arrowhead, and the yellowed fang, and was very careful not to spill any of the red dirt. But his fingers seemed to hesitate before touching the small curl of black hair braided and woven with colorful beads, and that was when Leigh could have sworn she heard him sigh. But when he saw the tiny silver dagger, the sun crowning its hilt, he placed his palm over it for a long moment.

As if he sensed her anger, he looked up, meeting her gaze for only a second before he looked back down at the pouch. He said something angry over his shoulder, instantly halting the other Comanche's tormenting of Gil. Without questioning his command, they pulled the lance from his jacket sleeve and quickly mounted their ponies, their expressions concerned.

The talismans that had belonged to a young Comanche brave known as Sun Dagger were returned to the pouch and were handed back to Leigh, her hand limply holding the soft leather as she watched the Comanche with the blue eyes vault onto his piebald pony and without a backward glance ride back into the cottonwoods, toward the west, the rest of the braves trying to catch him as he seemed to ride faster than a cold wind blowing through the mountain passes.

Somehow Leigh managed to reach Gil, who was still lying on the ground, his buckskin jacket stained with blood, his lip becoming puffy, his nose swelling from the blow he'd received.

. "I don't understand," he said dazedly, his blue-gray eyes darkened with pain. "We should be dead. Or at least I should. And you…" He felt the hot tears scalding his bloodied cheeks, unable to finish the thought, but Leigh's warm arms enfolding him in a fierce, comforting hug made him realize he was still very much alive, especially when she kissed his bloodied cheek.

"Why did they leave?" Leigh asked aloud, staring back at the cottonwoods, half expecting them to reappear, their attack in deadly earnest this time.

"What's that?" Gil asked faintly.

"The lamb."

"They didn't take it?"

"No, nor Capitane or Jicama," Leigh said in disbelief as she heard Capitane's neigh.

Gil shook his head, then wished he hadn't, because it made the world start spinning. "My God, Leigh. We're alive," he said, still unable to believe that he was feeling only the pain of an aching head and a slight wound to his arm, for the lance had just scratched him, he realized as he lifted his arm as he tried to rise.

Leigh grabbed hold of him and helped him to his feet, where he stood unsteadily, trying to keep his balance until her arm slid around his waist and he leaned against her.

"I still don't understand," Gil was mumbling as Leigh led him toward their horses, determined to waste no more time in this wretched place.

"What's that?" Gil asked, becoming aware of the leather pouch clutched in Leigh's hand. "It looks familiar."

"It's Neil's. He left it in my possession," Leigh said, grasping it tighter. "Jolie says it possesses powerful magic," Leigh heard herself saying. "She told me to wear it this morning," she remembered, thankful she'd heeded Jolie's warnings for once.

"*Neil's?*" Gil repeated curiously. "I wonder," he said, still unable to believe that their horses were really here. He managed to climb on Jicama's back, but nearly fainted while waiting for Leigh to find the lamb and climb on Capitaine.

"Leigh?" he said.

"What?"

"We mustn't ever tell what happened. Promise me, Leigh?"

"Why?"

"I was forbidden to come here. I could have gotten you killed. Don't tell my father, Leigh. Please? I just have a feeling, Leigh, that it would cause more harm than good to say anything. We're alive. They didn't really hurt us. Why cause trouble? It will just bring up old memories for my father. You see, I think those Comanche must have recognized that pouch of Neil's. They knew it belonged to a Comanche brave. They honored it, maybe even honored Neil. He might be remembered in the tribe. We can't say anything. If my father knew they were here, on his land, he'd go after them, maybe get killed. And what would that do to Neil? It's best forgotten. I'll say I took a tumble from Jicama. Leigh?" he questioned.

"All right, Gil. I'll say nothing," Leigh agreed, feeling a strange sense of foreboding, but then they were riding across the meadow, the sun shining down warmly on them.

Royal Rivers. Even in the darkness it was welcoming, she thought in growing excitement as they neared the opened gates. Then she realized why. It seemed as if the night were on fire, for countless torches were blazing across the grounds, the flames flickering eerily, with a smoky haze hanging low over the darker shapes of human and animal forms wandering about. Men and horses. They were grouping together near the corrals, ready to ride out in search of Gil and her.

Leigh caught Gil's pleading gaze on her, and she nodded. She wouldn't break her promise to him about what had happened. No one would ever know of their encounter with the Comanche braves.

She saw Nathaniel approaching out of one of the pools of darkness, his lean figure seeming taller than ever, the torchlight dancing around him as if he had stepped from the fires of hell, his long-legged, unhurried stride bringing him closer to where she still sat her horse. Even though she and Gil might have an uncomfortable few moments explaining themselves to him, she was glad she was home, she thought, closing her eyes tiredly.

Leigh never saw the arms that reached up and lifted the lamb from its snug perch across her lap, baaing loudly as it was taken from the warmth of its newly adopted mother. Leigh was about to dismount when the arms returned and easily lifted her from the saddle. She didn't think her legs would hold her when her boots touched the ground, but they never did, and instead she was swung up into the strong arms and held against the warmth of a broad chest as she felt herself being carried away from the corrals.

Leigh opened her eyes then, ready to protest that she could walk and Gil needed more help than she did, and she had things to do before she—but she found herself gazing up into a pair of cold, pale gray-green eyes. It was Neil Braedon who held her, not his father.

Twenty-two

Never seek to tell thy love
Love that never told can be;
For the gentle wind does move
Silently, invisibly.

William Blake

"LEIGH."

Her name came soft as a whisper to his lips, and even over the clamor surrounding them she heard his voice and glanced up into his face, still disbelieving that he was here, that he had returned to Royal Rivers, that he held her in his arms once again.

"*Once again*," he said, seeming to speak aloud her innermost thoughts, "we meet, and never as I would have imagined. But then you always have come upon me in unguarded moments, when I am most vulnerable," he murmured in greeting, the pale eyes becoming shadowed as his gaze rested on the pallor of her face. In the flickering torchlight, her flesh seemed as smooth as carven ivory. He reached out to caress the curving line of ashen cheek and was startled by its coldness. He found himself thinking of a stone effigy he'd seen on an ancient noble-woman's tomb—cold, unresponsive, forever lost to life—and his arms tightened protectively around Leigh's chilled body, holding her close against the wild beating of his heart as if he'd had a disturbing premonition of yet another parting that would separate them—and perhaps permanently this time.

Leigh felt the strength of the arms holding her, the heat of his body warming her, and she felt as if she, too, had somehow come home. For a long moment, she stared up into his face, the hawkish features so familiar, so beloved, yet his expression was strangely somber, and she wondered if he would always be a stranger to her. Would there never be a moment in time when they met with a singleness of mind, oneness of body and spirit?

Something of those deep yearnings must have crossed her

face, perhaps only for a fleeting instant, but Neil suddenly felt himself drawn into her as if he were already touching the warmth and softness of this woman he loved.

"Thank goodness, you have returned!" Camilla cried, hurrying up to them in a rustle of silken skirts that disturbed the silence that had fallen around them, holding them enthralled.

Camilla Braedon had never been considered beautiful. She was short, with dull reddish-brown hair that was turning gray and had been pulled back into an unflattering, albeit neat, chignon. Her features were unremarkable, and childbirth and the years of living a pampered life had added a slight plumpness to her face and figure, but it was not unsightly, and actually seemed to become her, for she was a warm and vibrant woman who loved to mother everyone.

That was why Camilla was considered beautiful by those who knew and loved her. She possessed an inner beauty that would never fade. It emanated from her, shining through her cornflower blue eyes and creating an aura of beauty that others with perfectly featured, cameo faces would never possess. "We have been so worried. When you did not return in the afternoon, I knew something tragic must have happened. And, *mon Dieu*, but it has been a long afternoon, especially with that Jolie so silent, pausing as if she heard voices none of us could hear, then she would begin to mutter those strange incantations as if death were lurking over her shoulder, and it very nearly did, because she walked up so softly behind Stephen she nearly scared the poor man to death. And the aunts have been in a dither all day long and I have been beside myself trying to calm the little dears down, for they have become so fond of you, Leigh. And you know how easily upset they become when their daily routine is altered.

"But Nathaniel was not worried. When you were not here by sundown, then, he begins to worry, because he knows his son would not disobey him and go anywhere other than the *pastor's* camp, especially with Leigh accompanying him into the high country. My son is no fool, and he fears his father's wrath. So, we wait a little longer, but still you do not arrive, and Nathaniel is about to set out in search of you when in rides Neil. I could scarcely believe my eyes, or my ears when

Jolie says she knew *he'd* be coming. Heard Thunder, she said, although I don't know how she could possibly have heard Neil's horse, Thunder Dancer, so far away. But I have come to believe she knows what she is talking about; *that one* has the gift. My mama knew their kind when she lived in Santo Domingo. You think she might be Haitian?" Camilla asked nervously, then smiled, touching their arms as if reassuring herself that they were both there beside her. "I was so happy to see Neil again, and always I remember that first time I saw him—and see!" she exclaimed, reaching up to touch the thick braid of golden hair. "It is the same as then," she declared, glancing over nervously at Nathaniel, who had not been pleased to see his son wearing his hair like a Comanche, even if he was a man full grown and could do as he pleased. For she also remembered the battle of wills that had followed for months afterward between Nathaniel and his fourteen-year-old son after Nathaniel had cut the damning braid from his son's golden head, but this time—if the braid was cut—it would have to be by Neil's own hand.

"It was not a happy homecoming for my poor Neil when he discovered his beloved wife is missing. I was so upset, and then the look on his face upsets me even more," she said with genuine affection for her stepson, although when she looked at him, she knew a deep sadness in her heart for the loss of her own son, her dearest Justin, who had resembled his father, and Neil, and would never return to Royal Rivers.

"I should never have allowed you to ride with Gil, not that he wouldn't have protected you, for my son is very brave, like his papa and his brothers, but it was not proper for you to ride so far from Royal Rivers. You were given into our protection by Neil, and it was our duty to see that no harm came to you. It was easy enough in winter Leigh, when you had to stay indoors because of the snows, but now it is spring, and you ride all the time, everyday, and never will you ride in the carriage with me when I visit my friends," she said, throwing up her hands as if she did not know what to do with so headstrong a young woman. "You will have to be very strict with this one, Neil, or you will never have a moment's peace—never knowing where your beloved is."

"I know exactly where she is," he said, not in any hurry to release the warm body in his arms.

"Let me down," Leigh said, loud enough for his ears alone, her heart pounding as she realized he had not denied she was his beloved. Although she protested, Leigh was happy to stay in his arms, their touch making it easier to forget the terror of the afternoon when another pair of arms had closed around her.

"But to have Neil arrive home at exactly such a moment, aah, I could not bear to face him, knowing how deeply in love the two of you are. And for Leigh it was tragic too. She should have been here to welcome you home, Neil. She has pined away for you, and thought of nothing but you day after day, and that is because she loves you so. And why should she not? I have heard of the romantic marriage at midnight, how you swept her off her feet with such fiery protestations of love and, to claim her for your bride, had to force that poor preacher man out of his warm bed. Ah, that Adam, I remember him. Always the jester. Ah, but he was a good boy, and we will always take care of his precious *bébé*. Ooh lah!" she said, laughing, for she had loved the romance of it all, and had exaggerated Leigh's story a trifle, and now to see Leigh's face flaming with embarrassment before she turned it away from Neil's gaze caused her no end of delight. "But true love will not be denied, and Neil is a man who will do as he sees fit. And he is the bold one. How could he leave his wife in danger, and not send her to us when we have such a big house and so much food, and so many brave men to protect us? And we have come to love her and her family so. Ah, and to have the little ones here, their voices filling the house with laughter again," Camilla said, wiping away a tear of happiness. "And soon, maybe, we will have more little ones in our home? And I will be their grandmama," she said, eyeing them hopefully. "I would never have forgiven you, Neil, had you not seen fit to marry this beautiful child. But why you did not do it four years earlier than you did, when in Virginia to buy horses, I do not know."

"Neither do I, ma'am," Neil said softly, holding Leigh closer, his grip becoming almost punishingly painful against her ribs, for they both remembered the reasons why he had not married her five years ago—she had chosen another. And they both knew the reasons why he had chosen to marry her a year ago—and they'd been anything but romantic.

"What? No kiss yet?" Camilla demanded over her plump shoulder as she hurried away, having caught sight of her son in conversation with her husband. "Do not mind all of us gathering around so. This time, it will be quite proper for you to kiss your wife in public, after all, you have been parted for so long. We shall be very discreet, and very disappointed if you don't," she warned, stopping for a moment to make certain they did as she requested, her hands held together expectantly.

Neil felt Leigh trying to struggle free from his embrace and a glint came into his eyes as he bent his head to hers. "For pride's sake, my dear," he murmured, his lips parting in the slightly curving smile that always made her nervous. "We cannot allow all of your efforts to go for naught, especially after that fairy tale you wove for my family's benefit—or was it for your own?" he asked softly, his lips lowering closer to hers.

"Mine, of course. As you say, 'for pride's sake' people will sometimes tell the most outrageous lies," Leigh told him with that cool, disdainful look, that look of Travers pride that always managed to get under his skin, sending a well-aimed shaft of anger through him as he felt challenged to force a different response from her.

Leigh frowned as his smile widened with purpose, then suddenly she felt his arms begin to fall away from her and she reached up around his neck to keep from falling into the dust at his feet—a place she vowed she'd never be.

But his arms hadn't fallen away completely, and now they tightened around her just before her feet touched the ground. He held her pressed against the muscular length of his body, his mouth finding hers without hesitation as she looked up at him in surprise, her soft, parted lips fitting perfectly against the hard, finely chiseled curves of his.

Why did it never change? Leigh wondered helplessly as she felt that same breathlessness and sudden twist in her stomach whenever he was near, the roughness of his unshaven chin heightening her sensitivity to his touch. His lips were warm and sensuous moving against hers, his arm around her waist bending her slightly backward, bringing her hips more firmly against his and she knew she was lost, and it frightened her, because she didn't want to give of herself again, not unless she knew there was love between them. The kiss deepened, his tongue touching hers intimately, and Neil sighed, loving the feel of her. Leigh's senses were so filled with his scent, she felt as if she were drowning in him, and she couldn't draw a breath of her own into her lungs. Her breath had become his.

Suddenly he felt her pulling, and none too gently, against his braided hair, trying to lift his mouth from hers, her slender body struggling against his, but her struggles only served to meld them closer, and he couldn't control the tightening in his loins, and when she tensed, he knew she felt his masculinity hard against her. He winced when she gave the braid a painful yank, refusing to lessen the pressure. Slowly, he allowed his mouth to lift from hers. She was breathing heavily, her dark blue eyes staring up at him triumphantly, then widening slightly when she saw the corner of his lips twitch slightly as he smiled, but before she could draw her breath to protest, he began to lower his mouth to hers again, ignoring the pain as she still clung to the braid—as if she sought to control him. While holding her attention, his hand moved from her waist, dropping lower over the soft buckskin of her skirt until he found the curve he wanted, and he lightly pinched her buttock in retribution, her indrawn breath and surprised look of indignation causing him to laugh aloud with the joy of having her in his arms again. "Always remember, my dear, two can play the game, and I like to win."

"So do I," she reminded him with a smile tugging at the corner of her mouth now, which gave him cause to worry as he wondered what she would do next.

But even Leigh was surprised by the odd expression that suddenly spread over his face as his nostrils flared slightly. Sniffing, Neil raised an astonished eyebrow as a very unsavory odor wafted to him from the lovely woman he held in his arms.

Leigh began to protest her innocence, realizing now what he had smelled as she felt the dampness of her leather jacket, but she never had a chance. Hardly having opened her mouth, she was rudely interrupted.

"Baaaa! Baaaa!"

Neil couldn't control his startled look as he stared at her, wondering how she had managed such a sound. But when he glanced down to find a damp, woolly lamb butting determinedly against his legs, trying to wedge itself between his and Leigh's, and bleating more and more loudly for its mother—which it thought it had found as it looked up sadly at Leigh—he grinned in resignation, laughing softly.

Leigh smiled in response. She had forgotten how wonderful the sound of his laughter was.

Neil sniffed again and Leigh found herself laughing, rather than finding offense. "Wet wool?" he queried, eyeing the closely buttoned leather jacket, and remembering now the lamb he'd taken from her lap when she'd ridden onto the *rancho*. Until now, he'd forgotten the creature.

"Pedro's herd was attacked last night and he lost several ewes. This little one became lost and we found it on the trail. If we'd left it alone, the wolves would have gotten it, and we were too far from Pedro's camp to return," Leigh explained, bending down and picking up the forlorn little lamb, cuddling it close.

"A lesson to be remembered," Neil said, holding Leigh's gaze meaningfully over the woolly head of the lamb.

"Ah," Camilla sighed watching them together after their passionate embrace, but her smile of contentment faded when she saw her son's split lip and swollen nose. "Ah, my sweet—" she began, hugging Gil's lanky frame close, even though he stood two heads taller than she, but he was quick to free himself from his mother's smothering embrace, ever-sensitive to the masculine eyes watching him, especially his father's. He was already uneasy, feeling the guilty pangs of conscience for having lied to him. Although, since they'd never reached Riovado, he could truthfully claim that he and Leigh had gone nowhere but to the *pastor*'s camp, and his explanation of having fallen into an arroyo while trying to catch the lamb sounded reasonable enough to him—and far less harmful an explanation for everyone concerned than had he mentioned the Comanche who had attacked them. Gil eased his conscience somewhat with the thought.

"I'm all right, Mama, please—" he said, a trifle impatiently, but he was tired, and he'd had a fright, and now he felt confused. His gaze drifted back to Leigh, where only moments before she had been held in her husband's arms and kissed and fondled so intimately. Irritably, he felt the rush of fiery heat that had flooded his face as he'd watched them together and wondered how he'd ever face them feeling what he did.

Neil was home, and Gil was experiencing both incredible happiness and jealousy by his brother's presence.

"Oh, my darling! Your arm is bloodied. Did I hurt you?" Camilla asked, tears beginning to fall down her already tearstained cheeks.

Gil's attitude softened somewhat and he managed to put his arm around her shoulders comfortingly, as if she'd been the one lost in the night. "Now, now, Mama, I'll be all right. It's just a scratch," he protested with manly dignity, sighing as his sister came racing up to him, ready to hug him all over again.

"You were lucky there was a full moon, or you and Leigh would never have made it safely down the trail," Nathaniel remarked, his gaze searching his son's young face. "You certainly took a tumble," he muttered, thinking his son had done well to get back to Royal Rivers in his condition, and without further mishap, and the lad had brought young Leigh home safely too. "You did good, boy," Nathaniel said gruffly.

Gil swallowed the painful lump in his throat. "Thank you, sir. Only wish I hadn't been so stupid, and careless," he said, cursing himself for having allowed the Comanche to catch him off guard, and he felt sick all over again as he thought of what had nearly happened to them—to Leigh. But Gil Braedon had matured that day, the near tragic consequences of his carelessness giving him a deep sense of responsibility toward others—and it was something he would remember and act upon for the rest of his life.

"Accidents happen, son," Nathaniel allowed, and generously for him, startling his son when he touched him on the shoulder.

"Tripped over my own big feet," Gil said quickly, feeling horribly ashamed of himself, "but not until after I'd delivered Pedro's supplies. He's being troubled by wolves," he told his father, hoping to change the subject. "That's why the lamb wandered off. Pedro said he lost a couple of ewes."

Nathaniel nodded, as if expecting as much. "We'll go hunting tomorrow," he said briefly. "You'd better get inside, you're looking a bit green," he advised, glancing at his son, then over to where his elder son now stood with his wife. He turned away, his voice carrying harshly as he began to give his orders for his men to dismount and unsaddle their horses. There would be no need for a search party tonight.

"Leigh! Leigh! Where are you?"

Leigh glanced away from Neil to see Guy coming toward her. Althea was holding onto one of his arms, while Solange held the other, their slow steps carefully guiding him along the uneven paving stones directly in front of the house, but their efforts were hindered somewhat by Noelle, trying to be helpful as she also held on to her uncle's arm, and Steward, who was tagging along behind, his hand tugging on the back of Guy's coattails.

"She's over there, Guy," Leigh heard Althea tell him.

"I'm here, Guy!" she called, handing the lamb to Neil as she hurried to her brother's side.

"Leigh, thank goodness you're home," Althea said, smiling with relief, although her brown eyes narrowed as they took in her appearance, seeing more than Neil had as she stared at Leigh's buttoned-up jacket.

"Are you all right? I thought I heard your laughter. Leigh?" Guy cried out again, never having felt so frightened as when he'd been told that she and Gil had not returned from their ride. And he hadn't needed to see the going down of the sun to know that it was dark; he could feel the coolness in the air.

"What happened?" Althea asked, still worried about Leigh, even though her sister appeared to have returned to Royal Rivers safely.

"We had trouble chasing a lamb. Unfortunately, Gil slipped down the steep bank of an *arroyo* and hurt himself," Leigh said, amazed at how facilely she seemed able to lie.

"Oh, no. Is he badly hurt?" Althea asked, searching for Camilla in the crowd, knowing she'd be close by her son.

"A lamb? Can I see it? Can I?" Steward demanded, his dark curls tumbling into disorder as he hopped up and down on chubby legs and peeked from behind his mother's back at the wide expanse of torch-lit yard that loomed like a frightening chasm before his small figure.

"I would like to see it too, but only after we have heard how Gil is," Noelle remarked in a far more civilized manner, her dark eyes reproving as she stared at her ill-mannered brother.

"I think he'll be all right. He'll have to have his arm tended to, and he may have broken his nose," Leigh said, thinking Gil actually looked even worse than it sounded.

"You will excuse me then? I should go see him, but just to make certain Camilla doesn't embarrass him too much. She does like to baby him so. She does not wish him to grow up, especially since—well," Solange said, having no need to complete her statement, for they all knew how Camilla hovered over Gil since losing Justin. Leaving them, Solange hurried across the yard to join the group around her nephew, stopping first for just an instant to pat the lamb and say something to Neil, leaving him grinning as she left him still holding the lamb.

"Leigh? You do know that Neil has returned?" Althea asked softly.

"Yes."

"Mama! Mama! When can we see the lamb?" Steward asked, jerking impatiently on her skirt to get her attention, for it was getting close to his bedtime and he was becoming grumpy.

"Did you manage to rescue it?" Althea asked, resisting the urge to smack a fat little rear end.

"Can't you guess?" Leigh replied, gesturing to her jacket, which Althea had been too polite to comment about. "It's right over there," Leigh said, taking a great deal of pleasure in pointing in the direction of a tall figure.

Althea nearly made an unladylike guffaw as she caught sight of Neil Braedon standing with the bundle of wool in his arms. "Oh, dear, we'd better rescue him," Althea said, schooling her features into a polite smile as she took a trying-to-maintain-her-ladylike-decorum Noelle and a giggling Steward each by the hand and led them forward.

"Thank God you're back, Leigh," Guy was saying when he heard a squeal behind him and took the precaution of stepping aside as Jolie barreled along the path, her long, thin arms outstretched to hug Leigh. Stephen, although more circumspect in his welcome, was just as relieved to see Leigh's slender figure standing on the path and he contented himself with a fatherly pat on her shoulder.

"I told him I heard thunder! My big toe! Hmmmph! Thought his eyes were goin' to pop from his head when he sees Mister Neil come ridin' in bold as brass," Jolie said, her yellow eyes not missing anything about Leigh's appearance, and her lips tightened accordingly. "Goin' to have to talk with Mister Gil for keepin' my lil' honey out so late. An' you're goin' to tell Jolie just what happened once I get you cleaned up. Lord help us, what've you been doin'?" she demanded, sniffing loudly. "Can't let you outa my sight for a minute, worse than your papa when it comes to gettin' into trouble. Reminds me of that afternoon he comes staggerin' up to the house smellin' like that ol' hound of Guy's that liked to roll in cow dung and would come trottin' back up to the house with the biggest grin on his fool's face I've ever seen," she said, grabbing hold of Leigh's shoulder and pulling her along with her toward the house. "We're goin' to get you cleaned up right away, honey," she vowed.

Leigh met Stephen's understanding gaze as he hurried to the door to hold it open. Leigh managed to glance back, seeing Althea in earnest conversation with Neil, while Noelle, down on her knees in the dust, and Steward, his rump placed firmly on the ground, petted the lamb.

Suddenly Leigh remembered Guy, standing by himself just off the path, and she called back to him, warning him not to move until she reached him.

But Guy didn't hear her; in fact, he hadn't been listening to anything around him for some time, so mesmerized had he been by the flickering torches, the reddish glow burning into his head like fiery brands. But he could see the flickering shadows, and the flaming color shooting like fireworks, although no image came into sharp focus yet, everything remaining shrouded in a haze.

But Guy knew a sense of hope, and laughed, turning to grasp hold of Leigh's arm, only she wasn't there and he missed his grab, his arms flailing in the air as he nearly overbalanced and stumbled across the path like the sightless fool he was.

"Lys? Lys? Where are you?" he cried out in panic.

Leigh called out a warning, but too late as Guy fell to his knees. Lys Helene, who'd been watching from across the yard, and had started to run at the first cry of her name, had almost reached him when he fell.

Leigh was just a step behind Stephen and would have reached him in another second, but then she stopped, waiting as she looked toward the yard, for it had not been her name that Guy had called out.

"Lys Helene?" Guy called out again, feeling that ancient fear of darkness spreading through him, and he wanted her by his side.

Lys Helene was stepping onto the path when Stephen held out his hand, helping Guy to his feet.

But to Leigh's surprise, Lys Helene just stood watching them for a moment, never coming closer. And Guy never knew she had come in answer to his cry for help, or that she stood so close by. And with a last look, to make certain he had not injured himself, she turned away without ever saying a word.

With Guy now safely in tow, Stephen followed them back inside the house. Just within the doorway, the Misses Simone and Clarice, the St. Amand sisters, stood, their parchment fine faces full of concern, lace-edged hankies pressed against their trembling lips as they stared wide-eyed at Jolie.

"Are the children safe?" they asked in unison, echoing the phrase they'd heard their grandmother ask a thousand times during the years following their family's flight from their burning home during the slave uprising in Santo Domingo.

Jolie loosed her grip on Leigh just long enough to take hold of the fretful misses and guide them back into the great hall, sitting them down on the silk-cushioned sofa, where they could usually be found sitting with their needlepoint, which even Jolie had to admit was superb—but then the Misses Simone and Clarice were convent-bred.

"She said there was danger today," Simone said in a quavering little voice.

"Yes, just like in Santo Domingo, when our house was burned," Clarice replied with a delicate shiver, for although they and their only brother had been young children at the time, they could still remember the fear of the adults around them, and over the years the stories had become of nightmarish proportions as with their grandfather's murder and the bloody massacre on their plantation; their grandmother's terrifying escape through the jungle with them bundled up and carried by a couple of house slaves who'd remained loyal; and, finally, their own parents' tragic separation while fleeing from the island.

"Well, there's no uprisin' here," Jolie told them, knowing exactly what was going on inside their heads as she handed them their neat little baskets of sewing.

"Oh, dear me, such a tragedy," Simone whispered.

"Yes, the bodies of *Oncle* Georges and *Oncle* Gilbert were never found, the murderers cut them up into so many pieces," Clarice elaborated.

"Our *maman* thought our poor *père* was dead too. We did not see him again until we were about ten and Pierre was eight."

"You were ten, I was twelve, and Pierre was seven and a half."

"Yes, and then to find *Papa* living in France," Clarice sighed, beginning to stitch a flower on a piece of fine linen.

"I still do not know why *Maman* was so displeased. I thought she would have been so happy to find him alive. Even *Grand-mère* was upset. Do you remember what *Maman* said, Clarice?"

"Yes, she was so angry her voice carried all over the house, and she never raised her voice, did she, Simone?"

"No, never!"

"And what was it she said? Ah, yes, 'thinking I have grieved for such a scoundrel for so many years while you've been safe in France, living with that—' what was the word, dear?" Clarice asked gently, selecting another strand of delicately hued silk and trying to match it.

"A *putain*."

Stephen's eyes grew round, for his father, Jean Jacques, had used the uncomplimentary term once when describing a lady who had been trying to break up Colonel Leigh's marriage to the lovely Miss Louise, and it was not a nice word, and certainly not a word nice ladies should be using.

"Ah, yes, *putain*, that was the word. And then she called *Papa* a *bâtard* and told him she never wished to see him again."

Jolie's mouth dropped open, for even she knew what that fancy French-sounding word meant in English.

"And we never did," Simone said as casually as if discussing the weather.

"*Maman* was always right, of course."

"Yes, as far as she was concerned, *Papa* died in Santo Domingo. She said she did not know this man who had betrayed her, who could have stayed away so long while she and their children lived alone, struggling to survive. She said she would never accept him back into her home. She would never forgive him for what he had done. She said he had made his choice, choosing another woman and this new family of his over her and their children, and the life they had led. He would have to live with his decision for the rest of his life. Even *Grand-mère* agreed, and she had grieved more than anyone for *Papa*. He was her only son. Such a *tragédie*. That is my silk, Clarice, please," Simone told her, gently slapping her hand away.

"Come on, Miss Leigh," Jolie said, shaking her head, for the sisters were harmless enough, even if they did ramble a bit now and again, but they were getting on in years and were a bit unhinged, Jolie thought, catching hold of Leigh's arm again.

"Must we?" Guy asked in a conspiratorial whisper. "This is fascinating," he said, unable to see Jolie's glaring look.

"No one comes back from the dead, Simone. That man couldn't have been our *papa*, and *Maman* was right not to believe him."

"I believe you are right, Clarice. I do not believe that man was our *papa*. How could he have been? If he loved us, he would have come to us sooner. How could he have stayed away, knowing how much we missed him, if he was our *papa*? *Non!* It is too cruel to think of all of the grieving we did, going to his crypt, which he was not even in, and placing flowers on his grave each Sunday, and he was not even dead. And I always caught cold in there. *Non!* That man was an impostor. Better our *papa* should be dead than to be that man," she said, nodding her head emphatically. "I don't believe that color matches, Clarice."

Leaving Guy to Stephen's ministrations, his scraped palms having to be cleaned and salved, Leigh allowed Jolie to hustle her into her room, knowing that she would not be able to lie to Jolie about what had happened, and she didn't want to. Jolie was the only person who would understand.

"Now, missy, you goin' to tell me without me havin' to pry each little detail out of you as if I was pullin' teeth?" she demanded, arms folded across her chest as she leaned against the door.

Leigh nodded, but the hot tears hadn't even started to fall before Jolie had her in her arms and was hushing her deep sobs as the terror of the afternoon came tumbling out. An hour later, Jolie was still bristling. The truth this time had caught her by surprise, even though she'd been having her feelings since hearing that thunder last night. But to have had one of her loved ones so close to death. Her long, thin fingers shook as she held the torn pieces of Leigh's linen blouse and thought of the savage hands that had torn the material apart—and what would have happened if Leigh hadn't been protected by the spirits.

If she hadn't been so angry, and scared still, she would have been smiling from ear to ear, for the spirits were watching over little Miss Leigh, Jolie thought, glancing to where Leigh was soaking in a tub of hot, soapy water, her hands furiously rubbing the dust and degradation from her tired body.

Next to her, on the small nightstand, was the leather pouch. Jolie nodded thoughtfully, firmly believing now that what had happened five years ago, that summer when Leigh had first had in her possession the pouch—and had first crossed paths with Neil Braedon—had been destined from the beginning of time. She shook her head, vowing she'd never question the signs again.

Leigh bent her head, dipping it beneath the water, then soaping the wet length of hair cascading over her slender shoulder. Jolie's lips tightened ominously as she saw the dark red welt circling the back of Leigh's neck, where the rawhide cord had been ruthlessly cut, leaving a painful abrasion against her soft skin.

"Honey, I'm goin' to fetch you a tray. You're goin' to bed early tonight. I already told Miss Camilla not to expect you for dinner, 'cause you're so tired, an' she understands. They've been sittin' in the hall drinkin' whiskey an' sippin' sherry, an' talkin' 'bout the war endin' an' what's goin' on back there in Washin'ton. So, you finish your soakin' an' I'll bring you somethin' nice an' hot to eat. But first, I'm goin' to burn *this*," she promised, wadding up the offending piece of linen and stuffing it beneath her arm.

Leigh nodded, opening her eyes and watching as Jolie left the room, and not for the first time did a member of the Travers family wonder what they would ever have done without Jolie watching over them.

Jolie's steps didn't carry her far along the corridor before she came to a sudden halt. Walking along the hall directly in front of her, and carrying a tray loaded down with dinner, was the object of her thoughts—and even up until an hour ago, not very pleasant ones.

Neil eyed the mulattress assessingly, as if a tigress had somehow found its way between him and the place he wished to be. And he wondered somewhat wryly if he was going to have a fight on his hands to bridge the distance.

But he had misjudged his enemy—onetime enemy—because Jolie startled him when she stomped forward, her yellow eyes looking like molten gold as they brimmed with scalding tears, her lips quivering as she tried to speak, then, to his uneasiness, she reached out a clawlike hand and grabbed hold of his arm, and Neil was surprised to discover his flesh hadn't been shredded. Staring intently into his face, the mulattress reached up and touched his chest, then his shoulder, then lightly touched his hard cheek with just her fingertips, the gesture of affection leaving him disbelieving.

She said something in a tongue that he recognized as Indian, but it wasn't Comanche or Kiowa, two tongues he knew, and then she nodded, rubbing her palm along his arm as if in some ceremonial gesture. Then she was gone, leaving the door to Leigh's room unguarded.

Shaking off his disquiet, Neil smiled. Half the battle had been won, he found himself thinking as he reached the door of *his* room—the room Leigh had chosen to sleep in. Balancing the tray, he opened the door and entered.

He was amazed anew at the transformation of his room. When entering it earlier in the day, when he'd first arrived at Royal Rivers, he had been astonished by the change, little realizing how much a woman's presence could alter the atmosphere of a room. Everything about the room, from the cheerful quilt across the daybed, to the small, feminine desk near the window, to the pair of lacy pantalettes thrown across the rocking chair, reminded him of Leigh. Opening one of the drawers in the dressing chest, the fragrance of lavender and roses had drifted to him and he had ached to see her again— the pleasure and promise of that thought keeping him alive through the last year of the war.

Now, she was here. And she was his wife. There was nothing and no one to keep them apart now. He stared at her bare shoulders, bent slightly as she rubbed the foaming soap through her hair, the herbal fragrance drifting to him. As he watched, she rose slightly from the tub, the soapy waters falling away from her body and revealing the slim contours of her back and waist as she tried to reach the pitcher of clean water to rinse her hair.

Setting the tray down on the dressing chest, he reached the pitcher first. Seeing the masculine hand taking hold of the pitcher, Leigh jerked her head and shoulders around, forgetting she half stood, and allowing Neil a generous view of her tip-tilted breasts, the rounded crests soft and pink, but before he could act on his amorous thoughts, she had sunk back into the soapy water. With a hand placed firmly on her wet shoulder, stiffening with outraged dignity, he poured the fresh water over the top of her head, grinning as she spluttered her protest of his rough treatment, although he doubted Jolie, in her finest moments of dealing with Travers pride, had been any gentler than he. There was a limit to a person's patience.

He stared down into her flushed face, the pulse beating rapidly in her arched throat fascinating him, but suddenly he stiffened, his gaze catching sight of the leather pouch as he set the pitcher back on the nightstand. Following his gaze, Leigh's hand moved quickly, automatically to grab hold of it, to keep it safe. Then, as if she realized she hadn't the right, she dropped her hand, lowering her head so she wouldn't have to see the expression on his face, not knowing whether he would be pleased or angry that she had chosen to wear it.

Neil picked up the pouch, which was so much a part of him. He glanced over at Leigh, his expression changing as he saw the angry welt marring the softness of her neck. Frowning, he noticed the frayed edges of the rawhide that had been retied into a knot—the width of the rawhide strap matching the irritated skin around her neck.

She had worn it. He had left it with her, hoping…but never knowing if she would care enough to wear it, if she would even believe. He reached up and touched the braid of gold. A piece of soft leather, tightly laced with a blue ribbon had been woven around it—his talisman, he thought as he remembered the day he had claimed the blue ribbon as his prize. Never realizing how fateful that encounter with a beautiful young woman, her unbound chestnut hair flowing behind her as she rode bareback across a summer meadow, would change forever his life.

"What happened?" he asked suddenly.

The harshness of his voice startled Leigh, who was already suffering from the guilt of her lies. And she wouldn't be able to assuage her conscience any—because she wouldn't be able to tell Neil the truth.

"What do you mean?"

"Your neck. It's raw. You've been wearing this, haven't you?"

Leigh watched as he felt the leather pouch, holding it caressingly in his palm.

"Yes, I have." She admitted that much of the truth. "It caught on a branch while I was trying to catch the lamb. I didn't lose it," she said, a defiant note in her voice. "I've kept it safe. It wasn't mine, even though you did forget it when you left Travers Hill that morning," Leigh said, watching him carefully.

"I knew exactly where I left it," he answered. "In your hand, tucked beneath your pillow."

Leigh glanced up in surprise.

"You left it with me on purpose? You hadn't forgotten it in your haste, then?" she asked, uncertainly.

"No, I knew you and your family had a long, perhaps

dangerous, journey ahead of you. I thought you could use all of the good luck you could find."

"Oh," Leigh said, stung, for his explanation sounded so impersonal, "then you have Jolie to thank for our safe arrival, because she believes in your Indian superstitions, and she saw that I didn't throw it away," Leigh added, turning a haughty shoulder to him as she began to squeeze the water from her dripping hair.

Neil smiled patiently at her smooth back, wishing he could reach out and run a finger along that stiff backbone of hers. His smile widened, for they had all the time in the world to get to know one another. Turning away from the tub, he noticed the cradle. Walking over to it, he leaned down and carefully picked up the wide-eyed baby, holding her close in his arms as he stared into the rosy-cheeked face, the big dark eyes staring up at him so trustingly.

Leigh watched as Neil touched one of Lucinda's dark curls, his hand so gentle against the tender curve of her head, his arms holding Adam's and Blythe's child, the creation of their love, as if she were as precious as his own daughter. And in Neil's eyes, she was, for Lucinda was special because of the sacrifice others had made for her—and, because of her existence, he had been given the woman he loved.

Had Neil glanced up, he would have seen Leigh's eyes full of love as she gazed at him, watching him press his lips against Lucinda's soft brow, then placing her back in her cradle, rocking it for a moment until she stilled, but when he turned around, she was busy rinsing soap from her shoulders.

"I've brought dinner," he said conversationally as he selected a warm plate from the tray and made himself comfortable on the daybed.

"Jolie is bringing my dinner."

"I met her in the hall, and, if I understood her correctly, she told us to enjoy our dinner."

Leigh couldn't hide her dismay at Jolie's defection. "I haven't finished bathing yet," Leigh told him, glancing over her shoulder in growing irritation as she saw him biting into a thick slice of beef, the tantalizing aroma drifting to her and causing her stomach to protest embarrassingly.

"Fine, you finish. Your dinner will keep warm for a while," he responded, apparently unconcerned. "But don't linger too long, or you might catch a chill in that cold water," he advised, dabbing his mouth with a linen napkin to hide his grin.

But still shy before him, Leigh remained in the water, ever aware of his warning as the water turned colder by the minute, until she was shivering noticeably and finally had to climb from the tub. Drawing on her pride, she stood, reaching for the towel on the back of the rocking chair. Wrapping it snugly around her, with stiff-necked dignity, her back straightened into haughtiness, her shoulders tilted at a lofty angle, her buttocks tight as if clad in buckram, Leigh stepped from the tub.

Turning around, she stopped in amazement. Neil was sound asleep. Stretched out comfortably on the daybed, his tall, broad-shouldered body almost too long for it, with one of his moccasin-clad feet dangling close above his empty plate set on the floor, he slept, looking as innocent as a child.

Sighing, for it had been a long day, Leigh unfolded the quilt and placed it over his sleeping form, tucking it around his shoulders, her hand lightly brushing his unshaven chin, feeling the obstinacy and strength that emanated from the man even while he slept.

Quickly Leigh pulled on her nightdress, and perched on the edge of her bed, she ate her dinner, but her appetite had fled, and she left most untouched as disturbing images and sounds filled her mind until she sought release in sleep. Climbing into her cold bed, shivering still from her bath, Leigh huddled beneath the blankets.

But the peace of slumber did not come quickly or easily for Leigh that night, and for hours she laid awake, tossing and turning as she sought something elusive that had been troubling her, tormenting her, until finally she fell into a deep, restless sleep, a pair of brilliant, sky blue eyes haunting her, hounding her into the deepest recesses of her mind.

When she awoke the next morning, Neil was already gone. Bleary-eyed, Leigh dressed, eyeing Jolie suspiciously as she hovered around the room, looking too smug for anyone's peace of mind.

"Now you get down the hall an' into the dinin' room,

missy," Jolie told Leigh, eyeing her approvingly, for she'd
chosen one of her prettier gowns today, a lavender-blue,
floral-printed muslin. "I saw your dinner plate last night, an'
you didn't eat enough to keep a bird alive. If you're goin' to
keep that handsome husband of yours interested, you're goin'
to have to have a lil' more flesh on those bones," she added
slyly, smiling when Leigh turned a cool shoulder to her and
left the room, but her smile would have faded had she known
that Leigh never reached the dining room.

Passing by Nathaniel Braedon's study, Leigh heard a
crashing noise from behind the closed door, followed by a
frightened whimper of fear. Remembering the incident the
day before in Guy's room, Leigh hurried into the room,
thinking Guy might have somehow stumbled into Nathaniel's
study. Entering the quiet room, Leigh stood looking around,
but the room was empty. Shrugging, Leigh was leaving when
a scratching noise sounded behind her, and she turned to see
one of Guy's hounds shoot past her, his feet spinning against
the wood floor as he tried to make his escape.

This time, Leigh looked around the room more carefully,
searching for something broken. It was a comfortable room, with
a large mahogany desk centered before the window, with a big
leather armchair positioned behind it, and from where Nathaniel
ran the everyday affairs of his ranch. Bookcases filled one wall,
and a high-backed leather sofa and upholstered chair had been
placed near the fireplace. A map of the United States shared
space on one of the walls with a map of Virginia and one of the
territories; another map, of a Spanish land grant, the land Royal
Rivers had eventually been built on, hung between them, the
focal point for all that Nathaniel had achieved in his life.

Fortunately, Guy's hound had only knocked over one
of the brass fireplace tools. Picking up the poker, Leigh was
replacing it when she glanced up at the portrait hanging on the
wall over the fireplace.

Leigh gazed at the portrait. She'd only seen it one other time,
for she didn't often enter Nathaniel's study—nobody did—but
she hadn't forgotten the beauty of the woman and child.

Neil's mother and sister. She was one of the most beautiful
women Leigh had ever seen, with her midnight-black hair

curling over alabaster shoulders that sloped elegantly to the lace-edged silk of her burgundy gown. Her mouth was soft and full and sweetly curved, the hand holding her daughter's slender and delicate. And the little girl sitting next to her in a pink gown layered with lace and tied with a burgundy silk sash, showing the beginnings of great beauty in the dimpled cheek, flushed with happiness, and the finely arched curve of a black eyebrow, her lashes long and thick.

Suddenly Leigh felt a strange coldness spreading through her as she met the brilliant blue eyes of mother and daughter, eyes she'd seen just the day before. There could be no mistaking that rare shade of blue. Eyes so bright, it was like gazing into the heart of the heavens. And that slight indentation in the chin…where had she seen that before? Leigh swallowed against the dryness closing her throat. Forgetting the overturned brass tools, Leigh backed out of the room, her steps carrying her down the corridor and away from the dining room.

Leigh paused uncertainly just outside the house, feeling the sun beating down on her and taking away the chill from the study. Without thinking further about what she was doing, except that she had to prove it wasn't true, she found her steps carrying her across the grounds.

Approaching Solange's studio, it appeared nothing more than a very small, weathered adobe shed for storing farming implements or feed stores. But once inside, a startling transformation occurred before one's eyes. The far side of the one-room shed was floor-to-ceiling windows with an expansive view of green pastureland, dominated by towering mountains, and, above, dazzling blue sky stretching away into the distant heavens, while the sunlight poured into the room like a golden stream of honey.

Paintings, portfolios, and rolls of canvas were stacked all around the room, except for a wide space before the wall of windows, which had been cleared of clutter, and where a lone easel stood facing the light, a half-completed canvas propped against it. Leigh stepped inside, the strong odors of linseed oil and turpentine assailing her, especially from a long, rough-hewn table crowded with jars full of varying-sized bristle-haired paintbrushes, spatulas, and pens, the quilled tips of descending degree in size and thickness, wads of paint-stained cloth, and boards dotted with splotches of paint representing every shade imaginable. Thinking it trash, she would have cleared the table of the broken sticks and short, coiled rolls of paper, but Leigh knew Solange used the odd bits to mix her paints and sometimes to apply the paint to the canvas. Molded sticks of chalky pigment were scattered across the table in a rainbow of color, and the shelves over the table were packed solid with small jars and packets of powdery pigments.

Slowly Leigh weaved her way through the jumble, careful not to brush against the fresco painted on one of the walls. Solange called it her *trompe l'oeil* because it "deceived the eye" into believing the room extended far beyond its dimensions. The imagery created a graceful arcade supported by fluted columns that led to a balustraded balcony overlooking the Tuscany countryside in its pastoral and mythical beauty, complete with a nude figure of a voluptuous woman reclining on a pillowed couch, a lute-strumming young pagan sitting at her feet in adoration, shepherds in the fields, and muscular gods in the clouds. Solange had created it from charcoal sketches and pen and ink drawings she'd made while on her honeymoon in Italy, and declared she'd felt inspired to create her own Renaissance fresco. Besides, Solange had added with a wicked wink, it brought back very fond memories of her honeymoon. But despite her apparent jest, her hand had lightly touched the silvery widow's peak above her wide forehead, as if being marked by it had brought true the prophesy of early widowhood, for Solange wasn't even thirty-five, the silver streak the only gray in her dark brown hair.

Leigh slowed her step to admire one of Solange's earlier oil paintings of a bazaar, which she'd painted when she and her late husband, Henri, Comte de Beaudecoeur, had lived in Algeria, the exotic setting rich in detail and vibrant jewel-like color, the figure cloaked in a burnoose in the foreground looking as if he could step right out of the painting and into the room. Another painting was from a vantage point high above the streets of Paris, with the panorama of the city spreading out to the edges of the canvas. Next to it was a painting of the Thames wending through London, the waterway crowded with ships and barges, the banks teeming with life. And there were other paintings of Edinburgh, Venice, Florence, Rome, Madrid, Amsterdam, Vienna, St. Petersburg, Budapest, Stockholm, and countless picturesque villages and rural scenes from across Europe—all the places Solange had visited during her colorful life as the wife of a French diplomat.

Some of the paintings had been painted in delicate, painstaking detail, the brushstrokes bringing the images into sharp, clear focus. Others, however, showed less realism, with broad strokes of the brush that swirled and splashed in brilliant, luminous color, capturing movement across the canvas in boldly contrasting light and shadow. Landscapes and portraits seemed to dominate the room, and the more recent additions to the collection were of the life Solange now found around her: the desolate landscape, wildlife, and people caught forever on canvas.

A *kachina* figure, arrayed in all its splendor, with a terrifying, hideous mask, stood surrounded by several young male figures. Wearing flannel breechcloths and beaded soft leather leggings, with pelts of gray fox hanging down in back, the men danced across the canvas to the beating of drums, shaking gourd rattles for rain and waving sprigs of evergreen for long life in the ceremonial ritual of the Green Corn Dance. Other paintings showed Deer Dancers and Buffalo Dancers, the women gowned in white cotton dresses, embroidered with colorful woolen yarn worked into geometric designs, feathers decorating their long, unbound hair as they swayed and chanted.

A portrait of Pedro and Soldado occupied a place of honor in the center of the wall, the shepherd's wizened face full of wisdom staring down at her, while Soldado's alert eyes followed her every step as if a sheep had strayed from the flock and was trying to sneak past.

An old Pueblo woman knelt in front of a *metate*, a sandstone slab in a shallow bin, her arms stretched forward, gnarled hands grasping a stone muller as she ground maize into meal day after day. She was dressed in a *manta* of dark brown woolen cloth tied over the right shoulder, part of a white moccasin showing beneath the blue-bordered skirt enclosed around her waist with a red, green, and black sash. The painting next to it portrayed a middle-aged man who was dressed in a colorful cotton shirt and short white trousers. He wore a leather belt studded with silver *conchas* around his waist and a necklace of turquoise stones dangled from his neck. He was sitting on a stool before a loom, his fingers busily weaving cloth into the same somber, narrow-striped pattern his ancestors, *The Ancient Ones*, had from the time of Christ.

A young Indian girl, of the Hopi tribe, Solange had told her, stared wistfully back from another painting, the thick butterfly twists of black hair over her ears a sign of her maidenhood, the chubby-faced baby she stood watch over not hers. But the perfectly formed corncob, placed next to the bundled-up baby strapped to the wooden cradle board, was her gift to the newborn child for a life of strength and health.

There were many more paintings: *Taos Pueblo*, the five-storied structure looking like a squat, sprawling pyramid rising from the earth with the help of the wooden ladders propped against the buckskin-hued walls; a *carreta* with big wooden wheels being pulled by oxen prodded by a small boy precariously balanced in the unsteady cart; a scrawny burro half-buried beneath a load piled high on its back; a small church, with its cross, bell tower, and cemetery baking beneath the sun; and the burnished ruins of a mission long abandoned. Mountain and desert came alive as hawks and eagles, wings outspread, flew toward the beamed ceiling of the studio, soaring through painted skies. A rattlesnake was captured coiled by a mound of rocks, while a kangaroo mouse hopped safely out of striking distance beneath a cactus adorned with a solitary pink bloom.

"Solange?" Leigh called out.

"Over here," a voice answered from behind a silk screen that partitioned off a private corner of the studio, where Solange kept a change of clothing, and other necessities for making herself decent before returning to the house each day. She claimed she didn't wish to offend, especially overly sensitive guests who might have arrived during her prolonged absence in her studio. But Leigh knew she did it for her sister's sake, although, she declared with a mischievous grin, she didn't know who was more easily offended, Jolie or her aunts.

Leigh walked to the windows, waiting politely for Solange. A small-boned, thin-chested woman suddenly appeared from behind the screen, a lock of dark brown hair falling over her cheek as she struggled with the last hooks of her gown. "Spilled turpentine all over myself," Solange said with a grimace as she quickly shrugged into her duster and pushed up the sleeves, ready to work. "It was one of my better gowns too, but I was in such a hurry to begin, I forgot to put on my smock. A good thing Henri left me well provided for," she said and sighed. "I have ruined six gowns this year," she added in self-disgust, throwing up her hands with Gallic emphasis.

Leigh, perched on the edge of a bench in front of the windows, glanced over at Solange and smiled, for although Solange seemed very extravagant at times in her eccentricity, she was just very French, and very practical, and Leigh suspected she knew exactly how much money she could afford to waste.

"*Ma petite*," Solange said, coming over and kissing Leigh on the cheek. "What brings you here so early?" she asked, feigning a scandalized expression. "*Mon Dieu!* Did I not see your husband, just returned from the war, arrive last evening? And what a kiss! Ooh, lah! Were I so young again." She sighed dramatically, her dark gray eyes alight with joy.

"He was already gone when I awoke," Leigh said, unable to hide the slight note of disappointment in her voice.

"Ah, men! Why do we put up with them?" she asked, patting Leigh's cheek affectionately. "You should have found a way of keeping him in bed with you longer," she said, watching in amusement as Leigh's face pinkened with embarrassment. "*Attendez-moi, ma petite*," she warned, shaking her finger at her to get her to listen carefully. "A married woman should never blush, not if she is truly married. If not, then I think she is married to a hen instead of a rooster. Ah, that is better," Solange said, hearing Leigh's laughter. "So, it is never as we wish, eh? He rides all through the night to be by your side, *ma petite*, looking forward to holding you close and making love to you the whole night long. And what does he find? His wife has vanished! He is beside himself when he arrives at Royal Rivers and finds his loving wife had not yet returned from her ride of early morning. I feared for the safety of my young, foolish nephew. I am afraid Gilbert does not think clearly when he is around you, *ma petite*. You have enchanted him, which is good for a boy his age, he needs to have a passion for more than horses and cows, as long as he remembers you are his brother's wife. Alas, had you not arrived when you did, and had Gilbert not been so sad-looking, I fear Neil would have skinned him and hung him up next to that buffalo skin. Never have I seen Neil so taken aback by something that has happened. What a homecoming for him, eh?" she said, not going on to mention her own disgust with Nathaniel's cool reception for his eldest son safely home from the war. Had he been her son, she would have hugged him until he had died from loss of breath. "You make life hard for this lover of yours, eh?" She laughed, but her gray eyes were narrowed as she watched Leigh nervously play with one of her dangling golden earrings.

"You do not smile, *ma petite*. So, what is wrong? I can tell there is something. But it is too soon for there to be trouble between you and Neil, and how can that be when there is so much love between you?" Solange said, going to stand before the canvas, her hands placed on her slender hips as she stared at it.

"I was wondering," Leigh began slowly, "if you could draw a sketch of a face if I described it to you."

Solange glanced over her shoulder curiously. "What is this? I do not understand. This is a face that belongs to whom?"

"I'm not certain who he is," Leigh said with a thoughtful expression.

"He? You dream of this man? It is good Neil returns to Royal Rivers, then."

Leigh shook her head. "No, no, it is not that at all!" she said quickly, the savage's face was still too real to her. Unconsciously, she put her hand to her breast, remembering the sound of her blouse being ripped apart and the rough touch of the man's hand against her breast. "No, it is a face I have seen, but I hope never to see it again."

Solange stared at Leigh as if she had become crazed. "You wish that I draw a face that you never want to see again?"

"Yes," Leigh answered, not meeting Solange's direct look.

Solange shrugged. "As you wish, *ma petite*. So, we shall see. You tell me about this face," she said, bending down to grab a wooden board with a large piece of thick vellum paper pinned to it. From the pocket of her duster, she produced a short stub of charcoal, the burnt sienna shade beginning to appear on the sheet of paper as Leigh began to describe the Comanche brave.

More than once Solange glanced up, her eyes wide as she listened, for lost in remembering, Leigh wasn't aware of how much she was revealing about the incident until she heard Solange suck in her breath.

"*So*, that is what happened. That is why you and Gil almost did not return to Royal Rivers. *Mon Dieu*," she whispered, thinking of the tragedy that had almost befallen them. Then she thought of her sister, and sent a prayer of thanks heavenward, for Camilla had already lost one of her beloved sons.

Solange glanced down at the face she had created with her charcoal on the page. "So beautiful," she murmured, "but so arrogant, and so savage," she added, looking up at Leigh, the pale sunlight bathing her in such a pure light she could have graced any Renaissance painting, and Solange realized how close they had come to losing her to that heathen devil.

"Will you paint the eyes blue?" Leigh suddenly asked. "And the same blue as the sky, Solange."

"Blue? *Mon Dieu!* Blue? A savage does not have blue eyes," she argued, but it also went against her artistic conscience to ruin her lovely earth-toned sketch by painting the eyes blue.

"This one did," Leigh said in such a strange tone that Solange frowned, but she found several shades of blue, holding each up for Leigh's opinion, but only after the fourth did she nod her acceptance, and Solange delicately shaded in the eyes—and even she had to admit the effect was quite startling.

"*Voila!*" she exclaimed, holding the sketch up to the light.

Leigh couldn't control her shudder of both repulsion and fascination as she stared at the bronzed face of the Comanche brave with the sky blue eyes.

"Thank you, Solange. And, Solange?"

"Hmmm, yes," she said, already busy mixing paints as she stared at the canvas on the easel with a critical eye.

"Please say nothing of this. I promised Gil, and now that Neil is home, I—"

"Do not worry. You and Gil returned safely, so—" she said with a Gallic shrug. "What is there to say, and certainly not for me to decide. It will be up to you if you wish to speak of this with Neil."

"Perhaps someday, Solange," Leigh said, knowing she could never speak of her suspicions to anyone.

Leigh glanced back at Solange, but she was already dabbing paint on the canvas, a paintbrush sticking out of the corner of her mouth as she stared at her work, and Leigh knew she needn't fear an indiscreet remark from Solange.

On her way back to the house, Leigh stopped when she heard a familiar bleating cry. Following the sound, she was led to one of the corrals, but by the time she reached it, the frightened crying had ceased. Peering over the railing, Leigh was amazed to see her orphaned lamb. It looked twice as big, but that was because it had been wrapped in the skin of another newborn that hadn't survived, the scent of the dead lamb clinging to its skin and fooling the ewe into believing that this one was hers, allowing it to nurse—and it was suckling contentedly, drawing all of the nourishment it needed to survive.

Leigh rested her arms on the top rail, frowning slightly as she watched the pair. She found herself thinking of a motherless eight-year-old boy and what he'd had to do to survive—and how, eventually, he'd come to accept the people who had kidnapped him as his family. And what of that boy's sister? What had she done to survive? And, had she, like the young boy, come to accept the people as her family?

Leigh closed her eyes tight, but the image on the rolled-up sheet of vellum could not be erased from her mind. Turning away from the corral, her lamb now safe, Leigh hurried back to the house, hoping she wouldn't see anyone. She had something she had to do: she had to prove to herself it couldn't be true.

Leigh let out her breath when she found the great hall empty, and running quickly across the room, she entered the corridor, pausing by the first door she came to. Knocking lightly, she waited, hoping no one would respond. When only silence answered her summons, she glanced around, assuring herself no one lingered nearby, then let herself into Nathaniel's study.

The room was as quiet as before.

Leigh walked over to the fireplace, where the gold-framed portrait of Fionnuala Darcy Braedon and her young daughter,

Shannon Malveen, hung above the mantel. Slowly, Leigh unrolled the sketch Solange had drawn of the Comanche brave.

Holding it up to the portrait, Leigh stared at the three faces, comparing them, her breath becoming ragged as she saw the stunning resemblance.

How can it be? she wondered, glancing between the brilliant sky blue eyes in Solange's sketch of the Comanche brave and the identical blue eyes of mother and daughter in the portrait, the chins, all indented so perfectly.

It couldn't be true, she thought. Shannon died when she was only fourteen. Neil told his father Shannon had died. As Leigh stood there staring up at the portrait, she heard again the conversation of the night before, remembering the shock and bitterness of a woman who'd thought her husband had died, leaving her and her children to grieve, to live an empty life without him—but he had not died. He had chosen another life instead. And they had never been able to forgive him for that betrayal of their love.

"My God," Leigh murmured, then her heart missed a beat when she heard a step behind her, then an apologetic cough.

Spinning around, Leigh found herself staring at a stranger. The man, who was in his mid- to late thirties, was of medium height, and rather slight of build, although there was a wiriness about him, a tightly coiled quality that was evident in the light-footed way he moved, and Leigh remembered Guy saying little men were sometimes the toughest to beat when in a fight—and harder to catch and quicker to fight dirty, he'd laughed.

"I beg your pardon, ma'am," the man said, removing his hat, a weathered gray slouch hat, his hair thick and a sandy brown shade. "I didn't mean to intrude, but I was told I'd find the master up at the big house. A little Mexican girl let me in. I was waiting in the hall, when a couple of white-haired ladies told me to come back here. They seemed rather offended that I was waiting in the hall while they were trying to sew. I'm looking for work," the man explained.

Leigh stared at the man in surprise. "You're Southern?"

The man's mouth thinned slightly. "Does that matter, ma'am? The war is over," he told her. "Or are only Yankees being hired?"

Leigh flushed slightly, her fingers fumbling as she rerolled the sketch. "You'll have to speak with Nathaniel Braedon about that. He owns Royal Rivers. But I don't think you need concern yourself about your former allegiance to the Confederacy. Nathaniel Braedon lost one of his sons, and a couple of nephews in the war, and they all wore gray."

"My pardon, ma'am," the man said contritely.

"I believe you will find Nathaniel Braedon in the north pasture. It's spring, and shearing time. Although we're expecting a number of shearers up from Mexico this year, you may be able to find work, ah, Mr.——?"

"Sebastian. Michael Sebastian," the man introduced himself.

"Yes, I believe Nathaniel might be able to find you work. You've missed the lambing by a couple of days, but after the shearing, we still have the dipping to take care of, then the docking, that is, cutting off lambs' tails, and then the wethering. And you'll forgive me for not explaining in more detail about that. Do you think you might be interested, Mr. Sebastian?" Leigh asked doubtfully, for she had taken a strange dislike to Michael Sebastian.

A slight smile flickered across Michael Sebastian's hard face as he felt her antagonism. "I think I might be able to handle that. I look at everything as having a purpose in life. Castrating lambs, distasteful as it may be to all concerned, improves the herd for better breeding and tastier mutton," he said, his brown eyes humorless. "Often, we have to take harsh measures to reach a sought-after goal."

Leigh stared at Michael Sebastian uneasily, sensing this would be a man who would be relentless in achieving a goal he had set for himself. "If you will come with me, I'll show you to the pasture."

"Thank you, Miss—ah?"

"Mrs. Braedon. Mrs. Neil Braedon," she said, glancing down at the roll of paper and not seeing the start of surprise that crossed his face as he heard her name. "Follow me, please," she requested in a cool voice.

They were walking along the corridor when Guy stepped into the hall from the gardens. Leigh glanced over at Michael Sebastian, for she could have sworn he cursed beneath his breath. Unfriendly man, she thought, moving slightly away from him.

"You're up early, Guy," Leigh said, thinking he looked pale.

"I couldn't sleep. I thought I'd find Lys Helene. Have you seen her? She's not in the garden."

"No, I'm afraid I haven't seen her. Oh, Guy, this is Michael Sebastian, Mr. Sebastian, my brother, Guy Travers," Leigh made the introductions, startled to see a strange expression, almost one of anger, crossing Michael Sebastian's thin face as he stepped forward, ready to shake hands with Guy.

Guy turned at the sound of a heel scraping the floor, seeing a hazy shape moving toward him. "Mr. Sebastian, an honor, sir," he said courteously, holding out his hand.

Michael Sebastian looked shocked, for until that moment, he hadn't realized Guy Travers was blind. He reached out quickly and grasped Guy's hand, shaking it firmly. "Mr. Travers, a pleasure, sir," he murmured.

"Indeed it is, sir, for unless I'm mistaken, you're a Virginian," Guy commented, smiling. "My family and I are from Virginia. Travers Hill, perhaps you've heard of it?"

Leigh was still watching Michael Sebastian and she would have sworn he suddenly seemed incredibly uncomfortable. "I'm sorry, you must be mistaken, I'm not a Virginian. I'm from North Carolina, although I am familiar, sir, with the name of Travers. Some of the finest Thoroughbreds came from your stables."

"Thank you, sir, that is certainly very kind of you."

"If you will excuse us, Guy, I'm taking Mr. Sebastian to the north pasture."

"Well, good luck. Hope you find what you're looking for," Guy said, holding out his hand again.

"Thank you, Mr. Travers, I hope so too," Michael Sebastian said, taking Guy's hand.

Guy stood for a moment listening to their footsteps fading along the corridor, a puzzled expression crossing his face. "Damn!" he muttered, straining to focus his eyes and put a face, perhaps a familiar face, to that voice—because he would have sworn the man was a Virginian. And he couldn't help but wonder why the man had lied about it.

Twenty-three

The fields fall southward, abrupt and broken,
To the low last edge of the long lone land.
If a step should sound or a word be spoken,
Would a ghost not rise at the strange guest's hand?

Algernon Charles Swinburne

MICHAEL SEBASTIAN PULLED A PIPE FROM HIS POCKET AS they walked along the corridor, politely holding the door open for Leigh to precede him, then following her as they entered the kitchens.

"This is the quickest way through to the grounds," Leigh explained almost apologetically, for despite the unflattering opinion she had of him, she didn't want the man to feel he was being shown out of the house through the back door.

A shadow of a smile touched Leigh's lips, for she never stepped into the kitchens without thinking of Travers Hill. It wasn't that the two kitchens were remarkably similar in appearance—for they were not—but the heart of a house was the kitchen, and this one beat with the same joyous intensity as had the kitchens at Travers Hill. The air was warm and redolent with steam rising from a dozen pots bubbling importantly over the coals in the big hearth. Lupe was busy scolding, her long black braid swinging as she scurried back and forth with unsolicited opinions concerning how thick to roll a *tortilla*, this chicken was too scrawny for the *patrón's* table, there wasn't enough parsley in the tomato sauce, and someone hadn't ground the *canela* fine enough. The sound of knife blades chopping, dicing, and mincing, wooden spoons beating against the sides of bowls, the sizzling of deep-frying fats, and good-natured gossip was a constant, companionable hum in the room.

Beneath a long table of planked pine pushed against one of the walls, *chayote*, and various other squashes and pumpkins were piled high, along with sacks of rice and flour. On top of the table were neatly grouped *tomatillos*, avocados, pineapples, melons, mangos, lemons and limes, colorful fruits from the *rancho* orchards, freshly picked cilantro, mint, and oregano, and peppers and chiles in so many shades that Leigh began to lose count, from large dark green chiles, to small light green jalapeño peppers, to fiery tiny red chiles to brick-red ones with wrinkled skins. Big jars of dried beans, nuts and seeds, pieces of candied pumpkin and sweet potato, and *pozole*, hominy, were grouped together at one end. A couple of woven trays layered with straw and packed with rows of fresh eggs, and a variety of cheeses, a *queso fresco* made on the *rancho*, several dark yellow cheddars, and a white cheese from Chihuahua were crowded together at the other end. Hanging from the overhead beams were strings of onions and garlic, culinary herbs and flowery *manzanilla*, drying for a fine blend of tea, and a brace of turkeys waiting for the stew pot, where the meat would be poached until tender.

A young girl was sitting beside a large basket of *nopales*, painstakingly removing the hard little eyes from the succulent cactus leaves with the sharp point of a knife, another was expertly placing *tortillas* on a red-hot *comal*, a greased cast-iron griddle, turning and lifting the flattened pancake-like pieces of dough one after another when puffed light and airy from the heat, while a third girl was bent over a *molcajete*, patiently grinding dried chile pods with a *tejolote*, the rough volcanic rock of the mortar and pestle making a fine-grained powder.

The cupboards were stacked with earth-toned pottery dishes of different size and shape, cups and saucers, cutlery, casserole dishes, great platters, and pitchers, wooden bowls, and baskets, while through another door into the pantry and scullery, Leigh could see the fine china and crystal filling the tall cabinets against the walls.

Leigh's smile widened in response as Lupe, a short, ample-bosomed, broad-hipped Mexican woman, dressed in a colorful skirt that hardly reached her bare ankles and a white chemise blouse with a gathered neckline stretched taut, called out to her. Her dusky round face was wreathed in a smile as she held up a hand. "Meez Leigh! You come and taste this," she said, turning around and grabbing a spoonful of green chile sauce.

"That *Holee*, she say it not hot enough! Not enough cayenne in it. What is this cayenne when I have *chile verde*? *Mi salsa*, not hot enough!" she repeated in outrage, sampling the *salsa* herself with a delighted rolling of her eyes, then shaking the spoon at two giggling kitchen maids. The pretty black-haired girls, her nieces, were busy spreading corn husks with *masa*, a thick, moist cornmeal prepared from *nixtamal*, dried white field corn soaked in limewater and cooked before being ground. Then they spooned a spicy filling of minced meat and onions on top before rolling the husks and sealing them, placing them on a board until they could bury the *tamales* deep beneath the hot ashes in the fireplace.

"Jolie was jesting, Lupe. You know she eats just about everything you cook," Leigh said, trying to soothe the little Mexican woman's quick temper, which was just as fast to fade—but she was afraid this time Lupe had met her match in Jolie. Lupe ran the kitchens with ironhanded single-mindedness, and even Jolie admitted she was a good cook, which was quite a compliment. Jolie, however, couldn't resist meddling—it was part of her bossy nature—and she'd run a household, controlling the lives of family and servants, far too long to sit idly by now.

"Hmmmph!" Lupe said, not realizing she mimicked Jolie to perfection, but a mischievous twinkle came into her black eyes when she picked up a long-handled flat wooden paddle, and it was fortunate Jolie wasn't around, Leigh thought. "You hungry, Meez Leigh? That Meezter Neil, he sure eats a good meal this morning before he leaves the *rancho*. I'm so glad he's home, and he's lookin' so happy too," she said, shoving the paddle into a small oven, then lifting it out with a tin of golden-brown corn bread sitting atop the wide board.

Leigh's eyes had widened slightly in surprise as she heard the news, thinking Neil had gone to the north pasture with his father. "Where did he go?"

Lupe shrugged. "Oh, he was in the big hurry. Ate in here in the kitchens, says he likes bein' 'round pretty girls," she said, blushing, even though she had five children and eleven grandchildren. "He says he has someone special to see, and don't expect him back for dinner. Took a couple of *burritos* and *churros*, 'cause he likes things that are sweet," she said with a wide grin, then shushing her giggling nieces.

"Are you hungry, Mr. Sebastian?" Leigh asked abruptly. "You've obviously had a long ride to reach Royal Rivers. There's always a pot of *puchero* on the hearth, and Lupe does make the best *burritos* north of the Pecos. They're far more practical than sandwiches, especially when someone is in a great hurry," Leigh offered, schooling her tone into politeness as she controlled her dismay at the news that Neil had ridden off in a hurry to visit someone very special.

"Thank you, ma'am, but I'll eat after I do a day's work. I don't accept charity," he said, chewing on the stem of his corncob pipe, which was still unlit and which he held cupped in his hand as if he liked the familiar feel of its shape.

Leigh bit her lip to keep from saying something she would probably regret. But too much pride—like Travers pride—had led them too easily into a war that had taken everything from them, except that pride—and a new sense of humility.

"As you wish, Mr. Sebastian," Leigh said, pointing toward the far door with the rolled-up sketch. "If you'll please follow me, we won't delay any longer," she requested, unaware of how haughty that Travers pride now made her voice sound. "No thank you, Lupe, Mr. Sebastian is anxious to see the *patrón* about work," she said, leading Michael Sebastian without any further delay toward the door.

"You come back through here, Meez Leigh, and I'll make you my best *torta de huevos. Holee* tells me you don't eat your dinner last night and I know you don't eat nothing for breakfast, so you come back. Don't want to get skinny as a jackrabbit, like when I first saw you, *pequeña*. Won't be able to keep a man like Meezter Neil in your bed if you don't have nothing for him to warm himself against. Never get the little ones that way, and you should have half a dozen by now. But Meezter Neil, he'll make up for lost time," she told Leigh with embarrassing bluntness, saying something in Spanish to her nieces, which had them giggling again and eyeing Leigh speculatively until Lupe got their attention by rapping a spoon on the edge of the table. With the deftness of long practice, even while she spoke over her shoulder to her nieces, she began to slice the corn bread into thick chunks, and Leigh knew the promised potato omelette would be waiting for her when she returned, and accompanied by further personal comments.

Leigh had avoided meeting Michael Sebastian's eyes, her cheeks a flaming rose, until she thought she heard a low chuckle from him, and she turned to give him a disdainful glance for being so discourteous, but he was looking quite innocent as he coughed, as if he'd been clearing his throat all along.

Once they left the kitchens, Michael Sebastian pulled his tobacco pouch from his pocket and began to fill the bowl of his pipe. Then he pulled the strings tight with strong-looking teeth and put the pouch back in his coat pocket. He searched the pockets for a couple of seconds before he finally found the matches. Striking one on the heel of his boot, he lit his pipe. The smoke, from an aromatic blend of tobacco sweetly scented with just a touch of rum, swirled upward above his head.

"The north pasture is just beyond that row of low sheds and the last fenced-in yards. Those long sheds are where they'll be doing the shearing and dipping in a couple of days. And if you're hired on, you'll find a bed in one of those houses," Leigh told him, pointing out several small, but well-built adobe buildings. "You'll have no difficulty finding Nathaniel Braedon," Leigh said, nodding a dismissive good day to the boorish man.

"Why, thank you, ma'am, you're too kind," he said, sounding overly obsequious as he put his hat back on with an almost insulting show of courtesy, and Leigh got the distinct impression he was laughing at her.

She stood for a moment watching as he walked off. He was limping slightly. Leigh's eyes narrowed thoughtfully as she noticed his trousers. They were an indeterminate color now, but at one time they'd been a beautiful shade of violet blue. She could see the darker color along the outer seam of his trouser leg, where the yellow braid had been removed, apparently in an effort to make use of an old uniform now that he'd returned to civilian life. He'd also removed the double-breasted row of gold buttons from his full-skirted smoky gray frock coat, sewing on plain ones instead, and discarding the broad black belt he'd once worn, and to which his sword had been strapped. The fancy gold braid frogging had been pulled from the sleeves, leaving a curling outline, and a darker gray collar had replaced the military-stiff yellow one that had been stamped with his rank. However, his coat branded him a cavalry officer as surely as if his insignia remained—and, in Leigh's eyes, so did the color of his trousers.

Guy had been wearing a pair of the extraordinary violet-blue trousers when he'd been wounded. He had been so proud of those trousers, Leigh remembered, for only his troop and one other in the regiment had received them—luck of the draw, he was to explain later. The dyers, having to make do as best they could under wartime conditions, had mixed the last batch of indigo they had, but they hadn't had quite enough and had added red to complete the order. Too much red, as it turned out, for the wool had come out a glorious color, but far more appropriate a shade for a silk pansy in a lady's bonnet. Jolie claimed they'd gotten the shade from mixing too much madder or bloodroot into the vats, since synthetic dyes were hard to come by, and the natural plant dyes were less predictable. At first the color had been cause for ribald comment by their comrades in arms, since most Confederate soldiers wore dull blue or light gray trousers. Guy's troop, however, always returned victorious from any engagement, suffering very few casualties. Wearing their violet-blue trousers like a badge of courage, they had effectively silenced any talk. And as the war had progressed and fine woolens and dyes had become even scarcer, coarse trousers of butternut had been even more common. And the violet-blue trousers of two troops of Virginia cavalry had stood out all the more—as they did now. Leigh wondered how the North Carolinian had gotten a pair unless he'd served in the Virginia cavalry, and those particular two troops had been made up almost exclusively of wealthy Virginians, the landed gentry, their horses some of the finest bloods the South had to offer.

Leigh was about to return to the house when something caught her eye. Bending down, she picked up the small packet of matches that Michael Sebastian had dropped in the dust. He was too far away now to call her attention to it. She'd leave the matches with Nathaniel, Leigh was thinking as she turned around. Glancing down at the matches, she frowned as she read the label on the paper packet:

FRICTION MATCHES
Manufactured by
LEWIS & CO.
For sale by
L. OLDHAM & CO.
RICHMOND, VA.

So, Michael Sebastian had been in Richmond too. Perhaps Guy had been right, and the man was a Virginian. But why lie about it? she speculated idly as she returned to the house, her steps dragging slightly as she finally allowed herself to wonder where Neil had gone. If the special person he apparently couldn't wait to see was Diosa, then he was in for a big disappointment, Leigh thought with little pleasure, for the lovely Spaniard had left Santa Fe some four months ago, traveling to Mexico City with her brother, Luis Angel, and Courtney Boyce. And they were not expected back for another week.

It was nearly half an hour later, after eating a meal that would have pleased Jolie had she been in the kitchens, and which Leigh had consumed beneath Lupe's watchful eye, that Leigh was finally walking back along the corridor, intending to leave the matches in Nathaniel's study—which gave her a good excuse to look at the portrait again—when she saw Lys Helene in the courtyard.

"Lys Helene, did Guy find you? He was looking for you earlier," Leigh called out as she crossed the courtyard.

"Guy? Looking for me?" Lys Helene repeated in her soft voice, a bland expression on her lovely features. "No, I haven't seen him this morning," she said with a shrug, sounding disinterested as she turned over a small clay pot, dumping the loamy dirt into a pile on a sheet of oilskin spread out before her.

Leigh stood uncomfortably for a moment, wondering what to say, because she suspected the reason behind Lys Helene's coolness. Thinking it best not to say anything, Leigh started to turn away when Lys Helene's voice stopped her.

"We missed you and Neil at breakfast," she said, glancing up beneath the wide brim of her straw gardening hat, her light gray eyes warm with humor, but her attempt at bridging the constraint that had widened between them only added to it.

"Neil was already gone from the *rancho* when I awoke. I don't know where he is. He was apparently in a great hurry to see someone special. I had to see Solange about something. I know she never has anything but coffee for breakfast, so I went to her studio. Then a stranger, looking for work, had to be shown to the north pasture," Leigh responded, trying to ease the stiffness from her voice.

"Oh," Lys Helene said, frowning as she stared up at Leigh's flushed face. "A stranger? What is his name?"

"Michael Sebastian. I have a feeling he is only the first of many. Now that the war is over, I think we're going to be seeing a lot of strangers, men like this Michael Sebastian. There is nothing left for them in the South. They no longer have anything to fight for, some don't even have homes or families left to return to. They're just drifting. But after the first day of shearing, I imagine we won't see any more of Michael Sebastian either. He'll ride out before sunrise."

"You don't like him, do you?" Lys Helene asked, surprised, because Leigh usually liked everyone. Sitting back on her heels, she pushed a loose strand of reddish-blond hair from her forehead, leaving a smudge of dirt across her lightly freckled brow.

"No, I don't like him," Leigh admitted with a rueful look. "I have no reason not to, except that he was rather rude, and I sensed a deep bitterness and anger in him. I think he lied to Guy too, about not being a Virginian. I'm just wondering what he has to hide."

"Everyone has something to hide, Leigh," Lys Helene said, her gloved hand clenched around the handle of the trowel. She sounded far wiser than her years, for she was only a year older than Leigh. "Aren't you judging the man too harshly? You just said many of these men have nothing. What if he had a family, a home, and they're all gone now? I'd be bitter too, and I wouldn't want to share my grief with strangers. I might want to forget the past life I'd led and just start over. We should remember that and try to be understanding, and—oh,

Leigh, I'm sorry," she said quickly, getting to her feet as she saw the flash of pain cross Leigh's face. "Sometimes I forget that you ever lived anywhere else. You seem to belong here, and I feel as if we've known each other for so long. Forgive me?" she said, and pulling off her garden glove, she held out a small pale hand.

"There is nothing to forgive," Leigh said, taking Lys Helene's hand in hers for a moment.

"Thank you. Although, I don't know how I can forget Travers Hill, when that is all Guy ever seems to talk about. Sometimes, I feel as if I know that house of mellow brick with its green-shuttered windows as if *I* were the one who'd been born and raised there. I could walk up to that green door with its pineapple-shaped brass knocker, and, without knocking, walk right inside the paneled foyer, where the painting of Charleston hangs and an Oriental carpet covers the pine floorboards. And over the door to the parlor is your grandfather's flintlock fowling piece and a powder horn engraved with a map of Virginia. And across the foyer, above the door to the reception room are a couple of swords, which Stephen claims nearly beheaded a couple of guests once. Then there's the bench along the wall, where your mama's garden hat is always hanging, as if she'd just come in from gardening, and there are fresh flowers in the Sevres vase on the small table, and the scent of beeswax is always strong. And from the dining room would come the cheerful singing of songbirds from the domed birdcage between the windows, and on the big table, if it were Sunday, we'd have one of Travers Hill's famous hickory-smoked hams, and chicken curry with rice, and your papa's bourbon pecan cake would be brought in by no less a personage than Jolie herself. And then, later, the melodic strains of a waltz would drift from the opened double doors of the great hall, where the ladies and gentlemen would dance beneath that sparkling chandelier," Lys Helene said, her voice dreamy. "And all of the linens would smell so sweetly of lavender and roses, and we'd have spicy geraniums in those kitchen windows again. But I think it's the rose garden before the house that I know the best. I'd bring your mama's roses back to life again, letting them breathe of the summer's soft, balmy air, pulling up the weeds choking them, and I'd find that damask rose you told me about, Leigh. And watching over us, the running horse weather vane. All summer long it'd swing in a southeasterly direction, toward the river, then as the days shortened, the evenings turning cool, it'd start spinning, warning us of a blue norther coming, and I'd have time to cover the roses," she said huskily, then becoming aware of the amazed expression on Leigh's face, her cheeks pinkened.

"Silly, isn't it. I know Travers Hill far better than I do Royal Bay, the home my father was born in, but he has never spoken of Royal Bay like all of you do your home. *Travers Hill*," she said slowly, knowing she'd never enter the house she so longed to see. "If my father hadn't left Virginia, and had stayed around Royal Bay and Travers Hill, then we could have been neighbors all these years. Grown up together."

"Best friends, even," Leigh said.

Lys Helene smiled shyly, because she liked to think they would have, for even though Leigh was a beautiful and accomplished young woman, who'd always had everything she wanted in life because of her privileged background, she wasn't like those other snooty girls Lys Helene had come to despise that year she'd spent at a Charleston finishing school. Small and quiet, her freckled face burning so easily with mortification whenever she'd made a social blunder, the other girls had sensed her vulnerability and loneliness and had cruelly exploited it, until she'd run away in tears, managing to find her way to Lexington, and the comforting arms of Justin, who'd been a cadet at the Virginia Military Institute. With the help of their Uncle Noble, he'd arranged for her return home to the territories, her stay at Royal Bay too brief to ever have visited Travers Hill, or met Guy Travers—until now.

And *until now*, she'd never wanted to go East again, to face those coldhearted women who ruled society and prove to them, and to herself, that she was every bit as good. But now... now she'd show them, she thought with a determined glint in her dove-gray eyes, knowing no one would ever again cause her to run away. "Of course," she added, forcing a cheerful note into her voice, her fair-complexioned face still bright with embarrassment as she tried to joke about something deep inside that was too precious to expose to anyone, "the roses wouldn't fare too well the first year, since we haven't any of that famous blend of manure to fertilize them."

"So Guy told you about that too?" Leigh said, laughing, touched by Lys Helene's loving description of Travers Hill, a place she'd never even seen, and wondering if she knew how much she'd revealed of her secret yearnings.

"Well, mostly about the stables, the horses, and his hounds," Lys Helene admitted, thankful Leigh hadn't ridiculed her about her sentimental talk of Travers Hill—after all, it had been their home, never hers. "Both you and Althea have spoken of Virginia, and your life there before the war. Although Althea never mentions anything that happened during the war. And I've heard absolutely *everything* about Travers Hill, and the Travers family, from Jolie and Stephen, and in letters to my mother over the years from Aunt Euphemia. We always wondered about the infamous Travers family, and then to have Nathan marry one of them, and now my own brother...well, you haven't any secrets from me. I even know about the Reverend Culpepper," Lys Helene warned, startled by the look that briefly touched Leigh's face.

"Your childhood indiscretions are safe with me," she added, grinning as Stephen came across the courtyard, his arms full of rose cuttings.

Leigh eyed Stephen in disbelief, remembering his offended dignity when they'd had to dig in the vegetable gardens, looking for anything edible that might have survived the long winter. And here he was carrying rose cuttings with a pleased grin on his face.

"Miss Leigh!" he said, momentarily returning to the old stiff-backed Stephen as he straightened his shoulders, and frantically looked for a place to drop the cuttings. Although he no longer wore the green livery, he'd managed to fashion a suit of charcoal-gray wool into as close a copy as possible, and as a free man he wore it even more proudly.

"Stephen has a gift for growing things," Lys Helene said, taking the cuttings from him and gently placing them on the brick floor of the courtyard. "He's going to plant these and raise them himself until they blossom into beautiful, fragrant blooms. He already has five cuttings that have taken root. Stephen selected the seeds, did the planting, and has tended the first sproutings in that window box without any assistance from me. And they're going to grow strong and tall," she said, meeting Stephen's pleased expression with an encouraging one of her own.

Stephen actually looked sheepish as he met Leigh's questioning glance. "Jolie's not pleased, Miss Leigh. Says I'm actin' like some sweaty field hand whose been out beneath the sun too long, says I'm tetched in the head, but I like the smell of roses. Reminds me of Travers Hill. They're such pretty flowers, very dignified an' proper. That's why Miss Beatrice Amelia liked them so. Never before had the chance to go into the gardens much, 'cause I had more important tasks inside Travers Hill. Wasn't proper for me anyway, Miss Leigh, 'cause I'm a majordomo. Hardly ever set foot out of the big house. Didn't want anyone to take me for a field hand. An' I didn't know anything 'bout gardenin' anyway, but now, I don't have anything to do, except takin' care of Mister Guy, an' he's no trouble. An' figured since Mister Guy an' me was out here in the courtyard with Miss Lys Helene all the time anyway I oughta give her a hand now an' again, she's hardly bigger 'n a mite. So, I started helpin' Miss Lys Helene, but now she's teachin' me an' lettin' me help her with her plantin' an' prunin'. Makes me feel real good to help these lil' sprigs an' seedlings grow into somethin' so pretty, somethin' livin' after all that dyin', Miss Leigh. I understand now, for the first time, why Sweet John loved them lil' mares an' colts of his. He was helpin' them to grow strong an' proud. Real proud of him, I was," he said, his hand gentle as he touched the delicate petals of several pink stocks and white alyssum, the honey-sweet fragrance reminding Leigh of warm summer afternoons at Travers Hill.

"Mama always complained that no one in her family would know an onion from a rose except for the smell. She would be pleased, Stephen," Leigh said simply, turning away before he could say anything—the look on his face enough. She left Lys Helene and Stephen to their gardening, Lys Helene's softly spoken instructions about the proper blending of soils drifting after her as she left the courtyard.

Leigh had nearly reached the end of the corridor when she saw Camilla sitting on one of the benches, a handkerchief pressed to her trembling lips, her other hand lost in the folds of her shawl. Seeing Leigh, she quickly dabbed at her red-rimmed eyes, then gave her short nose a trumpeting blow.

"What's wrong, Camilla?" Leigh asked, hurrying to her side and thinking some tragedy had befallen them. "It isn't Gil, is it? He hasn't worsened has he?"

Camilla sniffed, struggling to control her tears. "No, dear, he's full of aches and pains but he'll do just fine. At least he didn't lose any teeth, and he has such a sweet smile. I just don't know how he managed to take such a tumble into that arroyo. It's those big feet of his. When he grows into them, he's going to be as tall as his father and Neil...and Justin," she said, managing a watery smile.

Leigh sat down next to her on the hard bench. "What is it, Camilla?" she asked, still concerned. "Are you ill? May I help you to your room?"

"It's Neil," she said, starting to weep quietly again.

"Has something happened to him?" Leigh asked faintly, starting to get to her feet.

"Oh, no, child, no, he is fine. It is just that he has done such a wonderful thing. So dear of him to think of me. I never truly realized how kind a man he can be. Because of the misfortune of his childhood, living with those dreadful Comanche, people misjudge him. And he doesn't seem to care. He lets them believe what they want. It doesn't help him being such a loner, and so arrogant, but then that is a Braedon trait. I—I only wish his father could...well, perhaps that is not to be. Some things never change, and some people never can," she said more to herself than to Leigh.

"What is it, Camilla? What did Neil do?" Leigh asked quietly, sitting back down beside her and putting her arm around Camilla's shaking shoulders.

"We had a long talk last night, before he went to your room. He found Justin's grave," she said, pressing the damp handkerchief to her mouth, but a small moan escaped as she drew a shaky breath. "My boy was buried in a peaceful little village in the Shenandoah Valley. Neil said the valley is beautiful, a heavenly place, with rolling green hills, and softly murmuring creeks meandering through groves of willows and sycamores, and always in the distance are the Blue Mountains. And in the spring the apple blossoms are like a veil of lace over the land, and then in autumn the apples turn golden, then scarlet. Justin loved apples," she sighed, seeming to find some solace in that thought. "Neil promised me that one day he would take me there. He promised me, Leigh. He always keeps his promises. He's a good man. Better than a lot of people know. And sometimes, I think there is no reason for Neil to be so nice a man. He's had a hard life, too hard. But now he has you. I was so worried, when we heard he'd married again. His first marriage wasn't a very happy one. It was a terrible mistake. But when I met you, I knew everything was going to be all right. You are so warm and loving, I knew Neil would finally find his happiness with you. You do love him, don't you?"

Leigh swallowed. "Yes," she said softly.

"I knew you did. I could see it in your eyes when you saw him last night. You can't hide love," she said with a sigh.

But does he love me? Leigh wondered silently, then kissed Camilla's cheek. She was right, though, about Neil. He could be a kind man—when he chose to be—because he had spared Camilla the truth of Sheridan's devastation of the Shenandoah Valley. And in the eyes of Virginians, it equaled the savagery that followed in the wake of Sherman's march to the sea and the confiscation and destruction of anything of value to the Confederacy that stood between the Yankee general and Savannah, leaving Georgia, and later the Carolinas, in ruins. Sheridan's army had marched down the Shenandoah, burning barns, mills, fields, ravaging the land until there was little left. There would be no red and gold apples ripening this autumn, nor for many years to come. Adam had been right in his warning, and the Union had not allowed the Valley to continue to support the Confederacy with the bounty from its rich soil.

Slowly, Camilla withdrew a small box from the soft folds of her shawl, holding it close against her breasts. "Neil took a handful of earth from Justin's grave. He brought it to me, so I could be close to him, to know he is resting in peace," she said. Getting slowly to her feet, she suddenly looked tired and defeated.

Absentmindedly, she patted Leigh's shoulder, then walked

away, a forlorn little figure. Despite the family around her, Leigh knew Camilla would not be able to seek comfort from Nathaniel and would return to her room and grieve alone.

For a moment, Leigh remained sitting on the bench, wondering at Camilla's words about Neil. What manner of man had she wed? That night in the garden at Travers Hill, when he had dueled with Guy, she had seen the deadly side of the man, seen a man who could very easily have killed—had it suited his needs. Instead, he had chosen a revenge that had been deliberately cruel, striking out to hurt her by taking something she cherished—Capitaine. And there was another man, one who had laughed with her in the stables when they had fallen into the hay—but that was a face he had shown all too briefly.

Then there had been the man who had become her lover, touching her with a gentle strength that still took her breath away. He was the same man who had held Lucinda so gently in his arms, and the man who had brought a bittersweet happiness to a grieving woman. He was also the man who had led a group of raiders behind enemy lines with deadly intent, and now could ride off so callously the very next morning after coming home from the war—humiliating his wife because he longed to be in the arms of his mistress.

Of course, what did she expect? Leigh mused, getting to her feet and feeling as forlorn as Camilla. Like father, like son, she thought without bitterness, for she'd been under no illusions when marrying Neil. She had no right to demand anything else from him. He had already given her his name. Given her family a home. She wouldn't ask anything more of him.

Leigh heard a shuffling step and turned in surprise to find Guy walking hesitantly toward her, his arm held out, his fingers inching along the wall in front of him to guide his steps.

"Guy, you shouldn't be walking around without someone," Leigh cautioned, holding out her hand to him, and not even realizing at first that he'd grasped it without hesitation.

"Leigh, I'm glad it's you."

"Guy!" she breathed, staring at him in shock.

"No, not yet, my dear. I just saw a hazy movement in front of me and assumed it was your hand, since I could see a darker, human shape behind it," he told her, dashing her hopes. "I'll have to make certain I hear a voice first, don't want to hold out my hand to the wrong sort. Lord help me if I were to mistake a bloodthirsty Apache for Aunt Maribel Lu because I saw feathers sticking out of a war bonnet." He laughed. "My sight may never get better than this," he added warningly.

Leigh nodded automatically, then said quickly, "I know."

"We didn't have a chance to talk before, when the stranger was with you. It's wonder—"

"You were right about him, Guy," Leigh interrupted.

"What do you mean?"

"I think he lied to you when he said he wasn't a Virginian."

"What makes you think that?" Guy asked, more curious now than ever about this stranger, because something had been bothering him since being introduced to the man.

"Although quite faded, he's wearing what were once the prettiest pair of violet-blue breeches you could imagine—or maybe you remember a certain pair you used to wear?" she asked, enjoying the look of disbelief on his face.

"My old regiment?" he asked, shocked that the man would lie about something like that. "No North Carolinian was ever in either my troop or Pembroke's. Are you certain?" he asked, confirming Leigh's own doubts that anyone but a Virginian would have ridden with those two troops.

"Yes, I'd never mistake that violet-blue. And the color and cut of his coat is cavalry, Guy. He has removed the yellow braid, and the insignia of his rank, but you can see very clearly where they were sewn on. And I found this," Leigh said, handing Guy the matches Michael Sebastian had dropped.

Guy held the packet to his nose and sniffed curiously. "Matches?"

"Matches from L. Oldham and Co."

"Richmond? So he was there," Guy murmured, frowning as he held the matches to his nose again. "He smokes a good blend of tobacco. I can smell it on the paper. Never met a Virginian who didn't. Reminds me of something, though, but I can't quite place it," he said, trying to remember as he fiddled with the packet.

"He smokes a—" Leigh started to say, bending down as

Guy accidentally dropped the packet, spilling several of the matches onto the bricks.

"Leigh," Guy said excitedly. "Isn't it the best news we've had in a long time?"

"What?"

"About Travers Hill," Guy said, puzzled by her reaction. "Didn't Neil tell you? It still stands. The house is still there."

Leigh stood up quickly, grabbing his arm, the matches forgotten. "How do you know?"

"Neil told me. He rode through Virginia on his way home, and he went to both Royal Bay and Travers Hill. He said the house could use a coat of paint, but there has been no further damage," Guy told her, his voice thick with emotion. "Someday, we could probably rebuild the wing that burned, although I don't think we're ever going to have so many guests staying overnight at Travers Hill as we once were accustomed to putting up. Of course, I was thinking, if rebuilt, it might make a splendid servants' wing. No more slave cabins at Travers Hill," he said without regret. "And I don't think I could hire anyone but myself to muck out the stables," he joked, his voice threaded with an underlying excitement as he dreamed of regaining his sight and returning to Travers Hill. "It'll take a lot of hard work, and we won't have much at first, but we'll have the land, and our house, and if we can get a few mares and one or two blooded stallions, we can start up a stud again."

Hearing that note of determination, and hope, Leigh suddenly began to feel a strange, uneasy sensation in the pit of her stomach. She'd never thought about the full implications of Guy regaining his sight—but now she had to accept the possibility of what would happen if he did. Guy would never stay at Royal Rivers. He would return home to Virginia. He would never abandon Travers Hill, his birthplace, his heritage. He would never give up.

Leigh was momentarily relieved that Guy couldn't see her expression, because she wasn't proud of the brief flash of fear that had shown when she thought of him leaving her behind at Royal Rivers. When he'd spoken of returning to Travers Hill, a part of her had wanted to return with him. And to further

her unease, she wondered what Neil would say if she proposed such an idea to him. Would he want her to stay? Or would he, now that they might be able to resume their lives at Travers Hill, feel his promise to Adam had been fulfilled? Would he allow her to take Lucinda and return to Virginia?

Leigh pressed her slender fingertips to her temple, easing the pain of such a thought.

"I thought Neil would have told you last night."

"He was very tired. He fell asleep almost as soon as he'd eaten."

"This morning?" he questioned gently.

"I'm afraid I was still asleep when he left," Leigh explained, trying to smile. "I'm going to walk out to the corrals," she said hurriedly, before he could question her further. "I've a couple of apples for Damascena and Capitaine. Would you like to come with me?" she asked, not wishing to think further about what the future might hold for all of them.

"Thanks, Leigh, but Althea has another student in her class today," he said, bowing slightly. "I was supposed to meet her here, although I may lose my courage. I have the feeling I'm going to be placed in the corner to serve as a reminder to her pupils of what can happen to those who don't learn their sums."

"There you are," Althea greeted them as she walked quickly to where they stood, her arms full of lesson books. "I'm sorry I'm late, but I had to leave Noelle and Steward with the Misses Clarice and Simone. And I heard that," she added, laughing.

"Me and my big mouth. I suppose I've put ideas into your head," Guy said in resignation.

"If you will recall, talking too much was exactly why you so often found yourself perched on a high stool in the corner," Althea reminded him. "Dunce cap and all."

"Yes, I took a degree in duncery," Guy joked.

"Oh, Leigh, isn't it wonderful about Travers Hill. Neil did tell you?" Althea asked, a look of expectation in her eyes.

"Yes, I know," Leigh answered. "It is wonderful news."

Guy tipped his head slightly, as if listening to voices. "Is that Lys Helene's voice I hear?" he asked.

"Yes, she and Stephen are in the garden."

"I want to speak with her, so if you ladies are going to talk for a moment, I'll wait for you in the courtyard, Althea," he said, starting to turn away.

"Let me help you, Guy," Leigh offered, holding out her hand.

"No, I can find my way, thank you," he said, and if he saw the hazy movement of her hand, he ignored it this time.

Leigh dropped her hand, watching as he carefully made his way along the corridor, then through the opened doors to the courtyard. Leigh saw him shield his eye, as if the bright light bothered him. He stumbled slightly on one of the uneven bricks, then bumped his shin on the edge of a stone bench, his muttered imprecation hastily muffled as he heard approaching footsteps.

This time, Lys Helene did come to his assistance, her hand taking his arm firmly as she guided him the rest of the way, and Leigh saw the flash of naked longing revealed in Lys Helene's eyes when she stared up into Guy's face, but just as quickly the expression of loving tenderness was gone and she had released his arm to kneel back down by her cuttings, her back turned stiffly to Guy.

"I'm so relieved Guy finally met someone like Lys Helene. She is perfect for him. He would never have been happy with Sarette Canby. I have watched the love blossoming between them, just like one of Lys Helene's flowers. Mama would have loved her and been so pleased to welcome her into the family. I hope Guy won't wait too much longer to ask her to marry him," Althea said, watching with an almost motherly look as Guy hovered just behind Lys Helene, trying to get her attention and nearly tumbling over her shoulder in his impatience. "Guy has changed so from the man he once was. I believe the old Guy would have deserved someone like Sarette—well, perhaps not. I've never seen him so thoughtful, and gentle, especially when with Lys Helene. At one time, I don't believe he would have appreciated her, or truly seen her beauty, for her coloring is uncommon, and Mama would have despaired of all of those freckles. But I think it adds to her charm. They will be so happy together."

But Leigh wasn't as certain. Guy could also be very stubborn with pride, and if she was right and Lys Helene had overheard their conversation the day before, she might never forgive Guy for his scathing words, little realizing they had been feelings of frustration aimed at himself rather than her.

"I always hoped Travers Hill would somehow manage to survive. After what happened to Royal Bay, I didn't see how it could, with Richmond burned to ashes and the Shenandoah despoiled by that horrible little Yankee general. They say he was at Chickamauga, when Nathan was there, and he was the cause of Jeb Stuart's death at Yellow Tavern. And there sat Travers Hill, right in his path," Althea said, shaking her neat head in wonderment, a faraway look in her eyes. Then she closed them for a moment, as if banishing that vision from her mind.

Opening her eyes, there was a sparkle in the brown depths even if the words that followed sounded hesitant, as if she were still uncertain. "Guy and I were talking about Travers Hill, and the possibility of living there again. It is our home, Leigh, and we have a right to dream," Althea reminded her, her tone almost defiant. She could see Leigh's expression and anticipated the words of argument she was about to utter. "Of course, with Guy, that is all it is, a dream. But for me it is much more. I have a family to provide for. And now that I am well, I know I can do it. I didn't completely waste my years at finishing school. I am capable of many things, I've recently discovered, and I do know how to run a home. Mama taught us that much. I haven't made up my mind yet, but I've been thinking that if I returned to Virginia, I could either live at Travers Hill, or, perhaps even more practical, live in Charlottesville, where I could teach school, or…if there was no position available, I thought I could become a seamstress. I am a very accomplished needlewoman," Althea said, but not boastfully. "I will be able to support my family. Oh, Leigh, don't look like that," Althea said, touching her younger sister on the cheek in a gesture of loving affection. "You never have been able to hide your feelings. And you are absolutely horrified, I can see it in your eyes. *Whatever* would Mama think? Things have changed, my dear."

"I know things have changed. They will never be the same again, but it isn't necessary for you to have to change too, Althea. It isn't necessary," Leigh spoke huskily, staring down at the sketch she still held in her hands. "You have a home here. Lucinda and I are here. You can't leave."

"Oh, Leigh, you know I love you, but my home is in

Virginia, and it always will be," Althea told her, a note of
steel in her voice that Leigh had never heard before, and she
glanced up almost in desperation as she saw Althea slipping
away from her. "You have done so much for us. For me and
my children. Without you, without your unselfish strength,
which you shared with all of us, I would not have lived to see
the end of this war.

"I have the strength now to survive, and I want to raise my
children in Virginia. I intend to raise them the way their father
would have, had he lived," Althea said, finally speaking aloud
the words that had been so heavy in her heart for so long.
"We may no longer be wealthy, and I may not be able to give
them the life they would have had before the war, but they
will have a sense of honor and dignity, and what they achieve
in life will be because they worked hard for it. That will be
the heritage they will leave to their children one day. Nathan
would have wished us to stay in Virginia. So would Mama and
Papa. I would feel closer to all of them if I were back there. I
know we are welcomed here, and I have never known such
kindness. Living here, I have been able to recover my health,
and my courage. I can now face a life without Nathan. It is
something I have come to accept, as Guy has his blindness, and
if I'm to make that new life, I must have a home of my own
again. Can you understand that, Leigh?" she asked, searching
Leigh's face. "And you have to accept something too, Leigh.
You now have a home here. And you have a husband, never
forget that. You must try to make something of this marriage
of yours," she said. "You have a responsibility to Lucinda, to
the memories of Blythe and Adam. They both trusted you.
Blythe loved you so deeply, and I know she would have
approved of what Adam did.

"But my memories are in Virginia, Leigh. And what of all of
our family possessions, and those from Royal Bay? The family
heirlooms buried in that cave cannot be forgotten. Adam told
us where they were hidden. We can't leave our family's pride
hidden away in the dark. Guy wants to return to Virginia too,
but we know that would be impossible, at least right now. But
once I am settled in Charlottesville, and I am able to make
life comfortable for him, then he would be welcome to come

and live with Noelle, Steward, and me. Of course, it will be difficult, and we won't have much, but we will be together in our own home. By then, however, he and Lys Helene may have married and decided to stay here with her family. I do not know that he would have any other choice. He has no way to support her," she said, forcing herself to be realistic.

Leigh nodded, unable to speak, because she knew more than Althea how close Guy was to regaining his sight, and then, with or without Lys Helene, he would return to Virginia, to Travers Hill, and he and Althea, working together, would have a much better chance of beginning again—and succeeding in making a new life for themselves.

"We will talk more of this, Leigh. We have to. I want to consult with Neil about what I should expect to find when I return to Virginia," she said, sounding worried for an instant, but she'd already made up her mind and Leigh knew nothing she could say now would change it. "And I should speak with Nathaniel, because, although Steward is now heir to Royal Bay, Nathaniel was born there, and I would like to offer him the chance to claim any cherished possessions he might remember from childhood."

"And what of Julia?" Leigh asked, speaking her childhood friend's name for the first time in over a year.

Althea's face hardened. "She forfeited that right. I never told you, because it was far too humiliating, but I wrote to Julia. I knew where Julia was staying in Paris, Aunt Maribel Lu and Uncle Jay saw her there, although Aunt Maribel Lu would not speak with her. When I was desperate in Richmond, I wrote asking for help. Aunt Maribel Lu had written that Julia had been dressed in the height of fashion, draped in jewels, had a house and carriage of her own, and could be seen dining in the most elegant and expensive restaurants. I thought she might be able to send us money, or perhaps even a box of essentials, still easily bought in Paris. She wrote that she was preparing for a trip to Venice and did not have much time, and she was rather short of cash, having spent her allowance on clothes. But she did send us a box of chocolates, her favorites, she said."

"So very generous of her," Althea said, her voice quivering with the same repressed fury she had felt at the time.

"I never knew," Leigh said, unable to believe her friend could have been so selfish and uncaring, but as she thought back over the years, she knew that she'd always tried to excuse Julia's actions, to find a generosity of spirit where there had been none.

"Well, I must go now," Althea said, her silken skirts rustling as she took a step, then stopped. "Oh, and Leigh, I think you know that both Guy and I feel that anything you might wish to keep from Travers Hill is yours," Althea added, the scent of violets lingering long after Althea had crossed the courtyard to stand in conversation for a moment with Lys Helene.

Leigh watched them, feeling a strange sadness as Althea took Guy's arm and they walked away. Turning in the opposite direction, Leigh made her way to the study. Entering the quiet room, she walked to Nathaniel Braedon's desk and placed the matches in the center of the blotter. Taking a piece of paper, she took the pen from the inkwell and wrote a note of explanation, placing the paper beneath the packet. She had walked halfway back across the room before she glanced at the portrait of Neil's mother and sister.

As if compelled, Leigh unrolled the sketch and met the Comanche's blue-eyed stare, remembering again the terror she'd felt when they'd met face-to-face, and yet...

"So beautiful," Leigh murmured, glancing between the three faces.

"Yes, she was." Nathaniel Braedon's voice sounded so close behind her that Leigh drew in her breath in surprise, and guilt, almost choking on it as she spun around to find him standing just within the door.

"I'm sorry if I startled you," he said, watching her intently.

"Forgive me for intruding, but I left a packet of matches on your desk. That drifter, Michael Sebastian, dropped them when I was showing him where the north pasture was," Leigh explained, her hands fumbling as she tried to roll back up the piece of vellum. "I assume he found you?"

"Yes. I've hired him, so he'll have plenty of time to collect them," Nathaniel said as he came to stand beside her in front of the portrait.

"I was just admiring the portrait of your first wife and your daughter," Leigh said uncomfortably. "She was very beautiful. Fionnuala was her name, wasn't it? I have seldom seen such brilliant blue eyes," Leigh commented, glancing down instinctively at the rolled-up drawing in her hands.

"They were remarkable. Once you have seen eyes like hers you never forget them," he said, his gaze never leaving the two faces. "Fionnuala Elissa Darcy was her name when I first met her...a lifetime ago."

"It's a lovely name. And your daughter's name was Shannon?"

"Shannon Malveen. She was her mother's daughter. Even in that picture, when she was just four years old, she was exquisite."

"Fionnuala died in childbirth?" Leigh heard herself asking, then wished she hadn't when she saw the bleak look that entered Nathaniel's eyes.

"I'm sorry, I should not have asked," she apologized quickly.

But Nathaniel hadn't seemed to have heard as he continued to stare at the portrait of his beloved wife and child. "Died?" he asked, surprising her by the harshness of his voice. "She should never have died. She would be alive today, except for—" He broke off his words, as if he could not speak them. Then he said coldly, "I curse the day she told me she was carrying my son."

Leigh stared at him in shocked silence, the drawing dropping from her hand.

"Any time a woman dies in childbirth it is a tragedy, especially if the child she carried was stillborn, but you have a living part of her with you," Leigh said, thinking more of Lucinda than Neil in that moment. "You still have Neil, your son. And now he has returned safely from the war. You should be thankful, grateful that he is alive. That some part of Fionnuala still lives in him."

"Neil." He said the name almost as if cursing beneath his breath. "Neil always comes back. He always manages to survive. I knew he'd come back when Justin wouldn't. There is nothing to be thankful for. Neil is destined to survive."

Leigh felt as if she'd been slapped. She took a steadying breath, feeling a sudden, intense loyalty to Neil. "I never quite realized—or perhaps I refused to believe—how much you hated him. I think you must be the most hateful person I've ever met that you would not rejoice having your son return home to you, especially after losing Justin," Leigh said, two spots of angry color burning in her cheeks. "When I think of the loved ones I'll never see again, and here you stand sorry that your son lives, I-I could just...just—" she began, but Leigh couldn't find strong enough words to express her feelings and turned away, but his hand shot out, grasping hold of her arm and holding her in front of the portrait.

Nathaniel glanced down into the young, beautiful face staring up at him in such condemnation, and although her eyes were a dark shade of blue, they suddenly reminded him of other eyes. He couldn't bear to see such a look of loathing in them when they met his, and he found himself telling her what he'd never told another living soul.

"Hate Neil?" he repeated the words slowly, as if hard to comprehend. "No, I don't hate him. When I first saw him I knew such fierce pride, such love for this son of mine. No, I don't hate Neil. What I hate is myself and the curse I live with. Every time I look at Neil, at the son I loved, I see my own face staring back at me. Neil wasn't created in God's image, but in *my* image, in the image of a man who thought he was a god. Neil was to become a constant reminder to me of my arrogance. I was young and defiant, and contemptuous of everything but my own strength and will to hold on to what I had created, what was mine," he said, his voice sounding like it must have years ago, bold with self-assurance.

"Riovado was mine. I defended it against all who dared to challenge me. This land I'd conquered was my kingdom.

"Fionnuala was mine. I loved her as I have loved no other, and Fionnuala loved me as a man dreams to be loved by a woman. And we were blessed.

"Shannon was the symbol of our love, of our divine existence. But we were too close to the heavens at Riovado.

"I nearly lost Fionnuala when she gave birth to Shannon. We hoped it was just the difficulties of a first birth, but later we knew it would be dangerous for her to have any more children. She was never completely well after that. But our love was not to be denied, and I worshipped Fionnuala with my heart and my body. And I wanted a son. A son in my image. I was all powerful, and I challenged anyone to take Fionnuala from me, especially after she told me she was with child. I'd never seen her looking so breathtakingly beautiful. She laughed and sang, and sewed clothes for her son—because she always gave me what I wanted. You cannot have a dynasty without a son to inherit, to carry on the noble family name," he said with a bitter twist to his lips.

Nathaniel glanced up at the portrait. "She died in my arms, hemorrhaging away her life's blood. But my son lived, and every day he grew stronger and healthier, and his hair was golden like mine, and his eyes a pale grayish-green, and when he raised his little fist into the air, shaking it in defiance, as if at the gods above, as his father had before him, I knew then they were mocking me. They had granted me my wish, given me my son, but at what price?" he asked, glancing back up at the portrait. "Are you familiar with mythology?"

Leigh nodded, unable to speak.

"As a boy, I was always fascinated by the stories of the gods. In this land, despite one's Christian beliefs, it is easy to believe in those ancient myths. The Indians sense the power around them, they recognize the forces that influence their lives, and they are ruled by the beliefs that have been nurtured by what they cannot comprehend—what is beyond their reach, what they cannot change. Drought. Famine. Flood. Death. One comes to suspect that the gods sit up there on top of the mountains watching and waiting with infinite patience for some foolish mortal to challenge them, to change what has been proclaimed by them in their ancient wisdom. The myths are full of such tales, and of the gods' jealousy and anger, and retribution, against a mere mortal who would aspire to such Olympian heights and try to steal their power. There was a man who dared. And why shouldn't he? He was almost a god. There was nothing beyond his reach—except a son. And the gods smiled behind their hands, nodding to one another, then held them out, palms open, as if acquiescing.

"But nothing is given freely in this life, and you will learn that to your sorrow one day," Nathaniel said strangely, staring down into Leigh's widened eyes. "The gods gave the man a son. A golden son—gift of the gods. And they said they would watch over him, protect him throughout his life. But they had deceived the man. Every time they intervened, and saved the son's life, they sacrificed another in his stead.

"Both father and son were damned. For those who died were wife and mother; daughter and sister; and son and brother," Nathaniel spoke softly, his light gray eyes shadowed and sunken, his mouth, which once must have curled up at the corners when he smiled, like Neil's, was hardened into a thin line by the guilt that years of suffering in silence had caused.

But Leigh felt no pity for him, and she pulled her arm away, meeting his gaze angrily as she said in a low voice, "You haven't changed, Nathaniel Braedon. You're still an arrogant man. You've been so full of bitterness and self-pity you kept the love you could have shared with your son, and with others, to yourself. Hoarding it like a miser. How could you have truly loved Fionnuala that you could turn away from her only son? He is of her flesh. She died so he could live. Neil was *her* gift to you, the man she loved. How do you think she would feel to know how you had received it, how you had treated her son?" Leigh demanded, angrier than she'd ever been as she thought of how Neil must have suffered all of these years and how another man, a far better man, Adam, had loved the child whose life might have caused his beloved Blythe's death.

"My sister died shortly after giving birth to her only child, but did Adam turn away from that child? No, he loved his daughter more than his own life. He cherished the child born of the love he had for Blythe. To have turned against that child, for whatever reason, would have been a betrayal of that love. You may hate yourself for wanting that son, but Fionnuala gave her life so he could live. If you cannot see that, then she died for nothing," Leigh said quietly, turning away from him.

She'd almost gotten to the door, when his harsh voice stopped her.

"You forgot this."

Leigh took a shaky breath and turned around. Nathaniel was holding the rolled-up piece of vellum. Forcing herself to walk back toward him, her knees shaking, Leigh held out her hand.

Her eyes met his for a brief moment, while each held on to the roll of paper, then Nathaniel released his grip on the paper and turned away. He walked over to stand behind his desk, a lonely man with his back to the room as he stared out the window at his kingdom.

Leigh almost ran down the corridor to her bedchamber. Slamming the door behind her, she leaned against it, her breath coming in ragged gasps. Pushing herself away from the door, she went to her desk, opening the lid and searching through one of the small drawers for the small brass key to unlock the bottom drawer in the lower chest. For a moment, Leigh stood deep in thought, the rolled-up sketch balanced across her outspread palms, as if she were weighing its value.

The key clicked softly in the lock, and Leigh opened the drawer, carefully placing the drawing on top of Blythe's muslin shawl, next to the *brisé* fan and neatly tied stack of letters, the drawer holding all of Blythe's prized possessions—to be kept in trust for the daughter she would never know.

Leigh shut the drawer firmly, locking it. Placing the key back in the small drawer, she was about to close the lid of the desk, when her eye caught the gleam of the ornate silver frame that held the wedding portrait of Blythe and Adam. Leigh picked it up, her fingertip lightly tracing the curving line of the cold frame.

Blythe's smiling face stared back at her. She had been a beautiful bride in white satin and lace, a chaplet of orange blossoms, for chastity and fertility, adorning the dainty, shoulder-length veil, her bridal bouquet fragrant with flowers from the gardens of Travers Hill, the blushing pink rose buds, drops of dew still clinging to the petals, lovingly selected by their mother the morning of the wedding. The toe of Blythe's white satin slipper just peeked from beneath the lacy skirts of her gown, as if tapping with impatience for their images to be caught forever as the camera snapped. Leigh could still remember how long the photographer had taken in setting up his equipment, juggling thin metal plates, trays, and chemicals, his bald head popping up and down beneath the black cloth behind the tripod camera box, until finally there had been a bright flash that had sent Guy's hounds howling from the great hall, the flustered

photographer nearly falling in his haste as he tripped over the
stragglers as he rushed to his wagon, where he'd set up his dark
tent for developing the plates before they dried. The photographer had known his craft, however, for Adam appeared the
perfect bridegroom, standing somewhat stiffly in his somber
black tailcoat and trousers, his elegantly figured silver waistcoat,
white shirt, tie, and gloves impeccable. His blond hair was
neatly brushed, side whiskers trimmed close, but the devilish
grin on his handsome face was anything but appropriate for
the occasion, nor was the white satin drawstring purse over his
arm proper dress for a gentleman on his wedding day, but then
since Blythe held his top hat in her small gloved hand, Leigh
supposed it did not seem unusual, and knowing both her sister
and brother-in-law too well to have asked how the exchange
had taken place, it still remained a mystery.

Leigh was placing the photograph back on her desk when
she heard a gurgling noise behind her and went to the cradle.

"Hello, sweetheart," she murmured, bending over and
lifting the baby into her arms. "My, you're growing into a big
girl," she said, kissing Lucinda's chubby cheek and receiving a
tug on her ear in response.

"Ouch, don't pull on Mama's earring," Leigh said naturally,
not even aware of what she had called herself as she gently
pried the strong little fingers loose from the dangling earring
of lavender jade, then pressed a kiss into the tiny pink hand.

Big gray eyes, but a darker shade than Adam's, and fringed
with dark brown lashes, stared up at her trustingly, and Leigh
hugged her close to her breast, vowing this child would always
know love. "Your father loved you so," Leigh said huskily,
thinking of Neil, and the love he'd been denied because of the
untimely death of a mother and the bitterness of a grieving father.

But what of Shannon? Leigh found herself wondering as
she sat down in the rocking chair and began to rock Lucinda
back and forth gently, softly singing a lullaby well remembered
from childhood.

What had been the true fate of Neil's sister?
What had happened to Shannon Malveen?

❦

A lone rider approached a cabin in a clearing beneath tall pines. No welcoming smoke rose from the stone chimney, and the small windows were shuttered against the light. The corral was empty. Weeds grew tall before the big double doors of the ramshackle barn and a heavy tree limb had fallen from high overhead, crashing through the roof of one of the weathered outbuildings.

Densely forested slopes swept down low to the valley floor, where a broad sweep of plateau stretched to the low hills rolling toward the snowcapped peaks to the east.

A small mountain river with cool, clear waters meandered through the waving grasses of the meadow before tumbling into a ravine that narrowed into a rocky canyon. *Cañon del Malhadado* fell away to the south, the steep gorge descending through the cottonwoods and sagebrush to the desert floor far below.

The only place to ford the river was where it crossed the grassy plateau, where cattle, sheep, and horses could graze, and the mountains rose protectively around the valley.

Riovado. Vado del Rio. The ford of the river.

Neil Braedon had come home.

He dismounted, standing for a moment as he stared at his birthplace. Slowly, he walked toward the cabin, the big bay following a step behind.

Finding the rawhide strap, Neil pulled the latchstring, the bar on the inside of the door lifting. Pushing against the heavy crossbeamed door, Neil was momentarily surprised, for the door opened easier than he thought it would, even though the hinges creaked with age and disuse. His hand came to rest on his holster, the butt of his pistol comfortably against his palm as he stepped inside the cabin. He moved easily through the shadowy room to the window, lifting the bar across the shutters and letting the sunshine filter through the dirty panes of glass, and he wondered now why he'd bothered to replace the animal skins five years ago.

Neil glanced around.

Deer antlers hung above the door and held an old flintlock rifle and powder horn his father had carried with him from Virginia. The great stone fireplace almost filled one wall. A bear skin stretched before the hearth, where a black iron pot and a baking kettle swung from a long chimney bar, and a tin coffeepot sat on a trivet in the cold ashes. Other blackened long-handled pans and cooking utensils dangled from hooks nearby, and the long pine mantel held candles, lanterns, and an assortment of jugs and bowls. In the corner, a pole extending from the wall and held up with a notched log on the outer edge, then crossed with poles to the wall, held a soft mattress stuffed with leaves, sweet grass, and moss. A comforter and quilt had been folded across the foot, and feather pillows piled at the head. Next to the bed was a cradle. Across the room, a row of peg-like steps in the wall led to the loft above. A rough-hewn pine table and four chairs sat comfortably close to the hearth, as did a high-backed settle, while a corner cupboard held pewter dishes and cutlery. A long bench, a butter churn, and a spinning wheel had been placed next to it, and close enough to the window for light.

Nothing had changed during the last four years, Neil thought.

Nothing ever changed at Riovado. Walking closer to the hearth, Neil stared up at the painting above the mantel. It was a portrait of his mother, painted the year of her marriage. She could not have been more than seventeen or eighteen at the time. She had posed for the portrait dressed in a riding habit of dark blue cloth with a small ruff of lace around her throat and pinned with a cameo brooch. A black hat trimmed with a long ostrich feather and a blue veil was angled to expose the delicate line of neck and the luxuriant black curls that fell to her shoulder.

Neil stood staring at the graceful figure in the portrait for a long moment, meeting the brilliant blue of eyes the artist's palette had managed to capture, the expression full of warmth and good humor, the slant of the eyes alluding to a touch of impishness in the young woman's demeanor. "Mother," he said softly before turning away.

Neil pulled the shutters tight, unwilling for nocturnal visitors to make a shambles of his home during his absence. With a last glance around the silent room, he closed the door shut behind him, hearing the heavy bar slide back into place.

For a moment he watched the grasses as the breeze gently stirred them, the sound of the river drifting melodically to him across the distance. "Come on, boy," Neil said, patting the big bay as he walked by him toward a small copse of pine and spruce, the springtime air heavy with the sweetness of meadow grasses. Bending down, Neil picked up a pine bough studded with tiny cones, the spicy pungency of the pale sap sticking to his fingers.

Neil was about to stand, when he suddenly noticed the tracks; the hoof marks of unshod ponies. A number had been through here not more than a day ago, for the prints were still clearly marked, and had not been disturbed by even a pine needle floating down into the imprint.

But the tracks had not come from a herd of wild horses. These hoof marks followed in single file, and they were too deep for riderless ponies. Slowly, Neil stood up. Unhurriedly his narrowed eyes scanned the horizon.

Comanche rode unshod ponies. So did Apache.

Neil glanced back at the cabin, remembering the ease with which the door had opened. He reached automatically to touch the leather pouch at his throat, then dropped his hand halfway, remembering that it was still in Leigh's possession. His hand settled instead on his hip, close above the smooth butt of his pistol, and at his shoulder, Thunder Dancer walked beside him, the rifle within his grasp.

Reaching the shady copse of trees, Neil quickly searched the shadows for any that moved, listening for a distinct call to sound through the stillness.

But there was only the soughing of the wind through the trees.

Walking into the glade, Neil's soundless steps carried him to the small cross over his mother's grave.

FIONNUALA ELISSA BRAEDON
BELOVED OF NATHANIEL
B. 1805
D. 1829

This was the special person Fionnuala Elissa Braedon's son had wished to see. It had been four years since last he'd been at Riovado. Someone should stand by her grave, Neil thought, for his father, after burying his beloved, had vowed never to come to Riovado again. And he had kept his promise. Nathaniel Braedon had never again set foot on the mountain.

Gradually, Neil became aware of the footprints, softly implanted in the earth, as if others had stood beside his mother's grave. Neil's glance roamed over the area, finding the footprints that trailed away into the trees toward the meadow. Partly out of anger that anyone should trespass, and partly out of curiosity as to why, Neil followed the footprints into the deep shade of a stately pine close by, its boughs stretching to the heavens above.

Neil stilled.

At the base of the tree, overlooking the peaceful meadow below, the river a silver ribbon woven through the green grasses, was a cross. Neil didn't have to move closer to know who was buried there, for the softly spoken words came whispering back to him now, and he remembered his sister's words...

There was a beautiful white dove that flew in a sky so blue it had no end, the sun glinting on her outspread wings. She flew above a green field of wild flowers. She flew higher and higher and one day she flew too far. She flew through the sun, and was captured by the sky. Thunder surrounded her, and the white dove of the sky was frightened. The winds blew, and the world became dark, and the dove fell to earth, her proud wing broken. That was when she met the wolf, who stalked alone through the night. He protected the dove, healing her broken wing. But when the light came again, when the dove would have flown away, back to the green meadows, she discovered that the wolf was blinded by the light of day, and she could not leave him, for he had saved her when she had been lost. They roamed the lands together. She flew high into the skies during the day, guiding them, and he protected her at night. And they searched for the land where they would live together, where there was no light and darkness. But the land always eluded them, and their children flew through the skies during the day, and hunted at night, and knowing no other life, the children of the dove and the wolf, rejoiced in their freedom.

One day, when the dove knew she was dying, she found the passage through the sun, and she flew home, to the dancing grasses and the singing silver waters, where the guardian trees stood tall.

Neil knelt down beside the slender cross.

Shannon Malveen, She-With-Eyes-Of-The-Captured-Sky had come home.

Twenty-four

In a land of sand and ruin and gold
There shone one woman, and none but she.
                                        Algernon Charles Swinburne

STANDING IN HER STOCKINGED FEET, A SMOOTH LENGTH OF silken calf showing beneath the lacy, beribboned hem of her pantalettes, Leigh drew a deep breath, her waist becoming even smaller as she sucked it in beneath her ribs. "Hurry, Jolie, I can't hold it much longer," she said, beginning to feel faint as Jolie pulled the laces of the corset tighter, the front of the boned silk curving just beneath her breasts and lifting them upward, the pink-areolaed crests teasing the lace of her chemise.

"Don't know why you have to have it so tight all of a sudden. Figured you were goin' to stop wearin' one all together, along with your drawers, so forgetful of being lady-like had we become, 'course, we also got so skinny we didn't need a corset. But I've had this laced for twenty inches for the last five months, an' you've never complained before, an' why you want it smaller now I don't know," Jolie said, grimacing as she tried to hold the laces taut and tie them tight. "Goin' to break my ol' stiff fingers in two, honey child," she complained, wondering what had gotten into Miss Leigh. Then she remembered the tight lacings on Miss Beatrice Amelia's corsets, and close to thirty years *after* being courted, and, later, on Miss Althea's corsets, especially after giving birth to her first child, and she smiled knowingly.

"What are you smiling about?" Leigh asked suspiciously, catching sight of Jolie's smug grin as she looked up from straightening the lacy trim on her chemise, the silver hand mirror reflecting Jolie's coppery face.

"Hmmmm, just remembering, honey, just rememberin'. There's nothin' Jolie forgets 'bout," Jolie said, for Travers women were that proud when it came to their menfolk.

"Hmmmph, don't understand Mister Neil leavin' yesterday

mornin' an' not comin' back last night," she said, shaking her head in puzzlement. "You know where he went off to, honey?"

Leigh's jaw tightened slightly as she gritted her teeth. "No."

Jolie sniffed. "You didn't say something sharp-tongued to him, did you?"

"No."

"I know you, missy, you got a lot of your mama in you, 'ceptin' when it comes to common sense, then you've too much of your papa in you."

If Leigh could have drawn in her breath in indignation, she would have.

"No. I said nothing to him."

"Hmmmph! That's probably the problem. You've got to sweet-talk him."

"I didn't have time to say anything, he left so abruptly. And I'm not going to sweet-talk Neil Braedon," Leigh told a crestfallen Jolie. He'd laugh in my face, she thought privately.

"Well, you better be mindin' your tongue then, honey, 'cause a man doesn't like a sour-faced, vinegar-tongued woman 'round him. An' I've never seen such crazy goings-on in the rest of this household. Reckon everybody's actin' addlepated. Miss Camilla hasn't come out of her room since yesterday mornin'. Mister Gil's got the fattest lip I ever seen an' his nose is twice as big, an' that sure wasn't a little scratch on his arm. An' I thought those misses were goin' to have vapors when they saw him, jabberin' 'bout that *Oncle Gilbear* of theirs who was chopped up into so many lil' pieces. An' I swear that poor Mister Gil turned pea green when they said that. An' then there's Miss Lys Helene, who's not talkin' more than two words at a time to Mister Guy, an' Mister Nathaniel's hardly said even two words, an' they were hardly more than a growl. An' I don't like the way Mister Guy's been actin' lately, real sneaky, like when he was a boy an' didn't want me to find out 'bout somethin' bad he'd done, an' Miss Althea sashayin' over to that shed to teach readin' and writin'. Not proper. An' that lil' Mister Steward needs a hickory stick taken to that chubby bottom of his, throwin' all those tantrums when he doesn't get what he wants, an' Miss Noelle never smiles, an' she was such a sweet lil' thing, an' that Steban diggin' in the dirt like some bumpkin. I've never seen such goings-on."

"Tighter, Jolie, please. I can still breathe too easily," Leigh said abruptly, not wishing to think about what was going on— especially the goings-on she was partly responsible for—as she began to brush her hair, the heavy length looking like bronzed silk as it cascaded over one shoulder to fall past her hips.

"Well, you're goin' to have to stand stiller than you are, missy! Don't want me to lace your hair into this, do you?" Jolie said, frowning as Leigh bent slightly sideways, reaching out for the sapphire-blue perfume bottle on her dresser top. Removing the gold stopper, she dabbed the heady fragrance behind her ears and through several long strands of hair, then at the base of her throat and on the blue-veined pulse points of her wrists, before reaching back and dabbing a drop behind Jolie's ear, much to Jolie's mock displeasure.

"Scented soft skin and silken hair, satin and lace and laven- der," an amused voice commented from the door.

At the sound of Neil's voice, Leigh spun around in surprise, jerking the laces from Jolie's hand.

"Now, honey, look what you've gone an' done. I'm never goin' to get them so tight again."

"Allow me," Neil said lazily, straightening from where he'd been leaning casually against the doorjamb, his arm raised along the partly opened door, his tall body blocking any view prying eyes might have had into the room as he'd stood admiring his wife en déshabillé. His feet in their soft-soled moccasins made no sound as he walked across the room with his catlike tread.

"I don't think that will be—" Leigh began, only to be interrupted by Jolie.

"Nice an' tight now, Mister Neil," a traitorous Jolie told him, handing over the laces rather too precipitously for Leigh's peace of mind, especially when she felt the laces being pulled tight with such ease.

"If you don't mind?" he said softly, his hand gently forcing her head down so he could see what he was doing as he stood close behind her.

Leigh shivered slightly, then felt his hands around her waist, stilling her with their iron-band strength. "Jolie told you to stand still," he reminded her, his breath warm against her nape, and she could have sworn she felt a whispering touch of lips against the sensitive pink welt where the rawhide strap had grazed her.

"Don't you ever knock?" she asked, catching her breath as the laces were pulled even snugger around her waist.

"Not when it's my room, and my wife is within," he answered mockingly.

"You just get back, Mister Neil?" Jolie asked, eyeing him up and down critically, thinking she'd like to get her hands on those buckskins again. "We've all been wonderin' where you got off to in such a hurry when you just got home. I was askin' Miss Leigh, but she gets real uppity an' says she doesn't know," Jolie confided, much to Leigh's dismay.

"I rode in a few minutes ago," he said without revealing where he'd been.

Leigh's knuckles whitened as she stood, hands clasped demurely together, wondering angrily where indeed he'd been all night. He had certainly not been in any great hurry to enter his wife's room before now, she thought, remembering how endless yesterday had seemed, and how long the night had been as she'd lain awake listening for the slightest step outside her door—and finally falling into a restless sleep when none had sounded.

"You want something to eat?" Jolie asked, already heading toward the door.

"Thank you, Jolie, but that's not necessary," Neil said, smiling at the mulattress, and winning her undying loyalty, for she had a soft spot in her heart for handsome, sweet-smiling gentlemen.

"Quick like a fox, I'll fix up some food for you, *if* that Lupe'll stay outa my way. Interfering bossy woman, an' she still doesn't know how to fix grits properly," Jolie muttered as she reached the door, never glancing at Leigh's openmouthed expression.

"But I'm not finished dressing," Leigh protested, glancing around for her peignoir, unable to move, the laces still held fast in Neil's hands.

"Mister Neil can help you now, honey. Your papa was always sayin' it was goin' to take a firm hand on the reins to hold you, an' I've been thinkin' there's no better man for the job than Mister Neil," Jolie said, her wheezing chuckle coming back through the door after she'd closed it firmly behind her.

"Well, really…" Leigh muttered, trying to pull free again, but Neil's grasp held her fast.

"I don't want you leaving Royal Rivers," he said abruptly as he tied the laces, then releasing her, he sat down on the edge of the bed, her petticoats caught beneath his buckskin-clad thigh.

"I don't understand. Not leave Royal Rivers? W-why… w-whatever do you mean?" Leigh asked huskily, stuttering slightly, her eyes sliding away from his guiltily, for she had been thinking of exactly that since speaking with Althea and Guy the day before, and after her unforgivable words to Nathaniel, she thought it might be best if she left his home—at least before he asked her to leave. She still couldn't believe she'd said what she had to the man. Despite the provocation, her behavior had been unpardonable. She was a guest in his home, and her mother would have been horrified and ashamed of her. And now, suspecting what she did, she worried, glancing over at the bottom drawer of her desk where she'd hidden the rolled-up sketch, and not knowing what to say about it, she wished to be as far away from Royal Rivers as possible.

"I don't want you to leave the valley unless you're riding with me. It is too dangerous. Fortunately, you and Gil only had a stray lamb to deal with the other day, not the Comanche. Gil values his life too much to ride far from Royal Rivers, alone, and especially with a woman accompanying him. If he was so foolish to do such a thing, and he met up with a war party of Comanche braves, *and* he lived to return to Royal Rivers, then he would have to face my father and me. He has been taught since childhood what can happen to someone who makes a mistake," Neil explained, eyeing her thoughtfully as he noticed the rosy color staining her pale cheeks.

"I see, I thought you meant—well, I would think you wouldn't be overly concerned about the Comanche. You and your sister lived with them for many years," Leigh said, watching him carefully.

Neil smiled grimly. "That is precisely why I am concerned. My sister and I were lucky to be taken into a respected family of the tribe and treated as if we were of their blood. Others did not fare so well. You'd be better off to be killed during an attack than to be taken captive. Always remember that, Leigh," he warned her, thinking of what close proximity she and Gil had been to the Comanche who'd paid a visit to Riovado. If their paths had crossed, the depressing thought came to him, then Gil would be dead...Leigh would be lost to him—at least until he found her, and he would have, he vowed. And in that instant, Neil, because he loved this woman with all of his heart, felt for the first time the desperation his father must have had when his children had been kidnapped and knew the same deadly determination to reclaim what was his.

"B-but you and your sister lived a good life with the Comanche?" she questioned.

"A hard life, but a good one, yes," Neil admitted, his expression shuttered as he added, "because they were family to us and we were young enough to be able to adapt to their way of life."

"You were raised to be a warrior, weren't you? And your sister, Shannon, what was her life like? She was older than you, wasn't she? And she must have been very beautiful. I've seen the portrait of your mother and sister," Leigh said. "She died, didn't she? I mean," Leigh rushed on quickly, self-consciously, "quite a while before you were rescued?"

"Yes, Shannon is dead," Neil replied harshly, staring at Leigh with narrowed eyes.

"Oh," Leigh said almost disappointedly, but then what had she expected him to say? Why would he tell her anything different from what he had told his father all of those years ago? And, Leigh thought in growing confusion, he had sounded so positive. He would think her crazed, perhaps even be offended, if she told him of the Comanche brave who so resembled his mother and sister, and she would be betraying Gil's trust if she spoke of their terrifying encounter.

"And what exactly did you think I meant, my dear, when I told you not to leave Royal Rivers?" he asked, not having forgotten her initial start of surprise. "Where had you been planning on going?" he asked, and whether his question had been sarcastically intended or not, she couldn't be certain.

Leigh went to the wardrobe and searched through the row of gowns for her peignoir, using the time to gather her wits, even though she remembered Jolie had taken the robe yesterday to be laundered. Drawing a deep breath into her lungs, then wishing she hadn't as she felt a stitch in her side because of her tightly laced stays, Leigh turned to face Neil, forgetful now of her previous worries as her own problems became more important than what had or had not happened in the past. There should be no pretense between them, and she desperately hoped he would say the words she longed to hear—that he wanted her to stay with him at Royal Rivers.

"Virginia." She startled him with her answer. "Althea is thinking about returning home, now that the war is over. She feels she should raise her children there. She believes she will be able to support them. And now that you've told us Travers Hill still stands, I-I—" she paused, then admitted hurriedly, "I was thinking that I should return with her. It is my home, and she'll need me. And Guy is determined to return, also," she confided, her tone becoming excited as she thought of Guy regaining his sight, but in Neil's ears it sounded as if she could hardly wait to leave. "And your promise to Adam has been fulfilled. You managed to assist us out of danger, but the war is over," she reiterated again. "We are, of course, very grateful to you, but we can do quite nicely on our own once we've returned to Travers Hill," Leigh concluded, pleased with the way she had spoken her piece, her fingers crossed behind her back as she waited for his response and, hopefully, a stirring declaration of love.

"Adam's daughter stays here with me," he said coldly, his gray-green eyes unblinking as he watched her intently, as if waiting for a sudden move.

Leigh felt her heart take a painful tumble in her breast, for he had said nothing about wishing her to remain at Royal Rivers—only Adam's daughter. And she would never leave Lucinda, nor could she stay at Royal Rivers if she found out Neil was still in love with Diosa.

"That is completely unacceptable. She remains with me. She is my sister's daughter, or have you forgotten that?" Leigh asked, her anger taking over now that her hopes had been dashed by his coldhearted answer.

"I've forgotten nothing. And certainly not my promise to Adam, which you seem to have with very little show of conscience."

"How dare you say such a thing to me," Leigh said, her anger carrying her to within a foot of where he sat on the bed staring up at her, her blue eyes dark with indignation as she glared at him. "I loved Adam. And I promised him I would take care of his daughter. And that is what Blythe would have wanted too. And my mother and father. Lucinda is a Travers. And that is what I intend to do. I'll never leave Lucinda for someone else to raise," she warned, thinking of Diosa.

"Fine, then you stay at Royal Rivers," Neil said in a bored voice.

But in reality, he was tired. And he'd just had his hopes ruined by Leigh's casual suggestion that she would take Adam's daughter and return to Travers Hill with her family, and apparently, he would cease to exist as far as she was concerned, he thought savagely. Staring at her broodingly from beneath slightly lowered lids, he felt the sensual stirring in his loins that he always did whenever near her. No other woman, no matter how attractive, had ever had the effect on him Leigh did. She was so beautiful standing before him in her pure white underclothes, her breasts firm and high, the soft, pale flesh pressing against the delicate lace of her chemise above her small, cinched-in waist, her hips slender, but curving with womanly fullness to the triangle of dark hair outlined through the gauzy fineness of her pantalettes. He had known the loving warmth of her before, and he wished he could draw her down on the bed beside him and love her again, the harsh words spoken between them forgotten, even if just for a little while. She was the one person in his life who should be completely his to love, now that...

Neil closed his eyes, wondering if Leigh and he were destined to live out the fate of the *kachina* from the underworld who escaped into their world, but was fastened back-to-back with another person, a stranger to him; damned never to gaze upon the other's face—never to know and understand the other's thoughts. Their existence to become a hell on earth.

"I remain at Royal Rivers because of Lucinda?" Leigh asked quietly.

Neil glanced up. "Why ever else?" he asked in return.

"Yes, why ever else," she repeated, then squared her shoulders and raised her chin, unaware of how alluring she looked as her breasts rose, taut nipples outlined against the thin linen of her chemise, her unbound hair swinging around her hips. "I would have thought you'd be glad to be rid of the responsibility of raising another man's child. I am more closely related to Lucinda than you are," Leigh said, glancing over at the cradle where she heard gurgling baby sounds. "I will raise her out of love. Travers Hill is her heritage too. Now that the war is over—"

"This war is not over," Neil interrupted her, his voice hard. "At least for some people it isn't," he added, a thoughtful look in his eye as he ran his hand along his unshaven chin.

"Life in Virginia, Leigh, despite most of the fighting coming to an end, will not be easy. Adam was a farsighted man and he knew that when he made me guardian of his daughter. He knew the war wouldn't be over for a very long time, at least not in the hearts of many. The defeat and destruction will become a very bitter taste in the mouths of many Southerners. They will not forget, especially when they have to face the deprivations the years ahead will bring to them. But I can change Lucinda's future. I have the legal authority, but I also have the moral obligation. I gave my word to Adam that she would always be safe. And I will keep my word. And the only way I can assure the future Adam sought for his only daughter, is for her to be here with me. It is unnecessary for Althea to return to Virginia, for she and her family will always be welcomed here at Royal Rivers, as will your brother. But Althea is a grown woman, fully capable, now that she has recovered her health, of managing her children's lives. That is now her responsibility, and I think I can understand some of her reasons for wishing to return to Virginia, and I respect her for them. I will always be here for her should she ever need help," Neil assured Leigh.

"You have everything figured out, don't you?" Leigh said, her tone resentful.

"I always have."

"And what of Diosa?" Leigh heard herself asking.

Neil frowned. "Diosa?"

"Yes, Diosa. She is your mistress, isn't she?"

Neil sighed, remembering that Leigh had been at Royal Rivers for some time and would have met Diosa. And Diosa would have wasted little time in taunting Leigh about having been his mistress.

"Yes, she was," he admitted, wondering what else Diosa had told Leigh. "That was in the past. It doesn't concern us, Leigh."

"Doesn't it? She was your mistress while you were married to Serena," Leigh reminded him. "Am I to expect the same?"

"Would it matter to you?" he asked softly, watching with interest as her face became suffused with color.

Leigh licked her dry lips. "I have my pride," she answered, without meeting his eyes.

"Of course, your pride," he murmured. "Well, you are not Serena, and our situation is very different."

"I believe our situation may be very similar. I know that your first marriage was an unhappy one. And your marriage to me was to satisfy Adam's wishes," Leigh forced herself to say.

Neil shrugged, his strong fingers playing with the lace on her petticoat.

"A slight inconvenience, perhaps, but I'm willing to make the best of this marriage. Are you, for the sake of your sister's daughter? Because I warn you now, there will never be a divorce between us. We are married till death do us part," he said with a mocking smile that did nothing to soften the hardness of his face.

Suddenly Leigh was hearing again Diosa's venomous whispers about a first wife's tragic accident—or was it? Diosa had hinted knowingly, believing her lover might have killed for her.

"Adam wished us to marry because he was thinking of you also, Leigh. He knew you loved your sister's daughter as if she were your own child, but he knew I was the only one who could provide for her. He gave her to me, but he wanted you to be able to remain with her. He may have been misguided in his methods, but he saw this as his only chance, and he knew he was dying and had to take the risk, and trust that his faith in us had not been misplaced. Together, he thought we might be able to succeed in providing a home and family for his daughter. Do you think we can put aside our differences and try to fulfill that wish of Adam's?" he asked, his eyes never leaving her as she stood so proud before him, her face whitened to ivory.

Leigh swallowed the hard lump in her throat, wondering how he had managed to turn everything around, sounding so noble, while making her seem so heartless. Leigh turned away in confusion, biting her trembling lip and taking a surreptitious swipe at a hot tear about to fall.

"Leigh?" he asked, startling her when his voice sounded right behind her.

Leigh nodded her acquiescence.

"Good, then we might as well do it right," Neil said.

Leigh jumped nervously when his hand closed over hers, and she looked up into his pale eyes as he stood just behind her shoulder.

"You're my wife, so you'll wear my ring, not this mockery any longer," he said, his fingers closing over the gold and coral cameo ring she'd worn after returning Althea's ring to her as soon as the hasty wedding ceremony had ended.

Suddenly, for a brief instant, Leigh felt a deep, instinctive fear course through her, as if in some way this symbol of their coupling was robbing her of something precious—branding her as belonging to another. She'd already lost the proud Travers name, and the home she'd been born in, and now she didn't want to lose any more of herself than she already had. That had been her fear when engaged to Matthew Wycliffe, for she had known her life would be different in Charleston— and she would have had to change for Matthew's sake. Leigh tried to tug her hand away, but Neil's grip was punishingly strong as he held her hand, his fingers pulling the ring from her finger, then he tossed it onto the dresser.

"*This* is the ring my wife wears," he said, sliding a slender gold band onto the third finger of her left hand. Then, before she could protest, he'd placed another ring on her right hand. In amazement, Leigh stared down at the single deep blue sapphire surrounded by rose-cut diamonds; it was an exquisite ring, and must have cost a fortune. "Since our engagement was unexpectedly short, I hadn't the time to purchase the usual engagement trinkets my fiancée would quite naturally have expected to receive," he said, the scented fragrance rising from the warmth of her body tantalizing him as he snapped a gold bangle bracelet studded with sapphires around her slender wrist, vowing he would have her love one day, perhaps not as easily as he had captured her wrist with his gift—but he would have it.

Whatever it took, she would be his, his wife in every meaning of the word. He wanted to share his life with her. And one day she would come to love him as much as he loved her. But first she would have to want him as much as he wanted her. And she would again, Neil thought, remembering her passionate response to his lovemaking. She was not indifferent to him—if he believed that, he would have nothing. But he wanted more than the physical union between them; he wanted her heart. And he wanted her to come to him willingly. It was that damned Travers pride, and the circumstances of their marriage, that he had to overcome, for there had been an attraction, an affinity, between them from the very first instant their eyes had met, and he would find it again.

Very well, Leigh was thinking. She would stay at Royal Rivers as his wife, but she would be no fainthearted Serena, and if Neil thought he would ever be able to humiliate her by flaunting his mistress, Diosa, before her, then he was mistaken.

She had her pride. No Travers had ever given up. She had been raised to accept a challenge. Perhaps she could make Neil fall in love with her. She knew he found her physically attractive, Leigh thought, remembering his lovemaking on their wedding night. Yes, she would win Neil from Diosa. It had been too late for Serena when she had decided to fight. But she accepted Neil as her husband, and she would not share the man she loved with all her heart with another woman.

"Travers pride," she murmured inaudibly as she glanced up into his face, her cheeks flushed delicately, her lips parting slightly as she smiled. "Thank you, the rings are exquisite."

Neil felt his heart miss a beat as he stared down into eyes

that put to shame the deep blue of the sapphire ring he'd just honored her beauty with. The heady scent of jessamine floated around him, drawing him closer to the lips parted with such sweet enticement, almost invitingly, he suddenly thought, his hand touching her silken hair as he tipped her head back against his shoulder and slowly his lips lowered to hers, touching them, clinging to them as the pressure deepened...

Leigh felt the roughness of his unshaven chin scratching the corner of her mouth, then his callused palm moving beneath the curve of her breast, his fingers sliding around the firm roundness, the fine linen of her chemise of little protection against the heat of his hand.

Neil felt her trembling body becoming pliant in his arms as he pulled her against him, his arm enfolding her waist as he began to turn her around to hold her closer...

"Told you I wouldn't be long," Jolie said, sending the door swinging open, certain to crash against the wall with a resounding bang, but she caught the edge with the heel of her foot as she passed through carrying a loaded tray, then kicked it shut again. Years of practice making her timing perfect. "Aren't you dressed yet, honey? What've you been doin'?" Jolie demanded, placing the tray down on the dresser and pulling up a chair for Neil. "You sit down there, Mister Neil, an' eat. Now, we're goin' to get you dressed before you catch your death of cold. An' good thing, too, he's your husband with you sashayin' 'round in your drawers. Not that it makes it right, it just doesn't make it so scandalous. Your papa never saw Miss Beatrice Amelia in her drawers. Not decent," she scolded, grabbing up the petticoats. "An' you put on your slippers this instant, y'hear?"

Leigh quickly did as Jolie bid her, leaning deep into the wardrobe, and hiding her blushing face as she took her time searching for the pair of pale blue kid slippers she intended to wear.

Neil stared in appreciation at the very feminine curve of linen-covered thigh and buttock and smiled, for although he regretted the untimely interruption, he had at least settled the question of Leigh ever leaving Royal Rivers—or him. All they needed now was time.

❧

Leigh took Steward firmly by the hand as they walked toward the north pasture on their promised outing. Althea had already crossed the yard ahead of them, waving and blowing a kiss to them as she hurried toward the schoolhouse. Her neat, gray-suited figure had disappeared inside to the sound of young voices eagerly greeting her. An appreciative Solange had turned over all the duties of teaching the *rancho* children to an enthusiastic Althea, who welcomed each day with a new sense of purpose. Leigh knew she was preparing herself for the day when she would have to teach school in order to earn a living for her family, and not just as another of the genteel, charitable pursuits of a bored lady of leisure who might take on the challenging duties of a booth at the church bazaar, or the tiresome affair of the annual picnic at the county orphanage.

Leigh smiled thoughtfully, for yesterday she had accompanied Althea to the schoolroom, helping her with the lessons. And both she and Althea had decided there was no reason why she couldn't assume those teaching duties when Althea left for Virginia, which, hopefully, wouldn't be for some time, Leigh prayed. Although she knew Althea was anxious to return home and begin anew.

Leigh glanced down at Noelle. Her delicate-featured face was still turned toward the schoolhouse, where she'd last seen her mother's figure. She was a lovely little girl with her dark hair neatly plaited into two long braids beneath her porkpie straw hat, the cluster of scarlet cherries decorating the brim bobbing up and down. Her dress was of green-checked silk worn over a white guimpe, the long-sleeved blouse fashionably trimmed, while a green satin sash had been tied around her waist, the long ends almost reaching the ruffled hem of her skirt. Her demeanor was very ladylike as she walked across the grounds in her gaitered shoes; in fact, except for her dark hair, she was a small replica of her mother, but Leigh frowned slightly as she watched Noelle hug her doll tighter against her thin chest. Her solemn face showed no sign of interest in anything around her, even as they neared the long sheds and Leigh felt Noelle's small gloved hand grasp hers, tightening nervously as they heard the bleating growing louder and louder.

"Auntie Leigh! Auntie Leigh! Lookee, lookee!" Steward

squealed excitedly as he stared at the sheep filling the pens, his brown eyes round with wonder. Jumping up and down, dressed in a brown velvet suit, his stocky, white-stockinged legs revealed beneath the short full breeches, his short-waisted jacket worn over a linen shirt with a wide, ruffled collar, he looked the perfect little gentleman. And it was about time he graduated to pantaloons, as boys his age were supposed to, but when Leigh had suggested such a change to Althea that morning, she had looked startled, saying that Steward was far too young. He was just a baby still, she'd declared, smoothing his thick dark curls with a loving hand as she'd pressed a kiss against his apple-cheeked face.

His cap was now slipping from those pretty curls, and Leigh just managed to catch it before it landed in the dust, and would, no doubt, have been sent flying across the yard by one of his stubby little boots, accompanied by naughty giggles.

Leigh placed the brown velvet cap firmly on his curls, then tightened her grip on his hand, determined no disaster would befall them, for she had promised Althea she could easily handle her niece and nephew if she took them to see the sheep—the outing just as exciting for her since this was their first spring at Royal Rivers.

For the last week and a half, day after day, a thousand head of sheep had been herded from pens into the sheds, where the shearers clipped them of their winter coats, the thick fleece piled high into mounds by each shearer, collected and tied into neat bundles to be stored until the wool could be shipped back East on the first freight wagons loaded and formed into a train. Already the teams of bull whackers were showing up at the *rancho*, along with the wagon masters and herders. The cracking of the bull whackers' heavy, braided rawhide whips cut through the noise of braying sheep and cattle as they engaged in friendly competitions of flicking flies from fence posts while idling away their afternoons; for soon enough they would be facing the perils of the trail that lay ahead.

Leigh gave wide berth to the deep trough stretching before them, despite Steward's tugging on her hand to move closer. She would never have been able to explain to Althea about the premature end of her son had he fallen in—which, Leigh suspected, Steward, being a Travers, was certain to have accomplished with breathtaking ease. The trough was four to five feet wide and close to twenty feet long, and filled with sheep dip, a hot, noisome mixture of sulfur, tobacco, various pungent herb extracts, and medicines, the fumes rising on an overwhelming cloud of steam. Standing on the edge, with long poles with hooks on the ends, the shepherds and ranch hands ducked the bobbing heads of the sheep swimming along the gauntlet to make certain the sheep were fully covered by the fumigating coating that would protect them from mites, ticks, and other disagreeable creatures.

Struggling from the trough at the far end, up a cleated ramp, the sheep were dried off and branded with red dye from a wooden stamp. The double *R* of Royal Rivers' brand marking them even as their clipped woolly coats became fleecy again; and as an added protection an ear was notched for identification, the mark varying each year to identify the age of the sheep in the herd.

A few days from now, with the shearing over, the lambs would then be docked; their tails bobbed either by a knife on a chopping block, or with a docking iron hot from the fire. Then the wethering followed, with the majority of the male lambs castrated, for only prized rams were allowed to rut come fall, when the ewes were in estrus.

The daily routine of most of the *rancho* had been involved with the shearing, dipping, and docking of the sheep. And soon, once the sheep had been returned to their summer pastures high on the forested mountain slopes, the longhorns grazing the grasslands would be rounded up, the calves born of the winter months branded, then the herd sent back to the range to fatten up during the long summer months. Again in early fall there would be another roundup, and the cattle to be sold at market would be cut out and herded across rugged desert and prairie. As in the past, the inferior cows would be slaughtered for hide and tallow. But already, Nathaniel's herd was showing an improvement in its beef, the prized Scottish Durham bulls he'd crossbred with Spanish longhorns producing a sturdier beef cow that could withstand the hardships of the trail.

Leigh shaded her eyes, for even beneath the rim of her hat, the sun at noonday was blindingly bright. Despite that, Leigh raised her face to feel its warmth, the luminous blue sky directly overhead cloudless, but in the distance, jaundice-tinted thunderheads were climbing high over the mountains and promising an afternoon shower.

"Hey! Leigh!" Gil called out, waving to them from his position at the end of the trough, a long leather apron tied around his waist, his hooked pole held ready as he eyed any stubborn, shorn heads that refused to dunk beneath the strong-smelling mixture. And as an eye-watering whiff was carried to them on the breeze, Leigh found she really couldn't blame the poor creatures for trying to keep their heads up.

"Auntie Leigh! Auntie Leigh! Wanna go closer!" Steward cried, tugging harder on her hand.

"You don't want to fall in, do you?" she asked, refusing to be pulled closer. "Gil might have to pull you out with that big hook."

Steward stared at his tall cousin in amazement, and at that precise moment, the big hook dipped down as if in warning, followed by a loud baaing coming from the trough.

"I wanna sheep. Can I? Can I? Uncle Guy has hounds," Steward demanded, quick with another want.

"That is slightly different."

"Pugh! Don't smell different," Steward said, thinking that would make it acceptable.

Leigh sighed, for it was very difficult at times to convince Steward that he wasn't going to receive his little heart's every desire whenever he made a wish—which was frequently.

"I'll take you to see the lamb Gil and I found in the mountains. I will even let you pet it, if you like," Leigh said cajolingly, hoping to avoid the ear-splitting cries and stamping feet of one of his tantrums.

"Hey! Where you goin'?" Gil called out, nearly losing his balance on the side of the trough as he leaned forward too far, his grinning face, except for the bluish-yellow bruise high on his cheekbone, showing little sign of the mishap—the truth of which was still their secret. For which her silence was shown in almost embarrassingly fond glances whenever she caught

Gil's eye, which had caused Neil to raise a curious eyebrow more than once as he glanced between them.

"Over to the pens. I'm going to show Steward our lamb," Leigh told him, unable not to smile when he made a comical face and mockingly wiped his forehead of nervous perspiration, his knees shaking, for he could laugh about it now—now that they were safely returned to Royal Rivers. But despite his clowning, Leigh suspected Gil would never make the same mistake again.

Leigh waved to Solange, who was perched precariously on the top rail of the fence overlooking the sheds. To those unaccustomed to Solange's eccentricities, she must have appeared quite a bizarre figure sitting there on the fence rail in a very unladylike manner. And her choice of dress did little to dispel such an impression. Her gray skirt was designed to show her ruffled underpetticoat of Solferino cashmere. Worn with a Garibaldi blouse of the same bright purplish-red color, the paisley shawl she'd worn against the morning chill now tied around her waist gypsy fashion, the drooping white ostrich feather in her turban hat shielding her eyes from the glare, she was perfectly at ease with her small feet, in a pair of red Moroccan slippers she'd bought in Tangier, dangling high above the ground. Her stub of charcoal moved with quick precision across the sheets of paper she held propped on a drawing board across her knees as she caught the movements of the sheep in the pen, and of the dipping trough just beyond. And, Leigh guessed, Michael Sebastian, had he been privileged to view Solange's sketch pad, might have been surprised to find his own visage portrayed quite realistically upon those pages.

She had to admit she was surprised he was still here, and that he had proven a hard worker. He was standing slightly apart now, watching the sheep tumbling into the trough, his hook sending the shyest into the depths without further delay. Leigh had been uneasily reminded of his presence all week, after catching him skulking around the stables one afternoon when he should have been in the sheds loading bales of wool. Coming upon him unannounced, he'd turned in surprise, looking uncomfortably guilty at having been caught. But his explanation had come glibly enough, mentioning something about looking for more rope, before he'd walked away. When Leigh had entered the stables, she'd been startled to find Neil inside, his broad back to the door as he'd examined Thunder Dancer's foreleg, and unaware that Michael Sebastian had been just outside.

Leigh sought Neil's figure now, easily finding him as he worked in one of the sheds, shearing like any hired hand doing backbreaking labor for a day's wages. He still wore his Comanche braid, which was, Leigh suspected, far more practical than some of the other workers' untrimmed hair which hung loosely about their faces, sticky strands clinging to their sweat-streaked cheeks. The Mexicans, however, wore red bandannas around their heads, and were now dressed in plain overalls. When they'd arrived at the beginning of the week they'd been dressed as elegantly as the finest *caballeros* in town, with short black jackets fancily embroidered with colorful silks, trousers trimmed in gold tinsel, richly figured sashes tied tight around their waists, high-heeled boots with jingling spurs, and wide-brimmed *sombreros*. They were saving their finery for the festivities following the shearing on Saturday night when there would be a barbecue and fiesta with singing and dancing.

Slowing her steps slightly, Leigh continued to watch Neil as she, Noelle and Steward hanging on to her hands, crossed the yard, for this was one of the few times she'd seen him in the last week. Ever since the shearing had begun, he'd worked like a demon possessed. He fell into bed—the daybed—in their room each night, too exhausted to do more than mutter a perfunctory "'night" to her, before turning his broad back to the room—and her. And each morning, he was gone before she awakened, stealing away like a thief in the night, Leigh thought, for she was a light sleeper. And he took his lunch with the rest of the shearers, and dinner was not an occasion for private conversation.

As she watched him now, he finished clipping the sheep he held caught between his long, powerful legs, releasing the sad-looking creature shorn of his proud fleece and patting the bare rump to send him along the makeshift passageway to a pen, and then through another passageway to the trough waiting at the end. The mound of wool behind him was piled high, and with a nod to the young man quickly bundling it up into bales, he walked toward the pump, where a bucket of cooling water and a ladle awaited the thirsty. But as Leigh watched, Neil pulled the linen shirt he'd been wearing over his head, then bending down and pumping the handle vigorously, allowed the cooling waters to stream over his head, shoulders, and bared chest.

Standing up, he shook his head free of water. His buckskin breeches were slung low on his narrow hips, the wide expanse of chest rippling as he stretched aching muscles. As he stood there, drinking a long draft of sweet spring water, he happened to glance their way. Leigh's eyes locked with his, and for a breathless moment there was no one else in the world except the two of them.

Leigh inclined her head in polite acknowledgment of his presence, his slow smile coming in response as he watched them cross the yard.

As they neared the pens where the ewes with their newborn lambs were kept, Leigh's step faltered slightly when she saw Nathaniel. He was riding the big bay he'd ridden across the plains, the image of him riding alone, of searching the horizon as he sat silently on his mount, always to remain with Leigh—for that was the essential being of the man. Since that day in his study, when they'd stood before the portrait of his wife and daughter, and she'd accused him of such selfish cruelty, he'd been as courteous and polite as he'd always been.

As he was now, Leigh thought as he tipped his hat in greeting, stopping to exchange pleasantries with her before riding toward the grasslands where his cattle grazed. But he never smiled, and had anyone been close enough to see the expression in his eyes, they would have wondered at the coldness. And had they chanced to overhear his voice, they might have thought the tone rather stiff and impersonal.

They reached the pens, and Leigh lifted Steward up to the rail where he sat wide-eyed, watching the lambs suckling their dams or nibbling tender green grass shoots in the meadow, Leigh's hand hooked inside the waist of his breeches and keeping him from tumbling onto their woolly backs. When he tired of just watching, she led him and Noelle to another smaller pen where the lamb she and Gil had found was suckling at its adopted mother's side, its tail wagging contentedly. Entering the pen, they waited until the lamb had his fill of rich milk, the ewe wandering off to graze as the lamb stood staring dumbly at them with round brown eyes that looked a lot like Steward's as he returned the lamb's gaze. Steward's mouth dropped open as the lamb came tottering over to him, bleating a greeting. Leigh squatted down beside Steward, holding out his limp arm so he could pet the lamb as he'd been promised, his small hand patting the little creature on top of its woolly head as if it were a big puppy. Noelle stood close by watching, declining the privilege her brother was enjoying, but his excited squeals and giggles when the lamb licked his face with a rough pink tongue brought her a step closer, and Leigh could have sworn she heard an uncontrollable giggle from her when the lamb butted Steward, sending him sprawling backward, unable to maintain his balance on such short legs, his look of dumbfounded disbelief almost causing Leigh to laugh until she saw the tears beginning to well in his eyes at such an affront to his dignity.

"He didn't mean to hurt you, honey," Leigh said, picking up her little nephew, whose masculine pride had been deeply offended. "He was just showing you affection."

Dusting off his breeches, and setting his cap, retrieved by Noelle, back on his curls, she kissed his cheek. "Would you like to go to the barn? The mouser just had kittens," Leigh told him, smiling as his tears stopped miraculously and he hugged her tightly, turning a laughing face up to hers.

"Love Auntie Leigh. Pretty Auntie Leigh," he said, his dimpled smile and long-lashed brown eyes already showing promise of a masculine charm that would be a serious threat to feminine hearts one day.

They entered the first of the several barns on the property. The other barns held the stored hay, the cribs and bins of corn and grain, and the stalls for dairy cows, with room for newborn calves, prized bulls and rams, and any expectant brood stock or sickly beast during the harshest winter months.

But this particular barn served the family's immediate needs, for at the far end of the barn sat Nathaniel's Concord coach that had just been delivered to Royal Rivers by special order from New Hampshire. It was a shiny dark red burgundy with gilded scrollwork and a beautiful landscape of mountains and desert painted on its door. The polished brass of the side-lamps gleamed beside leather-curtained windows, and the running gear had been made of seasoned hickory, elm, and oak—the sturdiest wood for the best durability was the company's creed—and the seats had been upholstered in the finest buff leather. But the true comfort came of the carriage being suspended by two thoroughbraces, the leather strips absorbing the shock when wheels dropped into holes and rolled over bumps in the road, while allowing the carriage to rock as gently as a cradle, its passengers undisturbed. Nathaniel's best driver would sit on the driver's box, holding the ribbons, with a team of high-stepping Morgans pulling the conveyance, while a covered rear boot and railed area on the roof would hold all the baggage the family might find necessary for their journey.

In the stalls along the side, the six matched bays were stabled, waiting to be harnessed to the *patrón's* private stagecoach.

"That's strange," Leigh said, taking off her jacket and folding it over her arm, the walk across the yard beneath the noonday sun having made her uncomfortably warm. Glancing around the last stall, she shrugged, for it now stood empty. "I'm sorry, but the mother cat isn't here anymore. She and her kittens were curled up in that box when I was here the other day," Leigh said, pointing to an abandoned box in the corner.

"Horsey. Wanna ride! Wanna ride now!" Steward declared with a stamping of his foot as he heard the curious neighing coming from the stalls.

"Not now, sweetheart. Those horses are much too big for you. They pull the coach. Would you like to ride Pumpkin?" Leigh asked, thinking it high time Stuart Travers's grandson learned to ride, and that fat, grumpy little pony needed the exercise. In fact, she thought Pumpkin and Steward would get along splendidly.

"Pumpkin! Goin' to ride a pumpkin?" he asked in amazement, beginning to giggle, then he was racing around the barn, his short legs kicking up straw as he circled, neighing and pawing the floor while pretending to wave an imaginary sword over his head.

Leigh watched him in amusement for a moment, opening

her mouth too late to stop his cap from sailing through the air as she had feared earlier, the toe of his boot sending it high above his head and into the loft. He stood still for a moment, his giggles stopping abruptly as he touched his head where his cap should be, his shoulders drooping and his lips beginning to quiver as he looked over at his aunt. Leigh happened to catch her niece's critical eye on her. "It was only a suggestion, I had no idea he would become so excited," Leigh defended herself.

Noelle nodded understandingly. "One has to be very careful when handling Steward, Aunt Leigh," she said in a serious little voice. "Mama has spoiled him far too much. She never scolds him or takes a switch to him, but then I suppose it is because he reminds her so much of Papa. She cannot bear to punish him," she said, turning away.

"My cap, Auntie Leigh. Lost my cap," he said tearfully. "Bestest, most favorite cap ever, Auntie Leigh," he said, coming over to lean against her, burying his face in her leather riding skirt.

"Now, now, you haven't lost it," Leigh said, easily beguiled by him. "I'll get it right back for you."

"Should you really, Aunt Leigh?" Noelle cautioned. "The loft is quite high and that ladder doesn't look very strong," she said worriedly, sounding like her mother.

"Will so! Right now, Auntie Leigh!" Steward said, looking up at her brightly, for his Aunt Leigh could do anything. She was a lot more fun than his sister, he thought, making a face at Noelle, his dark head peeking around the slender curve of Leigh's hip.

Leigh nodded, looking for the ladder into the loft.

"It'll be all right, Noelle," Leigh reassured her, handing her niece her jacket to hold and walking over to the ladder, for she was an accomplished tree climber. "You watch your brother," she said over her shoulder as she began to climb the wooden slats that served as rungs. Halfway up, she had to admit that Noelle was right to have urged caution, for the loft was higher than most apple trees, and much higher than she'd thought when eyeing it from the safety of the ground.

With more haste than caution, Leigh quickly climbed the rest of the ladder to the top, standing on the top rung as she searched for Steward's cap. At first she couldn't find it, but eventually she spied it sitting atop one of the bales of hay stacked neatly along the edge of the loft. Sighing, Leigh left the ladder, crawling safely onto the floor covered thickly with loose straw.

"Where are you, Aunt Leigh?" Noelle called out worriedly, thinking her mother would never forgive her if she let anything happen to Aunt Leigh.

"Here I am. I found Steward's cap," she called down to her, having moved halfway along the edge of the loft.

"Cap! Steward's cap. Auntie Leigh found it!" he squealed excitedly, racing toward the ladder. "Come up too!"

"Come back here, Steward!" Noelle cried out, dropping her doll and Leigh's jacket as she ran after him, and catching him as he struggled to climb onto the first rung.

"Lemme go! Lemme go! Help Auntie Leigh! My cap!"

"You can't go up the ladder, Steward! Do you want to fall and break your neck?" Noelle warned, then hollered when he bit her hard on the hand. "You little brat," she said, slapping his hand, both beginning to cry.

Leigh heard the commotion, but had already climbed up on the second bale of hay, Steward's cap within inches of her fingertips. Making a grab, she caught it, and was hurriedly backing down, when she suddenly heard the mewing and the warning meow. Looking over her shoulder just in time, Leigh avoided stepping on the mother cat and her kittens, nestled warm and snug on a long-forgotten horse blanket wadded up between two of the bales of hay.

But by trying to avoid them, Leigh gave little concern to her own safety, missing her step and falling against another bale, sending it tumbling over the edge of the upper story. As she rolled into thin air, arms flailing, she managed to grab hold of the loft's rough-edged boards with her gloved hands, saving herself from falling all the way down to the ground, which suddenly loomed beneath her like a chasm.

Noelle's and Steward's screams from below nearly deafened her as she swung back and forth like a pendulum, her wrists beginning to ache as she hung on.

"Good Lord!" A deep voice came from somewhere far below, cutting through Steward's bellowing and Noelle's shrill cries for help and effectively silencing both.

Leigh managed to glance over her shoulder, then wished she hadn't as the floor of the barn spun dizzily, along with the tall figure outlined against the opened doors.

"Let loose, Leigh, and I'll catch you," Neil told her calmly, having come to stand directly beneath her. "Leigh? I said to let loose and I'll catch you," he said quietly again. "I won't drop you," he promised, staring up at the booted feet surrounded by a white froth of ruffled petticoat.

"I-I can't." Leigh finally spoke, her voice sounding tremulous.

"Auntie Leigh! Auntie Leigh! Doan drop Auntie Leigh!" Steward cried out lustily, his short legs carrying him to Neil's side. "Help catch! Won't drop!" he said, jumping up and down on top of the brown velvet cap that had floated harmlessly to the ground, his short arms held outstretched, his tears dried, his slapped hand forgotten as he giggled happily in the midst of this new excitement.

Neil glanced down at his little cousin. "Step aside, son," Neil told him.

"No. Help Auntie Leigh. My auntie. Love Auntie Leigh! Help her. Go away!" he said, pushing futilely against Neil's hard leg before stepping in front of Neil with audacious arrogance for one so young.

Neil eyed the velvet-clad figure more intently, wishing he had a switch handy. With little regard for the young man's wishes, Neil scooped him up and walked quickly over to the coach waiting in regal splendor for just such a princely being, lifting him through the window and placing him firmly down on the leather seat.

"You lift your bottom from that seat, and you won't sit for a week of Sundays, young man, because of the whipping I'm going to give you," Neil told him in such a deadly voice that Steward Russell Braedon's jaw would have fallen into his lap if it hadn't been connected beneath his small, bright pink ears.

Neil was up the ladder in seconds, his moccasined feet carrying him quickly and easily across the loft.

"Neil?" Leigh asked, not hearing him any longer beneath her. "Neil? You haven't left, have you?" she asked, her tone sharpening slightly, for she would have fallen into his arms eventually—she'd just needed a little more time to gather her courage. "Don't leave me, please. I don't think I can hold on any longer," she said in rising panic as she managed to glance down, but he was nowhere to be seen.

"That's all right."

Looking up, Leigh was startled to see his bronzed face and shoulders directly overhead.

"Let go, Leigh," he told her. "I have you now."

And he was as good as his word, for his hands gripped her forearms and she felt herself being lifted, his arms and shoulders undulating with sinewy, taut muscle as he easily raised her upward until her knees touched the straw scattered across the hard boards of the loft.

Leigh's arms reached for him as her knees buckled beneath her and she saw herself tumbling backward over the edge. Instead, however, with her arms wrapped around his neck, and his around her waist, they tumbled backward into the hay, Neil's laughing face staring up at hers as she found herself lying safe against his chest.

"Seems like old times," he murmured, enjoying the feel of her slender body against his. "You're my favorite maid to tumble in the hay."

Unable to pretend indignation where there was none, especially toward the husband who had just saved her from a nasty fall, a half smile curved Leigh's lips. "Odd, I should always associate the smell of a barn with you," she said innocently as she unlocked her arms from around his neck and placed them rather delicately against his shoulders, avoiding the patch of wiry golden hair covering his chest.

Neil's chest shook beneath her as he laughed, then she felt herself lifted high as he drew a deep, contented breath into his lungs, as if prepared to spend the rest of the afternoon lying in the hayloft, his arm heavy around her waist as he kept her where she was on top of him.

"Did I forget to mention that I approve of your riding habit. Although rather different in style, I find it quite attractive," he said, thinking of her long-legged graceful walk as she'd crossed the grounds in leather boots, short calf-length skirt split to form full-legged breeches, and a wide-brimmed hat tipped at a rakish angle, her long braid of hair moving sinuously with each step. He hadn't had a chance to see her properly the night she and Gil had returned late to Royal Rivers. But the first time she'd come sauntering across the grounds in her outfit, he'd stopped work and just stood and stared, along with every other man who'd caught a glance of her. He'd been aware of the admiring, lustful faces and known that had he not been standing there among them—and known to them as her husband—they would have been very vulgarly vocal in their masculine approval. Although perhaps not, Neil speculated, for the *vaqueros* were completely loyal and devoted to Leigh, and had anyone said anything ungentlemanly about her, they might as well have insulted the proud blood of the *vaquero* himself and prepared to defend his life. The *vaquero* would have been quick to defend his and Leigh's honor with the flashing blade of a stiletto. At first, that almost blind loyalty had raised his ire, until he'd realized that they respected her as a lady and even more as a horsewoman.

As it was, he'd received countless envious glances, some assessing, some speculative, some daydreaming, from the shearers, but when Leigh had ridden past astride Capitaine, handling the high-spirited stallion with ease, some of the glances had turned to pity as they'd shaken their heads—for it was one thing to dream about a beautiful woman, and quite another to be married to a headstrong one, no matter how beautiful she was.

"Do you ride Capitaine astride all of the time?" he asked. When she nodded, he said, "I don't know why I should be surprised, since I first saw you riding bareback in your wet chemise and lacy drawers," he reminded her.

"Then you don't mind that your wife's behavior would be considered very unladylike back in Virginia?" Leigh asked curiously.

Neil grinned. "We're not in Virginia, and there is a time and place for ladylike airs, which you have in abundance, my dear, but there is also a time for a lady to show some practicality, which you have. I'd rather have you causing a scandal than breaking your lovely neck," he drawled, his hand lightly clasping the slender column, his words echoing Leigh's to Jolie when she'd complained about her appearance.

Leigh sighed in relief, then she sniffed with ladylike disdain, causing Neil to laugh deeply as he realized his bare chest was sweaty and the odor of sheep clung to him like a second skin, and apparently to Leigh also, because she touched the linen of her blouse curiously. It was slightly dampened from the sweat coating his broad chest and the material was now sticking to her flesh.

"Forgive me, ma'am, but I hadn't planned on rescuing a fair damsel in distress, or I would certainly have put back on my shirt."

"Just returning the compliment," Leigh said mockingly, remembering his odious expression when she and Gil had returned to Royal Rivers with the lamb.

"That is what I like about you, Leigh, I can always expect you to even the score," he said, his pale eyes no longer cold, but glowing warmly with humor.

"Thank you. I do try," she said. "You don't suppose there is a pitchfork lying around here anywhere?"

Neil grinned with remembrance of their first roll in the hay, his hand moving slightly, almost caressingly, over her lower back.

"I wanted to ask you something," Leigh suddenly said nervously.

"Yes?"

"You don't mind, do you, that I'm riding Capitaine. I don't always ride him, sometimes I ride my mare, but when I leave the *rancho*, I—"

"He is your horse. He has always been your horse."

Leigh met his pale eyes for a long moment, noticing for the first time in a long time the little flecks of gold in the crystalline depths. "Mine?"

"Yes. I took him from you under circumstances I am not proud of. He is yours, Leigh. He has never belonged to anyone else."

Leigh closed her eyes. "Thank you," she whispered.

"I'm glad your little mare made it. I hardly recognized her in the stables. She looks quite different from the broken-down horse I saw at Travers Hill."

Leigh smiled. "She's showing her bloodlines," she said, thankful that Damascena now bore few of the scars of her ordeal.

"Aunt Leigh! Aunt Leigh? Are you all right?" Noelle's pitiful voice drifted up to them.

"Yes, dear. I'm fine. I'll be right there," she called back. "We'd better go," she suggested to Neil, glancing down at him.

"You haven't thanked me yet for saving you," he said, pulling gently on the long braid of chestnut hair. "You know by now I'm a man who always demands payment for services rendered, or for debts owed me," he said, raising his mouth slowly to hers, giving her time to draw back if she wished.

Leigh slowly lowered her mouth to his, meeting him halfway. Their lips touched. Softly. Almost tentatively, as if it were their first kiss. His hand slid up the long braid to cup the back of her neck, his fingers caressing the fine, silky hairs as he gradually increased the pressure, bringing their mouths closer together, parting them. His arm left her waist, his hand moving along her hip, then coming to rest on her buttocks, where he lightly fondled the soft curves beneath the leather of her skirt.

Still holding herself slightly away, Leigh now moved her hand to touch his cheek, allowing the swell of her breasts to come in contact with his bare chest. She felt him shudder beneath her, his hand leaving the nape of her neck to find the buttons of her blouse. His tongue lightly touched her lips, licking them, his teeth nibbling against the soft inner flesh, and she opened them wider, allowing him to touch her tongue, the kiss deepening as his tongue slid against hers, joining them together with the intimate contact.

"Aunt Leigh!" the plaintive voice sounded again. "Gil's bringing some people toward the barn. It's *that* Spanish woman and her brother, lil' Louie Angel," Noelle said, quoting her mother and uncle in both words and tone. "And that other man's with them. I don't like him, Aunt Leigh. He's always winking at me and tickling me beneath the chin. And his breath always smells like whiskey, but without the mint in it," she said, remembering the mint juleps of home. "Please come down," Noelle called out again.

Leigh lifted her head, breaking the intimate contact and a button off her blouse as she pulled free of Neil's hands and struggled to her feet, trying to button up the rest of her blouse and smooth her skirt as she walked carefully toward the ladder, her hips swaying as she tried to keep from slipping.

Neil closed his eyes for a frustrated moment, then got to his feet, his hand grasping her elbow firmly as he guided her the rest of the way. Their eyes met once, before Leigh glanced away in confusion, her fingers fumbling with one of the tiny pearl buttons, and Neil thought better of handing her the one he'd accidentally pulled off.

"Do you know, Leigh, I've always thought you had a very nice derriere," he said conversationally.

Leigh looked startled for a moment, then reluctantly, as if she were trying not to smile, her mouth started to curl at the corners.

"What?" he asked, uncannily able to read her thoughts.

He was caught off guard, however, when she eyed him up and down and said in the same conversational tone of voice, "And I've always thought the same about you."

She was glad they'd reached the ladder, for even though he was still laughing, the look in his eye warned her he would not let her comment go unchallenged.

"I'll go down first," he told her, easily stepping over the edge and onto the top rung, then down a couple of steps. He waited there for her to sit down and swing her legs over the edge, his hand guiding her as she turned and found her footing. Leigh felt his hand resting lightly against her hip until she'd gotten a little over halfway down, then, already standing on the ground, he caught her around the waist and swung her down the rest of the way.

"Thank you," Leigh said politely, her haughty tone not intentional, but it sounded to Neil as if she were thanking a footman.

Neil smiled crookedly. "You've got straw in your hair, m'lady, and you're missing a button," he said, reaching out and touching the pale flesh revealed by the gaping pieces of linen as Gil, still in his leather apron, entered the barn, followed by Diosa, Luis, and Courtney Boyce.

"Neil!" Diosa cried out in genuine pleasure, lifting her skirts to run to him, ignoring Leigh as she brushed past her. Throwing herself into Neil's arms, Diosa rested her cheek against his bare chest, her hands spread against his shoulders, as if feeling him to make certain he was truly there, before her arms slid around his neck and, standing on tiptoe, she pressed her mouth to his.

Breathlessly, Leigh—and Gil, who was staring at Diosa in slack-jawed disbelief—waited for Neil's reaction, but before he could do anything, Diosa had stepped back, glancing around with a fine show of flustered embarrassment, but Leigh would have sworn her lips were tight with anger.

"Please, forgive me," Diosa begged, gazing up into Neil's sun-bronzed face, her black eyes full of tears, "in my excitement I forgot propriety."

And his wife, Leigh thought.

"But my prayers have been answered now that Neil is back from that horrible war. If only he had never gone in the first place. Such a tragedy. Everything would be so different, *sí*?" she asked, not speaking of the tragedy that had befallen the North and South, but the tragedy in her own life—for Neil had returned from the war a married man. "Oh, but I am in despair that I was not in Santa Fe when you returned. I heard you were there," she said, meeting Leigh's eyes with a meaningful glance. "After such a long journey, how disappointing for you to discover that I had traveled to Mexico City and was not here to greet you. After all of this time, such a long separation, between friends, for we have always been such dear friends. I should have been here to welcome you home, *querido*." She added the endearment in a low voice, her eyes drawn back to Neil's face, and seeming to burn through him.

Leigh was staring at Neil too, but her gaze was icy. So, he had been to Santa Fe to see Diosa, she thought unhappily, realizing what a fool she'd been just minutes ago.

"One usually travels through Santa Fe coming from the east, or the south," he murmured, his eyes resting on Leigh's face for a moment. "Remember, Leigh, the trail you followed across the plains ended at Santa Fe."

Leigh nodded, wanting to believe him, for if he had been in Santa Fe the day he arrived at Royal Rivers, then he would have learned of Diosa's absence then, and not disappeared the very next day in order to see her, Leigh realized, her blue eyes warming a degree and Neil's mouth twitched slightly at the corner as if he had followed her train of thought to its logical, and favorable, conclusion.

But Diosa was fuming as she glared at Leigh Braedon, not having missed anything about her disheveled appearance; not the straw in her hair, not the button gone from her blouse, nor the telltale dampness that caused the linen to cling to her breasts and outline them most seductively. But her fury came from the scent of jessamine and lavender that clung to Neil's bare chest, the fragrance of which she had caught a whiff when pressing her cheek against his skin, as if he and this *wife* of his had been embracing, Diosa thought, snapping the quirt she carried against her knee as if barely able to keep from striking out at the other woman.

"Neil! It is good you are back at Royal Rivers, and apparently in good health," Luis said suddenly, perhaps having sensed his volatile sister's furious state of mind, and he held out his hand, his arm stretched between the two women. Neil took the hand offered to him, for he'd always found Luis a likable fellow.

"How are you, Luis?" he said, but his grip was perhaps too firm, because Luis grimaced slightly.

"Until now, quite well, thank you, Neil," he said with a wide grin, bearing his momentary discomfiture well, for Luis Angel Cristobal de la Cruz Martinez Sandovares de Jaramijos was a gentleman, from the top of his low-crowned, wide-brimmed hat trimmed in silver, to his high-heeled Spanish boots of cordovan leather. And like Diosa, he was very proud of his pure Castilian blood—blood of the *conquistadores*. Dressed in his customary black trousers and short jacket, with a ruffled shirt front, he was quite an elegant figure, although the boots allowed him more height than he actually possessed, but his aristocratic profile would have been envied by many a Spanish grandee, as would his faultless manners, which was where he and his sister differed, for Luis was soft-spoken and very genteel. "Ah, Leigh, a pleasure to see you again," he said, bending over her hand.

"Luis."

"But you have not met our friend and business associate," he said, sounding very upset at his unintended slight as he gestured to the stranger, as if about to introduce him.

"Oh, how remiss of me," Diosa said first, sidling up to the man, her gloved hands entwining around his arm. "Neil Braedon, my dearest Courtney Boyce," she introduced him in a soft, seductive voice, as if he held some special place in her heart.

Leigh knew what Diosa was up to—she was using Courtney Boyce to try and make Neil jealous. Leigh glanced back at Neil, wondering if he was still enamored of his Spanish mistress, for this was their first meeting in over four years, and dressed in a severely tailored black riding habit with a black felt hat, a diaphanous black veil framing her creamy-complexioned face, the only touch of color a crimson silk scarf around her white-collared throat, the Widow Alvarado was quite a stunning woman.

But Neil was looking at Courtney Boyce as he reached out to take the hand being extended to him.

"A pleasure to meet you, sir. I've heard a lot about you since I've been here in the territories," Courtney said with Southern courtliness, shaking Neil's hand.

"Mr. *Boyce*, was it? I knew a Charles Boyce when I was at Yale. Any relation to you?" Neil asked in polite conversation.

"Oh, no, sir, I'm a South Carolinian. Thought my Southern drawl would have marked me. Wouldn't ever catch me up North, no, sir, and certainly not at school," he said. "In fact, wouldn't have caught me at school at all," he added with a deep laugh. "Though, actually, sir, I attended South Carolina College," he admitted.

"Then perhaps you knew my cousin, Adam Braedon? He went there." Neil asked.

Courtney frowned thoughtfully. "No, can't say I did, sir," he said, looking sheepish. "'Course, my academic career is one I'm not overly proud of. When I did manage to attend class, bein' fonder, sir, of the racetrack and gaming tables, it was probably during a different year than when your cousin was there. Apparently, we just missed each other."

"Apparently, although there was a time when Adam enjoyed the racetrack and gaming tables more than his studies," Neil said, obviously agreeing with the man.

"Poor Courtney was also in this war you fought," Diosa said, leaning against the Southerner in closer intimacy and engulfing him in a cloud of heady perfume. "He was wounded most seriously when he arrived in Santa Fe, and I have helped him to recover, haven't I, *mi amado*?"

Courtney stared down into Diosa's upturned face, his feelings for the beautiful Spanish woman evident by the blatant manner in which he caressed her cheek, which was the delicate shade of a damask rose, the rosy blush of maidenly modesty, he thought with just a flash of a twisted smile.

"Ma'am, so grateful am I, I intend to make you my bride one fine day," he said with lover-like fervor, grasping her gloved hand possessively, but Diosa removed her hand to adjust her veil.

"I trust you have fully recovered from your injuries?" Neil questioned, thinking the South Carolinian must have for he looked in extremely good health. The man was of average height and build, although his waistline was thickening from too little activity and too much fine food and wine, Neil speculated, smelling the alcohol on his breath. With his black hair and carefully trimmed mustache and side whiskers, his eyes a tobacco brown shade, and his features of a classical mold, he would be considered quite handsome by most, although there was a flaccidness about his face; showing in the weakness of the line of his chin and the soft fullness of his lips.

"Why, thank you, sir; I have recovered completely," Courtney replied easily. "And you, Mr. Braedon? Not wounded, were you?"

"I was lucky. Not a scratch," Neil replied, automatically touching the blue ribbon around his braid of golden hair, and drawing several curious eyes to it.

"I had heard, sir, that you spent much of your youth with the Comanche, but I must say I hadn't expected to see you looking rather like one," Courtney commented with a smile. "After all, sir, you stand before me bare chested, wearing buckskins and moccasins, the shoes those heathens wear, and sporting a braid. Not the usual gentlemanly attire."

"You will find that Neil is not the usual gentleman but is *muy macho*," Diosa advised.

Courtney Boyce flushed a ruddy hue as he glanced down at her, only to find her gaze intent on Neil. "Quite the savage, eh?" he said, some of the good humor, and the refinement, gone from his voice.

"You must be familiar with the saying, Mr. Boyce, 'A leopard can't change its spots.'"

"Indeed, sir, and I trust no offense was taken by my comment. Well, I am pleased to hear you suffered no injuries in the war, for although I suspect we fought on opposite sides, I certainly wouldn't wish you ill. Last I heard, the war was over, except for a few foolhardy Southerners who won't give up," Courtney stated. "It's time to start over."

"Poor Courtney, he lost everything. He had a big home in a big *pueblo* called Charleston, and he had the very big *rancho* with hundreds of slaves. But, alas, all is lost," Diosa said pityingly. "And now he has had to go into business with my uncle. Courtney works for *Tío* Alfonso in the freighting business."

"I am a full partner, Diosa," Courtney corrected her grimly, then turned away, the ugly expression instantly replaced with a smile intended to charm. "Leigh, Miz Braedon," Courtney began, but quickly altered his address to a more formal greeting as he caught a flash in her husband's eye—something he was ever aware and careful of when flirting with a man's wife—but now it had his curiosity piqued and he wanted to know if Neil Braedon was interested enough in his wife to be jealous.

Glancing over at Diosa for an instant, there was a glint in his eye as he held out his hand to Leigh. "Forgive me, ma'am, but I haven't said a proper hello to you yet, lovely lady," he greeted her, stepping between her and her husband, and taking her hand in his, pressed a kiss against it, although some of the effect was spoiled since his lips came into contact with the leather of her glove.

"As beautiful as I remember," he complimented her, taking a good-sized step backward, and well away from Neil Braedon, for without ever glancing at the man, he had felt the tensing of the muscular body, and suspected the hairs on the back of his neck had been singed by the smoldering look he had just received from the lady's husband.

A smile of satisfaction curved his lips as he noticed Leigh pulling together her blouse, glancing at Neil as she did, and seeing the straw in her hair, he guessed what had just taken place between them.

"I'm not surprised, sir, you managed to get through the war unscathed, knowing you had a beautiful young wife awaiting your return. And not just any wife, but a *Travers* of Virginia, sir, that is indeed an accomplishment. I knew Miz Braedon's former fiance, Matthew Wycliffe, a fellow South Carolinian. Such a pity, he was killed. A fine gentleman, sir," Courtney said, knowing how to pour salt on a wound, and make a husband especially jealous and eager to convince his wife that *he* was now the only man in her life. "And, I suspect, sir," he said, making a point of glancing at Leigh, "that we have interrupted you folks at a rather delicate moment, not that I can blame you, for I am one of your wife's greatest admirers, and she has many," he said, glancing this time at Gil, who turned beet red in the face, then at Luis, who had just crossed his leg and nearly lost his footing on his high heels. "I'm certain, sir, you didn't linger long in Santa Fe," he said, glancing at Diosa's livid face, and having managed in a few short minutes to offend everyone present as he winked at Noelle, who had moved close to Neil's side. He started to reach out and tickle her beneath her chin, but thought better of it as he encountered the pale, grayish-green eyes of Neil Braedon as he placed his hand on Noelle's thin shoulder.

"Well, we really must be moseyin' on over to Alfonso's. We were already up at the big house. Had some refreshments," he said, confirming Neil's opinion that he'd been drinking. "But can't stay any longer. Don't want to be caught out on the trail after dark, not with a helpless lil' lady ridin' with us, eh, Luis?" Courtney drawled, knowing full well Diosa was very capable of defending herself, for he'd seen her whip out that wicked hat pin and jab it threateningly at some peasant who'd irritated her.

"Certainly not," Luis Angel answered, managing to smile, but only out of relief at being able to leave, because the atmosphere in the barn had become definitely uncomfortable. "We waited at the house for a while, enjoying our refreshments, talking with Camilla and her aunts, then Lys Helene came in, and then Guy, who, I must say, is in very good spirits and looking quite well. We hoped to see you, Neil, and Leigh, and your sister, Althea, but everyone seemed to have vanished into thin air, including Nathaniel. We could not leave without welcoming you home, Neil, and when we saw Gil, he told us where you were," Luis explained, much to Gil's continued discomfort. "So, until we meet again, *adiós*," he said, bowing slightly as he started to turn away.

"But we will be back soon, *querido*," Diosa promised, moving closer to Neil, her perfume floating between them and masking the scent of jessamine. "At the *barbacoa*, on Saturday, we will meet again," she said. "Of course, I do not think *Tío* Alfonso will attend. You know he has never forgiven you for Serena's tragic death. I fear he still believes Neil had something to do with it," she commented, meeting Leigh's wide blue eyes for a brief instant as she turned away, allowing Courtney to take her arm. "*Adiós*."

"Good-bye, Diosa," Neil said softly.

"Pleasure meeting you," Courtney said, nodding to Neil, his hand tight around Diosa's elbow.

"Yes, a real pleasure," Neil said.

Luis Angel stood indecisively for a second, an apologetic look in his eye as he caught Leigh's glance.

"Luis, come," Diosa called back to her brother.

"Please forgive her, Neil. Diosa sometimes speaks without thinking," he requested of him worriedly.

"No offense taken, Luis. I think we both understand Diosa," Neil told him unsmilingly.

"So, until then, *adiós*," Luis said, again, his handsome face looking troubled as he quickly followed them toward the doors, where just beyond they'd left their horses.

Gil shuffled his feet nervously. "Well, guess I better get back to work," he muttered, wishing he'd taken that tumble into the sheep dip; if he had, he'd feel about as welcome as he did now, he thought glumly. "Never did like that woman," he said beneath his breath as he stomped off.

Leigh started to take a step to retrieve her jacket from the ground, but Neil's hand reached out and grabbed her arm.

"Leigh, I—" Neil began, suspecting what she must be thinking because of Diosa's cruelly intentioned remark.

"No, please, you don't have to say anything," Leigh told him, holding his concerned gaze with an understanding one of her own. "I know the kind of man you are, Neil Braedon. And I know you'd never have harmed Serena."

Neil took a step toward her, his eyes locked with hers.

Leigh found herself stepping forward, almost reaching out to him, then she stopped. "Oh, my goodness. Steward!" Leigh said in a shocked voice, glancing down as she almost stepped on the little brown velvet cap and suddenly remembered her nephew. "Where is he? If anything has happened to him! Oh, how could I have forgotten him?" she cried, glancing around in disbelief, unable to find him anywhere. "The dipping trough! He's probably fallen in," she said, a horrified expression on her face.

"I know where he is," Noelle said calmly, gazing up at Neil as if he were a god, for he was one of the only ones who had survived the war—her father, grandfather, both grandmothers, an aunt, and three uncles, she counted, having all gone to heaven—and she had never seen anyone deal with Steward so strictly before. Somewhere in a haze of memory she remembered his also having dealt quite nicely with her Aunt Julia, whose name was no longer spoken in their family or polite society, so she must have done something far worse than pinch someone this time, Noelle thought wisely, pointing toward the burgundy coach.

But Neil had already started to walk toward it, Leigh hurrying to catch up with his long strides, and wondering where he was going. Neil stopped beside the door of the coach and looked inside, drawing Leigh close beside him so she could peer in.

His chubby rear end still pressed firmly to the seat, Steward Russell Braedon was sound asleep, his small mouth curved upward in sweet dreams.

❧

"I'm not dreaming. I tell you it was him. Major Montgomery Stanfield's brother. He was a captain in the cavalry. Hell, I know what I saw with my own eyes! He was standing there beside that trough of stinkin' sheep dip. I met the man in Richmond on several occasions, when he'd come by Headquarters to see his brother. I didn't see him much after his brother died, no reason for him to come callin'. Although I remember he was asking a lot of questions right after his brother died, then a couple of months later the Army of the Potomac crossed the Rapidan into the Wilderness in a new offensive, and his troop was sent into battle with Stuart's cavalry and Longstreet's corps. And I didn't see him again, because by then I'd dropped out of sight during the pandemonium when it looked like Sheridan was going to take Richmond. And now, I swear I have seen the same man at Royal Rivers.

"What was his name? Michael. That's it! Michael *Sebastian* Stanfield. Such a grand-sounding name. How could I ever forget one of *the* aristocratic Stanfields? Like the Washingtons, the Jeffersons, the Lees; all fine old distinguished families of Virginia. The Stanfields are a very wealthy, or should I say *were* a very wealthy Tidewater planter family. Stanfield Hall was burned to the ground during the war. The major said they lost everything. Montgomery Stanfield even lost his wife during the war. She was a frail thing, don't know what he saw in her, not much spirit. Guess she had the right last name though. That kind marries the same kind: blue bloods. Well, hers wasn't rich enough, because early in the war she fell ill and died. There weren't any children. And Michael Stanfield wasn't married. So it looks as if the Stanfields of Virginia are no longer with us—except for one."

"And we'll deal with him."

"You don't seem very concerned. Of course, it is *my* neck he wants in a noose, not yours," Courtney Boyce said, taking a hefty swig of whiskey.

"If you keep drinking like that he won't have to bother. You'll do it for him, probably by falling off your own horse and breaking your fool neck. Save the cost of a trial, twelve jurors' time, and a good rope."

"Easy enough for you to say, you don't have him breathing down your neck, Alfonso," Courtney replied, laughing harshly as he eyed the man sitting enthroned in the high-backed red leather chair near the fireplace.

Alfonso Jacobs did indeed look regal sitting there, his mane of white hair almost like an aureole encircling his head. He was a big man, with massive shoulders and bull chest, his features strong, but crudely formed, as if his face had been hewn from rock. But despite his rough appearance, he was a man who enjoyed the finer things in life, as was evident in the objets d'art, gilt-framed paintings, elegant English furnishings, and Oriental carpet that graced his study. He was dressed in a red silk smoking jacket with a red velvet collar, the gold of a watch and chain gleaming against the rich material at his waist, while the ashes on the end of a fine cigar glowed every so often as he drew on it, before taking a sip of the warm French brandy he swirled in a crystal snifter held negligently in his big hand, a gold and ruby ring winking from his little finger.

"Michael Stanfield is smart. The kind who relies on brains, not brawn. Know what he was before the war? One of these highfalutin architects. Designs fancy buildings. Even designed some in the capital, the federal capital, that is. What he designed in the reb capital got burned to ashes. Used to hear him and the major talking about New York, Philadelphia, Boston, the places he'd traveled to build those buildings of his. And they were always talking about the fancy friends he'd stay with in every town. Apparently his name gave him access to all the right people. Even went to Europe. Studied art, or something wishy-washy like that, in London and Paris. Wondered at first that he should be struttin' around in breeches, quite the fancy gent he is, but he's the ladies' man right enough. Saw him in Richmond with one or two of the most expensive harlots in town. Wish I could have afforded their kind. And I'll tell you this, even though he's one of these architects, he was raised as all gentlemen of Virginia are. From the time he was breeched, he could ride like the devil and shoot his granddaddy's fowling piece like a backwoodsman. And Michael Stanfield is out for revenge," Courtney said, emptying his glass and walking over to the sideboard and pouring another from the cut-glass decanter.

Alfonso Jacobs shook his head, hoping Courtney didn't get the brandy by mistake, and regretting he'd ever had to rely on the fool to help him. But Courtney had been in the right place at the right time. He'd had access to government and army forms, and most importantly, to dispatches; listing shipping dates, schedules, destinations, and how many troops would be needed to guard each shipment of gold. "Think, Courtney. Just try thinking for once. Why is this Michael Stanfield you seem to fear so much here?"

"He's after Captain Dagger. You know that," Courtney said, tossing off half the drink, and grimacing slightly, for he must have gotten the brandy by mistake.

"Yes, but you seem to have forgotten who Captain Dagger is."

"Of course I haven't. Neil Braedon is Captain Dagger," he answered, smiling grimly. "Lord, I couldn't believe I actually came face-to-face with the man today. And he's still wearing that braid and those buckskins. Have to admit, now that I've met him, I can believe half the stories I've heard about him— only half," he added, laughing wickedly.

"Yes, I've learned never to underestimate Neil Braedon, or his father. Now, why is Michael Stanfield after Captain Dagger?"

"Because Captain Dagger robbed that train of gold bullion near Gordonsville that Stanfield's brother was guarding. He murdered him."

"Exactly. And why does he think Captain Dagger is responsible for his brother's death?" Alfonso's voice came softly, patiently, as if taking a slow student step-by-step through a difficult lesson.

"Because, as one of Major Stanfield's men, and the only survivor of the massacre, I identified him," Courtney said with remembered pleasure. "You should know, you told me to put the blame on Captain Dagger."

Alfonso Jacobs smiled, causing Courtney to shiver, for it was a very unpleasant smile.

"Exactly, because I knew the true identity of this notorious Yankee raider, Captain Dagger. I was with the search party that rescued a young Neil Braedon, and I'll never forget his father's face when we saw the boy. I always wondered, when Nathaniel held out his arms, if he intended to embrace the boy or squeeze the life out of him. That's why I was surprised he saved Neil's life six years ago when I tried to hang him. Figured later he would have done as much for a stranger. You never know what Nathaniel's thinking. That makes him a tough adversary. I don't think I've ever met a more determined man.

And he tracked those Comanche until they left his son in the desert just to get us off their trail so they could live in peace. We found him wandering in the *Jornada del Muerto*. We found ourselves a young Comanche brave that day. One who wore his hair in a braid and would have knifed one of us as easily as spat upon us—and he did both. Later, we learned he could ride and shoot like nothing we'd ever seen, except when having the misfortune to witness a Comanche raid. This young buck's name was Sun Dagger. I always remembered that.

"Now, when I hear that there is a Yankee raider called Captain Dagger, who wears his golden hair in a heathenish braid, raids through Virginia like a Comanche on the warpath in Texas, and disappears into thin air as if riding a wild pony across the Staked Plain, naturally I thought of Neil Braedon, my former son-in-law. I knew Neil had chosen to fight for the Union. So I did a little checking, I have my informants, even in the Union army, and sutlers are just as money-grabbing on both sides in a war. I discovered that Neil was assigned to army intelligence and was stationed at Headquarters, Washington. For once the brass made use of a man's particular abilities when putting him in uniform, for their Captain Dagger was none other than Neil Braedon, and *he* is the man this Michael Stanfield of yours is looking for. That is why I planned it this way. If anyone became suspicious of me, of us, then what better than to have Captain Dagger, the notorious raider, who was raised by the Comanche, and who massacred those unarmed men in cold blood, living right here. And he is making it even easier for us. You say Neil is still wearing that braid, so your Michael Stanfield will have no problem putting a bullet in the right man."

Courtney had to admit Alfonso Jacobs's plan had been brilliant. But something still bothered him. "What if Michael Stanfield saw me today? What if he remembers me?"

"Maybe he won't remember you. You had a different name then, and no mustache. Men change."

"He'll remember," Courtney fretted, turning his glass bottom up.

"If Michael Stanfield can track down Captain Dagger, then why couldn't you have too? Why can't you be here to seek your revenge the same as he is? Who better, in fact, since you were nearly murdered by Captain Dagger and his bloodthirsty raiders? Always think of every angle, Courtney. Always have a 'wherefore' for what you do. You will never get boxed in that way. You will always have an exit for yourself," Alfonso advised.

Courtney laughed, raising his glass in toast to the man sitting in the big leather chair, frowning when he noticed it was empty. "My sincere congratulations, sir. You are one of the most devious men I've ever had the good fortune to meet, but remind me never to gamble with you."

"I never gamble, Courtney. And I never leave anything to chance."

"But what if Stanfield doesn't kill Braedon?"

"No matter. If he doesn't, then we will. A man can come to a tragic end in so many ways out here. It's a hard land, and at times, a lawless land. But when a man has been found guilty, justice is swift at hand. And once we've taken care of Neil Braedon, then we'll make certain the proper authorities discover Stanfield's body, for the courageous man, who has no family to care or question what has happened, will have been mortally wounded in his attack on Neil Braedon. We get rid of both of our enemies at the same time."

Courtney shook his head in amazement as he made his way a trifle unsteadily to the sideboard and poured himself another whiskey, and making certain he got the corn liquor this time.

Alfonso stared down at the fire as if mesmerized by the flames. He'd planned this from the very beginning, perhaps not in quite this manner, but the death of Neil Braedon had become a major part of his goal since his daughter had died. He held that young man responsible for the defeat of his carefully laid plans, and he would forfeit his life for causing him so much trouble. No one crossed Alfonso Jacobs and lived. He had placed a lot of time and effort into bringing that marriage about, which had joined more than a man and a woman—it had brought two great ranches together. Everything had been ruined when Serena had died. He had lost his chance to claim Royal Rivers. With his daughter married to Neil, the land would have become part of his empire on the death of Nathaniel and his eldest son—which could easily have been arranged.

Serena had been the only weak link in his chain. And she had disappointed him, nearly ruining all that he had planned by eloping with that Spaniard, when he had already planned her marriage to Neil. Fortunately, he had caught up with them and returned her to the ranch, and her lover back to Spain, where, under threat of losing his life, he had remained, never to contact his daughter again. The annulment had been granted. But because Alfonso didn't trust anyone, just to make certain the man had no second thoughts, a handsome allowance had been sent to him each month so he could live comfortably, especially after he had taken another wife and had a growing family to feed.

Alfonso smiled reflectively. People were tools to be used, the same way a carpenter used a hammer and saw to build a house. He had used Serena as part of his plan to build an empire. Just as he had used her mother before her, marrying the only daughter of a land-rich Spaniard, the land grant that Silver Springs Ranch now stood on becoming his for a tidy little sum—the man more than happy to sell out to his daughter's husband. And through marriage again, this time his daughter's, he'd planned to add to his empire. But Serena's premature death had cheated him of that goal, and of an heir to inherit both Royal Rivers and Silver Springs. He'd had such hopes for that part of his plan. He had miscalculated slightly at first, never realizing his daughter was so devout, but, finally, by telling Serena her first husband was dead, he had convinced her to accept Neil as her husband, and to consummate their marriage. He should have realized Neil was more savage than a white man, and whatever had happened between them had caused Serena's death. And he held Neil responsible. But now he had at hand another tool that would make it far easier for him to rid himself of Neil Braedon, and at the same time, cast suspicion from himself. For some might remember his attempt to hang his son-in-law after the questionable death of his daughter. And he had to admit he was ashamed of that moment when he had lost control. Never attack the enemy's front. Always try to flank him. That way he was caught off guard, and this way no one could possibly suspect him of Neil's murder.

But Neil had to die. It was part of the plan. He was a threat to him, even more so than Nathaniel, for Neil knew the Indians, especially the Comanche, and he might cause difficulties for him in the future if he tried to interfere when the trouble started, and it would start, Alfonso vowed. There were others too, powerful men like Kit Carson and Lucien Maxwell, over at the Cimarron, who might cause him problems, but he would deal with them the same way he would deal with the Braedons.

Courtney had already been in contact with the French in Mexico, who wouldn't mind seeing a republic just north of their *Rio Bravo del Norte*, and one not on friendly terms with the United States, and a republic of ex-Confederate soldiers still full of fight, and with nothing to lose. And he would see to it that they would have plenty to fight for. During the last two years he'd been selling rebel arms and munitions to the Comancheros, a group of half-breed raiders who existed in a no-man's-land between the Indian, Mexican, and white man's worlds, trading with all three while belonging to none. The guns, and liquor they would be well supplied with, would end up in the hands of the Comanche and Apache. With the trouble they would cause raiding in Texas and throughout the territories, the federal troops would have their hands full just to stay alive and protect the towns and isolated settlements. And in the meantime, with the help of the French, and the gold bullion from a score of robberies of Confederate banks and army shipments he'd planned and carried out throughout the war, he would establish his own republic in what was now the Territory of New Mexico.

That fool Jefferson Davis and his cabinet of fools had never had any hope of establishing another republic. They had their chance and they'd made a debacle of it, and all that had been left for them to do was turn tail and run. Of course they got caught, he thought contemptuously. They should have planned ahead, as he had. He had set his plan into motion over a period of years. It was a foolhardy venture for Davis to try and escape Richmond on a train loaded down with the gold from the

Confederate treasury, what with Union troops closing in, and rebel looters and deserters lying in wait along their path to halt their flight and seize the gold. The only smart ones, the secretaries of war and state, John Breckenridge and Judah Benjamin, hadn't been caught yet and dragged back to Richmond. But at least their flight, and the rebels he'd been hearing about who'd been traveling south toward the Rio Grande, had kept the Union busy tracking them down and worrying about what they were planning when they reached Mexico.

He glanced over at Courtney Boyce, who had just finished his drink and was getting slowly to his feet, and thought that everything and everyone had their uses, and the South Carolinian's usefulness was quickly coming to an end—and perhaps a very tragic one.

"Well, if you don't need me any longer," Courtney said, little realizing what a poor choice of phrase he'd used, "I'm dead to the world."

"Certainly, Courtney," Alfonso said, smiling benevolently. "You've done well. You truly deserve a long rest, and I want you to know that I'll always be very appreciative of your assistance," Alfonso promised, eyeing him thoughtfully.

"That's what I like to hear, along with the jingle of coins in my pocket," Courtney agreed, slurring his words slightly.

"Sleep well, Courtney."

But Courtney hadn't sleep on his mind as he staggered down the darkened corridor of Alfonso's mansion. And mansion it was, he thought in dismay as he managed to lose himself twice trying to find the south wing, where Diosa and the rest of the family had their rooms.

Blinking several times to clear his blurred vision, Courtney finally found the door he'd been looking for—and for what had seemed hours—but then a man was always impatient to be embraced by the soft thighs of a loving woman, he thought with a leering grin.

Since he knew he was welcomed, Courtney walked into Diosa's room without bothering to knock. Stumbling slightly, he let loose the door, not bothering to see if it swung completely shut behind him, worrying more about staying on his own two feet than whether the door had shut properly or not.

He'd always liked Diosa's bedchamber at Silver Springs, better in fact than her bedchamber in her own house in Santa Fe, which was too barbaric for his tastes, with grotesque, squat terra-cotta figures, one he particularly disliked, a dancing monkey she called the wind god, *Ehecatl*, whose breath moved the sun. She had adorning the walls devilish feathered masks of beaten gold and jaguar pelts that always made him want to look over his shoulder whenever he was in the room. She had a fascination for unnatural things, he thought, repulsed, as he remembered the sacrificial knife she'd held caressingly in her palm most of the long journey back from Mexico.

This bedchamber, however, had been furnished by Alfonso, as all of the rooms in his house had, and he had to admit that Alfonso had better taste than his niece. There were marble-topped commodes and silk-cushioned sofas in pale rose, delicate velvet-seated side chairs and a Grecian couch, a painted and gilt-trimmed bedstead and canopy, and white muslin, draped from the *vigas* in the ceiling, gave the room a light, airy feeling. Sometimes he felt as if he couldn't breathe when with Diosa, her perfume almost overpowering him when he lay with her, but it was part of the strange fascination of her, he thought, watching her now as she sat before the mirrored dressing table, brushing her long black hair, and looking like a pagan goddess.

He could see her reflection in the glass. Her eyes were closed dreamily as she pulled the brush through the strands with slow, lazy strokes, until he swore he saw sparks in the blue-black tresses. In her other hand, she held her usual *cigarrillo* with the delicate gold pincers, but as he sniffed, he thought it smelled slightly different tonight than the usual tobacco she smoked. It had an eye-burning pungency to it, and the smoke, mingling with her perfume, made his head spin. He glanced at her cluttered dressing table, where crystal bottles and jars of toiletries were crowded together at one end with silk ribbons, gloves, and the gold-encrusted coffer she carried her valuables in, and he knew she had a fortune in jewelry. But even that was pushed aside for the finely tooled leather box she always carried with her, and now occupied the place of honor on her dressing table. It looked innocent enough, until it was opened to reveal its contents: strange-looking little dried button-like things, from some cactus, she'd said when showing it to him for the first time, her sloe-eyes heavy-lidded and glowing with hidden fire as she'd held out some for him to sample, along with a piece of mushroom she called "flesh of the gods," and some bitter tasting powder, "seeds of the morning flower," she'd claimed, and he'd wondered later if she'd meant "mourning." And with good reason, for he'd never had such a nightmarish night in his life; in fact, he hadn't remembered anything for three terrifying days afterward, and to this day he still had strange, haunting visions crawling through his brain when he least expected, but Diosa had only laughed, saying he was not one of the chosen ones who could speak with the gods, as she did when she prayed to them and was given the magic of wondrous colors and images.

Swaggering as quietly as he could in his inebriated state, Courtney managed to reach Diosa's side without her having heard him, so lost in her dreaming was she, in her talking to the gods, he thought, grinning with pleasure as he stared down at her pale shoulders, the silk of her dressing gown having slipped to reveal skin just as smooth and silky.

Bending over, he pressed his lips to her warm flesh, his hand slipping over her shoulder to caress the bareness of breast. He heard her sigh with pleasure, then she raised her arm, the fur trimming the wide sleeve of her gown tickling his face slightly as she ran her fingers through his hair.

"*Querido*, I knew you would come, that you would not be able to stay away. You have flown down from the sun for me," she murmured huskily, her throat arched as she leaned back her head for his kiss. Their lips touched, and Courtney suddenly couldn't control himself as her cloying scent drifted around him and her smoky breath filled his senses, and he tightened his hand around her breast, his mouth opening hungrily against hers as he slavered hot kisses against her lips.

Suddenly Diosa's eyes opened wide, blazing with fury. "You!" she screamed, pulling away from him, and looking more beautiful in her rage than he had ever seen her.

"Me?" he asked, looking befuddled. "Of course it's me. Who else did you expect to find in your bedchamber?" he demanded, his whiskey-soaked mind finally beginning to realize that he may not have been expected.

But then…if he hadn't been, who had?

"How dare you!" she spat, pulling her dressing gown up around her shoulders as if offended by his touch, but it had been so rude an awakening that had shaken her, dreaming of Neil Braedon kissing her only to discover it was Courtney Boyce. Her god had turned into a toad before her very eyes. She pressed a shaking hand against her throbbing temple, easing the pain as the glare of reds and yellows filled her brain.

"Well, aren't we the high and mighty one all of a sudden. Never minded before," he said, two blotches of angry color marring his cheeks. "You thought I was someone else, didn't you? Didn't you!" he yelled, reaching out and grabbing hold of her arms and shaking her until her head fell back on her slender neck.

"Yes!"

"Who?"

She smiled, infuriating him as he saw the seductive light enter her black eyes, and suddenly he knew—and had since this afternoon, if he could have admitted it to himself.

"You were dreaming of Neil Braedon, weren't you?"

"Yes," she admitted, staring at him in disgust. "You are nothing compared to him. He is my love, and I am his. We were lovers. And we will be again, now that he has returned," she taunted him. "He is a god, and you are the dirt beneath his feet," she said, spitting on him.

"You think so?" he asked doubtfully. Her venom had struck deep, sobering him just enough to loosen his tongue too much. "Have you forgotten he has a wife?"

Diosa laughed. "What does that matter? It didn't with his first wife. I had him then, and I will have him again."

"Are you certain? Seemed to me this afternoon that we interrupted them at a very ill-timed moment. It was obvious to anyone who wasn't blind, or deceiving themselves, that they are lovers. He couldn't keep his eyes off her, or his hands, I saw him touching her when we entered the barn. Not that I blame the man, for Leigh *Braedon*," he said, drawling the last name, "is one of the most beautiful women I've ever seen. Neil Braedon must have felt that too, since he took the woman as his bride. He could have chosen another, Diosa, but he didn't," he reminded the sullen-faced Castilian. "He chose Leigh Travers for his bride. And now that I've seen the two of them together, I can see that they were meant for one another," he added, cutting deep into Diosa's heart with his carefully aimed words.

"You know nothing. Neil is mine. He has always belonged to me. To Diosa! We will be lovers again. It is our destiny to be together. I have loved him from the beginning of time. We will always be together. He cannot escape me. He will come to me again. He was meant to be mine. No one will take him from me."

Courtney was driven beyond caution. Diosa was his. He'd never known a woman like her. Until Neil Braedon had returned, she had been his, and she was going to become his wife. Nothing could change that. Nothing. He wouldn't lose her, he couldn't, he thought in numbing disbelief. Then, suddenly, he saw everything clearly, and he smiled as he realized that he wouldn't lose her—ever. How could he to a dead man?

"Neil Braedon is a man, Diosa, not a god, and he will die. And nothing you can do will stop that from happening."

"What?" she said, suddenly sounding groggy. "What is this lie?" she asked, drawing the smoke from her *cigarrillo* deep into her lungs, then a moment later the bluish smoke was wreathed around their figures.

"The truth, Diosa. It is the truth. Neil Braedon is a marked man."

"You lie!"

"Go ask your *Tío* Alfonso. It is his plan. And even you know he never fails in getting what he wants. Neil Braedon was a Yankee raider called Captain Dagger during the war."

"Dagger?" she said, glancing back at her dresser, her hand fumbling to find the sacrificial dagger, her hand closing around the bird-figured hilt.

"Yes, and he robbed and massacred innocent people during the war. There is a man, a Michael Stanfield, who is looking for him because Neil killed his brother. He will kill Neil. And if he doesn't, then Alfonso will. Because Alfonso has had it planned from the beginning. Neil Braedon is a dead man,"

Courtney told her, relishing the look of horror that spread across her face.

"No," she whispered. "He and I were meant to be together. He is *El Dorado*, the golden one. It is my destiny to be with him. I am Diosa Marina. I have been favored by the gods, as was the first Marina, *Malinal*, Cortés's mistress. She was his lover, and she brought him an empire of gold. I am a goddess, it is what my name means. I was sent by the gods. It has been meant from the beginning of time. The golden one is of the legend. We have waited for so long for the fair-haired man to come from the East. And he has come, and he is bathed in golden light. And now, Esteban is here," she said, her eyes wild. "The black-skinned Moor has come to lead us to *Cibola*, to the Seven Golden Cities. Esteban. I have seen him, spoken to him, and he has answered. He was sent to Royal Rivers, where he awaits my command. He will find the gold, and then he will die as a sacrifice to the gods. And I will become the woman of *El Dorado*."

Courtney saw his chance, for she suddenly seemed so lost and hopeless standing there, her black eyes unfocused as she tried to hold on to her dream. "Gold?" he asked, taking her unresistingly into his arms. "I can give you gold. So much we can travel around the world and never know we've spent a cent of it. Gold, Diosa, gold! It's hidden away—"

"Hidden?" Diosa asked curiously.

"Yes, Alfonso didn't want it here at Silver Springs, too dangerous, so he hid it where no one would think of looking for it," Courtney said, remembering his disbelief when Alfonso and he had taken the first load to be hidden away. "It's hidden in the ruins of some ancient pueblo."

Courtney saw again the ruins of the long-forgotten city, where the sandstone blocks fitting snugly together made the walls seem golden as they rose high above the desert, jagged where time had worn away the thickness and tumbled in a timbered roof, the doors and windows standing open to the wind and sky. He had seen the neatly laid out walls of *plazas* and the round chambers of the *kivas* with fire pits at the bottom, the ashes centuries cold, the circular benches emptied of worshippers. And in a ruin with a pine-beamed ceiling, they had hidden their stolen gold, piling the chests of gold bullion against the ancient walls where strange figures stared down at them, the Confederate seals unbroken and to remain so until they came back to claim their gold.

"There truly is a city of gold, Diosa, and *I*, not anyone else can show it to you," he boasted. "I will make you a queen. I'll drape you from head to foot in gold and jewels. Forget your legends, Diosa. With the gold I have, I can take you to Europe, where we'll be welcomed in all the fancy courts of Europe, kings and queens bowing down to us. You, Diosa, will become the legend," he promised, and he spoke sincerely, for he would make her his queen.

"Neil?" she whispered.

"Him?" Courtney spat. "What of him? Neil Braedon will be dead."

"No!" she screamed, jerking out of his arms with surprising strength, the malevolence of her expression causing Courtney to take a startled step backward, suddenly reminded of one of those hideous golden masks she collected.

"No," she said, the softness of her voice sending a warning shiver up his spine. "He will never die. No one can take him from me, or keep me from him. You can't, Alfonso can't, Serena couldn't, nor could that old man, my beloved husband, whose touch left me feeling as if I were in the grave, and I will deal with this blue-eyed *inglesa* soon enough, the same way I did the others."

"The others? You mean your husband and Serena?" Courtney asked, somehow managing to find his voice.

"Yes," Diosa said, her answer sounding like the hissing of a snake, her black eyes watching Courtney with the same cold, reptilian intensity. "Serena thought she could take him from me. But she did not understand. Neil was mine. He loved me. But suddenly she decided she wanted him, and she told me he was never going to see me again. He was going to go back to her, to try and make their marriage work. I laughed in her face. Then he came to me, and he told me it was over. He said Serena wanted to live as man and wife, and he had agreed. They were married and they had lost too much time already. He wasn't going to see me any longer. Leave me for her? Never! Luis had told me that her husband still lived somewhere in Spain. He had been sending the money to the man for years, because *Tío* Alfonso was gone so much he wanted to make certain the money always was sent so the man would not be tempted to write. But *Tío* Alfonso lied. He told Serena that her husband was dead. That was why she wanted Neil, but Neil was mine. I hated her. It was all her fault. I sent her a note telling her that her husband still lived and was waiting for her. I had her meet me in the canyon. *Cañon del Malhadado*. The gods were pleased that day, for I sacrificed her to them and left her there in the canyon. Poor Neil. His wife was now dead. And, later, my poor, sick husband died. A little *belladonna* in his *chocolate*," she said, laughing softly, "and I was a widow."

"You whore!" a voice roared from behind them.

Courtney spun around in shock to find himself staring at Alfonso, standing like a maddened bull in the opened doorway.

"It was you all along. You who ruined my plans. All this time I thought it was Neil Braedon who caused Serena's death. If it hadn't been for you, she and Neil would still be married today," he said, moving steadily closer to where they stood before the dresser. "And I would have Royal Rivers within my grasp. My plan would have worked except for you and your meddling."

Diosa eyed her uncle with dislike. "You old fool," she said, throwing back her head as she glared at him with narrowed, calculating eyes. "It would never have worked. Neil was mine. And he was from the time he married Serena. We were lovers. Serena was nothing. Neil was always mine. He has come back to me. And *I*, Diosa, will have Royal Rivers, not you," she challenged him, her voice low and strangely deep-toned as it vibrated with malice. "You and your stupid plans. You do not understand. The gods have controlled you from the beginning."

Her taunts snapped what little self-control a wrathful Alfonso had left after hearing her confession and realizing she had duped him for years, and with a mad bellow he grabbed hold of Diosa, his big hands finding her throat and tightening murderously around the slender stem, which he easily could have snapped, and would have, if Courtney hadn't attacked him from behind. His hard-hitting fists caused Alfonso to break off his attack and to release his strangling grip on Diosa's neck, and convulsed with rage, he turned to face this new assault, looking forward to sending Courtney Boyce to his maker, if perhaps sooner than originally planned.

Courtney saw the grim smile of satisfaction on Alfonso's face before he saw the flash of gunpowder or heard the accompanying explosion. He felt the fiery pain in his chest and glanced down; the last thing he saw before the black void of death enfolded him was the blood staining his shirtfront.

Alfonso stared down at the crumpled form, his back to Diosa for just a second, but it had been a fatal mistake, for he had underestimated his enemy this time. Diosa, struggling to draw breath into her burning lungs, her world shattering around her, raised her hand and drove the sharp blade of the sacrificial dagger deep into Alfonso's broad back.

Alfonso slowly turned around, the expression on his face one of disbelief, not pain, as he died at Diosa's feet, the madness in her black eyes the one thing he hadn't planned on.

"*Madre de Dios*," Luis Angel said from the doorway, feeling faint. He had heard the gunshot and come running from his room down the hall, and had stumbled upon this nightmarish scene. Forcing the stiffness back into his weak-kneed legs, he took a step away from the door and walked into the room, drawing on some inner courage he hadn't realized he possessed.

Her black hair streaming over her shoulders like a shroud, Diosa was slumped down next to the dresser, her eyes glazed, a thin trail of blood-flecked saliva dribbling from the corner of her slack mouth. Her breath was coming in short gasps, and Luis's eyes rested on her throat, the pale skin mottled with ugly dark purplish-red bruises.

Carefully, he stepped over the sprawled bodies of Courtney Boyce and Alfonso Jacobs, standing for a heartrending moment staring down at his sister, his eyes full of love as he saw the pitiful creature she had become. He glanced at the dressing table, shaking his head as he saw the finely tooled leather box and knew what it held. He had warned her, but she would never listen to him, kissing him on the cheek and telling him she was singing with the gods. Always, from the time she was a little girl, she had wanted to be a goddess. She always had been, he thought sadly, remembering the beautiful sister who had always cared for him, her little Luis.

"*Diosa*," he murmured, lifting her limp body in his arms and carrying her to the bed, where he placed her gently against the softness of the feather comforter, her ravings from the madness that had ended in murder chilling his blood.

He suddenly stilled as he listened to her disjointed ramblings, her eyes rolling wildly with tortuous visions only she could see. *God help us*, he thought, shocked as he heard her admission of guilt, knowing that one day, to ease his own conscience, he would have to tell Neil Braedon the truth about Serena—and this—but for now, he had to get Diosa away. He would never allow anyone to take her away to some madhouse—or, perhaps even to hang as she gloated about the murders of her husband and Serena, and now *Tío Alfonso*.

Luis sat down on the edge of the bed and began to think, his mind working quickly as he saw what had to be done.

What would it matter? Luis decided. What harm could it cause if he cleaned up this mess, then moved the bodies to *Tío* Alfonso's study, locking the door, then climbing out the window? Fortunately, *Tía* Mercedes was away visiting a sister in Albuquerque, and was not expected back for a couple of weeks. None of the servants would dare enter the room—even *Tía* Mercedes would not have had she been here. No one entered *Tío* Alfonso's study uninvited, and even then one did not care to, for it was only when *Tío* Alfonso was angry that one was invited inside. And before he and Diosa left, as if returning to Santa Fe, and then back to Mexico on business, as was often their practice, he would leave instructions for the servants, from the *patrón*, as if he and Courtney had planned to leave on a business trip—which, unfortunately, had been interrupted by tragedy.

And when someone finally would open that door, they would believe what they saw; that Alfonso Jacobs and Courtney Boyce had become embroiled in a violent argument and had killed each other.

By that time, he would have Diosa safely in Mexico, where they had many cousins. No one would ever find them, and he would be able to watch over Diosa. Yes, Luis Angel thought, it was a very simple plan. And it would work, because he had planned it very carefully. *Tío* Alfonso had always taught him to plan very carefully.

Twenty-five

And on her lover's arm she leant,
And round her waist she felt it fold,
And far across the hills they went
In that new world which is the old.

Alfred, Lord Tennyson

IT WAS THE NIGHT OF THE *BARBACOA*.

Pungent smoke, heavy with the aromas of cooking meats and spicy sauces of garlic and onion, floated through the air along with the melodic strains of fiddle, guitar, and mandola as gaily dressed musicians played a slow, lovely waltz or a fast-stepping *jarabe*.

Earlier in the day, a trench had been dug and filled with mesquite wood, which had burned down to the white-hot coals now lining the bottom and sides for the pit roasting and spit barbecuing of *cabrito* and *borrego*—suckling goat and lamb—along with venison, wild turkey, and whole sides of beef, which had been broiling slowly since late afternoon. Large frying pans of fresh mountain trout, stuffed with mint and wrapped in bacon, were sizzling over the coals as they cooked, while Lupe oversaw the basting of the meats with olive oil, garlic, and wild herbs, or tomato sauces fiery with hot peppers.

Great terra-cotta pots of beans, rice, and vegetables had been placed in the glowing ashes, the contents bubbling and steaming whenever the lids were lifted. Long tables had been set up and filled with warm breads and stacks of tortillas, *sopaipillas*, fried dough served with honey, salads, and sweet confections. Another table held the refreshments; bowls of fruit punch, pitchers of lemonade, bottles of wine and whiskey, and steaming urns of coffee.

The yard of the *rancho* was crowded with people. The diverse groups, friends and business acquaintances of Nathaniel, ranch hands, house servants, and *vaqueros*, and their families, the herders, shearers, bull whackers, and wagon masters, clustered around various fire pits and seldom strayed far from their own gatherings—even though it was a night where social status had been temporarily forgotten as Royal Rivers celebrated a successful spring season of lambing and shearing.

Guy Travers was sitting alone on a hard wooden bench brought from the house along with other chairs and tables, and arranged near the adobe wall separating the garden and orchard from the *rancho* yard where the fires in the great barbecue pits now glowed softly in the falling dusk. His plate balanced carefully on his knee as he ate, Guy listened to the sounds of music, cheerful voices, and laughter swirling around him, his foot tapping in time to the tune.

Guy reached out quickly for his wine goblet, his throat on fire from a chile pepper he'd accidentally speared, and heard the glass thud onto the ground as he knocked it over. Bending down, his hand groped in the darkness beneath the bench. Fortunately, the goblet had not broken. Guy sighed with frustrated relief, smiling as he felt one of his hounds give a quick lick to his hand, grateful no doubt for the wine just lapped up from his shoe, Guy thought, feeling a wetness seeping into his sock. Sitting back up, Guy suddenly stilled.

He sat unmoving for what seemed an eternity, staring with a wide green eye at the glory of the first sunset he had seen since being blinded in battle. Guy was afraid to blink, even to close his eye in thankfulness for the miracle that had happened. He had been so afraid it wouldn't. Gradually, his sight had been improving, but a haze had lingered over his vision, keeping it blurred and colorless until this moment. His hand closed so tightly around the stem of the goblet that he snapped it, unaware of the blood trickling through his clenched fingers. His lips trembling, he hastily wiped the hot wetness from his eye, the brilliant scarlet and gold of the sunset blurring momentarily, and as he continued to stare at the glorious light he was saddened to see the colors fade as night fell, for he had been in darkness far too long to welcome it now.

Almost shaking with anticipation, Guy slowly glanced around. He grinned with pleasure at the first thing he saw; a tall and thin, familiar figure in calico and startling white apron, the fire making her skin even more coppery than it was. *Jolie*. She was standing in front of a short, plump Mexican woman, shaking a big wooden spoon at her as they argued, the Mexican woman raising a turkey leg in defense. As he continued to watch, Guy saw a dapper figure carrying a couple of loaded supper plates approaching, and he frowned. *Stephen?* He hadn't recognized him at first, for he was dressed in a suit of dark gray and his hair was snowy white, but his step was just as brisk. The last time Guy had seen him, Stephen's hair had been grizzled, but when he saw the man pause, wisely changing direction to avoid passing where Jolie stood, hands on hips now as she prepared to do battle, he knew it was Stephen. And in a minute, he had reached the bench, coming to stand by Guy's shoulder in companionable silence for a moment.

"It's a beautiful night, isn't it, Stephen. Quite a sunset," Guy said, glancing up at the proud face he'd known his whole life.

"Yes, Mister Guy, it sure is. Nice an' warm an' I've never seen such a red sky," Stephen replied, thinking Guy had asked a question, never even realizing Guy had addressed him personally or how he'd known anyone was there since no word had been spoken between them until now. "What happened to Miss Lys Helene? She was sittin' here when I left. An' I saw Miss Leigh an' Miss Althea here a minute ago. You doin' all right, Mister Guy?" he asked, carefully handing him his plate of food.

"Yes, thank you, Stephen, I'm doing just fine."

Guy's eye roved the crowd of people, searching for three women; two he knew he'd recognize, the other woman he'd never seen before, but knew he would know when he saw her for the first time.

Immediately, his glance came to rest on two women standing side by side as they talked.

Althea. So lovely, and still as elegant and poised and perfect as ever, he thought with brotherly affection, although she was far more animated than he remembered. Althea had always been refined, possessing a politely detached quality that had held people at a distance, but now she seemed far more approachable, human even, as she stood there laughing at some remark, her classical features touched with warmth in the firelight.

Guy's gaze moved to the young woman in blue standing next to her.

Leigh. He frowned. How long had it been since he'd seen her? Two years? Almost three? He hadn't been back to Travers Hill for over a year before he'd returned a blind man. The last time he'd seen her was when she'd ridden down to the river road with him to see him off after his last furlough home. She'd been sitting astride her mare, her long chestnut hair in a casual braid over her shoulder, and she'd looked like the little sister he would always remember as she waved to him until he disappeared around the curve of the river. Although she had always been a beauty, he wasn't prepared to see the beautiful, vibrant woman standing across the yard.

Leigh, he thought proudly, was truly a woman now, and not that little tomboyish girl who'd always tagged along with him on his cross-country rides. And as he remembered the long days and nights at Travers Hill, and Leigh's strength of will, her courage and compassion, he wondered anew at the woman she had become—a woman born of gentle blood, who had found a nobleness of spirit during the darkest time of her life, when there had been no one to turn to except herself.

As he watched her, she bent down to pat one of his hounds as it crawled up to her with no show of dignity whatsoever and begged for food. He smiled as she palmed a piece of fried dough from her plate and handed it to the grinning hound. A thin, dark-haired girl who'd been standing quietly with them held up a doll to her, and Leigh kissed the cold porcelain cheek, which seemed to please the child. Guy was shocked. *Noelle.* The sad-faced child was his niece. She must be a foot taller than when he'd last swung her in his arms and she'd squealed for him to swing her faster. Now she stood as wooden as the doll she clutched, he thought, having worried about her quietness for some time, but he was even more concerned now, watching her for a moment longer as Althea put a comforting arm around her daughter's hunched shoulders.

Guy heard a voice and knew instantly the motherly figure weaving through the crowd was Camilla, and she looked just the way he had always imagined she would, and he was glad. He laughed softly as he caught sight of two little white-haired ladies sitting with heads close together as they whispered, trading bloodcurdling secrets most likely, for he knew without a doubt they were the Misses Simone and Clarice.

Guy's gaze continued to search the crowd. There were so many people; some held his attention for a second or two, until he glanced away, certain he'd not seen anyone familiar. But suddenly he did see someone he knew.

Guy stared in disbelief, wondering what Michael Stanfield was doing at Royal Rivers. No one had told him the man was here. How strange. Surely the man would have heard of his presence and renewed their acquaintance; after all, they were both Virginians, and they'd been in the same regiment, Guy thought, certain it was Stanfield as he caught sight of the violet-blue trousers.

And as he watched Stanfield take out a corncob pipe and tobacco pouch, the truth flashed brightly in his brain as Stanfield struck the match on the heel of his boot. *Sebastian.* He was the very same man Leigh had introduced to him—the man calling himself Michael Sebastian. But his real name was Michael Sebastian Stanfield. And when Guy had known him he had been a captain in the cavalry. And before that, he'd met him at the occasional social function, but Stanfield hadn't ridden to hounds much or frequented the race meets, so they'd never been overly friendly. In fact, Stanfield had been out of Virginia quite a lot during the years before the war. Guy believed he'd been an architect. But it was indeed the same man. Guy was puzzled, something bothering him as he tried to remember what it was about Stanfield he'd forgotten. But why on earth had the man not said anything when they met? Surely he remembered him, Guy thought, offended by the slight. Leigh had been right, and the man she knew as Michael Sebastian had lied. But why?

Stanfield continued to stand slightly apart from the crowd, just within the shadows of the wall as he leaned against it watching the people around him, his expression alert, as if waiting patiently. And Guy sat watching him, more curious now than ever, especially when he saw Stanfield straighten his shoulders, tensing as if he'd seen someone he'd been looking for. Guy turned his head, following Stanfield's glance.

He was staring at a tall figure in the crowd. Guy would have known Neil Braedon anywhere. He didn't look much different than he had the last time Guy had seen him, the night of the party during that summer a lifetime ago. The man was still a handsome devil, Guy thought with none of the former envy and dislike he'd once felt for him. Actually, the truth of the matter was he liked Neil very much. They'd had a long talk the other night, staying up past midnight as they spoke of the war and reconstruction, and the future battles that would test the strength of the nation as it tried to become united again.

Guy rubbed his jaw thoughtfully, wondering what Stanfield was up to and making a promise he would have a word with the man tomorrow and demand an explanation for the charade he was playing. Glancing back, he was surprised to see Stanfield had disappeared. He could hardly wait to tell Leigh who her mysterious reb was. As he looked around quickly, trying to find him, his gaze slipped past a small figure standing just along the wall a piece, near the gate, and he knew his search had come to an end.

Lys Helene.

Guy stared rudely, knowing he could gaze his fill at her without causing her to blush, because she didn't know he could see. He felt his heart begin to pound, for she was even more exquisite than he'd ever dreamed she could be.

She was standing in the light of the burning torches by the gate. Guy smiled, for it was the perfect place for her to stand to give him a clear view of her. Her hair was a deep, glorious red-gold, thick and curly and piled high on her small head, and Guy wondered that her slender neck could support such weight. Her face warmed his heart. It was lightly freckled, with a short, tip-tilted nose that he longed to touch with his fingertip, and her mouth was full and wide, made for kissing, he thought. She was a petite, delicate-boned woman with slender hips and small breasts, and reminded Guy of a fairy sprite in her frothy gown of white lace over cream satin. Just the right height for him, he found himself thinking, knowing the top of her head would fit nicely beneath his chin when they danced. And his arm would fit perfectly around her tiny waist.

If only she would come closer. He wanted to gaze into her eyes. She had told him they were light gray. But he wanted to see the expression—he had to know what she felt when she looked at his face, he thought nervously, remembering his disfigurement, his dreams beginning to crumble as he imagined leaning close to kiss her and a look of revulsion crossing her face as she turned away from him. She deserved so much better than he could ever give her, he thought, shaking his head and swearing beneath his breath, afraid now to face her, to learn that there was no future for them.

When he glanced up, she was gone.

"Lys Helene!" he called out, glancing around anxiously, for why hadn't she come to him? In fact, she had been noticeably cool toward him the whole week. Had he done something to offend? Perhaps she had sensed he was regaining his sight and was offended that he'd not confided in her. He got up, determined she would be the first to know he could see again.

"Mister Guy, where're you goin'?" Stephen asked, stepping forward to take Guy's arm.

"I'm all right, Stephen. I've got to find Lys Helene."

"Sure, Mister Guy, I saw her goin' through the gate a few minutes ago. I'll get her," Stephen offered.

"No, Stephen. I'll find her," Guy told him, placing his uninjured hand over Stephen's where it rested on his arm.

"Now, Mister Guy, you can't go walkin' 'round with all these strange folks here. You'd get confused, an' half of them aren't makin' any sense anyway when they talk. You let me guide you back into the house. It's been a real long day fer you. You need your rest."

"I'll be able to get there by myself, Stephen," Guy assured him, smiling as he met Stephen's doubtful dark eyes. "You finish your dinner. That slice of beef looks mighty good. Don't let it get cold," he said, gesturing toward Stephen's plate, where he'd set it on top of the wall.

Stephen glanced between his plate and Guy, then down at the hand grasping his tightly. Then he looked back up at the young gentleman's smiling face, the bright green eye gazing directly into his suddenly winking mischievously.

"You've a fine head of white hair, Stephen," Guy said.

"Mister Guy? You can't see my hair. Someone's told you it's white."

"Yes, I can, Stephen. And I saw the sunset tonight. You didn't mention the gold of the clouds. The first of many I hope to see with you, old friend."

"Mister Guy? Mister Guy, you can't see, can you? You're not foolin' me?" Stephen mumbled, searching his pockets with a trembling hand for a handkerchief, but Guy was faster and took the freshly laundered square of linen from his coat pocket and handed it to the old man, who took it gratefully.

"No, Stephen, I'm not fooling you. And do you know, the first person I saw was Jolie. A good omen, I think," he said, laughing. "Now, I've got to find Lys Helene. If you'll excuse me," Guy said, patting a shaken, still disbelieving Stephen on the shoulder as he turned and walked away without hesitation toward the gate where Lys Helene had disappeared only moments before.

Watching Guy Travers stride away so purposefully, Stephen bowed his head. "Never been so happy. The good Lord's blessed us," Stephen said, glancing over to where Jolie was still locked in deadly battle with Lupe, and he blew his nose, content to wait, knowing he knew something Jolie didn't. And she couldn't claim she'd heard thunder this time.

Guy followed the path without stumbling, finding his way through the big house easily, his gaze curious as he passed through the big hall that was familiar without being familiar as he looked around, seeing what he'd only been able to envision before. Guy thought he knew where he'd find Lys Helene, but he was suddenly uncertain about following her into the courtyard, not quite courageous enough to face her rejection. She was beautiful and had probably only pitied him. She was the kind to take in stray cats and dogs, and crippled men. Why should she care for him? What could he offer her if she did? he despaired, unwilling now to declare his love. The once proud Guy Travers frightened and humbled as he thought of the loneliness that awaited him if spurned by the one woman he loved.

Lys Helene was sitting in the darkness watching him. It had happened, just as she had prayed, and feared, it would. Guy

had regained his sight. She'd watched him glancing around the
barbecue like a small boy on Christmas morning, not knowing
what to look at first. She'd been so happy for him because she
loved him, but she knew she would never be able to hold him
now. Now that he'd regained his sight he wouldn't be interested
in her, he wouldn't even look her way, and she would lose him.
And he certainly wouldn't need her any longer. He would be able
to walk around on his own, and she would not have him pity
her. And he would, she had heard him say so. He didn't want her
hanging around, Lys Helene remembered, her cheeks flushing
in remembered mortification. He had even wondered what was
wrong with her for loving him. Well, he would never know.

"Lys Helene?"

"I'm over here. Is that you, Guy?" she asked, pretending
not to have noticed him.

Her voice came softly to him across the shadowy courtyard, the fragrance from her flowers drifting around him as
he walked the distance to where she sat in the trellised arbor,
suddenly feeling ill at ease as he approached her, as if she had
somehow gained the advantage over him.

"I can see, Lys Helene," he said simply, coming to stand
before her.

Lys Helene swallowed, ready to pretend ignorance, and
show great surprise, but she was not an accomplished actress,
and she was an even worse liar.

"I know," she whispered.

"You know? How?" he asked, startled. "It just happened.
Did you see the bolt of lightning that struck me? That was
what it felt like."

Lys Helene smiled despite herself. Even had she not overheard his conversation with Leigh when he thought he might
be regaining his sight, she would have suspected something.
He wasn't very good at hiding his feelings.

"You have been acting rather strange all week, as if you
were trying very hard to see, and then…tonight, I was watching you when you dropped the goblet. I saw the look of joy
on your face. Then you were glancing around at everything
and everybody, searching the crowd for faces. I knew."

"Why didn't you come over?" he asked, more worried than

before, for there was a politeness in her voice that hadn't been there since they'd first met as strangers. "I saw you standing there. I knew it was you, Lys Helene. I wanted you to know first."

"How very kind of you. And I am so very happy for you, Guy. I truly am. But I knew you'd want to share the great news with your family first, and I didn't want to intrude, to be hanging around," she said, not intending to quote him, but the hurtful phrase slipped out.

"Kind of me? Hanging around?" he said incredulously, having forgotten all about the words he'd spoken in frustration. "You?"

"Yes. Especially now that you've regained your sight, you'll probably want to ride all around the *rancho*. Meet people. You don't need me as your guide any longer," Lys Helene forced herself to say, thinking of some of the beautiful women at the barbecue tonight. She didn't want to see him gaze at them in admiration.

"Oh, I see. Please accept my apologies, for I have obviously been a pest to you since coming to Royal Rivers, but being a guest in your home, and a helpless cripple, you were far too polite to show your boredom and impatience with me."

"What a horrible thing to accuse me of. That's not true!" Lys Helene said angrily, unable to allow Guy to think that, for it stole from her the joy she'd shared with him this past year, and she would not lose that even if she lost him.

"Isn't it the truth?"

"Of course it isn't. I've enjoyed our days together," she finally admitted.

"You do care then?" he asked, raising his hand to wipe the perspiration from his brow, and feeling the black patch over his sightless eye. Perhaps it wouldn't matter to her.

"Yes, I care. We have become good friends, and I hope we always shall be," she answered, glancing up, then looking horrified. "Oh, Guy, what have you done to your hand?" she demanded, rising from the bench and stepping close as she took his bloodied hand in hers and stared down at the jagged cut across his palm. With quick efficiency she took her handkerchief and tied it around his hand, stanching the bleeding. "You must have this seen to properly."

She stood so close to him, her red-gold curls coming just beneath his chin as he had imagined, her perfumed body sweetly provocative.

"Friends," Guy said the word curiously. "Yes, we are friends, Lys Helene. That is very important to me."

"And to me too," she agreed, her hands clasped tightly. "Well, you must go tell Leigh and Althea. And I believe I'm promised to someone for the next dance. And, perhaps the next one after that. He has been very persistent this evening," she said, as if interested in this man.

Jealousy snaking through him, Guy felt as if his worst fears were coming true. He was losing her. If she walked away now, he knew there might not be another chance to declare his feelings, for as time went by they would drift farther apart. He could sense it already beginning. Desperate, his once great pride forgotten, he spoke from the heart, fighting for what he wanted most in this world. "I would have us become more than friends, Lys Helene. Much more. I love you, and if I were to lose you now that I've regained my sight, I would welcome blindness again. You've become the most precious person in my life, and I will not lose the deep friendship, and the love, that has grown between us. I-I am in love with you. I want you to become my wife." His words tumbled one over another almost incoherently; it was not the suave declaration he'd always dreamed he would make to the woman he loved as he swept her off her feet with masculine arrogance, certain the woman he chose would say yes. At one time, no woman would have said no to Guy Travers, but now…

Lys Helene couldn't believe her ears. *He loved her?*

Guy frowned. She was too quiet. He needed to convince her of his love and devotion, he mistakenly thought.

"I've wanted to regain my sight so badly, but I've been afraid. I almost did not want to see again. If I did, I thought I might lose you. I thought you might have been pitying me all this time. And, when I could finally see again, I was stunned by your beauty. I wondered if you could possibly come to love me. I had almost hoped you would be plain, and then I—" He paused, unable to continue, and perhaps wisely so, but he had already said too much.

"What you're saying is that if I had been so ugly I caused the milk to sour, then you might have taken pity on me and asked me to marry you?" she asked, but not angrily, for she'd seen the look of despairing uncertainty cross his face and now understood the reasons behind the conversation she'd overheard. Guy Travers was afraid. He'd always been handsome and wealthy, and could have any woman he'd wanted. But now, because he imagined himself horribly disfigured, and destitute, he thought only a homely woman would accept his proposal. No one else, and certainly not a woman with a fair face, could possibly be in love with him. There would have to be something wrong with her, Lys Helene thought, remembering his words.

Then she smiled, her eyes glowing with happiness. He thought she was beautiful. And she had been so worried he would not find her beautiful at all, that he would be disappointed by her freckled face and copper-colored hair, forgetting the friendship they had formed, not letting it develop further because he would not be able to love a woman he found unattractive. "And, had I been this poor creature you hoped, I would have been so grateful to you for rescuing me from my spinsterhood that I would have said yes with unseemly haste."

"Well, yes…no, I mean, that's not really what I meant at all, because I loved you without ever having seen you. I've never felt that way about anyone. I've never been able to talk to a woman as I have you. I've never been able to talk to *anyone* as I have you. You could have three eyes for all I care, but I thought if you were beautiful, as indeed you are, then you wouldn't want me and—"

"What are you so afraid of, Guy Patrick Travers?" she demanded. "Were you really so afraid that if you found I was not frightful, then I'd be the shallow kind of person who'd marry *only* a handsome, wealthy gentleman? How little you think of me. How little you know me," she told him. "I used to see that type in Charleston. Handsome, wealthy, and so callous. I would never marry a man like that," she told him. "And, at one time, had you asked me to marry you, I would have said no, because you were once that kind of man. You've said so yourself. Although the man you were then would not have asked me to marry him. The man you are today, the man you've become, is the man I am in love with and would be honored to marry," she said decisively, almost breathlessly, but she had to speak her mind, and leave him in no doubt of the kind of man she wanted. Standing on tiptoe, her hands on his shoulders, she pressed her lips against his in a soft, shy kiss. Then she pulled his head down lower, touching her lips to both his cheeks, then his eye, and finally, she gently lifted the black patch, and Guy felt her lips touch his scarred eyelid. "My love," she murmured.

Guy stood deathly still. She said yes. And she kissed his scarred eye. Still disbelieving, though, his hand closed around her slender arm and he pulled her into the light shining from the house.

"Guy, please, what are you doing?"

He tipped her face up to his, looking deeply into her light gray eyes for the first time. They seemed almost too large for her small face, and she could not hide the tenderness in them, or the love revealed in their depths. Yes, there was love. No pity. He knew her too well, she wouldn't deceive him. She wasn't that kind, and that was why he had fallen in love with her without ever having gazed upon her beautiful freckled face, or seen the glory of her red-gold hair—like his sunset tonight.

"My dearest heart," he said, touching her nose with his fingertip, then lowering his mouth to hers, his lips touching hers lightly, then when he felt the softness of them parting beneath his, his kiss deepened, his arms sliding around her waist as he lifted her easily against him, kissing her hungrily, and with all the expertise he possessed, determined she would always remember their first kiss of passion and never regret taking a disfigured man as her husband.

"You do realize what this means?" he finally asked, holding her slightly away from him.

"After kissing me and touching me like that, it had better mean you intend to make good that proposal of marriage," she said in a breathless voice, staring up at him in amazement, for she'd never dreamed a kiss could be so wonderful, and she was thankful he still held her in his arms.

"Just try to say no to me now," he warned, resting his chin on top of her head, her curls soft and fragrant. "I intend to return to Virginia, to Travers Hill. I'm asking you to leave here. And once we are there, it will be a long way back to Royal Rivers. You will miss your family. Knowing that, do you still wish to marry me? Will you come with me, Lys Helene? It will be hard at first, but it is my home and I want to live at Travers Hill and raise a family there."

Lys Helene rested her cheek against his shoulder and sighed with a contentment she'd never known. "Just try keeping me away," she said quietly, thinking of his mother's rose garden as she turned her face up to his to seal the promise of their future with a kiss.

❧

"This is quite delicious," Althea commented, biting into a warm corn tortilla she'd loaded down with chunks of grilled meat and garnished with *guacamole* and *salsa*. Leigh eyed her sister's plate in amazement, noting the pork strips that had been marinated in red chile sauce and cooked crisp over the fire, for Althea was the last person she would have thought would like spicy food.

Althea was careful not to drip any sauce on her gown. It was of mauve-flowered, pale amber silk trimmed with blond lace, and had been quite fashionable three years ago. It was the last gown she'd made when living in Richmond, intending to wear it to a grand, much-promised celebration ball, but she'd never had the opportunity—a festive occasion never having arisen. "I understand from the Parisian fashion magazine Solange received from her friend in France that cashmere shawls are considered quite provincial nowadays," Althea said in mock despair as she pulled the soft mauve wool over her chilled shoulders. "Of course, that magazine is almost a year old, fashion may already have changed again."

Leigh glanced down at her own gown of sapphire blue velvet. Like a magician, Jolie had somehow managed to unearth the bolt of material from one of the trunks they'd brought with them from Virginia. The soft blue velvet had been purchased four years ago, with the intention of fashioning a ball gown for her trousseau, but it had been forgotten during the ensuing years. Learning of the barbecue to follow the end of the lambing and shearing, with half of the territory invited, Jolie had gone through her wardrobe, a look that boded ill on her face as she realized Leigh had precious little to wear. From an illustration in Solange's French fashion magazine, she and Althea had made her a gown that even Beatrice Amelia could not have found fault with.

And it was beautiful, Leigh had to admit, and although not as elaborate as some of the *haute couture* gowns illustrated, it was fashionable with its square-cut, tight-waisted bodice and small cap sleeves.

In fact, Leigh thought uneasily, it might be a little too fashionable, the off-the-shoulder *décolletage* too revealing, but Jolie had shrugged, eyeing her critically, then had said with almost a smirk that she was a married woman and should dress like one, *if* she wanted to keep her husband interested.

Married? Leigh sometimes doubted that statement, wondering if Jolie knew Neil still slept on the daybed each night, and glancing down at the soft flesh of her breasts, lifted high by her corset, Leigh suspected Jolie had known exactly what she was doing when cutting the bodice so low; Leigh touched the triple strand pearl necklace with its sapphire and diamond pendant resting just above that tantalizing curve. Another gift from Neil. The glinting gold of her wedding band caught her eye as she raised her hand to push a stray curl from her cheek and frowned slightly in growing frustration, pride and passion warring against one another as she glanced across the yard to where Neil stood in conversation with several guests. He stood taller than those around him, except his father, who was in another group nearby, his head tipped slightly as if listening to what was being said in conversation behind him, where his son stood. And except for the braid, Neil would have looked like any gentleman properly dressed for an evening spent in polite company, wearing the expected black frock coat and black trousers, his linen fresh, his shoes shined.

"Do you know, I am absolutely amazed that Diosa has not made a very dramatic appearance yet," Althea said, taking a sip of fruit punch to douse the fiery heat in her mouth.

"Oh, my dear, haven't you heard?" Camilla said, overhearing the remark as she came hurrying up to them, glancing at their plates to make certain they were being well fed. "Leigh, dear," she said with maternal concern, "aren't you going to have any of the *borrego*? It is so tender and Lupe's garlic and herb sauce is perfect this time," she said, trying to entice Leigh to a helping.

But Leigh shook her head, remembering the lamb she had rescued, and that was still safely penned on this night of the barbecue, promising herself she'd keep it out of the pit.

"Now, what was I saying? Oh, yes, you haven't heard, have you? Diosa and Luis Angel left Silver Springs several days ago. They arrived in Sante Fe, then almost immediately left for Mexico. Whatever is this world coming to? All of this hustle and bustle. They just arrived back from Mexico at the beginning of the week, and here it is already the end of the week, and they are off again on business for Alfonso Jacobs. And he and that dear Courtney Boyce have left too. Somewhere into Texas, I believe. I really do not care, for I am quite offended, for I would have thought they could have delayed their journeys long enough to have attended our little *barbacoa*, not that I expected Alfonso to show up. You know I do like most people, but I have never cared for him, such a crude, argumentative man, always bullying people, especially poor Mercedes, and he did try to hang Neil," she added. "But I cannot understand Diosa not coming. She was so excited about tonight. She said the gown she was going to wear was of the latest French fashion. All black lace and gold-leaved rosettes, fashioned after a gown created by Mr. Worth for Empress Eugenie," she said, glancing around when she heard someone call her name, and giving them an apologetic glance, she hurried away, stopping half a dozen times for a tidbit of food or conversation before she reached the person who had greeted her, the old woman now sitting down and resting while she waited.

Hearing laughter, Leigh turned her head, the matching pendant earrings swinging back and forth over her bare shoulders, and sparkling with trapped firelight as they reflected the torches burning brightly into the night. She smiled as she watched several pretty young girls in their colorful skirts and pure white blouses race up to a group of handsome young men. Capriciously selecting the gentleman of her choice, one of the girls broke an eggshell filled with cologne over the man's head, leaving him in little doubt the young lady felt a tenderness for him, and in the next instant she was in his arms dancing the complicated steps of a contredanse.

Leigh's smile became slightly wicked as she wondered idly what Neil would do if she cracked an eggshell over his head.

"Just make certain it is one filled with cologne, my dear," his voice spoke softly beside her, startling her from her musings.

"Do you always read people's minds?"

"Only my wife's, especially when she has a glint in her eye, and I suspect is searching for me," he said.

Althea hid her smile, for they sounded like an old married couple exchanging easy banter, just as she and Nathan once had, she thought, glancing away as smoke caused her eyes to tear slightly.

"Do you know," she said to no one in particular, "I have been so pleased with Steward's behavior the last few days. He hasn't thrown one tantrum. And I must say, Neil, he seems especially impressed by you. Whenever he sees you, his eyes get as big as walnuts. He wanted to stay up for the barbecue this evening, but it was far too late. I was afraid he was going to become upset and make himself ill, but after I brought him out here earlier, letting him choose his own meal from the pit, he seemed contented to retire for the evening. That was after we saw you bringing in that long board for the dance floor."

"He'll grow into a fine young man one day," Neil said with a smile tugging at his lips.

Leigh glanced up at him, thankful Althea hadn't witnessed the earlier scene in the barn between them.

"You ladies finished?" he asked, and when they nodded, he took their plates and wove his way through the crowd.

Althea glanced over at her sister and smiled, for Leigh's eyes were following Neil's tall figure until the crowd swallowed him up.

"I do like him," Althea said softly. "The first time I met him, in Europe, when I was on my honeymo—" She hesitated, then continued, "when Nathan and I were on our honeymoon, I didn't like him. I hope you aren't offended by my saying that?" she asked, looking concerned as she glanced over at Leigh, but she was surprised to see her sister smiling.

"I didn't like him either when I first met him. Or when I married him," she said.

"Oh, yes, well, of course, I'd forgotten," Althea said, finding it hard to believe they had ever not cared for one another, for she couldn't imagine Leigh with anyone but Neil. "He was so silent and brooding. And I sensed such a ruthlessness about him. He never smiled. But now, he seems like a different man." And she knew the reason why. Leigh had made the difference. "There is something about him that reminds me of Nathan."

"Of Nathan?" Leigh said in surprise.

"Yes, I don't know what it is, but there is just some quality in Neil that Nathan possessed too."

Leigh nodded, understanding. "They have faith in themselves. They're Braedons. They're people you can trust. I used to think that if I needed advice, Nathan would be the man to turn to," Leigh admitted, for as much as she had loved her father, his judgment at times had been less than sound. "Although there was a time when I might have doubted it, Adam had that quality too."

Althea smiled sadly. "Yes, the Braedons. Do you know, Leigh, I don't think I truly deserved Nathan. I was a very proper wife, but I wasn't an exceptional wife. I just took from him, thinking it was my right, because I could not be faulted. But, sometimes, I think you must give a little bit more than what you receive, and more than what is expected. I would do so much more now," Althea said, a note of regret in her voice that she'd never have the chance now to prove to Nathan that he had not made a mistake in marrying her. "Yes, the Braedons."

"Did I hear my name mentioned?" Neil asked, coming to stand before Althea. "And as a Braedon, I think I have the right to ask another Braedon to dance," Neil said, holding out his hand to a momentarily flustered Althea, her cheeks pinkening with confusion and pleasure. She glanced over at Leigh uncertainly and Leigh pushed her forward, for it had been a long time since Althea had danced.

"I'm going to get some lemonade for Elizabeth. She's thirsty," Noelle said, gazing down into her doll's expressionless face. "Would you like some, Aunt Leigh?" she asked politely. "I may have some myself."

"No thank you, dear," Leigh said, watching as Noelle walked off.

"May I?" a baritone voice sounded close behind Leigh, and she turned in dismay, expecting to see one of the bull whackers, only to find Gil standing behind her nervously. "W-would you like to dance, Leigh?" he asked again, this time in his own voice.

"I would be honored," she said, allowing him to take her hand.

Clearing his throat, Gil led Leigh onto the dance floor, a platform of split logs carefully joined together to form a smooth surface, and guided her into the steps of the waltz now being played.

Leigh glanced up into Gil's thin face, watching as his lips silently counted the dance steps, his expression serious.

"You're a very fine dancer, Gil," Leigh said, and he was.

Gil glanced down grinning, then looked away, his face flushing with embarrassment as he said stiffly, "Thank you."

Leigh frowned. "Gil? Is there something wrong?" she asked, for usually they got along as easily as a brother and a sister.

"No, nothing," he denied, risking another quick glance, but he couldn't look away as fast this time, his admiring gaze resting on the creamy softness of her breasts, revealed so seductively by the blue velvet gown. He swallowed, for he'd never seen Leigh looking so beautiful, and it was making him uncomfortable to hold her so close and smell her perfume.

"Gil?" Leigh questioned.

"Huh?" he said, glancing up guiltily to meet her curious gaze and turning an even brighter hue.

"I hear you nearly set a record for shearing the most sheep in an hour."

Gil's grin returned as he easily answered her questions, forgetting his discomfiture as Leigh talked and laughed with him, and noticed the wistful gazes from several young ladies following his tall figure.

As Leigh glanced around, she saw a laughing Althea dance by in Neil's arms. She was startled to see Solange, in a gown of flame-colored satin, pass by in the arms of Michael Sebastian. They danced well together, Leigh thought, watching as their figures glided around the dance floor, but Michael Sebastian's dancing seemed automatic, as if his mind were on other, more important thoughts.

The dance came to an end, and Gil left her, his step quickening almost comically as he caught sight of a young girl with an egg trying to head him off before he could escape the dance floor. Leigh was watching in amazement as he bolted through the crowd, when she suddenly saw Guy walking toward her, sidestepping various people who happened to step in front of him, waiting patiently, then smiling and nodding when greeted by someone. He even stopped and retrieved a woman's fan when she dropped it.

She wasn't even aware of Neil approaching with Althea on his arm, until she heard his deep voice thanking her for the dance. Neil stared down at Leigh, a smile touching his mouth briefly as he thought of dancing with his wife for the first time. It was something he'd looked forward to for most of the night. He started to hold out his hand, when Leigh stepped away, her gaze locked on Guy walking across the dance floor by himself.

Neil's eyes narrowed intently as he saw Guy run the last few steps to meet Leigh, holding out his arms and lifting her off her feet in a hug as he swung her around, kissing her laughing face as they shared something wonderful that had happened.

"Althea! I've always thought you looked lovely in lavender," Guy said, coming over to where she stood in stunned silence, disbelieving of what she was seeing and hearing as Leigh, her laughing face tear-streaked, walked beside him, no hand on his to guide him.

"Oh, dear Lord," Althea breathed, glancing down at her gown, then back into Guy's face. He could see. "How? When? I had no idea," she began, then just shook her head and opened her arms to him.

With a sister in each arm, Guy turned around and smiled at Lys Helene, who'd been standing just a few feet away, watching their excited faces with pleasure. Leigh saw his glance, and held out her hand to Lys Helene, pulling her over and stepping aside so she could stand beside Guy, who glanced down and kissed her forehead.

He caught Leigh's glance on them. He mouthed the words

"She loves me," and Leigh thought only a blind man wouldn't have known that as she stared at them and saw the tender exchange of glances.

Neil held out his hand, still doubtful perhaps, but he had to believe, for Guy quickly reached out and shook it. "Congratulations, Guy. I'm very pleased for you," he said, glancing at Leigh's face, her eyes shining with happiness as they stood there talking, then he looked at his sister, who was held close against Guy's side, her wide-eyed gaze resting on his face lovingly, and he smiled, for it hadn't taken him long to see what was happening between his sister and Guy Travers. And there was a time when it would not have pleased him; in fact, he would have done his best to keep them apart, but now he had no reservations about their marriage. Strangely enough, in war, Guy had found his honor, and had become a man Neil would trust with his life—and his sister's.

As Neil stood listening to their excited talk, hearing the plans they could hardly wait to make for their return to Travers Hill and the future they would build there, he noticed the light fade from Leigh's eyes as she grew quiet, gradually withdrawing from their talk and standing slightly apart. She would not be returning to Travers Hill.

"Guy, I see Mama. She is looking this way. We must tell her the good news before she hears it from someone else. She would never forgive us," Lys Helene said, for a large group of interested people, sensing the excitement, had formed around them. Trying to find her father's figure in the crowd, Lys Helene was worried, wondering how he would react when she told him she intended to marry Guy and return to Virginia with him.

"If you'll excuse us," Guy said, kissing both Leigh and Althea on the cheek, before he hurried away, his gaze searching for the tall figure of Nathaniel Braedon, for he would ask the man for his daughter's hand in marriage as soon as possible.

"I do not believe I will be able to sleep tonight, I'm so excited. Oh, Leigh, isn't it wonderful," Althea said again, still unable to grasp what had happened. And, she had to admit, she felt slightly relieved. For now she would not be returning to Virginia alone. Even though she thought about it every day, she had dreaded that journey, and her arrival in

Virginia—afraid of what she would find. But now Guy, and Lys Helene, if she knew her brother, would be coming with her. "Well, I'll say good night now. I must find Noelle. It's getting late and she should be in bed," Althea said, looking for her daughter.

"She was going to get a glass of lemonade. I'll go with you. I want to check on Lucinda. Carmelita is so hard of hearing, I don't think she'd hear Lucinda if she started to cry," Leigh said worriedly, deciding she'd move Lucinda back into her room and stay with her, no longer interested in returning to the barbecue, especially when she saw Neil standing with a group of important-looking men, their voices carrying as they spoke of the latest news; the surrender of Confederate forces commanded by a General Watie, who also happened to be a Cherokee, in the Oklahoma Territory; the release of all Confederate prisoners of war; the lifting of trade restrictions and the blockade; the naming of provisional governors to the once rebellious states; President Johnson's policies for the restoration of peace in the Union, while others wanted the former Confederate states punished for their crimes of rebellion against the Union; and finally, the sentencing of the eight coconspirators found guilty of the assassination of Lincoln—four to be imprisoned, and four to be hanged, including a woman.

Althea didn't have long to look for Noelle, because she came running up to her, and was actually smiling. She had seen her uncle, or, rather, her uncle had seen her and surprised her by coming over to her. Leigh accompanied them to the house, Noelle still chattering. They entered Althea's room, where Lucinda was crying, while Carmelita sat sound asleep in a chair and Steward slept undisturbed in his bed.

Lucinda's lusty cries stopped as soon as Leigh picked her up, holding her close as she rocked her. "I'll be back for the cradle," Leigh said, taking Lucinda with her as she left the room.

"All right, dear. I'll help you with it," Althea said over her shoulder as she tried to waken the snoring Carmelita and send her to her own bed.

"I'll help you with the cradle, Mama," Noelle offered, and temporarily giving up on the sleeping Carmelita, Althea took her daughter up on the offer. Each taking an end of the cradle,

Althea the heavier covered part, they had just managed to get it through the door and had started down the corridor, when strong hands took the cradle from them.

Althea glanced up in surprise, then smiled when Neil lifted the cradle high, relieved they didn't have to carry it any farther, for it was heavier than it looked.

"Leigh took Lucinda back to your room and was coming to help with the cradle," Althea said, hiding a yawn behind her hand. "Say good night to her for us, will you?"

"I will," Neil said, bidding them good night.

Leigh was pressing a kiss against Lucinda's soft dark curls when the door opened and she said without looking, "She's asleep now. Just a minute, Althea, and I'll help with the cradle."

"That won't be necessary," Neil said, stepping inside with the cradle and quietly closing and locking the door behind him.

Leigh glanced up in surprise, looking for Althea.

"Althea said to tell you good night," he said, placing the cradle near the rocking chair in the corner of the room. "She and Noelle were carrying it down the hall and I gave them a hand," he explained, eyeing her thoughtfully.

"Oh," Leigh managed to comment, looking away from the glint in his pale eyes as she carefully placed the sleeping child in the cradle, taking a great deal of time and care in covering her, tucking the tiny pink hand beneath the soft downy quilt.

Leigh stood up, glancing around nervously for a moment before she turned to face him. She heard the strains of music drifting across the *rancho* yard and caught his eye. "I'm not going to return to the barbecue," she said, glancing at the door as if to say he was welcome to go.

But Neil had no intention of leaving. "I couldn't let this night end without dancing even one dance with my wife, especially since it has become such a night for celebration," he murmured.

"Oh, well…thank you, but I really don't want to go back out, I've already taken off my slippers," Leigh said, gesturing to the pair of bronze silk slippers by the bed, the long ribbons tangled as if she'd kicked them off.

Neil smiled. Suddenly he found himself remembering another pair of slippers, satin ribbons tangled, that he'd seen in her room at Travers Hill the night of their wedding—a night he would never forget. "That's quite all right," Neil replied, "because I thought I'd claim my dance right here."

And without waiting for her reply, he stepped forward and took Leigh in his arms, his steps shortened for the smaller space as he moved around the room, holding his wife in his arms. "Our first dance," he said, his words soft against her ear. "I've waited a long time for this."

"Yes," Leigh said, her voice a breath of a whisper.

"I never had the chance to dance with you in Virginia," he said. "You were very beautiful the night of Blythe's sixteenth birthday party; in fact, I'd never seen such a beautiful woman, and I wanted you that night, but you were beyond my reach then," he said, his voice roughening as he remembered the frustration of knowing she belonged to another man. "You are even more beautiful tonight, and now you are mine. We are husband and wife, Leigh Braedon," he said slowly, savoring the name as his lips touched the gentle curve of neck revealed beneath the long curls clustered with several thick loops of braids over her ear and held with tiny pearled pins. His mouth moved along the slope of shoulder, pushing the small cap sleeve from its anchoring position, the décolletage falling lower to reveal the perfume-scented curve between her breasts. He bent her slightly back in his arms, his lips touching the velvety softness of her flesh.

His hands moved from her waist, along her back, and in a minute she felt the bodice of her gown fall slightly. Then the fastenings at her waist gave way and the gown spread apart and was left on the floor as she was lifted free of the tangle of material and waltzed around the room in her petticoats, his laughter coming huskily.

"I've always had a fondness for you in petticoats," he said, his steps slowing until they stood unmoving in the center of the room, the lamp casting a golden glow over them. His hands slid along her arms, caressing her, his mouth following his touch, and Leigh shivered, feeling his lips on the soft inner flesh of her arm, in the delicate contour of her elbow, where she had touched the heady perfume of jessamine, then pressing into her palm, and moving along each finger. Then her petticoats landed in a swirl of lace and ribbons around her ankles. Suddenly she could breathe easier as his fingers unfastened her corset, the offending boned silk contraption landing on top of the petticoats and gown. He found the softness of her freed body, his opened hands encompassing her ribs, holding her captured between them for a moment, as if he sought to touch the heart beating so wildly, then they moved to her waist, his fingertips nearly touching around the slender width, then she felt them sliding up to cup her breasts, still hidden beneath a froth of lace.

But when they moved away from her waist, her pantalettes slid downward around her stockinged feet, the tabs loosened by a deft touch. Leigh drew in her breath as she felt his hand against the bareness of her buttock, then around the curve of bared hip and across her taut belly, his fingers briefly, tantalizingly touching the soft hair between her thighs before moving beneath the fine linen of her chemise to her breasts, his callused palms rubbing against the soft under-curve, then the hardness of her nipples. Leigh felt the coolness of the night air against her hot skin as he tugged against the drawstrings of her chemise and the gathered material loosened to fall from her, leaving her naked before him except for her silk-stockinged legs.

He held her away from him for a second, his searing gaze burning her as it moved over her, then he pulled her into his arms, his mouth finding hers, his kiss enticingly demanding, his hands moving over her intimately as his mouth opened against hers, parting her lips as his knee eased her thighs apart and she could feel the hardness of him pressing against her as his tongue touched hers.

Their lips clung, then separated, and Leigh felt his hand against her throat, then the necklace was removed, his hands gentle as they removed the earrings from her ears. Then his hands found the pearl-studded pins, pulling them one after another from her hair and scattering them as he tugged the braids and curls free, his fingers threading through the long strands until her hair hung in thick, shining waves over her shoulders. He picked her up, holding her close against his chest, staring down intently into her face, his lips seeking hers, tasting deeply of them before he placed her on the bed.

Standing before her, he slowly disrobed, his pale eyes never leaving her flushed face.

Leigh's breathing felt as restricted as if she still wore the punishing corset as she watched Neil disrobe before her, until he stood naked, his broad shoulders and muscular chest tapering down to the narrow waist, hips, and flat belly she remembered from the first time she'd seen him. His manhood was erect, and Leigh felt the stirrings of desire deep within her as she watched him come to the bed, his thighs long and sinewy with muscle. He sat on the edge of the bed, staring at her, then his hand took the lace-edged garters from her legs, his hand lingering and caressing the soft flesh as he slowly unrolled her stockings and pulled them off. Then she felt the fiery touch of his body next to hers when he took her in his arms, his mouth finding hers in long, breathless kisses that left her lips tender.

He moved to lie beneath her, liking the feel of her slenderness on top of him, the heat of her body burning into him. His hands moved over the delicate curving of buttock and thigh, sliding between and touching her, then holding her molded against him, his manhood caught between their bodies, pressing intimately against her thigh. He buried his face between her firm breasts, then his lips moved over the taut nipples, his tongue circling them, teasing the bud as he suckled it, increasing her desire as she felt his teeth bite gently against the sensitive flesh. His mouth moved lower, across the delicate curve of stomach and hip, his lips leaving a trail of fire until she gasped when she felt his fingers probing gently between her thighs, moving deeper as they sought the sensuous core of her. Leigh felt the sensations begin, moving through her in waves of delight and she moved against his hand, seeking a fuller satisfaction from the contact, a filling of the aching emptiness inside her. He moved lower, his hands against the trembling of her thighs, then his fingers moved closer, holding her apart. Shocked, she felt the roughness of his hard cheek against her inner thigh, the soft warmth of his tongue penetrating her, moving inside her, and she would have withdrawn from so intimate a contact, but his hands held her hips against him, and even when she writhed beneath his touch, coming close to pain as the feelings spiraled through her until she was almost crying with pleasure, he held her bound to him. She felt as if she would faint from the erotic pleasure he was bringing her and she reached out, grasping his shoulders, then his golden hair, pulling against him.

He rose above her, kneeling between her spread thighs, catching his breath when he felt her fingers trailing with a feathery touch across the flatness of his belly to the hair matted at his groin, touching him, feeling him gently as she held his manhood in her hand, her thumb sliding along its length as he throbbed hard and pulsing in the softness of her hand and she aroused him with her touch.

With a groan, he lifted her, her thighs moving around his hips with an instinctive knowledge as she fitted herself to him, allowing him the greatest access. He entered the tight folds, the physical joining with her robbing him of his breath as they became one, moving as one, the soft warmth of her surrounding him, holding him sheathed deep within her.

He remained slightly above her, his arms positioned by her shoulders holding him from touching her flesh, and gazed into her face, wanting to see her pleasure, the deep blue of her eyes, heavy-lidded with passion, her lips parted breathlessly, the delicate flush on her cheeks and light beading of perspiration on her forehead as he felt her muscles pulling him deeper inside of her, feeling her swelling around him and increasing his pleasure.

Leigh stared up into his face. His hair was golden, and his face was like a mask of bronze, with finely chiseled lips and high cheekbones, his pale eyes a bright silvery green. She felt as if he were a god, bringing such pain and ecstasy to her, and she raised to touch his lips with hers, unprepared for the passion of his kiss as he lowered himself until their burning flesh touched, igniting like wildfire until it melded together from the feverish heat of their coupling. He began slowly, thrusting into her, shivering as he felt her clinging to him, her hips moving rhythmically with his. Leigh felt the world beginning to spin around her as she felt him thrusting deeper and deeper inside her, gradually increasing the rhythm, the pulsating movement building until it became unbearable and she could not endure it any longer. She climaxed several times before he ever came, as he held himself poised, watching the enraptured expression flashing across her face, prolonging the intense pleasure of denial until he couldn't bear the tightly coiled, throbbing sensations and thrust into her with a final, powerful surge as he poured his seed deep, where he hoped it would flower within her womb and they would know the joy of having created a child.

Leigh would never leave him then, he thought, holding her coupled to him, feeling her breast pounding against his, her lips joined to his, her long, slender legs entwined with his. She would never leave him now, he thought triumphantly, remembering the look of sadness and longing on her face this evening when she'd thought of Travers Hill and the family that would leave her soon, and he vowed in that moment that he would make her forget. Someday he would know her full love, but for now he would keep her with him out of her body's need for his. He had seduced her, making her erotically aware of her body. And, soon, maybe not tonight, or tomorrow, but soon, she would be with child—his child. She could never leave him then.

He stared down at her face, her lips reddened and full from his kisses, her lashes fluttering against her pale cheeks. He slid his hand through a long strand of silken hair, pressing his lips against her breast, his arm like an iron band around her waist as he held her close against his heart until she slept, his own breathing becoming deep and steady as his eyes closed.

He took her again before dawn, their bodies pale in the darkness, moving together as one, their lips devouring and insatiable as they mated and formed a bond that would be hard to break, for even though unspoken, each knew love in their hearts, and their souls touched.

❧

"Well, 'bout time you opened those sleepy eyes," Jolie said, standing with hands on hips as she grinned down at Leigh.

"What time is it?" Leigh asked groggily, stretching lazily; then feeling the cool air against her bare shoulders and breasts as the comforter fell away, she jerked it up, huddling beneath the covers and staring at Jolie in embarrassment as if she'd done something that wasn't proper.

But Jolie's grin just widened, because in her opinion, a man's place was in his wife's bed, not some narrow daybed. *That* wasn't proper. "You've missed breakfast, honey, though that Mister Neil sure did have himself an appetite this mornin'. Hmmmm, hmmmm, he sure did. Reckon that man's been mighty hungry," she chuckled, beginning to pick up the stockings, chemise, pantalettes, corset, petticoats, blue velvet gown, and pair of silk slippers that were piled in the order they'd fallen the night before.

Leigh's face turned a bright scarlet as she remembered exactly how hungry he'd been.

"This is a mighty fine day we've got. I told Steban I thought I heard thunder yesterday afternoon, but that stubborn ol' man never believes me. 'Course, we've got the proof, honey. I've never see such a night as when Mister Guy comes walkin' over to me an' took that spoon out of my hand an' dips it into the pot like he can see an' takes himself a big spoonful of meat an' pops it in his mouth an' tells me it's not salty enough. Then he winked at me, lil' honey," she said, sniffing with the remembered pleasure of tears. "An' that ol' man says he knew first."

Leigh stared up at Jolie's figure as she busied herself with shaking out the wrinkled petticoats and gown and hanging them up, then putting the stockings, chemise, and pantalettes into a pile to be laundered.

"I've got your tray right here. Fixed you a nice breakfast, honey. An' already got the girls bringin' your tub an' hot water an' we'll have you up an' dressed in no time," she said, picking up the tray and placing it over Leigh's lap, then she walked away, then back, then away, then glanced over her shoulder at Leigh, who'd been watching her nervous pacing curiously, for she'd never seen Jolie so uneasy.

"You haven't been hearing thunder again, have you?" Leigh asked, smiling up at her, but Jolie's expression remained serious.

"Miss Leigh," she addressed her formally, which gave Leigh cause for worry, Jolie's voice suddenly shaking slightly as she came to sit on the edge of the bed, her coppery hand touching Leigh's arm affectionately. "Honey, you know Steban an' me loves you like we were your own mama an' papa. Couldn't love anyone more than we do you. You'll always be my lil' sweet baby. But, honey, Steban an' me want to go back to Virginia with Mister Guy an' Miss Althea. Honey, we belong back there, not out here. We want to go back to Travers Hill. That's home, lil' honey. That's where our Sweet John is. Want to be close to him. Wouldn't have thought of leavin', 'ceptin' now that you an' Mister Neil are sleepin' together proper-like, I figure you have a good man, an' I wouldn't leave you to no one else but him. He's meant for you, always has been since that summer you stole his breeches. You stealin' them, an' findin' that leather medicine pouch with them, that was a sign. An' his magic saved you, lil' honey. Nothing's ever goin' to hurt you. An' I've been watchin' him like a fox. He couldn't live without you. He loves you that much. An' he's a good man. He won't ever hurt you none. Wouldn't leave otherwise, you believe that, honey?" she asked worriedly, seeing the look of shock on Leigh's face, her wide blue eyes brimming with unshed tears as she nodded, knowing that there was nothing she could do to keep Jolie and Stephen here. They were free people, and could go where they wanted to, but even more, she knew they wanted to go home. If she'd said she wanted them to stay, she suspected they would, but they wouldn't be happy. She knew that and she loved them too much to keep them here.

"I love you, Jolie, and I'll miss you," Leigh said softly as Jolie's comforting arms went around her, holding her close.

Jolie sat back, dabbing at her yellow eyes, a smile crossing her coppery face. "Well, I'll tell you this, honey, that little Miss Lys Helene, she's goin' to need someone to help her clean that house. It's not goin' to be easy. We have a mess of work to do. An' she's goin' to need someone to help her with all the folks who start showin' up lookin' for work now that there's no war, an' there aren't that many houses left standin' to be hiring, 'specially no riffraff. No one's goin' to push Jolie 'round. I want to get back in my own kitchens again, honey. I sure have missed cookin' and gettin' my linens done proper-like. An' I just couldn't stand the thought of some other housekeeper running loose in my house.

"Mister Guy an' Miss Lys Helene, they asked Steban an' me to come with them, said they'd be honored if we wanted to go home to Travers Hill. Should have seen how tall and straight

Steban was standin' with tears in his eyes. He's always been so stubborn and stiff-necked with pride. Stephen Stubborn, I called him when we met. Never could budge him from his dignity. That's why I call him Steban—Stephen Stubborn," Jolie confided, full of pride for her beloved Steban. "Goin' to look forward to raising those lil' redheaded babies Mister Guy an' Miss Lys Helene's goin' to have comin' real soon."

Leigh wiped her eyes, nodding again. "Would you do something for me, Jolie?"

"Sure, honey."

"Get the key from my desk, and open that bottom drawer, please," she told her, waiting patiently while Jolie found the key then unlocked the bottom drawer. "Please take out that sewing kit. You know the one. It was Mama's."

Carefully, with great reverence, Jolie lifted the box covered in fine needlepoint from the drawer and carried it over to the bed. "I always loved this box," Jolie murmured, her thin hands holding it close.

"I know, and that is why I want you to have it."

Jolie glanced up in surprise, her yellow eyes wide. "Me? You want me to have it?"

"Mama would have."

"Oh, honey, I couldn't," she said, but her hand was touching it lovingly.

"Her favorite porcelain thimble and pin cushion, and the pair of silver scissors are inside, and even more importantly, the keys to the linen closets, the pantry, the cellar, and the front door of the house. You and Lys Helene should have them now. I won't need them any longer," Leigh said, staring down at her wedding ring. "They couldn't be in better hands."

"Oh, lil' honey," she cried, hugging Leigh again and nearly knocking over the tray. "I gotta go put this where it'll be safe. You finish yer breakfast now, an' I don't want to see anything but the plate left," Jolie said, hurrying from the room.

Leaning back against the pillows, Leigh sighed with both happiness and sadness. She would miss Jolie and Stephen, but they belonged in Virginia, at Travers Hill, the same as Guy and Althea. Leigh heard the chattering of the maids outside her door and threw back the covers. She bit her lip, trying to stop its trembling as she walked to the wardrobe and found her wrapper, and she was surprised at how tender her lips were, then she remembered Neil's kisses. As she pulled on her wrapper, she felt the soreness in her breasts, and glancing down she could see the pale bluish bruises on her hips, where his hands had held her against him when they had made love.

Leigh walked over to the cradle, where Lucinda was playing contentedly with her rattle. Leigh stared down at her, touching the sweet curve of head, then tickling her tummy as Lucinda laughed up into her face, her hand grabbing hold of Leigh's finger and tugging on it. Leigh placed her other hand against her own belly, wondering if she had conceived, and she prayed she had. She wanted more than anything else in this world to know the feel of Neil's child within her.

Leigh closed her eyes with the memory of their lovemaking, shivering delicately with the sensations it brought with it, her cheeks flushed with heat. The blue of Leigh's eyes was darkened with shadow when she opened them, for there was only one thing missing from her happiness and contentment—Neil had never said he loved her.

But one day—one day he would, Leigh vowed. An hour later, dressed in her riding habit, Leigh was walking along the corridor, her spirits high.

"Leigh!" Guy called out to her, seeing her from where he was sitting in the courtyard admiring the colorful blooms. "I always knew Lys Helene loved to garden, but I had no idea how beautiful her garden was until now. I can see the tradition of Travers Hill will continue once Lys Helene gets her hands into Travers earth. Mother will always be with us now, never forgotten," he said, thinking of the gardens that would once again bloom with fragrant life at Travers Hill, and he was suddenly anxious to see the pastures of bluegrass with the curve of river in the distance. He stared up at the brilliant blue sky overhead never having known such happiness to open his eyes after a night's rest and see the sky through the window, for he had not drawn the hangings last night, not wanting to be enclosed in darkness. "I cannot seem to get enough of this color," he said, laughing as Leigh sat down next to him on the bench. "Nathaniel has given me his permission to marry Lys Helene," Guy confided, his joy knowing no bounds this day.

"I'm so pleased, but I'm not surprised," Leigh told him, touching his hand. "I always knew you and Lys Helene should be together. I couldn't be any happier for you than I am. Lys Helene belongs at Travers Hill. Even though she has never seen Travers Hill, she loves it as if she'd been born there."

Guy grinned, grasping her hand tightly, then his smile faded. "Leigh," he began uncertainly, "have you, ah…have you spoken with Jolie?" he asked hesitantly.

Leigh knew what he was trying to say, and nodded. "Jolie told me she and Stephen will be returning to Virginia with you," Leigh said huskily.

Guy sighed, placing his hand on her slender shoulder comfortingly. "Leigh, I'm sorry. I wish it didn't have to be this way. It's going to be hard on you. I know you love them as much as I. It must seem with Althea and me leaving, and now Jolie and Stephen, that we are abandoning you. But it means so much to me, Leigh, to have Stephen and Jolie coming home with us. Travers Hill wouldn't be Travers Hill without them. And they come there of their own free will this time," he added softly.

Leigh nodded. "I know, Guy. And I also knew when I married Neil that my life would be here, not at Travers Hill. I have accepted it, as you advised me to do," she told him, smiling, but her smile was slightly wobbly, because even if she'd accepted what must be, she would still miss them.

"I would not leave you here, Leigh, be assured of that," Guy told her, tipping her chin so he could see into her face, "if I thought you would be unhappy with Neil. Tell me now, Leigh, that you want to return to Virginia with us, and you will. No one can keep you here against your will. I am your brother, and now that I've regained my sight, I can care for you, and for Lucinda. I will fight Braedon in the courts for custody of her, if you tell me that is what you wish," Guy told her without hesitation, staring deeply into her eyes as he searched for the truth.

Leigh took his hand in hers and kissed his cheek. "Thank you. That means a great deal to me, and I know you would never abandon me. But I know that I belong here, the same as you and Lys Helene, and Althea and her children belong in Virginia. This has been my destiny all along," Leigh said, suddenly believing Jolie's words.

"You do love Neil, don't you?"

"Yes, with all my heart," Leigh replied, getting up. "Well, I'm going riding. We'll have to find a horse for you now, Guy. Hope you haven't forgotten how to ride," she told him, eyeing him speculatively.

Guy laughed, then suddenly sobered, calling her back as she started to walk away. "Oh, Leigh, I almost forgot. I know who your mysterious reb is."

Leigh came hurrying back. "Who he is? What do you mean? His name is Michael Sebastian, isn't it?"

"To you, maybe, but the man I saw last night is none other than Michael Sebastian Stanfield. You were right about him. He is a Virginian, and he was in my regiment. I would have had a word with him then, but he disappeared. I saw him dancing, but that was when I crossed the floor to you, and after all the excitement, he was gone."

"Michael *Stanfield*? Why lie about his name?" Leigh asked, a thoughtful expression on her face as she tapped her riding gloves against her skirt.

"I'm not certain, although I have an idea. You won't like it. I meant to tell you last night about Stanfield, but in all the excitement I forgot, then I couldn't find you," he said. "But I hadn't remembered everything about the man then anyway, just that his last name wasn't Sebastian. I couldn't sleep last night, too much to think about, and as I lay awake, I remembered what it was about Stanfield that had bothered me."

"What?"

"He had a brother. An older brother. A Major Montgomery Stanfield. I met him several times when he came to our regimental headquarters from his department to visit his brother. Major Stanfield was the commanding officer of the troop guarding that shipment of gold bullion that was robbed near Gordonsville just before we left Virginia. Remember? The newspapers said it was Captain Dagger who robbed the train and massacred those unarmed soldiers. And remember that

Confederate troop that was scouring the countryside for Captain Dagger because of that incident?"

Leigh lost all of the color in her face, her blue eyes darkening into indigo with the fear she could feel sneaking up her spine. "But it wasn't true. Neil and his men didn't rob that train and kill those men. You know that."

"You and I know that, but most people don't," Guy reminded her. "When you have someone who becomes as legendary as Captain Dagger, instilling fear in the hearts of already frightened people, every act of violence is attributed to that mythical figure. It is far easier for them to accept Captain Dagger's almost supernatural feats than to think there might be another murdering raider roaming their lands. That would be too much to bear."

"Do you think this Stanfield knows Neil was Captain Dagger during the war?" Leigh asked, remembering Neil's words that for some, the war would never be over.

"Well, it is mighty odd, Stanfield showing up here. Of all the places he could drift to after the war, this is the last place I would have thought, *unless* he had a reason for coming here. And he lied about his name. Why the devil didn't he introduce himself to me? He knew me. But, if he somehow found Captain Dagger's true identity, which he might have been able to, and believing he killed his brother, tracked him down here, then…" Guy said, his words hanging in the silence that suddenly fell between them.

"Tracked him down?" Leigh repeated the phrase. "Tracked him down like an animal he was out to trap and kill?"

Guy met her worried glance. "Stanfield is a gentleman, Leigh," he said. "He's one of the Stanfields of Virginia. He may mistakenly hold Neil responsible for his brother's death, but I don't think he will do anything more than confront him, perhaps try to bring him to justice, or…"

"Or…?"

"Or maybe call the man out," Guy said almost in embarrassment as he remembered another hotheaded Virginian who'd done much the same thing. "He is a gentleman, Leigh," he said again, for he supposed that still meant something in this world. "He won't shoot Neil in the back," he added, only making matters worse as he got quickly to his feet, wishing he'd said nothing to her before he could have had a word with Stanfield. They could have settled it between them without Leigh ever having known. But now, as he saw the expression on her lovely face, he believed her when she said she loved Neil with all her heart, because she looked terrified.

"I have to find Neil and tell him about this man Stanfield. He has to be warned," Leigh said, already hurrying from the courtyard.

"Neil's already gone, Leigh," Guy called after her.

"Where?" she asked, damning herself for having slept so late.

"I don't know, out somewhere on the property. I'll try to find Stanfield," Guy told her, hoping she wouldn't do anything rash as he tried to catch up with her.

But Leigh was beyond listening as she hurried along the corridor, stopping briefly to look in Nathaniel's study as Guy hurried to the big hall, where he'd heard voices. Someone might know where Neil had gone.

The study empty, Leigh hurried on and found Guy in the big hall speaking with Solange, who was writing a letter as she talked with Camilla.

"What is it?" Leigh demanded, seeing the look on Guy's face.

"I don't know why you're so upset," Solange said, staring up at Guy in dismay.

"Solange just told me that Michael Sebastian couldn't come to her studio today to view her paintings because he was riding out with Neil to move a tree that fell across the creek during one of the last storms this winter. It's damming up the water," Guy said, glancing around almost helplessly as he stared at the whispering aunts, their furtive glances making him nervous.

"The tree fell during one of the winter storms, but it wasn't causing any trouble until recently, when the snows started to melt, and then it caused the stream to become only a trickle. Nathaniel saw it the other day when he was out riding beyond the north pasture and he gave orders for it to be chopped up. Neil offered to do it," Camilla told them, thinking nothing of it as she went back to her perusal of a fashion magazine.

"My God, I don't even know where the north pasture

is," Guy said in growing frustration, beginning to worry that Michael Sebastian Stanfield might not still be a gentleman.

"I know where it is," Leigh said, her steps carrying her quickly from the room. She reached Nathaniel's empty study, walking without hesitation to the gun cabinet in the corner, knowing what she must do. She tried to pull the glass doors open, but they were locked. Glancing around, Leigh grabbed one of the brass fireplace tools, raising the poker and breaking the glass as she wedged the pointed end between the two locked panels and, with a splintering of fine wood, broke the lock in two.

Reaching in, Leigh grasped a rifle, then fumbled through the drawers beneath to find the shells. Dropping a couple of the metal cylinders, she finally loaded the rifle, then hurried from the room, meeting Guy in the corridor, but she brushed past him.

"Leigh! My God, Leigh, what are you going to do?" he demanded, unable to believe his eyes, and remembering the reb deserters she'd shot, he almost wished now he couldn't see as he watched her running down the corridor with that rifle, unmindful of him as she disappeared out the door.

"Damn!" he swore beneath his breath, continuing after her and wondering what he could do. Not only did he not know where the north pasture was, he didn't even have a horse to ride to the north pasture if he did.

Leigh reached the stables, not bothering to get a stable boy to help saddle Capitaine. She had to disappoint him when she entered his stall and he greeted her with a welcoming snort, for she had no apple for him this time. Patting his rump, she led him from the stall, quickly putting his bridle on and saddling him, then adding the leather holster for the rifle, something she seldom rode with. Leading him to the mounting block, she was up and heading out of the stables within ten minutes of entering, Capitaine's hooves sending up dust as she rode across the *rancho* yard, not even seeing Guy running across the yard behind her, but Nathaniel did as he came riding from the opposite direction. He stopped just long enough to hear what Guy had to tell him, then he was riding after Leigh, the big bay traveling quickly across the grassland and through the streambed until Nathaniel caught sight of her disappearing into the woods.

Leigh paused on the soft bank overlooking the small lake that had formed where the pine tree had fallen across the streambed. Her breath caught in her throat when she saw Neil stretched out on the ground beside the fallen log, Michael Stanfield standing over his body, an ax raised high above his head—and held ready to swing down on Neil's unsuspecting back.

Leigh could already envision the blood pouring from Neil's back, cleaved in two by the blade of the ax, and she drew the rifle from the holster, raising it and holding it steady as she took aim on Michael Stanfield's head.

But before Leigh could pull the trigger, her forefinger just touching it, a roar split through the quiet, and Leigh fought to keep her seat, hold on to the rifle, and control a frightened Capitaine. Glancing around in surprise, Leigh saw Nathaniel sitting astride his horse in the stream below. Knowing Royal Rivers better than she, he'd taken a different, quicker trail along the streambed, where only a ribbon of water remained, and she'd never even heard his approach.

Leigh sent Capitaine down the slope, riding toward Neil and his would-be murderer, Michael Stanfield, both of whom were standing in amazed silence as they watched Nathaniel and his daughter-in-law come riding up, their horses lathering.

Michael Stanfield stared down at the ax handle, the blade having been blown clean off before he could swing it down.

"Neil!" Leigh cried out, hopping down with her rifle, and running toward him. "He was going to murder you!" Her voice came hoarsely as she swung the loaded rifle at a startled Michael Stanfield.

"He's not Michael Sebastian," Leigh began, looking surprised when Neil took the rifle from her and pointed it away from Stanfield's stomach. "His name is really Michael Stanfield, and he knows you were the Union raider Captain Dagger. He believes you murdered his brother, who was guarding a shipment of gold bullion he thinks you stole, and he has come here to Royal Rivers to get revenge," Leigh said, her story tumbling out breathlessly.

Nathaniel sat his big bay easily, his rifle held casually across his knee as he listened, his pale gray eyes never leaving Stanfield.

"So Guy Travers did recognize me," Michael Sebastian Stanfield said, glancing over at Neil with an almost comical expression on his face.

"Leigh, Michael Sebastian Stanfield rode with me from Washington. I've known all along who he is," Neil said, staring at Leigh as intently as his father had been staring at Stanfield. "He did indeed come here to find the man who murdered his brother, Major Montgomery Stanfield, and stole that Confederate gold, *but* he came as an agent of the federal government. Do you still have that photograph?" Neil asked, trying to hide his smile at Leigh's crestfallen expression.

Stanfield pulled a faded, dog-eared photograph from his pocket, handing it to Neil, who handed it to Leigh. "The man second from the right is one of the men who murdered my brother."

Leigh stared at the photograph of about ten men in Confederate uniforms, their grinning faces smiling back at her, and she glanced up in surprise. "That's Courtney Boyce."

"When he was a member of my brother's troop, his name was Clifton Butts. He was the only survivor of the massacre. *He* was the eyewitness who identified Captain Dagger as the raider. A couple of months after that, he disappeared mysteriously. I wanted to know why my brother was shot down in cold blood. Even though I was a reb, and had read about the exploits of Captain Dagger, I had never heard of him having committed such a heinous crime. He was no Quantrill. So I started investigating. I discovered there had been a number of robberies. And all very successfully executed. Not only had gold bullion been stolen, but guns and ammunition too. And all attributed to Captain Dagger. The only problem was that even Captain Dagger did not ride a horse with wings, and he could not be in two places at once, which it would have required for him to have been responsible for half of those robberies reported. The only man I could talk to, to confirm what he'd claimed, had disappeared. I started to look for the man, and my search kept coming back to one man, an Alfonso Jacobs. He was some official with the Treasury Department. This Alfonso

Jacobs and Clifton Butts, if they worked together, would have had the information necessary for planning these robberies. I ran into a dead end with Clifton Butts, so I tried to find out all I could about this Alfonso Jacobs, and the more I dug, the more concerned I became. He was a wealthy rancher in the territories, with a Spanish wife and close ties to Mexico, and he was a rabid Confederate sympathizer. He, also, disappeared shortly after the last robbery. The more I discovered about the man, I began to suspect that he was the mastermind behind the robberies, and that he might have aspirations to form his own republic in the territories after the South fell. He could not have been in a better position. He had guns and ammunition, gold to fund his ambitions, and the federal authorities would be busy fighting the last of the Confederate army that refused to surrender. I felt as if I could read this Alfonso Jacobs's mind. He had himself an empire out here in the territories. And he could very easily, after the last of the rebs were dealt with, stir up a problem with the Indians," Stanfield told them, his voice coming evenly, convincingly as he spoke. "I took my suspicions to Washington, to the federal authorities. Although I was the enemy, I had a brother who was dead, murdered, and I told them I knew it was not their infamous Captain Dagger who committed the crime. I told them I thought I knew who was behind those acts against the Confederacy, and what would soon become acts of treason against the Union, and they listened. It didn't hurt that I had friends at staff headquarters who could vouch for me. I had nothing to gain, except bring to justice the men who'd murdered my brother, and the Union had much to lose if they didn't stop this new rebellion before it spread."

"That is when I was called in to meet with Michael Stanfield. Headquarters wanted me to work with him," Neil said, not saying that his superiors might not have completely trusted the former Confederate officer, despite his convincing evidence. "I knew Alfonso Jacobs, and Captain Stanfield knew this Clifford Butts, or as he was known here in the territories, Courtney Boyce. I realized that when I recognized the man the other day when he arrived here with Diosa and Luis. The authorities knew I would have an interest in keeping peace in the territories, and I could also make certain Captain Stanfield had a legitimate reason for being here. Fortunately he arrived in time for the shearing and there was no problem getting him hired on at Royal Rivers. He could stay here without casting suspicion on himself while he investigated Alfonso Jacobs and Courtney Boyce. They have been making too many trips into Mexico and Texas for the government's peace of mind. Captain Stanfield's story was already being corroborated by American agents in Mexico. That is why he is here at Royal Rivers," Neil told them. "He is after Alfonso Jacobs and this Courtney Boyce, not Captain Dagger. We do not want another Civil War erupting here in the territories," Neil said.

"And if Boyce recognized Captain Stanfield, remembering who his brother was, then Stanfield and I agreed to let them believe he was here at Royal Rivers to find Captain Dagger. We know Alfonso knew I was Captain Dagger and was the source of many rumors during the war as to my identity. That is also why there were so many erroneous reportings of raids by Captain Dagger. Alfonso was already using Captain Dagger to hide his own activities. We thought to do the same thing, letting them believe Captain Dagger was again under suspicion. It would work to our advantage to mislead them, and perhaps they would become careless. We were surprised, however, that Boyce did not attend the barbecue last night, until learning he and Alfonso left abruptly for Texas. We intend to ride over to Silver Springs later today and do a little reconnoitering while they're away. I've already sent a couple of *vaqueros* to Fort Union and Fort Marcy, warning them to be on the lookout for Alfonso and Boyce, and for Diosa and Luis, who are heading into Mexico."

Neil glanced at the blown-off piece of wood still held in Stanfield's hand and glanced back at his father, then at Leigh, wondering why they had come to save him.

"Please accept my deepest apologies, Mr. Stanfield," Leigh said stiffly, walking back to her horse, and climbing into the saddle before anyone could assist her.

"No offense taken, Mrs. Braedon. Although I suspect I had better have a word with your brother, Guy, for I owe him an apology, as well as the rest of you for being here under false pretenses," Stanfield said smoothly.

Leigh caught Neil's eye for just an instant, then glanced away, pulling on the reins as she rode back up the bank.

"She must love you very much," Stanfield said. "Not many women would have the courage to do what she was going to do. You've quite a woman for a wife," he said almost wistfully, staring after Leigh's figure in admiration.

"Yes, I know," Neil said softly, an expression of revelation crossing his hard face as he realized what she had been prepared to do; the rifle he'd taken away from her had been loaded and cocked, ready to fire, ready to kill. No one, until Leigh, had ever loved him above everyone else. No one.

"Looks like you could use some help with this log," Nathaniel said, dismounting, and coming to stand beside Neil. "I'll give you a hand. And I'd be interested in hearing more about Alfonso Jacobs."

❧

An hour later, Leigh still couldn't believe it as she paced back and forth in her room. She would have shot Michael Stanfield dead. And he would have been an innocent man. If Nathaniel hadn't shot first, and carefully, sanely aimed his shot at the ax instead of Michael Stanfield's head, she would now be a murderess. What madness did love bring to a person, she wondered in despair, shocked by the savageness she'd felt when she thought Neil was in danger. She clenched her hands together, playing with her wedding band, the gold so pure. She pulled it from her finger, staring down at it. It was the first time she'd taken it from her finger since Neil had given it to her, and her finger felt bare without it encircling her flesh. Neil. She would have killed to save him. Leigh frowned, narrowing her eyes as she stared at the inside of the band. She was surprised to see an inscription. Neil had never told her.

"*For my beloved Leigh.*" She read the words softly aloud, words that proclaimed his love.

"I meant every word." Neil spoke from the doorway. "I've always loved you."

Leigh turned around, the ring sliding back onto her finger,

where it belonged. He stood so tall and powerful—and proud—before her. He flouted convention with his buckskins and golden Comanche braid, but there was a vulnerability about him that even his unyielding strength could not hide, and Leigh suddenly wanted to reach out and touch his bronzed cheek, see the hard curve of mouth soften beneath her fingertips, her lips…to see him smile down at her…to hear his laughter again. They faced each other for a long moment staring, a thousand words and declarations of love passing silently between them, but actions had proven their love for one another, and he held out his arms to her, and Leigh didn't hesitate, the proof of his love around her finger. She ran to him, feeling his arms enfolding her.

Their lips met and there was silence. Then Leigh felt herself lifted and carried to the bed. He sat down, cradling her against his chest, his lips tasting again of hers.

"I never dreamed until today that you loved me, or that you would have killed for me. To risk your life for mine. To want to save me. Do you know how much I love you? From the moment I saw you I wanted you. I loved your spirit, your loving laughter, your dignity, your beauty. And I wanted to possess you. I wanted you to be mine. I was tormented when I left Travers Hill, leaving you to another man. Knowing you hated me because I'd hurt you. Not only did I take something you loved from you, but I'd hoped you would never forget me, even if it was with hatred in your heart."

"Never that. I never hated you. Even when my pride told me I should, my heart spoke another word. Can you forgive me for not choosing you that summer?" she asked him, her hands caressing his face, touching his lips, his cheek, the strong column of his throat.

"I loved you all the more because you didn't, because you placed the needs of those you loved above your own desires. I think I was jealous of your family. You belonged to them. And you loved and cared for them. I was just an outsider. I knew you were physically attracted to me, and I set out to seduce you, and I would have seduced you, taking you from Wycliffe, but what I hadn't counted on was the deep, sacrificing love you had for your family, and that you'd marry the man because of them. I knew then I'd lost you. I couldn't fight that kind of love. A love I couldn't understand, yet wanted so badly. And I wanted to hurt you. Can you forgive me for that?"

Leigh pressed her lips to his mouth, healing the wound with her touch, warming to his.

"Everyone was telling me how important the right marriage must be, and that I must select the right man. I mustn't mistake infatuation for love. Or if there was no love, then how important friendship would be in my marriage, and that was why I must choose the right man, a man I had common likes and dislikes with, and who would be acceptable to my friends and family. Someone appropriate. And until I met you, a stranger who was everything a gentleman wasn't, I had thought Matthew Wycliffe would make the perfect husband for me. I didn't know what love was until I met you. And then, I was frightened to admit it, because I'd been listening to what everyone had been telling me. I listened to everyone but myself, what my heart was trying to tell me. You are the only man I have ever loved, could ever love with all my heart. But by then I'd learned that Travers Hill was mortgaged, and that my father was hopelessly in debt, and I couldn't turn my back on them, especially when I didn't truly know what your intentions were," Leigh said softly.

"Or trust me."

"And then you dueled with Guy and…"

But his mouth stopped the rest of her words, not allowing her to mention their parting.

"And then we had to marry under less than auspicious circumstances," he said, his breath hot against her cheek. "But I would do it again."

"Adam told me you refused at first," Leigh murmured, still remembering the hurt of that rejection, but Neil lifted her face to his, staring down into her eyes, no shadows between them now.

"I refused only because I wanted to come to you and win your love freely. I didn't want there to be misunderstandings between us. I wanted you to want to marry me because you loved me, not because you were sacrificing yourself to save your family. I wanted to have your love when I gave you my name. But I had no alternative, and I wasn't going to risk losing you forever. I took the chance, because I knew you would not have married me otherwise. You did not come willingly into this marriage," he reminded her.

Leigh glanced down at their clasped hands. "No, I did not, because I thought you were being trapped into marrying me. Adam's needs, and your men's, came before ours. I knew you desired me, but it wasn't enough," Leigh admitted, her cheeks flushed.

"Then why did you let me love you that night?" Neil asked quietly, still disbelieving of her declaration of love, for he had always wondered why she had lain with him and responded to him, hoping that it had been more than desire, more than wifely duty that had driven her into his arms that night—and last night.

Leigh looked up, meeting his searching gaze unblinkingly. "Because whatever your feelings were for me, I loved you, and I could not bear the thought that you would leave me and I might never see you again, and I would never have known your love because of some foolish, misplaced pride. If I'd lost you, then I wanted to at least have something more than a memory of you. I prayed that you had gotten me with child that night. At least I would have your son or daughter to love and cherish. But it wasn't to be," Leigh told him, unprepared for the fierceness of his response, little realizing how deeply she had touched him with her low-voiced confession as she bared her soul to him. His mouth found hers, his kiss searing, almost savage in intensity as he held her as if he'd never let her go, stealing the breath from her until they breathed as one.

"I do love you, Neil." He was her love. Neil Darcy Braedon. Sun Dagger. Captain Dagger, leader of the Bloodriders. He was all of those men and more. And now, with her love, he would become another man. He was her beloved husband.

"Leigh," he murmured, kissing her deeply, holding her tightly against him. He glanced away, staring through the window at the mountains, feeling a sense of power akin to the mountain gods', knowing at last that she was his. But Leigh knew there was still a part of Neil she did not know, that he had not shared with her, perhaps because he could not, because it was not his secret to share.

Leigh took her courage in her hands, determined there would be no more ghosts to haunt their lives. Before he could protest, she had pulled free of his arms, going over to her desk, where the bottom drawer still stood partly open. She opened it wider. Her hand hesitated a moment, resting indecisively over the rolled-up sheet of vellum.

"What's this?" Neil asked curiously when she handed it to him.

"It's the portrait of a man. A man I met. I couldn't forget his face, it haunted me, so I asked Solange to draw the face I described to her," Leigh told him, watching him as he unrolled the paper.

He was so silent, Leigh felt frightened, wondering what she had done. Why couldn't she have left well enough alone? Had she destroyed what had just happened between them? she thought in growing despair, afraid to move.

Neil looked up at her, a strange look on his face.

Leigh swallowed. "That night when Gil and I returned to Royal Rivers, the night you came home from the war, we had been riding to Riovado. That was why we were late."

"Riovado?" Neil asked sharply.

Leigh nodded. "Yes, but we decided to turn back halfway there, just beyond a stream crossing a wide meadow. In the copse of trees we found the lamb, and were trying to catch it. That much of the story we told you that night was true. What we didn't tell you was that we—" Leigh paused, her hand going to her breast nervously, almost protectively. "We were attacked by a group of Comanche braves."

Neil stood up, taking a step toward her, glancing from the drawing to her tormented face. "My God, Leigh," he said, knowing even more than she ever could the danger she'd been in, the life she would have faced had she been taken captive, and he felt his heart stop as he stared at her beloved face, his dearest Leigh.

"Gil tried to fight and was hurt. *That* brave was about to rape me when he saw this," Leigh said, gently lifting the leather pouch, which she still wore, over her head and holding it out to Neil. "He jerked it from around my neck and that was how I received the abrasion you saw that night. But when the Comanche brave looked at it more closely, he seemed puzzled.

He must have recognized the markings on it, and wondering why I had possession of something sacred belonging to the Comanche, he opened it," she said, doing the same now. "He was startled, Neil, when he stared down at the contents. He touched the tiny black braid, saying something softly, then he looked up at me as if sorry for what he had done. I could see it in his eyes, in his light blue eyes. He very carefully put the contents back in the pouch, but he seemed most fascinated by the silver dagger with the sun on the hilt. He held it for a long moment in the palm of his hand, as if he had heard the stories of a young golden-haired Comanche brave called Sun Dagger, and his mother's young brother, who had been lost to the tribe. Sacrificed, perhaps, so the others could live in peace. But never forgotten, Neil. Never forgotten, because of this pouch, he let Gil and me live. They rode off and left us."

Neil felt as if the breath had been knocked out of him. His secret, kept for so long, now spoken of by Leigh. How? he wondered, stunned. He stared at the beautifully sketched face. He could see Shannon in every line, in the incredible shade of blue of the eyes.

"The face of this Comanche brave seemed so familiar to me," Leigh said, twisting her hands nervously as she saw the expression on Neil's face. "I went to your father's study and compared the sketch to the portrait of your mother and sister. The faces were too similar not to be related."

"You've told no one?" he asked quietly.

"No, it was not my secret to tell. I suspected the truth after seeing the resemblance between the three faces, and then, something the Misses Simone and Clarice said made me realize that sometimes a person might want others to think they had died, when actually they had not. And I found myself wondering about Shannon, a young girl becoming a woman while she lived with the Comanche. What if she had a choice to make? Would she have come home?" Leigh asked gently.

Neil stared into her face, trusting her. "Shannon didn't die. I lied," he said in a low voice, his expression tortured. "She chose to remain with the Comanche. Shannon was four years older than I was, and as you've said, she became a woman during our captivity with the Comanche. And she fell in love.

Her Comanche name was She-With-Eyes-Of-The-Captured-Sky. She was very beautiful and a brave warrior of the tribe fell in love with her and claimed her for his wife. He was a good man and he worshipped her. When I was sent from the tribe she had given birth to a daughter and was with child again. She swore me to silence. She knew our father would never give up looking for her and would take her from the tribe, from her family. She also knew it would kill him to learn about her. She said it would be better if he thought she was dead. She was always so wise. She and her family, and the tribe, and our father could all live in peace if I said she was dead. I promised her, but I was young and I hated her and the rest of them for sacrificing me, turning me away from the only family I had known, where I had felt loved. I was alone again. I felt betrayed by her and the tribe. She now belonged to Hungry-As-The-Stalking-Wolf and her daughter, not to me. I've always regretted the things I said to her. I've wanted to tell her I was sorry, that I understood, to ask her forgiveness. I never saw her again. But now, finally, I know she forgave me, that she loved me. You've given me that by showing me this, and telling me about that young Comanche buck.

"It comes full circle, Leigh. Shannon's son saved you. He honored me, by honoring you. Shannon spoke of me, perhaps Stalking Wolf told the tales of our hunting days. They never forgot me. And he loved her enough to break tribal custom and have her buried in the white man's tradition at Riovado, where he first saw her, and where I found her grave when I rode up there the day after I arrived at Royal Rivers. She must have died just a year or so ago. The earth is still newly turned," Neil said, feeling a strange sense of release as he was finally able to speak of something he'd kept hidden deep for so many years.

"And all these years, lying to my father, I've felt something dying inside. I've never felt as if I could look him in the eye. But she was right. It would have killed him to know about her. My God, to think I've never spoken of this to anyone. To be able to share it, finally. Someday I would like to tell you about my life with the Comanche, about Shannon, about She-With-Eyes-Of-The-Captured-Sky. You would have loved her, and she would have loved you, Leigh," he said, staring out at the blue sky surrounding him. "And one day soon, we will ride to Riovado."

Leigh held back the tears, her heart breaking as she saw the young boy he'd been, caught between two worlds, feeling betrayed by one, rejected by the other, a desperate secret his alone to keep. But kept it he had, and because of his tortured silence, others had not suffered.

Leigh walked up behind him, her slender arms sliding around his waist as she enclosed him in her embrace, laying her cheek against his back. "That is what love is about. To be able to share. And I do love you with all my heart, Neil, my love." She said his name lovingly and he drew strength from her words, from her warmth touching him and he knew that never again would he be alone.

A month had passed since the night of the barbecue, but Althea still felt as if her tongue was numb from the hot chile peppers she'd eaten. She would never forget that night. It would be one she would long remember with Guy regaining his sight, and the plans they'd made together after that. And then, the following day the announcement that Guy and Lys Helene would marry, and with both her parents' blessing. Since then, they had made many plans, but the most startling to her had been the news that Nathaniel and Camilla, along with Gil, who'd never been out of the territories, would accompany them to Virginia. Once again they would be part of a wagon train carrying freight, but this time they would ride in style, traveling in the fancy red Concord coach.

A herd of cattle and sheep, and several wagons loaded with supplies, fruit cuttings and seeds, were destined for Travers Hill, where they would be used that first winter, the cuttings and seeds to be planted in the tilled soil that following spring, and hopefully the beginning of many a fruitful, bountiful year to come. But most important, were the two Thoroughbred stallions and several broodmares that had been given to Guy by Nathaniel as an investment in the future—the blooded horses returning to the bluegrass lands they'd been born of, destined to carry on the proud tradition of Travers Hill.

Althea smiled. A month ago, even up until the night of the barbecue, she'd had troubling doubts about leaving Leigh behind at Royal Rivers. But now she had no fears. Leigh and Neil were so much in love, it almost hurt her sometimes to watch them together, for their happiness brought back painful memories of her own happiness with Nathan. Althea's smile widened. Leigh had confided to her that she thought she might be with child. But she had sworn her to secrecy. Neil didn't know yet, and Leigh wanted to wait for a very special time and place to tell him. She wasn't certain, of course, but she had missed her time of the month—something that had never happened to her before, Leigh had told her, her dark blue eyes glowing with the cherished thought of giving birth to Neil's child. But Althea had a feeling Leigh was right in her suspicions, and she would not be disappointed, for she'd never seen her sister looking quite so beautiful. There was almost a golden radiance about her, a warmth and softness that came of the fulfillment of loving, of having given oneself to another. And she would never doubt that Neil loved Leigh. His love for Leigh was evident in every glance, warming the coldness of his eyes whenever he gazed upon her, and in every gesture, his hand becoming gentle whenever he touched her.

No, Althea thought, she would never worry again about Leigh, for she had found a love that was true and everlasting.

Althea stared at the blackboard and frowned slightly. Carefully, she spelled the word letter by letter. L-A-R-R-I-A-T. No, something was definitely wrong. It didn't look right, Althea thought, tapping the chalk impatiently against the board.

"There is only one *r* in lariat," a familiar voice said behind her.

Slowly, Althea turned around, her eyes widening in disbelief.

"Nathan?" she said soundlessly, her face paling so that the smile faded from the man standing just within the doorway. Thinking she was about to faint, he hurried forward, his arms outstretched to the wife he hadn't seen in nearly three years.

"Oh, my God! Nathan?" Althea cried, then covered her face with slender hands, shaking her head in denial. "No, no, it cannot be," she moaned, unable to believe her eyes. "It cannot be," she repeated again, her shoulders shaking with despair and the fear that she had gone mad.

"I *am* here, my love," Nathan spoke softly, his strong arms embracing her, holding her close against the warmth of a living body, not one cold with death.

Althea raised her tearstained face, breathless with the dawning realization that her husband still lived, that her dearest Nathan stood before her. Slowly, she stretched out a hesitant hand, almost afraid to touch him, to discover she was being cruelly mocked by an illusion.

"They said you were missing. We were informed. The War Department said you were missing. So many were killed. We waited and waited. Every day we waited. We never heard from you," Althea said, her voice husky with the grief she had borne for so long. "The days and months I sat there wondering what had happened to you, never knowing. That was the worst. My Nathan, lost so completely to me in death because I could not even grieve over your grave."

Nathan Braedon held his wife in his arms, his eyes searching her lovely face, then his mouth lowered to hers and they kissed, and he tasted the salty tears, and vowed never again would he be separated from her and his family.

"I had no idea I had been reported missing. If only I could have spared you that agony. I am not surprised there was confusion, nobody, whether reb or Yank knew where the other was near Chattanooga. I've never seen such dense woodland and impenetrable terrain. After the first battle, I returned to my troop having spent several days lost in the countryside trying to avoid being captured by federal soldiers swarming all over Missionary Ridge. We were in one battle after another, first in Knoxville, then in the Carolinas, and finally, home, to fight again in Virginia. When I finally had the chance to write, little did I realize that you had all left Travers Hill, or that there was no one at Royal Bay," he said, his eyes shadowed as he remembered his family home in ashes. "I was half-crazed with worry wondering how you were. After a while, no letter ever reached me, and I hoped it was because my regiment was on the move so often, and engaged in so many battles that any mail was lost. I fought on, until last fall, when I was seriously wounded," he said, pressing a gentle finger against her lips, silencing her fears as he said quickly, "but I am recovered. A little thinner, as you can see, but still all in one piece. I was one of the lucky ones."

Althea's eyes seemed to devour him, and she wondered that he could say he was one of the lucky ones, for he was just a shadow of himself, the black frock coat he wore hanging on his thin frame, his trouser legs baggy, his cheeks sunken—but at least he was alive, Althea breathed a thankful prayer, caressing his bony cheek with soft, healing fingertips.

"I was taken prisoner, but being badly wounded, I was sent to a field hospital. Fortunately for me, I was never put on a troop train and sent north to a prisoner-of-war camp. I would never have survived the journey, much less the winter that followed. Instead, a chance encounter saved me. A former Princeton classmate of mine who was visiting his brother in the hospital recognized me, and, as a high-ranking official in Lincoln's cabinet, saw that I was decently cared for. He and his family were uncommonly kind. I convalesced in Washington, but it was a long convalescence. They wrote letters home for me, but we never heard. When I finally got to Virginia, I found everyone had vanished into thin air. I made the mistake of inquiring of the Reverend Culpepper, thinking he, of all people, might know what had happened to members of his parish. Good Lord, Althea, the man nearly threw me from his newly built church. I thought at first it was because I had interrupted him, he was at the pulpit practicing his Sunday sermon, then I thought it could only be because of that unfortunate incident when Julia scalded the poor fellow years ago, which is carrying a grudge rather too long. But then he said a name which apparently had the power to chill or bring his blood to a boil, I'm not certain, since he became almost apoplectic. The name was Captain Dagger." Nathan said the damning name, glancing down curiously at Althea, who was looking anything but surprised by the news.

"I am afraid, my dear, the man had reason for his fears, although I will not forgive him for his rudeness to you. That was very callous and un-Christian of him," she said, telling him of Adam's midnight kidnapping of the good reverend in order to have him perform a wedding.

"Well, I am thankful, then, that he didn't send a load of

buckshot my way," Nathan said, a twinkle showing in his eyes for the first time, but then it faded as he remembered Adam.

Althea's arms tightened around him, knowing what he was thinking. "You saw the graves," she said.

"My God, Althea. I cannot believe they are all gone. My mother. Adam. And Blythe. Sweet, little Lucy. Whatever happened? She was so young and healthy, so full of life. I found myself seeing again Julia and Blythe in that cart, loaded down with blackberries, that fat pony pulling them up the drive, and Leigh riding like a wild creature around the side of the house. We were all there, that afternoon, sitting on the veranda. Your father sipping his juleps, your mother, glasses perched on the tip of her nose as she sewed, but keeping a watchful eye on everyone. And now, so many graves. I stood there at Travers Hill and felt as if I were in some horrible dream. And God forgive me for what I thought, but for a moment I was thankful, for I did not see your name, or either of those of my children.

"I finally learned from the Draytons what had happened. I will always be grateful to them for taking Adam in at the end and carrying out his wishes to be buried next to Blythe at Travers Hill. I'm not certain if I was relieved or stunned to learn that you'd gone to the territories, to Uncle Nathaniel. The thought of that journey left me shaken. I knew then, however, what the reverend had been damning me about. Yes, he actually cursed me," Nathan said, smiling at Althea's shocked expression. "He accused me of being no better than that infamous raider Captain Dagger. I'd always suspected Neil was this Captain Dagger, but when the reverend mentioned the name I knew for a certainty that Neil had been at Travers Hill and had somehow helped to get you out of Virginia. I had no idea until now that Neil had wed Leigh," he said in amazement. Then he suddenly gave a whooping laugh of great joy, picking Althea up in his arms and swinging her around until she pleaded with him to set her down before he hurt himself.

But Nathan just laughed, holding her all the closer. "Maybe Royal Bay is gone, and we've lost everything, but at least you and the children are alive and we are together again," he said, kissing her deeply.

Althea, finding her breath, stared down into his face with a look of incredulity.

"But we haven't lost everything, Nathan. Haven't you been to the cave?"

"The cave?"

"Yes, the cave where you, Adam, and Neil hid after you'd been particularly bad," she reminded him of his boyhood. "Had you, you might have been rather surprised to find what was hidden away there."

"The cave! Of course. My God, did Adam—no, he didn't? Did he?" he demanded, beginning to feel the stirrings of hope.

"He did, with help from my father and Stephen. Everything of value from Royal Bay and Travers Hill was hidden there. The only problem now is we will never find a home big enough to hold everything," Althea said, thankful that was the biggest of her worries.

"Adam," he said, shaking his head. "Now I understand why Travers Hill, although still standing, looked as if it had been looted. I was so angry. But you are mistaken," he added, his voice husky with emotion, "we do have a home. River Oaks, my mother's home, still stands across the river. I went there after visiting Royal Bay and Travers Hill, thinking you might have gone there. The house hasn't been touched. Hidden away beneath those oaks, and overgrown with creeper, and being on the far side of the river, no one even knew it was there. It'll need a lot of cleaning. I'm afraid bobwhites and nightingales have nested inside, but it has always been a fine home. Maybe not as grand as Royal Bay, no fluted columns, but it does have a lovely veranda and a splendid view of the river."

Althea nodded, knowing her family would find happiness in Euphemia's childhood home. Suddenly, she frowned. "How did you find me here?" she asked. "Have you been up to the big house? Do they know you're alive?" she asked excitedly, thinking of Leigh and Guy and the children.

"No, when I rode in, a small Mexican child came running up to me to help me with my horse. I hired it in Santa Fe," he said somewhat self-consciously, for he was a man who'd never had to hire a horse in his life. "I arrived by stage yesterday evening. And believe me, what I experienced in

the war was nothing compared to that ride across the plains.
I'm not sure I've a tooth left in my head, or a bone that isn't
broken," he said with a deep laugh, remembering the wild,
bone-jarring journey from Westport to Santa Fe in a few hours
less than fourteen days. Packed into the coach with eight other
gentlemen—and he used the term with deep reservations—
they had traveled night and day, existing on hardtack and salt
pork, the experience bringing back less than fond memories of
army life again.

"Did you lose your hat by any chance?" Althea asked,
laughing when he stared at her in puzzlement, and one day she
would explain to him.

"No, still got that," he said, looking around for it on the
floor, where he'd dropped it when entering the room. "I
asked for you, and the youngster's face lit up brighter than a
thousand candles and talking about the *muy bonita, muy rubia
inglesa* as he dragged me across the yard to this rather small
building. I was concerned at first about Nathaniel's hospitality to his nephew's wife, but upon entering I realized it was
a schoolroom. And you were the beautiful golden-haired
teacher the boy loved so," he said, staring at her as if seeing
someone different from the person he had expected to be
reunited with.

Althea closed her eyes for a moment, almost afraid to open
them again and find that he had vanished and she'd been talking to herself. But when she opened them, he still stood before
her and she found herself gazing into his warm gray eyes—eyes
that had always been so wise.

"I thought you were dead. Royal Bay was destroyed.
Travers Hill little better. I didn't know how we would live.
If it hadn't been for Leigh, and Jolie and Stephen, then we
wouldn't have survived at first. Guy was blinded," she told
him, hurrying on when she saw the look of pity cross his
face, "but we had our first miracle a month ago when Guy
recovered his sight. He lost the sight permanently in his left
eye, but he can now see perfectly out of his right eye. Cause
for celebration, Nathan, because it means he can now return
to Travers Hill with his bride. Yes, there is much for you to
learn," she said, smiling up at him, feeling as if they'd never

been separated. "And at least this time you will be here for the wedding. Guy is marrying your cousin 'Lys Helene. You will find Guy a changed man, Nathan. And one changed for the better. I think you may even find him interested in joining your law practice."

Nathan ran his hand through his hair in the old, familiar gesture Althea had remembered so well, leaving his hair standing on end, his expression thoughtful. "Well, well…" he murmured, then his gaze sharpened as he stared down at Althea's face, the glow of good health showing in the dewy softness of her rose-tinted cheeks. "And you, my dear? The Draytons said you were gravely ill. They truly thought you might die when you arrived at Travers Hill," he questioned gently.

"I had typhoid, and I am ashamed to admit that I lost my will to live. I was a coward, Nathan, when I heard you were missing in action. But Leigh pulled me through. She reminded me of Mama, always going after Papa to do this, or that, never letting him alone until she got what she wanted. And Leigh wanted me to live. Then thanks to Adam and Neil, and then Neil's father, we arrived safely here at Royal Rivers. We have been treated so kindly by your aunt and uncle. We have been welcomed as family, all of us," Althea told him, then added softly, "But I knew it was time to return home to Virginia, Nathan. I wanted Noelle and Steward to grow up near Royal Bay. I never wanted them to forget who they are, what their heritage was. But I also knew that I would have to work if we were to live there. So, I decided to teach school when we returned to Virginia," Althea told him with a defensive note in her voice, as if expecting a look of disapproval.

"I always knew you were beautiful, but I had no idea until now exactly how strong and determined a woman you were," he said, holding her tightly against him, his cheek resting against her soft golden hair.

"Let go my mama!" a petulant voice demanded from behind them.

Nathan turned around to find himself confronted by a chubby little boy with big brown eyes and dark curls, his short, white-stockinged legs planted aggressively apart as he faced what he sensed was someone to be reckoned with.

But the young girl standing just behind him suddenly gave a shrill cry that caused the little boy to squeal in fear, not having expected an attack from behind, especially when he was knocked down when his sister raced past him, flinging herself into the stranger's outstretched arms.

Steward Russell Braedon stared in disbelief as his sister was hugged tight. He eyed the tall man suspiciously, sensing now more of a challenge to his status as the only man in his mother's life than he did any physical danger from the man he'd never seen before—at least, did not remember ever having seen.

"Steward," Althea said, smiling understandingly as she walked over to where he still sat on the floor, tears welling in his fear-rounded eyes. Bending down beside her son, she took her lightly scented handkerchief and dried his eyes, wiping the tearstains from his pinkened cheeks, then pressing a kiss against his forehead. "Come and meet your father, dear," she said gently, holding out her hand to him, which he took shyly, his eyes wide with wonder as he stared at the tall man waiting patiently for him.

❧

There was a festive mood in the great hall at Royal Rivers that night. Lys Helene and Guy sat with their heads together, excitedly going over their dreams for Travers Hill, for their wedding was to follow on the morrow. Michael Stanfield had even drawn up a set of plans for the new wing they hoped to build one day—although that was some way off. But it did not hurt to dream. Stanfield was standing now in front of one of Solange's paintings, admiring it as he spoke with her, their conversation liberally sprinkled with foreign-sounding names of places both had visited during their travels, but even more incomprehensible was their talk of art, with both being very set in their opinions as they compared the merits of neoclassical and romantic painting against the new, unsentimental realism. Stanfield would be staying on at Royal Rivers for a while. He said he had nowhere else to go, and was willing to do a hard day's work. His quest for vengeance, or perhaps justice, was over. Quite a shock had reverberated across the territory when the bodies of Alfonso Jacobs and Courtney Boyce had been found at Silver Springs, apparently having killed one another during a violent argument. No one had been able to reach Diosa and Luis Angel to inform them of the tragic death of their uncle.

"This package arrived on the stagecoach with Nathan. He brought it with him from Santa Fe yesterday. I mistakenly opened it. It was addressed to Royal Rivers, and the Christian name, except for the letter *N*, was smudged. All that was legible was the Braedon," Nathaniel apologized as he handed a thick leather-bound volume to his son, who'd been half listening to the talk around him.

Neil raised a curious brow, wondering why someone should be sending him a book.

"It's inscribed," Nathaniel told him gruffly, a strange look in his eyes. "You'll forgive me, but I didn't realize it was intended for you until I saw the inscription, and since I'd already committed the error of opening your package, I didn't think you'd mind if I glanced inside the cover. The title was intriguing, and I found myself continuing to read until I'd finished the book. It was quite fascinating, and I imagine a very true account."

Turning the book over, an astounded expression crossed Neil's face as he opened the cover and turned to the title page.

THE DARING ESCAPADES OF
CAPTAIN DAGGER'S BLOODRIDERS
Or
A Partisan's True Account of Guerrilla Warfare
behind Confederate Lines
From a Diarist's Daily Record of Events as They Happened;
with Comments and Notes Thereof
By John Yates Chatham
Formerly of the Second Massachusetts;
Topographical Engineer and Cartographer on
General Meade's Staff
Army of the Potomac;
Also Former Member of the Federal Raiders
Known as the Bloodriders

ILLUSTRATED
With Ten Beautiful Color Plates and
Twenty-five Detailed Sketches
By the Author

The splendor falls on castle walls
And snowy summits old in story:
The long light shakes across the lakes,
And the wild cataract leaps in glory.
Blow, bugle, blow; set the wild echoes flying,
Blow, bugle; answer, echoes, dying, dying, dying.

Alfred, Lord Tennyson

BOSTON
JACOB ADAMSON
Printer, Bookbinder, and Stationer
1865

Neil shook his head in disbelief. Lieutenant Chatham. The young, bespectacled lieutenant who'd seemed to have more of a chance than anyone he'd ever met of *not* surviving the war. The soft-spoken, serious-minded lieutenant had actually written the book of his experiences and personal impressions, his memoirs, that he'd claimed he'd have published one day.

Neil smiled slightly as he noticed the portrait on the facing page. A fresh-faced young man with gold-rimmed spectacles, the round lenses giving him an owlish look, stared back at him. He seemed younger than ever without his beard, although he sported a fine-looking mustache and side-whiskers. His hair was neatly trimmed and combed, quite proper for Boston, as was the black broadcloth of his close-fitting frock coat and the starched perfection of his high-standing collar, but the casually knotted silk scarf and boldly patterned plaid waistcoat belied the fact that John Chatham had returned to his former life unchanged. He would never be quite as proper a Bostonian as he once might have been had he not ridden with the Bloodriders. The lieutenant had recovered from his wounds, his slow convalescence keeping him assigned to Headquarters in Washington, but his days as a Bloodrider had ended at Travers Hill. Which perhaps had been a blessing in disguise for all concerned, Neil speculated, recalling the near disasters caused by the lieutenant's sincere, but at times awkward, attempts to be of assistance.

Neil turned the page and read the following inscription:

These Memoirs
Of a Proud Bloodrider
Are Dedicated with Honor
To *NDB*,
Captain Dagger,
Who Cared More for the Lives of the
Men Who Served with Him
Than for His Own Life and Never Left a Man to Die
Alone and Forgotten in the Field

Neil stared at the page for a long moment, then turned to the Table of Contents, a grin spreading across his somber face as he quickly scanned several of the chapters listed. *The Hog Slop Polka. Schneickerberger's Breeches. Thunder Dancer; A Horse with Wings. Where the Last Rose Lingers. Long Winter Nights. Fire-breathers & Steely Beasts at the Gates of Hell. Scattered Butternuts; Or Skittle Alley. Angel of the Storm. "Open Sesame." Painted Faces and Ghostly Smiles. Double Trouble; Or Smoke against Gray Skies.*

Neil's smile faded as he read the last few chapter headings, for he remembered that winter when he returned to Travers Hill, and he and Lieutenant Chatham had stood outside the lighted window. And he remembered only too vividly how he and his men had hidden in the cave by the river, where three young cousins, boyhood friends, had hidden after mock battles, suffering nothing more serious than skinned knees and growling stomachs because they'd missed luncheon. And Adam. He would never forget the cousin and friend who had paid the highest price of all. Neil's gaze lingered on Jolie and Stephen, sitting on the woven pillows of the *banco*, Jolie holding Adam's and Blythe's baby daughter on her lap.

Neil stared over at Nathan and his family as they sat together on the sofa. His giggling son was sitting on his lap, while his daughter leaned over her mother's shoulder, laughing as she tickled her brother with a feather. Althea, her golden hair slightly tousled from the horseplay, was smiling indulgently, her brown eyes warm with contentment, and Neil knew that not everything had been lost.

Nathaniel stared at his son. For a moment they stood eye to eye, and Nathaniel cleared his throat, wanting to say something, but he couldn't find the words. There would be other days, and he rested his hand momentarily on his son's shoulder before stepping away to join Gil and Leigh as they stood by the pianoforte, where Camilla sat playing a lovely tune.

Neil watched his father for a long moment, seeing him look down into Leigh's face, then nod, a slight smile flickering briefly across his hard face at something she told him. It wasn't really surprising, Neil thought, that his father would like Leigh, but sometimes their glances met as if they had an understanding between them, as if they shared some knowledge the rest of them were not privy to. A puzzled expression entered Neil's pale eyes as he felt again his father's hand on his shoulder. Was he only imagining it, or was there something different about his father? Neil shook his head, still disbelieving of the gentle expression he'd seen in his father's eyes. Walking over to the window, Neil stared out at the mountains. As he stood there alone, he heard a step behind him and held out his hand without looking as Leigh came to stand beside him. His hand closed over hers as she reached out to him, her eyes meeting his in a loving, sharing glance.

His arm came to rest around her waist, holding her against him and she raised her face for his kiss. Their lips touched.

"Day after tomorrow we'll ride to Riovado," Neil murmured softly as Leigh rested her head against his shoulder, her cheek pressed against his heart as she leaned against him, the warmth of her body, shared with his, as necessary to his life as his own breath.

❧

The blackness of a star-streaked sky faded as dawn broke over the purple mountains. The sun rose resplendent, bathing the forested slopes in a golden light and gilding the outspread wings of a high-flying bird as it soared on the winds into the heavens.

Far below, two riders, a man and a woman, rode beside a stream, the silvered waters glinting through green woodlands. Across a high grassy plateau their horses galloped, toward a lone cabin nestled in a peaceful wood of tall pines. Neil Braedon, his beloved Leigh riding beside him, had come home to Riovado.

Read on for an excerpt
from another Laurie McBain classic:

Wild Bells to the Wild Sky

She shall be lov'd and fear'd. Her own shall bless her;
Her foes shake like a field of beaten corn,
And hang their heads with sorrow. Good grows with her;
In her days every man shall eat in safety
Under his own vine what he plants; and sing
The merry songs of peace to all his neighbours.

Shakespeare

"THE QUEEN IS DEAD. GOD SAVE THE QUEEN, ELIZABETH of England!" And with those fateful words, proclaimed on a November morning in 1558, Elizabeth Tudor, daughter of Henry VIII and Anne Boleyn, succeeded to the throne of England. The death of Elizabeth's half sister, the childless Mary Tudor, a devout Catholic and daughter of King Harry by his divorced Spanish wife, Catherine of Aragon, brought the Protestant princess, who had been declared a bastard and banished from the court shortly after her birth, the crown of a country that had yet to become the great seafaring nation that was to build a world empire.

The realm that the young queen inherited was facing bankruptcy, rising inflation, civil and religious unrest, and a heightening of hostility from its powerful Catholic neighbors, France and Spain, who saw England as an uncivilized island of heretics. Ever since Henry VIII had renounced the supremacy of the pope and severed all bonds with the Church of Rome, England had become the revolutionary symbol of the great Reformation sweeping through Europe and, in the eyes of the papacy and its zealous defenders, threatening the very heart of Christendom.

King Philip II of Spain, fanatic champion of the Catholic Counter-Reformation, ruled an empire that not only dominated the Continent but had conquered the New World. From her colonies in the Americas and Indies, Spain filled her royal coffers with gold and silver, precious stones, and the riches reaped from unrestricted trade with the Far East. By papal decree nearly a century earlier, Pope Alexander VI had established a demarcation line across the seas and lands of the newly explored western world, which forbade crossing by other nations, and allowed Spain and Portugal a monopoly on the wealth of the New World. And enforced by the unchallenged superiority of their well-manned and heavily armed fleets, the Spanish seemed destined for world dominion.

Across the English Channel, in France, Mary Stuart, daughter of Mary of Guise, a French princess, and of James V of Scotland, and the great-granddaughter of Henry VII—married the Dauphin of France. The marriage presented a grave threat to England and her queen. It united two ancient, Catholic enemies of an ever-growing Protestant England. And Mary Stuart, Queen of Scotland, and the future queen of France, also claimed the English crown. Under Catholic canon, which had never recognized Henry VIII's divorce from Catherine of Aragon, Elizabeth Tudor had been born out of wedlock and had no right to wear the crown.

Raised and educated in the French court, the devoutly Catholic Mary Stuart would find that her heretical English cousin would be a difficult rival to overthrow, and her native Scotland would be an even more difficult land to rule. The Reformation, which until then had been confined to England and the Continent, now took root in Scottish soil. The ancient faith found itself under attack by parish ministers, inspired by the soul-stirring speeches of the Protestant reformer John Knox, repudiating papal edict. And in the highlands and glens of Scotland, rebellious lairds and clan chieftains, aspiring for wealth and power through the dissolution of the monasteries and acquisition of church holdings, actively plotted the overthrow of their Catholic, foreign-bred queen.

In 1560, Mary Stuart had to meet that challenge, for in December she became a widow and, childless, lost her right to the French throne. In the summer of 1561 she returned to Scotland to rule an impoverished country of lawless subjects. Falling prey to the divisive politics of the time, as well as having ruled with her heart rather than her head, Mary Queen of Scots was dethroned by Protestant nobles only seven years after returning to her homeland. Her reign, which had been beset by murder and intrigue, was over, and fleeing for her life she sought exile in England.

Elizabeth was faced with a difficult decision. Despite her personal feelings for Mary Stuart, she was a staunch supporter of a hereditary sovereign's right to rule, and she would never willingly become a party to the shedding of royal blood. However, because England needed an ally on her unprotected northern border, she had secretly supported and aided the rebellion in Scotland. Mary Stuart had abdicated in favor of her infant son, James VI, who was protected by a Protestant regent. England need no longer fear a French-supported invasion from her northern neighbor. Elizabeth wished to preserve that alliance. She could not allow Mary Stuart the freedom to join forces with England's Catholic enemies on the Continent.

Queen Elizabeth would not sentence her cousin to death nor give her her freedom. And because Elizabeth Tudor never wed and had no heirs to inherit the crown, the Catholic Mary Stuart was heir-presumptive to the English throne. As long as she lived there would be those who would conspire to place that crown on her head prematurely and see the ancient faith restored to the heretics of that rebellious northern isle ruled by the Protestant usurper. The threat of assassination was an ever-present danger to Elizabeth and to the destiny of her kingdom.

During the following years of her reign, Elizabeth I sought to maintain peace with her neighbors while she restored order and stability to her realm and began to build a fighting force, especially a naval fleet, far superior to the might of her powerful foes. Elizabeth Tudor was a master in the fine art of diplomacy. Until she felt England could successfully defend her shores, she would not involve her people in a war. War was to be avoided at all costs. Elizabeth knew the end result would be far more devastating to her nation than a mere wrecking of the country's economy and a draining of the royal treasury. And tax her people to keep her armies fighting in a war on the Continent she would not do, for that would only promote further unrest and rebellion in the land, abetting the Catholic cause.

She would only engage in warfare to protect her people and defend her land from invasion. It was with reluctance that she allowed Englishmen to fight on the Continent, and it was with grave reservations that she even sent money and arms to her Protestant allies to aid in their struggle against the armies of Spain and France. Although she wished to keep the Netherlands in Protestant hands, she felt it would be only too easy for the papal-inspired armies of Philip II to cross the Channel and shed blood on English soil.

Elizabeth I remained stalwartly determined to keep her crown and her loyal Protestant subjects safe from the armies of Spain and the Roman Church's Holy Inquisition. She would not provoke Philip II's all-consuming ambition to make England a part of his empire or return her people to the orthodox faith. Despite increasingly strained relations, Elizabeth patiently continued to pursue a nonaggressive course and maintain an outwardly friendly diplomacy with Spain. But, privately, the queen and her council worried, knowing that it would be but a matter of time before the religious fanaticism of Philip II and his belief in a holy crusade of conquest in the New World would involve England in direct conflict with the Spanish crown.

Spain's aspirations for a world empire depended on her unchallenged supremacy in the New World. The religious and civil wars that had dominated western Europe throughout the century were bankrupting Spain, whose royal treasury financed the armies of mercenaries hired to suppress rebellion and restore the true faith.

Mountains of silver and temples of gold, masks studded and sparkling with emeralds and pearls were no longer legend when the *conquistadores* returned to Spain. Their ships' holds were filled with incredible riches plundered from a savage New World that existed beyond the western seas. This dazzling wealth raised Spain to its pinnacle of power. King Philip II came to depend on the great treasure fleets sailing home from the Spanish Main, a territory that stretched from Trinidad and the mouth of the Orinoco River at its southernmost point, to Cuba and the Straits of Florida at its northernmost, and encompassing Central America and Mexico to the west and the Bahamas to the east.

Spain's claim to all of the lands and seas of the New World would not go unchallenged for long. For years, French, Dutch, and English pirates, sailing along the coast of Europe, had been harassing the heavily laden Spanish galleons that had become lost from the well-protected fleet sailing home to Seville, but few sea rovers had dared to venture into the Spanish Main.

Now a few bold men, intent on winning a share of the plunder and wealth of the New World, sailed into these Spanish waters. Adventurers and privateers, backed by merchants hungry for access to the trade routes and natural resources so abundant in the New World, challenged the almightiness of Spain and Philip II's ordained right of sovereignty over the lands and seas of this once fabled terrestrial paradise.

Though Elizabeth was constrained by the precariousness of her position and vulnerability of her people to appear content with Spain's monopoly of the New World and its bounty, some of her more impatient and reckless seafarers now openly defied Spain's claim to a world empire. Seldom did these adventurers receive public support from their queen, in whose name they made their courageous voyages for gold and silver, honor and glory. But each captain and crew knew that they sailed with the silent prayers and good wishes, and some even with the private monetary backing, of Elizabeth Tudor. The white flag bearing the red cross of St. George flew proudly on the mainmasts of their trim ships. These enterprising, defiant Englishmen steered a course into the heart of the Spanish Main.

One

We must take the current when it serves,
Or lose our ventures.

Shakespeare

January 1571—West Indies
Fifteen leagues northeast of the Windward Passage

WHEN THE *ARION* HAD SET SAIL FROM PLYMOUTH SOUND
the church bells had pealed. It was the heart of winter and she
was not more than thirty tons, with fewer than forty hands man-
ning her. She made her way out into the Channel and turned
her prow into the fierce, storm-driven seas of the Atlantic.

Her captain was an English gentleman by the name
of Geoffrey Christian and one of Elizabeth Tudor's most
illustrious privateers. Also on board the *Arion* was Geoffrey
Christian's wife, the former Doña Magdalena Aurelia Rosalba
de Cabrion y Montevares. The captain of the *Arion* had met
Doña Magdalena eight years earlier when boarding and capturing the Spanish galleon on which she and her family had been
passengers for the journey to Madrid from Hispaniola, where
the Montevares family had a sugar plantation.

The Montevareses had been journeying to Spain to celebrate the birth of their first grandson. Their eldest daughter,
Catalina, had given birth to three beautiful daughters, but
until young Francisco there had been no male heir. Don
Rodrigo Montevares and his wife, Doña Amparo, knew
that the lack of a son to inherit his father's name and titles
was a grave disappointment to their son-in-law, Don Pedro
Enrique de Villasandro. Don Pedro was a scion of an ancient,
aristocratic family of Andalusia, and he exerted an influence
at court that few rivaled and many envied. For him to have
chosen a colonial for his wife, even one whose blood was
pure Castilian, had been the greatest honor and had filled Don
Rodrigo with pride and great expectations. Don Pedro was a

gentleman and a soldier and held in the highest esteem by all who knew or served him. There had even been talk that he was to be the next governor of Hispaniola. It would be the culmination of all of Don Rodrigo's hopes and dreams if his daughter Catalina were wife of the future governor, and her family were to take up residence in Santo Domingo. And he would no longer have to concern himself with trying to save the family's once thriving sugar plantation which now, due to his mismanagement, was failing.

It was aboard Don Pedro's ship, *Maria Concepcíon*, that the Montevares family was sailing to Spain. Setting sail from Santo Domingo, the *Maria Concepcíon* had joined the treasure fleet sailing from Havana and had made her way through the treacherous waters of the Straits of Florida without incident. The Gulf Stream carried them northward to Bermuda, where they caught the westerlies and the *Maria Concepcíon*'s bow swung eastward toward Spain. It was near dawn of the third day after they'd survived a sudden squall, which had blown them off course and separated them from the protection of the rest of the fleet, that the red cross of St. George was seen flying atop the mainmast of a ship bearing down on them.

Don Pedro had been momentarily stunned by the daring of the English captain. What madness was this? The *Maria Concepcíon* was a five-hundred-ton galleon with sixty bronze cannon and over two hundred seamen and soldiers defending her. Calling his men to arms, Don Pedro, from his exalted position of command on the deck of the towering sterncastle, fully expected to disable the smaller ship within minutes of firing a deafening volley of broadsides. Grappling irons would have brought the English ship close enough to have been boarded and the English captain to his knees before the unconquerable might of Spain. It was, therefore, with a look of incredulity that Don Pedro watched the royal arms of Spain fluttering at the mainmast-head of the *Maria Concepcíon* blown into the sea along with the mizzenmast and rigging.

The Englishman's ship seemed to sail out of danger almost magically, then, through some sorcerer's trick, or so Don Pedro would later swear, maneuvered to windward of the slower-moving Spanish galleon. With her long-range cannon, broadside after punishing broadside wreaked death and destruction on the crowded decks of the *Maria Concepción*. Listing dangerously, her quarterdeck in shambles, her masts splintered, the *Maria Concepción* surrendered when the English ship ranged alongside, her crew armed with sword and musket and standing ready to board.

Don Pedro Enrique de Villasandro's humiliation had only just begun. Catching sight of the frightened passengers, Geoffrey Christian insisted they come aboard the *Arion*. Unrepentantly he warned them that the *Maria Concepción* might very well sink before the rest of the Spanish fleet could rescue her. He felt responsible for their safety, since it had been the *Arion*'s cannon fire that had left the Spanish ship foundering. With a mocking smile that had Don Pedro reaching for his sword only to be bitterly reminded of an empty scabbard, the English captain informed the Montevareses that they need have no further cause for fear once aboard his ship, which was still seaworthy, for he would personally guarantee a safe, uninterrupted voyage to England. Once there, he assured them that they would be able to continue their journey to Spain.

The *Maria Concepción* was in far less danger of sinking, however, after her hold was emptied of its treasure and loaded aboard the victor's ship. As the *Arion* gathered way, the furious Don Pedro swore vengeance against the swaggering English captain who had caused him such mortification.

Geoffrey Christian's thoughts had not lingered long with the vanquished captain of the *Maria Concepción*. The Spanish captain might have lost his ship in the battle, but the Englishman had lost his heart. Doña Magdalena was an ivory-skinned, bronze-eyed beauty with hair of darkest Venetian red. Although it was the fairness of her face and figure which first caught Geoffrey's roving eye, it was the beautiful Spanish girl's undaunted spirit that finally captivated him. She had not experienced a fit of the vapors and been confined to her bed, as had Doña Amparo, nor had she remained in her cabin weeping or sulking. With exceptional grace, Doña Magdalena accepted the challenge of being aboard an English privateer's ship. Soon, even the most prejudiced crew member was enamored of the vivacious, laughter-loving young *señorita* who, despite the elegance of her appearance and her unfamiliarity with the English language, could mimic their captain to perfection as he roared his orders, much to the amusement of the crew.

The captain had shown unusual patience, even smiling at the jesting and good-natured pranks, for the game was his and, soon, so would be the lady. Pursuing the dark-eyed Castilian with all of the reckless determination that had so successfully marked his career as a privateer, Geoffrey captured the beautiful Magdalena's heart by the time the *Arion* reached the shores of England.

With a wrathful indignation that left him purple in the face, Don Rodrigo refused Geoffrey's request for Magdalena's hand in marriage. Thinking the unfortunate affair ended, he booked passage for himself, his wife, and his shameless daughter aboard a Spanish ship sailing for Spain. But Don Rodrigo's daughter had a mind of her own, and the heady memory of Geoffrey's kisses helped Magdalena to make the most important decision of her young life. Despite the vehement objections of her father and tearful protestations of her mother, Doña Magdalena eloped with her handsome, fair-haired inamorato. In a quiet ceremony performed by a minister and witnessed by several of Geoffrey's friends—without the blessing of her church and against the wishes of her family—Magdalena made her sacred vows to the man she loved.

The years passed in contentment for Magdalena. Never once had she regretted her decision to marry a man of a different faith and nationality from her own, even though it had resulted in a painful, inexorable rift with her family.

Although Geoffrey was often away for long periods of time during his voyages, Magdalena's life at Highcross Court was full of happiness. The house of gray-brown Kentish stone had been in the Christian family for over two centuries and was surrounded by meadowland grazed by sheep and cattle, deep woods thick with pheasant and partridge, clearwater streams full of trout, orchards of sweet cherry and purple plum flowering in spring, and golden wheat and hops ripening in late summer. It was a haven found appropriately close to the banks of the River Eden, which meandered through the fertile countryside southeast of London.

The fulfillment of Magdalena's happiness had come with the birth of her first child. As Geoffrey came to know his first-born, he proudly declared to all that the babe had been born laughing. Never had there been such a happy, healthy little girl who brought such great joy to all who knew and loved her. Lily Francisca had inherited her mother's dark Venetian red hair and cheerful disposition and her father's pale green eyes and love of adventure. She could never be found where she was supposed to be. An open window having beckoned her outside to explore, an apple on a branch having been just out of reach of her small hand until she climbed higher, a duck having paddled to the far side of the pond, his quacking a challenge to follow—all of these temptations and many more had resulted in misadventures that left her nursemaid, Maire Lester, feeling far older than her years.

The quince apples had been harvested and made into jams and preserves when Doña Magdalena, marking her eighth Michaelmas at Highcross Court, received a message from her father that her mother was dying. It was the first time her father had broken his silence since their bitter parting.

Don Rodrigo could no longer remain deaf to his wife's anguished pleadings to see her youngest daughter once again. Not even certain that Magdalena would respond to his entreaty, for he had greatly abused her character when she had defied him and he had banished her forever from his sight over seven years earlier, he sent her word of her mother's failing health. He asked, in as humble a manner as his pride would allow, if she would agree to come home.

Fortunately for Magdalena, Geoffrey was at Highcross Court, having returned in early summer from a voyage to Egypt and Africa, and soon the *Arion* was being refitted and provisioned for a voyage to the Indies. It had been over two months since the *Arion* had set sail from England. Running swiftly before the winds, their first landfall on the far side of the Atlantic had been the green hills of San Salvador Island rising up before them and looking little different than they had when sighted by Columbus seventy-nine years earlier. They had slowly threaded their way through the Bahamas, finding a port of refuge on the lee side of a small island, just northeast

of the Windward Passage, when storm clouds had darkened
the noonday sky. By evening the squall had blown itself out
without causing damage to the *Arion*, riding safe at anchor. By
dawn the sea would be calm and the skies clear, and the *Arion*
would continue her journey. Above the rain-washed deck, the
blackness of the night sky was already brilliant with stars.

"How many stars are there in the sky, Father?"

"'Sdeath, but you're up early, child!" Geoffrey exclaimed,
thinking he alone walked the quarterdeck of his ship just
before first light.

"At least a hundred, Father?"

"A hund—" Geoffrey repeated absentmindedly as he
measured the angle between the horizon and the North Star
with a cross-staff. "By my faith, child, but 'twould take us till
the crack of doom just to count all of these above our heads
alone, and then we would still have all of those we can't even
see," he said with a deep chuckle of appreciation, for it was an
inquiring mind that pondered such thoughts. And in a child
of seven, and a female at that, it was truly amazing, he mused
with fatherly pride.

Lily Christian continued to stare up into the early morning
sky. Above her head, beyond the tall, swaying and creaking
masts that stretched into the heavens, the sky was black with
myriad shimmering lights. The east, whence they had come at
noon of the day before and anchored in the cove to escape the
storm, was faintly illumined by a sun that still hid just beyond
the horizon. The sea and sky to the west were dark and silent
and seemed to converge mysteriously before the bow of the
Arion. Her captain now charted a course toward the channel that offered safe passage out of the dangerous waters of
the sunken coral reefs and hidden sand bars surrounding the
Bahama Islands.

"How can there be stars in the sky that we can't see? And
how can we count them if we can't even see them? And
what happens to the stars when the sun rises? Why do they
disappear? Where do they go? Do they fall into the sea?"
Lily demanded, her small brow knit with puzzlement as she

stared up at her father, certain he would be able to answer her questions.

Geoffrey's teeth gleamed whitely in his sun-darkened face as he grinned. "Ho! What devilment have ye got planned, my sweet Lily, with all of these questions to plague a man while he's about his measuring? Would ye have us run aground, then, on some heathen shore?" he exploded with a laugh that rumbled across the deck like thunder.

Lily's squeal of pleased fright filled the air as her father swung her up and tossed her high above his head. He caught her tumbling figure easily against his chest as she fell back into the safety of his arms.

"Well, fondling? Want to touch the stars?" he asked her with a gleam in his eye. "They're fading fast," he warned her as she giggled and hid her face against his shoulder.

"Yes, Father! Please! Let me touch them, please!" Lily said quickly, raising her face to gaze longingly at the few sparkling jewels that beckoned still from a sky streaked with the first glowing light of dawn.

"Wrap your arms around my neck and hold on tight, Lily Francisca. We're going to climb high into the heavens," Geoffrey declared loudly, defiantly, before he placed a reassuring kiss against his daughter's flushed cheek. "Just for luck, sweeting," he added softly this time.

"You do not need luck, Father," Lily corrected him. "You have always said that a man makes his own. And 'tis only a fool or a weakling who waits for good fortune to come to him or sits idly by while his fate is sealed," Lily solemnly repeated her father's philosophy of life.

"A mocking child, as I live!" Geoffrey said with a hearty laugh that threatened to shake the very timbers of his ship. "Do you never forget anything? I see I shall have to take great care in future, lest I look the pickle-herring should you repeat my most ribald comment as if quoting scripture. Now, up we go!" he said, his laugh fading as he set his mind to the task.

Sir Basil Whitelaw, a gentleman of unusual equanimity, which was why he was one of his queen's most trusted advisers, had come up on deck and was carefully straightening the elegant lace edging the high ruff about his neck when he glanced upward past the tangle of rigging overhead. He was thinking that it most likely would be another uncommonly warm day as he took note of the incredible color of the sky. Never had he imagined such colors, even in his wildest dreams. To an Englishman, especially one whose memory of rain-heavy gray clouds hanging low over the barren hills of a winter landscape were to be cherished, these colors were not natural; a plum-colored sky slashed with the brightest scarlet, molten copper, and aquamarine, which when it faded under the full light of day would still be the brightest blue of his recollection, seemed incredibly barbarous. Even the waters of this sea they sailed were unusually clear and bright, and warm, compared with the somber, unfriendly seas surrounding England. *Ah, England*, he sighed, and not for the first time since leaving those mist-enshrouded shores.

It was during the most nostalgic part of Sir Basil's melancholy reflections of home that a high-pitched giggle intruded along with a small velvet shoe that struck Sir Basil upon the shoulder, causing him more amazement than pain.

"What the—" he cried out, momentarily thinking the ship under attack by cannon fire from a Spanish galleon or a French corsair. "The devil!" he exclaimed in growing concern, for he suddenly realized that there had been no accompanying roar and flash of gunpowder; there had, however, been a giggle, and that he now remembered only too clearly.

Picking up the offending object from the deck, Sir Basil examined it, then glanced up into the rigging again, this time searching out with a keen eye what he disbelievingly sought.

"Oh, ho! We've been spied!" Geoffrey called out, his devil-may-care laugh having become only too familiar to Sir Basil during this voyage.

Although suspecting the worst, Sir Basil could scarcely believe his eyes. Far above him, in what seemed to be an endless crisscross of ropes, was the captain of the *Arion*, his nightdress-clad daughter clinging like a monkey to his shoulder as Geoffrey sat astride a yardarm.

Sir Basil felt sick, which wasn't unusual since he was not a good sailor, but this time it wasn't because of the motion of the ship. Should Geoffrey have lost his balance, Sir Basil did not even want to think of the tragic consequences of such a mishap. He prayed now that Lily Christian's mother still slept peacefully below.

"Ah, Sir Basil, 'tis a gloomy face you show to the world this fine day," Geoffrey called to the finely dressed gentleman standing in silent disapproval on the deck below. "Cheer up, then! All is not lost, for soon you will once again feel solid ground beneath your feet. Hispaniola lies not too many leagues distant."

Had England been the *Arion*'s next landfall, Sir Basil would have rejoiced of that sighting but the Spanish island of Hispaniola promised little pleasure for him. He feared that he was not the adventuring kind. Privately, he had to admit that he found it difficult to understand the desire to travel to faraway places, much less to venture into uncharted seas. In future, despite even the direst threats from his queen, he would leave the adventuring to the likes of Geoffrey Christian and to his own dear brother, Valentine, who actually seemed to enjoy the dangers of sea-roving.

"Ah! The sun comes, Sir Basil, and, unless I miss my guess, Mr. Saunders has prepared a most splendid feast for his captain and the stouthearted crew of this good ship," Geoffrey Christian declared with a wide grin. Then, spying a figure moving quickly along the port rail below, he called out in his sternest voice, "And God pity the fool who has yet to finish his ale and biscuit and get on deck."

"Aye, Cap'n, sir," Master Randall, the bos'n, answered without hesitation as he hurried below, determined to light a fire beneath the sluggards before his captain found need to repeat his command.

"Do I get stewed apples and buttered eggs, Father?" Lily asked hopefully.

"At the very least, my child. And, perhaps, poached chicken and sweet potato pie. We might even be able to find some sherry for Sir Basil," Geoffrey added, thinking Basil was looking a bit green.

Sir Basil inclined his head in acknowledgment of Geoffrey's kind offer. He even managed a slight smile, for he was not completely humorless, and despite their disparate views on life, he had been a good friend of the *Arion*'s captain for many years. He had even stood witness to the marriage of Geoffrey Christian and Doña Magdalena. And what a surprise that had been to the captain's friends and family, although, now Basil thought about it, it shouldn't have surprised any of Geoffrey's acquaintances, for he was a man who did as he damn well pleased.

Actually, it had been the taking of a bride at all that had been the surprising part of the affair, for they had all come to accept the fact that Geoffrey would remain a bachelor until his dying day. Hartwell Barclay, Geoffrey's cousin, and next in line to inherit Highcross Court, had not taken the news of his cousin's marriage at all well. It had been rumored at the time that he had taken to his bed for a week and had yet to forgive his cousin for his treachery in marrying—and a Spanish Papist at that.

Despite such a stigma, Magdalena had managed to become a favorite at court and had a large circle of friends and admirers. The fact that Geoffrey had always been a favorite of his queen, and had even managed to remain so after his marriage, had helped in Magdalena's complete acceptance at court. She had often accompanied Basil and his wife, Elspeth, to London, staying with them in their house in Canon Row, when Geoffrey was at sea. Magdalena and her daughter had even stayed with them at Whiteswood for months at a time until his safe return.

At the thought of London and the court at Westminster and his queen, Basil sighed again. Shaking his head in disbelief, he wondered with yet another sigh how it was he had ended up a passenger on board the *Arion* when she had set sail from Plymouth. After presenting his gifts to Her Majesty and enjoying the merrymaking and festivities so abundant in town, he had had every intention of spending Christmas through Twelfth Day in his own home, his feet stretched out before a roaring fire in the hearth of the great hall at Whiteswood, his wife and young son at his side.

However, it had been his incredible misfortune to have been in attendance to his queen the day that Geoffrey Christian had sought an audience with her. Basil had always experienced a certain feeling of nervous trepidation when conversing with

Her Grace, for Elizabeth was of a volatile nature, and one never knew exactly what mood she might be in.

Her regal appearance humbled the most arrogant courtier and silenced the most glib-tongued. With red-gold hair elegantly coiffed in curls and draped with pearls and diamonds, her dark eyes missing nothing, she swept into a room in a swirl of silk embroidered with gold and precious stones, her imperious commands ringing forth for all to hear and obey. She was quick-witted and short-tempered and spared none who displeased her, but with a smile of genuine warmth and affection she could just as quickly win the undying devotion of a recently admonished subject.

Geoffrey's request for permission to travel to the Indies, along with his wife and daughter, had been given careful consideration by Her Grace and by Sir William Cecil, secretary of state and Her Grace's most trusted counselor. Francis Walsingham, one of Cecil's proficient young protégés, had been summoned to join the discussion. It was a disquieting circumstance for Basil. Walsingham, now ambassador to France, had set up an intricate spy system on the Continent. He was personally involved in the apprehension and subsequent questioning of plotters against the Crown. Basil hadn't even known Walsingham was in London, which, he supposed, gave indisputable evidence of the man's capabilities at espionage.

Up until the moment it had actually happened, Basil continued to hope that Walsingham had been called in solely to advise Her Grace on Geoffrey's voyage to the Indies.

Walsingham was an avid supporter of such daring enterprises, having contributed heavily to many of the voyages of exploration into the Spanish Main—Francis Drake, Gilbert, and Frobisher, as well as Geoffrey Christian, having benefited from Walsingham's sponsorship. Her Grace had previously invested in several of John Hawkins's slave-trading voyages to the Spanish West Indies from Sierra Leone and had enjoyed a 60 percent share of the profits.

Basil wished to heaven that he'd had the foresight to excuse himself before he heard Walsingham's extraordinary proposal of sending someone along on Geoffrey's next voyage. He must be one in whom Her Grace and Sir William had the greatest confidence, and one whom they could trust implicitly. He must be completely objective in his impressions and observations of the Spanish Main, and, of course, whatever information he might accidentally overhear concerning the treasure fleet, future expeditions in the lands north of the Indies, the location of gold and silver mines, and anything else which might be of interest to the Crown would be most appreciated.

"I believe that your wife's brother-in-law, Don Pedro Enrique de Villasandro, is quite often seen leaving the Alcazar in Madrid," Walsingham murmured thoughtfully, his eyes meeting Geoffrey's for a meaningful moment, and if Geoffrey was surprised by Walsingham's knowledge of his wife's family, then he didn't show it. "It might be worthwhile to learn what your Spanish brother-in-law is about. He may have spoken boastfully, perhaps indiscreetly, to your wife's father. We must never lose an opportunity to learn. The information may prove useful one day," Walsingham said. "Sir Basil, you are fluent in many languages, including Spanish, I believe. And you and the captain are also longtime friends. Yes, that will serve quite nicely. And Doña Magdalena is a favorite of—"

"—of mine, Master Spy, and I know where your mind leads you and I want to hear none of it. Enough of treachery and deceit! They plague my very footsteps in my own palace," Elizabeth raged. "I am giving Geoffrey Christian license to journey to the Indies because I do not wish to have anyone's death on my conscience. Whatever else may come of this voyage is incidental," she proclaimed with a reproachful look at Walsingham. "However, *if* Sir Basil is determined to travel with his good friend, which is most commendable, then he might as well carry my personal good wishes to Doña Magdalena's family. And I certainly shall not turn a deaf ear to Sir Basil's report when he returns," she assured a stunned Sir Basil.

When all eyes turned to him, Basil felt himself growing pale, especially when Geoffrey's laugh rang out when he fully understood his queen's tactics.

"'Sdeath! 'Tis about time you saw some of the world you've only been reading about until now, Sir Basil," Geoffrey declared much to Her Grace's amusement, for Sir Basil Whitelaw was considered to be quite the scholarly gentleman, having taken a degree at Cambridge and studied law at Gray's Inn.

"Well, I—" Basil began, a blush of painful embarrassment appearing on his pale cheeks as he sought the proper words of refusal. He was slow to realize that he had been expertly outmaneuvered by Walsingham and the queen, who knew exactly what she was about.

"We cannot always choose how we would wish to spend our time, Sir Basil. God knows I fear the truth of that, but too often the best purpose is served when we put our personal wants aside," Elizabeth said quietly, earnestly, as if talking to a child.

Basil felt shamed and quickly spoke to reassure his queen of his loyalty, and unthinkingly so in his haste. "I would serve Your Grace through an eternity in Hell."

"By my faith! 'Tis where my enemies, especially His Most Catholic Majesty, would see me soon enough. Daughter of the Devil indeed!" she laughed, apparently finding more humor in Basil's unfortunate remark than had either Cecil or Walsingham, both of whom remained unsmiling.

"Good sir. You need not go that far on my behalf, only as far as the Indies," she added, her black eyes twinkling with mirth, and this time even Walsingham had to smile slightly.

Geoffrey, his laughter abating, couldn't help but feel sorry for poor Basil. He was such a sincere yet serious fellow that he never quite knew how to react to Her Grace's jesting.

"Rest assured you will have my most hearty thanks, Sir Basil, for the venture you are about to set out upon for the good of England," Elizabeth told him, holding out her hand for him to kiss.

About the Author

Winner of the Reviewers' Choice Award for Best Historical Romance, author Laurie McBain became a publishing phenomenon at age twenty-six with her first historical romance. She wrote seven romance novels during the 1970s and '80s, all of which were bestsellers, and sold over eleven million copies. Laurie lives in the San Francisco Bay Area of Northern California.